FIRESIDE

TRUE CONFESSIONS

TRUE CONFESSIONS

Sixty Years of Sin, Suffering & Sorrow

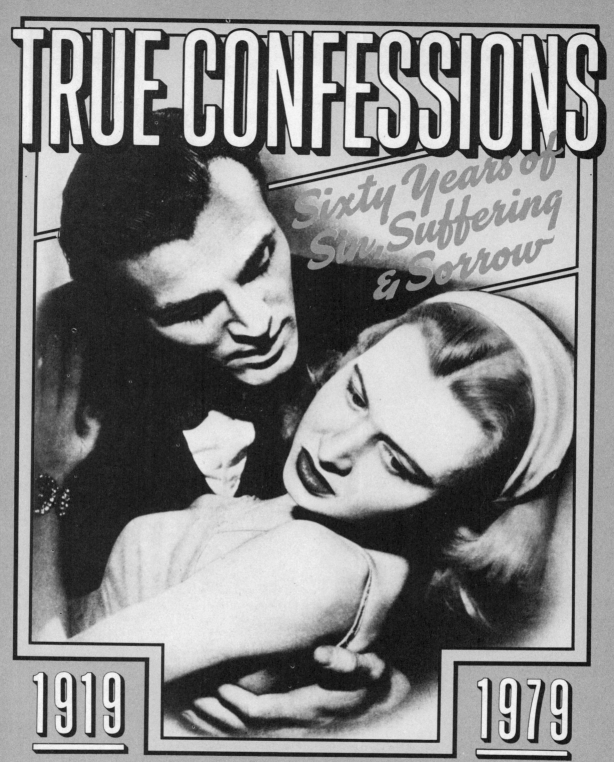

1919   1979

• FROM THE PAGES OF •

· TRUE CONFESSIONS · TRUE STORY · TRUE EXPERIENCE ·

· TRUE ROMANCE · TRUE LOVE · SECRETS · MODERN ROMANCES ·

Edited by Florence Moriarty, Editor-in-Chief of The Macfadden Women's Group

A FIRESIDE BOOK
Published by Simon and Schuster • New York

A Fireside Book
Published by Simon and Schuster
A Division of Gulf & Western Corporation
Simon & Schuster Building
Rockefeller Center
1230 Avenue of the Americas
New York, New York 10020

Designed by Joel Avirom
Manufactured in the United States of America

1 2 3 4 5 6 7 8 9 10
1 2 3 4 5 6 7 8 9 10 Pbk.

Library of Congress Cataloging in Publication Data

Main entry under title:
True confessions anthology, 1919-1979

  (A Fireside book)
  1. Confession stories.   2. Short stories, American.
3. American fiction—20th century.   I. Moriarty,
Florence.
PZ1.T755   (PS648.C66)   813'.085   79-16605
ISBN 0-671-24957-6
ISBN 0-671-24745-X Pbk.

Truth is Stranger Than Fiction

The 1950's — Truth is Stranger Than Fiction

The 1960's — TRUTH IS STRANGER THAN FICTION

THE 1970's — Truth is Stranger Than Fiction

TRUE CONFESSIONS Contents

THE 1920's

❦ *Truth is Stranger Than Fiction* ❧

One Awful Night

THIS is a tale of the half-way house to Asia—San Francisco—and of the mystery, fascination and terror of San Francisco's Chinatown. Reading this dreadful experience, one is brought to realization of the awful tragedy that ofttimes lurks behind the apparently innocent quaintness of Chinatown.

"BILL, it's up to you and me to stop this game, so let's go to it, old boy."

Little did I imagine that these would be the last words that my partner and gun-mate would ever speak to me. We had both joined the San Francisco detective force after making good in the lower ranks. Both being former Philippine Scouts during the Spanish-American war, we had little trouble to prove to the Chief of the Agency, when we applied for the promotions, that we had not purchased our expert riflemen's medals in some second-hand store. We had qualified with both rifle and pistol.

The white slave traffic had taken on very serious aspects. Chinese crooks gobbling up the girls by the wholesale and shipping them to the Chinese foreign markets as fast as they could smuggle them out of this country.

We had been working up clues for almost three months, when the Chief called us in one day and gave us a tip on a den of the worst and most notorious criminals of the whole gang of slant-eyed devils.

Pete and I had laid out our plan of attack and meant to advance upon the Chinese works right then and there. I need not bore my readers with the methods employed, but shall jump over a day's time and work into action at once.

I was to make my entrance into the slavers' den through one of the famous Chinese tunnels connecting practically all the buildings of Chinatown of that city. Many tales of terror the walls of these tunnels could tell, could they but speak. Three girls had mysteriously disappeared only the day before, and I would do all in my power to save them from sharing the fate of the other girls who had come and gone.

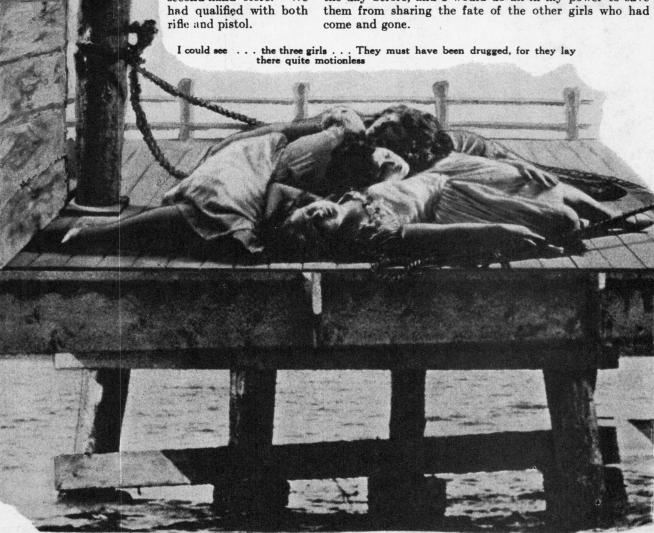

I could see . . . the three girls . . . They must have been drugged, for they lay there quite motionless

I turned the searchlight on the cold and rigid face of poor Pete. . . . and something I would rather have faced than a thousand Chinamen—a deadly adder

The tunnel through which I squirmed my way had evidently not been used lately, judging by the mouldy odor and the innumerable rats and mice who, like flashes of lightning, jumped over my face, body and legs as I crawled along. I did not dare make any noise for fear some lynx-eyed, long-tailed yellow devil would reach out from nowhere with a murderous grip, and deliver me into the other world without a sound. At last I could hear the familiar chattering of King Chang, the leader of the gang, and his associates, as I was only separated from my prey by the wooden ceiling of the coffin-like room in which I had arrived. Something was evidently wrong, for they talked in an excited manner, quite different from the sing-song usually employed by the people of their race.

ALL at once everything grew silent. I tried to find a way to the rooms above, and was afraid that I had been heard, when suddenly a shuffling of many feet took place and a panting could be heard as if the whole bunch were wrestling with the universe. Could Pete have arrived ahead of time and been detected, and was he now in trouble? I was not kept in doubt very long, for almost in answer to my mental query the familiar voice of Pete was heard, cursing with every breath. I tried frantically to find a way to the room above to help my buddy—but without avail. The shuffling gradually died out and I could hear a body dragged across the floor, then I knew I was too late to help poor Pete. I squeezed towards the wall to avoid a ray of light penetrating from a trap-door that had been opened from above and almost simultaneously heard a thud on the other side of the wall.

I gripped my gun tightly as I noticed the slim form of a Chinaman make ready to climb through the aperture. He landed on the floor only twelve feet away from me in cat-like fashion, and was soon followed by another, and the trap-door was closed again; however, not soon enough to keep me from seeing them make for the opposite wall, push a stone slab aside and disappear into the tunnel. I

I fired two shots, unconscious that two blue-uniformed pals of mine were behind me

quickly stepped over to the opening and listened to their chattering as they made their way out to the upper world.

MY time had come. I stepped into the opening of the tunnel and soon found narrow, stone steps leading into the room above. I slowly and carefully ascended, passed through the trap-door, and not hearing a sound, hurriedly threw aside curtains along the walls of the room hoping to find a trace of Pete; but Pete was gone. I drew aside another curtain and found myself in a small room with only a window-like opening. I stepped over and looked out upon a sort of hidden wharf.

Within a few feet from where I stood, I could see the three girls we had come to rescue lying in a heap, as though they had been passed through the very window from which I gazed.

They must have been drugged, for they lay there quite motionless, dressed in clothes they might have worn at some party.

I could not stop to conjecture further about this, nor could I attempt their rescue in their helpless plight with so many of their yellow abductors so near at hand. For at the very end of the wharf, at which was tied a motor boat, I saw a half dozen yellow-skinned devils. I determined to find some means of locating the entrance to their harbor of crime, and somehow to have their ship intercepted by our police boats.

I left, and had almost crossed the room through which I had entered, when I could again hear voices approaching. I quickly ran for cover, drew a curtain apart, and stepped in—and down.

HOW long I had laid just where I landed I cannot tell, but when I opened my eyes I found myself in a room, or rather, in a six by eight foot shaft, as my search-light revealed. My head ached fiercely, but my stupor slowly disappeared and I sat up. I was sitting on something soft and started to feel my way around. I touched a cold face and with a quick jump I was on my feet and turned the search-light on the cold and rigid face

I saw him roll over, and another Chinaman leap forward knife in hand

I jumped, grabbed the gun, and had barely steadied myself again, when of a sudden the entire room was illuminated and through a glass window in the wall, to which the snake had crawled, I could see the devilish grinning faces of three Chinamen. I quickly looked for the snake and new horrors crept up my backbone, for there, thrown against the wall in a heap, were the forms of two dead girls, still wearing an expression of pain on their faces. Another adder, much larger than the first one, I could see coiled upon one of the bodies, watching me with its small, diamond-like, hypnotizing eyes. I understood now the fate of the poor girls, and I could also see my own end approaching. Was I to die a slow death?

I TOOK aim and fired twice, the two snakes writhed in pain. A third shot spelled death to a Chinaman who had appeared from some quarter. I saw him roll over and another Chinaman leap forward, knife in hand. And then with a fourth shot I blew out the electric light, throwing all once more into grim darkness.

Come what may now, I had two shots left, one for my assailant and the last for myself. For rather than surrender I would kill myself.

of poor Pete, and at the same time on something that appeared a thousand times more ghastly to me. Right next to Pete's head, something slowly arose like a rapidly growing reed, and swaying back and forth, bowed closer and closer. It was a snake preparing to strike, and I would rather have faced a dozen Chinamen than this deadly adder. However, my clock of life was evidently not meant by the good Lord to have run its limit. I dared not move to reach the pistol which had slipped out of my hand while I had lain unconscious, for I knew it meant one quick little movement of those venomous fangs, a few minutes of intense agony on my part, and Pete and I would meet again. My suspense was, however, ended by a strain of monotonous music floating through the wall, which seemed to attract the snake and cause it to forget all about its prey. It began to sway gently back and forth and gradually moved towards the wall whence the music came. Now was my chance to jump for my gun.

Another noise reached my ears now. Heavy footsteps could be heard, shots rang out. Then I heard the gruff commands in a voice that I knew belonged to one of my friends on the Chinatown beat. My shots had been heard by the police. I fired two more shots, unconscious that two blue-uniformed pals of mine were just behind me. What happened then I don't remember, for the nervous strain had been too much for me.

When I opened my eyes again I was on the bed in my own room. I got up to strengthen myself with a good strong whiskey. As I raised the glass to my lips I stopped, stared into the mirror, and the glass fell to the floor.

Was that myself or somebody mocking me? I walked up to the reflection—and then I realized what had happened during those frightful minutes or perhaps hours. My hair had turned snowy white. ●

The Diary of a Lonesome Girl

Dear Diary:

April 12

I promised to tell you everything, Dear Diary, and I'm going to keep my promise. But it's awfully hard sometimes to write down just how I feel. For I am so discouraged. Met Edith Williams today on the car. She was going somewhere with Jimmy. And her clothes were so becoming that I envied her. Yes, I envied her clothes and I envied her sitting there with Jimmy. My hair is prettier than Edith's, isn't it? And my eyes—and my complexion? Then why am I always so lonesome—so much alone? Can't you help me, Diary? Bobbie's better today.

April 15

More trouble, Diary. Mother said today that the money she'd saved for my new dress would have to go to pay Bobbie's doctor bill. I'm trying to be brave, Diary, but I'm so disappointed. I wanted to go to a dance on the 26th. Shall I go, Diary? I wonder if I can fix up that white organdie from last season?

April 18

Went to church this morning. Walked home with Alice Browning. Saw Jimmy. He's always with Edith Williams. Oh, if I only had some pretty clothes—just a few of them! Mother tries so hard to save, but Dad never earned a large salary. And everything I earn goes toward keeping house. But I can still smile, can't I, Diary? Maybe, some day, my ship will come in and I'll live happily ever after.

April 23

I've decided to wear my organdie to the dance. I do hope none of the girls remember it from last year. That new sash may help. Do men ever remember dresses, Diary? Jimmy will be there with Edith Williams. Always Edith Williams. Oh, if I only had some becoming clothes!

April 27

I couldn't write to you last night, Diary—I just couldn't. I cried myself to sleep when I got home from the dance. Every girl had a new dress but me. I think Edith Williams' was best of all. Do you think Jimmy will marry her? Do you? He hardly looked at me last night. I came home all alone—so tired and discouraged. Isn't there something I can do to get pretty clothes?

May 15

Met Mrs. Feters today, with her two children. Poor woman—she hasn't had a new dress in years. She can't afford those in the shops and she can scarcely sew at all. I wish I could sew, Diary—then I could make my own clothes. Saw Jimmy walking down the street today while I was buying a magazine, but he didn't see me. I guess he was thinking of Edith Williams.

May 16

Remember that magazine I bought yesterday? Well, I sat up late last night reading it. I just couldn't put it down. For in it I found the story of a girl just like myself. She couldn't afford pretty clothes, either, and she was, oh, so discouraged. And then she learned of a school that teaches you, right at home, to make your own clothes for a half or a third of what you would pay in the shops. Do you think I could learn too, Diary? I'm going to find out, anyway.

May 18

More good news, Diary! You know Mrs. Devereaux, who has that dressmaking shop on Broad street? She is the best dressmaker in town. I asked her yesterday if she had studied in Paris. "No—not in Paris, my dear, but right in my own home. Everything I know about dressmaking and millinery I learned from the Woman's Institute." Do you hear, Diary—the Woman's Institute! Why, that's the very school to which I wrote the other night!

May 19

Early today the postman brought me a good thick letter from the Woman's Institute. I fairly snatched it from his hand. Guess he thought it was a love-letter. Why, Diary, do you know the Institute is the most wonderful school I ever heard of? Think of it, while I've been so unhappy, thousands of other girls have been learning right at home to make just the kind of pretty, becoming clothes they've always wanted, at oh! such wonderful savings. If they can do it, why can't I? I can, Diary, and I'm going to!

July 16

I know I've forgotten you for nearly two

Among the readers of "True Story" there are thousands of "lonesome girls." Yes, and just around the corner there are thousands of "Jimmys." There's a real and timely message here for every woman and girl who wants to know the happiness of having pretty clothes.

months, Diary, but I've been awfully busy since I enrolled with the Woman's Institute. Think of it, Diary, I'm learning how to make the pretty clothes I have always wanted. I've finished the first three lessons, and already I've made the prettiest blouse. Just think of being able to sew for yourself and have pretty things for just the cost of materials!

August 30

Well, it's happened, Diary. There was another dance last night and I wore my new dress. You should have seen the girls. They were so surprised. They all wanted to know where I bought it. And when I told them I had made it myself they would hardly believe me. And the men! Don't tell me they don't notice pretty things. My dance card was filled in five minutes. I've never had such a good time in my life. Jimmy and Edith aren't engaged yet, Diary. Jimmy's coming to see me on Wednesday night.

October 15

Here it is only the middle of October and already I have more pretty Fall clothes than I ever had in my life. And altogether they have cost me no more than one really good dress or suit would have cost ready-made. Oh, there's a world of difference in the cost of things, Diary, when you make them yourself and pay only for the materials. Besides, I've made over all my last year's clothes—they look as pretty as the new ones and the expense of new trimmings and findings was almost nothing at all. My friends are wondering at the change in me, but we know what did it, don't we, Diary?

November 8

Awfully busy, Diary. I've started to sew for other people. I made a silk dress for Mrs. Scott and a blouse for Mrs. Perry last week. Mrs. Scott paid me $10 and Mrs. Perry $3.25. Think of it, Diary—little me, who couldn't sew a stitch a few months ago, making clothes for other people. Mother just can't get over it. She's actually smiling these days. Says I'm going to earn $30 a week, soon. Do you think so, Diary?

P. S. Had the nicest letter from Mrs. Picken, the Director of Instruction of the Woman's Institute. She must be a wonderful woman, Diary. She's so sympathetic—so kind. I think she understands women better than any one else in America. She's taken a personal interest in me from the very start.

November 17

Remember mother's prediction that I would soon be making $30 a week as a dressmaker? Well, last week I made $35! We'd still be in the same old rut if I hadn't sent in that coupon. Isn't it wonderful what a difference a little thing like that makes? It hasn't been hard, either—everything is so clearly explained in word and picture. Oh, yes, Diary—I want to whisper something in your ear. I—I think Jimmy loves me.

November 20

The most wonderful, wonderful thing has happened, Diary. Jimmy has asked me to marry him. It's to be in the spring just as soon as I get my trousseau ready. It's going to be the best trousseau a girl ever had, every stitch of

it worked by my own hands. Jimmy wanted to know what had caused the wonderful change in me and I told him all about the Woman's Institute. He wouldn't believe it until I showed him my lessons. He said they were so easy and simple that he thought he would take up Dressmaking himself. Imagine Jimmy sewing, Diary!

November 26

Gladys Graham came in to see me today. I think she had been crying. Said she was discouraged because she didn't have pretty clothes. Then I told her all about the Woman's Institute. I think she's going to find out about it. I hope she does. Think where I would be, Diary, if I hadn't seen that magazine. Goodbye, Diary—Jimmy's here and I can't neglect him even for you.

WOULDN'T you, too, like to have prettier, more becoming clothes for yourself and your family for less than half what they now cost you? Wouldn't you like to have two or three times as many clothes at no increased expense?

You can do it by making them yourself. You can save at least $25 on a suit priced at $40 in the stores, for every item of material it contains would cost not more than $15. On a dress retailing at $20, you can save $12 or $14. Even on a blouse or a child's frock, or a little boy's suit costing $5, it is easily possible to save $2.50 to $3 by buying the materials and making it yourself.

Are such savings as these worth while? What would it mean to you to be able to save half or two-thirds of what you spend for clothes each season?

You *can* learn easily and quickly to make pretty, becoming clothes for yourself and others, and you can do it right at home, in your spare time, through the Woman's Institute. There is not the slightest doubt about it. More than 125,000 women and girls, in city, town and country, have proved, by the clothes they have made and the dollars they have saved, the success of the Institute's method. The State Superintendent of Public Instruction thinks so much of the Institute and its work that he recently called it "one of Pennsylvania's most valuable educational institutions."

Through the Woman's Institute, you learn how to make all stitches and seams; design patterns; use tissue-paper patterns; judge, select, buy and use materials; make simple, practical waists, skirts and dresses; perfect-fitting underwear and lingerie; dainty infants', children's and misses' clothing; afternoon coats, suits and dresses; evening gowns and wraps; tailored coats, skirts and complete suits; renovate, dye and make over garments; how to embroider, etc

It makes no difference where you live, because all the instruction is carried on by mail and it is no disadvantage if you are employed during the day, or have household duties that occupy much of your time, because you can devote as much or as little of your time to the course as you desire and just when it is convenient.

Send for Handsome 64-page Booklet

I prayed that God would have pity on those beloved ones who were suffering because of me

My Mad Elopement

"Are you afraid, little one?" he asked with his face close to mine. I drank deeply from that poisoned spring until—

TONIGHT as I sit by the open fire and gaze into the dying embers, my mind drifts back over the past, my years seem to have dropped away as a garment, my hair is no longer streaked with gray, my step is as light and elastic as in bygone days.

A sweet sound comes to my ears, the prattle of little children; their fairy forms flit past me in the firelight, and I reach out my arms, but always they are empty. Then comes vivid recollection—my pleasant dream is over. But because God has given me these moments, I am content to live.

Few know the real facts of my life-story, and from those

who do know, there is only censure and blame, but perhaps some kind reader may read between the lines and forget to blame, or some erring foot may be stayed by the story I have to tell. If so, it will not be told in vain.

Romance came into my life at seventeen. At twenty, perhaps it might have been different, but seventeen is ever heedless, and thinks not of tomorrow, but blissfully spends each golden moment of today.

It was at a gay little party that I met Horace Grant. He was somehow different from the usual men I had met. He was tall and dark, his voice was soft and caressing, and his eyes looked into mine with an assurance all their own. I was infatuated. Then I thought it was love; now I know it was only the infatuation of seventeen. Love came later.

The final, crashing bars of a waltz came to a close, and Horace was by my side. The room was lighted with shaded, gold-

I went to the bed and gazed in amazement down on the form of the sick man who lay there muttering incoherently

en lights. Outside, a big yellow moon smiled down in approval. The lilacs were in bloom, and their sweet fragrance came to us as we stood side by side in the open doorway. In a moment we were outside in the lilac scented garden and before I knew it, I was in his arms and he was whispering eager protestations of love in his caressing voice which, to me, was sweet music.

Early in September we were married. We settled down to the routine of everyday life and, although Horace's

salary was not large, we were comfortable. In two years Horace, Jr., was born, and a year later came Marjorie.

Life moved very smoothly for about four years. Then Horace had business worries, and he would come home with a frown on his brow which I tried to erase by a loving kiss. He always seemed too tired or too busy to take me any place, so I began to seek my own happiness.

The gay, reckless crowd I kept company with made me forget my troubles. Then I met Forest Harvey. We were attracted to each other at first sight. He was handsome and paid me marked attention. All I wanted was to be near him, to touch his shoulder, to feel his hand in mine. I was in love, I, a married woman with two children, was in love with another man who was not my husband.

At first the enormity of the idea made me dizzy, but the man fascinated me, and life with Horace had been so conventional, so commonplace, that I snatched at even a moment's excitement.

I MET Forest Harvey many times after that. One evening after telling Horace I was spending the evening at the home of a girl friend, I went to Forest who received me with open arms. With his mouth close to my ear, he told me of his love, covering my lips with kisses. I clung to him, caring not what happened as long as I was in his arms. Eagerly he urged me to run away with him. For a moment, thoughts of Horace and the babies came to me and I would not yield, but Forest's entreaties were so passionate that I promised tearfully.

"Sweetheart," he murmured, "meet me tomorrow night at my rooms," With my head on his shoulder, I promised.

Returning to my home, I looked in at my husband. He was peacefully sleeping. Poor, dear, unsuspecting Horace, who believed his wife faithful!

"But I love Forest," I murmured to still the voice of my conscience, "and love is ever paramount." With blinding tears in my eyes I stumbled from the room.

The next day dragged wearily away, but evening came at last. Somehow, I was not looking forward to my adventure as I had expected to.

At twelve o'clock, I slipped noiselessly into the nursery. The moon had risen and was silvering the room with its glory, caressing lovingly the forms of my darling babies. Don't think, dear readers, that I didn't love them. I did, but Forest's laughing, teasing face came before me making my babies' faces only a blurred vision.

SILENTLY I stood looking down on them. A salt tear splashed down on little Horace's upturned face and sleepily he murmured, "Mother" —just the one word, but it it was the key to my heart and I gathered him into my arms. For an hour I held him thus, then quietly disengaging his clinging arms from about my neck, I stooped and kissed my little daughter.

Blindly I staggered from the room, and groped my way downstairs.

Not giving myself time to think, I went to Forest's rooms where he was waiting for me.

I trembled as he drew me to him.

"Are you afraid, little one?" he asked, with his face close to mine. "Let us drink deep of this ecstasy while we have it and be content."

We left that night for a far distant city. Even yet, that night's ride is vivid in my memory.

At the end of three days, we came to our destination. Forest was as loving as ever; yet beneath it all, I sensed an unrest. I was tired and worn, and my thoughts flew back to Horace and the babies. I cried out sharply.

"Are you sick of our bargain?" Forest asked.

"No," I lied. I am only tired."

Horace, I supposed, would get a divorce; perhaps he would marry again. Somehow, this thought did not please me. Horace was mine. He must not belong to another.

I watched the papers eagerly, yet dreading what I might see. Glaring headlines met my gaze:

Strange Disappearance of Mrs. Horace Grant
Believed to Have Committed Suicide
Motor Coat She Was Wearing on Day of Disappearance
Found Near High Level Bridge

There was more but I couldn't see; the paper swam before me, and I sank down in a limp heap where Forest found me later.

When I regained consciousness, Forest was standing over me, almost roughly he shook me as he said, "You little fool, don't get weak-kneed now."

Tearfully I clung to him. "Oh, Forest," I moaned, "don't be cruel. Tell me, did you put my coat on the bridge to make them think that—that—" I couldn't finish the sentence.

"Of course," he answered indifferently.

She stood just inside the door watching me as if to read a verdict of life or death upon my face

9

My Mad Elopement

"I wasn't going to have the police on our trail."

Even then I admired Forest, admired him for the daredevil light in his eyes; the easy nonchalance of his voice. Still I was troubled. His love seemed forced, and then, unconsciously perhaps, I was comparing him with Horace, and Forest suffered by the comparison.

Months passed. Forest never seemed to be at home now, or if he was, he was moody and irritable, or often he would come reeling home under the influence of drink, bringing with him strange companions who in their drunken state would hint darkly of strange women.

Then one night Forest failed to come at all. All night long I lay in an agony of suspense, waiting for the stumbling footsteps I had so learned to dread. Morning came at last. At the first gray streaks of dawn, I stole from my bed. All of Forest's belongings were gone.

FOR a moment I was stunned, dazed, by what had happened. I could not reason or think. My mind seemed a blank. But through it all, the eyes of Horace seemed to be looking into mine. They were not accusing, but filled with the love-light of old, as on that lilac scented June night when first we met.

I tried to shut my eyes to exclude the vision, but ever those eyes danced before me, until I screamed and sank to the floor unconscious.

When I came to myself, some weeks later, I was lying in a hospital ward and a kind-faced sister with lustrous dark eyes was gazing at me pityingly.

Then I was alive, after all! Somehow, for the past week, I had had a vague notion that I was dead, and it didn't seem to matter. Life wasn't worth living. Horace's love for me was dead. Horace! Why must I ever think of Horace? I had forfeited all right to his affection, trampled his clean honest love under my feet; had left him for a worthless scoundrel who couldn't even offer me a name.

The silence of the hospital seemed to soothe my harrowed soul. Often I would kneel at the altar steps with the sisters, as they told their beads. I prayed that God might have pity on those beloved ones who were suffering because of me.

By the time I was well again, I had decided to make nursing my life work. Somehow, I felt that, in ministering to the needs of others, I would gain absolution from my sins, but I knew that only Time would heal my broken heart. Now I know that not even eternity itself is long enough, and but for my beautiful dream and the ethereal forms of my children, as they come to me at the evening hour, memory would be a hateful thing.

Nature seldom lets us die when we want to, so I took up the burden of life and, although my heart seemed to have frozen to stone I forced my lips to smile.

I spent three years at the hospital; then came a flu epidemic. Hospitals in every part of the land sent out all the nurses that could be spared, and I found myself one dark April morning, bound for a distant city in response to a call for help.

Arriving at my destination, I sought out the local Health Board and was given an address of a private home, whither I went at once.

The house had a desolate look as if it had been deserted. I walked up the steps and rang the bell. A gray-haired woman answered my summons. I soon discovered that she was the housekeeper.

"Oh, nurse!" she fairly sobbed, "we are in a bad way here. The two children are very low, and the master just raves day and night."

I tried to comfort her as best I could as she led the way to the room where the master of the house lay. She stood just inside the door watching me as if to read a verdict of life or death upon my face.

Something familiar about the attitude of the man made my heart beat very quickly and unprofessionally.

I went to the bed and gazed in amazement down on the form of the sick man who lay there muttering incoherently.

It was Horace!

FOR a moment the room seemed to reel while the housekeeper gazed disapprovingly from the doorway. One thought was uppermost in my mind. He was mine. Nothing could take him from me. No, not even death! And then came bitter recollection. He was not mine! I had cast him away as a child casts away a worn-out toy. I had wrecked his life and mine, too. I had renounced his love. I understood fully then that those who break the law are broken by it, and I sank on my knees and buried my face in the pillow beside Horace's dark head, now silvering at the temples, unmindful of the terrible disease that was racking his body.

Then my professional training began to assert itself, and I lifted my head, wiped away my tears, and set about making him more comfortable. Then I stole to the room where the children lay— Horace's children and mine.

Young Horace was much like his father. His hair lay dark and damp on his high, intellectual forehead. His eyes when closed were fringed with long lashes. One thin little hand stole listlessly outside of the covers. With my heart near to bursting, I took his burning hand in mine. His pulse was very weak. He had developed double pneumonia.

Oh! Was I to lose him in the hour of finding?

Sadly, with my eyes full of blinding tears, I went and looked down at my little daughter. She resembled her mother. Yes, I suppose I was still her mother. Nature had made me that. Her hair which had been cut short, clung to her head in clustering, golden ringlets. Her eyes were gray, and fringed with dark lashes.

"Oh, Lord," I prayed, "spare at least one of my darlings."

But I knew it was not to be. I had been led here only to be reminded of my mortal sin.

My thoughts were disjointed. I think, for a time, I was mad, but sanity came at last, and I sat by the bedside of my darlings, moving from one to the other at the slightest sound.

MARJORIE was the first to go. With scarcely a sigh she slipped away to the land where pain is not known.

With my grief almost more than I could bear, I closed her eyes and sat down by little Horace. His breathing was becoming labored.

I couldn't pray. In dumb misery I sat there, and my past sins came up before me. Truly the way of the transgressor is hard, and it was doubly hard for me as I sat with the wasted hand of my little son in mine.

Sometimes things are revealed to those who are about to enter the valley of shadow. I know not why, for God's ways are past understanding, but little Horace opened his dark eyes and looked full at me, while a smile of unearthly beauty lighted up his face. Then his hand stole into mine and he whispered faintly, "Mother." It was the last word I had heard him speak the night I had left my home, and it was the last word his tired lips would frame, for his head sank back and he was beyond recall.

The children were buried in the churchyard nearby. Alone with my grief, I went and sat by Horace. He was resting more easily, but he was muttering in his delirium. I bent close to hear the words.

"Margaret," he murmured, and his lips smiled. "Love is a priceless thing, because it brought me you." His voice trailed off into silence.

Involuntarily I started. It seemed he must know of my presence, but his breathing was heavy, and I knew he was still unconscious.

With my arms around him, I dropped to my knees. "Oh! Horace," I moaned, "I have come back to you," and the sorrow of my broken heart begged for liberation in confessional sobs. The feeling of my arms about him seemed to quiet him, and he dropped off into a deep sleep.

Flight was the next thought. I must get away. But my limbs refused to obey my will and I continued to kneel by Horace.

How long I remained on my knees, I do not know. I think I lost consciousness. When I came to myself, Horace was awake. For a moment he gazed at my face as if uncertain of himself. Then weakly he reached out a thin, transparent hand and clutched mine.

"Margaret?" His voice was filled with wonder. "Is it really you? I dreamed I was in heaven and you came to me—came as an angel of mercy."

"No, Horace, I have been in torment, but this is heaven," I said as I snuggled into his arms.

The strange story of my disappearance had been believed, and Horace, nearly heartbroken, had taken the children and moved to the place where he was now living. Horace had believed me faithful. He didn't ask for any explanation now. He was content to have me near him and with my sin and shame searing my heart, I could only wait until he was stronger.

Horace improved daily. One evening, just at twilight, I was beside him as usual when, with his face close to mine, he asked me a question which I knew must be answered. The mystery of the past years must be unraveled. My own lips must pass the sentence. The sound of my own voice must be the death-knell of all my hopes, for, of course, I could never stay after my horrible story was revealed. Horace would despise me, for the evil I had done. My head sank upon my breast and I cried aloud.

Then strength came to me and with my eyes averted I told the story of my sin and shame. No other sound was audible in the room except the rise and fall of my own voice. Horace seemed scarcely to breathe at times.

"Now I know," I finished lamely, "that you will hate me, but you cannot hate me worse than I hate myself." I paused. I had grown suddenly tired. Horace seemed scarcely to hear me.

I gazed out of the window. The twilight had deepened and a large, silvery moon was keeping watch over the world. The stars came out, one by one, and looked down upon us. I sat in silence with my soul bared, waiting for condemnation from the lips of the man I loved.

His words came at last, not like a torrent, as I had expected, but in the same caressing voice as of old:

"Margaret, love is stronger than hate, and when a man really loves, he wants to give only happiness. You have gone through a scorching fire and your wings have been singed, but your soul has soared, and remains pure. And love is of the soul."

The stars came out unheeded, the curtain of night was drawn close, the flaming banners of purple and gold had faded from the sky and we were alone with our love.

Six years have passed since our reunion; years filled with love and happiness, but my happiness is tinged with sorrow, for my arms are empty and my heart is hungry.

Often I visit the churchyard where the grass has grown thick and green on two little mounds, and there I kneel and ask forgiveness. And I know that I have been forgiven, for God has given me the priceless treasure of a pure, true love. ●

Her Morning After

Two Lives Transformed in One Night—Before the Volstead Act

I HOPE nobody will ever break loose through the same avenue that I did. In fact, that is the real reason for my telling this story: I want to save others from a similar experience. It is not good to be a drab, household slave to changeless routine, unbroken by encounters with real life. But let me say that such a life is better than certain other types of life of which I got a decided glimpse, and into which I—but I must not get ahead of my story. I simply want the reader to understand as I tell my story in detail, without interruption for moralizing, that mine is an example not to follow. Let nobody be stirred by the glamor of a certain part of my experience to attempt a similar adventure. What I went through of mental anguish afterward can be neither described nor imagined.

My mother was one of three sisters, born and brought up in a staid little New England town. They had all been brought up righteously by a very religious father. They had been taught housekeeping in the good old-fashioned way

SUPPOSE every natural, healthy instinct within you had been crushed down, starved out of your life, as was the case here. Would you have been brave enough to fight your way to freedom? Or would you have become as colorless as the human machines around you, going through life without hearing its wonderful human melody and never beholding its rose-colored joys? Read what this girl did and the startling result.

—which means that they spent hours and hours daily in making sure that no speck of dust or dirt remained in any spot in the whole house for more than a few moments at a time. The two older sisters had become settled at the time that a traveling salesman fascinated my mother and carried her off to New York with him. The only correspondence my mother had with her family after that consisted of a letter from Aunt Abigail, telling her of the death of both their father and mother through pneumonia. My mother had removed herself scandalously from their midst, and, more angered than grieved, they held religiously aloof from her.

MY father proved to be not merely just as gay and irresponsible after my mother's marriage as he had been fascinating before it, but also a hopeless drinker; and soon my mother found herself struggling to make a living for herself, and for me— soon to be born. My father had light-heartedly vanished, flitting to other parts, and

He . . . jerked the man suddenly away. "Leave the young lady alone," he said sharply

I knew that I was not acting like my usual self . . . I rose from my seat and danced gayly up the aisle

leaving my mother to shoulder the responsibilities of motherhood alone. What could she do but return to her two prim old-maid sisters. They took her back—after a long family conclave, I suppose. They never did anything without a long family conclave. But the strain was too much for my mother; and, when I was born, she died.

So I was left to Aunt Abigail and Aunt Sophronia. They had no liking for their task, but neither had ever shirked a duty yet; so they set grimly about bringing me up in the way I should go. All the drab precision that they worshipped, I was taught to worship. All that my mother had failed to be, they educated me to be. All that they were of primness, I was forced to be. And above all, the least sign of the reckless lack of responsibility which I inherited from my dashing young father, was crushed out of me as one crushes the cutworm in a garden. They never spoke of my father except once, when I asked directly about him. Then they told me in a hushed voice that he was a very wicked man and that I must never speak of him again.

THUS I grew up, bound hand and foot, body and soul, by the chains of righteousness. By the time I was twenty-two, I was almost as prim as my two aunts, and I looked at least thirty because of it. No man had

ever broken down the protective bulwarks of our home to pay me court, and it was evidently the fixed purpose of my aunts to see that none ever did so. My life was one quiet, orderly round of dusting, dishwashing, cleaning, cooking, preserving. The only break in the monotony was going to church on Sunday and listening to the details of hell-fire and damnation that were being prepared for all wicked sinners. I believe it was these vivid sermons on the wickedness of man that stirred my submerged inheritance. Certainly I was more my father's child after the sermon on Sunday than at any other time. And it was after a particularly vivid prohibition sermon that I finally decided to strike blindly for liberty.

Hardly knowing what it was that was within me, driving me, or what it was that I sought, I gathered together my few clothes and the two hundred dollars in money that I had hoarded patiently through close on twenty years, and I took the train to New York, leaving a colorless note for Aunt Abigail telling her what I had done, but not whither I was going. I found a cheap boarding-house, and obtained a position as salesgirl in a department store. Then I waited for life to burst upon me.

BUT my aunts had done their work only too well. I was still the prim, gray little old maid of twenty-two. My ways were the ways of Aunt Abigail, my appearance hardly less settled than that of Aunt Sophronia. The wickedness of the great city, upon which

13

the minister at home had dilated, failed to materialize. Life was just as dull a routine as ever—for me. But there was one difference: I could see others about me who were full of the life that I lacked, who spent their spare time in the idle gayety that I unconsciously yearned for.

Little by little, I began to follow them in my innermost thoughts, began to create an imaginary life for myself like theirs. I even went so far as to eat some little scrap now and then at a gay restaurant, so that I might see how these joyous creatures dressed. And then with all the cleverness that my aunts had taught me, I made myself an orange-colored gown that matched the most extreme mode I had seen. Ah! Shall I ever forget the wild, pounding thrill that went through me, when it was finished, and I put it on in the privacy of my own room!

THAT dress was the beginning of a new life for me—a secret life, in which no other human being had a part, a life that frightened me with its very thrills of wickedness, or what seemed to me to be wickedness. I stood in front of the mirror and gazed and gazed and gazed at myself. Then I took down my hair and put it up differently, but with an instinct that brought the desired effect at once. Then I looked and looked, and I knew that I wanted other things. The next day, after primly selling white goods to my last customer, I went to a certain store of which I knew, and bought powder, rouge, lip-stick and pencil for the eyebrows. I felt cold with horror at the thing I was doing, but I went on. When I got home I tremblingly took off my gray clothes and once more put on my wonderful orange dress. Instantly I felt differently. My pulses throbbed warmly, my cheeks glowed— and I used those accessories of beauty as they

had been meant to be used! I was a *young* girl at last.

But I did not go out. I had nowhere to go, no friends to go with. I simply looked at myself and let my mind run in a vague riot. Then I took off the dress and went to bed in a daze, to sleep placidly as I had never slept before.

THE next night I began the hat that was to go with the orange dress. Three nights later, I finished it. Then came the purchase of exquisite little slippers. The memory of the thrill that those shoes gave me lingers still. There followed silk stockings to match, and then a gradual replacement of each simple piece of underwear by some dainty thing that was meant for a countess or a daughter of wealth. Every cent that I earned went to the equipment of my "other self."

Yet during the day I was still the same prim, drab, little old maid as ever. My companions at the store laughed at me openly, and ceased frivolous conversations upon my approach, as if I had been as forbidding as the minister at home. They never invited me to join them in any of the gayeties that they talked of from morning to night. They never introduced me to the young men that met them outside the door. They treated me as one set apart by my prim manners.

I felt this all keenly, but in a way I was glad, for I did not like these flippant, shallow creatures; I felt nothing in common with them. Yet I yearned for a taste of the life that they talked of, waited all day for, and plunged into in the evening.

THEN, one evening, I simply opened the door of my little room, and walked out in my orange-colored gown and all the other wonderful things that went with it —walked out to try a little of the gayety that I longed for, even though I had to try it all alone. My ignorance and innocence of really wrong thoughts are best demonstrated by the fact that I really believed I could go out, in my radiant and eager girlhood, and be gay alone! I knew as near to nothing of men and their ways as a girl can. I knew vaguely that they were very wicked from the sermons of the minister; but that meant little to me. Moreover, I knew that such clothes as I wore and the places to which I intended going were wicked—from the same minister. But I liked the feel of the clothes, and I knew I was going to like the places. If the men were no more wicked than the clothes, I had little to fear. So I took no count of the men.

I went to a restaurant where there were many bright lights, and music,

I saw now Wally, the man I had just married, . . . was in a drunken stupor . . . Then the tension in me broke

and every now and then singing or dancing on a raised platform at one end, by some girl who looked very piquant and merry.

I had hardly seated myself, tingling with excitement from the roots of my hair to the tips of my toes, so taken up with a joyous trio at the next table that I forgot to think of what to order, when a pink-cheeked man slid into the chair opposite me with a self-possessed, "Hello, little one. What'll you have?"

HIS too sporty appearance, and his sleek plumpness struck just the wrong note; and his boldly leering eyes frightened me. I suddenly ceased to be the radiant creature of the orange gown who had set out seeking adventures, and became the very much terrified little old maid that Aunt Abigail had created. I looked helplessly about me, and my eyes caught the eyes of one of the two men at the next table. He was handsome and bold looking, but there was a cleanness about him too that appealed to me.

Just then the man across from me reached boldly across the table and patted one of my hands.

"Don't get nervous, little one," he said. "I'm not going to eat you. I'm offering to feed you." And he smiled with self-assurance.

I drew my hand away with a shudder. He chuckled.

"A bit shy, eh?" he said insinuatingly. "Maybe it's your first time? Well, don't be afraid. I like first timers. I'll show you some fun." He leaned as far across the table as he could, trying to reach my other hand.

I drew back, more terrified than ever, and not having sense enough to rise and go out. But my eyes once more caught those of the young man at the next table, and this time he understood my terror. He pushed back his chair without saying anything to the other man or girl at his table, and stepping over to my table, slid his hand down into the collar of the man opposite me and jerked him suddenly away.

"Leave the young lady alone," he said sharply, and gave the man a twist, flinging him toward the door.

"You damned young whelp!" roared the man, and

"I suppose I have been some disgusting kind of beast. Oh, Good Lord, what have I done?"

rushed at the young fellow.

MY protector reached out and struck him full in the face, sending him staggering backward. The plump man recovered his balance with difficulty, glared fiercely, made as if to rush again, changed his mind, and slunk out. My young defender dropped into the chair out of which he had just pulled the other, and smiled gaily at me.

"Good riddance to bad rubbish," he laughed.

Now this good-looking young man had no more business sitting down and talking to me than had the man from whose attentions he had rescued me. But his eyes were clear and honest and I never thought of objecting. I was instantly back in the personality of my orange gown, and I smiled back at him as boldly as he smiled at me. I had come out for adventure, and lo, here it was.

The proprietor of the place came briskly down the aisle, evidently bent on finding out the cause of the trouble. The young man grinned up at him.

"It's all right, George," he said. "This lady is with me. That rotter was bothering her. Send us a couple of Bronx's and forget it."

THE proprietor bowed almost obsequiously, and retired.

"You didn't really want that fellow around, did you?" asked the young man.

"No," I admitted in a low voice. I found myself eager to answer him in his own easy banter, but I somehow couldn't let go. The impulses of the orange gown were checked by the training of Aunt Abigail.

"But you don't mind my sitting here, do you?" he pursued with a self assured smile.

I didn't mind. I was strangely eager to have him stay. I wanted to say something which would make him want to stay, yet I didn't know how.

"I'm glad to have you stay," I finally said timidly, "if you want to and if—" I glanced

(Continued)

at the other table—"if they don't mind."

I noticed that his eyes lost a little of their gay assurance, and he looked at me with a slightly puzzled expression on his face.

"Oh, they don't mind," he said slowly. "I was one too many there." He paused, still looking at me doubtfully. "You're sure I'm not intruding?"

HIS very hesitation brushed away most of my own diffidence. I shook my head.

"Oh no," I confessed, "I came out for an adventure, and—and your sitting down here is an adventure, isn't it?"

He was still looking at me with that puzzled expression, as if there was something he didn't understand.

"Why—yes," he said. "I mean—is it really?"

"Of course," I answered naïvely, "this is the first time I've ever been here. I'm all trembly about it."

"Really?" he asked, and stared at me as if I were some strange creature.

It was little wonder that he was surprised, for though my clothes were those of a girl to whom such things are no adventure at all, my voice was the voice which had been trained by Aunt Abigail.

At that minute a waiter placed two cocktails on our table. I looked at mine interestedly.

"What is this?" I asked.

"Don't you know?"

I shook my head.

"Does it go with this kind of adventure?" I asked, smiling.

A funny look came into his eyes.

"I should think," he said slowly, "that it would help very much to make this adventure a success."

"Then I'm sure I'll like it," I said, lifting the glass to my lips and sipping it.

He laughed, with a strangely captivating twinkle in his eye.

"Oh, that isn't the way to drink it," he said. "You must toss it off in one swallow, like this." And he drank his with a flourish.

My first sip had suggested to me that this was orange juice with something else added that I didn't like quite so well.

HAD I known that my father was an alcoholic, I might have hesitated a long time before drinking it. But the orange juice made it pleasant, so I followed his example without question.

Then a queer thing happened. I felt the faintest, most elusive tingling start up in my whole body, spreading gradually to the tips of my fingers and toes. Things around me ceased to look strange and awesome. The thing that had just happened ceased to be a startling adventure, and became a delectable frolic. Even the incident of the leering man was just a huge joke.

QUITE suddenly, and without any intention on my part, I heard myself laughing—not Aunt Abigail's cultivated laugh, but a rippling melodious laugh that seemed just to fit the situation. I leaned forward on my elbows, looking with a surety of understanding into my companion's eyes.

"Wasn't he funny—when you punched him!" I cried in a gay, clear voice.

Once more the man opposite me stared. Poor man, he knew no better than I what that one cocktail had done in the way of liberating my suppressed inner nature. He did not even realize as I did, that at last the real me, that had made the orange gown, was in charge of the body that the gown adorned.

And then, awful as it really was, began the most totally exhilarating experience that I ever went through. Rose-colored glasses of joyous understanding seemed to have dropped before my eyes. In no time I was talking gaily, laughing merrily, enjoying every little incident that happened about me, catching the point of every slightest witticism that my companion ventured, and never failing to find a reply to match his sally and go it one better. I knew that I was not acting like my usual self; I knew that I had stepped into a sort of fairyland. But it did not trouble me, for I knew that I fitted the place perfectly.

The music struck up about then, and the girl on the raised platform danced pleasingly. When she ceased, I thought, "If she can do it, why not I?" So I rose from my seat and danced gayly up one aisle and down the other, humming a little tune at first and then singing the words. It must have been some perfectly sedate song, for I knew no others; but I must have given it an entirely new interpretation, for it fitted my ecstatic mood perfectly, and the other diners seemed to enjoy it immensely, for they clapped me again and again, till I repeated with another song and another dance.

Then we had something more to eat and Wally—I was calling him Wally and he was calling me Bettie by that time—Wally drank another bottle of wine. He beamed at me every minute, and I found myself gloriously happy.

Presently he suggested that we go somewhere else, and without a question I went with him by taxi to a still gayer place, where he beamed upon me some more, and I captivated the dining-room with another little dance, and he drank more wine. It was freedom itself that kept me intoxicated now. I did not drink any more. Then we went to a third place, and repeated the performance.

THIS time at the end of my little dance, Wally leaned across the table and laid a hand on each of mine. His hands were gentle and friendly. I enjoyed the pressure of them, gathering mine in protectively. He was now a little pale, and the smiles had given way to a complete dignity and self-possession.

"Bettie," he said slowly, and with a gravity that instantly held my attention. "Bettie, you're a wonderful little girl. I wish I had you with me always."

He looked at me very solemnly, as if he wanted me to understand the full meaning of his words. I had no experience to cause me to find his sudden solemnity indicative of anything but simple earnestness.

I felt a welling up within me of the same desire. How wonderful it would be to be always with Wally. How perfectly our personalities seemed to fit.

"Wally," I answered, with the same earnestness and with the frank ingeniousness that had dropped upon me with the drinking of that one cocktail two hours before, "Wally, I wish I could be with you always, too." And I added, "Why not?"

I KNOW that it sounds strange that I could say such a thing and say it quite unconsciously; but I vow it seemed the one sensible, natural thing to say at that time. Wally's eyes were fixed on mine. Slowly a gleam came into them.

"Why not?" he asked in the same slow, solemn voice. Then suddenly he rose. "Of course," he said with careful emphasis. "Of course, we'll get married."

He laid a twenty dollar bill on the plate, took my arm, and in the same solemn, dignified fashion, led me out and hailed a taxi driver.

"Listen," he said with great distinctness, tapping the driver on the arm to emphasize each word. "Listen, I want you to take us to some place where we can be married. We're going to be married tonight."

The taxi driver took us across to Hoboken by ferry, found a night court, and witnessed my marriage to Wally, the judge as unsuspecting as I—for he had no way of knowing that Wally's perfect gravity and dignified self-possession meant anything more than they seemed on the surface.

FROM the night court we crossed again to New York, and at Wally's direction drove to one of the big, luxurious hotels. By this time I myself was beginning to feel just the slightest bit different. I was still in an exalted mood, more exalted perhaps than ever, for Wally's earnestness had laid me by the very heart. But I was now looking about me with a suspicion of dazed wonder at what had happened.

Presently we were in a palatial apartment that added to my feeling of bewilderment. Wally regally tossed the boy a bill and held the floor majestically until the boy had gone out. Then he turned to me and held out his arms slowly.

"Bettie," he said, "you wonderful girl, you are now my wife."

"Yes," I said, lifted to a high spiritual level by my own emotions, "I am your wife." And I went to him.

He put his arms solemnly around me and bent his head to touch his lips gently to my forehead. His eyes closed, apparently with the sweetness of the thought within him. I closed mine too, and pressed my face against his breast to try to make myself realize the wonder of it.

THEN all at once I noticed that he was leaning against me heavily. The next minute, as I stepped slightly back, his knees gave way limply, and he slid to the floor, almost dragging me with him!

What had happened? I was terrified. I dropped to my knees and called him by name. I shook him slightly by the shoulder.

He opened his eyes half way.

"Bettie," he muttered thickly, "I'm sleepy. Put me to bed."

He sank to the floor suddenly. Then, and not until then, did the really terrible truth begin to come to me, that Wally, the man I had just married in the most exalted of moods, was in a "drunken stupor."

I stared at him in horror. I pressed my hands to my temples and tried to check the leaping fear in my blood. I brushed the back of my hand over my eyes and tried to drive away the sight of his limp figure and his now flushed face. But I could not drive away the frightful reality.

I stood there two or three minutes, just staring at him. Then the tension in me broke, and I dropped into a great, soft chair, crying aloud frantically little cries of anguished fear.

I must have wept there for half an hour or more. Then bit by bit my self-control came back—came back to Elizabeth Woolsey, niece of Abigail and Sophronia Endicott, not to Bettie of the orange dress. I went mechanically to the little bathroom and washed away the mess of tears and make-up. At length I felt like Elizabeth and could face things with Elizabeth's trained calmness.

Why did I not run away, back to my drab but virtuous little room in the boarding-house, and leave my drunken husband in his drunken stupor? It is a natural question to ask. Perhaps it may seem as if it would have been the natural thing to do. I had run away from Aunt Abigail and Aunt Sophronia· why not from this new encumbrance? The answer is, strangely enough, that I had not gotten as far away from those austere aunts of mine as I thought. In fact, in that moment of my dire misery, I felt their presence almost as keenly as if they had actually been there. I felt their presence—*and* their condemnation. But those aunts of mine had never dodged a responsibility. How could I dodge mine, and run away?

No, I realized that I must stay and face it out. I must take up the horrible burden that my recklessness had put upon me, and carry it until my responsibility had ceased. Certainly I could not go away and leave Wally lying there on the floor, with his head propped uncomfortably against the chair. I summoned all my determination and tried to lift him to the bed. But I could not. He was too heavy. Then I got a pillow and put it under his head, and a blanket, which I threw over him.

After that I stood gazing down at him, disgusted and bitter, and cold with the horror of my situation. And I began to realize that it was I myself that was to blame. Certainly Wally had not asked me to go adventuring with him. In fact he had simply stepped in to save me from something far worse perhaps than what had occurred.

He had been straight and square and kind and honorable. His one crime had been that he became intoxicated. Was I innocent? Had I not been intoxicated too? Had not I made a disgraceful exhibition of myself in public restaurants?

With a sickening sense of self-condemnation, I went back to my big comforting chair, and sat down to think it all over

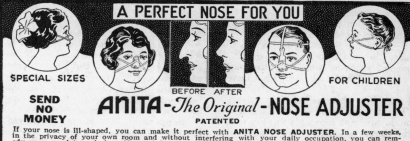

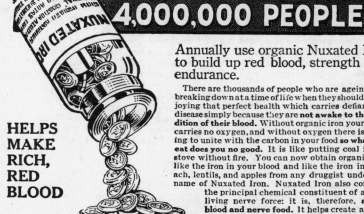

for the twentieth time, trying to find and face my duty. But the excitement of the evening had been too much for my endurance. The chair was soft and relaxed my taut nerves. Before I knew it, I was asleep.

I was wakened by a groan. It was broad daylight, and a beam of sunlight had lit full on Wally's face. He was waking up, and not enjoying the process. I turned away my head. I simply could not watch him.

HE suddenly gave a startled exclamation.

"Good Lord!"

I forced my eyes around to meet his astonished glance. He stared wide-eyed, with something as near terror as a real man can show.

"What the—" he began, and checked himself. Then, "How in the world did—" He broke off, thoroughly at a loss. I was too overcome to help him out.

For a moment we stared at each other blankly. Then he scrambled to his feet, brushing his tousled hair back.

"I—I don't know just what this means," he said in a strained voice. "I suppose I've been some disgusting kind of a beast. Oh, Good Lord, what have I done?"

I was very white and shaky.

"Don't you know—at all?" I asked tremulously, not moving from my chair.

He stared, and shook his head slowly.

"I suppose I got swinishly drunk," he said bitterly. "But what then? God! I don't remember anything—that would bring us two here. I remember that you and I started to have a glorious little adventure together. But I never meant to—that is—I—you quite evidently weren't the sort that—" he broke off in pained confusion.

I WAS having all I could do to keep from breaking down. In the cold light of the morning the thing seemed more than ever like some horrible, shameful nightmare. I bit my lip. I could feel my face growing hot with the shame of it. Wally's face took on a sudden horror.

"Did I—oh Lord, what haven't I done!" He dropped into a chair and let his face fall into his hands, his elbows resting on his knees. Then he looked up suddenly, his jaw set, his face drawn and white and grim. "I—give you my word I had no intention of—of—this happening," he said. "I—I'd give my right hand if I could change it."

I still sat biting my lip and holding back the impulse to break down. He stared at me earnestly, and went on.

"Won't you say something, Miss—" He paused, fumbling. "I don't even know your name. But, if you'd only say something, tell me what has happened; I'll—"

Then it came, the hysterical breakdown that I had been fighting back. I burst into tears, sobs, punctuated at sudden unexpected intervals with spasms of wild laughter that only made the weeping more heartbreaking. I was beside myself. I had no control.

SUDDENLY I felt his hand on my shoulder, then his arm slipping around me. Then I felt myself lifted to my feet as if I weighed nothing, while both of his arms closed round me, pressing me against his breast till I could hardly breathe.

"Steady, there. Steady," he was saying. "There isn't anything done that can't be helped. Stop crying till you hear what I have to—" He paused, evidently nonplussed, for I was still crying as hard as ever. "Oh, well," he said whimsically at last, "don't hold it in, then. Cry it out. But when you get through, just remember that I'm here, and that I've got a way out figured up." And he continued to hold me firmly in his arms.

Pretty soon I found myself taking a strange, incomprehensible comfort in the place against his broad breast that my head was pressed to. I continued to cry, but more softly, and finally I stopped. He patted my shoulder gently.

"There, now," he said with calm assurance. "You dry your eyes and we'll have a talk."

HE made no motion to put me away from him, though his hold on me had relaxed enough to show me I might step away, if I wanted to. But I felt strangely easier there, so I stayed. I had forgotten the hard, bitter thoughts of the night before, and remembered only the strength and gentleness of his arms and voice.

"Suppose we look at things straight," he said. "I guess we didn't either of us know just what we were doing, and I guess we don't know just what we've done. But here we are, and it's plainly something mighty serious. Now listen to my plan. I've enlisted to go to France—and Germany, I hope. Before I go, in fact today, we'll go and be married by a justice of the peace. Then—whatever happens—I mean on account of last night—you'll be all right. I'm well fixed—independent income. You'll be all right. Then when I come back—well, we can wait till then to decide about that. But I won't bother you. We'll do whatever you like."

He stopped, evidently waiting for my reply. I was strangely overcome. I had suspected already that he didn't remember about our midnight marriage. Now I knew it. And all the more I appreciated the thing he was proposing. Whatever he had done, he was on the square—facing his responsibility. I forgot about my recent misery, and thought suddenly of Wally on the firing line. Instinctively I clung a little closer to him.

"SO you see," he said, "it's going to be all right—reasonably all right, that is, and—" he caught his breath a little, "I'm awfully sorry I got you into this. Girl, I can't tell you how I wish I had had better sense. I wish I had a chance—" He stopped, and I could tell by his breathing that he was under great stress.

I drew slowly out of his embrace, and forced my eyes up to his. He was looking away, and his jaw was set very grimly.

"Listen," I said, and I know my voice was as strained as his, "you aren't to blame. And nothing has happened—such as you fear." His eyes flashed suddenly back at mine, with a great relief in them. I went on, wondering what he would say when he knew what had really happened. "I—I guess we both ought to be ashamed of—what happened last night. I—"

"But," he interrupted quickly, "you said—"

"Yes, I know. I mean our drinking and—all."

"Oh." Once more there was relief. "Yes, it was kind of awful—my part of it. But you needn't feel badly. You didn't disgrace yourself. I'm the only one to be ashamed."

We were still very near each other, and our eyes were studying each other silently all the time. I shook my head.

"No," I said, "I was worse than you—in a way. I let—" I broke off, trembling, but forced myself on again. "Something did happen, that I shouldn't have let happen. But you seemed to be all right then, though you don't remember now. I knew what was going on, and I—I let it go on. I— You—"

SOMEHOW I couldn't seem to tell him that he was tied to me by that crazy weakness of mine. His face took on a sudden concern and he took me swiftly by the shoulders.

"What happened?" he demanded. "What did I do?"

"You—married me," I cried, suddenly bursting into tears, and unaccountably stepping close and burying my face against his breast, "and I knew what was happening all the time—and I—let you. I—really I thought—you—knew too. Oh, I'm sorry. I'm sorry. I—I—" My shamed sobbing choked me then.

Once more his arms were about me, holding me tight. Once more I heard him say, "Steady, steady." Once more he waited till I was through. Then I heard him speaking.

"You say we were—married," he said slowly.

I nodded against his breast, trying to reach my eyes with my handkerchief.

"And you—knew it was happening—and let it go on because you thought I knew?"

Again I nodded. There was a long pause. A very long pause. Then,

"I don't deserve it," he said, "but won't you just let it stay like this, and—and when I get back—maybe give me a chance to—start fresh, and earn it?"

His voice was very low and very tender. A miracle had happened somehow or other. Foolish as I had been, wrong as we both had been, the thing was coming out right. As I stood there, and listened to him asking for a chance to start fresh, I knew I loved him, knew that he would never have to start fresh. Somehow I managed to tell him. Somehow we managed to grasp together the wonder of it all. And if ever two people breathed a united prayer of gratitude for forgiveness of sin, we two did that morning.

WALLY went away, and thank heaven came back—all a man, just as he was when he started, but with something new added, a certain extra steadiness in his eyes which told me that nothing was needed to make my cup of happiness perfect. That is, nothing except—something that is going to happen very soon, the thought of which has drawn us closer than ever.

●

OF ALL the lures which lead men and women to destruction none is more insidious than Dope. Its subtle influence begins as a beautiful dream, but before long the dream has become a hideous nightmare. Here are the facts from the life of a man Dope drove down to the depths.

I looked away as my fingers closed around the package

DOPE

SILENCE! A depressing, gloomy silence inside, while outside the green grass, the blue sky, the bright flowers, seemed to call to me to forget my sorrow and live. But I could not. For two weeks I had lived in a daze—hardly knowing what I was doing—wandering aimlessly about the house that had been the shelter of the dearest, sweetest woman God ever blessed the earth with—my mother. Two weeks ago she had died, and here I sat, elbows on the table, chin in my hand, staring, staring with apparently sightless eyes at the little framed verse which I had hung years before over her rocking chair where she used to sit and knit and darn my socks, when she was not doing the hundred and one other little things for my comfort that only a mother can do. I stared at the little framed verse and repeated to myself over and over again three of the lines:

"If I were damned of body and soul,
I know whose love would make me whole,
Mother o' mine, mother o' mine."

I could not suppress a groan as I arose wringing my hands helplessly. What would I do? What could I do? Her death had left an empty void in my life which I was sure could never be filled. I turned around with a start! I was sure I heard the soft rock, rock, rock, of the chair, and her sweet voice, softly humming as she knitted. But no, the chair was empty. I was going mad! I must do something, leave the house, forget, anything! Every little personal belonging of hers brought back her memory so vividly that I felt that I could no longer stand it. I must leave the house and forget, lest I lose my mind entirely. As soon as the decision was reached I started to fulfill it. Quickly and breathlessly, before I changed my mind, I packed a few necessities in my suitcase, brought it down stairs and left it on the table.

THEN I went around, fastened all the blinds securely and, with a sob that came from the bottom of my heart, I locked the door and walked down the white shell path to leave my old home and memories behind me. Diversion, sleep, forgetfulness; these were the things I craved and they were the things that eluded me. At night, in my bed, I would doze off, then suddenly wake with a start and stretch forth my arms for the phantom mother who smiled so sweetly at me from a vision.

So it went for two long months that seemed as years. From city to city I wandered, until finally I landed in the city of all cities, New York. Here, if anywhere, I would find forgetfulness. But a week in New York disappointed me, and one night, just at twilight, I found myself sitting on a bench in Central Park, my hands in my pockets, legs stretched out, carefully studying the toes of my shoes. I did not notice the stranger who sat down beside me until he spoke to me remarking that it was a wonderful evening. I looked up and saw a young man about my own age, twenty-five, smiling at me. I answered shortly that it was a nice evening, and resumed my brooding until finally he tapped me on the shoulder.

"Buddy, there's something wrong with you. You're up against it or something and I'm the greatest little joy peddler in the world. Let me in on the difficulty and I'll fix you up in jig time." I did not answer, but looked at him contemptuously.

"A woman?" he queried. I nodded
"Left you flat?"

I SIGHED, straightened up and answered simply, "My mother." He whistled softly and nodded. "I understand."

We just sat in silence for a few moments and then he spoke again. "I know just how you feel. Can't seem to pull yourself together. What you need is something to take your mind off it. Now, I'll tell you what I'll do. You give me the inside dope on the trouble and I'll guarantee to have you smiling and happy in a few days." His smile, his suave manner, his interest in my trouble, impressed me, and before I knew it I was telling him the whole story, how I had just received my degree of LL.B. from Yale, and was about to begin the practice of law when my only friend and relative, my mother, died. Finances? Well, there was a little home in Connecticut, and bonds worth about forty thousand in my safe deposit vault. He was so sympathetic and friendly that I was talking to him like an old friend before I knew it.

FINALLY he looked at his watch and, shaking hands, arose to go. "Well, I must toddle along, but before I go I want to put a proposition up to you. You meet me in the lobby of your hotel at nine-thirty tonight and I'll guarantee to take your mind off your troubles. Remember, there's a silver lining to every cloud. If you don't sleep, it won't be from sorrow, I'll guarantee that." I agreed to meet him in the lobby of the hotel at nine-thirty; in fact I would have agreed to anything under the sun that had the least promise of diversion in it.

At nine-thirty I went down to the lobby and found him smilingly waiting for me. Leon was his name and, offering me a cigar, he put his arm through mine and off we went like a couple of long-lost brothers, where or to what I did not know. He had a taxi waiting out-

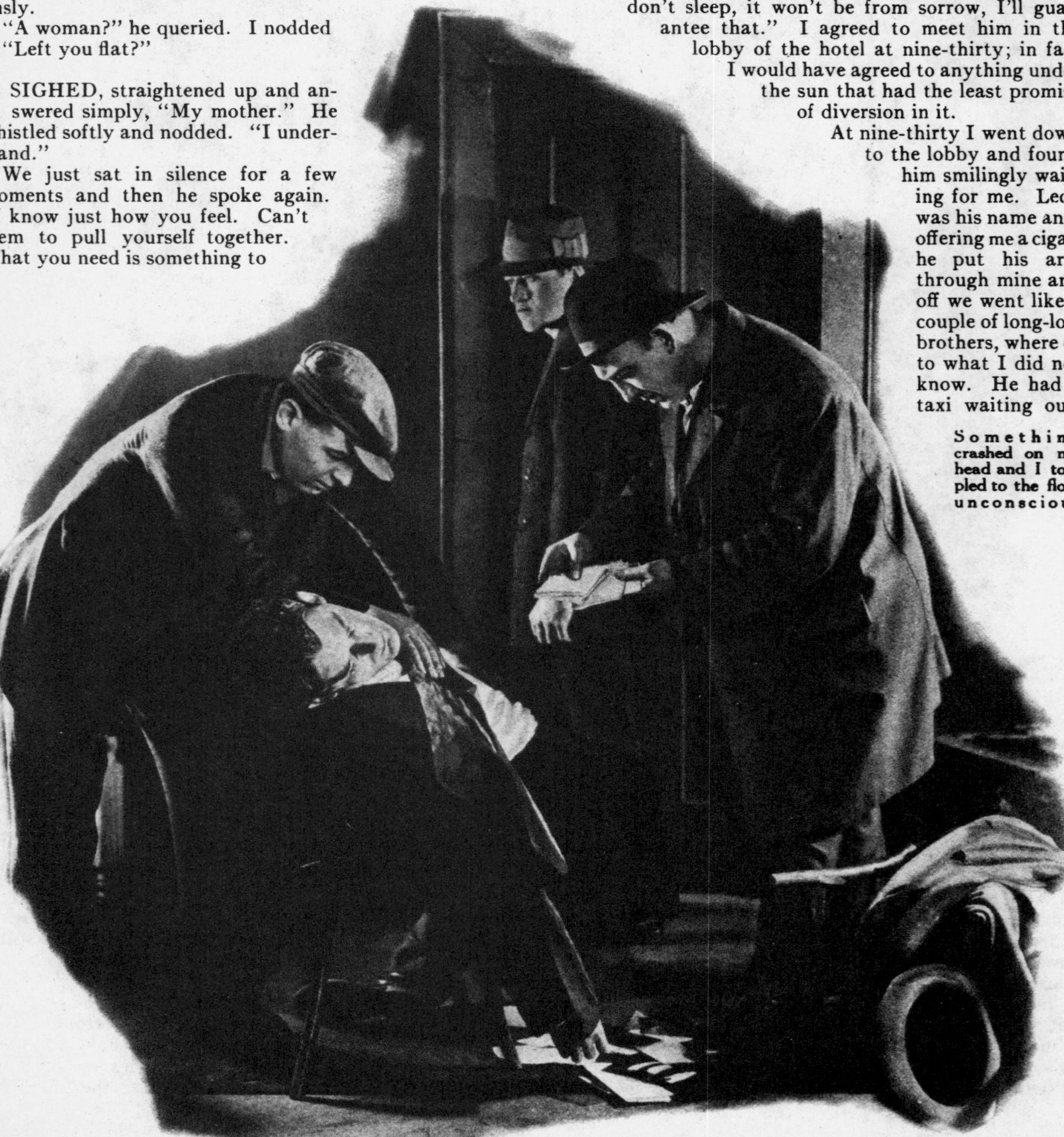

Something crashed on my head and I toppled to the floor unconscious

side and we drove for about ten minutes, when we stopped in a neighborhood strange to me. All this time I never gave a thought to the reason which would prompt a total stranger to take an interest in me, but I was soon to find out.

We descended a flight of stone steps into a cellar café, and as my guide opened the door we stepped into a dimly lighted room filled with tobacco smoke. I stood there blinking for a moment, and then gradually I could perceive the figures dancing around in a

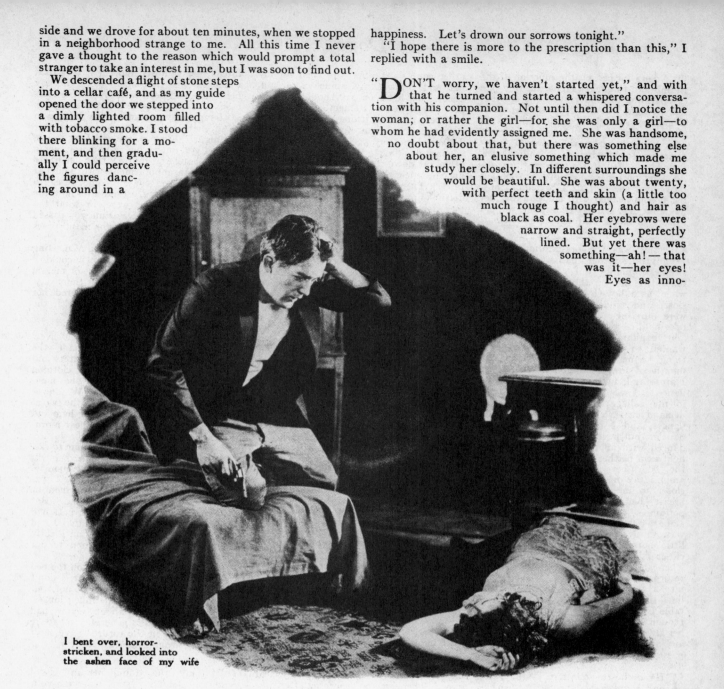

I bent over, horror-stricken, and looked into the ashen face of my wife

tiny cleared space in the center of the room, with tables and chairs clustered around it. Painted women smoking cigarettes; paunched men with jowls shaved to a beefsteak red; short-haired women and long-haired men; all were there, but none paid the slightest attention to us as we wormed our way through the chairs to a table at the edge of the dance floor near the orchestra.

I COULD hardly hear him as he introduced me to the two women sitting at the table, so great was the din from the jazz blared forth by the orchestra. Dancers in suggestive and almost motionless embraces slowly milled past us; portly gentlemen, evidently pillars of finance, danced with young girls whose set smiles and painted faces bore the unmistakable stamp of their trade.

I nodded, muttered something, and took the seat which he motioned me to. A whispered order to a waiter with a bartender's dirty apron tied around his waist, and Leon turned to me, rubbing his hands and smiling.

"Well, my friend, here we are on the first lap toward happiness. Let's drown our sorrows tonight."

"I hope there is more to the prescription than this," I replied with a smile.

"DON'T worry, we haven't started yet," and with that he turned and started a whispered conversation with his companion. Not until then did I notice the woman; or rather the girl—for she was only a girl—to whom he had evidently assigned me. She was handsome, no doubt about that, but there was something else about her, an elusive something which made me study her closely. In different surroundings she would be beautiful. She was about twenty, with perfect teeth and skin (a little too much rouge I thought) and hair as black as coal. Her eyebrows were narrow and straight, perfectly lined. But yet there was something—ah!—that was it—her eyes! Eyes as inno-

cent as a baby's, and yet in their depth there was a look of weariness, or worldliness—eyes large and clear, but eyes that might have seen fifty years of life, instead of twenty. Yes, it was her eyes that puzzled me, they were the mystery. She noticed me studying her, and with her chin on her hand, she turned her eyes full on me and smiled. "Well?" I found no adequate answer for a moment, then I blurted out, "I was just noticing your eyes. They are young, and yet they are old. They are the eyes of a perfectly innocent child, and yet they are the eyes of one old in the ways of the world."

SHE smiled and answered without taking her eyes from me, "Evidently you don't know New York. I am young, but a girl alone in this city is very apt to become sophisticated very soon."

Further conversation was interrupted by Leon tapping me on the arm. I turned around and he looked down at his right hand held just below the level of the table. My eyes followed his, and there in the *(Continued)* little delta formed by the junction of the thumb and forefinger reposed a tiny pile of sparkling white crystals. I started! I knew right away what it was—cocaine. There was no doubt about it. I hesitated for a moment, and then fascinated, drawn to it by some unknown power, I threw discretion to the winds and, bending over, I slowly sniffed it through my nostrils. Ah, I remember the look of horror on her face when she saw it; I remember how her bosom heaved with emotion and her lips went dry, and parted as if she wanted to scream out a warning but dared not!

So this was the prescription! Well, anything rather than weeks of more sleepless nights. I felt choked—it reminded me of the sensation I felt when, as a boy, I had been closed in a closet and suddenly released, my lungs were bursting. It was just starting to take hold of me. Then I felt light, jubilant, exhilarated. I wanted to sing. I wanted to dance, action, action, anything to make up for the weeks and months of slowly killing, brooding silence. I arose and, taking her by the arm, we danced. I was considered a good dancer in my college days; I was always in demand at the class proms and frat dances, and I have danced with good dancers, but never before or since have I danced with anyone like her. She was light as a feather and as we floated over the floor her arm tightened slightly around my neck. I drew her a little closer to me—her head rested on my breast—her hair touched my face, a faint perfume— This was living! We were alone as far as I was concerned, there was no one in that dirty smoke-filled little room but Lota and myself. Closer, closer I held her, entranced, enraptured. Then the music stopped. We did not return to the same table, but I drew her into a tiny booth, a number of which lined the room on one side, and across the table I took her hands in mine. I felt as though I had known her forever, had loved her always and she was mine, mine alone, and I took a fierce pride in the joy of possession.

The orchestra soon struck up a waltz, and I arose to dance again with her. As she held up her arms, she smiled a little smile as if to reassure herself, a smile of mingled fear and pity for me. She looked so beautiful at that instant that I could not restrain myself. I did not want to restrain myself—I put my arm slowly around her waist as if to dance, and then placing the other arm around her neck, I crushed her to me in a fierce, passionate embrace. She did not resist but lifted her lips to mine. They were cool, delicious, refreshing, then in an instant they were hot, burning, passionate; our souls seemed to be drawn from our bodies and welded together as one through our lips.

"Let's get out of here," I whispered hoarsely. "You don't belong here any more than I do. Let's go where we can be alone—anywhere—only don't stay here." She nodded and we danced across the room to the table where the

other couple sat. As I reached for my hat and topcoat my guide arose and, placing his hand on my shoulder, whispered in my ear, "Remember, that stuff will wear off soon; it doesn't last forever. Better let me fix you up with a supply." I reached into my pocket and pulled out a handful of bills. He went over to the table, sat down for an instant, and I saw his hand meet those of the girl at the next table. Then he turned back to me and deftly slipped a small package toward me. I looked away as my fingers closed around it.

Outside I hailed a taxi, and to the driver's query for directions, I shouted, "Anywhere," and in an instant we were out of the traffic of the city and racing, I knew not where. The memory of that ride will remain with me as long as I live. With my arms around her I told her that I loved her, that she was all mine, told her in crazy passionate words—and she a girl I had known only a few hours. For about an hour we rode, faster and faster, around curves! A large touring car came racing around a curve; a curse, the grinding of brakes, a shout in the dark as it whizzed by us, and I merely laughed and shouted to our driver to go faster. Then reaching into my coat pocket, I took out one of the little bottles and, with one arm still around the girl, I savagely pulled the cork out with my teeth and welded another link in the chain which later bound me so mercilessly.

The next morning I wakened with a strange feeling—not exactly a depressing feeling. I was in a strange room, and at the window a strange girl sat staring into space. She started at the noise of my movement and, with her hands to her breast, she watched me breathlessly as I stared at her, trying to collect my thoughts. Little by little I pieced together the events of the night before. There had been a ride, and—yes, there had been a marriage!

Then I remembered and reaching for my coat beside the bed I slowly and with almost a religious reverence, again breathed through my nostrils the burning cursed spawn of the devil which seared my soul. Everything was perfectly clear now. There was no "morning after." I was as good as new, and remembered everything. We had been married by a justice of the peace in a little town in Connecticut. I looked up at her and smiled. Reassured by my smile she came over and sat on the edge of the bed. "You are sure you're not sorry, Billy boy?" she asked, watching my face eagerly for any sign of regret. But I was yet young and honest and when I looked at her I was very, very sure that I was not sorry. "No, girlie, I'm not sorry. We're married and I'm glad. I remember everything very well and I'm sure neither of us will be sorry. I know you'll make a good wife and I'm surely going to try to make you take the place of my mother." With a little sob she fell into my arms, and I kissed her and whispered, "My wife." Most of the morning was spent in telling one another all about ourselves. She had made her own living since she was

fifteen, her widowed mother having died when she was that age. Until the day before she had been employed in the coatroom of the hotel where I was stopping.

"I suppose you wonder how I came to be in that terrible place where we met last night. Eleanor, the girl I was with, pointed you out to me as you were going into the hotel and told me that her friend Leon had an appointment with you that night and asked me to come along to complete the party. I didn't know the kind of people they were, or what the place was like, and every time you passed you looked so sad, I thought many times that I would like to meet you. So when she offered me the opportunity of meeting you, and talking to you, I just couldn't resist. You don't think badly of me, do you, dear, because I went there last night?" I kissed her and assured her that she was the sweetest little girl in the world.

Our honeymoon was spent in New York. For weeks we made the rounds of midnight shows, cabarets and suppers. I bought her jewelry, clothing —anything, everything that she mentioned I had sent to her. We never bothered with anyone else, just the two of us, going, going, dancing, flying here and there from morning until the next morning with never a thought of the future. There was no such thing as time to me, an hour was as a second, a second was eternity. I used the drug continuously, and buoyed by this stimulant, I was always ready for whatever excitement or adventure there was to be found. But with Lota it was different. Our path had been so reckless and headlong that I had not noticed the strain on her, until early one morning when we returned to our apartment from a cabaret.

She threw her cloak wearily on the bed and turned to me. "Billy, dear, I don't know whether you realize it or not, but things can't go on like this much longer. I'm worn out, and it's about time we had a talk about things in general. What are we going to do in the future? We can't be running around like this forever."

I put my arms around her and kissed her. "Don't you start worrying your little head about how things are going to be. This is our time to play and when it comes time to settle down I'll be ready to settle down with you."

"But, honey," she replied, "can't you see that things are getting worse and worse every day? You spend your money like a drunken sailor. If I look at a piece of jewelry, you buy it right away. If I look at a pair of shoes, you have six pairs sent up. You don't know how much money you have spent and you don't know how much you have. Every few days you write to your attorney and sell some more of the bonds your mother left you. What are we going to do?"

I pinched her cheeks playfully and tried to reassure her. I painted a beautiful picture of our future—how I would be a successful lawyer, and she should be a lady living in luxury. Dreams, dreams, that's all I had. Luxury and happiness for her, that's all I thought about. She walked over to the window and looked down at the street below. Then suddenly she turned and faced me.

"Another thing, Billy, that I simply must talk to you about. You have been using that drug now for weeks and weeks. At first I did not mention it, because I was afraid that was what held you; that if you stopped taking it I would lose you, but, Billy, you've got to know that I love you so much that, even if it meant my losing you, you've got to stop it! Oh, can't you see that day by day it gets a stronger grip on you? You use more and more every time, you crave it, you can't get along without it. Please, Billy."

I DROPPED my head in shame: I had never thought of it that way before. She continued, "It isn't too late if you stop now, but I am afraid to think of the future if you continue to use it." She put her hands on my shoulders and pleaded with me piteously to give it up, for her sake, for the sake of my mother's sacred memory. The mention of my mother touched a chord which had been silent for weeks. Again I could see the little framed card over her rocker with Kipling's immortal lines, and unconsciously I repeated them to myself:

"If I were damned of body and soul,
I know whose love would make me
    whole,
Mother o' mine, mother o' mine."

Tears began to trickle down my face. At last I realized that I was a slave—a slave to cocaine, and I was intelligent enough to know what that meant if I kept it up. I was experiencing a period of depression which follows the slowing down of the stimulating action of the drug.

I turned to her wearily. "What shall I do?"

"There's only one thing we can do, Billy, and that's to go away somewhere. I'm worn out, and as long as you can see Leon any time and get more, you're not going to cure yourself. Remove the temptation and you can do it. You're sure to experience a reaction sometime. You've often spoken of your mother's little country home. Surely, in such a place, with her memory, you can rid yourself of the habit before it is too late."

IT didn't take me long to decide. I was awake at last, and was afraid only that it was too late.

I put my arm around her. "All right, honey, we'll go back tomorrow. I want to do the right thing and I'm just beginning to realize that I've started off on the wrong track. We will pack tonight and be on our way tomorrow."

Taking my face in both hands she kissed me and then patted my cheek, "That's a good boy, Billy, we'll start to pack right away."

About that time my nerves began to bother me for another shot of the stuff. Just one more before we went, what harm could it do? Going into the next room I poured myself a dose of cocaine and after sniffing it, I returned to the room where Lota was busy hunting through drawers and began the packing operations.

I pulled out a drawer, and there, reposing in the corner under some linens, were two tiny bottles of cocaine. In a flash I

Is there a New Fashion in Rouge?

Emphatically, yes!—bright colors in costumes and settings are influencing the modern woman toward a more daring and colorful complexion.

A NEW fashion in rouge?—it is here! Appearing first in Vienna but a few months since, this new *mode* has traversed that swift, mysterious route that links smart women everywhere, from Deauville to the Riviera, to Paris, New York, Hollywood.

Decidedly, the modern trend of fashion in brilliant contrasts of pure color, in both costume and decorations is exerting its positive influence on the cheeks and lips of the modern woman.

And why not? Surely amid the colorful splendor of blazing fabrics and flaring lights, the soft rose tones of the complexion's natural flush fade into a totally unnatural pallor. So that the high color produced by the *modern rouge* merely restores the vivacity of nature.

VIVID—the New Shade in Rouge

For many months now, Princess Pat, Ltd., always alert to the latest modes and developments of beauty's toilette, has been apace with this newest trend.

Now, thanks to the countless experiments and tests conducted by the Princess Pat Chemists, a new and marvelous shade known as Princess Pat VIVID, has been produced, a deep and brilliant *intensification* of nature's own rose tone—so daring that its wearer will gleam with emphatic beauty amid the most colorful surroundings; yet so true to nature, that when sparingly applied and softly blended, even the most conservative need not hesitate to wear it.

Princess Pat VIVID is the chosen shade of the ultra-fashionable in these ultra-colorful days. Yet the vogue for Vivid Rouge has not by any means lessened the popularity of that other Princess Pat triumph, English Tint, whose bright orange in the compact, changes so miraculously to rose on the cheeks, and blends so delicately with nature's skin tones on blonde or brunette, whether in day or evening light. Princess Pat English Tint will always be widely popular because of its perfect harmony with all types of beauty.

There are some complexions so delicately childlike as to require only the softest wild-rose flush. For these Princess Pat Medium Rouge is particularly harmonious, especially with those dainty pastel shades of costume. But always remember—

The essence of beauty is the texture of the skin. Therefore, whether your preference is for the new and fashionable Vivid, the popular English Tint, or delicate Medium Rouge, *all* of the Princess Pat shades are *compact* or dry rouges. This means that their base is Almond, just as in Princess Pat Almond Base Powder—thus, not only beautifying but actually beneficial to your skin's fine grained texture.

The Princess Pat way of applying color. The Princess Pat method has won almost as wide acceptance among beautiful women as Princess Pat rouges themselves.

Apply in V-shape, the point of the V toward the nose—beginning at the temple, put the color on slanting forward and downward to the high point of the cheekbone, then backward and downward—leaving a space in front of the ear entirely clear of color. Blend softly, and you have duplicated Nature's own design. For lasting, even waterproof result, apply your Tint before powdering.

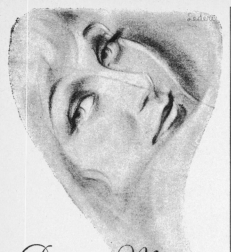

had put one bottle into my coat pocket and, holding the other up for Lota to see, I pulled out the cork, walked to the bathroom, and poured the contents down the waste pipe. "There, that's done. Now I guess I'll be all right."

I didn't realize I was cheating, not only her, but myself; I kept the other bottle because some devil from hell would not let me destroy it. I wanted to send it after the other bottle, but I couldn't. Oh, there was no struggle, no mental anguish, or anything like that. I just kept it.

The next day we went home. There was hustle and bustle and cleaning and dusting, and the excitement of opening up the house. My mind was occupied and it was late in the afternoon before I began to crave the stuff. Then my nerves began to bother me. It seemed as if tiny ants were crawling all over me. I yawned continuously, supplementing each yawn with a shudder. I wanted the cocaine, but I had resolved not to take it again and I kept my resolution—for about an hour. Then I went out behind the house, where with trembling hands, I took a dose and returned to the house. In a very few moments Lota's sharp eye detected the change in me.

"Billy, have you been cheating? Don't tell me you are starting again."

SHE was panic-stricken, and even now I can see the wildly appealing look in her eyes as she stood aghast, hands pressed to her breast, waiting for my answer.

I could not answer. I merely hung my head in shame. Then I lied. I told her that I had merely kept one little dose; that it was all gone and I was through with it for good. She did not question me, but took my word for it, apparently dropping the matter right there, although I could see she was worried, and I was worried too.

Little by little my supply diminished, until I found myself one day staring at an empty little bottle. Gone—all gone! Now I would have to leave it alone. I was glad, fiercely glad, and with a curse I threw the empty bottle out of the window. All that day and all that night my tortured nerves drove me nearly crazy. The next day I could stand it no longer, and going to Lota I told her that certain legal business would take me to New York for a day or two. She looked at me quickly, and right away knew what the trouble was. She knew I was going for more dope. "Billy, are you going to give up without a struggle? Don't I mean anything to you at all? Am I worth fighting for? The day will come when you will have to choose between me and that stuff. Don't give up without a fight, Billy, be a man."

I clenched my teeth as she continued, "You know, Billy, that I wouldn't leave you for anything in the world. I always dreamed of having a man like you, but I always met the other kind. I was almost discouraged when you came along. Your fight is my fight, and I'll stick with you through everything, but, Billy, for my sake and the sake of your mother, you mustn't give up so easily. Won't you try? Please."

I could not answer. All my world crumbled in front of me. I knew I was

licked. I knew that in spite of her I would go to New York again in quest of cocaine, and with a husky, "I'll try," I left the room.

That night, while she slept, I sneaked out and was on my way to New York. It would only be for a day or two I was sure, and then I would return. I had my two lovers to choose between, my wife and dope—and I chose dope.

Somehow I found myself again in the cellar café. I sat down in a dim corner, and hailed the waiter who now knew me. I asked him if Leon could be found anywhere. Could he be found? He should say he could! Leon just got a stretch up the river for peddling dope. I was panic-stricken. What should I do? I did not know where to go for the stuff; none of the others knew me, and a drive by the Federal authorities on dope peddlers had sent most of them scurrying to their holes. I pleaded with the waiter to tell me where to go. At first he was adamant, could take no chances but, finally, the sight of a twenty-dollar bill thawed him out.

"I'LL tell you," he whispered. "I don't know anyone who is handling 'snow,' there isn't so much call for it, but I can fix you up with a coupla decks of morphine. There's a guy here that handles it, but he won't do any business except in the men's room. He's a cautious bird, and if he gets the least suspicious, down the pipes it goes. You go in there and I'll tell him you're all right and send him in."

I went into the dirty foul-smelling room placarded, "Gents," and waited. In a moment a rat-faced youth shuffled in, looked around and then quickly motioned me into one of the stalls with him. "How much stuff do you want?" he queried.

"I'll take all you've got," I answered.

He stroked his chin and considered. "Well, I got a moll out there who has about twenty decks tucked away, and they go for five bucks a deck."

"I'll take it all," I hastily exclaimed and pulled out a roll of bills.

HE went out, returning in a few minutes and pushed a bundle of tiny paper packages into my hand. Without a word, I handed him the money and took the package.

"Tony tells me you've been hitting the snow. This is a little different, so I'm slipping you this needle and fixings so you will be all jake."

With feverish haste I made my way to a cheap hotel nearby and went to my room. I prepared the stuff as directed, and then injected it into my arm. It had the desired effect of soothing my nerves, although totally different in action from cocaine. Cocaine is stimulating, exhilarating. It makes one arrogant, superior, leader of everyone and everything. Morphine is soothing; it makes one calm, dignified, above the motley crowd.

After several days in that cheap hotel, I decided to make the acquaintance of several peddlers, so that when my supply ran out I would know where to go.

I thought of Lota in a sort of way, but Lady Morphia is jealous; she will not share you with another sweetheart and once she enfolds you, the soft white entwining arms that once looked so inviting

(Continued)

Grow Hair Quickly at Home—This new Amazing Way

In 30 Days~Or No Cost!

By ALOIS MERKE
Founder of the famous Merke Institute, Fifth Avenue, New York

I DON'T care how thin your hair may be now—I am guaranteeing this remarkable invention to bring a new growth of hair to you in 30 days—or it doesn't cost you one cent.

Even if one-third the thousands who try this successful method were dissatisfied—I could never continue in business. Yet every day, in all sorts of cases this wonderful scientific discovery is bringing back hair to people who despaired of ever having any again.

I'm not saying it will grow hair for everybody. There are cases that even my invention cannot help. Yet so great is the percentage of cases that are successful that I am

willing to make this offer. In 30 days you will be satisfied that your hair is coming back—or *the trial costs you absolutely nothing!*

Just 10 minutes a day!

My invention is scientific. It proves that when hair falls out it is usually because the roots are dormant. *Not dead*—just asleep. All they need is a stimulant to waken and nourish them. Formerly there was no way of getting down to these dormant roots. Tonics, salves, etc., failed to grow hair because they only treated the surface skin. But now, at last, there is a way to awaken and nourish dormant hair roots. And this method is embodied in the treatment I now offer you to try 30 days at my risk. It consists of a new invention which by the application of special light rays, opens the pores leading to the roots, enabling a highly nourishing food to get right down to them. Very often new hair is seen after the first few days use.

Remember—no one need know about it. The treatment takes place at home. On goes the cap for 10 minutes a day—in your own home. You'll enjoy taking the treatments, which are very soothing. No trouble or inconvenience of any kind. You keep it up for 30 days and then—if you are not amazed with the wonderful results—if you aren't simply delighted with the new hair produced—your money will be refunded completely.

Others Pay Hundreds of' Dollars

The Merke Institute, Fifth Avenue, which was founded by me has treated social and stage celebrities that paid as high as $500 for the results secured. Yet here—thru this latest invention, you get the same results by a few moments of daily home treatment—and the cost is only a few pennies a day. Treatment can be taken in any home in which there is electricity.

Free Booklet Explains All

If you are at all interested in your personal appearance, take the trifling trouble of filling in and mailing this coupon. It will bring you—absolutely free of cost or obligation—an interesting 32-page booklet "The New Way to Make Hair Grow," describing in detail my new invention.

This book contains very helpful information on hair health, and shows what my treatment has done for others.

No matter how bald you are—no matter what unsuccessful treatments you've had—this book will prove of invaluable interest. *Mail the coupon now.*

ALLIED MERKE INSTITUTES, INC.
Dept. 51, 512 Fifth Avenue, New York City

soon turn to gripping, choking, breaking tendrils that wrap themselves around you —body and soul!

I don't know whethere it was days, weeks or months before my supply ran out. I lived in a half stupor, but now that my reputation was established I had no difficulty in securing a further supply. I had just purchased a supply of five decks from a new peddler that afternoon, and was horror-stricken to find out that I had been tricked. Nothing but talcum— at five dollars a deck. I was raving and cursing my luck when a knock sounded on the door, and I opened it. There stood Lota.

OH, I've seen expressions of pain and expressions of sorrow but, to my dying day, I'll never forget the expression of indescribable agony on that little girl's face. I was speechless and backed away from her. She entered without saying a word, and closing the door stood with her back to it.

"Billy, I stayed away as long as I could. I hoped against hope that you would come back, that you had a little spark of love left for me. And night after night I have prayed that God would give you strength, but you never came. It was your answer to my query whether you loved me or not. But, Billy, whether you love me or not, I can't leave you. I have read somewhere, 'Man's love is of man's life a thing apart, 'Tis woman's whole existence!' Your battles are my battles, and I'll stay with you even if I have to sink into the stench and mire myself."

I didn't answer—I couldn't answer. I sat on the edge of the bed and wept and with her arm about my neck, she wept with me. I had lost—lost entirely and without a struggle.

WELL, she stayed there with me week after week, taking care of me, watching me sink lower and lower into the clutches of the drug, but never once did she whimper, never did she complain. I had lost all ambition now, I had no desire to break away from the stuff, and then again I was convinced that it was useless. I had been to the library and read all sorts of medical books on the subject, reports of the Smithsonian Institution on the psychological effect of drugs, the cure of the drug habit, and I was convinced that I was incurable. My will was dead. Day by day Lota looked worse and worse. I was killing her little by little, tearing the very heart out of her, but my mental, moral and physical condition was such that the thought of such things never occurred to me. I was beginning to attract attention on the streets. Once an officer approached me as if to stop me, and with my heart beating a terrific tattoo on my ribs, I rushed through dirty alleys and back yards back to my room. I realized that to be found with the stuff in my possession meant jail. Then and there I resolved to leave New York. I would cash in all the bonds I owned, take the money, put in a large supply of morphine and move to another city. California suggested itself and immediately I decided that California it would be. I would take Lota there so she could recuperate. In a few days, all the details were settled and the money was deposited to my credit in a New York bank. I had

the necessary letters of identification, and I had made arrangements with Peter, the rat-faced youth, to get me four large tins of morphine. That would be enough to last me for a long, long time, I thought. I never thought of concealing any of the details from Lota. She had been such a quiet patient soul that I never gave it a thought that she might object.

On the day appointed I drew every penny I owned in the world, about thirty thousand dollars, out of the bank and went from the bank to my room. I took off my coat and shoes and lay down on the bed to rest before I went out to meet Pete. I dozed off after an injection, and Lota woke me at a quarter of five. My appointment was for five o'clock and hurriedly putting on my coat, I rushed out. I met Pete as arranged, and he informed me that a deal of this size would have to be put over by his boss, who handled the large quantities. He asked me if I had the money, and putting my hand into my inside coat pocket I felt the envelope there and assured him that I had plenty of money.

WE got into a taxi outside and rode for about ten minutes through winding streets and dismal alleys, finally stopping at a dilapidated shack on the water front. We got out and I followed Pete inside. On the second floor he rapped at the door, and at a gruff "Come in" we entered. At the table sat two other men who, I surmised, were the ones who handled the stuff. They motioned me to a chair, and after talking over the price of the stuff, they sent Pete to a cupboard to get it. He passed behind me, something crashed on the top of my head, a streak of flame seemed to shoot across my eyes, and I toppled to the floor, unconscious. When I came to, I was alone. The room was empty, and my coat pockets had been ripped inside out in their mad search for money. I thought of the thirty thousand dollars which I had in the envelope in my inside pocket and, panic-stricken, I grabbed the envelope on the floor beside me. Gone! Every cent I owned in the world was gone. I was all out of the dope and now I had no money to buy more. In a daze I made my way back to the restaurant. I must have been unconscious for over an hour, for it was nearly seven o'clock when I got there. I called Tony and asked him if Pete had come back. He said that he had not seen him and did not know where to look for him. Then I told him what had happened, that I had been robbed by Pete and two other men of thirty thousand dollars in cash, that I had no money to buy dope and I needed it the worst way. He shrugged his shoulders, smiled in disbelief and walked away, saying there was nothing he could do. I buried my face in my arms and tried to collect my thoughts. Sick, broke, and craving drugs, I couldn't work, I had to get it somehow. In a few minutes Tony came back, and taking off his apron sat down beside me.

"Listen, kid, I've seen guys like you up against it before. I know that they'll go out and steal or kill or anything to get that stuff. You're in tough shape now, and I know it's hell. Tomorrow you'll be down with a 'Yen' if you don't get it tonight. Now, there's only one place I know where you can get it and that's off

Izzy Glantz. He gets it off the boats in big lots. Most of it is synthetic stuff from Germany, but what's the difference? He's got it and you need it."

"But I have no money," I answered listlessly.

"No, but you have something that will get to Izzy quicker than money. You know, he's the greatest fall guy in the world when it comes to pretty women. He's pretty fat now, and not so nice, but a good-looking woman can have anything he's got, and that dame of yours is a winner on looks. If you can get her to go see Izzy she can get the stuff from him."

I walked home wearily and threw myself on the bed. I had to have dope, that's all there was to it, if I had to kill to get it. Tony's way was to me the logical answer to the problem, Lota had to be sacrificed, if necessary. My soul was dead and I had reached my decision. I called her over to me and told her what had happened. She merely sat there and stared at me with tired eyes.

"YOU know, Lota, I'll go crazy if I don't get some stuff for my nerves. You always said that you loved me, loved me more than your life, and that you'd go through hell for me. There's only one place I can get that stuff and it's over to Izzy Glantz's. The only one he'll give it to without money is a woman. I leaned over and grasped her by the shoulder. "Lota," I whispered hoarsely, "You've got to go over to Izzy Glantz's and get me some morphine. And if you ever loved me, don't come back without it."

She sprang to her feet, eyes blazing fires of indignation. "I said that I loved Billy Manning—he was a man. I still love him, but you, you're not Billy Manning, you're a beast who would not hesitate to sell the soul of his wife, send her out on the streets just to satisfy his own vile craving for drugs."

"Then you won't go and get the stuff?" I screamed, grinding my teeth, and grasping her savagely by the arm.

"No, not for you, or any other foul beast."

I SAW red, I lost my mind, I could think of nothing but the fact that this woman who had it in her power to get me morphine had refused. She was not my wife, she was no one that I knew, she was someone or something that had denied me the drug I needed and with a curse I struck her with all my strength in the face. Yes, I had at last reached the lowest level, lower than a beast, lower than anything I could think of. Dazed, hardly believing my eyes, I watched her recoil to the wall, the tiny trickle of crimson from the corner of her mouth slowly widening and dripping to her bosom. Then her head dropped, the fire died from her eyes and she slowly turned and walked out of the room. I knew that I had killed the purest, greatest love on earth.

Now, indeed, I was alone! No! Not alone, for already the crazy phantoms produced by my sick and overworked body and brain were beginning to make their appearance. The excitement of the moment had been the last straw. I was mad. From the corner of the room there issued a blue smoke and from it appeared my accepted sweetheart, Lady Morphia.

He found her at last!

"FAIR STRANGER—I know who you are," he smiled; "you are a rose disguised as a Beautiful Lady!"

She was beautiful and radiant indeed, for she had learned from Madame Jeannette how to select the proper shade of Pompeian Beauty Powder and to apply it correctly for youthful beauty.

Pompeian Beauty Powder is used the world over by women who find that it meets every requirement of beauty, protection, and purity.

Mme. Jeannette's Beauty Treatment

First, a bit of Pompeian Day Cream to make your powder cling and prevent "shine." *Next,* apply Pompeian Beauty Powder to all exposed portions of face, neck and shoulders. It will give your skin that lovely effect of rose petal softness. *Lastly,* just a touch of Pompeian Bloom to bring the exquisite glow of youthful color.

Shade Chart for selecting your correct tone of Pompeian Beauty Powder:

Medium Skin: The average American woman has this type of skin, and should use the Naturelle shade.

Olive Skin: This skin generally accompanies dark hair and eyes. It is rich in tone and should use Rachel shade.

Pink Skin: This is the youthful, rose-tinted skin, and should use the Flesh shade. This type of skin is usually found with light hair, or red hair.

White Skin: If your skin is quite without color, use White Powder. Only the very white skin should use White Powder in the daytime.

At all toilet counters 60c. New thin-model compact $1.00. (Slightly higher in Canada.)

Mme. Jeannette
Specialiste en Beaute

Get 1925 Panel
and Four Samples

This new 1925 Pompeian Art Panel, "Beauty Gained is Love Retained," size 28 x 7½. Done in color by a famous artist; worth at least 50c. We send it with samples of Pompeian Beauty Powder, Bloom, Day Cream and Night Cream for only 10c. With these samples you can make many interesting beauty experiments. Use the coupon now.

Pompeian Beauty Powder

"Don't Envy Beauty— Use Pompeian"

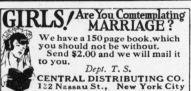

I watched, breatless as the apparition approached me. She was beautiful, oriental, bewitching, smiling sensuously at me as she stretched forth her white arms to me. I stretched out my arms to her and she changed into a terrible demon, with low slanting brow, snarling fangs dripping blood, her body covered with festering sores. I shrank as her long tapering fingers reached for my throat and, with a scream, lapsed into unconsciousness.

WHEN I wakened I was stretched on the floor of the room. I began to think feverishly. I had jewelry which I could pawn—what a fool I had been, why didn't I think of that before. I gathered together my watch, fraternity pin and a gold signet ring, and a few moments later slunk out of a pawn shop clutching fourteen dollars in my dirty hand. I made my way to the address given by the waiter and, after considerable dickering, I managed to wheedle three decks out of Izzy. I went back to my room, took a large dose and began to feel a little better. I could at least think. I had three decks of M., which would not last me very long, and I did not want to have the same thing happen over again. There was only one thing left for me to do, and that was to go back to Connecticut, sell my house and land, and I would again be on Easy Street. I took my suit case, packed everything I owned into it, and pawned it for enough to get me home.

What a difference between my homecoming and the day when I left, a young, clean, healthy youth. Here I was, returning broken down physically, mentally and morally. My soul was dead, and I pushed my way roughly through the door into the house that once had been the home of my mother. On the wall there was the little framed verse, and again I found myself repeating over and over the lines:

"If I were damned of body and soul,
I know whose love would make me
        whole,
Mother o' mine, mother o' mine."

Damned of body and soul! Yes, I was damned; I had not only ruined myself but had been willing to sacrifice my wife. I sat down in my mother's chair and thought. Suicide? I was too cowardly. I didn't even have the courage to take my miserable carcass out of the world. That was not the way out—there was nothing left for me to do but wait for the end.

FOR a week I did not leave the house. I ate hardly anything, and kept alive only by the ever increasing doses of morphine. My brain was weakened and night after night I would awake in a foul sweat and swear that the apparition which my diseased brain had conjured up was real. Night after night she came, the same horrible figure with the long tapering fingers clutching at my throat—and I would awaken with a scream; go rushing about the house, eventually to find quiet in a dose of morphine. I actually believed that the hideous figure was real—that she intended to strangle me. I found a revolver and loaded it, and kept it with me always. Darkness found me panic-stricken, and I never slept without locking and bolting my door. My reason was leaving me, nature was demanding her

price for the abuse I had heaped on her handiwork.

About two weeks after my arrival at the old home I had taken a dose of morphine and was lying on a couch in the kitchen with my revolver under the pillow. My supply was nearly exhausted and I was trying to make my poor brain function sufficiently to decide what could be done. I was on the verge of insanity and, unconsciously, I dozed off. I wakened with a start to find that darkness had overtaken me. I lay there in a half stupor when suddenly I heard the creak of the garden gate. Someone or something was coming! I listened and heard it hesitate at the door, then the creak of the hinges as the kitchen door was slowly pushed open and someone softly tiptoed in. My frightful visitor again! This time she would finish me. Panic, terror, terrible gripping fright such as only a diseased brain can know had me trembling in its grip. In the shadows I could perceive a figure approaching me. It was my Lady Morphia again. Soon she would assume her usual features and proportions and kill me. Suddenly my panic gave way to sly cunning. I had a revolver, fully loaded, under my pillow, and I would pretend sleep until she was close enough for me to settle forever.

THROUGH drooping eyelids I watched the form approach close and closer. I could see the festering sores on her face and her hands, hear the sibilant hissing of her breath through exposed fangs, and then as she reached her hand out to me with a quick movement, I jerked the revolver out from under the pillow and fired point-blank! She swayed slightly and with a thump fell sprawled on the floor.

The shock of the explosion brought me around. I had mesmerized myself with the drug and my constant thinking of this thing. Jumping from my couch I bent over, horror-stricken, and looked into the ashen face of—my wife! My brain, weakened by the drug had conjured up the terrible apparition and I could see nothing at the time but the repulsive, disgusting product of my own imagination.

The excitement was stimulation enough to make me think. What could I do? She required medical attention, and I rushed from the house into the street. An auto was passing and, heedless of personal safety, I rushed out into the street waving frantically for the driver to stop. He must have thought he saw a ghost by the way he looked at me, and my words, tumbling one over the other, finally made him understand that someone needed a doctor. He promised to get one and I rushed back into the house.

In a few minutes the doctor came and found a grotesque figure sitting on the floor muttering incoherently, and clasping an apparently lifeless and blood-smeared form to his breast. The events of the next fifteen minutes are blotted from my memory. The next thing I remembered was when the doctor shook me and looked at me sternly.

"Young man, it looks to me as if I had two patients here instead of one. From your appearance you won't last long yourself unless you pull yourself together and decide to do something. That woman is going to be a mother, and she says you are her husband! I'd hate to have any child born with a father looking

28

like such a wreck as you are!"

A child! The possibility of such a thing had never occurred to me. Lota was calling me to her. I was ashamed even to go near her. She had received a scalp wound which had stunned her, but the doctor said she was not seriously hurt. I realized the depths of degradation to which I had sunk, and with a moan of despair I fell to my knees and buried my face in my hands. She put her hand out and smoothed my hair. "Billy, I had to come back. I went to your room in New York and they told me you had gone. I thought of this place and came here because I knew you needed me more than ever, and oh, Billy boy, I need you so much now. I thought that when you realized you were to become a father it might straighten you out. Is it too late, Billy, can't we do something?"

I TRIED to answer, but for a minute the words stuck in my throat. Finally I managed to whisper:

"Lota, there's nothing I can ever do to make amends for the suffering I have caused you. I don't know why you bother with a beast like me. I know what I am, and I know I'm not fit to come back to you. For the sake of our baby, I'll do anything. I'll go through hell if I can only make him respect me. I don't know what I can do, my will power is gone, but if either you or the doctor can offer a suggestion, I'll do it if it kills me."

The doctor, once again the professional man, stroked his chin. "Hm, how long have you been using this stuff, young man?"

"About seven months," I told him. "But I've used an awful lot of it."

"I see you have, but you're not so badly off as many I've seen. Now, for instance, take the case of little Frankie Leary right here in town. Frankie was a good boy, but he got to hitting that stuff up, and went to the dogs for fair. Used it for a coupla years until they caught him with it in his possession. They sent him away for six months, and when he came out he had will power enough not to use it again."

HERE was the germ of an idea. If I could only go where I could not get it, no matter how hard I tried, I might cure myself. It was a case of kill or cure.

I had reached the point where I had to decide one way or the other. There was the easy way, to just stumble along as I was, dirty, degraded, and a physical wreck; and there was, on the other hand, intense suffering, untold agony but ultimate happiness. It didn't take me long to decide. I had caused the little woman lying there ready and happy to go into the Valley of Shadows more suffering that I could ever atone for, and she saw that I had made up my mind. She took my hand and whispered, "Oh, Billy, we have so much to live for now. If you can only do something, anything, to straighten out before the little one comes, so that you'll be a father to be proud of. And there's something else, Billy, all that money you spent on me, I saved most of it. Most of the things you sent me, I returned and got the money. I saved it, and the night you went out to meet that terrible man I took your money out of your coat pocket. I was afraid to let you

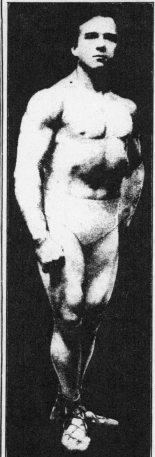

go out in that state with all that money; someone might kill you for it. It is all saved, Billy, and we can begin all over again. Please, Billy, do ·something." The tears were trickling down her cheeks. She was pleading, fighting desperately for something that all women ultimately desire, a home, a husband and a baby. Her entire happiness, the entire course of her life lay in my hands.

I MADE arrangements with the doctor to have her taken to a quiet home where a kindly old lady would take care of her. Then I kissed her hand, and told her that I would be back before the baby was born—that I would come back a new man. I knew what I was going to do. It was a drastic act, but with all I had at stake I would have risked anything. I had four months to do it in before our baby was born and, walking to the mirror, for the first time in months I looked at myself. Horrors! Was that William Manning, the erstwhile gentleman? What I saw was a face with no flesh, weeks' growth of stubby beard, bleary eyes and running nose. My hair was matted, my linen was filthy—not soiled, but filthy and dirty. Bah! I spat at the reflection in the glass, and putting the little framed verse into my coat pocket, I opened the door and walked into the moonlight once again to seek salvation.

Unconsciously I walked toward the railroad track, and just as I arrived at the freight yard, a freight train was pulling out. I saw the open door of an empty box car, and in an instant I was inside, and huddled in the corner while the train gathered momentum. After several hours of riding the train stopped at what appeared to be a fair-sized city. I crept cautiously from my hiding place and went

scurrying across the tracks to the street. I had not gone far when I met a policeman. He looked at me suspiciously, and then, taking the bull by the horns, I walked up to him and asked him the penalty for vagrants in this city.

"Three months to a year," he answered. "Would you like to try it out?" I never saw a more surprised man than when I answered, "Yes," and asked to be directed to the police station. He directed me, about two blocks away, and as I walked up the street I could see him following me, still wondering, I suppose, whether or not I was sane. I walked boldly into the great brick building and soon found myself facing the night lieutenant. I explained the circumstances to him in a few words, and asked to be sent to the county jail for three months. He stroked his chin and looked at me. "Well, your request is an unusual one, but you look as though you needed straightening out. You won't be much good for a week or two from the looks of you, but they're short of help out on the farm, and I guess maybe we can arrange it."

I was confined in the station lockup that night, and in the morning I was in bad shape, I had what they call a "Yen" and the oxidization of the drug in the body sends forth a foul smelling sweat. My nerves were trembling and I had to be helped into the patrol wagon which conveyed me to the courthouse. I soon found myself facing the judge. The lieutenant had explained the circumstances to him, and after he finished reading the charge, that I was an idle person of questionable character with no visible means of support, in a trembling voice I said, "Guilty," and was escorted to the basement of the courthouse, and again put in a cell. Shortly after, with other prisoners, I was sent out to the county jail. The first

thing they did after taking our finger prints and "history," all of mine being fictitious, was to clip our hair and take our clothing from us. We were then ordered to take a bath and were outfitted with prison garb. At last I had burned my bridges behind me and started in to serve my sentence of three months.

WHO can adequately describe the sufferings of a drug addict deprived of his goddess? The thirst of the traveler lost for days in the desert without water is a feeble comparison for the indescribable sufferings I went through. Outraged nature was exacting her toll. For three days I lay in my cell without eating, with my tortured nerves crying out for the drug I craved, pains, as if the fiends of hell were tearing out my entrails with red hot hooks, shot through me. I begged, pleaded for a dose, but there would be no drug for me for three months. After three or four days I began to get a little relief. I developed a craving for sweets, and my food consisted principally of bread and molasses. The warden, understanding my condition, fed me into fairly good condition on this fare. Days went into weeks, weeks into months and, finally, came the day of my departure. My system had been cleared of the poision left by the drug. I was clean, smooth-shaven and tanned by my work in the fields. I was given a cheap but new clean suit, and with a handshake from the warden, I started home.

I HAD no desire for the drug; I had steeled my will against it. My thoughts ran to purer, higher ideals. I had a wife waiting for me, and soon we would be three. We had kept up a regular correspondence while I was in jail, and I knew she would be waiting for me with a smile and a kiss on her lips.

In my pocket I had the little framed card, and as I trudged down the road away from the prison my heart sang over and over:

"If I were damned of body and soul,
I know whose love would make me whole,
Mother o' mine, mother o' mine."

I knew she would see me up there, and somehow I seemed to understand that she was glad that I had won, that she had been helping me, urging me on, lending me courage.

It is not so many years since all this happened. I am now a small town lawyer with a fair practice, the greatest wife on earth, and a son who is proud of his daddy. But I have pledged my life to the task of bringing him up with the idea instilled in his mind that there can be no other person so good and beautiful as his mother; I have made it a religion with him, so that through him I can atone for the suffering I caused her.

We are happy in our peacefulness, and many an evening when the little fellow is tucked away in his crib, and I sit before the fireplace with Lota's head on my shoulder, I kiss the faint scar on her forehead and look back on it all as a terrible nightmare, and cannot repress a shudder. But God is good, and although at times we cannot understand His ways, we doubt Him, still, if there is the will and the incentive, there is no pit, no matter how deep or how filthy, from which we cannot extricate ourselves, especially with the helping hand of a good woman. ●

My Own Story of Love

He drew me closer
and I did not draw
away

*S*HOULD a
woman tell her
husband all the secrets
of her past? Should she uncover
things gone—but not forgotten? Read
what this woman did—and then decide
this problem for yourself.

*L*OVE has brought me the deepest misery and despair.
It wrecked my life, left me stranded, hopeless,
abandoned. If this first part of the story were all
of it, I would not tell it. There are no redeeming features
to give hope or courage to an unhappy girl. But there is
a second part. Just as love came bringing sorrow, it also
brought happiness. It has shown me that there is no
depth of degradation that cannot be purified.

I must give a brief history of my childhood before telling
the story of love. I was the only child of doting parents.
My mother was a beautiful woman who flitted through
life as a coquette. She went out of this world when I was
ten as she lived in it, with a gay little laugh. She left as a
heritage for me the gifts of beauty and wit, but nothing else.

My father, who had loved
madly this fragile piece of
frivolity, did not attempt to
supply me with the wisdom and
the stability which should be the
companions of beauty. I was left
entirely alone to do as I pleased. I
thought of life in the terms of dancing,
flirting, excitement; yet I stayed a girl with a clean mind
and an untouched heart.

As I look back upon those years, I now realize that I
was lonely.

Soon after the death of my mother, my father started
to forget his grief in drinking and gambling. While he
was drunk one night his automobile skidded, and he was
brought home dead.

I was left with several thousand dollars, a pretty face,
and a keen desire to know life. I learned it only too soon.
I wish I could erase from memory those pictures of what I
did learn from life—but I am ahead of my story.

*M*Y uncle, who was appointed my guardian, decided
that I should go away to school and so, for two
years, I attended a boarding school. I was happy there
in a carefree way. Boys had never been lacking, and they
were not now. I enjoyed the companionship of boys more

31

than I did that of girls, but I never could return the ardent affection they bestowed upon me. I wondered if I were different from other girls in this respect when I heard them discussing their violent love affairs. I longed for the thrills they described, but an occasional caress left me cold and unfeeling.

MY restless nature craved something new and after two years of boarding-school, I persuaded my uncle to allow me to take a business course in a city. I little dreamed that the city was to offer tragedy rather than business training. I soon made friends and became more interested in social engagements than in a career. I felt that my guardian would not approve of the social set of which I had become a part, but this thought did not disturb me in the least. We had never agreed on many points, and moreover I would soon be twenty-one.

On the night of my twenty-first birthday I went to a dance. It was a night made for romance, tender and beautiful. Nature had staged her most effective setting for the little drama. However, I anticipated no unusual thrill. Settings equally

I was placed in an insane asylum

lovely had left me perfectly indifferent to the dancer. I loved the dance, but never took any particular interest in the partner. Sometimes I longed for that feeling of intoxicating thrill described in books. These thoughts were passing idly through my mind when I noticed a friend coming toward me. With her was a man. At this point Philip Harden entered my life.

WE were introduced and we danced. It sounds commonplace enough but it did not seem so to me. I had the sensation of floating. I was afraid to speak for fear the spell would be broken. But—the spell was not broken. If it only had been!

The evening passed as in a dream. I came down to earth once to go into the dressing-room to arrange my loosened hair. I frowned at the disarranged hair, for a hair unbecomingly out of place seemed a tragedy for that night. I wish those who called me bad later could have compared the face that greeted me in the mirror then with the face of a year later. Perhaps they might have hesitated in their condemnation, and wondered if sorrow, rather than sin, had not taken away the look of girlishness.

PHILIP HARDEN became very attentive and I lived my days for him. My friends called me lucky, telling me that Phil was the most sought after man of the set. I agreed with them, for I considered myself the most fortunate girl in the world to have won the ardent attentions of handsome Phil.

MY studies were sadly neglected in those days. Business seemed remote and cold, a thing of the future. The present was alive and warm. My money, handled carefully by my uncle when he was my guardian, began to dwindle. Neither parent had endowed me with the slightest knowledge of the value of money. I spent recklessly on evening gowns, wraps, slippers, for Phil never failed to comment on my appearance.

Glorious, romantic days were those, and they passed as on wings. Phil was not only my love but my confidant. As I look back I realize how clever he was. He knew that my emotions were new to me; that I must awaken gradually to their call.

His method was not the modern one of argument. He knew me too well. If he had tried to convince me of the right of unrestrained affection, he would have failed. No, his method was the primitive one of playing with the emotions. As I dined and danced the days and nights away with him, I felt his tones become more tender and his embrace more possessive. I thought his love was deepening as was mine and I answered his caresses in the way they were given.

ONE night we drove during the intermission of a dance. Instead of turning back for the rest of the dance, we kept on. It was a magical night, such a one as that when I met Phil. Several miles out from the city the car refused to move, with the stubbornness of a mule. I believe now there was a reason, known only to Phil, why that car stopped. As I drank in the beauty of the night, I felt the pressure of Phil's arms. His lips were on my hair, my throat, my lips. He drew me closer and closer until I felt smothered in his embrace. I did not draw away. I would have taken passage with him that night to the ends of the earth, if he had suggested any such wild idea.

There was little sleep for me that night. I lay awake out of sheer happiness. I planned our future together. I pictured an elaborate wedding one moment, and an elopement the next. One point was fixed. The marriage would take place soon. It was inevitable with such an overwhelming love as ours.

The next time I saw Phil, marriage was not mentioned, nor the next; but a week later I talked of it. He interrupted me with a kiss.

"LET'S not be serious today," he exclaimed. "We will talk about it tomorrow." On several occasions my sentences were similarly interrupted with a caress and a light remark. I was a little hurt, but I said no more about it for a few days. Then a chance remark brought up the subject again and this time Phil listened to me.

"Why couldn't we be married while I'm taking my business course? We could do light housekeeping. It would be fun. If I wait until I am through and go back to my uncle's, I will have to have a wedding and — why you look so queer!"

He answered lightly. "Queer, child! I am listening. Go on with your plans."

BUT I had become sidetracked from the details and came back to the main point.

"Can't we be married soon, Phil—why put it off when we love each other?"

"Jean, why must we talk about marriage? We are enjoying life as it is. Why spoil it all?"

"But, Phil," I answered, "Why does it spoil anything? We must marry and why—" I stopped, for the first time doubting. "Look at me. You want to marry me, don't you?"

When I had finished there was an overwhelming silence

This, his answer, was not lightly spoken. It came after a moment's silence.

"I hadn't intended telling you now, dear girl, but I shall never marry."

"You will never marry!" I repeated stupidly.

"Exactly. We love each other now, but it would pass away after we were married. Love never lasts. Today I love you more than anyone in the world but, a year ago, I felt the same way about someone else. A year from now we may both love other people. I don't want you for a wife. I don't want anyone for a wife."

I SAT perfectly still. There was nothing to say to this stranger who had been talking. Senseless little details of the room impressed themselves upon my mind—the small hole in the curtain, the figure in the paper. I felt numb. Then, as if out of a fog, there came the remembrance of all that we had been to each other. Surely he had been joking.

"Phil, you can't mean what you said."

There was a sneer in his voice   (Continued)

33

as he replied, "You may feel cut up, my dear, but I do not. You should have thought of all this before, if it meant so much to you."

It was true, horribly true, and I made no protest. He talked on, but I heard nothing of what he said. I wanted to be alone and I asked him to go, and not to come back. He looked surprised.

"You really mean that, Jean?"

"I DON'T want to see you again. Please go," I replied, still dazed.

He walked out of the room without another word and I was left alone to think and feel. It is woman's lot to think and to feel. If only we could divorce our thoughts from our feelings, or our feelings from thoughts, as does a man!

The next morning I went to classes for the last time.

In the afternoon I tried to make plans. I opened my bank book and found the amount of my balance surprisingly small. Yet there was enough to last a year. I decided to go to a city several hundred miles away, for no reason in particular. Just to get away. The idea haunted me.

A week later I was in that city looking through the newspaper advertisements of help wanted. I wanted to work hard in order not to think. Here, in this strange city, where I intended to forget the existence of Philip Harden, I had a most inexcusable longing to feel the arms of the man I ought to despise. I had left him a note saying I was going out of his life as he probably desired. I had also written a brief one to my uncle.

Without much effort I obtained a position as office girl for a doctor. Then days wore on, insufferably long. I made no friends, for I wanted none. My apathy gave way to fear when I realized that I was to become a mother.

FOR three months I went to the office in the morning tired before the day had begun. Each evening I returned to my room, too exhausted to care about eating. I was too tired to worry about what would become of me.

One Monday I was too ill to get out of bed. For a week my landlady cared for me. I am sure she realized my condition, but she said nothing. She was wonderfully kind. Her care was the first tenderness I had known for years. She insisted upon writing my uncle and telling him I would be unable to continue work for the present.

Very soon my uncle arrived with the intention of taking me back with him. When he announced this, I had a moment of wild confusion. It was utterly impossible for me to have him learn the truth. To escape going with him was just as impossible. I came to a decision over which I had been wavering. I would write to Phil.

I did write as soon as possible after arriving. As I wrote the words, much of my old love came back. I lived again those moments of joy. I had no misgivings now. Phil, the lover I had known, would respond at once. He would save me even at a sacrifice to himself. I even forgot his last words in anticipation of his coming.

He did not come, but a letter did! I have not the letter now, but I remember every word:

DEAR JEAN—You speak of atoning for our sin. As I told you before, I do not consider our love a sin. The consequences are unfortunate. I am sorry for you, but I am not sorry enough to marry you.

To be brutally frank, I have received similar requests before and I refused, as I am refusing you now. I shall send you money if you need it.—PHIL.

Merciful heavens! I had loved the man who wrote that! My last hope was gone. I was frantic. There was no one in whom I could confide. My aunt had never cared for me, and she resented my convalescence in her home. What would she say when—but there must be no when.

I WAS utterly unable to sleep in my anxiety to plan some way out of the trouble. Each day increased my dread, for my secret could not be concealed much longer. I felt my aunt watching me and talking to my uncle about my strange actions. Frantic with fear, I resolved to take my life. This decision brought no dismay. I had nothing to live for. The method I planned. To give as nearly as possible the appearance of an accident, I said one afternoon that I was going to take some medicine for my headache and lie down.

I cannot accurately describe what happened. I remember the panic-stricken sensation as I put the poison to my lips. I remember excruciating pain and then more pain. Later, I realized my aunt and a doctor were with me. Toward night I fell into a broken sleep. I awakened to see my uncle sitting by my bed. His face looked tired and I had my first feeling of tenderness for him. It accounts for what I did.

In spite of my pain, I was anxious to tell him my story. At the end of it, I said to him, "I have made a miserable failure of my life since I became of age. I wish you would become my guardian again." My uncle did not reply to that request. Instead he spoke tenderly and tried to get my mind off myself.

THE next day I asked him again and I gained my point. The doctor insisted I must be quiet and he realized I would not until the matter was disposed of. A few days later, I legally became my uncle's ward. Just why in those days of illness I desired that, I am not sure now. I remember a feeling of belonging to no one, of too great a weariness to manage the remnants of my fortune, or my life. After I had signed the papers, I became less restless. A calm settled over me. Even when the doctor told me there would be no baby, I had no feeling either of elation or disappointment.

My aunt was kinder during my illness than I had ever remembered, but as I grew stronger she became her old self. Her remarks were cutting, but they bothered me little. During this time I began to have frequent nightmares. Always the face of Phil appeared, sometimes beckoning me to follow him up a cliff; sometimes forcing me into deep water.

I would waken screaming. Naturally, this new development was most disturbing to my aunt. I once overheard the remark that she thought I was in danger of losing my mind.

Several weeks after I had recovered sufficiently to walk around the yard, I sat down by an old well. I had not conquered my depressed feelings and this spot was my accustomed place to brood. This day I unconsciously removed the board from the well and looked in. Was it Phil's face I saw in that well—the face that haunted my dreams? No, it was my fancy—but I looked again. There it was, sneering. I jumped up and ran toward the house, but before reaching there an irresistible force pulled me back. I stood at the edge of the well and looked down. The face was there. It spoke to me. In my delirious fancies, I was not careful of my position. My foot slipped and I fell in.

I KNEW no more until I became conscious in my own bed. No bones were broken; almost a miracle. But I was so badly bruised that I was unable to rise for days. While in bed my aunt asked me sharply why I had tried to kill myself again. I was surprised at the idea and tried to explain. The more I talked the more queerly she looked at me. I wondered at her.

I learned the cause of that expression too late. The hard part of my story begins here. True, the first part was hard, but the horror of it does not linger in my memory as vividly as this next step in my degradation, which was so unnecessarily cruel.

I must say it abruptly. I was placed in an insane asylum. The charge that put me there was two attempts at suicide. My uncle, my mother's own brother, made the charge, but I know he did it only after several scenes with his wife. I do not know which is my stronger emotion at present, horror of that place or hatred of my aunt.

I knew I was sane, but I became obsessed with the idea that I might lose my mind through association. Day after day I had to look at faces that stared vacantly. I had to hear curses and shrieks. I longed for and still dreaded the night. The dark shut out those pitiful faces, but it brought rats that ran across my bed and pulled at my hair. There was never any privacy. I dressed, undressed, even bathed, in the presence of other patients.

MY salvation was that I was allowed to read. Only then could I shut out the prying eyes. Letters came from my uncle, but I tore them up unread. Could it be possible, I cried to myself, that in a civilized country such a crime against a helpless person was permitted? It was possible, because it had happened, not only in my case, but in hundreds of others.

Two months of unbearable existence dragged by before I was freed. Those in authority explained that I had to leave

35

with my guardian, or I would have refused to see him. I stayed in his home one night, and left. He could have detained me legally, but he was as glad to see me leave as I was to go.

I went to a city not far distant, and obtained employment. I had to work, not only because of my diminishing income but also to try to forget. I performed my duties faithfully and well, but I was told at the end of two months that I need not return the next week. The ugly story of attempted suicide and insane asylum, decidedly exaggerated, had reached my employer. I had some difficulty in getting another position and that one lasted just about as long as the first one had.

MY funds were becoming exhausted, for I had not been as economical as the circumstances demanded. Because of my love for pretty clothes, I had drawn frequently, even when working, on the money in my uncle's care. He had never refused to send the amount I requested, but he wrote nothing concerning my financial condition until the end of six months in this city. Then, I received a letter stating that I had been very waste-

ful of my money and now that it was gone I must not expect help from him. He need not have written the last, for I would not have accepted a penny from him. However, I realized my position more intensely. I was alone in the world except for a disagreeable past.

With a feeling both hopeless and helpless, I decided to try for employment in another city where, perhaps, my story would not travel. Without delay, I went to a more distant city. My story arrived several months later. It was then I became most bitter. I had honestly tried to go straight, and I had paid dozens of times for my one mistake.

IN a hardened mood I counted my assets. I had business ability, but it did not stand up against a past. I could sing and dance, but not well enough to try for the stage. It seemed that the only weapon of livelihood left was my beauty. The horrible experiences had not taken my looks as toll.

I packed at once and left for another state; I selected a city at random. The selection of that particular place seems providential. I little dreamed then of the happiness so soon to be mine. I did not even know, or more truthfully, I had forgotten that there ever lived a man like Jack Curtis.

I met him the second day after my arrival, in a restaurant. Providence again seems to have directed me to that particular restaurant, one of hundreds in the city. We had not seen each other since school days, but we recognized each other at once. The sight of a familiar face was like a tonic. I forgot the fear of the asylum in the pleasure of renewing our friendship. Jack helped me to find work and to select a convenient boarding house. I soon found that he had heard nothing of my life, and I offered no information. He did not seem to notice that I evaded his questions.

It was only the week following our meeting that Jack asked me to be his wife. I was genuinely surprised for I had learned not to trust men. My experiences had not placed me with men who were the marrying sort. I had not expected a frank proposal of marriage.

Although I was not in love, that proposal was the sweetest moment of my life. Much of the bitterness disappeared, and I forgot for the moment I was not what he thought me. Presently remembrance returned and with it conscience. I was not able to give an answer then but begged for a week. During that time conscience played an important part, but it did not win out. I realized how utterly unfair it was to marry Jack without telling him of my past, but I was afraid. The advantages of marriage were too great to be thrown away. Upon marrying, my uncle would have no legal power over me. This fact outweighed all others and, at the end of the week, I said yes.

Jack's desire for an immediate marriage suited me exactly. Within two weeks I was Mrs. Jack Curtis. We honeymooned in a truly conventional style. I was happy for the first time in months. Amid the pleasures and excitements of a resort, I forgot to think about the past.

THE honeymoon had to end and with it my peace of mind. I loved our little apartment and every piece of furniture. I enjoyed cooking inviting dinners for Jack. I was most thankful for a protector. In spite of all these reasons for contentment, a dread began to hang over me. Running through my thoughts was the ever constant question, "What if Jack should find out?" Each day I decided to tell him as soon as he came in. He came and I would put it off until bedtime. The words came to my lips dozens of times only to be repressed. Before marriage, I had wanted to insure my safety. Now I wanted to keep his love.

The strain culminated when Jack was out on a business trip. During his absence I could neither eat nor sleep. Suppose some one told him while he was away from me? By the time he returned, I was in a hysterical state. The moment he entered with the same happy look of love, I started to cry from sheer relief. Alarmed, he drew me down in a chair and tried to soothe me. As I became quieter he said, "Jean, something has been worrying you and I want to share the worry. There is no trouble in the world that you need bear alone."

THE story came. I told it without keeping back a single detail. Probably the agony of those weeks and months crept into my voice, but I honestly tried to state facts without offering excuses. When I had finished there was an overwhelming silence. The extent of my love came upon me while I waited for that silence to be broken. All other emotions faded into insignificance beside my love for this man. Life apart from him would prove the most bitter punishment of all.

I longed to touch his hand where it rested on the chair, but I waited. His head had been turned away, but now he faced me. In his eyes was not the reproach that I had feared, but tears. I shall never forget what he said then:

"Poor little girl, life has been mighty rotten to you, but it hasn't spoiled you. We will erase the memory of that unhappy past together, you and I, except when it can teach us how to help others."

The love of the man who spoke these generous words was worth all the heartaches of years. The real romance had come and with it the desire to help those whose feet strayed in the paths mine had.

I WANTED them to learn that just as truly as love can cause tears and tragedy, it can also create laughter and inspiration. Happy as I am in the glow of real romance, I am not content to forget the past entirely. Jack has agreed with me that my misfortune has placed upon me a responsibility. Perhaps I can show someone that love is able to surmount all foolish mistakes of the past.

So I have told my story. I could not have written it had not my husband given to me a love that proves the greater value of a future over a past.

Love may find you battered and bruised in body and soul but it also heals the wounds and scars. It beautifies living. It did for me; it will for you. •

The Curse of Beauty

I AM a cripple, a hopeless cripple. I drag my feet along like a toad. When I go on the street people look at me with pity. If people would only realize how terrible it feels to be pitied—I hate it!

And to think that only two years ago I was beautiful. Now I don't know; I scarcely ever look in the mirror. My beauty was a curse, look what it made of me! There are times when the mere sight of a man almost drives me frantic, and then at other times I watch them in bitterness, and yet I know truly that there are as many good men in this world as there are women. I am a good girl and I was always a good girl, but there is no man on this earth for me now. No man who could feel anything for me but pity, and the only peace I can look forward to is the time when I shall close my eyes forever.

HOW many thousands of girls have wept bitter tears because they were not beautiful! Yet here is the heart story of a girl who wished she had never been beautiful and of the day that came when she was afraid almost to look in her mirror.

Think of it, and I am a young girl not yet twenty-five. But read for yourself; I need no judgment.

I WORKED for a thirty-eight million-dollar corporation that had agencies in all the large cities of the United States and representatives in all the principal foreign countries. Another thing, I worked among men—big men, men of enviable position. And, working as I did among men and coming in contact with more every day, I learned to dissect a man almost at a glance.

As my work was confidential, I think I knew more about some of these men than those nearer to them by ties of blood, and there were some things that they couldn't be very proud of, either. Most of the salesmen had their money spent before they got their checks, and some days I didn't do much but wire to the main office for money. It was little wonder that I grew callous, as it seemed at times that it was just one hard luck story after another from some of these men.

I had been with the firm approximately three years when T. M. L. joined our sales force. He

"Let this nonsense stop once and for all," I said

had gone through our school for junior salesmen at the expense of the company and was praised for his quickness and brilliancy, and noticed by the high officials of the company. He was a young man, just thirty-one, single, had gone through one of the best colleges in the country and, as could be expected, he made a splendid start in the field.

STRANGE, but I never liked him even from the very first, although everyone else in the office did. I don't really know why I didn't care for him; perhaps, however, it was due to his over-politeness.

More depends on being polite, and then too polite, than most people think. Somehow, his manners struck me as if he had known plenty of women, and his clothes, too, at times, just reeked with perfume. I'm sure he didn't use it himself, but it came from being in contact with those who did. I'm peculiar in that I hate perfume; I could never bear it since an incident in my childhood when I snuffed the contents of a bottle of cologne up my nose. It drugged me and for a number of days I was ill, not in any pain, but I just lay there in a stupor and, even to this day, I have but to think of that incident and the vile odor is revived and a weakness comes to my stomach.

Then, one day, I had occasion to go through his desk for a memorandum, and I came upon a large, full-length photograph of a scantily clad woman—it was inscribed to him. I was so disgusted that I couldn't bear the sight of him for a long time—he might have had the sense to know that someone would come upon anything like that in his desk. His standard of morals was revolting. I had overheard enough of his talk to know how little he thought of women, so naturally I didn't believe a really nice girl would go with him.

I ANNOYED him, I know—because I paid no attention to his somewhat pointed compliments to me. He mimicked me and finally called me "stuck up," just because I wouldn't have anything to do with him.

In spite of all this, he asked me to go to the opera with him one evening, and as it was between three and four in the afternoon when he asked me, it was evident that one of his so-called lady-friends had disappointed him at the last minute.

The poor fool, even if that were the only chance I ever had to go to the opera, I wouldn't have gone with him. The worst of it all was that he really couldn't be convinced that I was in earnest and had refused his invitation.

I am an orphan and all I had in the world came from my own labor. I maintained myself and, in addition, I

"Another word from you and out I go," I panted wildly

was trying to give myself a musical education, and still save something for a rainy day. So, though I was poor and couldn't afford many luxuries, still, just for the sake of a good time, I was mighty particular not to go with the kind of man I knew T. M. L. to be.

His arrogance after my refusal amused me highly, and I made no effort to conceal it. Still, I'm sure it was his last thought that he himself was the objection, for a number of days later he asked me to go to the theater and condescended even to let me select my own evening. However, when I thanked him kindly, still refusing, he got an inkling of what I was driving at and he gave a short laugh.

"SO I'm not good enough for your highness, eh? Pray what the deuce are you waiting for, a duke to marry you?"

"I hope I'm not to consider that as a proposal, Mr. L.— as I'd have to refuse that, too," I answered sweetly, and he took himself out of my presence, to my great relief.

Then came flowers on my desk every morning; not a huge bouquet but just some pretty posies. Of course, flowers on my desk were not a novelty to me—I got them frequently; but one morning as I came in earlier than usual, I found T. M. L. arranging the flowers in my vase and, in answer to his customary politeness, I greeted him with:

"Oh!—so you are the kind donor of all the pretty flowers!· Thank you so much, they are indeed lovely, but I wish you wouldn't bring them, for they wilt long before I get them home and I really have no room for them on my desk."

So ended the episode of the flowers, but something else came up which annoyed me still more. He started to comment on my personal appearance, and he never left the office in the morning until I arrived. This morning I was charming and the next, sweet; then I was beautiful, he could just eat me up, I drove him wild, and all such nonsense until I really began to detest him. Had he left me alone, unnoticed, I might have even liked him; but with his pretty speeches and devouring looks, he grew repulsive to me. I hated the very nearness of him at times. Still, I must say he was a gentleman; he did not try to touch me. Some rainy days he wouldn't leave the office, but would content himself with pretending to read the paper, but all the time watching me. It grew so irritating at times that it was little wonder I didn't throw something at him.

One morning, after I had handed him his letters, he tore the whole batch right through the center without even opening them. I looked at him aghast and he came over to me with his face flushed darkly and I really was afraid of him for the first time; we were alone.

"It's all your fault—do you understand?" he breathed heavily. "I love you, I do! Why are you so cold to me?" He was coming closer. "You beauty, you lovely little thing!" I gritted my teeth, I mustn't let him know I was afraid, and with outward calmness I seized the ruler that lay on my desk, and struck him swiftly in the face. It was about the last thing he expected and he looked at me with a curious, in fact, almost an admiring, look in his eyes. It makes me laugh now, but I think he rather liked that blow.

"And now let this nonsense stop right here once and for all," I said and went on with my work without another glance at him. Next day, he declared that I had knocked out one of his back teeth. I know he lied, but I certainly wished to heaven I had knocked out all of them.

Several mornings later, after a rather turbulent staff meeting, when I had finished typing the records, T. M. L. interrupted the general conversation with:

"I have a proposition to make—here with Miss—and I wish everyone to witness it." I stopped my work and wondered what under the sun he was going to do now. He came to my side and dared to take my fingers in his, and then continued, "If I make one hundred and fifty per cent of my quota for six consecutive months, will you marry me?"

I snatched my hand out of his, swallowed hard and, looking him square in the face, I said, "If you were the last man on earth, I wouldn't marry you."

Everybody laughed; they thought it a joke. He stayed after the rest were gone and then he gave a short laugh—his characteristic short laugh (I think I shall know that laugh even when I die; I can always hear it ring in my ears, even now, as I write) and then the corners of his lips went straight while a hard glint crept into his eyes and his words were deliberate:

"Listen! When I want something I always get it. I want you, no matter how, but take it from me, you'll be sitting on my lap within six months," and with those words he left me alone, but I was still too angry to be afraid or put thought to his words.

AFTER that, he was almost a stranger to me—and I couldn't help but notice the lines of dissipation returning to his face and his clothes again gave forth that vile perfume that I had not noticed for a long time—he had gone back to his old friends.

Suddenly, he left us to work for a competitive firm, and you can imagine the relief that his departure gave me. However, upon leaving our company, he failed to return the company's samples, and though we wrote him and gave him ample time to return these things he gave no heed to our communications until, finally, our patience exhausted with his attitude, we turned the matter over to the bonding company and let them proceed to collect.

They handled the matter so slowly that I had almost forgotten it. But one evening, as I was coming out of the Conservatory of Music, I almost collided with T. M. L. Naturally I couldn't be rude to him, so we spoke of trivial matters and I permitted him to see me to the bus, and I was somewhat surprised that he did not ask to take me home. The next Monday evening, I met him again, and when, on the following Monday I met him for the third time, I grew angry. I knew the first time was accidental, and perhaps I might have overlooked the second, but the third, never! He was meeting me intentionally. Still, I made no comment, but instead I rearranged my schedule and went for my music lesson on Thursdays. And the following Monday evening as I sat alone in my little room, I couldn't help but laugh, because I knew he would be waiting for me.

A number of days later the bonding company had a warrant sworn out for his arrest and Saturday morning they took him. Nobody at the office was any too happy about it; but after—well, we all agreed that he had been given all the chance in the world to return the machines or make good for them, but evidently he thought the company would do nothing toward straightening the matter up; this time he had thought wrong; too bad!

I had to go to the hearing as I had delivered the machines to him. He pleaded guilty and kept his eyes on the floor. Of course I was sorry for him, and I hoped he did not think I was glad anything like this had happened to him. He was put under fifteen hundred dollars' bail, to await the Grand Jury. I thought he would have to stay in jail, as I did not believe he could raise the money for his bail, but I was wrong.

It was a little over a week later that I came home to find that the old couple from whom I rented my room had gone to be with their daughter, who was ill, and I was left all alone in the house. Of course I didn't mind; it wouldn't be the first time I had stayed alone, so, after washing the dishes, I went to my room to read,—but a restlessness seized me. I couldn't concentrate, I don't know—I don't think I was really afraid, but I just couldn't remain in the silent house by myself, so, slipping on a light jacket, I roamed the lighted streets until almost midnight and then, tired, I returned to the lonely house and wished dully I had not been left alone.

AS I climbed the stairs wearily, I was startled at seeing a light streaming through the crevices of my door. I had left no light—it had still been daylight when I had gone out.

My heart thumped heavily, and then I gave a reassuring laugh. The old couple must have come back and Mrs. — was waiting for me in my room; she had often done so when I came home late, poor soul, afraid that something might happen to me. Dear heart, she was the only mother I knew! I ran up the rest of the stairs lightly and burst open the door, but the laugh of welcome on my lips died into fright. T. M. L. was leisurely reading one of my books. He looked up at my entrance, finished the paragraph and returned the book to the shelf.

"Sorry to frighten you," was all he said. I had got myself in perfect control and confronted him.

"How did you get in here?" I demanded.

"All roads lead to Mecca," he gave a light laugh.

THEN, "You couldn't have torn up my receipt, could you, and got me out of all that mess?" His mouth was hard, he shrugged his shoulders, "Well, never mind about that now. What I want to know is, whether you are going to marry me, yes or no is sufficient?"

"It wasn't necessary for you to come way up here for that—you've always known I wouldn't be so foolish!"

"I think you will," he drawled, but I wasn't afraid now. The angry blood beat in my head, as I read his motive.

"Now that I've answered your question, you will be so good as to get out." But in another instant, he swung me around with an oath:

"Listen, didn't I promise that you'd sit on my knee in six months? Well, I've come," he was laughing again, "I believe you were glad to see me behind the bars, but I've cleared the slate and I've come for you—to be mine from this moment on!"

I started to scream, but, with a soft laugh, he crushed me to him, his eyes devouring me.

"Why scream? We are alone, save your breath. There's no one to help you," he mocked. And he smothered my screams with savage kisses whose baleful fire scorched my soul. I slipped out of his arms to his feet and begged for mercy. I'd marry him, yes, if he'd only let me alone now; my face was blistered with tears. He swooped me into his lap, I think it was a satisfaction for him to see me cry, then:

"Do you think me such a fool as to believe you?" He kissed my eyes, my hair, my throat. I struggled but he held me like a vise, and just continued to laugh, softly, softly, until I thought I'd go crazy.

SUDDENLY I seemed endowed with superhuman strength and I leaped to the window.

"Now, another word from you, and out I go!" I panted wildly. He said something, I don't know what, and made a spring to catch me. Too late—too late! I had gone and he came crashing down after me. Then it grew dark and all was chaos!

It was only after I was better that I was told that he had been killed, while I— oh! Why hadn't death taken me, too?

For months I lay on my back in mortal agony, my feet in plaster casts. If I had had a chance I would have taken something to end it all.

They saved my legs, but that's all! They are dead—no life, no nothing—I drag them along. It would have been more merciful to let me die, and yet I wonder! Perhaps, some day, who knows? I slave for a paltry twelve dollars now— and live in a hole in a garret where I freeze in the winter and broil in the summer. I am writing this—not only for a lesson that beauty is not all, and at times is a curse; but also it may bring me some money and even a few dollars will be a blessing from heaven to my meager purse.

●

He Wanted Children

Bob said, "That's too melancholy for tonight, dearest. Let's have something jolly."

A Powerful Story of a Woman's Supreme Sacrifice

SHAKESPEARE said: "There is a divinity which shapes our ends, rough hew them how we will," but I believe that the man who put the comma after "rough" instead of before it, was not such a fool, after all.

Many years have passed since the events related here occurred, and yet it is with a real feeling of trepidation that I am now, for the first time, setting down these facts which, hitherto, have been locked away in the treasure-box of my heart, too sacred for any one to know.

No one could have guessed my secret; no priest, physician, or lawyer has had my confession, and no friend my confidence, I had thought.

I had thought indeed to carry my story untold into the Great Beyond where, we believe, all things will be made right. Why then, am I writing it? That is a thing which I cannot explain even to myself. Possibly, to relieve an overburdened heart; or it may be just weakness coupled with the long repressed hope that it may carry a message of love to the only one who of all those most vitally concerned in this narrative will have the power to supply the rightful names and places.

It all started the summer I was eighteen and had just been graduated from the fashionable girls' school at Elmcliff.

Mother had been making elaborate plans for bringing me out the following winter. She dearly loved the social whirl and was never so happy as when the season was at its height. In fact, there was just one thing that gave

The next thing I remember I was sitting on my own bed, my locket open in my hand

mother a bigger thrill than a well filled engagement calendar; that was to see her name in the paper the day following some big society event as "among those present."

But a few weeks after my graduation, just as we were ready to leave for a month at the seashore, dear old Dad had a sort of nervous breakdown and the doctor prescribed a sea voyage. So we canceled our reservations and mother and I decided we would accompany Dad. The plan was to go first to England, and then for a cruise through the Mediterranean. How little I dreamed that my whole future was to hinge upon that trip!

We sailed on the fifth of August—a never-to-be-forgotten date—for it marked the day that I first met Bob Williams. There was nothing unusual or romantic about the meeting itself; it was uninterestingly conventional, or conventionally uninteresting, whichever way you choose to put it. But from the first handclasp, time, for me, just naturally ceased to exist, and I lived in a rosy haze not measured by hours, minutes and seconds, but by the coming and going of a certain well set up, gray-clad figure. It was love at first sight with both of us, and before the boat docked at Southampton we were engaged.

FATHER and mother were inclined to be a bit unpleasant about it at first, but that was natural, considering that I was their one and only and that they knew next to nothing about Bob. Though how any one could talk five minutes with him without knowing that he was ab — so — lutely all to the good, was beyond my comprehension. At that time he was an agent for a very old and conservative firm of merchants in London. So Dad lost no time in looking them up, and after a half hour's conversation with them, all his objections to our engagement were withdrawn. He even won mother's reluctant and tearful consent. Poor mother! All her plans and dreams for my coming-out party had to be given up, though the prospect of a big church wedding did much to assuage her grief.

"Well, if it had to be, it couldn't have happened better, Kathy," she said. "Now we can run over to Paris and buy your trousseau."

Which we did.

Dad went on his Mediterranean cruise alone, while mother and I spent much time and money in the Paris shops, with frequent—very frequent—visits from Bob.

And so the summer passed, and at the end of September we all returned to New York.

Bob and I wanted to be married in November, but mother was hoping we would wait until spring, for she always hated to do anything in a hurry; and since my wedding was to be the greatest achievement of her social career, she not only wanted time to enjoy it in anticipation, but also to feel sure that nothing should be overlooked that would make for its success.

But Bob had to take another trip to England early in November and we simply couldn't think of being parted so soon. So the date was set for November third, and preparations for the great event went ahead. Oh, the teas and dances and luncheons that were given in our honor! How tired we were of them! But the time was short and all of my friends wanted to meet and entertain my fiance. So poor Bob and I had no time to see each other alone, and we missed those delightful heart-to-heart talks so vital to the newly engaged.

One night, driving home after a dance, Bob had a happy inspiration. "I tell you what, sweetheart," he said, "let's get up early tomorrow morning and go for a canter in the park. I'll call for you about seven and we can ride for an hour before breakfast. What do you say?"

"Splendid!" I cried. "Why didn't we think of it before? Just think of my having you for a whole hour, dear, all to myself!"

"You little witch," he laughed, kissing me; then, very tenderly, he added, "Oh, Kathy dearest, if anything should happen to keep us apart, I shouldn't care to live."

The next morning, bright and early, found us in the park. Our mounts, procured from a nearby riding academy, seemed to realize the importance of good behavior on their part, for they walked sedately side by side along the bridle path under the crimson arches of the trees. What a glorious day—and what a short hour! I could scarcely believe it when Bob, looking at his watch, announced that our time was up.

"Let's do it every day," I cried, and as Bob readily acquiesced, each fine morning thereafter found us in the park at seven, where we would ride until eight or eight-thirty, sometimes ending our lark with breakfast at some hotel in the vicinity. And so the days flew by until the wedding was only a week off, and mother dear put a veto on the early morning stuff.

"You're beginning to look sallow, Kathy," she remarked. "You know you can't burn the candle at both ends. I'd advise you to give up the rides and get a little beauty sleep."

"Just one more, mother," I pleaded, though I knew she was right, for the days were getting so strenuous that most of the time I felt like a mere rag.

"This is the last time, Bobby," I said sadly as we turned our horses in at the entrance to the park.

"PERHAPS the last for Miss Abbott," he laughed, "but just think of all the rides Mrs. Williams and I will have together."

I started to reply, but at that instant the thing occurred which changed my entire life—such a little thing, too—a puff of wind—a pedestrian's hat blown under my horse's nose—a rear—a plunge. Then a moment of terror as I felt myself falling—then—blackness!

Hours afterward I woke in terrible pain. Strange faces were bending over me. I was dimly conscious of hushed voices. Where I was, or what had happened I did not know, and was too weak to care. All I wanted was to sleep and forget the horrible agony that racked my poor body.

Weeks passed which I cannot even now recall without a shudder. But I will not torture you nor myself with a recital of my hospital experiences. It is sufficient to say that it was well after Christmas before I was considered

The desires to perpetuate ourselves through our children runs high in most of us. To live on in our offspring is the only way we can really cheat death.

Doubly blessed is the love match which results in healthy and happy babies. But occasionally, through no fault of the man or woman, children are denied a loving couple.

Will love eventually die if it cannot achieve its natural end—children? What is a woman to do if her husband craves an heir, and an accident has eternally robbed her of the privilege of motherhood? These questions throbbed through Katherine's brain. Her answer was a startling decision. Did she act wisely?

strong enough to be taken home. Then it was Daddy's strong arms that carried me down to the carriage where dear, fussy mother waited with enough pillows and blankets to supply an army of invalids.

It was good to be home again among the dear familiar surroundings after all those tedious weeks. The only fly in the amber of my happiness was that Bob was unable to be present to share in the joy of my homecoming; but he had had to take the long-deferred trip to England. During the weeks when my life hung in the balance, his firm had been most considerate, but when the danger was over and it was just a matter of gaining strength, he felt that he could no longer postpone the trip which was to be a short one. He was due home very soon now, and I was impatient to see him.

"Well, mother dear," I said one morning when we were sewing together in my cozy sitting room, "you will have your way, after all."

Mother looked puzzled. "What do you mean, Kathy?" she asked.

"Why—the wedding, of course," I responded. "You wanted a spring wedding, and that's what it will have to be—now."

To my surprise I saw her eyes fill with tears.

"MY dear little girl," she said, laying down her work and coming over to put her arms around me, "I have not dared to tell you before, you were not strong enough to bear it, but I am afraid that you must give up all thought of marriage. At least, you ought not to consider it without first having a very frank talk with Bob so that he will understand just how things are."

"How things are!" I repeated. "Why, aren't they just the same as they were before my accident?"

"No, dear, not quite," faltered mother. "You see, you were injured internally when the horse threw you, and an immediate operation was necessary if your life was to be saved. It was a very serious operation—very serious—and now it will be impossible for you ever to have any children."

So that was it! I knew of course, that there had been an operation, but I had been kept in ignorance as to its nature. So the enlightenment came as a considerable shock. Rising unsteadily I walked into my bedroom and closed the door. I wanted to be alone to think things over.

For more than an hour I lay on my bed fighting the thing out. And I always came up against the same blank wall— I *could not* give up Bob—and yet I felt that I must!

I had always been fond of children. My own childhood had been a lonely one, and I had often longed for a brother or sister to share in my play; so it was not strange that, with the thought of marriage had come also the half shy longing for children of my own.

And yet, they would not be mine alone. Our children! What a splendid father Bob would be! What were his feelings in regard to the matter? I was sure that he felt as I did, for though those reticent days young people never discussed such topics, I could judge by chance remarks and by his great tenderness for the little ones. He could never see a child in trouble

(Continued)

43

without stopping to inquire the cause, and doing all in his power to chase the tears away.

If I were his wife he would look to me for this happiness. Had I the right to marry him, and so forever snatch it from him? And loving him as I did, could I stand aside and see some other woman fill the place which I so gladly would have filled, but which, through no fault of my own, was denied me? I could not decide the matter. I would leave it to Bob.

As soon as I had reached this determination I got up and went out to where poor mother was still sadly wondering if she had done wrong in telling me.

"Mother dear," I said, sitting down beside her and taking her hand in mine, "I have decided not to see Bob again until he knows everything. When he comes tomorrow, father must tell him—or Dr. Gibbs. If he still wants me after hearing what they have to say, why, I shall do everything in my power to make him happy. If he decides otherwise—I shall never blame him. Please tell Daddy to make that very plain. But the decision rests absolutely with him."

ALL that night and the next morning I was in an agony of suspense. Bob's steamer was due early in the day, and father had promised to see him at once. So, at the very latest—if things went my way—he ought to be with me by noon. But—would he come? I paced the floor, drummed on the piano, tried to read—anything to divert my mind from the awful doubts which thrust themselves upon me.

At ten o'clock he came! It was too wonderful! Gathering me into his arms he held me close and whispered, "It's only you that I want, Kathy darling. Do you understand?—only *you*!"

And so a month later, very quietly with only father and mother as witnesses, we were married.

It would be impossible for me to attempt a description of those first years of our life together. Father's wedding gift to us had been a piece of property out on Long Island, and all our interests were centered in the new home which we were building. We were so happy in just being together that the cloud which had seemed to threaten us at the start was quite dispelled. At any rate we both were much too philosophical not to realize that in this life one must always take the bitter with the sweet. We never alluded to our disappointment and, after a time, I began to console myself with the thought that perhaps after all Bob didn't care as much as I had feared he might.

But one day, going through some trunks up in the attic, I came across an old photograph album which contained a picture of myself taken at the age of two. I ran gleefully down with it to where Bob sat writing at his desk. Laying it down in front of him I asked, "Do you recognize your wife?"

For many moments he sat staring at the round baby face with its serious

eyes and fluff of curls without saying a word.

Then abruptly he threw both arms around my waist as I stood beside him, and buried his face in my dress. "Oh, Kathy!" he cried, and I could feel his shoulders shake.

"What is it, darling?" I asked, alarmed that he should display such emotion over an old photograph. At that he let me go and sat back, a trifle shamefaced; but his mouth was bitter, as he quoted, "Of all sad words of tongue or pen—" and I understood.

It was shortly after this that my dear father died and mother came to live with us. Prior to this I had always accompanied Bob on his periodical trips to England. Now, however, I felt that mother must not be left alone; so that meant a separation for Bob and me—the first since our marriage.

It seemed strange for him to be starting off alone, for we had enjoyed these excursions together so much that we laughingly called them our semi-annual honeymoons.

How vividly I recall our last evening together! Mother had retired soon after dinner, and Bob, stretched at full length in his favorite place on the bearskin rug in front of the fire, begged me to sing to him. Without turning on the lights I went to the piano and with tomorrow uppermost in my thoughts, started the old song:

"What would you do, love,
If I were going with white sails flowing
The seas beyond?"

But the second verse was too much for me:

"What would you do, love,
If distant tidings thy fond confidings
Should undermine?
Should I abiding
'Neath sultry skies, should think other eyes
Were bright as thine?
Oh, name it not!
Though guilt and shame were on thy name,
I'd still be true.
But that heart of thine
Should another share it, I could not bear it.
What would I do?"

BOB heard the tears in my voice, and coming over to the piano he put his hands on my shoulders tenderly, saying as he did so, "That's too melancholy for tonight, dearest. Let's have something jolly."

So I dried my eyes and we spent the remainder of the evening singing some of the hits from the musical comedy we had both seen a few evenings before.

The next morning, as he was leaving, Bob slipped a small packet into my hand. "Just so you won't forget me," he whispered.

When he had driven away, I took it to my room and opening it, discovered an exquisite gold locket set with diamonds. A tiny spring in one side released the cover. I pressed it, and there—smiling up at me—was his dear face. I placed the precious trinket next to my heart and there it has hung for nearly thirty years.

The month of Bob's absence seemed

an eternity to me, but at last he was back and with the good news that he had been made general manager of all the business in the states east of the Mississippi. That meant fewer trips to England, though it would necessitate considerable travel about the country, and the establishing of headquarters in Detroit. "Still, there won't be the whole Atlantic Ocean between us," I remarked happily.

But, ocean or no ocean, the next three years took Bob away from home more than ever, and if it had not been that mother was in extremely poor health, I should have closed the house and gone to Detroit so as to be near him.

As it was, he got home for a few days only every three weeks, but even then his time was not free, for he spent most of it at the telephone or in conference with business associates. At times I almost resented his promotion, though you may be sure I was proud of the honor conferred on him. But I could not help longing for the good old days when we had been constant companions.

Then came the exposition in a Middle Western city and that kept Bob away for the entire summer. He had all the responsibility of arranging for the company's exhibit, and that necessitated frequent conferences with the western manager as well as the representatives from Canada.

AT the end of the summer he was simply worn out; so instead of spending his vacation at home as had been his custom, he went for a month's hunting up into northern Quebec with Tom Bisby of the Montreal office. Their camp was miles from any railroad, so letters were out of the question, and I often lay awake nights thinking of all the dreadful things that might happen to him so far away from civilization. But the change and outdoor life did him a world of good and he came home hard and brown, and handsomer than ever.

The following summer mother fell and broke her hip, so that she was confined to her bed. I had to be with her constantly, for she suffered a great deal and depended more on me than on the nurse for care. So when vacation came again, and Bob asked wistfully "if I would think him a selfish beast if he went hunting again with Tom," I could answer quite honestly, "Not a bit of it, dear."

To tell the truth, it was something of a relief, for had he remained at home I should have been able to give him very little time and that would have been an aggravation to us both.

Isn't it strange how things happen? I sometimes feel that we are all just marionettes. Fate pulls the strings—we respond—it's all a matter of destiny. In reviewing my life I cannot detect a single instance in which my misfortune was the result of my own misdoing. It is as though everything had been carefully planned beforehand, like a play, and all that life required of me was to walk through the scenes, quite powerless to change the action.

Just a week after Bob's departure dear mother died. The end came quite suddenly and peacefully, and I was thankful for her sake that it was so; for aside from her intense physical suffering her grief over father's death had been hard to bear. It was impossible to get word to Bob and I doubt if I should have tried, anyway, for there was nothing he could have done and he needed badly the rest and change.

WHEN all was over I let the servants go, and closed the house for two weeks. I wanted to get away, for I couldn't stand the loneliness and felt that a change would freshen me up so that Bob's return at the end of the month would find me quite my old self. I could not help thinking that now, at last, our life would revert to the old lines once more. Bob and I would be real pals. Why, it would be almost like starting life over again!

But a difficult problem confronted me. Where could I go to get the rest and quiet which my jaded nerves demanded? It must be a place where there would be no social obligations whatsoever; where I could come and go as I chose and be beholden to nobody.

Such a place seemed hard to find until suddenly like a flash came the memory of a beautiful lake in western New York where, as a child, I had spent one of the happiest summers of my life. I recalled with delight the quiet beauty of the place, seeming almost to hear again the lapping of the water upon the pebbly beach. Immediately I decided that of all places in the world Owago Lake was the one for me now.

So one bright morning a few days later found me sitting on the porch of the little Elsmere Hotel overlooking the sparkling waters of Owago Lake. The air was like a tonic; already the charm of the place had me half hypnotized. It was far lovelier than I had remembered it to be. My magazine lay with pages uncut as I watched the children frolicking on the beach and in the water.

And as always on such occasions, my heart yearned for them in all their happiness and innocence and for the little one which might have been.

In fancy I chose one from the laughing group and called him *mine*. He was a sturdy youngster of perhaps three years—chubby and brown and with a mass of golden ringlets which bobbed with every motion of his small body. It amused me to hear the children call him "Bobbin"—it fitted him so well.

Just here my reverie was broken by an old lady from the "rocking chair brigade" who detached herself from her comrades and charged down upon me. She was a friendly soul whose chief aim apparently was to impart all the gossip of the place while inadvertently finding out all she could about me. I inquired about "my" baby.

"Oh, you mean Bobbin," responded Mrs. Crosby. "Ain't he cute? That's his mother down there on the dock with the pink parasol. She's nothing but a kid, herself. They come from out west somewhere—been comin' here three years, now. Last year her husband came, too—awful nice man—thinks the world of that boy. Did you say your name was Williams? Now, ain't that funny? They're Williamses, too. Mebbe you're related."

"Possibly," I replied. "My husband's people come from this part of the country though he has no immediate family."

THEN the gong for the noon dinner sounded and we all trooped into the dining room. To my delight Bobbin and his mother were my table companions, so we soon became friends, though the mother being extremely shy had little to say, devoting herself almost entirely to her young son. Dinner over, Bobbin slipped his small hand into mine and proposed that I let him show me his five crabs which were in a pail on the dock. "I yike you," he confided as we bent our steps beachward. "You're nice!"

From then on he was my shadow, following me everywhere and, to everyone's amusement calling me "his yady;" while I simply adored him with all the latent mother-love which hitherto had been suppressed.

"Oh, Bobbin," I exclaimed one day when a quaint remark of his had set me laughing, "I wish your mother would give you to me."

He regarded me gravely. "Well," he responded after due deliberation, "I dess my daddy wouldn't let her—'less you take him, too." Then, clapping his hands he gurgled, "You ask him. He's tomin' tomorrow. Muvver's goin' to take me to town to meet him!"

But Bobbin was doomed to disappointment, for next morning, while in wading a sharp stone cut his foot which made the town trip an impossibility.

"Let me take care of him, Mrs. Williams," I begged when I found that she hesitated about leaving him. She accepted gratefully, and hand in hand, Bobbin and I watched her train pull away from the little station behind the hotel.

That was a day to remember! For six hours Bobbin was mine! Nap time brought difficulties, however, for he was in a fever of impatience to see his beloved daddy who was not due until supper time. But I held him in my arms out on the cool piazza, and sang some of the songs I had loved as a child until gradually the warm little body relaxed and his eyes closed. Lifting him care-

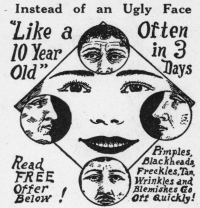

The Beast In Men

A Powerful Story of Primitive Passions. Read it in

February TRUE STORY

On Sale Everywhere January 5th

45

This New
BEAUTY BATH
is astonishing in instant results

THE Linit Bath is an outstanding beauty secret — because not only is it amazingly economical, but the soothing, luxurious results are *immediate*.

Merely dissolve half a package of Linit (the remarkable starch sold by grocers) in a half tubful of warm water — bathe in the usual way, using your favorite soap — and then feel your skin — soft and satiny smooth!

This soft, velvety "finish" comes from a thin coating of Linit left on the skin which is invisible to the naked eye.

You will notice that Linit adheres well — never comes off on the clothing — eliminates "shine" and absorbs perspiration.

Starch from corn is the main ingredient of Linit — and being a pure vegetable product, is absolutely harmless to even the most sensitive skin. In fact, doctors recommend starch from corn to soothe the tender skin of young babies.

You May Not Believe

that a fine laundry starch like Linit also makes a marvelous beauty bath. So we suggest that you make this simple test:

After dissolving a handful or so of Linit in a basin of warm water, wash your hands. The instant your hands come in contact with the water you are aware of a smoothness like rich cream — and after you dry your hands your skin has a delightful softness. You'll be convinced — INSTANTLY!

Corn Products Refining Co., Department T. S., 17 Battery Place, New York City.

fully, I tiptoed down the hall to their room. The key had been left in the lock, so I had no difficulty in entering. As the door swung open, I stood transfixed upon the threshold. There, facing me on the dresser, stood a framed photograph of my husband!

I placed Bobbin gently on the bed and covered him with a quilt. I even kissed his dear dimpled hand.

The next thing I remember I was sitting on my own bed, my locket open in my hand. There it was — the same face — the same picture even. Slowly, very slowly, I tore the beloved face to bits, saying to myself, over and over, "No one must ever know — no one must ever know."

WHAT could I do? He was coming. He must not find me here. Though the prior right was mine, I am thankful that the idea of claiming it never occurred to me. They were so happy — the three of them. Even if I should destroy their earthly paradise, what would there be left for me? And what had I to offer the man I loved that could compare with his precious little son?

In my heart there was no bitterness toward my husband — I understood so well why he had done this thing.

Five o'clock! He would soon be here! I went in and waking Bobbin, I dressed him. He was wild with excitement; his cheeks like roses, every curl on end. With my manicure scissors I snipped off one of the bright ringlets — then he went whooping off down the hall — and out of my life forever.

Dear little boy!

Does he ever think of "his yady?"

I heard the train come. I heard Bobbin's ecstatic cry, "Daddy, my daddy!"

I HEARD my husband's voice with a note in it that was new to me exclaim, "Well, old man, you look good to me!" And I prayed for strength to do the thing that I felt was right.

That is all. Next morning I took the milk train into the city. It left so early that I avoided seeing any one except the sleepy landlady to whom I explained that I had had bad news and must start for home immediately.

I went to a western city where an old school friend had lived since her marriage, about the time of my own. I felt I must know some one, and Bess was a sweet understanding soul who would never try to force my confidence, or to find out more than I chose to tell her about myself.

My lawyer back home was the only person who knew where I had gone. Just at first he forwarded a lot of letters from Bob, but I burned them all, unopened, and after awhile they stopped coming.

I have never gone back east. I broke absolutely with the old life and all its associations. But one thing remains which binds me irrevocably to the past — my treasured locket.

Yes, it still hangs above my heart, just as on the day Bob gave it to me — and it always will. But within that secret place, instead of the face which I still love — did I not sacrifice my life's happiness for him? — there lies a tiny curl of golden hair.

CHARIS

Within this woman's soul burns still the flame of her desire for charm and beauty. Not grinding toil nor bitter heartbreak may quench its fire. Hers is a spiritual triumph over all adversity. This woman is your friend . . . your neighbor . . . an acquaintance . . . a stranger. She is every woman.

She is . . . you!

Flame of Desire

CHARIS brings a priceless gift to the woman who wears it. Every day you admire women whose supple, youthful figures are achieved by adjusting this light, supporting garment so that bust, hips and thighs are fashionably molded without physical restraint.

And the wonder of CHARIS is this: its wearer is younger in fact as well as in appearance! The Adjustable Inner Belt, exclusive with CHARIS, gently lifts the abdomen and its delicate organs into normal position and holds them there without discomfort or injurious pressure. Lost vitality and wretchedness are replaced by new strength and happiness.

Will you let CHARIS answer your desire for personal charm and health? Will you send *us* this coupon, *today,* so that we may send *you* all the wonderful story of CHARIS?

CHARIS *is never sold in Stores*

THE FIFTH AVENUE CORSET COMPANY, Inc.
Allentown. Pennsylvania

© F.A.C.Co.Inc., 1928

Playing with Fire

AS I sat before the open fireside in my comfortable living-room, one bitterly cold February evening, I strove in vain to keep my thoughts upon the book before me. My husband was away again and I was all alone. Suddenly a strange thought took possession of me. I found myself saying in an undertone, "I am lonely, desperately lonely. Oh! for some excitement!"

IT was only a little indiscretion caused by loneliness so long-continued it made her desperate, but that one indiscretion led her into another and still another, until the climax came and she found herself caught in a whirlpool of her own creation. Through it all her husband never knew, never even suspected. This is a story with a moral, a story in which the intensity of the drama enacted serves to accentuate the lesson.

The young man paused . . . In a low, pleasant voice he asked if I intended taking the Meltown car

Many times in the course of events which followed, I had occasion to wish most sincerely that I had been content with my solitude and had gone to bed rather than to have done what I did. Glancing at the watch on my wrist, I figured that with great haste I could catch the seven-forty-five car and could thus spend the long, tiresome evening at one of the various vaudeville houses in Marshall, three miles from home.

I did not experience any great alarm as I realized that I would have to go alone, for I knew no one whom I might ask to accompany me had I wished. In my great hurry to catch the car, I gave small heed to the biting, cold wind. My thoughts were all centered in discovering a way of escape from an evening which, like many another, began in solitude and ended in solitude.

AS I emerged from the small theatre several hours later, I saw to my great disgust the car I had planned upon taking, far in the distance — its tail-lights growing dim in the semi-darkness. Thrusting my cold hands further down into the deep pockets of my fur coat, I stood for a moment at a loss.

I was alone on the wind-swept corner except for one individual, a young man about my own age. As I walked briskly to and fro in a vain endeavor to keep myself warm, the young man paused in his striding and calmly, smilingly regarded me. As he glanced at me I turned and walked some distance away.

Back and forth, he came past me, each time bringing his steps a little closer until at last he boldly paused beside me. A smile of amusement curved my lips for an instant at his childish behavior. Thinking I meant it for a smile of encouragement, he spoke in a low, pleasant voice, asking me if I intended taking the Meltown car. Not wishing to appear rude, I told him such was my intention.

"May I ask if you live in Meltown?" he asked me, as he buttoned his coat more closely about his throat.

"I do," I replied briefly as the car I had been so long waiting for came into view. We were the only passengers to board the car at this point. Hurriedly I took a seat far down front, faintly wondering where the young man would seat himself, but scarcely surprised when I heard his voice at my side inquiring softly if he might sit with me.

IT must be remembered that I said I was lonely, and human companionship then seemed the most desirable thing upon earth. Without a word I nodded my head in assent, perfectly well aware of what I was doing. With a smile he seated himself by my side.

"I live in Meltown also," he remarked. "It is strange that we have never met in so small a town."

"There is nothing strange about it to me," I replied. "I have only lived in Meltown about a year and have been about very little. I know scarcely anyone." Before the car reached the end of my street I had promised to meet the young man the following Saturday evening to attend the theatre. Emphatically I refused to allow him to see me home. To his low-whispered "Good-night," I responded with a cool little smile and hastily left the car.

With a strange feeling of guilt I entered my warm, silent home.

"Lillian Crawford," a faint voice within me seemed to say, "what do you intend doing? You, a respectable bride of a year. What would Jim, your husband, say were he to learn of your behavior?" With a shrug I murmured, half-aloud, "I do not intend doing wrong; but I can't stand this solitude any more, this will at least give me a diversion for one evening—Jim need not know."

"Do you think," asked the small voice, "that Saturday evening will end your friendship with this man of whom

you know nothing further than his name?" "I am sure it will," I whispered, as I undressed for bed.

Jim was an employee in Uncle Sam's railway mail service, and was gone from home two, and sometimes three, evenings in succession. Consequently my life was spent almost entirely alone.

AS I kissed my husband this particular Saturday afternoon, before his departure for New York, my guilty conscience whipped me mercilessly. I really loved the tall, handsome man whose name I bore. Never before had I spoken to a strange man, and I had always regarded women who carried on such a practice as low and vulgar.

"Good-by, dear. God willing, I will see you Monday, and I do hope, darling, that you won't be too lonely during

As I kissed my husband . . . my guilty conscience whipped me mercilessly . . . "I do hope, darling, that you won't be too lonely during my absence," he said my absence," he said, as he went down the front steps.

After Jim's quiet departure, I leisurely dressed myself in my very prettiest clothes and slipped into my fur coat. As I closed the door of my home I noticed for the first time how feverishly hot my face and hands were. Slipping my wedding-ring off, I placed it in a corner of my handkerchief and tied a knot to hold it in place, and thrust it deep into my pocket. "For," I mused, "I am supposed to be single this evening." A wave of remorse swept over me at this. Here was I playing the part of a "vamp"—a part which was really exceedingly distasteful to me, and against my nature.

As I turned the corner I saw Henry Alston, the young man, awaiting me. I was halfway minded to turn back; but, after all, I meant only to find amusement for awhile. Trembling with the excitement of my extremely perilous position, I scarcely acknowledged his warm greeting. As in a dream, I found myself walking by the side of this strange man. He might also be married, I thought. At this I glanced, half-frightened, at his strong, good-looking face, but it told me nothing.

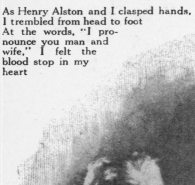

As Henry Alston and I clasped hands, I trembled from head to foot At the words, "I pronounce you man and wife," I felt the blood stop in my heart

IN my enjoyment of the play, I forgot for a time my companion who sat silently by my side. After the theatre he accompanied me to the corner of the street where I lived, but firmly I refused to allow him to go farther. As I was about to leave him with a hasty good night, he put forth his hand and touched my arm.

"You haven't yet told me your name and you have spent a whole evening in my company."

"Is that necessary?" I asked, uneasily. "I may never see you again, so why bother to know my name?" His eyes rested upon my face for a moment before he spoke. An uncontrollable shiver passed over me at the look in his handsome brown eyes. It was not the look of a human satyr, but rather the look of a wounded animal pleading for kindness. At this I had not the heart to refuse my name. "My name is Lillian—" I paused abruptly. I could not tell him that I was married. "Lillian Bailey," I finished, using my maiden name.

"Thank you, Miss Bailey," he replied. "You said a moment ago that you might never see me again. Will you tell me why? Surely you will meet me again or allow me to call on you?"

"No! no!" I exclaimed, hurriedly, "I must not see you again and neither can I invite you to call on me." I started away, but his voice stopped me.

"Is there any reason for this?" asked my companion, earnestly.

"Yes," I answered, "there is a reason which I cannot reveal."

"Miss Bailey," he went on, "do you remember telling me at our first meeting that you knew no one here in Meltown?"

"Yes," I replied, briefly, "I do."

"WELL," he went on more slowly, "I, too, am lonely and know scarcely anyone. Since meeting you the other evening I have looked forward to this evening, and have hoped that we might become good friends, for"—he paused and looked at me half-questioningly—"do you know I was very much drawn to you? Never before have I spoken to a woman without an introduction, but there seemed something about you that made me speak. I couldn't help it."

I really felt a genuine sorrow for him and told him so.

"Won't you let me

see you again?" he pleaded.

After his confession I had not sufficient courage to tell him my secret, thinking he would despise me. My conscience told me I must never see him again, but the voice of the Tempter whispered, "Surely you can do him no harm in seeing him once more?" And with a smile I told Henry Alston that I would meet him once more the following Thursday evening.

At that he grasped my hand with a joyous exclamation. Then bidding me a quiet good-night, he left me, and I slowly made my way home.

The following Thursday evening I met Henry as I had promised to do. Each week I met him twice, at least. During the bright spring evenings we spent many happy hours together. Each day I became more certain of his love for me and of the wrong I was doing in allowing him to think of me as single. Several times I had tried to break with him, and had even gone so far as to seek a quarrel, but to no avail, he simply would not quarrel with me.

Several times I was on the point of revealing to him my guilty secret, but something seemed to hold me back. Perhaps it was the inevitable look of pain I knew I would see in his honest brown eyes.

Little did my loving husband suspect what a despicable creature I was, and of what duplicity the woman he loved so ardently was capable. Someday, sometime, I knew it must all end as all such things end—in woe for someone.

ONE warm summer evening as I sat alone upon my spacious veranda, my husband having departed for New York a few moments before and Henry being away for a few days on business for his firm, a messenger boy came whistling up the broad walk and inquired for "Lillian Bailey." With a quaking heart I informed him that I was the person.

How thankful I was that my husband was not there. With a fast-beating heart I read the telegram:

"Henry Alston seriously hurt. Come at once to M— A— Hospital, New York."

Dizzily I entered the house. My benumbed brain refused to take in the seriousness of the strange situation. I was like one stunned. In a half-dazed way I searched for a time-table and found there was no train for New York before midnight.

Although I did not love Henry Alston, I was fond of him in a sisterly way, and knowing he was alone in the world and needed me now, I knew I must go to him. Slowly the tortuous hours dragged by until train-time. My one thought was to reach the hospital before it was too late.

All through the long hours of the night, as the noisy train thundered on its way bringing me each minute nearer and nearer to the man who loved and believed in me, the awfulness of the situation kept ringing through my mind. How was I to face this man? This was no time, I realized, to reveal my wickedness. He would not die happier knowing that the woman he loved was a sinful creature, not worthy a good man's love.

AS the train came to a standstill in the New York terminal I was weary in mind and body.

Slowly I dragged my tired feet to the hospital. At the door of Henry's room I met the doctor and was told that Henry was not expected to live more than a few hours.

Then a nurse took me into the room. She spoke to him quietly, and immediately his tired eyes opened and fell upon me standing motionless by his bed. He put forth a bandaged hand, and painfully and weakly grasped my icy fingers.

"Lillian," he gasped, "I am going to die. Will you marry me before I go? It will make me happy," he breathed.

Startled, I drew away, but paused as I saw the bright color dye his cheeks. Reaching for my hand again he said in a reproachful tone, "Why, Lillian, I was so sure that you would marry me that I took the liberty of sending for a minister to marry us; and I expect that he will be here any moment."

"I MUST have time to think," I replied, dully. Turning quickly away I walked unsteadily to the window and dropped down into a chair. "Oh!" I thought, "this is what my sin has led me to! Why, oh why did I ever do this thing?"

A soft knock at the closed door seemed to punctuate the stillness. A tall, elderly minister entered the room. As my eyes rested upon his serene face I came to a sudden decision. Rising, I crossed to the doctor's side and asked him in a low whisper how long he thought the injured man would live. He replied kindly, "I am afraid not more than two hours."

"Is there the faintest doubt in your mind?" I asked.

"No, there is not. I do not see how he could ever recover," he answered quietly. Quickly I turned from him and stepped to the sick man's bedside.

"Henry," I whispered, "I will marry you."

With a glad smile overspreading his pain-drawn face he motioned with his hand for the minister to come close.

AS Henry Alston and I clasped hands, I trembled from head to foot. Cold drops of perspiration stood out upon my face. As one in a dream I heard the minister's low, monotonous voice as he read the marriage ceremony that united Henry Alston and myself. At the words, "I pronounce you man and wife," I felt the blood stop in my heart. Every inch of me seemed to grow icy cold. Weakly I tried to speak, to protest, but not a word came from my lips.

"Now, Mrs. Alston, you may kiss your husband if you wish," the kind-faced man said as he closed his Bible. Smilingly, with hands that trembled in their eagerness, Henry Alston gently drew my face down to the snowy pillow, and our lips met in a first kiss. Then I went limp in his arms, and I sank down upon the floor in a heap.

Several moments later I opened my weary eyes and found myself in a sort of reception-room upon a couch.

The doctor bent over me as I stirred

and said, kindly, "Poor child, it was too much for you. I feared as much when our patient broached the subject yesterday."

Throwing the blanket that covered me to the floor, I sat up rather unsteadily, and in a weak voice asked, "How is Mr. Alston now?"

"WELL," replied the doctor, heartily, "he is no worse, but is rather anxious for you. You will want to see him again, no doubt, before you leave."

"No, no!" I cried excitedly.

The doctor eyed me with a keen glance of surprise.

"Very well, Mrs. Alston, it shall be as you wish," he said coldly.

Summoning all my strength I arose and crossed the room to the table where my hat, coat and bag lay. Picking up the hat with shaking fingers, I said in a firm voice, "Will you kindly telegraph me when the end comes?"

"Yes, Mrs. Alston, I will," he replied, briskly, a shade too briskly, I thought.

Somehow I managed to find a taxi to take me to the depot. During the few moments' drive I sat with my throbbing head clasped tightly in my cold hands. Suddenly a terrible thought flashed into my weary brain. Supposing he shouldn't die? What then? With a shudder I resolutely sent that thought from me. I would never have gone through the marriage ceremony with him if the doctor had not said positively that he would not live.

UPON my arrival home I found the telegram I had so anxiously awaited. Hastily I tore it open, but instead of the words I expected to see, I read in their place: "Henry Alston will recover. Wants you."

With a low moan I dropped the paper. In despair I wrung my hands as I paced the floor.

"Oh," I cried, "what will I do? I am a bigamist and have ruined Henry Alston's life as well as my own!"

I despised myself heartily. I felt as though I stood alone upon a great desert with no one to share this terrible secret. I wished for nothing so much as to die, for never could I bear my husband's reproaches, to say nothing of those of the man with whom I had just gone through a marriage ceremony.

"There is nothing I can do but wait and see what Henry Alston will do," I murmured, half-frantically. My secret seemed to burn within me like a living coal. I must share it with someone—but with whom? I could not tell my husband.

Then I thought of Helen—dear, unselfish girl that she was—I knew positively that she would come to me if she knew I needed her. In a few moments I had my sister on the 'phone. As soon as I heard her soft, musical voice I felt better.

She promised to come to me as soon as possible. True to her word she came in the early evening with Jim.

THE following morning I was too ill to leave my bed. Jim sent Helen to me, and in broken sentences I told her my secret. Her sweet sympathy was like balm to my storm-tossed soul, sympathy not alone for me but for Henry Alston as well.

"I have ruined his life," I cried, in my bitter misery.

"But surely, dear, there must be a way out," she replied, as she gently stroked my burning forehead. "Try and get some sleep now and later we will see what can be done." Although Helen was the younger, I felt then, if never before, that her soundness of faculties far out-balanced mine. Taking her advice, I lay perfectly quiet for several hours. At noon, when she brought me a light lunch, she said in a low whisper as she bent over my pillow, "I am going to the hospital to tell Henry Alston your story, dear." I opened my lips to protest, but she stopped me.

"No, let me finish," she said, firmly. "You don't want Jim to know, and you cannot have Mr. Alston coming here to claim his wife when he is well. Leave this to me, Lillian," she pleaded. "I feel certain I can adjust things in a satisfactory manner."

"Very well," I said, at last. Something must be done, it was plain.

EARLY the following day Helen went to New York. My heart ached with tender compassion for Henry Alston, and as I lay there in bed, I resolved that if things did adjust themselves rightly I would try in every way to make atonement for my sin.

Two days later I was up and about again, although still weak and pale. Jim had been gone but an hour when Helen came. As she entered the house I saw instantly from the expression of her face, that her errand had been a successful one. And I breathed a silent prayer of thanksgiving.

"Lillian," she exclaimed in a happy voice, "was there ever such a man as Henry Alston? He has forgiven you, dear, and," she hastened on, breathlessly, "he has promised never to mention the hateful affair to anyone."

"Dear God," I cried, the tears coming to my eyes, "you are too good to me!"

"There, dear," soothed my sister, "have a good cry and you will feel better."

"Helen," I asked, chokingly, "do you like him?"

"Do I like him?" she cried. "My dear, I simply fell in love with him. I really can't blame you for holding his friendship until it became dangerous." Suddenly a sadness came into her dark eyes.

"Do you know, Lillian," she said in a low voice, "he will always be lame. He will always have to walk with a cane now."

Several days later Helen went home leaving me with a deep sense of gratitude and peace in my heart—a sweet peace such as I had not known since that February evening that seemed so long ago.

SEVERAL months later I went on a visit to my father's home.

That evening, as I sat alone upon the veranda, a handsome limousine drew up to the curb, and from it stepped a tall young man. I saw instantly the slight limp as he came up the broad walk. Long before he reached the house I knew him. As he paused at the steps I arose to meet him.

"Henry," I cried passionately, as I extended my hand, "can you forgive me?"

"Lillian!" Henry Alston gasped. "Is it you?"

"Yes," my voice trembled a little—I was so ashamed.

Before he could speak the screen door opened and Helen came out. Henry Alston's eyes fell upon the beautiful girl before him; then he turned to me and said, gently, "Of course I can forgive you. If I had not known you I might not have met Helen. Do you know, when she came to plead your cause, I fell instantly in love with her. And I love her more dearly the longer I know her."

I took both my sister's hands in mine. "I wish you every happiness," I said, earnestly. "You deserve all the world can give you."

Then I went away and left those two alone together. ●

Why Not Help Us Edit True Story?

PERHAPS you know that our readers are welcomed to our editorial staff.

Why don't *you* help us edit TRUE STORY Magazine by sending constructive letters of criticism on the various features appearing in each issue? We are asking you to write and tell us:

First—Just what articles you like the best, and why.

Second—Just what articles you do not like, and why.

Third—How do you think the magazine could be improved?

Fourth—Whether you find errors, typographical, grammatical or otherwise.

GIVE a percentage rate for interest-holding qualities of features and stories as follows: Poor, equals a rating under 79 per cent; fair, equals 80 to 89 per cent; good, 90 to 93 per cent; very good, 94 to 96 per cent; superlatively good, 97 to 100 per cent.

Number each article to correspond with the page on which the story appears, and give its percentage of interest.

WE are offering a prize of $10.00 for the best letter, $5.00 for the second best letter, and $2.00 each for the next five best letters.

This is your opportunity to make your magazine as you like it, and, incidently, to turn your ideas into cash.

And your letter must be mailed sometime during February.

Please remember that comment and criticism of TRUE STORY'S contents are invited from its readers.

The 1930's

oo Truth is Stranger Than Fiction oo

Diary of a

JUNE 3 --- Donald kissed me --- sensual, seeking kisses that filled my soul with loathing

The confession of a beautiful woman who made the discovery that there are no light play-days for an ex-wife unless she pays for them dearly.

JUNE third—

Why does everything seem so changed since Martin went away? It shouldn't have made such a difference because it has been a long time since I've really loved him, and his going brought only a sense of freedom and release.

I, myself, have not changed. I am the same woman, with the same ideals and longings. Perhaps the only difference is that now I can dare to think of love and romance again, just as I did when I was a girl. Those five years of marriage with Martin, bitter and disillusioning as they were, did not cure me of that.

I'm still young, only twenty-four, and I feel a renewed sense of life and vitality. I'm glad that the struggle is over, that I don't have to try to love Martin any more, or to make him love me. I'm glad, too, that it was he who deserted and not I. I can try to be happy again without that conscience prick.

I had known during those years of our marriage that there had been other women for Martin, but I had not let myself have other men. Now I shall, for his going has released me. Someday, as soon as I can afford it, I shall get a divorce. I have plenty of grounds. Right now I am content just to let my heart search for the right man.

Oh, Martin, I did try so hard, and once I thought I loved you terribly. But it's over now. You've gone, and I can't be sorry. Life opens up before me, and I want it, all of it.

Tonight I have been with Donald Breen. I was forced to realize with a new bitterness just what it means to be a discarded wife. For years I had thought of Don as my friend, although it had been Martin who first brought him to the house. There had seemed to be a strong mutual attraction between us, but never a trace of love-making. I had believed it was because he respected me too much. Lately I've been thinking of Don a great deal. Perhaps, who knows, he may be the one man. Something in me always stirs to life whenever I am with him, and his eyes

Discarded Wife

follow me with a strange intentness. He is thrillingly handsome and I could so easily let myself love him.

When he asked me to drive out to his Summer camp and have dinner there, I didn't feel a bit uneasy, even though I knew that the season was closed, and the whole place deserted. I'd made such a habit of trusting Don that I felt utterly safe in his hands. He'd always treated me just as a woman likes to be treated, sort of repressed, as if there were lots of things he'd like to do and say, if he could. But I'd always known that he'd never over-step.

And now, tonight, to go with him alone like this, with no husband waiting in the background, made him appear all new and sparkling and strange. And yet, so sweetly safe. To me, a friendship, mellowed through the years, brought no sense of danger.

So it was with a singing heart that I dressed for the long drive to his camp. I put on the white knitted trouser suit that Martin said was so shocking, and one of those cocky little white wool caps that perch on the side of the head. As Martin's wife that rig would have seemed too frivolous, but as Connie Faber, on her own again, it was just the thing. I felt a sort of inward swagger as I walked down the driveway with Don. It was glorious to be young and free and open to all adventure.

"Pretty darned cute," he whispered, and pressed my arm close

I made a decision. I would go away. Pose as a girl, unmarried and unkissed.

OCTOBER 12

Are all men alike? Must all ex-wives expect propositions?

against his side. "You don't look over eight-een."

"And that's just how old I feel," I laughed.

The camp was really a large ten room house, shut off from the road by a thick grove of trees. There was a huge living room in the center, with a fire-place at one end, and four bedrooms open-ing on each side. I knew that Don had given some pretty wild week-end parties there and that his reputation was a bit shady, but everything always had been de-cent enough when our crowd came.

It was Don who lifted the absurd little cap from my head and tossed it on the table. "Queer things—wom-en," he said, "the clothes they wear, the thoughts they think and the silly little tricks they play. Don't be like that, Connie—with me. Get into something soft and clingy for tonight, won't you?" He led me toward one of the bedrooms and opened

MAY 4

*No man seems to value
much what some other
man has possessed
and thrown away.*

dressing table. I'd played with Don before, clean, honest fun, and this need be no different, it seemed to me, just because Martin was—gone.

And so I came out to him, smiling and radiant, and stood poised for a moment in the doorway so that he might get the full effect of the feminine lure he had demanded.

I saw his eyes kindle and blaze; then he strode toward me and took me in his arms. "That's better," he said. "I knew you could look like that. You're the most exquisite creature I ever saw."

I was glad he didn't kiss me then. He let me go the moment I pushed him from me. He was again putting on that mask of repression which I always had found so fascinating. Without it a man can't even be a charming play-fellow.

"I had Jean come out and fix dinner for us early this evening," he said. "It's here, ready, in the cooker. No, you can't work, dressed like that. Just sit there and let me wait on you."

He had drawn a table in front of the fireplace and was arranging the food before me as he spoke. He moved with a sure, lithe strength that always gave the impression of forces held in leash. His face was alive with charm and power. His teeth gleamed firm and white and his eyes glowed with vital fire. But a woman mustn't let herself love a man like

the door. "You'll find a lot of things in there, feminine things. Dress up for me."

"You don't like the trousers, then?"

"Sure. I told you they were cute. But not for—tonight. Change will you, while I build a fire and make some tea?"

SOMEHOW, as I stood looking at the lovely things hanging in the closet, I knew suddenly that Don never could be the One Man. This meant that there had been women, too many women, in a way that shut me out. Oh, I'm not a prig. I know men, I've had reason to know, yet somewhere, sometime, I'm going to find that One Man who'll be all mine, who'll want me to be all his, and he never could have his closet filled with women's clothes, or want me to wear them if he did.

But this was adventure and my heart could still thrill to it, even though I knew now that it couldn't be love. Tonight would be just—tonight, a moment to laugh about, and then to forget.

If Don wanted to play, all right I'd play. Why not? He was tremendously attractive and my laughter had been leashed so long.

I chose the most feminine and alluring of all the soft negligees, sprayed myself with perfume that I found on the

Don. I knew that, even as I felt my heart beats quicken. Just this moment—lightly—and then—pass on.

We ate, eyes clinging, hands touching, and lips holding back our thoughts. But, at last, when the meal was finished and the table had been pushed back, the barriers crashed and I was in his arms.

"You're lonely, Connie," he whispered, "and you're hungry for kisses."

I drew away, one hand pressed against his breast to keep him from me. "No, not just for kisses," I denied, "but for—love."

"For love, of course, that's what I meant." His lips were on mine, hot and hard.

"This is not love, Don."

"But it's sweet. Let's take it while it lasts."

"No, there's more for me than that, Don. There's everything. I'm not going to be content ever again with just a part."

"Don't be silly, Connie. I've wanted you for so long. Let's take tonight. It's ours."

He lifted me in his arms and carried me toward the bedroom beyond. I made no effort to struggle. I waited until he had placed me on the pillows; then I rested there, silent for a moment, looking up at him.

"No, Don," I said, "there mustn't be any more—tonight. Let me go now. Just because love failed me so terribly in my marriage, I needn't lose it forever. And I would be losing it, if I came to you like this tonight."

"Nonsense!" he cried, and drew me to him roughly. "What difference can it make to you now? You've known all there is to know. You're through with sentiment. It isn't as if you were a silly girl."

"But I'm no different than I was the last time we came here. You wouldn't have wanted me like this then."

"Of course not. There was Martin. He was my friend."

"But now," I cut in bitterly, "Martin is gone. That makes me fair game. It doesn't matter so much what happens to just—me."

"But you came here alone with me," he accused. "You're here in my arms, dressed like that—"

I laughed then, and the hot color streamed over his face. "Oh, no, Don, not dressed like this—that lets you out. The feminine lure was your idea, remember."

It was my laughter which cooled him. Quick anger took the place of his desire. "Anyway," he flared, "you knew what it meant."

"How could I know?" I demanded. "I'd been here before and it didn't mean anything then but a good time. I was willing to play a little tonight, and then to let it go. But this you're asking is—different."

"Sure it's different, and you shouldn't have started it at all unless you intended to go through with it."

"You mean that just because Martin has gone, just because I'm left sort of stranded and on my own, I mustn't play any more? If I were a young, unmarried girl, or if Martin was still waiting for me there at home, you'd stand guard, just as you did before. What you're trying to tell me now is that a man is careful of a woman only when he knows she has someone else to protect her. And that is being a pretty poor sport, Don."

"Oh, quit stalling!" He spoke with a brutal harshness and I saw the ugly veins commencing to stand out on his forehead. Anger and passion were running wild in him and anything that I might be saying or feeling could not reach him now.

I had struggled to my feet and was using all my strength to keep him away. "Then all this time it was only Martin that stood between me and—this? It wasn't something fine and sweet in me that you wanted to cherish. You don't even love me. Do you want me to believe that men are like this—all of them? I thought you were so fine!"

Don wasn't listening or caring. His kisses were bruising my lips, his strong arms seemed almost to be breaking my slender body. In those next few moments nothing seemed to matter greatly except the wave of horrible soul sickness which swept over me.

"No, no, Don, not after our years of friendship, of really liking me, guarding me, not this, just because I am—alone!"

"Just because you are so damnably tempting!" His voice was hoarse and unnatural. "You've made me want you, and I'm going to have you—just why, you can figure out tomorrow. This, my sweet, is tonight!"

And now, standing here alone in my room, I'm wondering if Don was worse than most men, or if that is really life. I've got to find out. Love must be there somewhere waiting, clean and fine, just as it always has been. Tonight has killed something in me, just as did those five years of marriage with Martin. But not my faith in love. That is still there. I'll find it someday.

OCTOBER twelfth—
It has been four montsh now since I've really had courage to sit down and face the truth. But I'm forced now to realize that Don was no worse than most men. Being a discarded wife has seemed to make me a target for every unfair proposition that a man can make. I guess all men are alike and an ex-wife must expect such proposals.

Perhaps it was my own fault. I don't know. I do realize that I've been deliberately searching for love, wanting it, needing it. Maybe I've attracted men by that longing, stirred them too much. Yet most of them are willing enough to court a young, unmarried girl, aren't they? Willing to wait, to woo, and to protect. I am young in years, young really in that sort of experience, yet not once since Martin left me have I escaped disaster. I realize now that as Martin's ex-wife there can be no more light play-days for me, unless I want to pay dearly for them.

I can no longer even try to figure out why this is so, but I know what I am going to do. I am going away where I am not known. I shall take my own name, Connie Faber, leaving Martin's name, and all the past behind me. I can't afford to get a divorce yet, but I have a right to my freedom and my happiness, without carrying this brand of a discarded wife.

APRIL first—
AND it worked gloriously! I am here in a small Southern California city, as Connie Faber, unmarried and unkissed.

And I've found The Man. Surely I should have known why no other man could have been The One. I should have known why I could not really love Martin, or Don, or any of the others. Because they were not—Brian, and only Brian could have made me realize that when a woman loves, nothing else counts. After I found him I didn't have to force myself to forget Martin, and all the scars that came afterward. They were wiped out, as if they had never been. This was a new life, a new world.

It's hard to describe Brian. His charm to me seems to rest so much in the spirit of him, the strength and the tenderness of his mouth, the clear, keen honesty of his eyes, and the firm sturdy vigor of his tall, slender body. I seem to sense, rather than see him, and he seems a part of my very self.

I wish now that I hadn't deceived him in the beginning. On the very first day we met he asked me if I were married, or if there was any other man. Without hesitation I had, at once, replied: "There is no other man." Perhaps it wasn't a complete lie, yet I wish now that it had been the complete truth. But I hadn't known then that Brian was to be for me the end of the quest. Afterward, when I tried to tell him, I couldn't. I hated to spoil the wonder and the beauty of this new love I had found. Yet experience had been so bitter, and this was so heavenly. I drifted on without telling.

I have a tiny income, left by my mother, just barely enough to live on, and if I can find work here in California, perhaps I can before long save money enough to get a divorce.

APRIL eighteenth—
How can any heart hold such a wealth of happiness. I have learned that I can get what they call a Mexican mail-order divorce for fifty dollars. A lawyer assured me that it would be legal, and that after the papers went through, I could immediately re-marry. I found a job in a gift shop and at the end of six weeks was able to save the fifty dollars.

I wrote to Martin asking him to sign the necessary papers and to make it as simple for me as he could.

Before long now I shall be free to marry Brian when he asks me. And I know, oh, so happily, that he will ask.

APRIL thirtieth—
He did, this very night. We were lying on the beach in our bathing suits. It was one of those gorgeous California nights, when the moon seems like a great ball of fire in the sky and the water a vast gilded carpet.

"It has been so wonderful," he said. "I've wanted to keep it just like this. But I can't any longer, darling. I've got to have you, all of you, for my own."

"I've wanted to keep it like this, too," I whispered, "every sweet minute of it, every touch of you, every look in your eyes. And I'm so glad we stopped to pick all the lovely flowers along the way. We didn't miss any of them, did we, Brian? You remember them all, the first time you touched my hand, the first kiss. Then all the precious words, too, the first time you said, 'I love you,' remember—?"

"That was the Springtime garden, Connie. I wanted you to have it. But now—it's Summer. There'll be even lovelier flowers in our new garden, for I'm saying now, I want you, I must have you. Marry me, beloved."

"Oh, darling, darling Brian. Marry you—yes, just as soon as—I can."

Now the moment to tell of Martin, the divorce, the ugly shadowed past. But the moment came—and went. I could not spoil this night. Soon, of course, he must know it all. But not until I had the papers, until I was really free. Then I'd tell him, and surely love, his and mine, would make it right.

MAY third—
The lawyer tells me now that I am free. The fifty dollars has been paid, the papers are in my hands. Strange that it should be so simple. And now, tonight, I shall have courage to tell Brian. Later. . . .

Tonight has come—and gone. Perhaps the most breathlessly glorious night of all my life. We had gone out in Brian's little motor boat. The bay was as quiet as a lake and the far off lights along the shore blinked like watching eyes. We had anchored in a cove and had found a great flat rock upon which to sit. We seemed alone in a little world of our own. Just sky, and water, and the warm, fragrant night.

I was in Brian's arms, my head pressed down close against his steadily beating heart. I loved to listen to that beat, it seemed like part of my own life throbbing there. I reached up and drew him nearer. I must hold to him close like that, while I found courage to say all that must be said.

"Brian," I commenced, at last. "There's a lot I have to tell you, but first I want to know what it is that makes you love me most. It's the real me, isn't it, that part deep down which no one else has ever touched?"

"That's it, darling, you've found my answer. I love you most because you're so unspoiled, so untouched by life. You're different from any girl I've ever known. I expect every boy, even if he won't admit it, keeps that ideal, and has that secret desire to know that when his wife comes to him, no other man has ever had her. I didn't hope ever really to find that ideal, until you came—so I think I love you most for that sweetness, darling, all the fragrance of our Springtime garden that will blossom first for me."

"No, no, Brian!" My voice rose in a quick fear. "That isn't what I mean. It isn't for that you love me most—it's something deeper, the spirit of me, the soul, that no matter how long I had lived, or how much I had known, could never have been touched except by you, by your love and mine together. Tell me, it's that, darling—"

"Of course, that's what I've been trying to say—"

"No, Brian, you don't understand. Suppose there had been some one else first—"

"Hush, darling, there wasn't. You have told me there wasn't. 'No other man,' you said. And it meant a tremendous lot to me."

"But you would have loved me, wanted me just the same, even if there had been—other men?"

"Nothing could make me stop wanting you. It would just have been—different—that's all. Not this perfect thing we have now."

"But we'd still be married and—happy?"

"Of course. But—" Suddenly he drew back and looked deep into my eyes. "But, Connie—you don't mean—" His voice broke off and, as if in protest against his thought, he drew me fiercely close. "Stop trembling, sweetheart, and stop talking nonsense. Don't spoil our lovely night. I have known you through and through, way down to your soul. It's all sweet, and all mine." His lips were pressed close again. So once more the moment came—and went. I'd tell him, oh, yes, the words must be spoken sometime, but not tonight.

MAY fourth—
This morning I woke with a sense of heaviness and depression. Brian's words kept ringing in my ears. "Every boy, even if he won't admit it, keeps that ideal, a girl who will be all his own." And again. "All the fragrance of our Springtime garden, that will blossom first for me."

What if he could have known of those horrible, torturing nights that I spent by Martin's side, the fever of his passion that had felt no love? What if he had known of Don, that night when all the garden had been trampled, and those other men who had destroyed my life's illusions?

If he knew would he blame me so much for wanting to wipe it out, to start all fresh and new as Connie Faber, the

girl I once had been, that I longed so intensely still to be?

I had to make sure. I couldn't put it off any longer. I was to have dinner with Brian in my own little apartment. I had made up my mind that after the meal I'd tell him.

I could hardly listen to Brian's words because I was so intent upon finding words of my own with which to tell him all that he must know before I could marry him.

"Brian," I leaned forward and drew his hand up against my cheek. "I wonder if you, or any man, can realize some of the things a young and pretty woman has to stand if she's once married and then—has been left alone?"

He laughed. "I expect she has to stand a lot. But don't worry, darling, I'll never be leaving you alone one single night after we're married."

No, that wasn't the right start. Those weren't the words. I'd have to commence again.

"But Brian, I'm serious, and I want you to listen. I know, oh so bitterly, just all she has to stand. Men don't seem to value much what some other man has possessed and thrown away. It doesn't give a girl a fair chance to start again if a man knows—" My words ended in a sharp cry and I sprang to my feet. I had looked up to see Martin standing in the doorway.

I spread out my arms instinctively as if I must keep Brian from him. "No, no, Martin, wait—not now, not here—"

Oh, what was I saying, guilty words, as if there was so much to conceal. But Brian mustn't hear it first like this, not as if the confession had been wrung from me. I had meant to tell him, the words almost had been spoken, and now—

Martin's voice, cutting through the twilight of the room, darkening it, making everything so ugly.

"So this is why you were so anxious for a divorce! I thought that might be it when I got your letter so I ran down to see." Yes, the words were being spoken. I could not stop them. They went on and on. I stood rigid, listening, unable for the moment to move or to protest. "But I'm afraid I can't let you go so easily, my dear. I've found out that one woman is about as bad as another in the end. I can't live alone, so I want my wife back. We'll both have plenty to forgive, so let's call it quits and go on from where we left off."

Then Brian, moving forward, his face white and stricken, his hands gripping my shoulders. "Connie, what is this man trying to say?"

"I'm trying to say that this is my wife you've been playing around with," Martin cut in. "And that I'm taking her back home with me where she belongs."

I realized then that Martin had been drinking. Oh, this mustn't go on. My bright new happiness mustn't be crushed like this, and that look must somehow be driven from Brian's eyes. It was too terrible, and the hurt of it would tear at my heart as long as I lived.

"Brian, Brian darling, listen to me, try to understand. Yes, it's true, I was his wife, but, oh—don't you see—"

What use were the words now? For a moment Brian's hands reached out, then fell heavily to his sides. "His wife—but you said—God, no, Connie, this isn't true, it isn't happening. You couldn't have lied to me like that, let me think—not that it would have mattered

so much, if you just hadn't—lied." He jerked back his head as if to shake off an evil dream, then slowly his eyes narrowed and he looked from Martin to me. "You—Connie—and I thought you were —all mine."

That was all, incoherent, broken words, and I helpless now to take that stricken look from his eyes. Then, before I could stop him, he had gone. Better so, perhaps, for the ugly blight of Martin's presence in the room had withered all our lovely garden.

I don't want to remember that scene with Martin after Brian had gone. All the ugly shame of it, his words and mine. But I had to make him know that it was the end, to make him realize all that he had done to me and why I never could come back. Once I had tried so desperately to love him and now I tried as desperately to pity. But all I could feel was this new terrifying hate.

But perhaps I should not, at this moment, have blamed Martin so much for that, or hated him so bitterly. He had been the wrong man for me, that's all, had despoiled the garden, trampled on all the flowers. Only for Brian could they have truly have bloomed, and Brian has gone. Martin has gone, too, forever. I made sure of that before I closed the door.

OCTOBER thirty-first—
Then those long hours of trying to pull myself together, to reconstruct my little world again, and somehow to go on. Should I go to Brian with my pitiful little plea for understanding, or should I wait until he came back to me? For surely he would come.

Yes, he came, grave-faced and heavy-eyed, but with arms held out to enfold me.

"No, let's not talk about it," he pleaded. "I've been over it all in my own mind before I came back to you, and now I think I understand. You had learned a lot of bitter lessons and you were trying to forget."

"But, Brian, tell me just this: If you had known that I had been married, that I was a discarded wife, that other men had kissed and wanted me, and in the end had made me hate it all, would you have loved me—just the same?"

"Darling, how can I answer that? I remember that you tried to ask me some such thing once before. I knew only that I fell in love with one girl, the girl I thought you were, but I know, too, that I love that other woman, also, the woman you really are. Perhaps, after all, we can be glad that we had the Springtime. If you had told me the truth right at first, you might have robbed us both of that. Maybe if I had known in the beginning, I'd have been no different from those other men. I'd have gone on searching for the Springtime, and would have missed our—Summer."

Brian, my lover, only you could have understood my heart, or could have put into words like that my own most sacred thoughts. Yes, we'll go on together into our lovely garden, trying to forget that other hands have picked the first rare blooms.

But first, before we were married, Brian insisted upon a more regular divorce. "For the sake of—our children," he reminded me.

It will delay us perhaps a year, but Brian is showing me, oh, so tenderly, that he is willing to woo and to—wait. ●

Top Honors go to Rubber Suits

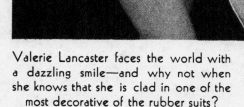

Valerie Lancaster faces the world with a dazzling smile—and why not when she knows that she is clad in one of the most decorative of the rubber suits?

June Clyde's rose and white crinkled rubber cap may not keep the hair dry or the curl in, but it's grand for loafing on the beach

Phyllis Barry, they tell us, is getting in trim, (very trim) for the strenuous vamping she has to do in the new Wheeler and Woolsey comedy, "In the Red". And being a smart young lady, she does it in the fashionable way, clad in bathing garb

Barbara Barondess, left, who is as blonde as the classic boy of Ancient Greece, chooses heavy green rubber with a rubber bandana top in which to greet the beach crowds. If you, too, are blonde, follow her example

BEACH LIFE OF 1933

When I Learned

One impulsive moment, one impetuous kiss . . . and their marriage was shattered! Would you do as this wife did, if your husband strayed?

TO SOME love comes suddenly and but once—burning on to the end of time in an all consuming flame. And if we deny it or try to destroy it, there is heart-break, anguish and sorrow which follow as relentlessly as the wrath of God.

Love was like that with me!

I was overjoyed when I got the position of under-secretary in the big offices at the Waverly plant. It was a move up in my profession. A move that I needed badly. I didn't dream that it was the opening of a new life as well.

Bending over my desk that first morning, struggling with the unfamiliar detail of my new work, I was unaware that any one had entered the room until Grant Worth's husky, deep-throated voice came over my shoulder. Startled, I looked up, straight into the darkest, most lustrous eyes I ever saw.

"Take a letter, please, Miss Brown," he said.

Something deep down inside me clutched at my heart. I gasped: "Certainly."

I knew even then that I had fallen hard. But I kept telling myself over and over— "Things like this don't happen to girls like me. You simply musn't fall in love with the boss' son. When *he* picks a wife she'll have to rate a place in the social register."

He lingered a few moments to consult me about my notes. His fine head was bent low, thick, dark hair almost brushed my own ash-gold curls.

What a wave of emotion swept over me! I could scarcely breathe. Oh—how can I make you see this man—little more than a boy, really, as I saw him that day? The most utterly lovable human being anyone could imagine.

I couldn't bear to let the other girls guess what had happened to me for it looked to me as though I were headed for nothing more than a big ache. I tried to keep my chin up and my eyes smiling.

But it wasn't very long until the whole office force knew that Grant was going for me in a big way, too.

For a while we just drifted. Then, there was one night in my apartment. Grant had called for me early. I had to keep him waiting. When I stepped from my dressing room, all powdered and fresh and fragrant, he gathered me into his arms and I knew from his manner that his mother had been bringing pressure to bear against me. I saw the deep hunger of desire in his dear, dark eyes. And, for that moment, my heart stood still.

If he wants me, I thought, longing for what happiness I could grasp, he can have me any way he'll take me. Then

# of His Folly

I saw the stain of hot emotion sweep my husband's face as he stooped to take Nan's kiss. It was ghastly to look at—jealous as I was.

two together before someone would cut in on us.

We were starting a heavenly waltz when Grant complained: "Here comes another." His voice was cross. "It'll be the end of everything."

"Are you going to—let it be?" I whispered back audaciously.

Laughing happily, Grant held me closer to his heart. "You darling!" His lips brushed my ear. "Let's beat it then and let them boil."

The French windows to the wide terrace stood open. We fled to Grant's car, parked under a tree at the edge of the grounds.

"You're awfully sweet to come out here with me," he whispered.

And then, without quite knowing how I got there, I was in Grant's arms and the distant orchestra sounded like harps in heaven.

Silently I let my face press softly against his. He turned his head. Our lips met. I'll make him stop in a minute, I thought.

But I didn't. I couldn't!

Laughing a little I stretched up my arms to tangle my fingers in his thick, dark hair. With a half-cry, he buried his lips in the curve of my throat.

After *that* kiss, a creature I had never known existed sprang to life inside me, overpowering my senses with the terrible hunger that tortured it. I was a person spellbound—helpless—anything might happen. . . .

THIS can't have happened to me! That was the first frightened whispering of my awakening conscience. It positively can't!

The damp sweet smell of spring came in the open car window. And a little patch of moonlight glistened on young leaves overhead. Below us the water murmured softly.

"Don't worry, darling. I'm going to marry you," Grant declared. Then with a half-shamed, boyish chuckle—"I just can't wait for the whole world to know that you belong to me alone. I'm sinfully proud."

I lay quite still in his arms, thinking ahead. Oh—I wasn't afraid that Grant wouldn't do the right thing. It was there in the worshipful look on his face when he took me. His eyes were loyal and clean—if you understand. But I was thinking of the time when we would be married, when I'd take my place in Grant's world as Grant's wife. Accepted as something I was not. He and I knowing. Would we still feel this way about each other? I, too, had my pride.

Suddenly I wished that we hadn't. That our love had not been so swift, so insistent, so impatient. I was afraid!

Grant's arms tightened about my trembling body. "What's the matter, honey?" he asked gently. "Don't you really love me? Don't you want me as much as I want you?"

"You know I do," I gasped. "But right now I'm positively stiff with fear."

a flush of shame for my weakness stained my cheeks. Gently I drew away.

"I wonder if you know exactly how sweet you are?" whispered Grant.

"That's a good line, too," I answered, picking up my wrap as I slipped past him and through the door.

It wasn't until that night at the country club that things got completely beyond control. How suddenly some things can happen! There was a terrible jam. The stag line wound along one wall and clear across the end of the room. It seemed impossible to take more than a step or

"Fear?" echoed Grant. "Why fear?"

"I'm afraid of the things this secret knowledge will do to our confidence and trust in each other. I wish we weren't getting married like this, Grant. I wish we had . . . waited."

"Don't be such a gloom, darling," he begged. "Nothing's going to happen to us."

"But we're almost strangers, Grant. And after we're married—when I meet your friends—will I be wondering if every girl is possibly someone that has been before me? Will you see in my friends possible lovers? We couldn't build faith on a thing like that."

"IT'S no use, Grant," I said, "I'm going back to my desk where I belong. But let's part friends, can't we?"

He took my chin in his strong, tender fingers to look at me searchingly. "I couldn't have believed you so simple," he said wonderingly. "You talk as though we were the very first. I'll wager that ninety per cent of the couples that marry—loving each other as we do—have tripped over this same step."

"Small comfort to us if, losing our faith, we stumble over the next one, too. And," I repeated stubbornly, "I still wish we hadn't."

"Snap out of it, sweet," Grant laughed and tried to kiss my fears away. "The words we'll say before a minister will be only a—second marriage."

I DON'T know if I planted the seeds of mistrust myself that night, or if things just had to be. At any rate, it wasn't very long after our wedding before Grant and I encountered rough sailing. This, with each of us loving the other dearly.

I didn't really fit into Grant's crowd and I guess that made things a lot worse. All of his set had been friends together since childhood. I was the outsider.

We were both frantically jealous. I, of everything and everybody and of Nan Daws, in particular—the girl Grant's mother had wanted him to marry. He, of every man I met. To make matters worse, there was that overwhelming pride in each of us—making words difficult.

One night at a dancing party, Nan Daws deliberately set out to entice Grant with her charms. She succeeded. Coming in from the terrace where I had gone to cool off a bit, I saw them. He was holding her closely; her bare shoulders gleamed white against his dark coat. Her lifted lips were soft and very close to his. Then, with an unintelligible murmur, my husband stooped to take the kiss she so freely offered. He crushed her to him as though he could not bear to ever let her go. Even at that distance I saw the stain of hot emotion that colored his face.

It was ghastly to look at—eaten with jealousy as I was. Grant couldn't help it, maybe, men being what they are, but he might have held off, I thought.

I didn't tell him I had witnessed the scene. *I couldn't.* But next night, at a beach party, I swam out to the raft, anchored about a hundred and fifty feet from shore, with Nick Ash. It was my way of paying Grant back in his own coin.

Nick had a vile reputation regarding married women. He was a gorgeous animal. Conceited and proud of his manly form. Poison to many husbands. But he could be frightfully sweet and sympathetic. And he wasn't dumb.

"Never turn your back on the enemy," he said, drawing himself up beside me. "Face her and fight."

I turned over without answering and lay looking up at the mere shadow of a moon—my heart breaking within me.

"Besides—you're too simple," he continued in a judicial tone. "You take small trifles much too seriously. Things like that mean nothing in our crowd. It's just—paprika—sprinkled over our salad."

Leaning on his elbow, he bent close above me. "You're lovely. You could drive us all ga-ga if you'd come out of your medieval shell. I'm half mad about you as you are."

He was comforting. I found myself wondering if his theory of life was true after all. If to let him kiss me would mean nothing—be simply pleasant and harmless and healing to that terrible pain in my heart.

He must have read my thoughts for, the next instant, his lips were on mine. His heart pounded wildly. I could feel its savage beating.

And right then I made a startling discovery. The kiss was pleasant—but far from harmless! I liked it. I wanted it to go on. It was forbidden and shocking and thrilling all rolled into one. And I didn't want him to stop.

I don't know what might have happened if, just at that moment, someone on the beach hadn't cupped his hands and shouted, "Break!"

Probably it did look pretty bad from that distance, in the dim light of the new moon—but I give you my word that there was only that one kiss between us—then. But one kiss is oftentimes enough to knock marital bliss for a loop.

THAT night Grant took his injured pride and his business suit into the small back bedroom. I followed him. Stubborn pride forced me to say: "It's no use, Grant. We might as well cut our losses now. I'm leaving tomorrow anyhow. Going back to my desk where I belong. But, please, let's be decent about it. It's been a wonderful experiment."

His eyes remained frozen. He turned his face to the wall without speaking. "I'm not guilty of the thing you think," I went on, as steadily as I could. "But in my heart I know I could be. I guess that's almost as bad. I'm not staying to be driven into something that'd make me despise myself forever. We can call it incompatibility and wash everything up clean. But—can't we be—good sports—respect each other as—friends?"

"Suits me." Grant's pride-stiffened words were curt. "Fix it any way you like."

I went back to my room—not to sleep but to pack. I went stubbornly forward from that point, step by step, until I stood before the old judge and took the paper he handed me—my decree of absolute divorce.

Then suddenly I had a complete revulsion of feeling. The divorce I had been determined to have seemed now a hateful thing. Nausea of it shocked me almost into insensibility. And I knew that I'd never again know happiness unless I could destroy it and everything could be as it was before.

Queer, how one can feel and not feel. I was like a person completely severed in half [Continued]

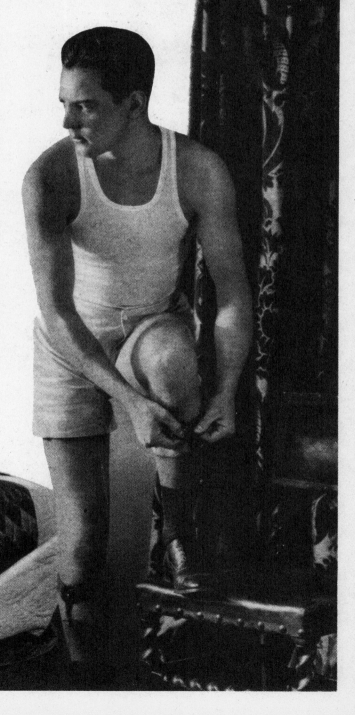

"SUITS me." My husband's pride-stiffened words were curt. "Fix it any way you like."

The Untold Story of Joan Crawford's Past!

When I Learned of His Folly

yet somehow able to move through space. Queer, too, how one may be free yet bound a million times more securely by that very freedom.

Looking neither to the right nor left, I made my way into the open and climbed into my little roadster. The car lunged forward under the pressure of my foot and I felt cool air sting my face. Corners slid past. I hardly noticed for now that everything was settled I was sorry. And it was too late. I wanted Grant with every fiber of my being, would always want him, but he wasn't offering me a second chance. It was his move and he was going in the opposite direction. He and Nan were to be married this very afternoon.

My hands clenched the steering wheel. I half hoped, as I hurled the car forward, that I wouldn't see a curve ahead in time. That there'd be a crash. Oblivion.

Nothing happened. After a while, I headed back to town, back to my desk to try and find oblivion in work. . . .

LONG days stretched into weeks, broken only by Nick Ash's persistent attempts to make love to me. I guess the hope aroused that night on the raft didn't die easily. In spite of his natural charm and the fact that I was now free to accept his attentions, I couldn't endure his caresses.

Six months passed; six months of dreading the future; of wondering why Grant and Nan had not returned from their honeymoon; of hoping they wouldn't knock around too much in my way, for I knew I'd have to go on acting like a good sport and it was breaking my heart.

Then one day, in a narrow booth at the Green Gate, I was munching a sandwich and sipping a glass of milk for lunch when someone slipped into the seat opposite.

Glancing up, I looked straight into the cool, green eyes of Nan Daws Worth. I shrank back—hating her. She must know that she was torturing me. Wasn't it enough that she had my husband? Need she openly gloat over me?

"You despise me," she stated matter-of-factly, without any attempt at greeting. "And quite right. I rather hate myself—now."

She went on. "It was rough work, Avis. We were cats—all of us. Particularly myself. And you, poor kid, with all the cards stacked against you."

"Don't waste your pity," I answered stiffly. "Highway robbery can be very amusing at times."

"That's exactly what I want to talk about. Grant and I having been paired off since childhood I got to thinking he belonged to me. When you came along and married him, I thought it was highway robbery—myself, the victim. I found it anything but amusing. I thought you were a common chiseler. And I was darned sore." She bit her under lip and drew a long breath. "Afterwards—I found out it was I who was the chiseler—taking what never could have been mine in any other way."

Reluctantly I scored Nan's side of the sheet. Her utter honesty and frankness demanded that.

"Let's let bygones be bygones," I begged, trying hard not to cry.

"Thanks, Avis. You're more than fair. I'm even less deserving than you think. I haven't the excuse of an undying love for Grant. Oh, I'm not denying that I felt his sex-appeal all right." She gazed at me ruefully. "But it wasn't a death-dealing blow. I never really loved him. No more did he me."

There didn't seem to be any answer to that either, so I pushed my glass away and started to rise.

"Wait!" Nan said sharply. "I want to be the one to tell you that I have never lived in your house. And I'm not Grant's wife. We were divorced in Paris. That's why we've been gone so long."

My knees folded up weakly. I sank back into my seat. I knew then how a soldier must feel when the war is over and the enemy suddenly becomes his friend. I found myself admitting that I had no corner on sportsmanship.

Grant came to see me right away and my hopes flew high—then were dashed to the ground.

I couldn't figure him out. He was friendly and protective and affectionate toward me, but he seemed more than ever like a person within a person. It was the outside Grant only that I was able to reach.

Strange as it sounds, the three of us—Nan, Grant and I—became good friends. We went about a lot together although people thought it shocking. They never tired of pointing us out and whispering—"Grant Worth and his two divorcees!"

THAT was how things stood the night Grant took us both to dinner at Harper's Inn.

He leaned across the corner of the table with a light for my cigarette. The knuckles of his smooth brown hand bumped my chin. Even at that slight contact my heart did an upward plunge, only to slide down again, leaving me quite faint.

"Don't suppose you girls have the least idea why I asked you to dine with me tonight?" He looked from me to Nan and back again. His right brow raised quizzically.

Nan shook her head—"No."

Snubbing his cigarette on the side of his saucer, he squared his shoulders and plunged. "Wanted to tell you about my new girl." He chuckled self-consciously and paused. Then: "Crystal Farnsworth. A recent importation of Dad's. I'm pash about her."

My throat pinched together. Grant—and *another* woman! I wanted to scream. I wanted to pound on the table until my fists bled and the dishes rattled drunkenly to the floor. I wanted to forbid it. But I couldn't. I had no right.

I wondered what was to become of me. Of Grant. I sat there quivering with the wild, torturing hunger that had filled my every dream and waking moment since we parted—wondering if it was always to be like this. I wondered if a woman ever forgets a man she's really loved and lived with . . . if only the man is able to forget. . . .

Nan had, I told myself, but she said it was because she didn't really love Grant and she'd felt all the while that he was looking through her at the ghost of me.

I straightened—suddenly alert. The

thought struck me that perhaps that was why Grant was considering this third marriage. Perhaps he did still love me as I hoped and prayed he did. Perhaps, thinking it useless to let me know, he wouldn't risk another hurt and was merely trying to find the ghost of our love in another woman.

If this weren't true, then he was simply a sensation seeker, playing at love. I positively knew he wasn't that.

An idea slowly formed in my mind. It filled me with a thrilling terror—terror, that trying, I might fail. I told myself: It's a darned poor rule that can't be worked both ways. If jealousy and hurt pride took Grant from me—why can't they bring him back?

I glanced up to meet his unreadable gaze. "Splendid!" I cried, imagining he seemed a bit surprised. "It's bound to be the talk of the town. Let's make it a bit more original though. Give the gossips a really novel sensation."

"Sounds 'sthough you were hatching something," Grant grunted. "Spill it."

"Well—everybody thinks it's such a scandal that Nan and I are good friends —we three knocking around like this—I was thinking that it would be pretty good if we got together and threw a party to introduce Crystal. Open up the lodge, Grant. Let Nan and myself be hostesses. We'll make up the list—arrange everything." I laughed as lightly as I could to hide the deep anxiety that filled me. "I think it would be fun."

Grant's glance strayed to his coffee cup. I saw the muscles of his jaw stiffen. Suddenly he reached into his pocket and drew out a bunch of keys. Detaching one from the ring, he pushed it across the table to me. "Go ahead. Guess I owe you two all the satisfaction you can get out of it."

I HAD to take Nan into my confidence. We talked things over but she was doubtful.

"Nick's bad medicine," she said, shaking her head.

"Granted—but sometimes," I pointed out, "it takes poison to kill poison. Besides—what have I to lose?"

The list of guests was arranged carefully. After everyone had accepted, Nan and I went out to open the house, put things in order and receive provisions.

At last the stage was set. Nearly time for the guests to arrive. Nan was arguing with the bootlegger at the back door. I stepped into the bedroom—the room Grant and I had occupied—and slipped off the smock I had been wearing, took my party dress from the bed and dropped it over my head. It was the prettiest one I possessed. Grant's favorite color, too— pale green and silver.

Taking my divorce decree from my bag where I had carried it always, I slipped it inside my brassiere. To feel it there gave me courage. I needed plenty of that. I hadn't the least idea what this Crystal girl was like—I only hoped and prayed that she wasn't too absolutely devastating.

Finally, by ones and twos, the gang arrived. Almost the very last to put in an appearance was Grant, with him, Crystal. My hopes lifted when I saw her. She was cheap, like a gilded clock. She wore her clothes with an air of insincerity that plainly labeled her "gold-digger."

Since a pow-wow on the beach was out of the question at this time of the year, we gathered in front of the wide fireplace. We pushed back the furniture, piled tables in corners, scattered mats and pillows over the floor. The great log on the hearth settled down to a steady glow—its warm red light filling the room.

Before long couples were pairing off into dark corners.

Nick and I settled down to an exciting flirtation in a corner of our own. Glancing amusedly around at the affectionate couples, he leaned closer. His liquor-laden breath nearly stifled me.

"Divorce has improved you, innocent," he murmured. "You've certainly learned how to throw a wicked party."

I smiled. "You'd be surprised how one can develop under—proper conditions."

His hand slid expertly under my arm. "You've been so darned stand-offish I came near passing up this party tonight. Wouldn't I have been sore if I had?"

"M-m-m. Specially since I had you in mind when we arranged it." Then, freeing myself from his embrace, I got up. With a provocative smile over my shoulder, I moved off. I crossed the hall and stepped into the bedroom. Nick followed.

He was much too excited to kick the door shut—and I noticed with a little shiver of hope and fear that the red glow of the burning log in the grate across the hall fell full on the deep window seat.

Sinking into this cushioned corner, I leaned my head against the cool glass. Nick promptly settled down beside me and transferred it to his shoulder.

His mouth closed over mine. I felt myself go limp in his arms. As I've mentioned before—Nick knew his kisses. I responded in spite of myself. Then I realized with a queer, sick feeling at the pit of my stomach that he didn't intend to waste too much time in preliminaries. His hands were moving with soft caressing strokes—but in a quite business-like manner.

Suddenly, over his shoulder, I saw Grant crossing the hall. His chin jutted out pugnaciously. His shoulders were squared with unmistakable intent.

Before I could wriggle out of Nick's seeking clasp, Grant thrust wide the door. Grasping Nick by his coat collar, he lifted him and, for all his size, fairly hurled him into the hall.

Then he closed the door and locked it, turning to glare at me. "Is *nothing* sacred to you? Not even this room?"

I struggled to my feet, shrank back trembling from the fury in his face. And without in the least intending to do so burst into sobs.

The next instant his arms were around me. Lifting me bodily, he carried me to the bed and put me down on the pillows. Cradling me on one arm, he reached for his handkerchief to dab gently at my tears. He said: "For God's sake, darling, don't cry. I couldn't stand watching that bounder paw you." He choked so he could hardly speak. "Damit—I love you."

For answer I reached up my arms and pulled his head down until his lips pressed hard in the hollow of my throat.

"Darling, darling," he groaned, "I thought it would never be like this again."

The last shred of my stubborn pride was swept away. Slipping my divorce decree from my breast, I tore it into shreds and let the pieces flutter silently to the floor. "It'll always be like this," I whispered. "Take me, Grant. I can never belong to anyone but you." ●

Here is the confession of a modern girl who thought she could make her own love code. And then she learned that you can't have love without honor.

I Said It Could Never

THE red light flashed. I opened the key and someone's voice said softly, "Love me, Beautiful?" Clay Morel's voice. It tingled along my nerves in little shivers of ecstasy. I knew that I was a fool to let my feelings run away with me. Clay was "class" in Blairsville. The upper strata, while I was just Rosanna Best who ran the telephone exchange. We, that is, Mother, Bill, my little sister Becky and I, lived in a small frame house on the wrong side of the tracks. My brother Bill was a lineman for the same company I worked for. He was a good-looking boy, democratic to the core, and he turned up his nose at my qualms of conscience.

"What have the Morels got that we haven't got?" he asked me once. I said, "Just nothing, Bill, nothing—but all the money in the world; the key to the town, and ringside seats when they get to heaven."

A small town can be the last word in snobbery and although Clay had been giving me a rush, I had no romantic illusions concerning his parents. Mrs. Morel was a cold, sharp-featured woman with snow-white hair. "Old Hatchet Face," my brother Bill called her. Clay's father was a contractor who got all the plums that fell from the county tree.

Just now Blairsville was building a new grammar school and my little sister, Becky, was all excited about it, for the good citizens had dug into their pockets to the extent of a gym and a swimming pool. The old school was about ready to fold up, anyhow. It had been there ever since the town came into existence.

"Sanna," Clay coaxed into the mouthpiece, "how about meeting me tonight—corner of Oak and Vine?" It was a dark corner which made our meetings seem a little clandestine, but, I told myself, Clay was probably right. Why set all the old gossips talking? They wouldn't see anything good in my running around with Clay. I wasn't a marriage prospect. I was only a girl who was hopelessly in love with him.

"Okay. I think I can make it." I hated myself because my voice was all out of control. Mary Skidmore took the exchange over at eight o'clock, which left my evenings free; free for the long moonlight rides, the dances at quaint little roadhouses, the thrill and splendor of stolen kisses and Clay's headlong, passionate love-making which found such a dangerous response in my hungry heart.

"Oh, Sanna," my mother worried that night, "are you going out with Clay again? I'm afraid you're only storing up trouble."

I never lied to Mom—she was such a swell person—so I only nodded, pulling my green, linen frock down over my slim hips and brushing my dark hair until it shone like satin. My eyes were wide and black with excitement. Half an hour—fifteen minutes—I thrilled for the moment I would be with Clay, nestling down against his shoulder while his car licked up the road in a trail of dust.

"Take me along?" Becky asked wistfully as she watched me dress with wide, interested eyes.

I patted her tumbled curls with an absent gesture.

"Not tonight, sweet." She *was* sweet; dimpled, sunny and adorable. Smart, too, because she was in fourth grade although she was only nine. "Some day you'll have a boy-friend, darling, and then you'll have lots and lots of dates."

THE tail light of Clay's car winked at me from the shadowy corner and I climbed in breathlessly, my heart thumping in that crazy fashion as it always did when I was close to him.

"Gosh, darling," he whispered, "I thought you were never

coming." Our lips clung in the darkness, parted and clung again. There were no half measures when Clay and I were together. We lived at the very pitch of our emotions, as though each moment might be our last.

"There's a dance at Bender's," he said. "We'll run over for a round or two." Bender's was a new roadhouse a few miles from town. They had a hot swing band and a revolving dance floor and if you were dizzy when you went in, you were wound up like a top by the time you left.

Dancing with Clay was like floating on air; a dreamy, delicious sensation which lulled you into a feeling of false security. We had a cocktail—just one—I saw to that—and afterward we drove back to Barney's Thicket, which was a popular rendezvous for petting parties.

Clay drew me close into his arms and held me there.

"Sanna," he whispered against my lips, "don't get me wrong. I'm nuts about you but—right now—just starting in the business with Dad, I depend on him for every cent and he'd fly right off the handle if I suggested marriage. Can you wait, darling, just a little while? We'll break it to the old folks gradually—use a little tact, understand? They'll love you when they get to know you—"

I said to myself despairingly, "I hope, I hope, I hope," but in my wildest flights of fancy I couldn't see Old Hatchet Face opening her arms to me and calling me "daughter." She'd be more apt to call me an "adventuress" or a "little so-and-so."

A few weeks later my brother Bill confided in me. "There's some nasty rumors going round about the new school. Looks as though your fancy boyfriend's old man might get his ears pinned back. It would do those snobs good to have some of their smugness peeled off 'em."

A curious little chill went over me.

"What do you mean?"

He threw his climbers into a corner and bending over, unfastened his leather puttees.

"Don't quote me—but that inspector of his, Baldy Wyers, smells to heaven and the workmen are talking. You can't stop them on a job as big as the school. They say Wyers is raising the devil with plans and specifications and old man Morel hasn't raised a finger to stop it." Bill jerked off a legging with a violent motion. "Grafting on a school!" he muttered. "Death's too good for the lot of dirty grafters

THE red light flashed. I opened the key and someone's voice said softly, "Love me, Beautiful?" Clay Morel's voice. It tingled softly along my nerves in little shivers of ecstasy. I knew that I was a fool. Clay was "class" in our town while I was Rosanna Best who ran the telephone exchange.

Happen to Me!

that'll grab off a few dollars at the expense of little children!"

"But—but Bill," I stammered, "Mr. Morel wouldn't do a thing like that! He's been in the business for years and he has a reputation for honesty."

"Yeah? Well, if you ask me, Morel's slipping. He's getting old. He isn't going to be hauling down the fat, juicy jobs that used to be handed him on a silver platter much longer. There's so much smoke about this school affair, there's bound to be a little monkey business somewhere. Better drop your boy friend a hint. He seems like a decent kid. Too bad if he got mixed up in his father's dirt."

I couldn't believe that Mr. Morel would wilfully fall down on his contract, yet if anything did happen, Clay would be involved and it wouldn't matter at all that he wasn't to blame. I felt I ought to do something to warn Clay about the gossip—but what? I couldn't just say to Clay, "Look here, people claim that your father's a crook. How about it?"

I WAS still debating how to tell Clay about those hideous rumors when Mrs. Morel sent for me, calling me on the exchange and asking me to drop in after work that night. I remember how excited I was; how thrilled at the idea that Clay might have spoken to her about us—though I might have known that it was a whacky notion. A leopard doesn't change its spots and Mrs. Morel's prejudice against me, and what I stood for, was so deeply ingrained that it bordered on fanaticism.

When I knocked off at eight o'clock and turned down the tree-lined avenue toward the Morel's White Colonial mansion, I had a complete case of jitters. A girl in a neat cap and apron showed me into the living room and I looked quickly around for Clay but of course, he wasn't there. Leave it to Mrs. Morel to pick a time when her son was out of the house!

She stood on the hearth rug when I came in, her lorgnette raised, looking me over as though I was something right out of a zoo.

"Miss Best, I believe?"

I hated to antagonize her but I hated her condescension more. My voice went all stiff on me.

"Yes, I'm Miss Best. Rosanna Best. Why did you want to see me?"

Her brows were a pale arch over her cold blue eyes.

"Because I wanted to warn you. You're seeing too much of my son and it's got to stop. If your own mother can't control you—"

I interrupted her rudely. I was in for it, anyhow, and I didn't intend that she should carry off all the honors.

"Leave my mother out of it, please. If that's the way you feel about me, why not speak to your son? Tell him to leave me alone. Tell him to stop calling and inviting me out—tell him to stop making love to me—"

She shook her white head.

"Of course, you would try and throw the blame on him. It's true that Clay's impressionable and you're an unusually pretty girl, but deep down he's level-headed like his father and if you think that you can rope him into a scandalous marriage, you're very much mistaken. I've tried to save your pride for you but if you're bent on your own destruction, there's nothing more that I can do. You may go now." She folded her useless white hands in her lap and tightened her mouth to a straight, cruel line.

A furious anger swept over me. I was so burned up that I could scarcely talk.

"You can't send me away like a maid you're dismissing, Mrs. Morel. And while you're throwing stones, you might remember that your own windows are made out of glass. How about the school Mr. Morel is building? If you're hunting for scandal, look into that. Maybe I won't want to marry your son after the storm breaks. Maybe he won't be good enough for me—"

It was silly and childish, that display of temper, but it

MY sister was lying limp and still, a nasty bruise on her temple. "Let me carry her," Clay said hoarsely, his lips white as chalk.

kept me from breaking into tears and I slammed out of the door without looking back at her. I'd broken the news all right —broken it with a vengeance but I wasn't sorry. Not then! I was still seeing red.

CLAY'S car was parked by our curb when I reached home. Perhaps if it hadn't been, if I'd had a little time to pull myself together, that night might have turned out differently, but when he sang out, "Hop in, honey. I've been waiting around for ages," I did as he told me, the frantic desire for reassurance outweighing everything else—even my anger.

"You're late tonight, Sanna." He flung an arm around me as we started off. "Yes," I whispered, but I didn't say, "I've been to see your mother." If she wanted to tell him, that was her affair. He chuckled softly close to my ear. "Guess what? I've planned a surprise. We're going out to the cottage and have a corn roast—just you and I." The Morels had a whole lake to themselves a few miles out of town and a log cabin that they used summers, but I'd never been there because even to my inexperience, it seemed like looking for trouble; Clay and I with a little place all to ourselves, a little house with beds and chairs and tables that might almost have been a home. . . . Yet I didn't have the heart to say "no" that night. I wanted his arms and lips as I'd never wanted them before. Just to have him hold me close and still the terrible fear that was riding me— give me a hope, however faint, for a future that would find us still together.

A dirt road wound off the main highway to the cabin, up hill and through a stretch of forest. You could almost feel the stillness and the loneliness, and the stars were so near it seemed as though I could touch them with my hand.

"Gee, honey," Clay murmured, "I've dreamed of bringing you here so often— but you always put the jinx on it. Must have caught you at the psychological moment." He laughed unsteadily, and looking down, I saw his long, brown fingers tighten on the wheel. Oh, Clay! Clay! He did love me. He must care! This irresistible attraction between us must mean something more than mere sex hunger. It had to! It was something as big and breathless and immortal as two souls uniting. It had to be something that would last. When we reached the cottage, Clay built a fire down by the edge of the lake and after the flames had died down, he thrust the ears of silky corn into the glowing embers. There was ice cold beer, *[Please turn page]*

I Said it Could Never Happen to Me!

*Specially posed by
Florence Rice,
M-G-M star*

crackers and fancy cheese and for a little while it was fun, yet when the feast was cleared away, that sick sense of desolation came back over me again with renewed intensity.

I was stacking the dishes in the small rustic cupboard when I felt his hands on my shoulders, turning me around and gathering me hard and tight against him.

"Sanna, if this were real—if this were true—you and I keeping house together—" His mouth crushed mine with sudden violence and I thought wildly, "Oh, love me, love me, Clay! Make me know that what your mother said about you isn't true—that you do want me—forever and ever. . . ."

The flame of the small oil lamp flickered unsteadily for a moment and then went out.

"I forgot to fill it," Clay whispered, "but it doesn't matter. It's—nicer—here in the dark. Listen, darling! Hear the peepers down by the lake! Doesn't it give you a swell creepy feeling? Kiss me again! You're the loveliest thing in all the world —and you're mine. Say it, Sanna! Tell me that you've never loved anyone else but me."

"You know I haven't." It seemed so right to be there, my heart warm against his own—so natural and so unutterably sweet. Outside a little wind was soughing through the tree tops, rocking in my mind like a lullaby. I only half-realized that Clay had lifted me and was carrying me across the threshold of another room where the faint glow of the dying fire flickered through the narrow panes. I saw the tense white outline of his face and the way his lips were shaking, uncontrollably, as though all his defenses had crashed. Then darkness blurred it over and nothing made sense but that blind, terrific need of him which left me helpless and trembling in his arms.

IT WAS three o'clock in the morning when Clay let me out at my own front door.

"I'm sorry, darling," he whispered. "I made you cry and I hate myself for that, but oh, Sanna, it's so wonderful to know that you belong to me—that nothing in the world can ever take you away."

My lips met his but the fervor was gone now and only remorse was left. Clay's mother had insinuated that I was a tramp and now I was one. Oh, why, why had I given in when down in my heart, I knew how wrong it was? A moment's happiness—then tears and this agony of regret. I was sick with shame—I, Rosanna Best, who yesterday would have said, "This could never happen to me."

Clay's mother told him about my visit, for he called me at work the following day and asked a single question.

"Sanna, just what did you mean—that crack about Dad and the new school?"

I suppose Mrs. Morel had put me in the worst possible light—glossed herself over and claimed that I'd deliberately insulted her under her own roof, yet the coldness of Clay's tone struck me like a blow between the eyes. After last night—how *could* he? The burning blood rushed to my cheeks. Maybe he didn't respect me any longer. Perhaps he thought of me now as a girl lightly taken and just as easily forgotten.

"I—I can't discuss it over the phone, Clay. I'm sorry. I shouldn't have said it—"

"You're darned tooting you shouldn't have said it—not about a man like my father. Why—why the building's all finished . . . They're opening next week. You know, Sanna, that I stand or fall with Dad and when you slam him, you're slamming me, too. It makes me feel that I don't quite know you any longer—"

I switched off the connection because another word in that changed icy voice would have killed me. I'd been wrong, of course, even to mention that the school wasn't being built according to Hoyle. You had to prove an accusation like that and all I had to go by was an ugly bit of gossip which might very well be untrue.

For the rest of the week, Clay ignored me and the pain of it was like a knife in my heart. He meant to break with me. Why—why? Because Mrs. Morel had talked him over or because that glamorous night in his arms had completely changed his opinion of me? I felt lost—betrayed by that passionate surrender. Oh, he might have given me a fighting chance! He might, at least, have let me explain about his mother.

I was sick with worry when Baldy Wyers put in that long distance call to Chicago; so worried that I forgot to close the key and Baldy's voice reached me plainly, "I'm givin' you the low-down, Gyp. It don't look so good to me. They're gettin' darned nosey about this job we just finished—"

Then another voice, low and carefully controlled.

"Keep your shirt on, punk. You're only Morel's hired hand. You're in the clear. Who's going to get anything on you? Just sit tight—"

"Sure," Baldy interrupted passionately, "just sit tight and get left holding the bag. It's oke for you. You're Gyp Sauggerty—"

"Shut up! I've told you never to mention my name and not to call me unless it was a matter of life and death. How do you know but what that operator's listening in? Come to think of it, the wire doesn't sound just right to me—"

I left the key open because I didn't dare to close it then. I scarcely dared to draw a quivering breath. Baldy was talking to Gyp Sauggerty, Chicago's "big shot" racketeer, and the significance of the fact went screaming through my brain. Then there was something c r o o k e d about Morel's contract. Someway, somehow, Gyp Sauggerty was behind it. Gyp Sauggerty was building the Blairsville school, the school that had gobbled up our taxpayers' money and was opening tomorrow with a triumphant flourish, a band from Muncie, speeches, games and refreshments. Mother made Becky a lovely little dress to wear and she and the other children were to have wreaths of flowers in their hair.

I didn't know what to do with the stupendous information after I had it. Go to the district attorney, perhaps. Yet the thought of involving Clay's father, maybe Clay himself, in a State investigation turned me sick all over.

SO FOR the moment I didn't do a thing. Mary took over the exchange the following afternoon and although I longed to skip the school opening, I went to it because Becky had begged me to be there. Mr. Morel sat on the improvised platform in the yard with the mayor and important men of the town. He looked dignified and kindly but people were murmuring behind their hands and I knew what that meant. A whispering campaign would ruin him; insidiously, but just as surely as any direct evidence could have done.

Once Clay passed me, his head averted. Possibly he didn't see me, for there was a terrific crush of people and my five foot two was almost lost in the crowd, yet my throat ached intolerably and my eyes smarted with unshed tears. I loved him so terribly that the mere sight of him was exquisite torture. How could I crush that intensity of feeling out of my life and act as though nothing had ever happened between us?

I only half heard the program, the mayor's speech and Morel's, the shrill childish voices which sang the *Star-Spangled Banner* as the flag was raised in the yard. Perhaps that stealthy fear in my mind had developed to a premonition. Something was so vitally wrong that I could sense it—feel it . .

A shudder went over me when that ominous cracking sounded. The children were just marching into the building, the smaller ones first. Becky had already gone in. A woman shrieked hysterically, "Look—the wall—it's shaking! Dear God, it's going to fall—" I lifted my eyes in an agony of terror while that shining line of new red brick swayed and shivered, then suddenly popped outward as though pushed by a giant hand, collapsing in a shower of dust and flying debris.

"Becky, Becky!" I was sobbing frantically under my breath. The mad stampede toward the building carried me along like an atom; mothers and fathers, distracted like myself, not daring to think, just pushing, struggling, ready to claw away the ruins with bleeding hands. The portion of the wall which had given way was on the east side of the building and I had no notion where Becky's room was located. I could only pray, "God, God, don't let her be hurt! Keep her safe until I get to her!"

It was a miracle that the entire building didn't collapse under that rush of frantic feet. We had no adequate police protection, just a few picked men who were helpless against that surging tide of humanity. The paper came out next day with a list of the injured; seven children and one teacher hurt but no one was killed because, mercifully, the small procession was still in the hallway when the accident occurred.

When I found my sister, she was lying limp and still, a nasty bruise on her temple, blood trickling over her forehead and staining the waxy pallor of her face. A voice said hoarsely, "Let me carry her, Sanna," and I looked up dully into Clay's tortured eyes. But he didn't mean a thing to me—not then—not with that childish form cradled in my arms.

"You did it!" I accused him on a shrill high note. "You and your father and Big Shot Sauggerty!" I didn't know nor care that Baldy Wyers was wedged in there with the crowd. I'd have shouted it out to Sauggerty himself—with a gun in my ribs—it didn't matter.

Clay's lips were white as chalk.

"You're crazy," he muttered. "I don't know what you mean. Darling, please let me carry Becky—" but I struck at him when he tried to lift her and another man, a neighbor, took her out to his car and over to Dr. Monroy's office.

After Becky was home in bed, bruised and whimpering, one small arm in a sling, I told my brother about that telephone call, while he whistled sharply between his teeth.

"You should have done something about it yesterday, Sanna. Maybe—maybe they wouldn't have opened the school. Oh, I know, I'm rubbing it in, but because you're in love with a guy is no excuse. It's a cinch that Morel's all washed up, anyhow, so we'll go to the D. A. right away and get it off our chest. Tangling with crooks is dangerous business but no one knows that you're hep, so you'll be safe enough."

"I can't go today," I answered dully. "I swapped places with Mary in order to get off this afternoon and she made an appointment for this evening in Muncie about a job she's been wanting for a long, long time. I wouldn't have the heart to do her out of it and there's no one else to handle the switchboard. I'll have to stay."

"Tomorrow then," Bill said grimly, "and I'll go with you."

It wasn't just a question of making a local visit, for the D. A. lived in Allentown and that was several miles away, but Bill and I made our plans for the next evening.

I HAD no way of knowing that Baldy Wyers put in a call to Chicago just before Mary went off duty. Night operating in our town was a tedious job because there wasn't enough work to keep you busy, yet you had to stay awake—or else. At ten-thirty a call went through to the Morel's and I closed the key hurriedly, thinking what a dreadful day it had been for all of them—even Old Hatchet Face. They'd held their heads so high and now they were humbled to the dust. Mrs. Morel had treated me shamefully, yet I was sorry for her now. What would happen to them—Clay and his father—when the investigation of the school disaster got under way?

For ten minutes after the Morel call I sat with my hands locked tightly together in my lap. It was lonely there in the exchange, an office building deserted for the night, the shops along the block closed and shuttered and only an occasional pedestrian passing in the street. Once a car purred along and stopped somewhere close at hand, giving me a faint sense of companionship. I wasn't afraid—exactly —but the accident had left me jittery. The shock of it was still in my numbed fingers and ragged nerves, so that when those pounding feet sounded on the stairs, I stiffened, every muscle in my body tense as a strung wire.

I don't know whom I expected to see—certainly not Clay—white-faced and anxious, with haggard, burning eyes. He burst into the room like a whirlwind and stopped dead still when he saw me sitting quietly there at the switchboard.

"Sanna, why—" he swallowed convul-

sively, "I came just as soon as I could— when your brother called me. Sanna, what's wrong? Why did you send for me?"

The room went round for a moment, giddily, then slowly righted itself. What was this, anyhow? A joke? A trick? That call I'd put through—who had made it?

"But—but I didn't send for you and Bill is out of town—" I rose to meet him, the palms of my hands suddenly cold and my knees shaking. "I'm afraid it's all a mistake—"

"No mistake" The snarling voice from the doorway went down my spine like a trickle of ice water. Baldy! Baldy Wyers! What was he doing here?

"Get on your things," he grated. "We're going places. It ain't healthy for little girls who listen in on phone calls— specially when they spill the works out in public like you did this afternoon, blabbing it to your boy friend here." His narrowed eyes turned to Clay who was tensing for a spring and I saw the bulge in his pocket where his hand closed tightly. "Don't try any monkey business, squirt! I've got you covered. Just get out here in front and go along quiet. My car's down there at the curb."

I found my voice somewhere in the bottom of my shoes.

"But—but I can't leave the exchange." His mouth twisted to a sneer.

"Now ain't that something! Such a sense of duty! Get going, you sneaking little fool, if you know what's good for you. You sure put me in one hell of a jam with the Boss by sticking your nose into our affairs. Too bad! You're a pretty kid and you mighta lived a long, long time."

I WENT down the stairs with Clay beside me, his arm pressing me tight. I only half-remembered what I'd said to him that afternoon but I'd mentioned Gyp Sauggerty's name and that was enough to involve him. I'd placed him in danger and there wasn't a thing that I could do about it—only walk along, faint and trembling, out to the waiting car.

"You're driving," Baldy told Clay gruffly. "You and the dame in front and me in the back with my gat handy. One false move and I'll drill the girl friend. Get going! Straight out Main and turn right at Orton. I'll tell you what to do next."

I huddled down beside Clay, my cheek against his coat sleeve. Once I bent and pressed my quivering lips upon his hand which clutched the wheel.

"I love you," I whispered. "Oh, Clay, do you hear—do you hear? I'd give my life to get you out of this."

"Hush!" he said gently. "It's one of those things and we have to face it. Let's be sports, you and I! We've been so foolish about the little things that didn't matter—you getting sore at mother and me grouching because you repeated a bit of gossip . . . How silly it all seems now! We might have had a few more wonderful hours together and we threw them away. Oh, Sanna," his voice broke, "at least, wherever we're going, we'll be together."

"Turn right." We moved along as Baldy directed, through the town and out into the open country. We must have traveled thirty miles before we stopped, turning in at a squat, white farm house whose

shutters flapped a little in the rising wind. "Get out!"

There wasn't any help for it. Those low brutal commands were like the crack of a whip, putting us through our paces. I stumbled from the car, clutching at Clay's hand with stiffened fingers. Above us the stars shone, clear and close and friendly. It wasn't fair that we should die like rats in a trap. For I hadn't the faintest notion that Baldy would show any mercy. He was Sauggerty's henchman and human life is cheap to a racketeer—all except his own.

The door swung open on rusted hinges and we walked into what had once been a parlor, a large front room facing the road. Baldy pulled a piece of paper and a fountain pen from his pocket.

"Here," he told me, "this is the set-up. A suicide pact between you and your boy friend. You're to write it down just as I tell you. Young Morel can't stand his old man's disgrace and you can't live without him. So you're going together—" he grinned evilly— "just like you said a while back."

I looked at Clay. His hands were clenched and his eyes were blazing.

"My dad wasn't mixed up in your dirty work. You know that he wasn't. He trusted you and you signed for everything—"

"Oh, no, I didn't," Baldy said softly. "He just took my word for it and put his John Henry down on the dotted line." His desire to brag got the best of him. "Sauggerty owns the Spalding Brick and Cement Company where your father bought materials. He's backing a lot of concerns that the public ain't wise to. He bills, say for argument, two thousand bags of cement, and your old man signs for it. 'Cause I tell him it's oke—see? Who's the wiser if we only get a thousand? You can make up the difference with sand."

"You—you swine!"

I caught Clay's arm in a frenzy of fear. "Don't—don't! He's only baiting you. He'll shoot you if you make a move." The paper rattled in my hand and Baldy, tired of his sport, growled, "Well, get on with it! I ain't no scholar. You'll have to choose the words."

A SUICIDE note! While every drop of blood in my body clamored for life and the right to existence. When love was waiting, the love that I'd savored and found so sweet; Clay's tender arms, his lips seeking my own that mingling of fire and rapture which had been ours for such a little while. How could I sign it all away—like that—with a stroke of the pen? I put the sheet of paper against the peeling wall but my hand shook so badly that I couldn't write and my whirling brain kept saying, "Stall—stall—as long as you possibly can. He's got to have that note. He doesn't want it to look like murder."

But it was written at last, with Baldy's gun boring into the small of my back, and my name, Sanna Best, leaped at me in letters of blood-red terror. After Clay had put his own name beside it, it would be all over.

Turning, I stumbled toward him. Just once more to feel the human warmth of him; the pulsing of young blood and the

beating of our hearts. so soon to be stilled!

Our lips were clinging together when the kitchen door crashed open. I heard a single shot followed by a fusillade of barking revolvers and when I turned, half-fainting in Clay's arms, Baldy lay quite still on the splintered floor, his glazed eyes staring at the dirty ceiling, while half a dozen policemen clustered around him and a familiar figure in a leather jacket and puttees came striding toward me, his face working in a curious fashion. as though he was going to cry.

"Bill," I whispered, "oh, Bill, how did you ever find us?"

He tried to be jaunty about it but he couldn't make the grade.

"What's the use of being the best lineman in the county," he asked shakily, "if you can't turn it to your own advantage when you want to catch a crook? I tapped Baldy's telephone wire and heard him get his orders from Sauggerty—to bring you here with young Morel. He said the old Brewster place on the Plainsville Road. So I gathered me a handful of cops and we got here first." His hand fumbled lighting a cigarette. "I'm sorry, kid. I hated to let you in for so much agony but the police insisted. They wanted evidence and I guess they've got it. We were listening in the other room while Baldy talked."

Clay gathered me up in his arms and carried me out to the car as though I were a child.

"I'll take you home," he murmured, "home to my people where you belong. I've been a coward, darling. I should have settled this marriage question right in the very beginning but you can write your own ticket with Mother now. She may be cold and overbearing to the outside world but she worships my father and you've saved him from disgrace that would have been worse than death to him. He's so proud of his record. He's good, Sanna. If I could only be like him—"

I touched the outline of his cheek with tremulous fingers. "If—our sons—could be like you—" After the shadow of death, the world was so beautiful—so full of glorious promise.

CLAY often laughingly remarks that we're a mutual admiration society, his parents, our two selves and little Jimmy who is just past his second birthday. We live a block from the Morels and "Gramma" always plays nursemaid when my husband and I go out for the evening. It seems strange that I could ever have been afraid of her, although Bill still refers to her as "Hatchet Face."

Mr. Morel was exonerated from all blame in connection with the school disaster. They might have brought a charge of negligence but his unblemished reputation balanced the scales in his favor, so Clay and his father are carrying on, building up a business for the "little tyke."

After all, that's life; building up—tearing down whatever doesn't seem good to you and starting all over again. Clay and I made the mistake so common to lovers, snatching at a joy which wasn't rightfully ours, but our marriage is founded on our faith in each other. Please God it will stand forever!   ●

COLLEGE KISSES *Lie* !

I lived those days only for the hours with Steve, when we were tearing up the miles in his roadster. It's dangerous to love like that . . .

And college men don't marry the town girls! They date them —make love to them—and then, as this girl learned in anguish, they go back to marry girls in their own social set.

I WOKE up, the morning I was twenty-four, thinking ruefully about the play I'd seen the night before. It was a revival of a very old favorite, "The College Widow." And I lay there looking at the sunlight on my shabby wall paper and remembering one line, spoken with bitter wisdom, by the girl who'd been running around with college boys for years and years.

"College boys don't marry," she'd said. "They just fool 'round!"

Well, I'd been going with college boys myself for seven years. And my kid sister, Beth, had married six months ago. Beth, who'd never had a date with a college boy or been invited to a fraternity dance or house party, happily married; and I, who'd been rushed by dozens of them, not even engaged!

Seven years! I'd need the fingers of both hands and then have to start on my toes, to count all the boys who'd said to me, on sundry moonlit nights, "Gosh, Di, I'm crazy about you, but you know how it is, honey-chile—I've got two more years in school. Just wait till I get out of college!"

But I wouldn't have needed any fingers at all, not even one thumb, to count the ones who came back to lay their hearts and fortunes at my feet after they were out and earning their living. Because there hadn't been any.

I sat up in bed, and my own reflection stared back at me from the mirror across the room. I looked at the disordered, dark curls and the big, purple-pansy eyes and the curved, scarlet mouth. No, she didn't look twenty-four, that girl in the mirror, not even this early in the morning. She still looked a college freshman or sophomore. But she wasn't, she wasn't—and the years were slipping by so fast! When you're seventeen, you can't really believe you'll ever be anything but young. But when you're twenty-four, you've begun to realize that it won't last forever.

At seventeen I'd been wildly excited over my chance for contacts with a college community. Now I'd begun to wonder, a little bitterly, if it weren't perhaps the unluckiest move of my life. You see, our town is a small Southern city where caste lines are somewhat more closely drawn than in more cosmopolitan places. The social life centers very largely around the beautiful and aristocratic university, which sits enthroned on its lovely campus in the stately glory of marble buildings, ivy-clad, and tall trees, and bright grass and flowers.

There was no chance that I could ever attend it. I'd never even dreamed of such a thing. I knew that my parents were doing very well indeed to put me through high school. My folks are grand folks—understand that. But my dad carries his lunch in a pail, when he goes to his factory job, and my mother doesn't always do right by the King's English. They don't belong to the class who are able to send their kids to college. They're the salt of the earth—but socially they're utterly obscure; and content to be so.

I was a bright youngster, and I made good grades in high school. In my senior year I took the business course the school offered; and it happened that one of my teachers left the school at the end of the year to accept a job as alumni secretary and all-round publicity man for the university.

"How'd you like to go with me as my stenog, Diane?" he asked, one day.

Just like that! As casually as if he weren't offering me the world and all on a silver platter. For that's the way it looked to me. My family were just as tickled. Mother bragged to the neighbors and Dad proudly told his co-workers.

It reconciled me to being a business woman—this getting to work on the university campus. I hadn't wanted to be one, originally. I'd wanted to be a musician. Music was my big passion, and I knew I had talent. But though Mother had managed to squeeze in money for lessons for me for years, a thorough musical training was about as attainable as the moon. Still, I kept up my practice; and after swing music came in, I discovered that I had quite a special gift for that.

I had built a hundred rosy, shining dreams around this campus job, and at first it seemed to me they were all being realized. I liked the work and did well at it, and to my delight the boys and girls at the U. apparently liked me. So, because the girls begged me to come to their sorority houses and play for them, and the boys dated me up enthusiastically and made love to me, it took me quite a while to realize that, in spite of this, I wasn't really one of them at all. I was in the college halls; I was surrounded by the college atmosphere, and I loved it. *But I never belonged to it!*

A dozen things, little and big, forced the realization home. The fact, for instance, that the girls were only carelessly kind to me, and invited me places just when I could be of use to them as pianist and no other times; the fact that the boys seldom asked me to the important formals or bothered to introduce me to their mothers and sisters when they came visiting. . . . Oh, so many signs, so many, that I was just the pretty, little girl who worked in the Alumni office—"you know, the one who plays so marvelously"—but not a girl in their own social group.

When this finally dawned on me clearly, I think I grew a little bitter. These boys who rushed me—what they were after might be just an entertaining evening, or it might be some hot kisses, or it might—yes, and sometimes was—something more serious than kisses. But it wasn't marriage. Not even vaguely and in the distance. Sometimes, being young and very human, I felt unhappy and reckless and asked myself if there was any special use in trying to stay straight, after all. I think it would have shocked my blessed mother profoundly if she had ever guessed that I was tempted. But at least she would have been glad that, this far, I'd always held on to my ideals. . . .

SO NOW I'm back to that morning of my twenty-fourth birthday when I woke up rather unhappy. Oddly enough that happened to be the day when Steve Denton stopped me on the campus and asked me for my first date with him.

I'd known him for three years. I'd danced with him a hundred times. I admired him tremendously because he was handsome and brilliant and prominent and attractive. But I'd never thought of him in connection with myself, for I believed he belonged to pretty, dashing Betty Cavenaugh, who had graduated the year before in Liberal Arts and had gone home. Certainly he'd been with her constantly during her last two years. He was graduating himself this year, in law, and I had supposed he was engaged to Betty.

I even teased him a little about it, that first night. But he shrugged his shoulders, and answered, his blue eyes looking down into mine, "That was a boy and girl case." Then he added deliberately, and now there was a blaze in those brilliant eyes, "I'm older now."

He was wonderful to be with! He had a charming kind of deference, a way of talking to you, of bending his handsome, corn-colored head toward yours as if the thing you happened to be saying were just the most important thing in the world, that was intoxicatingly flattering. I told myself every day, "I won't fall in love with him— I won't, I won't!" And every day I fell in love with him a little deeper!

He was giving me a marvelous rush. Flowers, candy, dates, telephone calls. I lived in a kind of rosy haze, shot occasionally by dark flashes of misgiving. And then one night he kissed me . . . and after that I didn't even try to fool myself any longer about what I felt. I knew I was madly, wildly, in love with him. I *had* to believe him when he said he loved me, too. I had to, or go crazy with grief it seemed to me. I couldn't bear not to!

Besides, why shouldn't I believe him? He said it so well and so often! And how he could kiss! I lived, those days, only for those hours with him. I seemed to myself just a sort of efficient automatom, a kind of robot, during work hours. I only came to myself when I was with Steve again, tearing up the miles in his roadster; when I could look·at him, drinking in his bold, masculine young beauty—could talk to him—could listen to him. And oh, I flamed into rich, full, glorious living when he caught me in his arms, holding his lips on mine in long, burning   [*Please turn page*]

AS Steve led Betty back to their table, the contrast between their happiness and my utter misery made me sick. Suddenly the band leader said firmly, "Buck up, go back to the piano—don't let anyone get wise!"

kisses, murmuring broken lover's phrases between each kiss.

It's dangerous to love like that! I knew it, of course. I wasn't surprised when Steve groaned one night, that he couldn't stand this much longer—that he wanted me so—that he ached with wanting me. I wasn't surprised, but I was troubled and a little frightened. I said, my arms around his neck, wide eyes on his, all my heart in them, "Darling, darling, I want so to give you whatever you want! But, oh, Steve, I'm afraid we might be sorry!"

"I'd never be sorry!" he answered violently. "It would be—oh, Di, it would be the most wonderful thing that ever happened to me!"

"Can't we get married as soon as you graduate?" I faltered. "That isn't very long."

"It's months," he answered reproachfully. "And I won't have a bean even then except what Dad gives me."

"You'd think less of me—" I stammered, and at that he caught me close, protesting passionately that he couldn't understand how I could say such a thing.

I wasn't experienced enough then to realize that this discussion was the first step toward an inevitable end. Because when two people in love begin to argue about whether they will or will not belong to one another, the step between talking of it as a possibility and making it an actuality grows shorter and shorter.

IT WAS one blowy March evening that the climax came for Steve and me. We had been out, and he had been moody and silent, quite unlike his charming, chivalrous self. Mother and Dad were sound asleep, their lights out, when we came home. In the living room, the firelight flickered. It was very quiet and sweet, and we spoke in whispers.

"Diane!" His lips were on mine. "Di, my lovely, darling—must I wait? Oh, Di, I can't—I can't! Be good to me—please, please!"

I loved him so! But even now, for a moment I held back, wanting him dreadfully, longing to be his, but half-terrified by the sense that if I gave myself to him it would be something I could never, never undo whatever the consequences.

"Aw, Di, don't draw away, sweet. Oh, you're so beautiful—and mine, mine!"

He was gentle—but oh, he was ruthless, too, in the way a girl in love loves for her lover to be ruthless! I said his name, once, on a frightened sob . . . and then the mounting crescendo of rapture, so keen, so poignant as to be almost intolerable, drowned out every other feeling, every other thought. I knew only that I loved him, and that in belonging to him I seemed to be fulfilling all my womanhood. . . .

I did a lot of arguing with myself, in the weeks that followed. I told myself a hundred times that our great love justified everything; that we had, after all, only anticipated our marriage by a few months, that what we had done was—it was, it was —right and good and pure! But I never faced the fact that when one is really secure in his consciousness of being right and good and pure, he doesn't need to argue with himself about it.

I considered myself engaged, of course —married, really; and I was very eager for Steve to tell his people about it, very eager to meet them. But he said, when I mentioned it, "Better go slow, I guess, honey. Mother and Dad—well, they're apt to disinherit me or something if I don't please 'em. They're that sort."

"Will they be displeased about me?" I asked, troubled.

But he kissed me and laughed and said, "Let's don't worry our heads about parents just now."

And it was spring, and I loved him. Parents didn't, after all, seem so dreadfully important . . .

The first time things began to go wrong was the first week in May. That week Steve didn't come to see me at all. He only telephoned that he was busy. The next week he took a flying trip home, for five days, since his work permitted it; and he didn't write me except a postal card. I got quite panicky before he came back. I remembered that Betty lived in his town, and thought of unbearable possibilities, for which in the next moment I reproached myself.

However, he came to see me immediately when he did get back; and I knew one evening of rapturous relief, for he was quite his charming, affectionate self. But then—another week went by when I waited and waited and he didn't even telephone.

And now I had a real reason for being frantic . . . I had begun to be sick in the mornings. And this, taken with other signs—well, I'd seen my mother have a baby, and I *knew*.

What *could* be the matter with Steve? I fought against terror and wild dismay. Nothing was the matter, I told myself severely. He was going through his last exam, that was all. Didn't I trust the man I was going to marry? I hated calling him at his fraternity house—I never had, but I'd do it right away, and ask him to come by, and then I'd tell him about myself, and of course we'd be married, and that was that.

As soon as I heard his voice over the wire, a gush of relief swept over me—for there was no constraint about it; it was just the same, warm, affectionate, sweet-tempered.

"Di, how sweet of you to call, honey! I've been so confoundedly busy—"

"I know, Steve, I understand, honestly I do! But—there's something rather special I want to see you about. Could you possibly run around a while tonight?"

His answer came promptly, with his usual charming courtesy; he was studying, but that didn't matter. If I wanted to see him, he'd come, of course . . . I hung the telephone up shaking with relief, absurdly happy.

I had studied how I would tell him, and had thought up just the right approach; but when he came up the walk and to the vine-shaded porch where I waited in the shadows for him, I forgot it all. I simply flung myself in his arms and hid my face on his shoulder and gasped, "Steve, dearest, please don't be too upset, but—oh Steve, we're going to have a baby!"

I felt the arms that were holding me go perfectly rigid; and the tone in which he echoed: "A—baby? My Lord, Di, are you sure?" was frankly and utterly appalled.

"I—I'm afraid I am. Oh Steve, please don't mind too much! We'll pretend we were married two months ago—it'll be sweet to have a baby, darling."

I was pleading, though I didn't quite realize it; talking against the persistent rigidity of those arms. Then they loosened. He said seriously, "Sit down, honey. We'll have to talk this over. You'll have to go to a doctor and get yourself fixed up, Di— I'll get the money for you."

"You mean—? But Steve, it's murder— and it's terribly dangerous—it—oh, Steve, you can't mean that!"

"Now, sweetheart, you're such a brave kid—you're not going to pieces over what I've got to tell you now. Nobody will ever be so fond of you as I, Di, but we can't get married. You see, while I was home those five days, Betty and I fixed things up again. After all, she had a sort of prior claim, you know. I'll always care for you, and I'll always be grateful to you, but honestly you wouldn't be happy with me, dear. My parents—well, they're pretty keen on family and all. They're strong for Betty, always have been, and I'm afraid they wouldn't treat you quite as I'd want them to. You do understand how it is, don't you? And you'll let me give you a hundred dollars to get straightened out—and you know I'll never, never forget you—"

If he had been rudely cruel, if he had jilted me violently—why, I think that would have been easier. But no, he was talking in the same affectionate tone he had always used—his attitude toward me seemed not to have changed one bit! And that made it all so utterly fantastic, cheapened everything so unspeakably, put our love on so light a basis, that it gave me the oddest sense of nightmare unreality. Why, it was funny! Yes, it was tearingly funny—but I mustn't laugh, for if I started I couldn't stop!

I got to my feet unsteadily. I said, "How nice of you. I'll not be likely to forget you, either. You ought to have a grand career as a criminal lawyer—you're fine at making black seem white. Goodby, Steve."

"Di!" His tone was actually reproachful. "Please don't be that way—please—"

I couldn't stay, I couldn't stay! I *would* begin to laugh in a minute—or to cry—and in either case, I was gone! I fled into the house, slamming the door behind me; and I ran upstairs, glad that Mother and Dad were at the movies, and shut myself in my room.

Maybe if I live to be a hundred or so, I will forget that night! Maybe—but I don't think so. . . .

I don't know how I got through the next few days. I really don't. Mother thought I was sick with a cold, and I encouraged the notion. For her sake, and Dad's, I held myself together somehow. But only on the outside. Inside—inside, I think I went a little bit crazy. Crazy with wild, tearing grief, and mad, intolerable pain.

There seemed to be so many different ways that I suffered—so many different facets that my agony had! There was frantic remorse, and the anguish of betrayal, and searing humiliation, and outraged love; and most of all, perhaps, there was terror. Panicky fright that turned me cold and sick; that made my hands shake and my stomach gripe, at the thought of the suffering and disgrace I was going to bring on my family. Yet Steve's way out seemed an utter impossibility to me. I had been taught that such an act was murder; I couldn't commit murder and endure to go on living afterward. Oh, if I could only just die! That would be so much the easiest solution. I didn't want to live any more—I didn't . . . what was there to live for? I'd flung my life away; I'd got myself into a frightful mess; I'd lost everything I had built all my hopes around, and now I was going to break the hearts of the people who loved me. When I thought of all this, I felt as if I were going quite crazy. An iron band seemed to be tightening 'round my temples, and I knew I couldn't stand things much longer. Something was giving 'way inside me, and before long I was going to smash—just shatter in jagged bits like crystal from a broken bowl.

THE University offices were closed the last few days before graduation, and that was why Mother brought me Steve's letter in bed that morning, two days before graduation. It was special delivery and her smiling archness as she handed it to me was almost more than I could bear. When she had left, I tore it open with ice cold fingers, and a blue check for one hundred dollars fell out. I tore it up violently, and crumpled it in my hand viciously before flinging it in the wastebasket; and then I read the letter with hot, smarting eyes.

Di, darling, I'm terribly sorry you felt as you did, but of course I understood. I'm hoping you hate me less, now that you've had a chance to think things over. You wouldn't be happy with me, Honey. I do want you to know, though, that I'm grateful to you, and that the memories you have given me are among the loveliest of all my life.

Please try to understand when I tell you that tomorrow night I'm flinging a big graduation party at the frat house at which my engagement will be announced. My family, and Betty and her family will be there, of course. I didn't want to do this, Di. It probably seems to you a kind of insult to you. The truth is, it is an effort to protect you. You see, people have gossiped to Betty about you and me, and when she said she wanted her engagement announced here, and I objected, she said right away that it was on account of you. So naturally I gave in, because of course I don't want her to start any talk about you. She's a grand kid, but you know how it is when a girl gets jealous.

Once more, I'll never, never, forget you.

Steve.

IT WAS incredible! That he could be so charming, so easy, so darned chivalrous and gallant about having broken my heart, seduced me, betrayed me, and then deserted me! What kind of a man had I given my heart to, anyway?

If there was a lower depth of bitterness than I had already plumbed, I reached it now. I no longer believed that Steve had ever had the faintest idea of marrying me. I did not even believe that his engagement to Betty had ever been broken at all. Doubtless this party had been planned for months . . . and I—I, twenty-four and modern, had been as easily fooled and betrayed as any simple village maiden of fifty years ago!

Well, this was all! I wouldn't answer his letter; I wouldn't go to the Commencement exercises even, and I'd never again hear the hateful music of his lying voice,

or look up into those brilliant eyes that could seem so tender but had no heart behind them. Never . . .

But I was wrong. Steve telephoned me the next morning, much perturbed.

"Di! Gosh, I hate worrying you about this, but I've got Kerry Gallant and his orchestra here for the party tonight, and the blasted pianist has gone and smashed his hand in a door. There isn't anybody who can take his place but you—of course it will mean something to you financially, and then, too, I've been thinking that maybe when Kerry hears you play, he'll get you some big musical chance."

"Don't bother to keep on lying to me, Steve," I said wearily. "You weren't thinking of me at all. But I'll come—because if I don't the people who know you've been rushing me will probably guess why . . . funny, but I still seem to have a little pride left."

"Di, don't be like that, please—"

"I'll come," I repeated, and hung up on his reproachful voice. It sickened me.

Half an hour later Kerry Gallant himself telephoned me, and said he would call for me after lunch so I could run over some of the numbers with the orchestra. At any other time, I'd have been rather thrilled with it all—the chance to meet this promising, young orchestra leader for whom a brilliant future was being predicted, and to play with his band. I'd often heard them on the radio, and the fact that Steve's parents had gone to the big expense of importing the Gallant outfit from the city, a hundred miles away, showed me what a very swanky affair this engagement and graduation party was to be.

Today—well, today it was just one more feverish activity which might keep me for a little while from going to pieces; might

postpone that inevitable moment when the unbearable future would be upon me!

Young Mr. Gallant, I realized dimly, was an engaging chap. Lithe and agile, with a quick, boyish smile, a shock of red hair, and friendly, gray eyes.

"They tell me you're a whiz, and probably a lot better than my regular pianist," he said, smiling down at me. Which was nice of him, because he was probably secretly worried to death about the substitution, and fearing I was awful.

And then he began to talk music to me; almost the only subject he could have selected which would have taken me out of myself even the least little bit. For I could still respond, at any rate to a small extent, to what had been my major passion, before Steve came.

The practice went off quite smoothly. I caught on quickly to what he wanted, and his orchestra was perfectly trained. It was wonderful, the extent to which he seemed to carry every single instrument with him; watching him and working with him would have been awfully exciting, musically, at a happier time.

Afterward, driving me home, he said, "Well, you're just as good as they said you were. Even better."

"So are you," I answered sincerely.

"But what are those clever little fingers of yours doing pounding typewriter keys?" he demanded. "It's a crime when they can make music like that."

"I don't pound typewriter keys in a down-town office," I replied, a little bit stiffly. "I work at the university."

"Oh!" he drawled, and somehow his tone made me flush, angrily.

I think it was while I was dressing for Steve's party that night that I suddenly and definitely decided that I had come to the end of my row, and that I couldn't, and wouldn't, stand it any longer. I was going to quit, that was all. I was getting out, and getting out that night! I couldn't make up my mind to kill my baby, and go on living myself—but I could kill myself and take the baby with me when I went. I knew exactly how I'd do it, too. In such a way that the family would never suspect it was anything but an accident. Oh, it would be easy! I was taking our shabby little car, and when I came back home across the high railroad bridge—why, I'd skid, and, instead, the car would miss the narrow bridge and slither off the steep embankment, a good fifty-foot drop. Everybody in our end of town would cry, "We always knew there'd be some terrible accident there!" It was really a dangerous place and would seem natural.

A sort of wild relief welled up in me. Two bright spots of color came into my cheeks, my eyes were unnaturally brilliant, and the family fondly commented on how pretty I looked as I kissed them goodby. The eyes of the group of young men who saw me come in, at Steve's fraternity house, told me the same thing. And Steve, coming forward to meet me, looked surprised.

"You look awfully well and blooming," he remarked almost reproachfully.

At that, I laughed; clear laughter, that rang out, and made several people look at me with appreciative smiles, as if they enjoyed spontaneous, girlish gayety. Only Kerry Gallant (and this was funny) frowned. I saw him. He frowned and winced. Well, he was a musician, accustomed to detecting "sour" notes; and maybe the laughter didn't sound spontaneous and girlish to him. Maybe it sounded macabre; like the last wild gayety of a lost and doomed soul.

IN ALL my life, I'd never played like I played that night. I suppose, really, it wasn't the sort of playing that Kerry wanted. Because I didn't accompany the orchestra; I dominated it. I couldn't help it. All of the selections were the very best, of their kind—trust Kerry for that. And somehow, the knowledge that this was the last time my fingers would ever wander over those beloved black and white keys. That this was my swan song; that life was ending tonight for me, put a wild fire and passion into my music.

Even the dancers (who don't often listen to music) noticed it; and sometimes they stopped dancing, and stood around, just listening and watching my fingers race across the keys.

The plan, I knew, was to announce the engagement while refreshments were being served, during the intermission. Rising from the piano, very tired all of a sudden, I saw Steve and Betty, he bending his handsome head over her with that flatteringly devoted air of his, she glowing and sparkling; and just behind them, smiling indulgently at young love, the four parents, solid, dignified, aristocratic, prosperous. The contrast between their happiness and security, and my own utter forlornness—the sudden stab of wild pain—turned me white and sick for a moment. I staggered to my feet just as Steve led Betty back to their table. I couldn't play any more! I had to get out—away. I'd cave in if I didn't. In that instant a voice said firmly in my ear, "Buck up. Don't let anyone get wise . . . I'm taking you out in the garden."

I knew the voice—Kerry's. But I couldn't see his face, for my world was dancing and wavering. Blindly, I let him propel me out—and found myself sitting on a bench in the fraternity garden, with a fountain tinkling in front of us, and the many lights of the big house gleaming beyond.

"Now then!" The tones were almost harsh. "What is it?"

"What is—what?" I gasped.

"You know! My Lord, I never heard such playing! You swamped the whole orchestra—you were leading, not I! Once I thought you must be full of dope—then I decided it wasn't that, after all, but—"

"But—what?"

"That you were the most desperately frightened and unhappy person I'd ever seen in all my life," he said. There was a long silence.

"I—I'm not, though . . . not any more, I mean . . . not like I was. Because I thought there wasn't any way out—and now I've thought of one!"

"What do you mean?" he asked sharply.

"If life is unbearable, a person doesn't have to go on living, does he?"

"Unless he's a coward and can't take it."

"Then I'm a coward and I can't take it."

He said quietly, "It can't be that bad—you're young and talented and beautiful."

"What has that got to do with it?" I cried passionately. "It never got me anything! Money and social prominence—they're what get you places! It's because I haven't got either one, that the man who said he loved me, the man I loved, is—is—"

Kerry finished it for me. "Announcing his engagement to another girl tonight, eh?" he said, still in that quiet tone.

Just for a second the realization of the extreme delicacy and sensitiveness of his perceptive powers pierced even through my misery. "How did you know?" I asked dully.

"I don't know how," he answered simply. "I feel things, somehow. But let

me tell you, young lady, it's the other girl that's unlucky, not you!"

It was queer; I'd only seen him for the first time that afternoon. Yet I felt absolutely no restraint with him. I shook my head.

"No. You wouldn't say that if you knew. He's worthless, all right—a light-weight, selfish, cruel. But—but she'll at least be married. And I—I'm going to have a baby . . . his baby . . . and I'm not married. So now you know."

His hand fell over mine. "I knew before. I guessed that, too. It wasn't just pain I saw in your eyes—it was terror, too. Now listen—can I call you Diane?—now listen, Diane, we're going to work this thing out somehow! I'll help—you aren't going to do anything wicked and foolish—why, it would be—"

Someone was calling him; two of his orchestra members were looking for him. He said hastily, "I'll see you later . . . remember, we'll find a better way than yours!"

It was warming, somehow; his understanding. And though you felt instinctively that he was clean and good, there was no condemnation in his attitude. Just sympathy and a desire to help. I thought, "I'm glad I knew him and talked to him tonight. There isn't any other way, and there's nothing he can do. But I'm glad that somebody understood, before I went out—it makes it less lonesome."

The hideous nightmare of an evening wore on. All my hysterical exaltation had left now. I was playing more soberly; following. There was left simply a fathomless despair, and the chill determination that I would not live to smash the hearts of my parents and disgrace myself.

I slipped away by a side door, after the "Home Sweet Home," a little bit afraid that Kerry would try to stop me. I was shaking as I climbed in the little car; already I felt half a ghost. Just for a second, in the fragrant June air, so wild a regret for all the sweetness life might have held if I hadn't messed it up, swept over me, that it seemed to me my heart was literally breaking in two. With trembling fingers, I turned on the ignition and started the car; and I said out loud, "Just a little longer now! I can stand it fifteen minutes longer . . . then—just one bad second, and it won't hurt any more, nothing will hurt any more!"

As I turned out of the great gates at the end of the curving driveway, I thought I heard someone behind shout my name. But I did not stop. My whole being now had crystallized into one definite and final purpose. . . .

There was the bridge! Another car was close behind me, coming very fast. Its headlights glared through my back window. I heard its horn. Well, it would pass me on the left, and I would swerve to the right, the steepest side, just as I reached the bridge. Now!

I gave a sudden, violent wrench to the wheel . . . and at the same instant, with incredible quickness, some big, dark object rushed past me, on the right, turning sharply so that we collided . . . and sight and sound went out . . .

SOMEONE was calling my name from a long way off. Sharply. "Diane! Diane!" I opened my eyes, and for an instant saw nothing at all. Then I realized that I was bent across my steering wheel, my head against the glass of my windshield. I put my hand up stupidly and felt blood on it; there was a terrible pain, where the wheel had rammed into my stomach. [CONTINUED]

HOW ONE GIRL FOUND ROMANCE

ARE YOU FLAT-CHESTED?

Give Me 30 Days To Prove I Can

INCREASE YOUR BUST MEASURE

LOVE, Romance, Popularity—all are attracted by *feminine charm*. And the outstanding charm of beautiful womanhood is a full, shapely bust. Lovely, rounded curves are the vogue. The straight-line figure is hopelessly "out."

Do you lack the allure of a shapely, well-developed figure? Is your bust small, flat and drooping? Are you embarrassed when you appear in a low-cut evening frock or a bathing suit? Let me show you how to fill out your form to fascinating curves. Let me show you how to add inches of firm, rounded tissue to your bust. No matter how small and undeveloped your bust may now be, my famous Miracle Cream treatment will quickly increase its size and mould it to lovely, arching form.

ADD 1 to 3 INCHES

One woman writes: "My bust was so thin and undeveloped that I was positively ashamed of my figure. I had tried everything without success. Then I decided to make one last try with your Miracle Cream treatment and I am certainly glad I did. My bust soon began to fill out nicely and now it has increased to attractive size and shapeliness. I never dreamed that a well-formed bust could make such a difference in one's appearance."

DEVELOP YOUR BUST THIS NEW, EASY WAY

Thousands of women all over the world have used this safe, simple home treatment to develop the bust. Will you give me 30 days to prove that I can give *you* a full, beautifully modelled bust? Take advantage of my special offer now. Mail the coupon below and see how easily you can add one to three inches of shapely beauty to your bust measure. Sagging contours are lifted, flabby tissues are made firm and rounded. Soon your breasts will stand out in exquisite beauty.

FREE: *A Beautiful Form*

My new illustrated book tells all about this new easy way to develop the bust. It is yours free. And here's my great special offer that brings you the Miracle Cream treatment to try for yourself: send only $1.00 for large container of Miracle Cream and valuable instructions—free book included. Don't delay—mail the coupon or write TODAY—before this wonderful offer is withdrawn.

NANCY LEE, (Dept. P-7) 816 Broadway, New York, N. Y.

WHEN ANSWERING ADVERTISEMENTS PLEASE MENTION TRUE CONFESSIONS

"Diane!" said the voice again. "Oh, my God! *Diane.*"

I answered then; weakly. "Kerry, it's you?"

At that I heard him sob; distinctly. He said, "Thank God!" But where was he? I was in the car alone; and it was rammed against something, it seemed. Then his voice came again. "My front wheels are trembling over the edge of this ravine—I'm holding her here with the brakes and I don't dare move for fear of jarring her over. Listen carefully, Di, for God's sake . . . I think your front fender is locked with my back one, there at the side—I'm afraid if I go over, I'll drag you with me. Can you crawl out very cautiously, not jarring at all, and prop up both cars with rocks under the back wheels? There's a big pile over there where they've been working on the roads . . . do you understand?"

I didn't know whether I did or not. I was sick and dizzy and my head was whirling.

"Diane!" said the voice again, and now there was a mixture of tense command and appeal in it. "You've got to be a real woman—even if you're badly hurt; you'll have to manage it, or we both are going over this edge together . . . get out and get to work and don't move an unnecessary muscle while you're getting out!"

The last sentence had the crack of a whip. My numbed brain responded almost mechanically, and very carefully, moving a bare inch at a time, I managed to get the door open and found myself outside with the cars both still in place. For a moment then I thought I was going to faint. My head was throbbing from the cut place, and there was a violent pain inside me somewhere. The world was wavering, and I wavered with it, when the voice from the dark mass of the car in front of me spoke again.

"Brave kid, Di . . . the rocks are just behind you there!"

And as if that voice had been a stimulant that stung me into a kind of automatic, nearly unthinking, action, I began to move again, this time with a sort of feverish haste. I dragged huge rocks and placed them in front of the back wheels of Kerry's car; I brought more, and built almost a high little wall, all around those wheels. Then I did the same for mine. I've no idea how long it took. I only know that at last it was done; that I cried, "It's all right—they'll have to hold now!" and keeled over on the grass . . .

Jumbled, confused, memories, then. A nightmare of pain . . . someone groaning—myself? Someone carrying me . . . riding in a car, held in someone's arms . . . then bright lights, white halls, strange faces, firm, efficient hands taking me in charge.

Later . . . many hours later . . . I found

out that I had lost my baby; and I found something else—that Kerry, when he brought me to the hospital, had told the doctor my story in deepest confidence, begging that my family not be told of my condition. And they never were. To them, still, what happened that night was a queer accident, in which I suffered some temporary internal injuries and in which, they thanked God, I had not lost my life.

WITH youth and a good constitution in my favor, I lay there getting well fast, but not much interested in whether I did or not . . . trying not to think, but doing a good deal of thinking, nevertheless, and liking myself less, the more I thought.

One afternoon, they told me that Kerry was there and wanted to see me.

It had been just ten days since the first day I'd met him; it seemed twenty years or so.

He came in a little diffidently. He said, "I've been 'phoning long distance every day and I drove over this morning. You're looking fine." I started to answer, "Thanks, so are you—" But midway in the speech my voice broke, and I turned my head on the pillow, tears in my eyes. Then, with a little rush, I found him beside me, holding my hands, his own voice husky.

"Don't cry—please don't cry! You were fine—you were the bravest thing ever—"

"Brave! I've been a weak coward—it would have been better if you'd let me die—"

"Being weak once doesn't mean you'll never be strong again, does it?" His hands were so warm and strong on my shaking ones! "You didn't really love that rotter; you couldn't have, a grand girl like you! No, you were just dazzled because he was rich and socially prominent and because you were tired of feeling left out. Oh, Di, it doesn't get you anywhere - pretense and social climbing! Things will come to you, if you just go

along being yourself, not caring about all that or trying for it. Me, I'm nobody—I was raised on fire escapes, just a slum kid with some music in my heart and my fingers . . . But I know the difference between what's real and what isn't."

I clung to his hands, as if they alone were holding me up. I whispered huskily, humbly, "Thanks . . . I'll—remember . . ."

"Gosh!" he said. "Gosh!" He bent an instant and laid his cheek on mine, just the barest touch. Then he straightened up. "Are you all set on going back to the college job? I'm afraid Bill—my pianist—has ruined his hand for a long time. Anyway, his folks want him to go into his dad's business, and he's been wavering about whether to quit or not all year. I thought—I thought I'd offer you the job—if you're interested."

"If I'm interested!" I gasped. "If I'm interested!" I began to cry in dead earnest. . . .

Later I asked him tremulously, "How in the world did you guess what I was going to do that night, and how did you manage that car business?"

"Why, you told me—that afternoon. Practically. Don't you remember? When we crossed that bridge, I said, 'This is a dangerous place,' and you said, 'It would be a fine place to commit suicide. That steep bank right there—you could twist your wheel or go over the edge, and everybody would think you'd skidded or missed the bridge in the dark.' So naturally when you hurried out that way, and started hell-for-leather in your car, I guessed what you were up to. I followed, and the only thing I could think of—" he hesitated. "Well, it was crazy—it might have killed us both, I guess. I passed you on the right and tried to turn in front of you—and there wasn't quite room."

He must have moved with incredible, superhuman skill and quickness. I didn't, I never will, understand the force and the courage and the decision it must have taken. I simply bowed in spirit then, and still do, and always will, to a character far stronger and finer and braver than mine.

I laughed a little—shakily, the tears not far away. I said, "If—if I ever get married and have any children, I think I'll try to raise them all on fire escapes. It—it seems to be a grand place to raise children."

And then—oh, and then!—the room turned rosy pink and swam a little before my eyes, dazzled by sudden, intolerable brightness, by the shining hope I glimpsed of a happiness I'd never even faintly dreamed of before. For Kerry was smiling at me; not trying to kiss me, not "making love"; but saying, with his voice all gruff, "I guess I'll have something to say about that . . . think I want my kids brought up on a fire escape?" ●

Love's Lesson

Whatever I know about poetry
I learn when you walk down the
street,
Whatever I know of adventure
I follow in your twinkling feet.

Whatever life holds of content-
ment
You hold in your soft, little
palm,
Whatever of melodic singing—
Your voice is my favorite psalm.

Whatever the meaning of beauty
The smile on your face is a sign,
Whatever the meaning of rapture
I know when your dear lips
meet mine.

By RAMON YBARRA

We danced as no boy or girl ever did before. The clamor of drums and brass beat through our blood, sweeping us on and on in a fury of motion.

I F YOU saw that picture of Danny and me in the newspapers, you must have wondered what sort of girl would be willing to get married like that, as a sensational publicity stunt. And yet, to us, it was so much more than that.

No one could have recognized us from those awful pictures and our real names were not given. In fact my own mother might have skimmed over them in the morning paper without a second glance. But I think if she had known that those glaring headlines referred to her own seventeen-year-old daughter, she would have died right then with shame and heartbreak.

Danny and I were really desperate that day when we happened to see the big red and white poster ballyhooing the dance contest.

HONEYMOON TRAILER AND FIVE HUNDRED DOLLARS GIVEN AWAY TO WINNING COUPLE

The rules, printed underneath, were as sensational as the poster itself. The contest was to run six nights. There were to be fifty contestants, all engaged couples, and the winners were to be married on the dance floor at the end of the sixth night. A honeymoon trailer and five hundred dollars would then be theirs and they were to drive two thousand miles to California, arriving finally at the San Francisco Exposition where they'd be given a six months' contract to dance in one of the Gayway shows.

Danny and I stood in

JITTERBUG WEDDING

If only young people could learn the discipline of waiting for marriage, how much misery they'd save themselves!

front of the poster for a long time, hands clasped and hearts pounding. Everything had seemed so utterly hopeless until then, and here was a possible answer to all our prayers—romance, adventure, a job, and most breathtaking of all, a chance to get married.

I looked up at this tall, handsome boy that I had grown to love so recklessly, and saw that his eyes were dancing and that the dare-devil grin I knew so well, was spreading over his face.

"Get a load of that!" he cried out. "Right there in front of you!"

I saw then that the honeymoon trailer was hitched to a new coupe and parked outside the big hall where the dance contest was to be held. It was attracting a lot of attention here on the West Side. One glance at its silver sleekness, its modern gadgets and shining perfection, set our blood to racing. Imagine gliding along in a marvel like that toward all sorts of wonderful adventure! That in itself would have been enough, but actually to be married, to have five hundred dollars in cash, a place to live and a job for six whole months in a glittering wonder world was more than we could imagine. Perhaps we can't be blamed too much for going a little mad!

Just that morning we had made up our minds that we'd have to wait years before we could get married. Both Danny's folks and mine were so terribly against it. They said we were too young, and Danny didn't even have a job. I was seventeen and Danny was only a year older, but we were desperately sure we couldn't bear to wait.

Danny's father was a retired naval officer, and passionately determined that his son should enter Annapolis. Danny already had been appointed and had planned to go there as soon as he graduated from high school. But that was before he fell in love with me, and now, although I'm afraid he still had Navy in his blood, he refused to go.

"That would mean we couldn't get married for years," he declared. "Perhaps never, with all this war scare. There are plenty of other things I can do." But he couldn't seem to find them, and I know his father hated me for standing in the way of a cherished dream.

Mother was bitter about early marriages. She had lived through one, but my heart wouldn't listen to her. She wanted me to stay at home for at least eight more years and to keep away from love affairs. "A girl's a fool to marry before she's twenty-five," she told me over and over, "and I need you here with me." But I didn't believe she really did, and to me at seventeen, eight years seemed eternity.

Dad had left her a generous annuity to be paid as long as she lived and I was the only thing she had to worry about. She fussed almost constantly over nearly everything I did, and things were pretty dismal for me at home. She wouldn't let me go to work, even if I could have found a job. She said there always would be money enough to support us both.

All that might not have been too unbearable if Danny and I hadn't fallen so desperately in love, or if on one mad, moonlight night, we hadn't so nearly lost our heads. I had stolen away to meet him in our secret little place under the stars, and our flaming young love had swept us on to those unknown heights.

"Danny, I'm scared—"

"No, Virgie, darling," he whispered hoarsely, "I love you too much for that! They'll just *have* to let us get married. I want you so terribly! They think we're too young. But why are we? You're as much a woman now as you will be in ten years, and I need every minute of you. Why do we have to waste three whole years, until I'm twenty-one?" he cried rebelliously. "Dad could give me the money that's coming to me now just as well as he could then. It's a trust fund left by my mother, and it's more than enough to set me up in some good business. But do you think he'll listen? Not while he has this Navy bug, he won't. Navy's swell, if it's what you want, but right now all I want is—you!" he whispered fervidly.

I shivered a little, even then, with a sense of premonition. I wondered if after he gave up the Navy for me, I'd always

be enough. For, of course, a man can't go to Annapolis if he's married, nor can he marry during all the years of his training. I tried to put the question into faltering words:

"But will you always want—just me, Danny?"

"Listen to the child!" he jeered. "Haven't you any idea at all how sweet you are, with your brown eyes all dotted with gold stars, and your red hair and turned up nose. You're all fire and softness, and your mouth—it's like liquid flame. I never want to stop kissing it."

And again as he tottered on the brink of desires too strong for us to fight, Danny pulled me to my feet.

"Listen, we'd better go home, Virgie, before something happens. Tomorrow I'll try to have it out with Dad and you'd better have a talk with your mother. It's time she realized you've grown up. Make her understand why we want to get married, and what might happen—if we don't."

But somehow we couldn't either of us find the right words to make them understand. Mother wept and told me I should be ashamed to talk of marriage at my age. She declared that if I ever tried to see Danny again she'd lock me in my room. Danny's father stormed and blustered, and cut off his allowance. There was some danger that Danny might be taken away to Washington, even against his will.

"I won't go, Virgie," he told me fiercely, the next night. "Nothing can make me leave you. I'll find a job somehow."

But there didn't seem to be any jobs in town for an eighteen-year-old boy whose father had taught him nothing but Navy. If Mother had let Danny come to the house, or

if we could have met openly without that sense of guilt, we might have stuck it out. But as it was, we were filled with a sort of panic, as if every moment we spent together might be our last.

AND then we saw the exciting red and white poster, with its dazzling promise of a way out.

"It would be a cinch for us," Danny boasted. "We can out-dance any couple in town."

We'd already won two silver cups in the high school contests, but that had been among our own crowd on Maple Hill. We didn't know these West Side kids, and the dancing might prove pretty rough.

"What do we have to lose?" Danny urged. "And gosh, Virgie, suppose we should win! We could get out of this town, with a job and a place to live. After that we'd be able to manage somehow, until I'm of age and Dad *has* to hand over that trust fund."

It didn't take much persuading, even though I realized how hard it would be for me to steal out of the house without letting Mother know. But one look at the shining trailer, and I was lost.

"Come on, then, before I lose my nerve," I cried out, and led the way inside the big, barn-like hall.

A fat man with little sharp eyes was explaining the rules to a group of boys and girls gathered around the platform. First, he told us, the contestants had to be of age, the girls over eighteen, and the boys over twenty-one. Danny and I exchanged quick, questioning glances, and he made a warning gesture. "Who says we aren't of age?" he whispered. "And remember, we'd better not give our full names or correct addresses. They'd be ballyhooed all over town."

And so began our first deception. There was some sort of application blank to make out, and Danny wrote his age as twenty-one, and mine as eighteen. He signed his name Daniel James, leaving off the Carter, and told me to sign my first and middle names, too. So I wrote just Virginia May, and the first address which came into my head. We really did look much older than we were, and no one would be likely to recognize us in a West Side dance hall. None of the Maple Hill crowd ever came down here.

In our state a couple could be married on the same day they received the license, and it was arranged that on the morning of the sixth day, the three couples who had received the largest scores were all to take out licenses, and in case they won, be prepared for the big prize at the close. Only these three would compete on the final night, and the couple who received the most votes would be married by a justice of the peace, right on the dance floor. This was part of the publicity stunt and each couple had to sign an agreement to carry it through.

If our [*Please turn page*]

Unluckily, Danny heard Carlos' words. "If you weren't right," Danny choked, "I'd punch your head in."

need hadn't been so desperate, and we hadn't felt that gnawing sense of guilt against Mother and Danny's father, it might have been just mad, exciting fun. But as it was, I felt as if I never could live through it.

First there was the sneaking out the back door at night, and the constant fear that Mother would find out I had gone before I returned home. Luckily for us, the contests didn't start until nine o'clock, and I could make some excuse to go up to my room early. Mother usually was in bed by that time, anyway. She complained of feeling tired most of the time. But what worried me most was that she had queer fainting spells whenever I did anything to displease her. Danny said she was just putting on an act so she could have her own way. But I always had dreaded them a hundred times worse than if she had given me a good spanking.

And those wild, swing-mad dances through the long hours of the night! If you've ever seen a jitterbug contest you'll know what I mean, and if you haven't, no words of mine could quite describe it. The clamour of the drums and the brass beat through our blood in a rising tide, sweeping us on in a very fury of motion, on and on, tirelessly, arms and bodies swaying, swerving, whirling—there is nothing else in modern youth quite like it—so wild, so free, so unexplainable, and yet so completely a part of life, itself.

Danny and I danced during those six nights as I believe no boy and girl ever danced before, for *we had to win*. And we did win. Don't ask me how, for I shall never know. Sometimes by midnight, I was so utterly worn down I could scarcely get home, and I crept sobbing into bed. It was only by some miracle that Mother did not discover what was going on. I'd sleep as much as I could through the day, trying to save my strength, and then creep out secretly at night. And at last came that sixth morning when Danny and I found ourselves up there among the three winning couples who must go to the City Hall for their licenses.

We realized then that this was, indeed, pretty serious business. We gave the same ages and names that we'd written on the application, but stood in fear and trembling lest someone there should recognize us and shout the news from the housetops. But again, nothing and no one stopped us, and by midnight we were standing there in front of the applauding crowd, almost too tired to realize just what the justice of the peace was mumbling over our clasped hands.

There was shouting and laughter and a jumble of rough jests. Newspaper men took pictures and asked questions which we did not even try to answer straight, and then at last the hall was cleared and we stood there alone with the manager to receive our final instructions. The five hundred dollars had been given to us just before the ceremony and was now tucked inside my own purse where Danny had insisted upon putting it. We were to have the whole month of April to ourselves and on May first we were to report for work at the Exposition Gayway. The show, evidently, was to be called Dance of All Nations. The man wrote a scribbled introduction on his card and this, too, with my marriage certificate, I tucked inside my bag.

At last, clinging together like two tired children, Danny and I stumbled out to the trailer. It had been taken around to the back of the building and parked there away from the curious crowd.

"It isn't real," I whispered, and slumped down in a crumpled heap on one of the cushioned seats. "It can't be, and I'm too dead tired even to think."

"So am I," Danny groaned.

We sat for awhile longer dazed and sort of let-down, with every bone and muscle in our bodies aching.

"I'm glad I wrote my letter to Mother this morning," I said, "for right now I couldn't think of a single sane thing to say. We'll mail it as soon as we get far enough along the road. I don't want her to worry too much—and gosh—I hope she doesn't have one of those fainting spells."

"Dad won't find my letter until he gets back from Washington," Danny said. "That will give us a good two days' start. Even if they try to come after us, they'd never think of looking for us in a brand new trailer. I had such a wide grin on my face when they snapped those pictures, that I'll look as if I'm being tickled and I never saw one of those flashlight pictures that could be recognized, anyhow."

Perhaps we were just young and reckless, or maybe we were callous and cruel. I don't know, but at least they never could say that we hadn't given them fair warning.

We were too utterly worn out to risk traveling far that night and parked behind a deserted barn just a few miles outside of town.

We slept for hours in complete exhaustion, and I woke with a start to find Danny bending over me, his eyes eager and glowing.

"Wake up, darling," he cried out, "we mustn't waste another minute of our first day. Have you forgotten just who you are?"

"I'm your—wife!" The words came from my lips in a sort of song, and I felt myself gathered into his arms.

IF ONLY we could have kept the sweetness of those first hours, the breathless sense of fulfillment after long months of waiting. I was Danny's wife, and his strong young arms held me fiercely close. I felt protected, and shut away from anything that ever could harm me.

"Always let me be enough, Danny," I whispered. "Don't ever want anything or anyone else."

"As if I could, little silly!"

My heart kept up its wild singing. Everything was going to be all right. We were really married—I didn't have to be afraid now of what might happen. Nothing mattered now but that Danny and I should love each other always.

After awhile we came down to earth, and eagerly, like two children, began to explore the trailer. Last night we had been too tired even to realize that it could be truly ours. A honeymoon trailer, indeed, with shining aluminum pans, gay yellow and white dishes, knives and forks with bright blue handles, and even a blue luncheon cloth with a wide yellow border. There were new sheets and blankets on the bed, and when these were tucked away, the bed folded back into a breakfast nook. Our little cook stove had been filled with gasoline, and there was water in the tank over the sink. But I think what delighted us most was the bathroom, unbelievably tiny, yet complete in every shining detail.

"I still can't believe it's true," I cried "and that it's all our own."

"This, and all the world!" he exclaimed, and again whirled me around in his arms.

We stopped at the next town to stock the trailer with provisions and to mail our letters home. Then we got our first meal in the little doll-house kitchen. I was glad that Mother had taught me how to cook.

"Who says this isn't the life." Danny grinned. "And now we're on our way to the Fair."

The Fair! Why, just a few days ago, not in my wildest dreams, could I ever have believed that I might see it, and now, by some miracle, Danny and I were really to work there. They hadn't told us exactly what the job would be; just that we were to see a Mr. Sam Flowers, at The Dance of All Nations.

"Imagine us turning into a pair of hoofers," Danny burst out, as we started to wash the breakfast dishes. "Some difference from being a naval officer."

I winced and turned around to face him. "Maybe you'll hate it, Danny."

"Maybe," he shrugged, "but anything to get by for these next three years, until we get that trust fund. It's quite a lot of money, Virgie. As much as twenty-five thousand dollars. We could buy a real business with that, and settle down anywhere we want to live."

I loved the way he said "we" and my heart felt all glowing with pride. "What sort of business, Danny?" I asked eagerly.

"I don't know. What do you think?"

"A store, maybe, or perhaps a trailer camp."

"Now that's an idea," he laughed. "There seem to be a million of these things on the road. We'd have something different, with a lot of new ideas. Anyhow, it's worth thinking about."

After that, every time we parked in a trailer camp, we'd compare it with our own rosy visions.

The idea grew as we drove farther west until it became an obsession. "When we get our trailer camp—" was the burden of our song.

OUR one shadow was the thought of Mother and Danny's father. They'd probably be searching for us by now. They might even have called in the police. It was certain by this time that if they'd recognized those newspaper pictures or learned of our part in the contest, they'd have caught up with us before now. The trailer idea seemed to have completely covered our tracks. The last place they'd ever think of looking for us would be in a thousand dollar outfit, headed for California.

If only those weeks could have lasted forever; the bright, sunshiny days, and the sweet, starlit nights. Often we wouldn't go to a regular camp, but park off the highway in some sheltered spot all our own. And those nights were sweetest of all.

But it had to end, for our month was

nearly up, and we had to report to the Gayway show.

I'll never forget my first glimpse of the Fair. It was indeed, as the ballyhoo proclaimed, a magic island, lighted by some modern Aladdin. We had crossed the great Oakland Bridge just as it grew dark and Treasure Island blazed across the Bay like some brilliant wonderworld. It seemed to float on crystal clear water, and was bathed in a stream of liquid color—gold, green and amber. It didn't seem possible that we really were to work in this fairyland of breathtaking enchantment.

We left the trailer at a camp not far from the grounds and drove the rest of the way in the coupe. We parked in the huge ramp, then went on, scarcely able to take in all the beauty of this man-made miracle. We passed through the Portals of the Pacific, into the Court of The Seven Seas, and on to the Lake of Nations. Even the very names seemed to spell sheer magic.

Then we had to leave the beauty behind and go on to the great sprawling Gayway. This was the Fun Zone, where barkers screamed in front of gaudy doorways, and where there was a reek of wet paint, hot dogs and popcorn. Nothing seemed quite finished here and the din of hammers and saws almost drowned out the clamoring voices of the spielers and the shouts of merrymakers.

There were rollo planes and giant wheels, and all sorts of miniature foreign villages. And at last, in one of these we found the gayly decorated front of the Dance of All Nations.

"This is it!" Danny exclaimed, "but look at the picture of that girl. She makes Sally Rand's Ranchettes and the famous Stella seem over-dressed. If that's the sort of dance we have to put on, we just aren't having any."

The card in my hand called us as the Honeymoon Kids. The rough, garish building was already packed, and we could hear the loud laughter of the audience. There was no glamour here, just tawdry scenery and a glare of red and purple lights. We found Sam Flowers in a small bare office near the front entrance, and he stood looking down at us with a broad, good-natured grin.

"So you're the Honeymoon Kids," he said. "Well, that was a swell publicity stunt, and I've got a spot waiting for you. No, don't let those posters fool you, that's just the come-on. Our show's decent enough. It has to be with the cops swarming the place like flies. Why," he chuckled, "they even made Sally's Ranchettes wear bandanas. Come on, let's go out back and see what you can do."

He hadn't asked us any questions, or let us say a word, but led us to a big room at the back where a girl in green and gold tights was rehearsing a snake dance.

"Our show," Flowers explained, "is just what the ballyhoo says, The Dance of all Nations—Spanish, Russian, Hula-Hula—the whole works, but I figured it couldn't be complete this year without a couple of jitterbugs. That's where you come in. So now let's see you do your stuff."

"Swing it," he shouted to a three piece rehearsal orchestra, "and make it plenty hot."

So Danny and I swung into it with all we had, and heard his loud, laughing applause. "That does it!" he cried. "And for costumes, you'll wear kid stuff, white slacks and a silk polo shirt, both of you. Swing and Strip Tease don't mix."

Danny's eyes met mine in quick relief. "The pay," Flowers went on, "will be fifty dollars a week for the team, three shows a day, seven days a week. That's the best I can do right now. We'll bill you as the Honeymoon Kids. It's a natural, but we won't sign any contracts until I see how the act turns out. We'll get you fitted for costumes, and schedule you to dance on Monday."

On our way back to the ramp I saw that Danny's face was pretty glum. "Well, we're in for it, honey," he said, "and I'm afraid we'll take an awful chance of being spotted by someone back home. A lot of folks we know are coming to this Fair."

"But what could they do, Danny, even if they found us? We're married now." And that, to me, seemed the answer to everything. I was Danny's wife. No one could separate us now.

The trouble did not wholly leave Danny's face until we were out on the road again, rolling along in the trailer.

"We sure can cut expenses living like this," he said. "Let's find some camp, not too near the city, yet not too far from the Fair, and with a view of the bay. Then we can sort of settle down."

Out across the big bridge, and on toward Oakland, we came upon just the right spot. "Take a look at that," Danny exclaimed. "It's almost as swell as the one we dreamed of!"

Back from the highway was a rolling stretch of field that skirted a canyon and overlooked the bay. It evidently had once been part of a great redwood forest but now it sheltered fifty or more cars and trailers. It was partly hidden from the road by a long row of the towering trees, and at the entrance was a huge redwood gate. Over the gate a Neon sign blazed out the words REDWOOD CAMP.

85

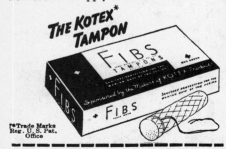
Inside we could see that each trailer was surrounded by its own grove, and had a view of the Bay.

"They're stealing our stuff," Danny declared gleefully.

"It's exactly the place for us to stay," I exclaimed. "We can keep the trailer here and get out to the grounds in our car in less than half an hour."

There was a long, rambling pavilion near the entrance, made of redwood logs, and one door was marked "office." The rest of the building seemed to be a dance hall and restaurant. The tables were crowded and an orchestra was playing Spanish music.

A pretty girl in a gay Spanish costume opened the door for us, and Danny asked to see the proprietor. She led us to an inner room and we were greeted by a tall, dark-eyed man, who looked as if there must have been Spanish blood in his veins. He couldn't have been much over twenty-five, yet there was about him a sort of grave pride that made him appear much older.

I never had seen any one just like him. His skin was bronzed by sun and sea, and his face had a handsome, clear cut strength that would be impossible ever to forget.

For some reason I found myself trembling, and yet his eyes, after that first quick, searching glance, had scarcely met my own. I think Danny must have sensed something of that strange turmoil, for I felt his hand, almost as a warning, pressing my arm. I jerked myself back, as from a great distance, and tried to listen to what they were saying.

Danny was telling him that we'd be working at the Exposition for about six months, and would like a spot with a clear view of the bay, and cut off as far as possible from the others. "It happens to be," he ended boyishly, "our honeymoon."

The man's name, it seemed was Carlos Madero. And, just as I had sensed, the land once had belonged to his great-great grandfather, and for years had been eating itself up in taxes. He was the last of the line, and had hit upon this idea to pay off the heavy mortgages.

I don't know why he was telling us all this—I'm sure he didn't, usually—perhaps it was something he sensed in me; a quick, warm sympathy, that had surged almost instantly between us.

Yes, he went on, he had just the spot for us, not far from his own rancho. The estate, really, reached out to that clump of redwoods at the far edge of the canyon, but he was using only this corner of it for the camp. He led the way as he talked out beyond the group of trailers to an isolated grove of trees. A gravel road extended to the edge, and there was room between the towering trunks to park the car and trailer.

We finally agreed to thirty dollars a month and Danny went for our outfit, while Carlos arranged to have the electric wires run down from his rancho. For a moment we stood there together after Danny had gone, and I felt again that strange inner turmoil.

"You are terribly young to be married," Carlos said very gravely, and I wondered why I felt no resentment. "And you're different from those others."

And so, I wanted to say, are you. But I did not, and felt a quick relief when I saw Danny returning with our little caravan. The trailer fitted snugly under the first row of trees, and was entirely out of sight from the rest of the camp. If it hadn't been for our work on the Gayway, we might have hidden right here for the rest of our lives with no danger of being found.

Danny was growing impatient again and tugged at my arm. Carlos walked slowly away.

"I don't like that chap," Danny growled. "He talks too darned much about himself."

"He reminds me of the redwood trees, somehow," I said softly.

DANNY and I sat at the edge of the canyon a long time that night, looking out across the bay. He was strangely silent, and all the boyishness seemed gone from his face.

"Everything would be fine," he said at last, "if it wasn't for that blamed Gayway show. It was all right to swing it out back there at high school, and all right, perhaps, to do our darndest to win the contest, but to become regular jitterbugs. Gosh, Virgie, we'll hate it, especially when we look at all that out there, the battleships, the navy planes."

I shivered a little and drew closer. "Perhaps we can get out of it, Danny—the dancing, I mean."

"Not when it's the only way I know of right now that we can earn a living," he growled. "That five hundred isn't going to last forever, and we'll need the fifty a week. Three years can be a long time, Virgie, and we've got to hang on somehow till I get hold of that trust fund."

"Maybe dancing for six months won't be so bad," I tried to soothe him. "It might even be fun."

"For you, perhaps, but imagine a Navy man earning his living doing the shag."

A Navy man—there it was again! Once more I shivered, and drew him back toward the trailer. "I'm tired," I whispered, "and still a little scared. Hold me close, Danny, it seems so strange and different out here under the redwoods, and I feel so small, and sort of lost."

His arms reached out to hold me close—but did I imagine it, or was something missing from their tenderness? I tried to feel brave and reckless again, but my throat was dry and choked, and there was a sting of tears in my eyes. Yet nothing really had changed. I was Danny's wife—everything was all right—no one could separate us.

I kept telling myself these same things over and over, as if to convince my own heart.

I found myself clinging to Danny almost wildly. "Don't let anything happen to us," I choked, "and don't keep looking at those ships."

"If that's what you're thinking," he said a bit moodily, "you needn't. I made my choice, didn't I?"

I don't think I realized just how much I hated it, myself, until that night when I saw Carlos Madero watching us from the audience. He had asked me the day before where we danced, and now his eyes seemed to sweep over me like a reproachful lash. He went out before our dance was finished, and I did not see him again for several days.

Danny was beginning to get more and more restless. Although we had our mornings free, he spent little time inside the trailer. He'd wander down to the waterfront and sit for hours gazing at the passing ships. The newspapers were filled with scareheads about the war, and I'd find him reading them with clouded eyes. "All that going on," he'd rip out fiercely, "and I'm dancing swing to a lot of brass horns."

We'd come home at night so tired that all we could do was tumble into bed without even trying to talk. And now that the first wild flame of our love had died, Danny took me less and less often into his arms.

It was Sunday morning when we had our first real quarrel. I had just washed my hair and was drying it in the sun. It hung around my shoulders in a flaming mass. Carlos suddenly appeared on the graveled walk and stood looking down at me with his grave, dark eyes.

"You're just a little girl, after all," he said in a soft, low voice. "You ought not to be out here in San Francisco alone."

"Alone!" I laughed. "I'm with my own husband!"

"If I were your husband, or your—brother," he said more sharply, "I wouldn't let you dance like that in front of a Gayway mob."

As bad luck would have it, Danny came back from the waterfront just in time to hear the stinging words. His face turned dead white and he lunged toward Carlos with clenched fists. I sprang quickly between them and caught Danny's arm.

"No!" I cried out. "Don't do that, Danny."

"I'm sorry," Carlos said, "and I suppose I should be minding my own business. But I can't take back what I said. That show is no place for a sweet kid."

"If you weren't so damned right," Danny choked out, "I'd punch your head in. Of course it's no place for her, or for me, either. Don't you suppose I know that?"

Carlos started to speak, then checked his words, and strode abruptly away through the trees.

Danny turned to me savagely. "Why do you let that guy hang around you so much?" he demanded. There was a look on his face I never had seen there before;

a hard, cold anger that seemed to close me out of his heart.

"He doesn't hang around me," I flared.

"Well, put on some clothes," he growled, "and let's go for a ride. I'm fed up with this place."

AFTER that first quarrel it was too terribly easy for us to quarrel again. All the beauty of our lovely camping place seemed lost in a new bitterness. I began to realize for the first time how really young Danny was. He acted these days like a sulky little boy who'd screamed until he got some forbidden sweet, then found that it made him sick. Could it have been, after all, just those first few nights of sweet madness he had wanted, and now that the thrill of adventure was over, did he wish we could turn back?

Sam Flowers was beginning to look at us with sharp-eyed displeasure. "Your act hasn't any 'umph,' he complained. "Remember you aren't putting on a church festival. If you don't pep things up, I'll have to find someone who will."

"I wish he'd fire us," Danny muttered as we swung into our dance. Perhaps if he had, right then, everything would have been different. But it was several nights after that, just as we had finished our dance, when Danny rushed me off the stage and out the back door. I saw that he was white and trembling, and his eyes were filled with a sort of little-boy terror.

"Dad's out front," he whispered in quick panic. "He was with old Cronkheit, his lawyer. I saw him just as we went into that last crazy whirl. I thought I'd fall down dead right there on the stage. Listen, you go back to the camp. You'll have to take the bus, and wait there until I come. I don't dare leave until I'm sure

he isn't following. No one here knows where we live, not even Sam Flowers and it's a cinch if we once get out of here, we're safe. Get going now, and don't leave the camp until I tell you it's okay. Even if I can't get back there tonight, you stay right in the trailer. It's the one place they would never think of looking."

"But, Danny, I'll die waiting, not knowing what has happened," I cried.

"Well, would you rather face Dad, and perhaps your own mother? Quick, Virgie, it's your one chance, unless you want to be forced to go back with them. I'll come as soon as I can."

As I ran away and slipped into the crowd I saw Danny's father striding toward him. I had a quick impulse to turn back and face it with him. I felt a sudden heartsick desire to know how my mother was, even if it meant the end of our wild adventure. But the crowd hemmed me in, and by the time I had struggled free, I could no longer see where Danny had gone. I groped for a moment uncertainly, then made my way slowly to the Oakland bus.

I'll never forget those next few hours of waiting. It was after midnight when I reached the camp. The bus did not go directly past the gate and I had to walk several blocks through the darkness. I was white-faced and shaken and I tried to run through the trees when I realized that Carlos Madero had seen me come in.

"Virgie!" he cried out. It did not seem strange that he should use my name. "What has happened? Did you have an accident?"

"An—accident, yes," I faltered, and leaned weakly against the trunk of a giant redwood.

"You're white as a ghost," he said. "Come, let me get you a drink." He tried to lead me toward the rancho, but I drew back.

"No, I must go to our trailer. Danny might come, and not find me there. He'd worry," I gasped.

"Then I'm going with you. You look as if you're going to faint. Listen, Virgie, it's more than just an accident, isn't it? You've been frightened of something for a long time. I knew that the first moment I saw you. I haven't been able to get your little face out of my mind. It hasn't been a very happy honeymoon, has it?"

"Oh—don't!" I cried, and burst into sudden weak tears.

"I've had an idea," he went on, "that you plunged into this thing before you realized just what it was all about. You seem like such a baby, you can't be much over seventeen."

"I knew exactly what I was doing," I sobbed, "and you'd better not be here when Danny comes."

"I don't want to leave you—not while you look like that. Won't you try to tell me what happened? Perhaps I could help."

"No, and please go. I've got to think."

He turned away then and walked slowly toward the rancho. I flung myself down on the bunk and buried my head in the pillow. I felt sick all over, and more afraid than I ever had been in my life. Yet even in my terror there was a wild relief that we never would have to dance in that place again. I had grown to hate it with all my soul.

I don't know how long I lay there crying. Once I heard a footstep on the gravel and rushed to the trailer door. But it was Carlos there at the edge of the trees, as if standing guard. I didn't want Danny to come back and find him there like that, and yet I felt a strange sense of comfort in his nearness.

It was dawn before I finally took off my dance costume and put on my camp rig. I walked down to the edge of the canyon and looked out across the bay. The great grey ships still lay there at anchor—Danny's ships, that had such a pull on his heart. Behind me the great redwood trees were silhouetted against the sky like watching sentinels. I'd hate to leave this beautiful spot.

But he didn't come that day nor the next day either, and then when it seemed as if I could stand it no longer, and must somehow go in search of him, I saw him coming slowly along the walk. There was no eagerness in his step, and no light in his eyes.

With a cry of relief, and yet with a sense of premonition, I ran to meet him. "Danny, it's been awful, waiting. Tell me, has he gone? And Mother—does she know?"

"COME inside, Virgie," he said in a strange, husky voice, and lifted me up the trailer steps. "This is the first chance I could get to come here, unless I wanted Dad and the lawyer on my heels. Gosh, I'd rather be shot than tell you. I don't know where to begin, but I suppose you've got to know the whole of it. It's pretty awful. . ."

"Quick, Danny, tell me! I can take it—"

"I wish you didn't have to, Virgie, not all of it. Well, here goes—Dad is going to have our marriage annulled. It seems that it wasn't legal, anyhow. We lied about our ages and didn't gives our right names. We thought we were pretty smart, but I guess we weren't, really."

"But, Danny," I cried out, "they can't do that—we've lived together—I've been your wife. They couldn't separate us now."

"It seems they can, Virgie, until we're of age. If we stayed together now we wouldn't even be married and they could have us arrested—"

"You mean you'd be willing to leave me, and go back—" I gasped.

"What else can I do?" his voice rose sharply. "Even if we got married again, they'd only annul it. We're up against it, Virgie."

"But—what are we going to do?"

"Dad says there's still a chance I can get into Annapolis. If I wait, there might not be."

"You mean—oh, Danny, you can't mean—"

"Listen, Virgie. We weren't really happy, you know that. We've hated it, most of the time. We were too young to know what we did want. But no real harm has been done if we go back now—"

"No real harm!" My heart turned sick, and I could hardly speak the words. "Not for you, perhaps. You'll have what you really wanted most all the time, your navy. But do you suppose I could go back to that town, when they know I haven't even been really married to you? Don't you realize that Mother would never let up on it—"

"Virgie, wait," he cried out quickly, and I saw the white drawn look on his face. "Don't say any more about your mother, because you'll be awfully sorry afterward, if you do. I've been trying to tell you, and just couldn't but—your mother . . ." He broke off, and for the first time since his return, took me into his arms. "It's tough, Virgie, and I couldn't stand it if anything like that had happened to Dad, too, but on that day when she got your letter, your mother had one of those spells—a sort of heart attack the doctor said—and she never got over it. She's dead, Virgie."

"Danny, no! Oh, no! No! It can't be—It mustn't." I clung to him in tortured unbelief. "I couldn't have done that to her."

"Listen, Virgie, it might have happened anyway. Remember, she always used to have those fainting spells whenever you did anything she didn't like. We used to think it was just so she could get her own way."

"Oh, Mother," I sobbed. "She did need me, then, after all, just like she always said, and I wouldn't believe her. I can't bear it. She died, and I wasn't there! I was the only thing she had in the world. . . And she was all I had, too, really. You've made me know that, now," I wept brokenly.

"Virgie, don't cry like that, honey. What's the use. You'll only make yourself sick. . . . Stop sobbing and listen. You've got to be practical! Dad says your mother's annuity stopped when she died, so there wasn't any money left for you. But he wants to make a settlement on you— Look, I have the check with me now."

He took it from his pocket, and I stood looking down at the figures with blurred, shrinking eyes.

"Five thousand dollars," I said in a husky whisper, "to buy me off. And so now, what am I supposed to do?"

"We want to look after you, Virgie, to make sure you're all right—"

"But you don't want to marry me or have me in the family—not any more and this—this five thousand dollars, is to

pay for your mistake. Well, it can't." My voice rose shrilly in a very panic of pain, and I tore the check into tiny pieces.

"Virgie, you're crazy! All the money you have in the world is what's left of that five hundred dollars. I don't want any of that, of course."

"Sure, I'm crazy," I wept wildly, "but not as crazy as I was when I believed you really loved me."

"I guess Dad was right, Virgie, a boy of eighteen doesn't know what love is. And marriage— Gosh, look what it got us into! And now, Dad's waiting for me at the hotel. He's going to take me on to Annapolis. I'm leaving the car with you, of course, and I never want to see another trailer as long as I live."

"You mean you're just going to walk out, and leave me here?" I gasped.

"Dad and I are moving to Washington, but there's no reason why you shouldn't sell the trailer and go back to Maple Hill. You have plenty of friends there, and Dad will insist that you take the five thousand dollars. He'll send another check. You could use it to go to some college, then in three years—" He hesitated and flushed in quick confusion. "In three years," he stumbled on, "I'll be of age—"

He didn't finish. I faced him with blazing eyes. "Are you trying to say that in three years we could be married again? Then you haven't any idea at all how much I *hate* you!" I cried.

"Of course," he began sullenly, "if that's the way you feel—"

I turned on him wildly. "Get out," I panted. "I never want to see you again. If your father, or you, ever dares send me any money, I'd kill myself before I'd use it."

"I guess that washes us up, Virgie. I'm sorry—" His voice grew husky and he

took a step toward me— "Will you, kiss me goodby, Virgie?"

I tried not to burst into weak tears then; tried not to feel anything. Spent, I could only moan softly. When he took me back into his arms and pressed his young, hard lips to mine, I was too spent to resist. I felt nothing at all—only dull pain.

"Don't let's blame each other too much, Virgie. We were just a couple of crazy kids, that's all, and maybe we did have a little fun—while it lasted. No one can ever make me believe we didn't really love each other, and perhaps it would have lasted if we'd started right, and given it half a chance."

He turned away then and the next moment I heard his footsteps crunching along the walk. I stood for a long time, just where he had left me, unable to move or to think. Then I flung myself down on the bed and let the dam of my misery wash over me. Harsh sobs, that shook my body, seemed to come from my very soul.

"Mother, oh, Mother, darling, you did need me, just like you always said, and I wasn't even there. You were so terribly right about everything, and I was so wrong," I moaned. "Mother, if there is any way at all that you can hear me, forgive me. Forgive me!"

I cried on and on until I had sobbed myself out, then I lay very still, scarcely able to breathe. Suppose—my heart turned deathly sick—suppose, I were to have a baby? Danny hadn't even thought about that, or asked me one question. Well, if it should happen, never in the world would I let him know. If he had loved me, he would have stayed to fight it out in spite of a million annulments. But he hadn't even pretended to fight.

True Confessions at the World's Fair

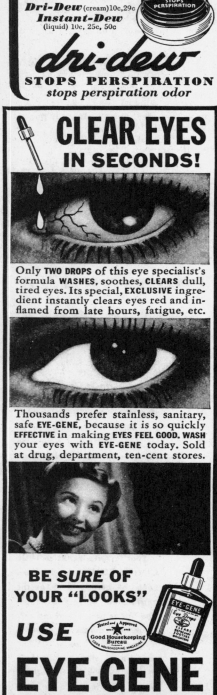
To him marriage was just something you wrote on a paper, and if it wasn't legal, or if you got tired of it, you could just tear it out of your heart and throw it away.

Suddenly I felt a strong, cool hand pressed against my burning forehead. "Look," Carlos demanded, "how long do you think I'm going to stand out there listening to you tear yourself to pieces?"

"I've stopped crying now," I choked. "I have no more tears left."

"That's fine," he declared, but I saw that his eyes were very grave and filled with a deep compassion. "There's one thing I'd like to tell you, though," he went on. "I've wept some bitter tears in my own life. I've known what it means to have everything and everyone I loved, taken away from me. You don't have to tell me that kid has run out on you. I saw him leave the car on the lot and take the bus back to town. I knew he wasn't coming back. What I want to know now is, if by any chance you'll be needing a job, or are you going back to the Gayway?"

My head came up with a jerk. "I never want to see that place again," I declared fiercely, "as long as I live. They still owe me fifty dollars but I'd rather lose it than ever go back there."

"That suits me," he said. "It happens I have a job for you if you'd like to stick around here for awhile. The girl out in the front office is getting married next week. I can't afford to pay much, but I could let you have this parking space for your trailer, free, your meals in the dining room, and ten dollars a week. You'd have to act as sort of a hostess, helping folks get settled, taking phone calls and showing the lots. In the evening you might get the dancing started in the main hall—but we don't put on any jitterbug stuff. Well, what do you say?"

And then I found myself bursting into tears again, this time in sheer, incredulous relief. It was such a wonderful, unbelievable way out. To be able to stay here in this place I had grown to love, and to earn my own living by helping to keep it alive. For what was there to go back to in Maple Hill?

"All right, don't answer me now," he said gently. "I'll be back."

"But I want to answer you," I choked out. "I'd love it, of course. It's just that it seemed too good to be true."

"Then, it's a deal. You don't have to start work until next week, but in the meantime you can sort of nose around and get the hang of the place and watch how we handle the guests. The rest of the time just swim, hike, and lie in the sun and if you possibly can help it, don't do too much thinking."

Before I could thank him, he had turned and walked away. When he had gone I jumped to my feet and dashed cold water on my face. Then I sank to my knees and prayed. I prayed to God and my mother for forgiveness and offered humble thanks of gratitude for my second chance. That little dream of the perfect trailer camp had been just a passing game to Danny. He had forgotten it almost over night, but here was my dream come true.

DURING those next few days, I found myself talking to my mother as I never had been able to talk when she was alive. And somehow, I felt, for the first time, that she could understand. The ache in my heart was deep, but in some strange way she seemed closer to me than she ever had before. Of Danny, I would not let myself even think.

Then suddenly I realized that the little girl who had loved Danny, and had wanted to be his wife, had died that night when he left her. There was nothing in my heart that ever could ache for him again. And from far off I seemed to hear my mother whispering: *"Don't you understand, then, why love shouldn't come too soon? At seventeen how could you have known what marriage meant? If you had loved truly and everlastingly, as only a woman-heart can, your pain now would be beyond all your power to bear—and yet, here you are—feeling nothing!"*

Throughout those days I felt the eyes of Carlos almost constantly upon me. Sometimes he would follow me to the edge of the canyon, and we'd stand looking back over the ranch. Once when I tripped against a rock he reached out his arm to steady me, and I remained there for a moment so close to him that I could feel the strong beating of his heart.

"No, Virgie," he said, very low, as if in swift answer to some question our hearts had spoken, "that's one thing I've never done—made love to another man's wife."

"I'm not anybody's wife," I whispered brokenly.

"You mean," he cried out, "that young devil brought you here, and didn't marry you! If you are not his wife," he demanded with a sudden new fierceness, "then come here to me where you belong —where you've always belonged. I know you're far too young to get married. If that damnable thing hadn't happened to you, I'd want you to wait a year or two and work here along with me and grow to know me—and yourself—better. But as it is, you've been hurt too much, and if you think you could love me enough, I want us to get married right away."

"You mean." I whispered, "that even though you know I wasn't really Danny's wife, that we weren't of age and his father had the marriage annulled and made him go back home—you mean, even then, you'd want to marry me?"

When I said that word "annulled" and he realized that I had at least thought I was married, I saw the swift change that came over his face, like a blinding light. In it was relief, joy, and then an utter tenderness of compassion.

"Oh, you poor, little lonely, heartbroken kid," he said in a low, husky voice. "So it was just a lovely little adventure, and they smashed it all up. Oh, my dear, if I can somehow make it up to you! I'd like to try, for all the rest of my life."

He did not speak for a long time after that, but I shall never forget the gentleness with which his arms reached out to draw me closer. He lifted my head until his lips rested against mine. It was a kiss almost like my mother's kiss might have been if I ever could have made her understand—so very soft and tender.

"My dear," Carlos said gently, "we aren't going to get married for awhile, perhaps not for another year. We're going to have a bit of old-fashioned courting first, the kind your mother might want her little girl to have, with not too many kisses. Marriage can wait a bit until all those hurts are healed. But believe me, after that, my sweet, I can stand a lot of loving."

And that, please God, is how it will be, I hope. And it is for that day, drawing closer and closer, that I live for and yearn for.

♥ ♥ ♥ ♥

You may have gone through a similar experience.
... Or you know of someone who has.... Won't you
help this girl find the answer to her anguished cry:

"MUST I BREAK MY ENGAGEMENT?"

IN SPITE of all the talk about women having achieved the double standard, I think things are still pretty different for women and for men. You read a lot of letters in the various columns from men wondering whether they ought to forgive their fiancees for dead-and-gone indiscretions. But I don't, at this moment, recall a single one from a girl asking whether she should overlook her lover's past or not.

Now I'm going to break that record. What I want is not advice about my own past, but advice about the past of the man I've been planning to marry.

I'll try to explain . . . Rocky and I grew up within a few blocks of each other, and he was one of my heroes when I was a kid. But he was four years older than I, which meant that we were in entirely different sets. He was in high school when I was in grammar school. He was going off to college, a resplendent freshman, when I was just starting high school.

He was home summers and vacations after that, for the next four years. But for at least two of those years he was rushing Alice Brewster. Allie was the only child of a widow, an awfully nice lady, who lived in a quiet little house on a side street and took in sewing. Their family had been a good one and everyone in town was sorry for Mrs. Brewster and respected her.

As for Allie, she was a gentle, pretty, sweet little thing, not overly gifted with brains, as far as books went. It took her five years to graduate from high school. And after she got out she kept getting first one job and then another in somebody's office or somebody's store, and losing it because she couldn't spell and couldn't get her arithmetic straight. Finally she just settled down to keeping house for her mother, and at that she turned out to be a perfect whiz. She was a wonderful cook, and she was efficient at everything connected with a home.

She and Rocky were constantly together during his sophomore and junior years, whenever he was home. And everybody thought they would get married. But something or other happened in his senior year, and things were broken off. I was enjoying the whirl of my own popularity about that time and really paid very little attention to any of it, though I do recall hearing somebody say that Allie had "had a nervous breakdown" just before I went away to college.

Then I dropped out of the local scene myself. I went to State U. and joined a sorority and had a gorgeous good time. Rocky was still there, because after he got

his B. A., he started right in on a law course.

It was when I went home in my sophomore year that I found Allie working for Mother. Mrs. Brewster had died in the spring, leaving nothing at all for Allie. And Allie had very sensibly decided that the only thing she was good at was domestic work, and had gone in for it. Mother was easy to work for, treated her like a daughter, and paid her unusually well.

THEN, when I was a junior, and Rocky was a Law School senior, he began to rush me. By spring we were head over heels in love, and by Commencement we were engaged. He had a very good place in his uncle's law office waiting for him when he got home, so we planned to be married the following autumn. I'd break it to my family in the summer that I wasn't going back to the U. for my degree, and we'd have a lovely fall wedding.

Of course I asked him about Allie and he said, "Just a kid love affair that all parties outgrew, honey."

I didn't realize that she still cared, however, until I began to notice her after I got back home that summer and Rocky was underfoot every night. Mother said, "I think Allie isn't very well," but I was dreadfully afraid that it was seeing Rocky rush me that was making her look like a heartbroken little ghost. And I was right. One night I heard Allie sobbing so wildly in her room, that I couldn't stand it any longer and went to her.

She hadn't known I was home. She had thought I was out with Rocky and that she was alone. She was caught off her guard and she sobbed out the whole story, under my questioning. How she had belonged to Rocky, been "all his" for two whole

A PROBLEM STORY

summers. How there had been a baby who never saw the light of day. "And that broke Mother's heart," she sobbed softly. How Rocky had promised to love her always, always, and she had thought it was "forever and ever," or how could she have been so wicked? And her heart was broken, it was broken, and she'd never love anybody any more! She didn't blame Rocky—he'd been ready to marry her when he thought there was going to be a baby, but she wished she was dead.

At white-heat, on fire with pain and anger, I went to Rocky. I told him Allie was really his wife. I told him he'd betrayed her and seduced her—I hardly know what I did say!

Rocky took it, tight-lipped and white. Then he gave me his side. He said it wasn't a "seduction." They had both been kids together, she a year older than he, and it had "just happened." He said he was sincerely in love with her at the time, truly meant to marry her, had been on his way to marry her when the news came that she had lost the baby.

"I just outgrew her, that was all," he said earnestly. "What would you have had me do? Do you think marrying her, and coming to hate her, would have made her any happier? I offered to marry her, for that matter. But I had to admit I no longer loved her, and she herself freed me then. For God's sake, Virginia, don't wreck my life and yours for a boyish sin which I've bitterly regretted? I'm a man now and I love you with a man's passion. This is real—and big! Are you going to sacrifice it for something that's dead?"

"Why didn't you tell me the truth when I asked you about her?" I cried.

And he answered, "Not because I thought you wouldn't forgive. I thought you'd be big enough to understand. But it was Allie's secret. Not mine."

Then he broke down and pled passionately, tears in his eyes, holding me in his arms, his big, athletic frame shaking. And I—I promised, at last, to think things over before breaking the engagement off.

But oh, I don't know what to do! All he said sounds so plausible, so true! It's all so reasonable and logical. And yet—and yet—I keep hearing Allie's voice sobbing, "He promised to love me always, always, I thought it was forever and ever, and so it seemed right to be all his!"

And I keeping asking myself, "Will a man who has proved himself untrustworthy to one girl, be the sort whom another girl can trust?" Should I break up all the plans I have made for our life together? Must I break my engagement?

PRIZES FOR YOUR LETTERS

A Debutante Tells

You, who think a society girl's life is all velvet, will be appalled and shocked by the inside story of what goes on in her set.

M Y MOTHER scurried into my room in a fragrant mass of cloudy chiffon draperies. She perched on the side of my bed and said, "Tell me everything, darling. I was so excited I could hardly sleep. How was Peggy Melville's party? Was it as large as yours? Was everybody there? Did Montonet do the catering? And of course Peggy's aunt, the duchess, was there!"

I stared at her sleepily and wished vaguely that she'd go away and let me alone. There had been too much champagne last night. Too much of everything, as a matter of fact. Gordon Lambert had brought me home. He was tight and horrible and I had ended up by slapping him. Mother would have a fit if I told her that! I thought, with a touch of humor, just how shocked she'd be. Gordon Lambert's father had too many millions to count and Mother would consider that no one with the Lambert name and money could possibly be horrible.

"The party was all right," I answered drowsily. "The usual gang was there. All the girls who came out last September. It was a brawl. I'm simply dead."

"My poor baby," Mother purred. "But that is the price one must pay for popularity, darling. And you must get up, pet. Miss Bessell has so many things she wants to talk over with you. Zebelene's want you to pose for some pictures for them in those new gowns we bought there. They're going to use them in the Smart Review magazine. Isn't that thrilling? That's the magazine that always features pictures of royalty. Think of Mother's baby with her picture right across from Princess Marina's!"

My head ached and I preferred not to think about it. I rolled over but I couldn't drown out the sound of Mother's voice or the urgent pressure of her plump, jeweled hand on my shoulder.

"Now! Now!" Mother said, coyly but firmly. "Mustn't go back to sleep, baby. Charles is so pleased about the write-ups you've been getting that he's going to get you that string of pearls from Carster's. They'll probably want your picture, too, dear. After all, you're the most beautiful debutante of the season. All the papers agree on that score!"

Charles was my stepfather. He had money enough to buy out Carster's if he'd wanted to. Twenty years ago Charles had been simply Charlie Ryder. Some

Nan came in with a gown I was to fit;

92

of the newspapers still annoyed him by remembering it. He had had the ranch next to my father's in Texas. Then one day Charles had struck oil. I was a year old when my mother left my father and came east with Charles and now Mother and Charles were Mr. and Mrs. Charles Newton-Ryder. I don't know where they picked up the hyphen, but Charles was very pompous and exacting about it as became a millionaire oil man and he and Mother were anxious to forget those early days in Texas.

I will say that Charles had always been grand to me. He couldn't have given me any more or done any more for me had I been his own child. I had nurses and governesses and went to the best schools—but sometimes I had the feeling that I was just another pawn in the game Mother and Charles were constantly playing to secure social recognition.

Their ambition was so whole-hearted and ruthless that it was a little terrifying. And in twenty years Charlie Ryder had become the most fearful sort of snob. From my earliest days he and Mother had instilled in me the idea of knowing only the "right" people and it was only since I had grown up that I had begun to realize that they were using me as a wedge to push themselves into the charmed "inner circle." Through the contacts I made in the fashionable schools to which they sent me, they were able to meet the kind of people to whom their money alone could not introduce them.

The girls I went to school with made me part of their crowd and unwittingly their parents were forced to accept

Clara was ready for my manicure and Bessell started listing my appointments—and I hadn't even had breakfast!

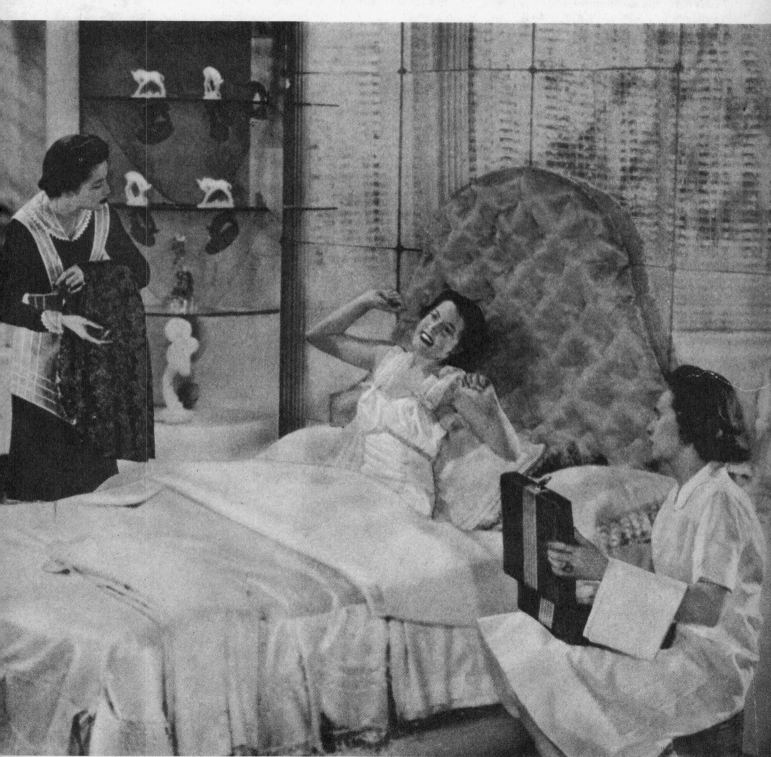

Mother and Charles. Oh, I was a valuable asset all right, I was beginning to realize with a touch of bitterness, and more and more I found myself resenting the way Mother and Charles were exploiting me.

And now Mother gave me another little shake. "Clara is here to do your hair and nails, dear, and Miss Bessell with the lists. You simply must wake up, Zelda. You have a very full day today and the Waterman party tonight. Charles and I have been invited, too."

I sat up protestingly but obediently. Clara sat down and began getting her manicuring equipment together. Behind Mother loomed Miss Bessell, Mother's secretary, her long, aristocratic nose quivering efficiently. Bessell always reminded me of a hound anxious to begin the hunt and I loathed her.

Mother stood off and looked at me rapturously. "Oh, Miss Bessell," she sighed happily. "Isn't she beautiful? Wasn't I the most blessed of mothers to have such a beautiful baby? That mass of black curls with that white, white skin and those gorgeous grey eyes! Oh, darling! No wonder those naughty playboys are so wild about Mother's baby."

"Oh, Mother, please!" I protested. "Stuff like that is sickening at any time, but it's worse before breakfast after a hard night."

"So modest!" Mother murmured and went into my dressing room to look over my wardrobe.

Miss Bessell looked at me curiously. She knew as well as I did that Mother wasn't nearly as big a fool as she sounded. There were plenty of sharp, calculating brains under Mother's carefully dyed black hair. But she believed in keeping the people she was using good-natured.

And then, Nan, my personal maid, came in to have me try on the gown I was to wear tonight at the Waterman's and in which I was to be photographed as a special concession to the modiste who designed it for me. This photograph was to be slipped into the magazine as a very special favor.

There they were, secretary, manicurist, maid, ready to start my day, each one trying to get my attention first. I hadn't had a bite of breakfast yet, and I was so darn sleepy, I could have slept on a board, but Mother had set the machinery clicking and there was nothing I could do but get on the merry-go-round and act as if I enjoyed it.

While Clara did my nails and I ate a hurried breakfast with my one free hand, Bessell read me her lists.

"Appointment with photographer for Zebelene pictures at eleven. Luncheon with young Mr. Lambert—"

"You can cut that off," I broke in casually. "We had a little disagreement last night."

"I am sure," Bessell said coldly, "that your mother would not like you to break a luncheon engagement with Mr. Lambert."

"It won't be necessary for you to even mention it," I assured her.

"Mrs. Newton-Ryder is having tea with Mr. Lambert's mother this afternoon," Bessell said portentiously.

"All right. Let it stand," I answered crossly.

Bessell looked pleased. The social register was her bible and the Lamberts rated highly there.

Mother came out of the dressing room. "Wear your silver-fox jacket today, darling. It's so becoming to you, especially with that little French hat with the silver fox pom-poms. You know, dear, I'm afraid Gordon Lambert has serious intentions regarding my little girl."

"You mean you hope he has," I thought bitterly. "And there's not a bit of sense telling you the kind of passes Gordon Lambert makes and the sort of filthy suggestive stories he tells and the kind of propositions he offers because all you can think about is the Lambert ancestors and the Lambert yachts and the Lambert names in the society columns. Oh, I suppose with a little diplomacy, I could turn his mind toward matrimony instead of his present ideas—but it turns my stomach to think about him!"

But there wasn't any use telling Mother any of that, and so I held my tongue. But definitely I was not going to lunch with Gordon Lambert! If she wanted to think that I was, it was all right with me.

Zebelene sent the best society photographer in town to

take my pictures in the dresses we had bought there. They took me from every possible angle. They bowed and they scraped and they told me that if I hadn't been one of the wealthiest and most beautiful debutantes of the year I could have been a wonderful model. And when they finished the man in charge said, "And we hope you will use our firm exclusively, Miss Newton-Ryder, and persuade your friends to do the same."

I had known that was coming. Everybody wanted something, I thought wearily, and they all handed you a line to pave the way for what they wanted. Mother and Charles wanted me to make a socially successful marriage to make their own position impregnable. Zebelene's wanted me to advertise their clothes. The photographer wanted me to get him more business. Gordon Lambert wanted to carry on an affair with me. I was more than a little tired and disgusted with the whole set-up.

When the photographer left I went up and Clara helped me change my clothes. Mother and Charles had gone out but I knew that Bessell would be watching to report to Mother whether I left to keep my luncheon appointment with Gordon.

I dressed in the simple, printed redingote dress Mother had suggested, pulled the tiny black hat with its silver fox pom-poms down over one eye and slid into the silver-fox jacket. Quite the proper costume for luncheon at the Colony, I assured myself ironically. Only I didn't happen to be going to the Colony!

It was good to be outdoors. The day was fragrant with the promise of spring and I sniffed the air greedily. Idly I turned toward the park. It was nice to be out. Nice to have nothing to do for a few short hours. It amused me to think of Gordon Lambert, tall and handsome and sure of himself with his hot, seeking eyes and his possessive hands, sitting there at the Colony waiting for me.

The day was much too warm for my silver-fox jacket, particularly since my dress had a long coat which I was carrying because it was too warm to wear. I dropped in the side door of the Plaza and checked my fur jacket. The check-room girl knew me and smiled pleasantly: "Almost too nice a day to have luncheon indoors, isn't it, Miss Newton-Ryder?"

"It certainly is," I agreed. "And that's just why I'm not doing it. I just wanted to check this for awhile, Molly. It's too hot to wear it while I'm walking. I'll pick it up this evening when the crowd drops in for cocktails or else I'll send Stevens for it. Just hang onto it for me."

A few blocks from the Plaza I passed a little hatstore. *EVERY HAT IN THIS STORE $1.89* the sign in the window said. Some of them were cute. A little black straw turned off the face caught my eye. I had never owned a hat that cost a dollar eighty-nine. The bill for the one I had on had been thirty-five dollars.

I went into the little shop and bought the hat. It was far more becoming than the one with the pom-poms, I thought.

"I'll wear it," I said. "Send the other one home for me

stand they have some new baby monkeys—so don't forget your peanuts."

There was something warming and human about his smile and his voice. I found myself thinking about him as I left the shop. There had been admiration and a pleasant twinkle in the blue eyes that had looked at me. I found myself comparing that glance with Gordon Lambert's gaze when he looked at a girl. There was always sly speculation in Gordon's glance. He seemed to be undressing you mentally. I shivered a little in the warm sun. "Maybe I should have worn my fur jacket after all," I thought.

The zoo was fun. I saw the bears and the tigers and the snakes and finally I found my way to the monkeys. The man from the florist shop was there and he seemed frankly pleased to see me.

"I wondered if you'd been here yet," he said.

Even to myself I wouldn't admit that I had been hoping that I would see him here—that I had saved the monkeys for last for that reason.

"There was so much to see," I laughed, "and so many hungry squirrels and birds on the way that I've run out of peanuts."

He grinned. "I brought a double supply," he said.

The baby monkeys looked so much like humans that it was a little startling. We laughed at their antics and at the solicitude of the mother monkeys.

As we turned to walk away he said casually, "My name is Jack Bonner. My uncle owns that little flower shop and someday I'm hoping to be able to save enough to buy him out. Then I'd like to get a little place in the country and have my own greenhouses. I went to the state agricultural college, but I believe there's more future in flowers than there is in farming. I'm a little crazy on the subject of them both, however."

"You don't look a bit crazy," I assured him. "You look nice. And I can't think of any nicer way to make a living than to produce as lovely a crop as flowers."

He talked easily and well. He told me about his uncle's business which was good but could be made so much better with a few more modern ideas. He spoke a little scornfully of some of the wealthier customers. Most of them were people I knew intimately—people of Mother's charmed "inner circle." He considered their lives empty and useless.

We sat down on a bench in the sun and ate the rest of the peanuts. "And now let's talk about you," he suggested. "I've been wanting to talk about   [Please turn page]

when you get around to it. I'll give you the address." Back on the avenue I determined to continue on to the park. I might even go to the zoo, I thought recklessly. I hadn't been to the zoo for years. Not since one of my nurses had taken me. Mother had been furious. She said that I simply reeked with the smell of the animals and that none of the better families permitted their children to go to such places. Well, I knew better—but as I have said, there was never any sense in arguing with Mother!

THERE was a flower shop along the way. You could tell by a glance that it wasn't a very fashionable one. There wasn't an orchid in the whole window but there was a riot of spring flowers that were strangely appealing.

I went in. "I'd like a bunch of violets," I said.

The clerk grinned down at me. "It's the time of year that people begin thinking about violets, isn't it?" he said.

His voice was nice. Pleasant and deep and a little drawly. I looked at him more closely. He was nice-looking, too. One of the nicest looking men I had ever seen. He didn't look like he belonged in a florist shop. He was tall and broad and tanned with clear blue eyes in a sunburned face and dark, unruly hair. His tweed suit fit him well, but I noticed that it was shabby.

I found myself smiling back at him. "Yes," I agreed. "It's the time of year you begin to think about violets and new hats and the zoo. I'm going to the zoo now."

Now why on earth, I found myself wondering amazedly, should I confide such perfectly nonsensical things to a perfectly strange young man!

There was a flash of white teeth as he grinned at me again and then he said gravely: "The new hat is very becoming and I'm going to the zoo myself this afternoon. I under-you ever since you walked in the door of the shop, but I thought I'd better lead up to it gradually."

His smile was so sweet and boyish and his blue eyes so warm that I felt the strangest sort of emotion creeping over me. I had never felt quite like this about anyone before. I wanted to reach out and smooth back that dark wave that insisted upon separating from the rest of his hair. I wanted to put an inquiring finger into the deep cleft in the square sunburned chin. I wanted to touch him, just to feel the clean masculinity of him. It was a little terrifying to feel this way about a man you had only known an hour or so.

"There isn't much to tell about me," I said evasively.

"Oh, there must be!" Jack Bonner insisted. "Girls don't look like you for no reason at all. I'll bet you're a model. Or perhaps you work in one of those too, too ultra shops on the Avenue and this is your day off. You haven't even told me your name," he added reproachfully. "Here I bare my soul to you and tell you all my rural and greenhouse ambitions and you haven't told me where you live or what your name is or when I can see you again. I'd like to, you know."

I knew without a doubt that I wanted to see him again, too. I had enjoyed myself more this afternoon than I could ever remember enjoying myself before. Sounds a little cracked, doesn't it? But it was true.

I wanted to lie to him. I wanted to tell him that my name was Zelda Garth. It really was. Newton-Ryder was only my stepfather's name that he insisted that I use. I wanted to tell Jack Bonner that I worked over on the Avenue and that we could meet some place and go to the movies any time he said. Because I knew that as soon as I told him who I really was, there would be a barrier between us. Jack Bonner wasn't the type of man who made a play for wealthy debutantes. In fact, from what he had said, I gathered that he thought them a pretty addle-brained, empty-headed lot.

But on the other hand there was something about that direct blue gaze that would have made me ashamed to lie.

"My name is Zelda Newton-Ryder," I said in a low voice and I told him where I lived. "I wish you'd come to see me," I added honestly.

BUT the blue eyes had changed. They were dark and opaque and expressionless. "I suppose I should have known," he said quietly. "I thought you looked familiar. Lord knows, there've been enough pictures of you in the papers. 'Miss Zelda Garth Newton-Ryder at Miami Beach,' 'Miss Zelda Garth Newton-Ryder in Bermuda' or aboard her father's yacht or going into the Ritz or coming out of Twenty-One. But you've always been wrapped in furs or exposed in evening clothes or a bathing suit. I guess it was the hat you're wearing that put me off the track. My sister came home with one like it yesterday. Of course she doesn't look as well in it as you do. The papers were right about one thing. You've certainly got what it takes."

"Oh, please," I begged. "You were so nice before. Don't spoil it all. I've had such a swell time today. You don't suppose I like being spread all over the papers, do you? Yes, I guess you do. I guess I'd have hard work making anybody believe I didn't. But you can take my word for it, Mr. Bonner, I've had more fun today than I've had in heaven knows when." And to my embarrassment my eyes filled with silly, senseless tears.

It was those tears that softened him. "I believe you mean it," Jack Bonner said wonderingly. His blue eyes were puzzled.

"And I meant it when I asked you to come to see me," I added firmly. "You won't have a good time. If Mother's home she'll look at you with a fishy eye and our place is just about as cozy as the British Museum—but I'd like to see you just the same."

The nice grin came back to his good-looking, young mouth. "I don't think I'll risk it," he told me good-naturedly. "And you're so far out of my sphere, Miss Newton-Ryder, that if I had any sense I'd grab my hat and run like hell right now. But if you're not doing anything tomorrow night, I'll park my ancient chariot outside your palatial homestead and wait for you. There will be a full moon and we'll ride along the Drive and look at it."

"It's a date!" I cried gaily.

Tomorrow night was Sue Butterfield's dinner in the Rainbow Room, but I didn't give a darn. Tomorrow night I had a date with Jack Bonner to look at a full moon!

I was glad that Mother and Charles had dates for the evening before the Waterman party. It kept Mother out of my hair. Miss Bessell was disapproving enough. "Mr. Lambert called three times this afternoon," she said primly. "You evidently did not keep your luncheon date with him, Miss Zelda. He said to tell you that he'd have it out with you tonight when he called for you for the Waterman party."

"That was a nice gentlemanly message to leave," I returned acidly. "And it happens that I am going to the Waterman party with Ned Griffin and to cocktails at the Melville's first, so I won't be here when Mr. Lambert arrives."

"Your mother will be displeased," Bessell warned me, thin-lipped.

Ned Griffin was about one degree better mannered than Gordon. He didn't paw

as much and his jokes weren't as filthy. But he wasn't as handsome as Gordon either, nor did his parents have as good a rating in Dun and Bradstreet. Charles and Mother and Miss Bessell knew all about the ratings and the other things didn't bother them.

All of the younger crowd were at Peggy Melville's for cocktails. Some of them were already tight from previous cocktail parties of the afternoon. Gordon came in late and raised an unpleasant scene about our broken luncheon date and the fact that I had come with Ned. I saw Peggy watching him with sultry eyes. I knew that Peggy had been crazy about Gordon ever since they had gone to dancing school together and she hated me because she thought that I had taken him away from her. Well, she was welcome to him as far as I was concerned. I tried to tell her so, but she wouldn't believe me.

But somehow, nothing seemed to bother me tonight. I kept thinking about Jack Bonner and the fact that tomorrow I would see him again.

MOTHER and Charles were at the Waterman party, Mother hung with diamonds and purring contentedly and Charles strutting pompously about looking for Big Names to engage in conversation.

The stag-line gave me the usual rush. The society columns tomorrow would mention it and Mother would be properly gratified. But I couldn't have told you whom I danced with. I passed from one pair of arms to another. Automatically I answered the usual lines. But my thoughts were back at a sunny park bench and a boy in a shabby tweed suit and clean blue eyes.

When it came time to go home, Gordon Lambert appeared from the bar with Ned following in the rear, looking shame-faced and sulky.

"I won you in a crap game," Gordon told me with a broad grin. "You're in my power again, gal!"

"The rewards of popularity," Peggy Melville sneered from behind me, "to be the object of a crap game."

"And don't you wish it were you?" Gordon jeered. He reached out a casual hand and pulled Peggy toward him and leaning over kissed her on the mouth, long and lingeringly. Her fingers clutched his coat convulsively and her eyes were shining. She cast a triumphant glance over her shoulder at me, but just then Gordon gave her a push and laughed loudly. "Just to show you what I could do for you if I wanted," he told her coarsely, his handsome face flushed from too many cocktails and stupidly arrogant.

Then he took my arm. "The most beautiful deb of the season," he announced loudly. "And what I'm going to do to you on the way home, sister, will be nobody's business! I'll teach you to walk out on me!"

My face was flaming and everyone in the hall was laughing. I looked up and saw Mother and Charles in the doorway, Mother wrapped in her ermine coat, Charles, very elegant and correct in his evening clothes.

Now let them see the kind of boys this "inner circle" produced, I thought scornfully! But Mother was beaming and Charles looked gratified. This was just another proof of my popularity to them— that a son of the wealthiest and most socially-prominent family in the country should so patently desire me.

"I'll have to get my evening coat," I told Gordon and pulling away from him

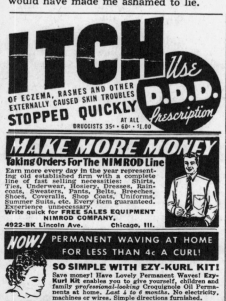

fled toward the dressing room. But after I got my coat I slid out a side door and caught a taxi home. I knew it meant another battle with Mother but I was too tired to stage another wrestling match with Gordon Lambert on the way home.

I don't know how I managed to cut Sue Butterfield's dinner party the next night, but I did! And it was worth it! Jack Bonner was quite as nice as I had imagined him. He was a little wary about me at first. He was afraid, he told me afterward, that this was just sort of a game to me, something new to relieve the boredom that assails most girls with too much social position and not enough real things to fill their lives.

But after awhile he forgot that I was Zelda Newton-Ryder of the society columns and began to regard me as just an attractive girl whom he liked, and who liked him.

THAT date was just the beginning of many. I sneaked away whenever I could. Jack had an afternoon off a week and an hour for luncheon. I would drive down at noon and wait for him and we would take a little walk together and have a hasty lunch at some little tea-room near-by. And soon we both realized what we must have known from the first—that this thing we felt for each other was much more than liking. It was love, breath-taking in its sharp sweetness.

"I knew it the moment you came into the shop," Jack told me humbly. "I didn't know who you were or I probably would have stopped right then and there. But I said to myself: 'This is it, Jack! That big moment that you always knew would arrive. This is why you've been as clean and decent as you knew how to be. This is the thing they write about in books and poems.'"

"I felt it, too," I whispered.

When he kissed me, parked there in the shadowy dusk of the Drive, it was so sweet that I felt that I couldn't bear it. I knew that this was why I had hated Gordon's kisses and Ned's and all the other kisses of the boys in our crowd. I had been waiting for this.

My blood pounded in my veins and I felt limp and a little frightened.

"And what are we going to do about it?" Jack asked me somberly lifting his dark head and looking at me. "Would you marry me and take a chance on making a go of it? Would you give up all these things you've had all your life and not mind it?"

"Oh, I would," I whispered tremulously. "You know that I would. Mother will be furious but I don't care. I don't care about anything, Jack. Only you—us!"

But when it came time to tell Mother, I lost my courage. It would be better, I thought, for Jack and me simply to run away. It would save all the scenes and bitter recriminations that I knew I would otherwise have to face. I was a little afraid of Mother and Charles and the lengths to which they might carry this driving ambition of theirs.

I knew that Jack considered this cowardly of me. "Might as well face the music and have it over with," he told me. "I don't like to do things underhandedly, Zelda. I'm funny that way. Let me come to the house and meet your mother and stepfather. I'll probably be scared to death of 'em but I'd rather do it that way."

"You're just an old mid-Victorian," I teased him, but I loved him even more for his courage and his straightforwardness.

Well, I'd rather not dwell on the night

Jack came to see me and met Mother and Charles. It was a nightmare. Charles was patronizing and ruthless. His attitude and his voice dismissed Jack as the lowest sort of tradesman. Mother was overpowering. Jack had very little opportunity to say anything and certainly not to broach the subject of matrimonial intentions. Mother shot questions at him concerning his family, his past, his present, his future, and scarcely paid attention to the answers since she patently considered his answers to be of little importance. Before she and Charles swept off to the opera, she kept up a running patter concerning my expensive schools, my tremendous social success, my popularity among the boys of my own set. Mother emphasized that "own set" stuff.

"And I guess that's that!" Jack said as soon as Mother and Charles were gone. His face was pale beneath his tan and his mouth was tight and thin-lipped with anger and humiliation.

"I—I told you how it would be," I whispered. "I tried to spare you that, Jack."

"Do you still want to go through with it?" he asked grimly. "Do you still love me after you've seen them make a worm out of me?"

"They didn't make a worm out of you!" I cried. "Y—You were wonderful. They just showed themselves up for what they are. I love you, Jack."

"Let's get out of here," he said impatiently "This place smothers me. Let's get out and take a ride and talk things over."

THE roads in the park were dark. Parked in the shadow of the trees Jack turned and took me in his arms. His arms swept around me like bands of burning white-hot steel. His lips crushed mine for a long, hungry moment. All the misery and humiliation that he had endured that evening were in that kiss. All his hopes and his uncertainty and his desires. I was limp in his arms, deliciously faint as the storm of his kisses rose with fierce tenderness.

"You're mine," he said. "They can't take you from me."

"Oh, no," I whispered in drowsy ecstasy. "Don't let them, Jack. Don't let them take me. You're all I want."

His kisses grew longer. He couldn't help himself—and I couldn't either. We belonged together and we were afraid of what fate and life might do to us. Neither of us meant to be swept away like that We just couldn't stop—and finally it was too late.

"Oh, darling," he whispered huskily. "I—I didn't intend to. I—never meant to. Zelda. Believe me, darling, I love you so. Now you're really mine, sweet. Now you'll have to marry me, dearest, but I didn't mean to take you in that way."

I buried my head against his shoulder I was crying a little. I felt very young and very frightened and filled with a dim ecstasy that was shot through with shamed terror.

I had thought I was so sophisticated. I had believed I knew all the answers Why, I could manage Gordon Lambert in his most obnoxious moments! But this was different.

"How soon will you marry me, Zelda?" Jack was asking anxiously with his lips against my hair. "Tomorrow? Next day? We can manage, sweet. We'll take a little apartment somewhere at first. You won't have all that luxury but—"

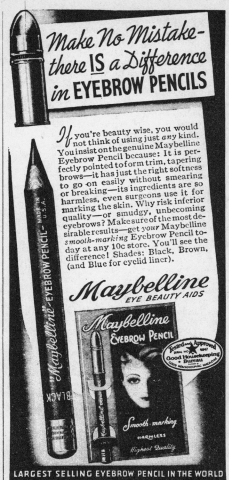

97

"But I'll have you," I finished for him and lifted my head for his kiss.

Mother came into my room late that night to discuss with me the seriousness of making the wrong contacts. "That young man you had here tonight," Mother said. "A clerk in a florist shop! How could you, Zelda? Suppose the Melvilles or the Watermans or the Butterfields should hear of it. A girl with your background and your opportunities! I'll admit, my dear, that he was very handsome. And of course, you're too young to realize that he is obviously a fortune-hunter, too."

I was too tired, too weary, to argue. What difference did it make what she said now, I thought with a sense of relief. I was through with it all. Tomorrow I was to let Jack know when I would marry him.

I COULDN'T sleep that night. I kept thinking of Jack and what had happened. I was ashamed and frightened. Yet we loved each other. We were going to be married. That was all that mattered.

And yet would Jack think perhaps I was cheap, a moral lightweight, shoddy for giving myself before marriage? Had I stripped the beauty from our relationship by my wild, abandoned response to his ardor? Suppose Jack, thinking over in cold blood what had happened, decided he wouldn't marry me after all? Perhaps he would think I was like the rest of my set—indifferent to the decencies of life, intemperate, promiscuous. Cold terror seized me and I was in a sweat of agony. I didn't close my eyes all through that long, terrifying night. I could hardly wait until morning when I could phone him and hear his voice and reassure him that I wasn't like that.

But the next morning Miss Bessell was in my room bright and early. "The fitter is here for your dress for the Junior Cotillion," she said. "I told her you would be down in half an hour. And Mr. Lambert called and said he was dropping in for lunch as he had something he wanted to talk over with you."

"There is plenty of time for my fitting," I said crossly. "The Junior Cotillion isn't until next month." I didn't add that I wouldn't be here for it anyway, that I'd be Mrs. Jack Bonner by that time, but I did add that I would not be at home to Mr. Lambert for luncheon and she could call and tell him so.

"Your mother has already told him that you would be here," Bessell said triumphantly and marched out in the hall to take my breakfast tray from Clara.

I felt hemmed in and trapped. The more desperately I tried to reach a phone, the more obstacles there seemed to be in my way until I was a nervous wreck. I wondered if this was the beginning of a clever campaign of Mother's to see that I had no time to myself for young interlopers who threatened to upset her plans.

The fitter stayed until almost noon. Part of the time Bessell was in the room and when she went out Mother came in. When I went upstairs to change for luncheon Mother went along babbling happily about Gordon Lambert's mother and father and his sister, who had married a prince, sitting in the next box to them at the opera last night. "Mrs. Lambert was *so* cordial!" Mother said joyously.

"Such lovely people. The prince is cross-eyed but every inch royal. Blood will tell, I always say. Now, darling, do be nice to Gordon today. I'm having luncheon served in front of the fire in the library for you. It will be cozier and more private. He's so crazy about you, baby. I believe he intends to ask you to marry him."

"Listen, Mother," I said hopelessly. "If you knew Gordon like I do you wouldn't want to be cozy and private with him. He's awful! And I wouldn't marry him if he were the last man on earth."

"He's very handsome," Mother said. "You would probably be presented at Court. You can overlook a lot of things, Zelda, when you're marrying a Lambert."

"But I'm not marrying a Lambert!" I cried desperately. "Mother, I have something to tell you—"

But Clara tapped discreetly on the door. "Mr. Lambert is here, Miss Zelda," she said.

"She'll be right down," Mother said.

I WONDERED if Mother could possibly know how I felt about Jack and if that was why she was using these high-pressure methods. Oh, I didn't underestimate Mother's intelligence any. She was smart. Too smart.

Gordon was waiting for me in the library. He was sober for a wonder. He paced up and down, tall, handsome and sure of himself.

"Hello, beautiful," he said when I came in. "I suppose it doesn't matter to you that you're driving me nuts. Who were you out with last night? It wasn't Ned Griffin or Holstead or Peter Lassen. I

checked 'em all. And when I start doing things like that, it must be love."

"You're wasting your time, Gordon," I told him coolly. "Why not concentrate on Peggy? She really goes for you in a big way."

He grinned down at me sardonically. "Are you telling me?" he asked with a sneer. "I know all about Peggy. I've been out with her, you know. In fact I definitely recall a certain week-end we spent at her folk's winter lodge. Maybe that's why I'm so crazy about you, Zelda. You're hard to get."

I DON'T know what I intended to say to him. He was coming toward me and I knew he would try to take me in his arms. I felt that I would kill him if he tried. But at that moment there was a scuffling sound outside the library door. The door opened and Leech, the footman, stood there, flushed and disgruntled and Peggy Melville swept by him impetuously.

"He wanted to announce me," she said scornfully. "But I told him I'd announce myself." Her eyes blazed at Gordon and she ignored me. "I heard you were coming here for lunch," she said, "so I thought I'd come, too. I told you I wanted to talk to you today, that I couldn't wait any longer. Well, I'd just as soon talk to you here in front of Zelda, because I want to talk to her, too."

I said, "You may go, Leech. And close the door behind you."

Peggy stuffed her hands into the pockets of her fur sport jacket. "Everybody says Gordon is crazy about you," she hurled in my direction. "They say he wants to marry you. Well, I suppose you and your trashy family would like nothing better. But he isn't going to marry you. He's going to marry me."

Gordon took a step toward her. "Why you dirty little—" he flared. "What do you mean by coming here and starting something like this! Why, I'll—"

Peggy looked at him with scornful eyes. "You'll do nothing. You'll marry me or you won't marry anybody. I went to see your sister yesterday." Peggy's voice rose hysterically. "I told her about us. And do you know what she did? She laughed. Said we'd have to settle the matter between us and that she was sure your mother and father would say the same. So I decided to settle it."

"Listen, Peggy," I cried. "I have no intention of marrying Gordon. I—I'm in love with someone else. I—"

"You bet you won't marry Gordon," Peggy said levelly. "I'm going to have a baby and it's his. He knows it is. And I don't care who else knows it now."

Gordon began swearing at her. He made a lunge toward her. Her hand came up out of her pocket and there was a sudden sharp explosion and Gordon was lying there on the rug between us!

It was horrible! I felt as though the whole thing must be some terrible nightmare. Peggy standing there pale and dazed and that still figure lying there on the carpet in a widening pool of red.

I screamed. That and the noise of the revolver brought Leech and Bessell with Mother and Charles close behind. I think it was Mother who hurried me out of the room and when we got outside I fainted.

At any rate, the next thing I remember was that I was lying on my bed, alone in my room.

With trembling fingers I reached for the telephone. I called Jack. "Come and get me!" I begged. "I'll be ready whenever you come."

I packed my bag. Just a change of underthings and a nightie and a sweater and skirt. I slipped into the simplest thing I had, the black wool dress I had worn the first day I met Jack.

Mother came up. She looked old and tired and frightened. "Peggy's folks came and got her and Gordon has been taken to the hospital. He is badly wounded but he will live. What an awful thing to have happen in our house, of all places! Oh, that wretched child Peggy. It will all be hushed up, of course. We have talked to the servants very sternly. The Melvilles and the Lamberts will see that it is kept out of the papers. They are going to send Peggy away for awhile. Such a little fool to get us all in a mess like that!"

"She was in pretty much of a mess herself," I said grimly. "The whole rotten structure is a mess, Mother. All this build-up, and veneering and pretense of glamour. None of us are really happy. Peggy sought escape in one way—I'm going to seek it in another. I'm getting out. I'm going to marry Jack Bonner, the boy you met last night. He isn't a fortune hunter. Neither of us want a thing from you or Charles. We just want to be let alone to seek happiness in our own way."

"Zelda" Mother screamed hysterically. "You shan't leave this house. I won't permit you to wreck your life this way. You can't! I forbid it! You mustn't! Charles! Miss Bessell!"

I felt sorry for her. I wanted to put my arms around her and kiss her. But I didn't dare hesitate. I was afraid they might try to hold me by force. I grabbed my bag and pushed by Mother, evading her plump, jeweled arms that attempted to hold me back. I ran down the stairs past Charles and Miss Bessell.

I didn't stop running until I was tucked pantingly into Jack's shabby roadster.

WE WERE married that night in a little town in Connecticut. The papers wrote it up gleefully.
GLAMOUR GIRL OF THIS YEAR'S DEBS ELOPES WITH CLERK
But there was nothing in the paper about Peggy having shot Gordon Lambert! Money and social power can do a great deal. But it can't buy happiness.

Mother and Charles have washed their hands of me. But next year we are going out to visit my father's ranch in Texas. He has written us the sweetest letters and would like Jack to come out and look over the country and see if he wouldn't like to help run the ranch and use part of the land for his greenhouses and flowers.

I have never been happier in my life. We live in a tiny apartment and Jack's mother and sisters have taught me a great deal about housekeeping. We're expecting our baby next month and we can hardly wait!

I read in the society columns the other day that Gordon Lambert and Peggy Melville had been quietly married at his sister's villa in southern France. Poor Peggy! Poor little debs whose names appear daily in the gossip columns and society pages!

I wouldn't exchange the peace and ecstasy I have found in my young husband's arms for any part of that empty world I left behind me. I have found the true meaning of life at last.

♥ ♥ ♥ ♥

RUTH ETTING'S

By Peter Levins

WILL there ever again be peace in this world for Ruth Etting? Will she yet find the happiness and contentment she has sought so long, or will fear and frustration continue to shadow her life?

Only a few months ago it seemed that an unkind Fate had at last relented. She had freed herself from a fiercely jealous husband after fifteen nightmare years, and she had met another man as different from Martin Snyder as it was possible to imagine.

With her divorce she had escaped from a world in which she had been a prisoner, and found peace. A new life, a life of tranquillity and companionship, was beginning for his beloved songbird of stage, radio and screen.

But Fate would not let her live in peace. This was but the calm before a gathering storm.

Until that storm broke, the world knew nothing of Ruth Etting's real story. To the millions of radio and movie fans she was a woman to be envied, for she had won fame and fortune, struggled from nowhere to the very heights of popularity. The public did not know how she had been enslaved by her own success. They did not know about the years of drudgery and dread she endured while chained in marriage to Martin (Moe the Gimp) Snyder.

Thus the outside world was stunned when the headlines exploded with the news of the shooting at Beverly Hills, California, on the night of October 17. According to the police, Snyder had waylaid Myrl Alderman, 34-year-old musician friend of Miss Etting, and shot him before her eyes.

Snyder had kidnaped Alderman, said the police, while the musician was on his way home from a National Broadcasting Company studio. Mad with jealousy, Snyder had forced his captive into the house at the point of a gun, then threatened to kill not only Alderman but Ruth and his own daughter, Edith, twenty-one-year-old child of a former marriage who had become Ruth's secretary.

Only the most fortunate of accidents, Ruth said later, saved them from death. Snyder fired twice. One bullet missed, the other struck Alderman in the abdomen, and he collapsed to the floor of the music room. Ruth believed that Snyder intended to turn the gun on her and Edith, and then perhaps himself. But at that moment the concussion of the shots loosened an electric light bulb, and the room was plunged into darkness.

WHAT happened then must ever remain a nightmare to Ruth Etting. According to the story she told the police and the reporters, she dashed into the bedroom to get a gun of her own—a gun she had bought for just such a terrible emergency. Snyder followed her and wrested the gun away from her. It fell to the floor. Then Edith and Ruth both struggled with him for possession of his gun.

It was Edith who found the gun on the floor, and fired the one wild shot that sent her father fleeing into the night.

Snyder, arrested a few minutes later, was charged with kidnaping, attempted murder, and with a violation of the

AT the pinnacle of her fame—Broadway and her name in blazing electric lights! Ruth Etting as she appeared in 1927 when Ziegfeld starred her in the Follies and when she was a Number One favorite on stage, screen, victrola records and over the air.

TRAGIC LOVE STORY

LEFT: Ruth Etting pictured as she visited Myrl Alderman in the hospital where he is recovering from bullet wounds afflicted by "Moe" Snyder, Miss Etting's former husband. Right: A favorite portrait of Ruth taken at the height of her fame and popularity. Below, left: Col. Martin "Moe the Gimp" Snyder, divorced husband of Ruth Etting who was released on bail after the shooting of Alderman.

state firearms law. Ruth wept frantically at Alderman's beside at St. Vincent's Hospital, not knowing whether he would live or die. But it soon developed that he would live; the bullet had touched no vital part.

Ruth first declared that she and Myrl had been married since July, and that she had been "ecstatically happy" in this new marriage. Later, however, she admitted that there had been no ceremony as yet; Alderman's divorce from his second wife would not become final until December 2. The singer explained that she had wanted Snyder to believe that she was now married, hoping he would then become resigned to losing her.

Two days after the shooting, Mrs. Alma Alderman, divorced second wife of the musician, filed suit for $150,000, charging Ruth with having alienated Alderman's affections. Through her attorneys, Ruth denied this accusation, adding that even if she had stolen Myrl's love it was legally too late for Mrs. Alderman to collect.

Alderman in turn sued Snyder for $225,000 as the result of the attack. Snyder in the meantime was freed on $25,000 bail pending his trial.

Thus Ruth Etting once more reached a crossroads of her life, just as she did years before when she met Snyder. She faces a future of lawsuits and trials which threaten to drain her hard-earned fortune. She has already paid Martin Snyder well for her divorce—and now there were to be greater costs to pay for knowing him and letting him become the savage proprietor of her career.

RUTH ETTING, descendant of pioneers, was born in David City, Neb., a typical mid-western farming community as far from Broadway—and all that Broadway means—as it is possible to imagine. She was the only child of Colonel P. G. T. Etting, a leading citizen of the town. Her grandfather, Elax, built the first grist mill in the region; her uncle, Alexander Etting, was to become Mayor.

When Ruth was five years old her parents took her to San Diego. The blue-eyed, blonde-haired child did not know it but her mother was very ill; that was the reason for the shift to the milder climate of Southern California. Ruth attended school, played the games of childhood, and became a little nurse to her mother.

Then, when she was seven—

Ruthie lay in bed one tragic night, wide awake and frightened because she knew that something terrible was happening. The doctor had been coming frequently; she had noted his air of helplessness, the sorrowful shake of his head when he talked with her father. Once she caught the words, ". . . nothing anyone can do."

And now. . . .

Her father was sitting on her bed, holding her small hand in his, and saying quietly that she must not cry, that Mommy was not in pain any more. Mommy had "gone to Heaven."

This was a tragedy which affected Ruth's whole life. In later years, when the outer world was calling so insistently, when she burned with an ambition that could be realized only amid the glitter of a great city, when Martin Snyder entered her life and assailed her heart in those vital years she desperately needed a mother's counsel and guidance. Yes, it seems certain that if her mother had lived Fate would have dealt the cards quite differently.

Father and daughter returned to David City after Mrs. Etting's death, and Ruth went to live on the Etting farm with her grandparents and an aunt. Colonel Etting had to be away on business a good part of the time.

Grandfather Etting taught the child the lessons of thrift and hard work. Of course she had her periods of play, but often she had chores to do, like the other farm children of that region.

So this sweet-faced child grew into girlhood, and a great yearning grew in her lonely heart—a yearning that stemmed from her talent for drawing. All during her school years she drew constantly, whether in class or at home, and by the time she was fourteen she was designing and making her own clothes.

It was this talent, and not any flair for singing or music, which sent Ruth Etting out into the world. It was this ambition for an art career which, in the course of Fate's strange machinations, brought her rich fruits in another field. Rich fruits, but bitter.

While still at school in David City she broached the subject of studying art in Chicago, knowing even before she heard the answer that she faced stern opposition to any such unconventional plan. An Etting an artist? No woman of the

RUTH ETTING as she appeared in the offices of Attorney Hahn where she faced Myrl Alderman's estranged wife, Alma Alderman who is suing Ruth for $150,-000, for alienation of her husband's affections.

RUTH accompanies her throbbing songs on the piano. The photographer has caught, in this wistful pose, something of Ruth's warm, wholesome charm and the appeal in her eyes that have known secret tears.

THE golden voice that thrilled millions—Here's Ruth singing before the microphone in a career that reached the heights in meteoric brilliance and reached the depths in heart-break and despair.

EVEN as a baby, there was something "extra special" about Ruth Etting. Here is a rare picture of the songstress taken in David City, Nebraska, where the Ettings lived and where Ruth grew up.

Ettings had ever worked for a living, much less dabbled in anything so unusual as art.

But the year after her graduation from high school the family gave their consent. Her aunt accompanied her to Chicago, installed her in the Y. W. C. A., and enrolled her in the fashion designing class at the Academy of Arts.

THE next twelve months passed very happily, even though she had to watch her pennies constantly in order to make ends meet. Then she got a part time job in a costume shop. She designed, sewed and cut patterns. And sometimes she hummed at her work in a voice that was low and throbbing.

"You have a strange sort of singing voice," a fellow-worker remarked one day.

Ruth laughed. "As a matter of fact, I haven't any voice at all. I don't know much about music but I do know that my voice hasn't any range. The high notes are simply beyond me."

Thus she spoke of the voice which one day was to charm millions of radio listeners, sell carloads of phonographs, and send Ruth Etting to the topmost peak of the entertainment world.

Her journey to fame was long and devious. It began when Ruth's employer was asked to suggest some costumes for the new girl show Mr. and Mrs. Eddie Beck were staging at the Marigold Gardens, a popular cabaret. Ruth drew some designs, and the Becks liked them so much that they suggested she come and discuss the matter with them. Thus the Becks found themselves admiring the fresh young beauty of the farm-bred Nebraskan.

"How would you like a job here in the chorus?" Beck asked, noting the engaging smile, the perfect skin, the slim figure.

"Oh, I have no stage ambitions!" she laughed.

"The girls get twenty-five dollars a week," he coaxed.

"But I have no experience—none at all!" she exclaimed.

"Doesn't matter. You've got the looks and a personality that's not easy to find. What do you say?"

She pondered. Twenty-five dollars a week was a lot of money to her. It meant that she could live better, buy new things she needed. She would be able to support herself completely, rather than depend upon her father for assistance.

"All right, Mr. Beck," she agreed. "I'd like to try it."

And so she entered the chorus at Marigold Gardens, wearing costumes she herself had designed. Although she had no training for this sort of work, she had a natural sense of rhythm, along with her characteristic eagerness to learn and willingness to work. Meanwhile she kept her part-time job, not knowing how long she might last at the cabaret.

That she might be called upon to sing never occurred to her. But she soon discovered that, during certain numbers, the girls were required to sing together.

"What am I going to do about that?" she asked one   [Please turn page]

Specially posed by Ann Sothern, United Artists' star.

of the others in the line. "I can't sing the way we're supposed to."

"Well, you can move your lips, and hope nobody notices."

So that's what she did. She was actually *afraid* to be heard!

She did not take this cabaret venture seriously because she could not see any career in it for her. She did her steps, flashing her naturally winning smile, simply for the twenty-five dollars they paid her every week. Fashion designing was still her real life work.

Then the management engaged a baritone for the show, a soloist. As a result the songs were pitched lower and Ruth began to join in the singing.

Ruth's career hung in the balance at this point. Had she obtained a better-paying job in the dress designing business, she would have quit the show without a further thought. But the day came when Ernie Young, producer at the Marigold Gardens, heard her sing during rehearsal. That low, throbbing quality struck his ears at once, and gave him an idea. When the rehearsal was over he told her to learn the baritone's songs because the first time the fellow failed to

appear she would have to take his place as soloist.

"You're the only one in the company that has that type of voice," he said.

Then he regarded her, asking, "Where did you sing before?"

"I never sang anywhere before!"

"Well, one of these nights, when that baritone drinks too much, you'll make your debut right here. I think you might do all right."

Again she did not take the matter seriously. It sounded fantastic. Nevertheless, she studied the baritone's songs, adjusting them as well as she could to her own restricted range. The other girls liked to listen to her, which at least seemed encouraging.

WEEKS later her chance came. She arrived to find the dressing room in a turmoil. The baritone would not be singing tonight.

"You're it, Ruthie," Young told her. "And if you do all right you can have a solo spot regularly."

Considerably dazed, she found herself getting into the man's costume—white trousers, white polo shirt and polo hat. She had to stuff wads of cotton into the toes of the shoes so that her feet would fit. The other girls, noting her nervous-

ness, hugged her reassuringly and told her she would get by all right. But she wasn't so confident of that. When it came her turn, Young all but pushed her onto the floor.

Jauntily she waved a polo mallet as she pranced out in front of the chorus. And for the first time Ruth Etting was singing a solo. She had no consciousness of how she was doing; all she could think of during the number was how big her feet must look in the baritone's shoes. But she "got by." The crowd showed its approval with generous applause. Ernie Young told her the spot was hers.

Here was a turning point, although she did not recognize it at the time. Now destiny was definitely leading her away from the career on which she had set her heart so long. This business of singing and dancing in a smoke-filled, alcohol-reeking cabaret was anything but a career to her; it was just a job, frequently a very distasteful job. She looked ahead to the time when she could quit the sordid and sometimes degrading environment of Chicago's night life.

Nevertheless, step by step, without her being conscious of what was happening, fate moved her farther and yet farther away from what had been her dream and her ambition.

Young gave her several more songs to sing after her first effort. In one of the numbers she sang and danced with Danny Healy, now a producer in New York. She worked nightly from eight in the evening until four or five in the morning, and saw the sun only briefly each day before she dragged herself, in complete exhaustion, to bed. The job required so much of her strength that, before long, she had to give up her studies at the Academy as well as her part-time work in the costume shop.

But there was one thing that buoyed her up during this period—the fact that she was allowed to design various wardrobes and sets for the cabaret. Her good work in this respect strengthened her ambition all the more. She wanted to earn a lot of money, and save a lot, so that she might one day devote herself entirely to designing. She yearned constantly to get ahead, to free herself from the nightly slavery of the chorus.

OTHER girls have scored successes overnight, and moved on to fame and fortune. Not so Ruth Etting. She sang on almost unnoticed in those early Chicago days. Friends told her that she should have an agent or manager with influence. What she needed, they told her, was some good publicity, and some opportunities.

But she knew no such person in Chicago; that is, none she could trust. From time to time she met men who undoubtedly could have helped her, and indeed did offer to help her. But the price, she invariably discovered, was too high for her to pay. Come what might, she was resolved not to make any more compromise in order to better herself. To her way of thinking, that would only mean a far more degrading servitude.

And then, one night in July, 1920, she met the man who was to become her slave as well as her evil genius—that strange, mysterious fanatic, "Colonel" Moe (alias Martin) Snyder.

The date was July 17th. One of the other girls introduced them between shows, and Ruth was struck at once with the burning, driving vitality of the man. His voice seemed to explode as he spoke, and he spoke very flatteringly.

"You don't belong in this joint," he told her. "You rate a better spot."

"Thanks," she responded with her friendly smile. "I hope to do better."

"I'm going to see that you do better."

He was so positive, so final about this, that she laughed.

"You can laugh," he said, almost resentfully, "but I'm going to prove it fast. I know everybody in this racket."

"That helps, I'm told."

"You bet your sweet life it helps. You can't get anywhere without influence. I know Al Jolson. I know Eddie Cantor. I know all the big shots in this town."

"And you want to help me?"

"That's right."

"But why?"

"I think you got what it takes. I knew it as soon as I laid eyes on you—soon as I heard you sing."

"I've had to turn down other offers of help," she said. "I have to be careful about accepting favors from men."

He grinned. "You needn't worry about that. I'm not one of those on-the-make guys. You just stick to your singing here," he urged, "and it won't be any time at all before you'll be going places!"

Ruth thought this piercing-eyed, fanatically confident man one of the most unusual personalities she had ever met. Yet she remained doubtful about his boastful claims, until she mentioned him later to the girls. They told her it was true. "Colonel" Snyder did have influence, and did know all sorts of people. The right people.

There were other things about him that they did not know. They did not know that he had been associated with underworld leaders. They did not know that he had acquired bullet wounds in the course of his thirty years. In fact, they knew very little.

Moe Snyder—he changed the Moe to Martin in later years and also gave himself the title of "Colonel"—emerged from Chicago's West Side to become, as an old acquaintance has picturesquely put it, "one of the toughest apples in the toughest apple orchard in the world." Just what he did in his youth remained as much a mystery as how he acquired the limp which earned him his nickname, "Moe the Gimp."

He had driven taxicabs in the Loop, and had worked from time to time as a strikebreaker. Recently his practice had been to visit other cities, pose as "Mayor of the Loop," and promise protection to actors fearing extortion and possible death at the hands of gangsters in Chicago. Thus he had served as bodyguard for Jolson, Cantor, Ben Bernie and other luminaries and had built up a formidable list of important, and grateful, theatrical acquaintances.

His political connections, in that glittering and violent prohibition era, were rather impressive, too. Much of his influence, as well as his income, grew out of his association with Dennis J. Egan, powerful leader of the old Twentieth Ward, later to be known as the "Bloody Twentieth." When Ruth met him he was on the payroll of the municipal Sanitation Department. He was described as an "investigator."

Purely from the standpoint of getting ahead in the entertainment field, this man was precisely what Ruth Etting needed at the time their paths first crossed. He knew everybody worth knowing, and he knew how to influence certain people in underworld ways at which he had long been a master. Added to this was his utter belief in Ruth's genius, and his fanatical determination to push her along.

SNYDER became a regular visitor at the Marigold Gardens after that first meeting. He was married at the time but separated from his wife. It soon became obvious that he idolized Ruth, worshipped her with a devotion so complete as to be almost pathetic. The fact that he stirred no answering spark in her heart seemed to mean nothing at all to him. Just to be near her, to be able to fight her battles, to protect her from possible insult or harm—that was all he asked. In his eyes, she was a creature out of a world he had never known.

He strove ceaselessly to fulfill his promise to her. He boosted her at every opportunity. He made influential people come and see her and listen to her. He got her name in the theatrical weeklies, never tiring of pestering editors to "give Ruthie a slug." Before very long he was getting results. He cajoled, wheedled, bought and fought for her from the chorus into the limelight. Sometimes, in this campaign on her behalf, he resorted to threats. Because he was known as a "nasty man to cross"—his temper could be very frightening—theatrical people were careful not to offend him.

Ruth went from the Marigold Gardens to the Rainbow Gardens, then to the Green Mill Club. She did not find any of it any fun. As she said years later, "I worked in every low cellar in Chicago. It was terrible drudgery. Sometimes I had to sing as many as forty songs a night." Lots of times she had to sing to a table of half-drunken, lascivious-eyed patrons. Frequently she had to dance with men whose only purpose, it seemed, was to insult her.

"Yeah, you're too good for all this," Snyder would agree. "But some day you're going into big time. One of these days you're going to see your name in big lights—on Broadway!"

"You always seem so sure about that," she sighed, "and I'm always wondering whether it will be worth what I must go through here."

"Sure it'll be worth it! Once you're a star, you're all set!"

So she drove herself on, aided and abetted constantly by Snyder. Though she became well known in Chicago, and though there were theatre engagements from time to time, life was still arduous and uncertain. She looked back on her early ambitions now with sadness, knowing that this other life had claimed her and trapped her. She found herself imprisoned in a cage which was to be lined with gold—but a cage nevertheless.

More and more she came to depend upon this man who had made her success his life work. Although he accepted no money for his services, he actually had become her manager, as well as her press agent and bodyguard. In time she became fully convinced that he was just about essential to her—a conviction which he himself had long held.

The story that Snyder terrified her into marrying him could be true, but it isn't. Their marriage, two years to the day after their first meeting, grew out of a combination of circumstances and emotions. Ruth's gratitude and dependence played a large part, as well as Snyder's adoration of her, and dependence on her. Moreover, he had monopolized her from the start, stuck to her constantly and faithfully. With Moe the Gimp hovering near, no other man had ever dared court her. It simply wouldn't have been healthy.

"It was a grave mistake," she has said since. "I didn't know what I was doing."

However, knowing Snyder and his all but pathological passion for Ruth, one wonders what would have happened—to him and to her—had she tried to shake herself loose from him in Chicago. One wonders, too, if that thought might have occurred to her during the courtship.

The ceremony took place at Crown Point, Indiana. There could be no honeymoon because Ruth had to appear for her nightly singing. They went to live in a hotel room; and they were to live in hotel rooms for many years to come. For this girl there was to be no real home of her own, no family life, no children to bear and worry over and hug and laugh with. For this girl there was to be "success"—fame and fortune—and heartaches.

Snyder continued to fight and snarl and chisel for his "sweet little singer." He became her manager and shared in the proceeds. The time came when he did nothing but labor in her behalf, and spend the proceeds. Then he learned that radio program producers needed talent. Radio was then struggling for recognition in the entertainment world. He wangled a spot for her at WLS. She sang her first song over the radio in that station's makeshift studio and reached another milestone in her career.

She was an instant hit on the radio.

The microphone caught and intensified the throbbing melody of her haunting voice. Fan mail poured in, asking that she be a regular feature. After that first appearance she sang twice nightly at the station for more than a year. Her income steadily mounted, as well as her hours of work.

RUTH ETTING was now fast approaching the popularity which won her the title, "Chicago's Sweetheart." She sang as a featured performer in stage shows, then began making records for the Columbia Phonograph Company. Her singing of "Remember," "Looking at the World Through Rose-Colored Glasses," "Thinking of You," "No, No Nora," "Ramona," and many other hits of that period brought cheers from every audience. Soon, as sales of her phonograph records steadily climbed, the whole country was thrilling to that voice of which she herself had once been unaware.

The one-time Nebraska farm girl might be said to have "arrived" when she was engaged to sing at the swank College Inn in Chicago's Hotel Sherman, where Abe Lyman and his band were playing. The predominantly collegiate crowd packed tightly around the bandstand whenever Ruth came forward, and they swayed to the soothing caress of her singing. In fraternity houses and dormitories all over the land she became the Number One favorite.

To say that she was working overtime would be putting it mildly indeed. There was never any let-up. She had to snatch her meals more or less on the run, between rehearsals or engagements. Life seemed to begrudge her even the blessed periods of sleep.

The reader might wonder why she did not call a halt somewhere, so that she might have more leisure. That was where Snyder's influence figured. Although he continued to worship her, it was much the sort of worship that a racing man bestows upon his favorite winner. Moe did not want Ruth to miss any opportunity to enhance her prestige and increase her income. There were races to be won and he wanted to win them all.

Ruth left everything to him in that respect. He got her the jobs and she did them. He haggled and stormed over contracts. He battled with producers, orchestra leaders, rival stars for her. "You just be my sweet little Ruthie, and I'll do the beefing," was a favorite admonition of his. Thus she remained in the background in all matters of this kind. Snyder even handled her interviews with the press. No reporter ever dared talk to her when Manager Moe wasn't around—not twice, at any rate.

So this strangely-matched couple approached the next turning point in Ruth Etting's career.

In the Fall of 1926, soon after the death of her father, a Ziegfeld agent, Stanley Sharp, visited Chicago for the purpose of scouting Ruth Etting. Irving Berlin, then engaged in writing the score for the Ziegfeld Follies of 1927, had heard one of Ruth's records and tipped off Ziegfeld that she might be the singer they needed for the new show.

Presently Sharp telephoned his boss. He reported that Ruth Etting would do—decidedly. She had a grand figure, a lovely face, a most unusual voice, and an ideal personality. "That girl's got everything!" Sharp exclaimed.

Now, as it happened, Ruth had already begun to pack for a trip to New York. She had been engaged to sing with Paul Whiteman's band at the great Paramount Theatre on Broadway. Then Ziegfeld's

wire came. He wanted her to join the Follies at once.

Here, indeed, was success.

When they reached New York, she and Snyder called at the Ziegfeld office. The celebrated producer had a contract all ready. He signed her without even trying out her voice—and he never regretted his haste.

Ruth made a great hit at the Paramount, and later with the Follies in which one of her songs was "Shaking the Blues Away." She began making movie shorts for Paramount Pictures; got $4,000 a week for personal appearances; and starred on the radio at $1,500 a performance. In "Whoopee" she played the feminine lead opposite Eddie Cantor. That was the show in which she sang:

You say the night time's
The right time for kissing;
But night time is my time
For just reminiscing—
Regretting instead of forgetting
With somebody else.

That song, the plaintive wail of a lover forsaken, thrilled audiences from coast to coast. It was a natural for Ruth and some of her own heart went into it.

Another song she made famous was the "Ten Cents a Dance" number in Ed Wynn's show, "Simple Simon."

But still life wasn't any fun. Her routine never changed; it was work—go home to a hotel room—get up—rehearse—work—and then the same procedure over again. She wouldn't have minded it so much if there had been something to fall back on in the way of companionship with her husband. But Snyder could never be a companion to her, for all his devotion. Living with him was like living with an uncouth child who never could be trained.

IN NEW YORK he continued to snarl and fight with everyone. He could not seem to realize that Ruth's employers were now of a higher class than in their Chicago days. The consequence was that he made enemies right and left, and embarrassed his "sweet little singer" continually. Snyder was absolutely uncontrollable. He popped off, as Broadway puts it, regardless of his surroundings. His attitude was habitually uncompromising, his language was the language of a hoodlum. He became a hindrance rather than a help, so far as his wife's career was concerned, but no one would ever have been able to convince him of that.

Broadway abounds in instances of his jealous guarding of Ruth's interests. Sometimes this went to ludicrous extremes.

Richard Himber, the orchestra leader, has told how Snyder behaved in a radio studio when Miss Etting was about to go on the air.

"He'd get on the platform before a

broadcast and draw chalk lines to keep the musicians a safe distance from the microphone where she was singing," said Himber. "He ordered them to stay behind that chalk line—or else. Of course this was utterly unreasonable. The only way the orchestra could get the music across was to have the microphone slipped up closer to them just as the broadcast began."

Snyder even tried to intimidate Ziegfeld. Once Helen Morgan, a great blues singer in her own right, was paired with Ruth in the Follies. Snyder decided that Ziggy was discriminating against Ruth. He marched around to the producer.

"You ain't gonna shove that little lady around—not for a minute," he snapped in his best Chicago manner.

Ziegfeld ordered him barred from the theatre. The Colonel stood in the adjacent alley, grimly smoking a cigar and muttering to anything who would listen. "Nobody's gonna shove us around," he growled. "My little lady don't need no Ziegfeld. One more crack outa him and I'll yank her out of the show, contract or no contract."

An another occasion, during a matinee, a pair of comedians playfully sought to make a date with Ruth. They gave her a playful shove in the course of the act.

Snyder was waiting for them.

"So you're comedians, are you?" he said. "Well, I'll make you funny enough so you can be comedians."

Then he waded into them with flailing fists.

The next audience that saw the comedians howled at their appearance. Spectators believed that their mashed noses and purple eyes were make-up. Always thereafter the pair used make-up to stimulate the battered faces given them by The Gimp.

Ziegfeld asked Ruth time and again why she stuck to Snyder. So did others. They could not understand how this gentle, unassuming, untheatrical young woman could endure life with such a creature. But she had her answer: *"If I ever left Moe, he'd kill me."*

Years later, the day came when she was free of him—or thought she was. Broadway wondered how he ever agreed to a divorce. But Broadway was not surprised when, raging with jealousy, suspecting that another man had won his sweet singer, Moe Snyder began to crack.

"There's nothing for me without the Little Lady," he told his listeners time and time again at Lindy's Restaurant on Broadway. "I go home and come right out again. I walk the streets all night. I can't sleep."

One night he suddenly smashed his fist against the restaurant wall until it was mashed and bleeding.

"That's how my heart is," said Moe the Gimp.

And Broadway held its breath. ●

———

Broadway held its breath because it feared what might happen to Ruth Etting at the hands of the man she divorced. Many believed that he would kill himself. Others were sure that he would never leave this world without taking her with him.

Don't miss the second installment of the amazing true story of Ruth Etting's tragic career in March TRUE CONFESSIONS On Sale February 1st.

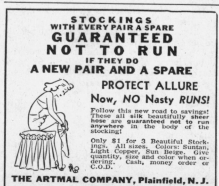

ANY lonely reader wanting a pen pal may write to The Skipper of The Port of Lonely Hearts, 529 South Seventh Street, Minneapolis, Minn.

PORT OF *LONELY* HEARTS

By SALLY O'DAY

DEAR Pen Pals: *Does life seem hum-drum, prosy, uninteresting? If that is so, you are in a rut. Get out of it! Pick out a pen pal and see how much fun you can have. I'll help you as much as possible. Don't forget to read the rules printed below:*

1. I cannot enter into personal correspondence with anyone, neither can I give out addresses, but I will be glad to publish your letters asking for pals as soon as possible.

2. Letters to pals must contain a three-cent stamp for postage and ten cents to cover clerical costs.

3. Your first letter must go through the Port. After that, correspondence between pals is direct.

Sincerely,

SALLY O'DAY.

Searching for his ideal.

I AM twenty-two; have dark hair and a small mustache. I am looking for my ideal, but as yet, haven't found her. Come on, you modern girls, give me a break.

Nate, Africa.

Two modern Scotch girls.

WE ARE two Scotch girls, modern, and fond of dancing. We should like to hear from Americans and would appreciate it if photos were sent.

Billie & Grett, Scotland.

He's a wheat farmer.

I AM a wheat farmer living in Colorado. I am very lonely and blue. I am thirty-eight years old but look twenty-five. I want pen pals between the ages of twenty-five and thirty-five.

E. O., Colo.

She teaches school.

WOULD anyone care to write to a lonely Newfoundland girl? I am teaching school in a small settlement in the north. I like the work well, although at times it's a bit monotonous. I am twenty-two years old and am fond of outdoor sports. I have a camera and would exchange snap shots. Here's hoping to receive a shower of letters.

School Mar'm, Newfoundland.

This is interesting.

I AM a young man just over twenty-five and have traveled extensively all over India. I do not drink nor smoke and am a vegetarian. I am keenly interested in literature and am very fond of tennis and swimming. I long for pen pals and will exchange photos and souvenirs. I would like to hear from everyone. Will someone write to me? I will answer all letters received.

Montgomery, India.

A secretary joins the port.

I AM nineteen years of age and employed as a secretary. I love all outdoor sports and would like to hear from pen pals in foreign countries as well as my own.

Terry, D. C.

Don't keep her waiting.

I AM a girl of seventeen, living in a steel city and longing for pen pals. I promise to answer every letter I receive. I will exchange snap shots. Don't keep me waiting.

Ets, Ind.

Who will show her?

I'M A stenographer, English and twenty-one. My hobbies are photography, hiking and reading and I'm wondering what sort of letters Americans write. Come on, give me a break.

Curious, England.

A middle-aged man.

I AM a middle-aged man and am very lonely at times. I am very fond of writing letters and will answer everyone who writes to me.

F. H., Ore.

Her mother is ill.

I'M A girl twenty-one years old. My mother is ill and I have to stay with her. I get awfully lonesome. I'll send a photo to the first girl and fellow who write. I love to dance, swim, play tennis and drive a car.

Ginger, Mass.

Want a photograph?

I AM British, twenty-one years of age. I am fond of reading, can dance, swim and play golf. I would be glad to hear from girls and boys all over the world and will exchange photographs. I promise an answer to every letter.

Milt, Scotland.

A stranger in America.

I AM a Lithuanian girl of twenty. I came to this country five years ago and am very lonely. My parents are dead and I haven't any relatives or friends. Won't someone please write to me?

Helen, N. Y.

He's so all alone.

WON'T someone write to a five foot, nine inches tall, gray-headed man of forty-eight? I am so lonesome.

Louie, Wis.

Ruth Etting's Tragic Love Story

She wanted only simple happiness—love, a home, children. After disillusion and tragedy, she stands near her goal. We hope, as the conclusion of her dramatic story here promises, that she will find it!

HAPPINESS at long, long last! At Las Vegas, Nev., Ruth Etting and Myrl Alderman were married, dashing away during the trial of "The Gimp." Bliss is mirrored in Ruth's face.

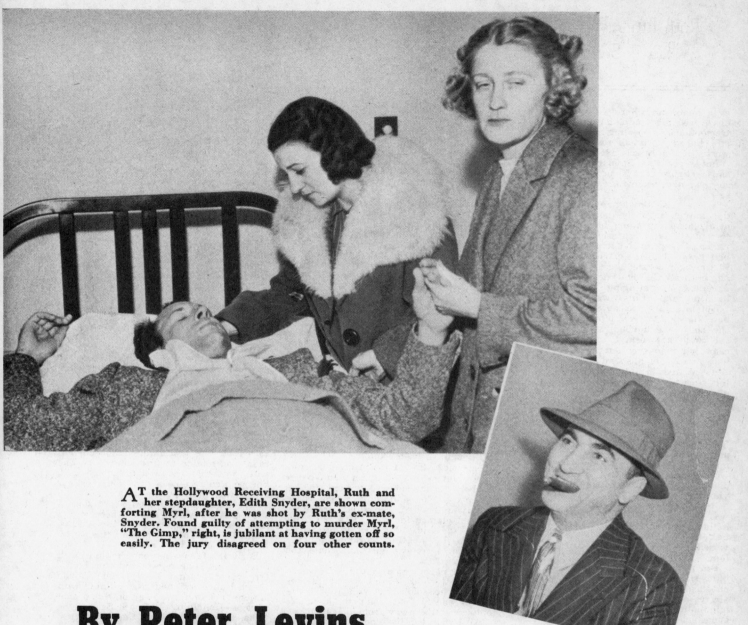

AT the Hollywood Receiving Hospital, Ruth and her stepdaughter, Edith Snyder, are shown comforting Myrl, after he was shot by Ruth's ex-mate, Snyder. Found guilty of attempting to murder Myrl, "The Gimp," right, is jubilant at having gotten off so easily. The jury disagreed on four other counts.

By Peter Levins

TRUE CONFESSIONS concludes in this issue the tragic story of Ruth Etting, star of stage, radio and screen.

Chained in marriage for fifteen years to Martin (Moe, the Gimp) Snyder, insanely jealous husband-manager she dared not divorce for fear he would kill her, Ruth found love in the person of Myrl Alderman, handsome young Hollywood musician. She took her life in her hands to divorce Snyder—and when this savage, violent product of the Chicago underworld learned that another man was to have her, he went berserk.

Snyder's rage reached its climax on a night last October when he invaded a peaceful Hollywood cottage and shot the man Ruth loved, but whom she had not yet married.

Now the case has ended, for the time being at least, in Snyder's conviction of the attempted murder of Alderman. But as this is written Ruth still faces a future of lawsuits accusing her of love piracy—suits which threaten to drain the fortune she worked so hard to amass.

THE great tragedy of Ruth Etting's life, without any question, is that she ever met this man Snyder. But for him, her life would have been altogether different from what it turned out to be. Had Snyder not become interested in her, while she was appearing in a cabaret chorus in Chicago, she might never have attained the heights she did in the entertainment world. But she most certainly would have had a happier future.

Ruth never had any stage ambitions. To this day she feels that her real career was in fashion designing. When, as a young girl, she left her farm home in David City, Nebraska, for Chicago, it was to study designing, at which she had shown definite talent since childhood. She accepted the job in the Marigold Gardens chorus because she needed money to finance her art studies.

This beautiful, gentle, ambitious girl saw no future for herself in the amusement world. She knew that she had been hired simply because she had a lovely face and figure. Neither she nor anyone yet knew that she possessed one of the most unusual singing voices [*Please turn page*]

Ruth Etting's Tragic Love Story

ever heard anywhere. Even after she discovered this completely untrained but tremendously appealing vocal talent, she still hoped to break away from stage work. It simply was not her sort of life.

But then Moe Snyder, that limping, sinister figure, that Nemesis from a world she had never known, entered upon the scene.

In one sense, Snyder rescued her. This dominating, savagely possessive product of a violent era swept her along on the torrent of his enthusiasm and his infatuation. He pushed her ahead, won her better jobs than the cabarets she sang in in Chicago, boosted her and fought for her until all Chicago knew her, until all America was swaying to the husky, haunting voice of his "sweet little singer."

But in another sense, Snyder enslaved her. He spun the web of success in which she became entangled, and from which she could not seem to escape. He became her manager, her press agent, her bodyguard—her husband.

As related in the first instalment of this story, the marriage in 1922 grew out of a combination of circumstances. Ruth in the two years since she had met Snyder had come to depend upon him entirely in all matters pertaining to her career. Even though she still had no affection for the constant drudgery of rehearsals and performances, she felt grateful to the man who had made her success his life work. Besides, no other man had ever dared court her, knowing the Gimp's violent nature.

Ruth was one day to say her marriage was "a grave mistake." But there was nothing, really, that she could do to save herself. Divorce? Her answer never varied: "He would kill me if I ever left him."

During subsequent years, when the blues singer attained the greatest success on stage, screen and radio, this strange, always angry man made her life one of humiliation and embarrassment. Snyder's gangster methods of intimidation, terrorism, and threats of bodily harm, had gotten results in Chicago. But when Ruth invaded New York—at the urging of Paul Whiteman and Florenz Ziegfeld—her husband became more a liability than a help. She no longer needed that sort of exploitation; she had reached the crest and now was being carried along on the current of her hard-won reputation and her nationally recognized ability.

But Moe the Gimp never realized that. He thought she still needed his crude, ruthless and often unreasonable methods of managership. Chicago, New York—they were all the same to him. Big shot Broadway producers were no different, in his eyes, from the small fry cabaret operators he had snarled at in the old days. He could not change his hoodlum ways.

Though she soon was making thousands and thousands of dollars a week, Ruth Etting got no fun out of life whatever. Rehearsals and performances—stage, screen, radio, phonograph recordings—consumed almost all her waking hours—and at the end of every weary day there was Snyder, always angry, always suspicious of his fellow creatures, always

burning with rage about one thing or another, usually imaginary.

She never could go anywhere, except with him. No one ever saw her in a night club or at a party. No man dared even to smile at her in Snyder's presence. As Jack Miley once wrote in his Broadway style, "Snyder is a rugged hombre from Chicago. He is likely to bend anybody into a hoop and roll him home if he catches him slipping his frau a sly ogle. That is one of the reasons why Ruth is the most un-ogled girl on Broadway—the boys all know the Gimp."

Meanwhile the money rolled in. Ruth herself had little spare time to enjoy the riches she was making. Indeed, she preferred to spend her leisure hours designing and making her own clothes. But Moe, an inveterate gambler since his early days in Chicago, discovered lots of ways to play with their income. He dabbled in the stock market, which was booming then, played the horses, and also bet heavily on ball games and prize fights. It has often been said that the "Colonel" would bet on anything.

BY 1929 just about everything they possessed was invested in "sure thing" Wall Street stocks—and when the financial crash struck the country they were completely wiped out. Moe, it appeared, had made a few more wrong bets.

This blow hit Ruth particularly hard because she had just about decided to quit show business. She had made more than enough on which to retire. Now she must start anew. She gritted her teeth and told herself that when she made $300,000 she would thumb her nose at Broadway and go back to the farm she had bought in Nebraska.

She voiced this ambition often in subsequent interviews. (Snyder would never let her be interviewed except in his presence.) She would quit as soon as she had made enough, she said: Broadway held no glamor for her. "It's hard, it's tiring," she said. "It's a world of throat-cutting. It's not my world, and never was. I'm a country girl, and that's the life I want."

Snyder never could take this seriously. "That's all right to tell the dumb reporters," he told her, with that ever-present sneer, "but don't think you're gonna drag me away from this town!"

"All I want is a little peace and quiet—some leisure to do the things I've always wanted to do," she said. "I never was meant for the stage in the first place. As soon as I can I'm going to get away from it—far away."

"Meanwhile," he growled, "you've got plenty work to do."

Ruth sighed. That was only too true. Three hundred thousand. . . . It would take years to make all that, years of living in hotel rooms, years of driving, exhausting work. And even then—what of her hopes for peace, what of her dreams of a home?

The precious years slipped by, and that dream of happiness still hovered like a will o' the wisp over the horizon. Youth had disappeared long since, though she still retained that freshness of face and loveliness of form which had won her such admiration in Chicago. Happiness . . . peace . . . love . . . were these jewels of great price ever to be within her reach?

Meanwhile success piled upon success. In July, 1932, she was voted "Queen of Radio" in a popularity contest. She went to Hollywood and starred in million-

dollar musical productions. She—and Snyder—bought a magnificent estate on Ambassador Drive, in exclusive Beverly Hills. A home of her own? Well, hardly. It never could rate that description so long as Snyder stalked and stamped about, ever angry, ever suspicious, ever raging against someone about some fancied slight or wrong.

The "rugged hombre from Chicago" never relaxed in his campaign of "carrying the torch" for Ruth. Whether he was in Lindy's on Broadway, a favorite hangout with him, or in the Brown Derby in Hollywood, she invariably became almost his sole topic of conversation. It was plain to everyone who met him that Ruth was the be-all and end-all of his existence. He seemed incapable of thinking of anything else for more than a few minutes at a time.

"He eyed everyone with mistrust," wrote columnist Ed Sullivan, "and he limped through the world with a cigar in his mouth, a sour look in his face, and the 'little lady' in his heart."

Ruth watched desperately for some change in him, some sign of recovery from this almost insane devotion. If only he would come to his senses and see how much she wanted her freedom! If only he were to fall in love with some other woman! But there seemed no chance of any such happy eventuality. If Snyder ever dallied with other women, they were merely passing fancies. His wife and his gambling remained his two consuming passions in life.

IN THE spring of 1935 Ruth admitted to reporters that she wanted to retire—that she would definitely retire early in 1936 after she had fulfilled her current radio and motion picture contracts. The truth was that she was tired, she said. She wanted to take a long, long rest far away from show business.

"It's been almost fifteen years since I started in the chorus and it's been lots of hard work," she sighed. "All my life I've wanted to take a trip around the world. I've never even been abroad."

Early the following year she and Edith Snyder, her sixteen-year-old stepdaughter, would board a ship on the Pacific Coast, Ruth continued, eyes shining with anticipation, and sail away on this dream voyage—Honolulu, the South Seas, Java, India, Siam, South Africa, South America, New York. They would probably travel on freighters because she wanted to dress as she pleased during the trip.

"I've been dressing up for fifteen years," she said, "and I'm tired of it."

She and Edith by this time had become great pals.

That summer of 1935 Ruth starred in a thirteen-week radio program staged at the N.B.C studio in Los Angeles. Her accompanist and arranger was a young man named Myrl Alderman.

Ruth found working with Alderman extremely pleasant. Handsome, well-built, with a very attractive personality, he was as different a sort of person from Moe Snyder as it was possible to imagine. Had she met someone like him, years ago, someone nearer her own age, life surely would have been something else than drudgery. . . .

The musician, at that time twenty-seven years old, had just recently contracted his second marriage. His first wife had been granted an interlocutory decree on the previous January 7, and two days later, despite the fact that re-marriage in California is illegal until one year has expired, he had married Alma Mott, an attractive young singer, at Tia Juana. He and Miss Mott had met a few months before their marriage, while he was playing in a band at a Long Beach R.K.O. theatre and she was singing in a trio on the same bill.

Ruth's radio contract expired in October, 1935, and it was to be two years before she again laid eyes on Myrl Alderman. They met by accident on Hollywood Boulevard, and they had lots to tell each other.

Alderman's second marriage had failed, he told her. He and Alma had been separated since the previous May. As for Ruth, she admitted that life had not changed much for her. True, she had just about retired now, but Moe was still carrying the torch, still snarling at everyone, still making life miserable. She had realized one ambition and gone abroad, but thanks to Snyder the trip had been a nightmare.

Manager Moe had contracted for her to star in a London musical production, then alienated everybody in sight with his uncouth tactics. She had been mortified as she had never been before in all her association with him. Finally the production had been abandoned and she had returned home, resolved to have nothing more to do with the theatre.

Had she and Edith made that wonderful voyage around the world, Alderman wanted to know. Sadly she shook her head. The nearest she had come to realizing that particular dream had been a lovely vacation with Edith at Honolulu.

"Edith is my secretary now," she added.

"What about your music?" he asked. "Surely, you're not going to quit that!"

"I'm not so sure I could!" she laughed.

Myrl told her that he would like to do her arranging, as he had two years before. He recalled how pleasant had been their association then—and so did she. As he talked, so full of enthusiasm himself, he aroused new ambitions within her. For the moment, at least, that trapped feeling seemed to dissipate. She found herself agreeing that she could not give up her singing.

"We must get together," he said, "and talk all this over."

She thought that would be very nice.

As it happened, Snyder was out of town. He'd gone to Chicago to see his ailing mother.

Ruth and Myrl met again—and again. They had dinner engagements. There were evenings at his apartment when they talked about teaming up in their music work. Delightful, comfortable, tranquil evenings.

How charming he is. . . . How sweet she is. . . .

When next Ruth saw her husband she knew that, come what might, she must have her freedom. Though she took her very life in her hands, she faced him and told him that she wanted to go her own way, that there must be a divorce, that she would pay him well for her freedom. They no longer had mutual interests, she pointed out, since she preferred a quiet retirement in Hollywood, and possibly later in Nebraska, while he preferred Broadway, the race tracks, the sporting, gambling world in which she had never moved.

Snyder raged and wept, stomped about and shook his fists, but in the end he gave in because, as he put it, he wanted her to be happy. She was still his sweet little lady—whatever she wanted he wanted for her. Nothing else mattered. Then he

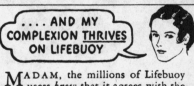

A ticket of admission to previews of all the big hit pictures! That's what the ten cents you pay for MOVIE STORY Magazine buys you. These previews are in the form of thrilling, full-length story versions of the films, and are generously illustrated with beautiful pictures from the movie itself. This month Clark Gable and Norma Shearer are first on the program, in their new dramatic smash hit, "Idiot's Delight." And there are ten other movie stories and features for you to enjoy! You'll want to buy MOVIE STORY this month—and every month!

MOVIE STORY
MAGAZINE

March Issue Now On Sale!

brought up the question of a settlement. After all, he'd been her manager; he'd discovered her, he'd fought for her and got her onto Broadway. He rated plenty for what he'd done for her, didn't he?

So Ruth paid his gambling debts totalling $50,000, turned over to him some $25,000 in stocks and bonds, and also gave him a half interest in their Beverly Hills estate. The divorce was granted in Chicago, November 30, 1937, the grounds being cruelty. Incredible as it seemed to her, Ruth Etting was at last free of Moe the Gimp.

OR SO she thought—so she hoped. . . . After the divorce, Ruth moved with Edith into an apartment (the Ambassador Drive estate having been rented for $400 a month) while Snyder returned East with his bankroll. He began gambling heavily.

Early in January he read in Ed Sullivan's column that Ruth had a new "boy friend," and immediately went into a tantrum. He telephoned Ruth via long distance, with the result that she hastened to the office of District Attorney Buron Fitts to ask for protection. Snyder, she related, had telephoned her, apparently from New York, and told her that he would take a plane out to the coast and kill her. Fitts assigned two investigators from his office as bodyguards for her.

Moe failed to show up. Nevertheless, she bought a revolver, determined to defend herself should he attempt to carry out his threat. Snyder was questioned by the authorities in New York, regarding his alleged threat to kill his former wife, and he assured them that it "didn't mean a thing." Why, he'd never harm a hair of her head, he said.

He continued to carry the torch. Indeed, he seemed more obsessed than ever. To lose Ruth was bad enough; to lose her to another man was unendurable. "I go home and I come right out again," he told anyone who would listen to him. "I walk the streets all night. I can't sleep."

When his money ran out, he raved on, he would "hit myself in the topper with a coupla slugs and call it a day."

At Lindy's he would smash his fists against the wall until they were bleeding, then he would all but sob, "My heart is bleeding just like that—for her." Associates who witnessed all this were agreed that Ruth would not have to worry much longer, because the "Colonel" would soon find a way to end things for himself. They didn't see how it could go on much longer.

Moe the Gimp "blew his wad." And then headed for Hollywood.

On Saturday evening, October 15, Ruth and Edith were preparing supper in Alderman's blue and white cottage on Lake Hollywood Drive. Myrl, employed at the NBC studio, would be home any minute—and this *was* his home, although shortly it would be Ruth's, too, as soon as his divorce became final early in December. She sang softly to herself as she attended the pots on the stove; she was at last a happy woman. The future stretched out ahead of her like a magic carpet, a rosy vista of peace and contentment with the man of her dreams.

Here is what happened within the next few minutes, according to the story she told over and over to the authorities:

Above the sound of the radio in the music room, where Edith sat, Ruth heard the sound of the car. Then Myrl's dog began to bark. She went to the kitchen door and opened it.

To her horror she saw Snyder, gun in hand, pushing Myrl ahead of him toward the house. Myrl's face was white. He kept shaking his head negatively at her, as though to warn her to get back into the house. But she could only stand there, petrified.

The men entered the kitchen. Ruth noted a wild, almost insane glare in Moe's eyes.

"Well, I've caught up with you two at last," he growled. "I've got you at last!"

She tried to pull herself together, to face this dreadful emergency. "Now, Moe, what is the use of doing anything foolish? We all have our lives to live, and if you kill us what good is it going to do you?"

"Whose car is that in the garage?"

"Edith's."

"Call her."

His daughter came. He snarled, "You're in this with them, and I'm going to bump you off, too."

He ordered them to line up. He herded them into the hallway, then into the music room.

"Sit down—all of you!"

Alderman sat on the piano bench, Ruth on the divan. Edith stood facing her father, back against the wall, betraying no fear.

"Sit down, damn you!" he shouted. "Sit down or I'll drill you!"

"Go ahead," she retorted. "If you want to shoot me, then shoot me!"

Ruth cut in. "Please sit down, Edith." The girl did so. Ruth continued, trying her hardest to be calm and persuasive. "Moe, what is the use of all this nonsense? Why don't you look at this the smart way?"

He sat down, glaring at her. Alderman began to say something.

"Shut up!" Snyder all but screamed the words.

And then he fired twice.

Ruth saw Myrl slump to the floor. She believed he had been killed. She believed Snyder would turn the gun on her and Edith.

Fortunately, at the very moment that Alderman fell, the one light bulb in the room flickered out. The concussion of the shots had jarred it loose. For the moment, at least, she was protected by the darkness.

"Where are you? Where are you?" she heard Moe shout. "Now you can call the police!"

Ruth managed to get out of the opposite door from the one Snyder barricaded. She dashed into a bedroom and got her own gun out of a drawer—the gun she had bought for just such a horrible moment. She turned on the light, and then he found her again. She held the gun behind her back.

"What have you got there, you——!"

He closed in on her. He wrenched the gun out of her hand.

Now, indeed, the end seemed at hand. But then Edith rushed in. She gave her father a shove that enabled Ruth to break away and run for the kitchen. Moe threw Ruth's weapon into the hallway as he hastened after her.

Again he reckoned without Edith, who had found the gun in the hallway. She fired one shot, the bullet striking some dishes in the kitchen cupboard. Snyder ran out the back door, knocking over the garbage pail.

By this time Ruth was outside, too. Edith pulled her back and slammed the door in her father's face.

They called the police, then tried to

administer first aid to Alderman, who had been struck once in the stomach. When officers arrived, Snyder was pacing back and forth in front of the house. They placed him under arrest and took his gun, a .38 calibre short-barreled automatic whose serial numbers had been filed off.

THE prisoner was charged with kidnaping, attempted murder, and with violation of the state firearms law. At the Hollywood police station he demanded an attorney and refused to make a statement.

Now the ambulance came. Ruth wept frantically as Myrl was carried out. Would he live? Would he live? They couldn't say—yet.

She told the police that Snyder had waylaid the musician as he left the NBC studio, and forced him at gun-point to drive to the cottage. "He was insanely jealous," she said. "He couldn't stand the thought of me having happiness with anyone else." (She said at this time that she and Myrl had been married since July.) "I've been ecstatically happy. Moe just couldn't stand it. He called me on long distance last January and told me that if I didn't come back to him he would kill me."

An examination at the hospital soon disclosed that the bullet had touched no vital part. It had merely passed through the abdominal wall. Ruth wept for joy. She took a room in St. Vincent's Hospital to be near the patient night and day. Gladly she posed for pictures stroking Myrl's hair and clasping his hand tightly in hers. "I'm lucky to be alive," she said. "If it weren't for Edith I'm sure he'd have shot me, too. Edith saved my life." Told that Moe had been locked up, she exclaimed, "Thank God! I feel safer now."

Edith sobbed, "I don't know yet whether I'm sorry I missed my dad or whether I am glad."

Meanwhile, the accused man gave his version of what happened. "I shot in self-defense," he insisted to the police. "Alderman pulled a gun on me when I went to talk to my former wife about some business problems. There was plenty of shooting going on that I didn't do at all. Ruth knows what happened and she won't prosecute me. I have to laugh at the story that my daughter fired a shot at me. That's ridiculous. Do you think she would shoot me after all I've done for her?"

Ruth, told of this statement by Snyder, declared Alderman had never had a gun in his hands in his life. "It all happened exactly as I've told it," she said. "The only offence that boy committed was that he was a good husband to me and made me happier than I have ever been in my life before."

Still maintaining the pose about having married Alderman in Tia Juana the previous July, she explained the simplicity of the seven-room cottage—a strong contrast to the Beverly Hills estate—by saying that she wanted to get back to the simple life. She wanted to do her own housework and cooking.

"I was all through with big city life," she said. "I wouldn't go back to Broadway if you gave me the street. That was what enraged Snyder. New York to him is the whole world. He's gone through everything and is probably about broke. He threw away everything I gave him. He has already had more than the average man has in a life-time."

Later she denied that she had been

"My Make-Up Secret"

BETTE DAVIS
Star in Warner Bros. Feature Picture, "Ex-Lady"

"The secret of perfect make-up I learned from Hollywood's make-up genius, Max Factor...that my powder, rouge and lipstick must be in color harmony to blend with my own complexion colorings. You know that for years Max Factor has created make-up for the stars and studios of Hollywood, so it is only natural that I follow his advice for both screen and street make-up. Perhaps these suggestions will help you to find new beauty with make-up."

Now the luxury of color harmony make-up, created originally for the screen stars by Hollywood's make-up genius, is available to you at nominal prices... Max Factor's Face Powder, one dollar; Max Factor's Rouge, fifty cents; Max Factor's Super-Indelible Lipstick, one dollar. Featured by leading stores.

For your own personal make-up color harmony chart, mail coupon to Max Factor.

1. "For my colorings...blonde hair, blue eyes and fair skin...I use Max Factor's Rachelle Powder. Its color harmony tone is perfect for me...and it creates a satin-smooth make-up that clings for hours which every screen star depends upon. And here's a hint about powdering...always pat it on, removing surplus with the face powder brush."

2. "Pat on a touch of rouge following the natural curve of the cheekbone... and then soften the edges by blending with the finger tips. To be sure of correct color harmony, I use Max Factor's Blondeen Rouge...its delicate texture and creamy smoothness help a lot in blending a beautiful, soft coloring."

3. "Always dry your lips and keep them dry when applying lipstick. Make up the upper lip first and trace this lip contour on the lower lip by simply compressing the lips together; then fill in. Max Factor's Super-Indelible Vermilion Lipstick completes my make-up color harmony...it's moisture-proof, permanent in color and lasts all day, which are three good reasons why I use it."

P. S. "Of course, in my new picture, "Ex-Lady" I use Max Factor's Make-Up exclusively, too. In fact, in every feature picture from every studio you can actually see how perfect Max Factor's Make-Up is."

Max Factor's *Society* Make-Up
Cosmetics of the Stars ★ HOLLYWOOD
Face Powder...Rouge...Lipstick...*in Color Harmony*

living at the Lake Hollywood Drive address. She said the house wasn't even furnished yet, that Alderman was living there alone. "There were just a few things there," she said.

"Oh, yeah?" Moe snorted. "What was her sewing machine doing there? I saw it. Besides, she said she ran into the bedroom to get her gun. She was living there, all right! She was waiting for Bill Bacher's lease to be up at our house in Beverly Hills so she could take enough furniture out of that house to furnish this place she bought on Lake Hollywood Drive!"

Still later Ruth was to say that the cottage was being furnished for Myrl and his mother. She denied that she had bought it.

Reporters checked the marriage records at Tia Juana, and could find no trace of the purported ceremony. Ruth, worn out from her constant vigil at Myrl's bedside, smiled wanly and wistfully and hinted that everything would be cleared up early in December.

Two days after the shooting, Alma Alderman, divorced second wife of the wounded man, filed suit against Ruth for $150,000. She charged that Ruth had alienated his affections. Alderman in turn sued Snyder for $225,000 as the result of the attack.

Ruth denied that she had stolen Myrl's love. Through her attorneys she stated that, even if the accusation were true, it was now legally too late for Mrs. Alderman to do anything about it. Subsequently, on October 29, the harried songstress submitted to questioning by Alma's attorneys in the latter's office. Alma sat nearby, listening in.

Ruth admitted, first of all, that she and Myrl had not married.

"Did you sign any papers as Mrs. Alderman?" attorney S. S. Hahn asked.

"Yes," she replied. "I did the night of the shooting. Everyone was calling me Mrs. Alderman and I was so excited I didn't know just what I was doing. So I signed my name that way at the hospital."

"When people called you Mrs. Alderman didn't Myrl object?"

"We just laughed," was her reply. "I think the main reason Myrl didn't deny or affirm it was because he thought if it were believed we were married, Snyder wouldn't carry out his threats."

"Did you ever have marital relations with Mr. Alderman?"

"Absolutely not!"

She denied that she had ever spent the night with him at the cottage, or anywhere else. On the night of the shooting she had simply been preparing supper. It was her practice to cook the evening meal two or three times a week.

As a matter of fact, she had become infatuated with Myrl, had she not? Ruth managed to answer this question ambiguously, saying, "I don't know. I felt a great responsibility for the shooting and

we'd had many happy hours together after the divorces."

The wounded man recovered rapidly. Soon he was able to leave the hospital. As Snyder in the meantime had won his freedom on bail, Alderman remained in an undisclosed retreat, pending the trial.

MOE the Gimp exuded confidence as he went on trial early in December on five felony counts. If convicted, he faced prison terms totalling more than the average lifetime. He seemed perfectly convinced that he would not be convicted, that he would win his freedom with his story of sacrifice and struggle on Ruth's behalf, and his version of what happened at the cottage on Lake Hollywood Drive. He had retained to defend him none other than Jerry Giesler, perhaps the most celebrated criminal lawyer in Los Angeles.

ARE YOU MARRIED—AND HAPPY?

—Do you warn young people to have a good time before it's too late?

—Do you enjoy having strangers think you're single?

—Do you mind having your husband show up when you're talking to an attractive man?

—Do you talk about how much you gave up for marriage?

—Do you tell people that no one understands you?

—Have you made up your mind not to have children?

Answer these questions honestly, and test yourself. The more "no" answers you have—the more likely it is that you are glad you're married!

Six men and six women filled the jury box on December 9, and then Prosecutor U. U. Blalock opened his case.

Ruth, Edith and Myrl told their stories. There was no variation from the stories they had already told the authorities. They insisted repeatedly that Snyder had been the aggressor, and they repeated their belief that he had intended to kill them all, and would have done so had he not been frustrated. They merely wished to be left in peace, they said—and Snyder had come with a gun in his hand and blasted away their hopes.

Having testified, Ruth and Myrl then managed to accomplish a very much desired item in their plans for happiness. Early the morning of December 14, with the trial still in session, they flew to Las Vegas, Nevada, and were married there in the chambers of Judge William E. Orr. Then they flew back to Los Angeles—and sat holding hands while the defendant wept his way through his story.

"We're too happy to be angry at anyone," Ruth sighed. "We'll be happy forever!"

Snyder, on the witness stand, told how he had worked and slaved for Ruth all those years, from the time he first met her in Chicago in 1920 until she had reached the peak of the entertainment world as a high-paid star of stage, screen and radio; how she had discarded him

when she no longer needed him. He repeated his story of going to the cottage to discuss some business matters, and insisted that he had shot Alderman purely in self-defense.

Moe wept some more, later, when Giesler, in his final plea to the jury, likened his client's love for Ruth to that of "the Hunchback of Notre Dame" for beauteous but fickle Esmeralda.

Giesler pointed out that Miss Etting had departed from the Esmeralda role by marrying her crippled protector and living with him for fifteen years. "As long as she could benefit from this union, she kept this cripple," the lawyer shouted. "But when she was all through with her public life and wanted to play, she cast him out and looked about for a younger man.

"Esmeralda, too, wanted a younger man —a man who was physically whole. When she found him she left the cathedral, where she was sheltered and safe, and was hanged. They found the Hunchback dead at her bier, finally reunited with his love."

Referring to Ruth's romance with Alderman, the lawyer continued:

"She went out on the market and bought a playmate, for I tell you as surely as we are standing in this courtroom that Myrl Alderman sold himself for gold. He is a used article. This is his third marriage, and although I wish them all the happiness in this world, I do not think they will get it."

He referred to the elopement, then added, "I ask you not to give Ruth Etting the wedding present she wants. The wedding present that would make her the happiest would be the conviction of the defendant."

But Giesler did not do all the name-calling in those final appeals. Prosecutor Blalock in his closing rebuttal called the defendant everything from "gangster," "fingerman," and "gambler," to "libertine" and "kept man."

The case went to the jury late the afternoon of December 20. They wrangled for two full days. According to unofficial reports, some were in favor of sending the Gimp up for a heavy stretch; others held that he had shot without premeditation. Finally they agreed upon a conviction upon one of the five counts —the attempted murder of Myrl Alderman.

Free at long last from the domination of the Gimp, Ruth Etting and her husband stand on the threshold of a new life—a life more in line with Ruth's heart's desire. What matter if other lawsuits are pending against her? With the Gimp in jail—no matter how long or short his sentence—she can breathe easier.

Hand in hand with the man she loves, even Moe Snyder can no longer touch her. That chapter in her life is closed out—and the new chapter should bring her the happiness she so richly merits.

●

THE 1940'S

· Truth is Stranger Than Fiction ·

The next day the campus was agog with the latest sensation—about Les Saunders! "Did you know he was going to do it, Sue?" the girls exclaimed. "You were with him yesterday."

I WALKED with a little swagger these days, not just because I wore a becoming navy blue uniform and had passed the rather stiff requirements of the Waves—which as everyone knows by now stands for Women Assigned for Volunteer Emergency Service — but mostly because I had finally got Lester Saunders out of my blood—or so I thought.

I tried not to think about it any more than I had to, and that wasn't hard, because to be an ensign in the Waves means hard work. I was sent to school first, then delegated to train other Waves. Life was new and interesting, and I thought, "That other part of my life is finished and done. I need never think of it again."

It had happened at the university when I was twenty. Lester had been handsome in a tall, tantalizing way with a quick mocking grin and a reputation for being dangerous.

There are so many different kinds of love that you sometimes wonder how you can know the real thing. It seems like the real thing at the time, and then, when it is over, you wonder how you could have been so blind, so stupid.

I thought that I was so irrevocably in love with Lester that if anything happened to that love I wouldn't want to live any more. Things that he did could hurt me with an unbearable agony, and I know now that he knew it and gloried

I stood there completely icy, frozen. How could they guess that it was guilt that held me silent?

Interrupted Elopement

She could, and did, turn her back on his love, but was there anything that could make her forget him?

in it. There was a streak of cruelty in him and I recognized it vaguely, but nothing seemed to matter but our love.

When we planned on getting married, my parents begged me to wait. They didn't like Lester, I knew, but they gave as their reason that we were both too young and that it would be wiser if we waited until we were through college.

But Lester was impatient with anything that thwarted his desires. To have someone try to keep me from him made me seem more desirable.

Sometimes in his arms I couldn't think, couldn't reason. But when he asked me to go on a week-end trip with him, every decent instinct within me revolted. I thank God now that I was that sane. There have been too many girls to make that fatal mistake and live to regret it.

I tried to put Lester out of my life then, telling myself that he couldn't really love me or he would never have suggested such a thing to me. I wouldn't see him for several weeks. The college newspaper's gossip column said: "What well-known campus couple have pfft—as our Big City rival columnist would say? And how soon will they make up?"

Well, it wasn't long. He came back and told me how sorry he was, that he had wanted me so much that he had risked everything to get me. He had an irresistible charm. There was something in him that stirred girls and thrilled them—and I loved him. It was my first love—

young, ardent, crazy. He hadn't been able to get me one way, and so he tried another.

"Run away with me, Lil," he pleaded. "We can drive to Doversville after the football game, get married there, and no one will be the wiser. We'll come back to school, and our parents needn't know about it until we graduate. In that way we'll both keep on getting our allowances and we can be together when we want, with everything all legal and proper, and no one will know but. us. Please, darling!"

The lips that pressed mine were eager. The arms that held me were tight and possessive. Things began to swim, to spin around just as they always did when Lester held me like that.

I tried to be sensible, tried to realize that this thing we were about to do was wrong. But that Saturday, tucked in beside him in the front of his car, I let his pleas overcome my reason. He had the ring in his pocket, the license. He had got them many *(Continued)*

Interrupted Elopement

days before. He was that sure of me!

We left before the football game was over. We drove toward Doversville, Lester's arm around me, holding me close. There was a funny feeling in the pit of my stomach. "Stage fright!" I told myself scornfully. But somehow it seemed to go deeper than that. I had never planned this kind of a wedding. There was to be a church, a white satin gown, my kid sister Madge as maid of honor, and my mother and father, proud and distinguished, in the front pew.

I wanted to cry, "Oh, let's not do it, Les. Let's turn around and go back. If we really love each other, it shouldn't be hard to wait."

But I knew that he would only laugh at me, only kiss me into a helpless ecstasy. And then there was the thought that I might lose him for good. He was young, popular and there were other girls on the campus who looked at him yearningly and whom he had regarded with a speculative eye.

THESE thoughts were spinning crazily through my brain when I saw a country wagon drawn by a horse ahead of us. Les was going too fast. He always drove too fast, but he never paid any attention to you when you cautioned him—not even to the campus special officers who had threatened to take away his license.

"Watch it, darling," I warned now.

Les laughed. "I'm going to scare the devil out of the old guy," he said. "Some of these farmers never get a thrill from one year to the next. I'll swerve just as I get to him."

"Les! Don't!" I said sharply and pulled away from his arm.

He meant to get as close to the horse as he could. I'd seen him do it before to horses and other cars. Then, just when the other person thought that an accident was unavoidable and was probably terrified out of his wits, Les would pull out with a fair margin of safety and grin mockingly back over his shoulder.

That's what he meant to do now. But he missed! Oh, dear God, will I ever be able to forget that horrible, sickening crash, the sound of the splintering wagon, the rearing horse—and then, in the road, the crumpled, shabby overalled figure of the old man! It lay very still.

Les had jammed on his brakes, but now he put the car in reverse and was backing out of the wreckage of the wagon. It was evident that we were unharmed except perhaps for scratched and dented fenders and bumper.

I had screamed and hidden my face, but now I had my hand on the latch of the door. Lester's voice was harsh, his face white and scared. "Sit still, you little fool!" he commanded. "We've got to get away from here as quickly as we can."

I was crying, but now I stopped in sheer horror. "Get away!" I gasped. "Are you crazy, Les? We've got to get out and see what we can do, get that old man to a doctor as soon as possible!"

"And have a charge of manslaughter slapped onto us and a devil of a mess with our families and be expelled from school!" he retorted hoarsely. "Don't be a dope! If we get away before anyone sees us, we're okay."

"You do what you want," I said wildly, "but I'm going to stay right here and do what I can. Oh, you utter coward and rotter!"

My hand was on the latch again, but Les jerked me back. He slammed the car in gear and headed down the highway at such a speed that it would have been suicide to try to leap out. I screamed at him. I tried to tear his hands from the wheel. I think I went a little crazy at the thought of that still figure lying back there in the road.

But Les, physically stronger than I was, kept me away from him with one hand while he drove furiously with the other. And finally I subsided, crying bitterly, tragically, in a small heap in the corner.

When Les finally spoke in that new harsh voice, I thought that I couldn't bear it. He said, "We couldn't bring him back to life, could we? We'd only be getting ourselves into a mess. I'm sorry. But if you go to the authorities, if you drag me into it—"

I think he threatened to kill himself. I don't know. I was too steeped in misery and fear and horror.

He drove me back to my sorority house. I tried to drag myself to the telephone, tried to call the police, but I couldn't. God help me, I couldn't do that to Les!

THE next morning the campus was agog with the latest sensation—about Les Saunders. He had left college the night before and driven into town and enlisted in the Army!

"Isn't he marvelous!" the girls exclaimed. "Did you know he was going to do it, Sue? You were with him yesterday! Did he tell you then?"

They probably thought that I was angry about it, hurt, because I stood there so completely icy and frozen. How could they guess it was guilt that held me silent? I was still hearing the crash of the wagon, still seeing that frail old figure thrown into the road. I went to a pay station that day and called the town nearest to the spot at which the accident had happened. I knew they wouldn't be able to trace the call, and I had to know. I had to know.

Yes, I was told, a hit-and-run driver had wrecked a farmer's wagon on the road and knocked the farmer off the seat into the road. No, he wasn't dead, but an arm and leg and some ribs had been broken, and bones heal slowly when you're old. The police were trying to locate who had done it—and who was this calling, the constable asked. I hung up then, but I had already learned the old man's name and his rural free delivery mail route number.

I had some money saved up for a fur coat. The family had given me gifts of money on birthdays and Christmases so that it would swell my fund. I sent every bit of that money to the old man anonymously, and every once in a while I would call the village store in the town near his farm to find out how he was getting along. They never traced the calls or the money. I was careful about that. But even when I knew he was on the road to recovery, I had a hard time forgetting him.

No one ever connected Les with the accident. Although he never came back to school, he became a sort of campus hero—one of the first boys from college to enlist. And everyone wondered why I never spoke of him and thought I hadn't wanted him to go into the Army.

He wrote to me. That was how great his assurance was! He wrote and said he was sorry it had happened, but that I could see the spot he was in. Even if the old guy wasn't dead, there would have been ructions about the whole thing. "Unless they send me overseas right away, I'll come home on furlough and we can talk things over," he wrote. "I'm sure you've calmed down by now and can see my side of it."

BUT I didn't hear from him after that, and I was glad. I finished my year and a half more of school and, eager to do my bit, put my application into the Waves. I'd had a grandfather who was a rear admiral and a brother who was a naval lieutenant, and my kid sister Madge had just married a young Navy flier. So I thought that the family might as well be completely seagoing.

I was just beginning to feel like a human being again—that's what a man like Les can do to you! But I knew definitely that I was afraid of love. It was all right for everyone else, but a burned child dreads the fire. Suppose, I'd think, that accident had happened after Les and I had been to Doversville and got married instead of before we reached there! Suppose I had married a man like that and hadn't found out completely what he was until too late!

You can't blame me for feeling a little doubtful about men and love. And then I met Dick Raedy at a Service dance!

He was Lieut. Richard Raedy of the Army Air Corps, and he pointed out to me that first night that Waves were permitted to marry—that is, anyone except a Navy man. "Which makes me pretty darned glad I picked the Army," he said, grinning down at me.

There were a lot of physical differences between Les and Dick. While Les had been almost too handsome, Dick wouldn't be called handsome in any conventional sense. He had nice cool gray eyes under well-defined brows. His mouth was too wide, with a lift to the upper lip and a rebel corner that tilted even when he was grave, and was mischievous and boyish when he laughed. The nose was a good nose, long and straight, and his chin firm and square with a scar that was like a cleft set crooked. But he was merely a well-tanned, well-exercised and trained young flier at the peak of his physical fitness. Yet there was an attraction between us so strong and so tangible that I felt a helpless wonder.

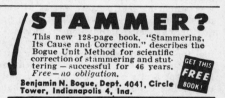
We saw a lot of each other, considering the fact that we were both putting in many hours a day in the service of our country. And I think my little swagger and the proud tilt of my shoulders under my uniform became even more pronounced, because I was happy now—happier than I had ever been in my life. I was completely over my bitterness about Les Saunders, although I still had the feeling of waking, cold and clammy, from some horrible nightmare and knowing it was a nightmare and still not being able to throw off the dread and shock of it.

And then one night I found myself in Dick Raedy's arms. The aroma of tobacco filled my nostrils as my chin pressed hard against his shoulder until he lifted it with a brown hand and found my mouth with his own.

This wasn't like loving Les had been. This was peace and heaven, glorious understanding, and happiness. We made plans to get married when we could both get a few days' leave. It still wouldn't be a white-satin-and-bridesmaids sort of wedding, because I would have to be married in my uniform. But my mother and father would be there, and they liked Dick and trusted him.

AND then, in the midst of this happiness Les came back. He had changed. He was older-looking, stronger-looking. His eyes were clearer, more direct, his shoulders straighter. I almost didn't recognize him when I saw him waiting for me in the street in back of the drill grounds. I don't know how he had found out where I was. But there he stood!

He said, "You have every right to hate me, Lil, but please don't. I've changed. I'm not like I used to be. I've changed a lot in the Army—and a lot about square-shooting. You don't have to tell me what a heel I used to be. I know."

He had foreign service stripes. "Australia," he told me quietly. "And I saw a little action there." There was a wound stripe, too. "I'll be going back," he said. "But I had to see you—had to tell you that the memory of you has been with me everywhere I went. I'm still carrying the ring and a marriage license that has grown a little battle-scarred and frayed, but we could still use it, sweet."

"That's over," I said sharply. "You have no business carrying that license. Give it to me or burn it up. I—I'm different, Les, just as you are different. We've both changed—grown up. Everything's different. I—I'm going to be married as soon as we can both get leave. Now, please go away and let me alone."

He wouldn't believe that I didn't still love him. He threatened to go to Dick, to show him the ring and the license, to tell him that I had belonged to him first.

He caught me in his arms in back of a clump of trees where no one could see us. He was fighting now with the only weapon he was sure of, his charm. Tipping my head back, he kissed me long, expertly, as only he could kiss and despite my struggles.

When he let me go, I was weak and shaky. "You still love me!" he said triumphantly. "Whether you know it or not, you've never got over me. You never will. Just as I'll never get over you. You can't hold the past against me, Lil. I was a crazy kid. I didn't know what I was doing. I've changed. You've got to give me a chance."

But, free of his arms, I turned and fled. Over and over I told myself that it was Dick I loved—and I knew that it was true. But what would I do about Les? He still had the ruthless determination to get what he wanted, and I knew he would make trouble between Dick and me if he could.

All my new-found happiness was clouded by the shadow of Les. He phoned me. He waited for me. I did everything I could to avoid him, told him again and again that everything was over between us. I didn't want to tell Dick how Les was bothering me, because I was afraid there would be trouble. I didn't want to go to Les's commanding officer unless I had to, because that would be embarrassing for me and would be a permanent mark on his record which he seemed to have kept pretty good. But finally I had to tell Les if he didn't let me alone, that was what I was going to do.

He looked down at me. "If you can kiss me and then still tell me that everything is over between us, that you love someone else, I'll go away—for good," he said harshly.

He gripped my arms, his muscles tensing under his khaki jacket, his face dark with pain. I found myself remembering how I had loved him all those gay, young college days, our quarrels and then the wild sweetness of our kisses when we made up. Even remembering now brought back that confusing, tearing ache.

"You've been my reality, my everything," he said. "I knew what you must think of me, and I made myself over just for you. And now you let me down as casually as though I had never mattered to you at all."

Suddenly I wanted to laugh—wildly, crazily. I had let him down! He dared stand there and say I had let him down. Oh, yes, he had changed, but how could that erase the past, how could it bring back the freshness and the ecstasy of a love that had been torn to shreds? He was taking advantage of his knowledge of women—knowing that we cling more to the past, that we are sentimental and

soft. But were we? I had been weak once in my love for him, but I had learned strength—and I had met Dick!

There was a love that demanded and took, never gave—that was Les. There was a love that enveloped and protected —that was Dick. How lucky that I had found out in time! A little old man lying in the road had changed the course of my life. The little old man was all right now. He was back working in his fields.

But Les didn't know that. He didn't even care. It was something that hadn't caught up with him. Did people ever change underneath? Even if they did, wasn't there still a price they had to pay for the things of the past?

I knew now what was in his mind, that now in his extremity, he might dare try to waken me to that wild, unreasoning

❀❀❀❀❀❀❀❀❀❀❀❀❀❀❀

My Heart Is Sure!

I've been in love before, my dear,
    I really must confess,
But oh, this time I'm very sure
    I want to answer "yes."

For I have quite forgotten now
    Those other lads that I
Was sure I loved so dearly when
    A summer moon rode high.

But you have held my wayward heart
    In summer, spring and fall,
And all the passing seasons have
    Not changed my love at all.

If time is not the final test
    That romance will endure,
My heart's a better reason,
    Because oh, my heart is sure!

Catherine E. Berry.

❀❀❀❀❀❀❀❀❀❀❀❀❀❀❀

emotion people often mistake for love. Manlike, he believed that my lips must answer him if he demanded fiercely enough. To kill that belief forever I closed my eyes and took his kisses.

At last he drew a long breath and released me. "You—you weren't there, Lil," he said wretchedly. "You never would be there, no matter how closely I held you."

"I warned you," I whispered through pale, shaking lips. "I no longer love you, Les."

"I never believed you till now," he said

and turned and walked away, his broad shoulders slumped in utter defeat.

As I stood there and watched him go, I think something of me went with him, something that had been young and gay and heedless. But I had gained something, too, and I knew it. I had gained a new strength, a new self-respect. I could face things and conquer them. Maybe it was my uniform, maybe it was Dick, or maybe I had grown up at last.

WELL, Dick and I were married a few weeks ago. We each had three days' leave, and you'd be surprised how much happiness you can pack into three short days and nights! I knew that ours, come what may, was a marriage that would last as long as we both should live, because neither of us would ever let the other one down. It was a marriage where spirit and mind and body had found their perfect mates.

I knew that in a few days Dick would be sent away, but I had learned that nowadays you send your man away with a smile. That takes strength, too. But when he drew me into his arms to say good-by it was with a devotion that was not the fancy of a moment, but the kind with strength to last a lifetime. I was glad that God had let me wait for this.

Having a job to do and doing it well helps, too. I knew that by being in the Waves, I was doing almost as much for my country on this side of the water as Dick was doing wherever he was.

I got a letter from Dick yesterday— and I got something else, too. Both of them are here before me on the desk. Dick's letter was filled with love and strength and plans for the future. The other was a package done up and addressed in an unknown hand. It had been sent to my home and finally forwarded to me here at the Wave training center. In the letter was a frayed and soiled piece of paper with strange darkish spots on it— and a wedding ring. The piece of paper was a marriage license made out to Lilian Lloyd and Lester Saunders. Its date was four years ago. A marriage license that had not been used and a wedding ring that had never been needed!

The letter also contained a note that said, "If anything happens to me, please send these to Miss Lilian Lloyd at ——." And the letter explained that Sergeant Lester Saunders had been killed in action, and these articles had been found on his person.

I think that Les paid his debt to life bravely at the end, because we do pay for everything in one way or another. We pay for knowledge with tears, for love with pain, for life with death.

I cried a little over the memory of a boy I had loved, and the bitterness is gone. And now I shall burn the marriage license, and thank God that it was never used!

The ring I shall give to some Service Relief fund. My own small ring gleams on my finger as I write this. If anything should happen to Dick, I don't know how I could go on. But somehow I would, because he wouldn't like a coward. And I would have the comfort of knowing that I had found real love at last. ●

This is a picture of an eviction. Remember?

We don't think there will be any more pictures like it. But there *might* be. Yes, there *might* be if American families muff this greatest opportunity to put money aside in War Bonds.

Why?

Just this. We're all working now—and making good money—because there's a ready customer for what we make . . .WAR. He drives a hard bargain, that customer. In return for high wages he takes our sons, and husbands, and brothers, sometimes for keeps.

Families all over America are asking now if WAR is the only buyer big enough to make jobs enough. The answer is *no.* To have good wages and enough jobs after the war simply means that there must be a peacetime "customer" equally as big, with equally as much cold cash to spend. *And the only customer big enough is the American working public—you and your neighbor, his neighbor, and his.*

THIS WON'T BE YOUR FAMILY . . . OR WILL IT?

War Bonds today are the soundest, safest, surest way for American working families to have cold cash to spend after the war. That's why we say:
Every War Bond you buy now **WAR BONDS TODAY ARE JOB BONDS TOMORROW**
will be *cash* later on. You'll be able to buy some of the things you've had to do without—a car, a washing machine, or a new radio. And nearly 80 cents out of every dollar you will pay for that car, washing machine, or radio will go to *people,* as wages. Then *they* will have money. They will be able to buy what you make. *You* will get paid.

And it doesn't even stop there. For as *long* as people buy, people work. As long as people work, people buy. And if you and enough of your neighbors *have* that ready cash, there will be no more pictures of evictions or breadlines. No more "made work". No more handouts. Instead, there will be jobs, bank accounts, security—the America we all want.
—TRUE ROMANCES MAGAZINE

Suddenly cameras flashed and reporters were saying, "Any statement, Private Putnam? Does your mother know of your marriage?"

Shakedown

TODAY I got four letters from Putt in Sicily, every one of them full of love and faith. They make me happy and sad, too. I say to myself, "Fern, quit worrying. He can't find out. Nobody knew but you and Doris, and she probably has forgotten already."

I'll never forget, though, and I only pray I get a chance to make up to Putt—not for anything that happened, but for what might have been.

It all began last fall in Atlantic City. I, Fern Foster, was dancing in the chorus of the floor show at the Atlantic Club. Nineteen, red-headed, talented and pretty, I realized after two years in show business I wasn't pretty enough nor talented enough to get very far.

I was voted the prettiest girl in my high school class in Brooklyn, and my routine stopped the show at Elks' Hall, but there were prettier girls from other high schools and faster, trickier dancers from all over the country, and a lot

of them could sing, which I couldn't. Any doubts at all were settled when the New York agent shipped me to this third-rate night club where I was the youngest in the line.

A girl who called herself Doris Downes—copper-haired, hard, and past thirty—invited me to share the apartment with her. It wasn't much of an apartment, dingy, damp, and smelling of last year's wet bathing suits, but it was better than trying to find a rooming house or hotel with space, what with the Army taking over everything. The Army also took over the chorus. Doris talked to me about that.

"Look, Fern, a sweet, wholesome kid like you ought to get

out of this racket. Get yourself a nice soldier and marry him."

"And get one more headache?" I asked miserably. "I tell you I've got to make money. Mom needs my help now with Nan and Bernadette still in school, and Jim in the Navy."

"They'll get by. Families always do. Think of yourself."

But I did have to help Mom. Besides, these home-loving soldiers Doris talked about weren't so easy to find. All the boys I met at the club were looking strictly for fun, and most of them were being what Doris called "basically true" to a girl back home.

I sent Mom all I could, but the cost of living was going up in Atlantic City, too, and I had to eat. Lots of the girls got men to buy their meals, but I always met up with the kids who barely had the price of a cup of coffee.

When a showgirl down on her luck meets a naive lad in khaki on a 36-hour leave, a lot can happen—and does!

Marriage

Then, early in November, a new worry cropped up. Mickey Daley, who ran the club, said he was changing the show and putting in all specialties. Any girl who had a specialty could stay in the line; otherwise she was out.

I went to his office after the show, a tiny cluttered room with an old-fashioned roll-top desk and walls covered with pictures. Mickey was an unhappy-looking man with bags under his eyes and a hat perpetually on the back of his head.

"I haven't got a specialty, and I need the job," I said.

"You ain't as bad as you think," he said. "You're just losing your nerve." Those poached-egg eyes rolled over me.

"Why don't you do a strip? We got to be careful down here, but you could get away with a little one."

"A strip?" I felt my cheeks burn. "I—I wouldn't like that."

Mickey shrugged. "It's your funeral, kid. We got to put new pep in the show for the holidays. I'll give you a break if I can, but there it is."

I climbed down the long iron staircase, my hands icy on the rail. Strip tease! If Mom ever heard about that! Funny enough, she was proud of me. She thought it was nice to have a daughter in show business, and was always writing about when Hollywood "discovered me." I didn't tell her I photographed like a freak. Now what could I tell her?

I walked quickly along the dimmed-out streets, my hands thrust in the pockets of my windbreaker, my thoughts a deep indigo.

"Pardon me, boy, but do you have a match?"

I looked up quickly at the soldier standing under a shaded street light. "If this is a gag, it's not funny," I said curtly, and then I saw his face.

He was so young and looked so startled. He took off his peaked cap and smiled. Even with a GI haircut I could see his hair was curly, and he was actually blushing.

"I beg your pardon, miss, but in those slacks you do look like a boy."

"Okay, soldier," I said, and then as I dug a paper of matches from my pocket, "are you English?"

"I? Oh, no. My father's family have been in this country since before the Revolution."

"You still have the accent."

He offered me a cigarette, and I took it before I realized it was from a leather case and not a crumpled pack. "Strange about that, a chap in our outfit calls me Limey. You know that's an English expression. I did go to school in England for a while, a long time ago."

"It couldn't have been too long," I said, "since you started school."

"Ten years," he said. "You see I had a governess at first."

He was walking beside me then, and talking in that funny earnest way. I laughed. "You really have a line. I have to hand it to you for originality. How long can you keep it up?"

"I don't understand," he said blankly.

"Skip it," I said. "I won't cramp your act. It's a change but I've got to be getting along. It's late."

"I say, mayn't I see you home? It is too late for a girl to be out alone."

"Shouldn't you be in, too?"

"I've got a thirty-six-hour pass, but I had no place to go. I thought it would be rather fun *(Continued)* just to stay around, looking at things."

If this was an act, it was tops. We were passing a diner. I said, kidding, "Have you ever been in one of these?"

"I like them," he said earnestly. Then rather hesitantly, "You wouldn't want to go in there, would you?"

"For a hamburger and coffee? I sure would. What's your name?"

"Alexander Putnam," he said. I repeated it, trying not to giggle. After all, my right name was Veronica Madeline O'Hara. I said:

"I'm Fern Foster, from the show at the Atlantic Club and I'm going to call you Putt."

Elbow to elbow at the counter, we got better acquainted. I found out his full name was Alexander Prescott Putnam, III. He was twenty-one and had been in the Army three months. He had monograms on everything, wrist watch, cigarette case and a wallet that cost more than a private's monthly pay, and had at least the amount of a yearly pay in it.

"Why didn't you apply for a commission?" I asked.

"Actually I didn't have sufficient education. We traveled a great deal when I was a child. I spent part of my time in schools in England and France. Mother and I returned to this country three years ago. I found I could barely make the grade in a prep school. I worked hard—I really did—but I was so much older than the others, it wasn't very pleasant."

His smooth boyish face looked unhappy as he said it. Unconsciously I put my hand over his. "You're funny," I said, and then, "I don't mean funny. I don't know what I mean."

I smiled to make up for it, and he smiled back. He said, "I like you ever so much, Fern."

We walked home slowly. Once an MP stopped us to look at his pass, and I could see when Putt spoke to him, the MP wasn't sure whether or not he was being kidded. Putt was like that, but I knew then it was straight. He was just different.

Doris was asleep when I came in and gone when I woke up next morning. I wanted to talk to her, not only about Putt, but about the show. I'd almost forgotten that in the pleasant late hours. But it was still there and I was going to have to make up my mind in a hurry.

There was a letter from Mom that morning, saying Pop's back was worse and he was lucky to work two days a week. "Just when wages are good, too," she wrote unhappily, "but it cheers me up to think of you, having a good time and making money. I know you'll be a good girl and make the most of your fine chances."

Fine chances! To do a strip tease! I was doling out coffee into the one-cup pot when the bell rang and there was Putt. He had orchids, a five-pound box of candy, and an invitation to the movies and dinner. We had a grand time. He was so sweet, it was like going out with a kid brother. He didn't even hold my hand in the movies.

Over dinner, he told me a little about his mother. He had wanted to enlist in the Navy, but she objected. She objected when his draft number was called, too, but it didn't do her much good.

"She's still fuming," he said with that little boy smile, "but she accomplishes nothing. I'm very glad, because I like it quite well."

He took me to the club in a cab and shook hands at the door. His properness irritated me. I was sick of wolves that were all paws; but, at the same time, you do want a man who makes you feel desirable. I just couldn't take Putt seriously and I needed somebody to take seriously. To add to the general depression of the day, I put my toe through my last pair of nylons and Mickey stopped me on the stairs to ask if I'd made up my mind. The first rehearsal call was for the next Monday.

THAT night Doris and I got home together. She asked where I'd been all day. Then she spotted the huge box of candy. "What did you get?"

"I don't know what I've got," I said disgustedly, then laughed in spite of myself. "I picked up a big, sweet overgrown kid last night. He's like nothing you ever met."

"Another private?" she asked, as she took a bottle of beer out of the nursery icebox, handed me the container of milk and gasped at my orchids, while I explained.

"Not even first class, but he's got a first-class name. Alexander Prescott Putnam, III."

"What?" Doris stopped with the bottle-opener raised.

I repeated the name.

"No wonder you never met anything like him. Don't you know who he is?"

I shook my head and Doris told me, full steam ahead. It seemed that his father and grandfather had made one of the great fortunes. "They belong to the old four hundred, or however many it was. This, Fern, is your big chance."

I laughed. "Not with Putt. He's big, Doris, but he is only a baby. He is two years older than I, but I feel like his grandmother."

Doris got the cap off her beer bottle and sat beside me. "Now, listen to me, Fern. You know what Mickey's got you slated for—a strip act. You take it or out you go. You're not so hot and you know it."

"I know it all right. I try, but—"

"It's not a matter of trying. It's a certain touch of brass, liking to show off and strut your stuff. You just don't have it. I've been telling you all along you ought to get married, and this is it."

"Not Putt!" I think I said it fifty times that night while Doris argued and cajoled and said she wished somebody had talked to her like that when she was my age. I let her do most of the talking because I didn't think Putt had any notions about marrying anyway, and I'm not the kind who can get a man to do whatever she wants.

However, before we were out of bed next morning there was a dozen roses from Putt and a note, asking if he couldn't see me for a couple of hours before the show. Doris danced around in her pajamas.

"You'll really be fixed up, hon. I'm tickled as though it happened to me"

"But I don't love him!"

"You won't have to. The Army will take him away and so will Mother. She'll buy you a nice Reno divorce. You'll be fixed. You can go back to Brooklyn and marry some guy you really like, and help that family of yours besides."

If you hear anything often enough you begin to believe it. I began to believe that, especially when I was out with Putt that night. I could feel something tightening up inside of me. He was so soft, so kiddish, he was fair game and it wouldn't cost him anything.

His family would pay and never miss it, but what it would mean to mine and me— the difference between decency and downright poverty, the rent paid and food in the house and warm clothes for the kids! I knew what it was to feel the sidewalk through your shoes. I knew what it was to eat oatmeal for supper or go to bed hungry. You get a big box of the stuff for a dime —and I loathe it. I've heard it's good with cream, but we never had cream.

I thought of all those things when Putt bought me more orchids and expensive gewgaws from shops on the boardwalk, strode beside me, his eyes shining like a kid looking at a Christmas tree. But he never touched my hand or tried to kiss me.

AT last it was Friday night, a week since we met. In the early evening, Doris gave herself a facial and me a lecture on making a big load of hay in a hurry. The rehearsal call was only three days off. I was glad when the doorbell rang to interrupt her, but surprised when I opened the door to Putt.

"I hope I'm not intruding," he said.

"Come right in," Doris sang out. "I was just getting ready to leave, but Fern doesn't have to go for an hour."

"I'm terribly glad," he said, looking down at me. "I only have an hour and I just wanted to see you."

Doris went so fast I didn't know how she got her clothes on. Impatiently I turned to Putt. "Well, what did you want to see me about?"

"Not about anything," he said gently. "I just wanted to see you. You're upset. What has happened?"

"Nothing's happened yet," I said, curling up on the faded cretonne covered lounge. "But it's going to happen next week. I'll either be out of the show or have to do a strip tease."

I was almost surprised he knew what it meant. He stood over me, looking grave and huge and rather handsome in his uniform. "You don't want to do that, do you?"

"No, I don't. You see, I've never done that sort of thing. I can't."

Suddenly, before I knew what was happening, he was kneeling, actually kneeling in front of me. "Fern, will you marry me? Let me take care of you. I can't actually, of course, being in the Army and all that, but the money would be here. There's a great deal of it. I love you, Fern. I have never loved anybody in all my life before. Please marry me."

I kept thinking, "This can't be happening! I'll wake up any minute now."

I said, "But, Putt, you scarcely know me, and your mother wouldn't approve. I'm nobody—less than nobody."

"Mother's run the show until now, but it's going to be different if I come back. I've changed already in the past three months. I don't want the kind of life Mother leads anyway. I want a special life for us, a farm perhaps, or an orange grove in Florida. Fern, will you marry me—tomorrow?"

EVEN when we stood in the city clerk's office, I couldn't believe it. This was tomorrow, my wedding day. Doris and a pink-cheeked corporal stood up for us. Doris had said the price of my wedding ring alone would probably keep me for months, but as we entered the door, Putt took two boxes from his pocket.

"I hope you don't mind," he whispered, "but I always like this idea—double rings."

I went cold looking at them. The ring was exactly like my mother's, a plain gold band. So was his! It was the kind to stay married with. I could hear Doris's deep breath as he said, "With this ring—with all my worldly goods." My hand was shaking as I put his ring on the long brown finger. Then there were other words, and "I pronounce you man and wife."

Putt drew me to him gently as if I would break, and for the first time, kissed me. His mouth was warm and sweet, like a child's. I wanted to cry, to run, to get away from there.

Suddenly cameras flashed and reporters were saying, "Any statement, Private Putnam? Does your mother know of your marriage?"

Putt was strangely at ease with the reporters, because, as I guessed, it was an old situation. His family had always been news. The corporal was pulling his sleeve. "Remember we've only a four-hour pass. If you want to have that wedding breakfast—"

The wedding breakfast was in the bridal suite of the best hotel, with a wedding cake and champagne, and a flower pin set with diamonds that made her eyes bulge. "Baby, is this commission!" she breathed.

But I was getting sicker every minute. Then Putt's time was up and he had to leave. "I'll meet you here tomorrow night, darling, for our honeymoon."

He kissed me again, gently, as he had at the altar, and Doris and I were alone with the remains of the wedding breakfast. "That's class," she sighed. "Gee, Fern, am I happy for you."

For answer I buried my face on my arms and sobbed. I went home with Doris that night. I couldn't stay in that suite. I wanted to send back the ring, end the whole thing right then, for I realized I loved Putt as I never could love anyone else, and I hated myself for using marriage to him as the way out of my difficulties.

"You can't—you're married," Doris pointed out. "At least you've gone through the ceremony. Don't lose your nerve. In twenty-four hours his mother will be here to blow everything."

Marcia Putnam made it in less than that. I got her telegram at ten the next morning. She was at the hotel—in our bridal suite for all I knew. She wanted to see me immediately.

"This is it," Doris said triumphantly. "You won't have a thing to worry about. She'll break it up and Putt will never blame you."

"This is it." I kept repeating that as I put on my black tailored suit and my black coat with what Doris called the "almost fox." I certainly didn't look like a showgirl or a gold digger on the make. I would have felt more confident if I had. This way I was sure his mother would see right through me—she a grand lady and I just Veronica Madeleine O'Hara from Brooklyn. She'd be able to detect every patch I'd ever had on my underwear. Why had I ever let Doris talk me into this?

I was shaking so that I had to make a real effort to cross the lobby. The clerk smiled. "Good afternoon, Mrs. Putnam." He was a little bald-headed man with thick glasses, but I'll always love him. "I'll call Mrs. Putnam's suite."

A moment later I was being whisked up in an elevator, and then a maid opened the door and I was in a sitting room exactly like the one where we'd had the wedding breakfast. Then another door opened and there she was.

FOR a moment I was too startled to see clearly. There was a blurred impression of a woman, of a husky voice. Then slowly my vision cleared, and my breath came easier. Marcia Putnam was a tall woman of about forty. She wore a black satin negligee and held a cigarette in a long, scarlet-nailed hand. Her voice was sharp as cracking metal. She reminded me of someone, but I couldn't place her.

"So you are Fern," she said.

"I am," I answered, my eyes fixed steadily on her. I suddenly felt warm and tall as I watched her. My head was spinning too fast to think clearly yet, but I had the feeling I was close to something.

She surveyed me with chill, prominent eyes. "You quite obviously took advantage of Alex. I expected something of the sort to happen. He is utterly unworldly and inexperienced."

"He's very sweet," I said.

She frowned. "We may as well get directly to the point. How much do you want?"

Suddenly I knew whom she reminded me of—a hostess at the club. This woman was smoother, but they were alike, just as hard, just as glassy, only Marcia Putnam cost more.

"How much do you want?" she repeated.

"Why are you so sure I want anything?" I asked.

"Why else would you marry Alex? He's not ready for love. He's a baby."

My right hand moved over the little gold band on my left. I could hear him saying, "I have never loved anybody in all my life before. I'm changing—I don't want her kind of life."

I suddenly laughed, and she demanded, "What do you find so amusing?"

"Me, I guess," I said ruefully. "I came up here scared at the idea of meeting you. I thought you'd be like a queen or—"

"Well?" she said, as if she thought she was.

"You don't really love Putt, do you? He's been a nuisance to you. Yet there must be a reason, a money reason, for your trying to hold onto him. But as he said, you couldn't argue with the United States Army, and you can't argue with me. I'm going to stay married to him."

I think I was as surprised as she was when I said that, but it was said and I meant it. She sprang up.

"You'll regret this! Alex, or Putt as you call him, does not come into his money until he is thirty—nine more years. As executrix of the estate, I saw that he got a very liberal allowance, but without my approval he will get nothing."

"So there was a tie-up, and you get some extra concession if he doesn't marry before he is thirty? When I thought you loved him, I could have made a deal, but we can't both be on the same side of the fence." I walked to the door.

"Where are you going?" she demanded.

"Up to our suite and wait for Putt."

HE came at seven. I was sitting in the dark room, looking out over the ocean. According to Doris, I'd messed things up properly, but I didn't see what else I could do. I hadn't expected his mother to be like that! I knew that kind of woman. That was what I was thinking when I heard Putt's key in the lock. I ran to meet him. I was frightened and a long way from happy, but I concealed it.

"You're here, Fern!" he said softly. "You're really here, and mine!"

Then I was in his arms, and suddenly his kisses came to life, mad and sweet and glorious, and my own were answering them. We ordered champagne and we danced to the radio and got drunk on joy and love.

"I knew we belonged to each other," he said, "from the first moment we met, but I'm so bad at saying things, perhaps because Mother used to laugh at me."

"You can tell me anything," I said happily.

"Even that I talked to Mother?"

I stiffened a little, but I said he could.

"She said she sent for you, but you weren't for sale—just as I knew you wouldn't be. We'll be poor, darling. You'll have only my Army pay and maybe two or three hundred a month—"

"And what?" I whispered.

"Two or three hundred from my grandmother's estate. I tell you, we'll be poor."

"There are all kinds of poor," I murmured, and kissed him. "Why, we're rich!"

I'M home with Mother for the duration. We have a nice apartment in Brooklyn, and I do Red Cross work and civilian defense. I write letters to Putt every day of my life, and think of him every minute.

I've learned a lot about his family—his father's will that forbade his mother to marry again, and provided a limited income after Putt's marriage gave him control of his own money, providing the match met with her approval. After thirty, Putt was to come into his money—married or single. She's paid high for all that money, robbing herself and her son of love. But I'll make it up to him. I will—I will! ●

my G.I. Joe

Julie tried not to fall in love with Joe, and he tried even harder not to fall in love with her. Maybe they tried too hard

THEY lay there in a little pool of light on the cocktail table, Tommy's things. There was the brown leather case that we knew without opening held tinted miniatures of Mary Sue and the baby. There was the little Bible he had written he read every night—hard to imagine, that. There was the good luck penny he'd carried ever since I could remember, dull now but I could see right now the way he used to shine it on his pants when he was a kid. ("Look, Sis—I got a gold piece!") There were a few other things, but nothing of much intrinsic worth.

Lieutenant Carter, the "Joe" of Tommy's letters from Africa, had hesitated a little before putting them on the table, but no one had made a move to take them, not Mother, not Mary Sue, and so, very carefully he had put them down.

"Like I wrote you, he gave me the things to bring you when he—when he knew he was going. Somehow or other he didn't seem to want the things sent home in the regular way. He said this way maybe it'd be easier for you. I guess neither one of us thought it would be a whole year before I'd get here."

Mother spoke. "Tommy was always so thoughtful—he never wanted to worry anyone. We're very grateful to you for your trouble—"

His blue eyes went to her face. "It wasn't any trouble, Ma'am. I'm out at the Field for a few months' additional training. I requested I be sent here when they sent me back to this country, but I never thought I'd be that lucky. Tommy was always bound I had to meet you all."

Mother smiled politely. "We hope we'll be seeing you often." I saw her look furtively at her watch. At any minute now her bridge guests would start arriving.

Mary Sue bent forward, her head gilt-bright in the light. For a moment I thought—I guess I hoped—she was reaching to pick up one of the things on the table, but instead she opened the silver box that was there and took out a cigarette. She murmured, "It's very kind of you, I'm sure." She lit a match, but her hand stopped in mid-air at the sound of a car out in front. The car went on by, and she finished lighting her cigarette. Then she, too, stole a glance at her watch. She was expecting Captain Harker who was taking her to a dance at the officers' club.

Upstairs Nicky cried. He was two now, and the darling of us all. No longer was he the dimpled baby of the picture, but stretching up into the lean ranginess that had been his father's. Mary Sue, who usually was content to let Lobelia go to him, murmured an excuse and hurried from the room.

There was an awkward silence. Mother, who was an expert at keeping conversations going, didn't say anything. And the tightness which had come to my throat at the sight of Tommy's things wouldn't let me speak.

The soldier's eyes went from Mother to me, and I saw now a baffled look on his young face which was burned to a bronze much darker than his light hair. He had a cowlick that even the G.I. haircut couldn't subdue. But there was an oldness in his blue eyes that I had seen before in the eyes of even very young soldiers who had come back from one of the several hells where they fought our war. Aware that I had been staring, I dropped my eyes to the pathetic little heap of things on the table. And suddenly they went out of focus, swam together in the blur of my tears.

I felt in the pockets of my red gabardine suit for a handkerchief. Oh, there was no reason in the world why, after nearly a year had passed, Mother shouldn't have started having bridge parties again. No reason why Mary Sue shouldn't be having dates again, getting ready, perhaps, to marry again. She was

"Oh, so you're being practical!" Joe said. "Is this your idea of practicality?"

—things there. Put them somewhere, will you, dear?"

Out in the mild April evening as we walked towards town I could almost have believed it was Tommy who walked beside me—he had been tall, too. How many times we had walked down Hillyer Avenue towards town in the frequent intervals when there had been no money for gas. Tommy would have loved this night. The white dogwoods were heavy on the trees, and the spring moon was a curved thread of silver in the sky to the west.

The soldier said, "Tommy always said there was no place like North Carolina in the spring. He said the dogwood and redbud trees together were a sight. Well, I guess he was right. It's nice down here." We walked for a while in silence and he said, but with an edge to his voice now, "He was always talking about his family, too. About his mother, how young looking, what a good sport she was. About his wife—how sweet, how beautiful, how everything she was. His last thought was to make things easier for them—"

Passionately I said, "You mustn't think they didn't care! You don't know how they grieved. But Mother says there's no sense in trying to live in the past. Or to be morbid—that's the last thing Tommy would have wanted. He'd have wanted us to be happy. Everyone thinks Mother has taken it wonderfully. Mary Sue, too."

"Yeah, I guess so." He looked down at me. "But you're the only one who's the way I imagined you."

"What did Tommy say about me?"

"Oh—that you were tall, with black hair and gray eyes. Pretty—"

"What else?"

"That you laughed at the same things."

I swallowed to rid myself of the sudden ache in my throat. "Did he say that? Bless him. That's what's been so hard about having him gone—not having anyone to share the funny things with. I was always cutting out cartoons to send him. I reach for the scissors even yet before there is time to think—"

"YOU could send them to me. I miss those cartoons. Remember the one of the guy running towards the empty swimming pool looking back over his shoulder saying, 'Last one in is a sissy'?"

My laughter was sudden and free. He caught my hand and laughed, too. We had reached Miller's drugstore and the bright lights from the window shone on his face, showed his teeth square and very white and even. Instead of the soldier who had said, "Yes, Ma'am," to my mother and had seemed somehow at a disadvantage in our living room, I saw the Joe of Tommy's letters, the gay companion. And, for the first time since Tommy's death, the feeling of emptiness lessened a little.

"Let's go in here and have sodas. That's what Tommy and I would have done." I wanted to prolong the feeling of warmth. "And tell me everything you can remember. All the funny things he ever said, the things he did—"

Joe rubbed his chin and thought for a minute. "You ever hear about that time in Casablanca?"

For two hours we sat in the back booth

so young, and Nicky needed a father. It was only the timing that was wrong. These things of Tommy's shouldn't have had to come at a time when we were too busy to look at them, too busy to think for a little while about the warm-hearted, laughter-loving boy we had lost. Tommy —my brother, my brother—

The doorbell rang, and Mother rose with a barely audible sigh of relief. I met Joe Carter's eyes, not caring that my own were brimming. "I haven't anything to

do. I'll walk back downtown with you. I'd like to talk to you."

"We all would, of course, Lieutenant." Mother looked back over her shoulder with a little distressed frown between her brows. "Perhaps you can come to dinner soon if you're to be stationed here for a while—"

"Thank you, ma'am." He got to his feet.

At the door, her hand on the knob, Mother turned again. "Julie, dear, those

at Miller's. I heard about the time in Casablanca. I heard the story of the little scarab ring he had sent me which I wore at that moment. I heard for the first time the crack he had made that got into *Stars and Stripes*. By the time the place was ready to close for the night I could understand why it was that Tommy had written, "Sis, I've got a guy for you."

Six weeks later I told Mother I was going to marry him. It was a warm morning for May, almost hot, and I sat on the end of her bed in a white silk nightie and waited, my arms clasped tightly around my hunched knees while Lobelia let down the legs on the little breakfast tray over Mother's knees. Lobelia de-

parted and Mother smiled at me as she tied the bow of the pink flowered bed jacket under her chin. She was still pretty. She would always be pretty, but little lines had come around her eyes in this last year.

"Well, dear?"

"Mother—I'm going to marry Joe."

She had reached for her orange juice but she set it back down.

"Julie!" Her laughter tinkled. "You're not serious, pet."

"Terribly."

"My very dear child, it's ridiculous." She laughed again. "I've been meaning to speak to you about seeing so much of that boy. I see now that I should have —but I thought, of course, you were just being sweet to him on account of Tommy. Now here you've gone and let the fact that he knew your brother in Africa sweep you off your feet."

"Mother, they were like brothers. You remember Tommy's letters—"

"Indeed I do. I remember all that Tommy told us about his background— an orphanage upbringing. Wait—I quite approve of him as a friend for my son, but not as a husband for my daughter." She smiled reprovingly at me. "Julie, I'm surprised at you."

Her tone was the one she had used when I was ten, but I noticed that the hand she reached out for her orange juice was shaking. Bart Cottrell— Mother had counted on my marrying Bart Cottrell eventually. He was the easygoing son of a family that had about run itself out. One of the decadent families of the South that the Northerners were always talking about. But they still had plenty of money, and I really had thought I'd end up by marrying him. He had proposed to me every time he came home on furlough for the last two years.

The lines between Mother's eyes were deeper. I put my hand out towards hers and said, "Darling, you don't know how I wish it could have been somebody who could have made things easier for you. I—I was trying to fall in love with Bart. I tried not to fall in love with Joe. Truly, darling. And he tried not to fall in love with me. He tried just as hard as I did."

Mother stabbed at a piece of bacon and tried to smile. "I guess neither of you tried very hard."

He had, though. And if I hadn't shamelessly urged him on he never would have asked me to marry him. There had been an evening when the two of us played gin rummy in the little room at the front of the house that had been Dad's office. It had been the one occasion when Mother had invited Joe to dinner. For some reason or other all the big silver pieces, platters and tureens, and the goblets and fingerbowls, and things that ordinarily didn't come out except for special occasions, had been used. I had seen the way Joe watched and hesitated before picking up a fork, and because I was so terribly in love with him, I had been more than a little bit relieved when the dinner was over. He was more at ease when the two of us were alone in the shabby little office, surrounded by the bookcases full of the out-of-date medical books Mother hadn't been able to sell. I remember that it crossed my mind that it had been too bad a few of the securities hadn't been too out-of-date to sell!

Shuffling the cards aimlessly after our interest in the game had waned, I said, "Tommy'd have liked knowing you had dinner with us tonight."

Joe's face lit up. "Wouldn't he? He was always planning how after the war I'd come down. He said your family would take me in." The swivel chair at Dad's desk creaked as he leaned back, looking up at the ceiling. "He wanted me to start practicing here if I ever got to be a doctor. He planned a lot of things that never could be."

"Such as?"

"**Y**OU and I." He leaned forward and his big hands covered mine. "You were my pin-up girl, Julie. Surely, you knew that."

"He wrote me you had my picture—"

"And I used to think—oh, well. I see now that it never could be."

"Why not, Joe?" I held on to his hands when he would have withdrawn them. "Why on earth not?"

"You're rich, for one thing. That dinner tonight—everything done up in such style. I was like a fish out of water. You should have seen the enamelware dishes we used to have at the orphanage. The spoons left a brassy taste in your mouth. You can't imagine the difference. You've always had plenty of money, a servant—"

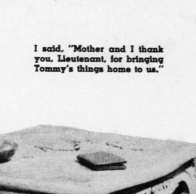

I said, "Mother and I thank you, Lieutenant, for bringing Tommy's things home to us."

He stopped because I was laughing. 'What's funny?"

"You darling dope—we're poor as church mice. Poor old Lobelia gets paid about half the time. Mother even borrows it back from her when she loses at bridge. We never have a cent left over, and if we do we spend it."

He was looking at me as if he didn't believe me.

"It's true." I laughed at his puzzled face. "This dress—" I plucked at the white sharkskin dress that I wore. "This dress isn't even paid for, and I bought it in February. Our accounts are all frozen all the time, and when one gets unfrozen it freezes right up again."

He said slowly, "Then how come you don't try to get a job, Julie, if you need money?"

"I don't know. I'm just no account, I guess. Spoiled. Joe, you could help me amount to something. I think maybe that's what Tommy had in mind—"

He had pushed the table between us aside then, stood up and pulled me with him. I lost myself in response to his kiss; it was as if I had never known a man's lips before. He buried his face in my hair. "Oh, Julie, Julie, if only some day after this mess is all over you can be mine—"

"Some day" had been enough for us until last night. It was Lobelia's night out. Mary Sue and Mother had gone out to dinner and to a movie; Joe and I had looked after Nicky. I guess it was the domesticity of the scene that did it: romping with Nicky in the back yard, and then putting him to bed, together hearing his "Now I Lay Me"—an imp of an angel with flushed cheeks and tousled, dark hair; cooking hamburgers together, then, over the back yard grill. The stars came out, and the fireflies, and the smell of roses grew heavy and sweeter the way it does after dark. And, standing by the embers of our fire, Joe had taken me in his arms and said, "I thought it was going to be enough, honey, remembering you over sodas, remembering the way you look in your white sweater and skirt—times like this, kissing you. But it's not enough. I want you for my wife, Julie. I want those memories, too."

Just the memory of those words now made my heart pound. I got off of Mother's bed and walked over by the window. I looked down into the bright garden, where dew flashed in the morning sun, where a mocking bird sang like crazy. Like my heart.

Mother had been saying something. I said, "What did you say, Mother?" I turned to her dressing-table because I didn't want her to see my face, the telltale color there. I glanced at my reflection in the glass—my arms and shoulders were very brown in contrast to my white gown, my hair still sleep-tousled. Joe would see me this way. With an effort I tried to listen to what she was saying as I fingered her throat strap, moved about the little jars of throat and rejuvenating cream.

She said, sharply for her, "Oh, I know you're thinking it doesn't matter—your differences in background. Nothing I can say, probably, will make you see how important it is." I heard her sigh. "Well,

if you just won't rush into it, child. When does he want you to marry him?"

I turned to her, my hand against my throat. "This afternoon, Mother."

We took a room and bath in a third-rate apartment hotel—the best place we could find in this town of soldiers and their wives. We didn't mind the shabbiness, the soot on windowsills, the spotted walls. Sometimes when I would remember that I could have had the high-ceilinged grandeur of the Cottrell mansion and half a dozen servants I would think, oh—lucky, lucky me!

THERE was a bus that took Joe out to the Field at such an ungodly hour in the morning that I made no attempt to do more than look up sleepily at the tall, khaki-clad figure, kiss him, and then fall asleep for two hours more. In those days he only laughed at my laziness, and seemed amused at my explanation that the only way I could bear the day without him was to sleep part of it away.

Not that there wasn't plenty to do. I went to the Red Cross afternoons and rolled bandages and swapped Field gossip with other Army wives instead of playing bridge at a tenth, because Joe approved of the former and not of the latter. He said we couldn't afford to risk our money on any except a very sure thing. I learned to take care of my own clothes—which surprised me by requiring a great deal of time. I washed and set my black shoulder-length hair, feeling virtuous when Joe applauded my economy. I even found you could get pretty good nail polish at the five and ten, and learned to do a passable job on my own nails.

Five o'clock was the high spot of my day—the moment towards which every daily act was directed. Someday, when Joe had been sent back overseas, it would be the zero hour, but now I crowded that thought deep, and made the most of the unimagined happiness that was the present. Even carrying our trays at night in a cafeteria and trying to see who could get the most for under seventy-five cents was an exciting game. And every Tuesday—Joe's one day off from the Field each week—was like Christmas and Thanksgiving and all the birthdays I'd ever had rolled into one. All that summer when the weather was fine and not too hot we pushed a cart in a chain store, carefully buying sandwich makings and ten-cent bottles of olives and such for a picnic lunch. And then we took a bus to the country and walked and talked and made dreamy, wonderful plans for when the war was over and Joe could be a doctor as he'd always planned. We'd have a houseful of children. The oldest boy would be Tommy.

Maybe it would have gone on indefinitely being wonderful—I've often wondered if it might not have—if I had not found out that Joe had over four thousand dollars in the bank.

We had been married three months. It was a Tuesday morning, and we had been lying abed making lazy plans as to how we should spend our day.

Joe kissed me and sat up and began to feel around with his feet for his slippers. "Better get a move on, punkin. It's almost ten. We've got to get our breakfast before they quit serving."

"We can go to the tearoom," I said, not moving. "They'd serve you breakfast in the afternoon if you wanted it."

"A dime for a cup of coffee? Not on your life."

"I know what I ought to do." From the bathroom came the sound of his razor blade sharpener—he'd get dozens of shaves on one blade—and I had to raise my voice to be heard. "I ought to buy a dress. I really hate to embarrass you by going to the fall dance out at the Field in the rags I've worn all summer. If they're going to make you a captain, I ought to help you along by looking like a captain's wife. Psychology, darling."

There was no (Continued)

My G. I. Joe

sound from Joe, I said anxiously, "Of course, I know you probably can't afford it."

He appeared in the doorway rubbing lather onto his face. "I guess I can. You go shopping this morning. I've got a lot to see to anyhow."

"But have you got any money in the bank?"

"A little."

"How much?"

He was looking at me in a very funny way. After a moment he said, "Four thousand, two hundred and thirty-two dollars."

I fell back against the pillows with a shriek that was only half put on. "We're rich! Oh, my soul, Joe Carter, why on earth didn't you tell me?" Abruptly I sat up. "You're kidding."

He grinned. "No. It's the truth. Want me to give you a check for what you'll need?"

I LEAPED from the bed and began to tear into my clothes. "No, darling, no. I have charge accounts simply everywhere." I sang, "Oh, what a beautiful morning—" "Joe, honey, you don't care if I get a few other little things I've been needing?"

He caught me and kissed me and got lather on my chin. "Just don't spend it all, punkin."

I had no idea I was spending as much as I did. All the new fall clothes were in, and there were marvelous specials on summer things. The boxes covered the bed and overflowed onto the floor of our room that afternoon when things arrived by special messenger. Joe's face, when he walked in and saw everything, was something to see.

I turned before him in the flame chiffon evening gown. "Sixty-five dollars, darling, but—reduced to half price! Did you ever hear of such a buy?"

He glanced briefly at the dress and walked past me to the bed. "What's this?"

"Another evening dress—but that's for winter. I—I guess maybe I was a teeny bit extravagant on the one, but look—" I lifted the silver brocade from its tissue. "The colonel's wife will die when she sees it."

"Is that good?" His face was impassive.

"Dearest, don't be cross." I stood close to him, but he moved away and picked up a pair of shoes. The sales slip fluttered to the floor. He caught it in mid-air. "Fifteen thirty-four?"

"That's with the tax. There's a terribly high sales tax in North Carolina. Three percent. Imagine."

"But Julie—I've seen windows full of shoes that look just as good as these for five or six dollars."

"And heaven knows what they'd do to your feet. You wouldn't love me with bunions, would you? I was trying to be practical." I pushed the play shoes under the tissue, but not before he had seen them.

He held one up by a red strap. "This your idea of practicality?"

"No ration coupon, though, darling!"

He ran his brown fingers through his light hair and turned away. I followed him and burrowed my head against his shoulder. In a small voice I said, "You shouldn't have told me how much there was in the bank, Joe. Four thousand dollars seemed like such an awful lot."

"It seemed like a lot of money to me, too—before today. I see now that it wouldn't last you a year if I were sent overseas." I would have pulled away then, but his arm restrained me. "Listen, Julie, I worked my way through college. It's not just a phrase—to me it's thousands of trays of dirty dishes, thousands of shovels-ful of coal, miles of snowy walks. I started in with out a dime and finished up with a little in the bank. Not one guy in a thousand ever does that."

"You must have had a whirl." I laughed a little but his mouth stayed grim.

"After college I got a job and buckled down to save for medical school. I had one good suit—good enough for me, anyhow—and I ate on four dollars a week. I practically never bought myself a beer or took a girl out. When the war came I had about enough saved, but it didn't seem right not to join up, somehow. Since I've got my commission I've added to it—but we'll need it, now that there are two of us. I won't be able to add much to it now that I'm married."

"That's tough." I twisted out of his arms.

"No, that's okay. But we've got to live on my pay, Julie. That bank account is for us to live on during medical school after the war's over. It's got to be there. It's not to be touched for anything. Ever. Is that clear?"

"For pity's sake, why don't you draw me a diagram?" A tear splashed down on the tissue paper I was folding back around the shoes with wooden soles. Any of the men I'd ever known had always been glad to indulge the women they loved. They hadn't acted as if spending a little money was a crime. Dad had always been amused by silly things when Mother bought them. Tommy would have got the moon for Mary Sue. "I'll take these back. I won't ask you to buy me any clothes! I'll—I'll get a job at—at the munitions plant!" I named the most unlikely place I could think of.

He looked surprised, and then to my consternation, pleased. "Julie, I think that's a very good idea!"

I kept the clothes and Joe paid for them, but since he seemed to think I had meant what I said about getting a job at the munitions plant, I went out and applied for one. Almost at once they put me to work operating a pelleting press. It sounds dull. Actually, it wasn't. I had never worked before; my pay check, which, some weeks with overtime, was fifty dollars, seemed like a miracle. Joe made me buy a bond every week, but the rest I spent with the return of my former abandon in money matters. One penny-pincher in the family was enough!

THE quarrel, eventually, was made up, but for me the thrill in little economies was gone. Joe, seeing my tendency, watched his pennies more closely than ever, which infuriated me into even greater extravagance. There was no relaxing even when a lieutenant's single silver bar gave way to the two bars of a captain. Many of the boys gave "promotion parties" when they were upped in rank—nothing fancy, just cigars and drinks, but not Joe.

Looking back, I see that, sadly enough, the best way to chronicle our marriage up to the time I left is by recording our quarrels. Even then I could see they weren't just the money fights so many couples survive. They had their roots in our vastly different backgrounds. Mother, apparently, had known what she was talking about.

Our second quarrel of any consequence was when Lobelia quit and Joe made no attempt to cover the fact that he was tickled to death.

I told him about it one night while we ate. "Imagine—leaving Mother flat now when help is impossible to get!"

He said, "Name one good reason why Lobelia should fetch and carry for an able-bodied woman who sits at a bridge table all day."

With an effort I held my temper in check. "But hasn't she any gratitude? She's been with us ever since I can remember. We've treated her like one of the family. She

knows Mother always would have taken care of her—"

Joe laughed a little and raised a quizzical brow as he emptied the sugar envelope into his coffee. "With what?"

My control snapped. With more heat than logic I said, "I'll have you know we've taken care of our darkies since before the Civil War! You wouldn't understand. You don't understand Mother or me or our way of life. The only values you know anything about are the ones represented in dollars and cents. The art of gracious living escapes you completely!"

He slipped a dime tip under his plate and made ready to leave. Angrily I shoved a quarter across the table. "There's an example! I'm embarrassed to eat in public with anyone as tight as you are!"

He bowed. "Sorry, Mrs. Astor."

The man at the next table was taking it all in. I rose and Joe followed. Over my shoulder I said furiously, "I'd rather skip my next meal than leave a dime tip!"

"Really?" His voice was pleasantly conversational as he came alongside me. "That's because you've never skipped one. I have—"

OUR last quarrel was when I quit my job at the plant. One of the girls working in the room with me was seriously injured at work. In our room I waited for Joe, still wearing my blue coverall uniform. On the verge of hysterical tears I gave him the details. "It could have been me!" I said. But to my hurt surprise he wanted me to reconsider.

"I won't!" I unpinned the identification badge with my picture on it and dropped it with a little click of finality in the pin tray on the dresser. "You wouldn't care, I suppose, if I were mutilated. Or even killed. That job is dangerous!"

"Not very. But suppose it is, and suppose all of the women in your department run home whining now that this has happened—"

"All right." I was crying now. "I'm scared. I'll admit it. And Tommy or Father or any of the men I've ever known would have wanted to protect me from danger. You would if you loved me—"

"I'd love you more if I thought you had the stuff in you to stand up to a crisis—"

"Well, I haven't. I'm never going back there and there's nothing you can say that will make me. I—I'm going to Florida with Mary Sue and Nicky—"

She had asked me to go with her but up to that moment I hadn't even considered it because I couldn't afford it. She couldn't either; the trip would take the last of Tommy's insurance money, but light-hearted Mary Sue would worry about that when the time came. I raised my head and looked at the spotted wallpaper, at my grim-faced husband, and thought defiantly that I could do with a little lightheartedness for a change.

"Florida?" His voiced cracked. "Are you out of your mind? With the trains so crowded and the government requesting civilians not to travel—You haven't the money anyhow—"

"I have my bonds."

"You wouldn't cash them."

"Why not? They're mine." I flung back my black hair.

"All right." His blue eyes went hard. The smile on his lips went strangely with the hardness of his eyes. "Then go, Julie. But if you go—don't come back."

The Florida beaches were hot with sun, and Mary Sue and Nicky and I got back our summer tans and more, too. We didn't stay at the Roney Plaza, but we went there often for cocktails. Everything was very high—even a soda was seventy-five cents—but there was a lot of drinking and gambling and the dog races were jammed each night. You kept hearing people say comfortably, if somewhat defensively, that it did us all good to forget about the war for a while.

It should have been fun. I went through all the motions and laughed a lot and wore my wooden soled shoes and all my other pretty clothes, and knew, because there were plenty of men around to tell me so, that I was desirable. But deep in my heart I knew, with a sickness and despair, that it didn't matter how desirable other men found me if Joe didn't want me any more. Times when I should have been having fun, I'd see his face as it had looked that afternoon in our room. Times when I should have been sleeping, I cried because my penitent letters had brought no reply.

OUR money didn't last nearly as long as we had thought it would, and so in mid-December we were heading north again. "What day shall we go back?" Lazily we discussed it. And Mary Sue shrugged and said, "See if we can get reservations for some day next week. It doesn't matter which day. . ."

Maybe that's what they all thought—nearly a hundred people who died, scores more who were injured on that night of ice and death and horror in that little North Carolina town. Buie, North Carolina, a whistle stop. I'd never heard of it—you'd never heard of it either, most likely. But you heard of it last December when a southbound train blocked the track—a minor wreck—and a northbound flyer tore its screaming way through, making a shambles of them both.

I hadn't gone to sleep yet, although it was between one and two o'clock, as I recall. I was lying there listening to the sleet against the windows, thinking about Joe, when the quiet of the sleeping car was, between one second and the next, split a thousand ways with the sound of steel on steel, splintering wood, and shrieks so terrible they return in nightmare to haunt me still.

Maybe you read about it in the papers and know more about it than I do. I couldn't bear to read about it, and so I know only what I could see and hear from under the wreckage where I lay pinned from early morning hours until after daybreak. Merciful unconsciousness blacked out some of that time. My shoulder was deeply gashed, but I remember the bitter cold that streamed into the broken car worse than the pain.

Sometime during those confused hours a WAC crawled through the wreckage and put her coat about me as well as she could. "They're bringing blowtorches to get you all out," she told me. But she could tell me nothing of Nicky and Mary Sue whose berth had been at the other end of the car. And when at last they got me out I remember that someone bared my arm for a hypodermic. But the solution that held the pain-killing drug was frozen in the syringe.

I have no clear memory of being taken to the hospital at Fayetteville. Blood loss and shock account for that, I suppose. I do remember that they told me Mary Sue had minor head injuries, but that their evasiveness regarding Nicky shocked me into wide-awake, awful fear.

A family conference took place in the hospital still later that same day, I believe. Beyond the heart-stopping announcement that one of Nicky's legs was so badly shattered he might never walk again, I recall little of the orthopedic surgeon's technical explanation of what bones and nerves and muscles were affected. But I remember quite clearly that

Mother was wearing brown gloves with her black suit; that Mary Sue looked like a nun with her hair shorn under all the bandages and adhesive tape. And better than any of the intelligent questions Joe asked when the doctor discussed the possibilities of a nerve transplant, I remember the hard, hurting way he clung to my hand.

But this is the part I remember best of all. The doctor said, "It's not a sure thing, but there's a fifty-fifty chance that the child might walk again. If anyone can give him that chance, it's a man in New York. I'd like to see him do the job. With after care and all, it would come to fifteen hundred dollars." He looked appraisingly at the three of us women, all of us expensively dressed. "There would be no difficulty there, I presume?"

Mary Sue wet her lips. "Fifteen hundred dollars?"

And at the doctor's nod she covered her face with her hands and wept.

Mother patted her shoulder, but her eyes looked bleak and old.

Joe cleared his throat.

"Fifteen hundred dollars, sir? We can manage that."

Mary Sue raised her tear-wet face. "But how—who—?"

I looked at Joe, my brain in a whirl. A fifty-fifty chance, the doctor had said. Joe, who never gambled. Joe, whose voice had cracked when he said, "That money is not to be touched. Ever." But now his hand was tightening on mine, and his voice was gentle as he said to Mary Sue, "I can let you have whatever you'll need. I—I'll never miss it."

Last night I walked again down Hillyer Avenue. The sights and scents and sounds are the same as a year ago, the dogwoods sheaves of white under the spring moon. This spring I walked alone.

In my pocket was a V-mail to Joe in England. And I smiled to myself in the darkness remembering its contents. Twice, although she tried to appear casual, Mother had reminded me to tell him she had been made a supervisor out at the munitions plant. And did he know they had received the Navy E Award? Mary Sue, I told him, was at the hospital learning to be a laboratory technician. Nicky was learning to walk again. We were letting the nurse go next week. "Thanks to you, his leg will soon be sound and strong again."

AND on the last page, "I've quit my job at the plant again, darling. But this time you'll be glad. Remember our dream? Next fall I'll hold that dream in my arms."

Outside Miller's I picked up the fifty cent magazine I have always bought. And put it back. To the new boy at the counter I said, "A nickel limeade, please." I took it to the last booth in the back and made it last a long time.

This was the booth Joe and I had sat in a year ago. How little I had known of him then—how well I knew him now. On a night three weeks before we had walked slowly down the street to a place where one of the sergeants from the Field was to meet him and take him and his luggage out to the plane. A child on the corner was selling arbutus. Fifty cents for a good, big, fragrant bunch.

Joe reached into his pocket and drew out a coin. He looked over the flowers and made his choice with care. Then he turned to pin them to my coat, pleased with himself, the expression on his face that of a little boy who expects approval. •

"OUR investigation shows, Mrs. Benson, that your home background and the influences of your early life were unfortunate. . . ."

Judge Burton was speaking to me. I looked up at him, sitting there all decked out in his black robe and looking smart enough to tell the world what was wrong with it, and I almost laughed in his face. Home background? Influences of my early life? Where I grew up, we wouldn't have known what the words meant.

That was over in the factory district where the rickety frame houses are so black from chimney smoke they never need painting. You'd be surprised how many people can live in a four-room house if they've got to. Or wouldn't you call it living? Freezing in the winter, panting for air in the summer, never quite clean, never enough food in your stomach. That was the way I spent my first 14 years, crowded in with the rest of Aunt Mame's kids.

Maybe you think it was pretty kind of my aunt to take me in when my mother faded out of the picture about the time I was 6. Well, maybe. On the other hand, could be Aunt Mame had an eye to the amount of work and baby tending even a scrawny 6-year-old kid can do. It's considerable, believe it or not, and that's the way things worked out. Oh, I liked some of the kids, sure. They were cute when they were babies. But I had to take some stiff pushing around from Aunt Mame and Uncle Frank, who figured they were doing me a big favor by keeping me out of an orphan asylum.

At first Aunt Mame just used to bawl me out if I didn't do the dishes fast enough or if the stew didn't taste good, but then she got to hitting me, too. That was after she started drinking—first sour red wine and beer and then cheap whisky—whenever she could get the money for it. That meant we had less to eat, and Uncle Frank started fighting with Aunt Mame because he thought he was the only one in the family who had the right to spend money on liquor. Oh, it was some happy home, believe me!

I guess nobody'll be surprised to know that I jumped at the first chance to get out of there. The chance came when I was 14. Al Benson, who lived down the street, asked me to marry him. Al was 18 and his house was a lot like Aunt Mame's except that there weren't so many kids in it.

Uncle Frank was furious when I told him. "The idea of a girl as young as you wantin' to get married and leave a good home! Ain't your aunt been a mother to you? Ain't I tried to be like a father?" There were walrus tears in his eyes.

A father to me! That was a good one. That was just the thing to say to me. I haven't mentioned my own father. Could be I like to forget that he ever existed. Aunt Mame said he went down to the corner saloon for a beer one night and forgot to come back. That was after he'd heard I was slated to arrive. So you can see Uncle Frank didn't do any good for himself talking about fathers. Anyway he and Aunt Mame weren't kidding me. They just wanted me around for the work I did.

So I decided to do everything wrong. I stayed away when it was time to cook the meals and I hid Aunt Mame's whisky bottle. I figured they'd be glad to let me go after that, but the beatings became more severe, and sometimes I was so hurt I could hardly move. I'd sneak down to the cellar and hide, crouched miserably in between a pile of litter in the filthy, rat-infested

ALL HER SORRY, PITIFUL LIFE IVY LONGED

FOR SOMEONE TO CARE, ANYONE! YES, EVEN

CLINT...BUT HE WAS ALREADY MARRIED!

the girl they called BAD

Hiding! Hiding! Hiding!
Would it always be like this?
The footsteps came closer . . .

corner where it was real dark and they couldn't find me.

I knew I couldn't stand it much longer. The day I was so tired that I accidentally spilled scalding soup on Uncle Frank capped everything. I'd been cleaning and scrubbing all morning, dodging Aunt Mame's abuse, and I was dead on my feet. Uncle Frank had come in, yelling for something to eat. He sat down at the table, his battered hat still on his head. I filled a bowl with hot soup, and rushing over to put it before him, I tripped and the soup spilled all over him. He jumped, cursing, picked up a heavy iron skillet and slowly came over to me where I stood motionless, horrified at the terrible, cruel gleam in his bloodshot eyes. I came to life as he raised his arm to strike. Quickly I spun around and fled out the door. I took the stairs at a jump. I could hear his heavy tread coming after me. I don't know why I didn't rush into the street except that I might have met Al, and I didn't want him to see me this way. I darted to the back of the hall, opened the cellar door and rushed down into its inky blackness. I just had time to press myself up against the wall by the stairs when the cellar door opened and the light from the hall streamed in, lifting the darkness. My heart was pounding furiously. I knew what would happen if Uncle Frank found me. It would be worse than anything before! *Hiding. Hiding! Would it always be like this?* I wondered frantically. The footsteps came closer, stopped. I could hear Uncle Frank's labored breathing. The first step creaked under his weight, and I thought, *This is it. This is the end!* My body was clammy, my breath coming in strangled gasps. Then, miraculously, the footsteps stopped halfway down the stairs. I could feel Uncle Frank peering into the darkness. He shuffled, turned around, and started running up the stairs. He must have decided I'd run into the street.

I stayed down there huddled in a heap until nightfall, then sneaked out and up the street to Al's house. I knew I could never go back to Aunt Mame's. Al's mom let me stay a few days, then talked to Aunt Mame and Uncle Frank. They finally gave in, and Al and I got married.

"*I understand that your marriage, contracted at an early age, was unsuccessful, and that after your estrangement from your husband, your son was shifted about from place to place. . . .*" Judge Burton's voice went on.

You understood right, Judge. Here's what happened. Al got a job washing cars in a garage, and we moved into two rooms up above—no bathroom, and a gas plate to cook on. We furnished it with sticks of furniture and odds and   [*Please turn page*]

The Girl
They Called Bad

ends of junk that we picked up cheap in the open-air markets.

Like two kids playing house, we were. But marriage isn't meant for kids, is it, Judge? Some days I kept the place clean and shining, like a little girl in her doll house. Then other days I'd be pouting, maybe because Al wouldn't give me any more money for movies, and I'd let the place get in a mess. That made Al mad and he'd slam out of the place and spend the evening in a pool parlor.

Al didn't like my cooking either, and I was too stubborn or too lazy to try to do it any different.

"Ivy," he'd yell, pushing his plate across the table, sometimes knocking over his coffee cup, "is this the kind of grub you used to cook for your aunt and her family? No wonder they were glad to get rid of you! I'm surprised they didn't *pay* me for takin' you offa their hands!"

"That ain't so!" I'd yell right back, really ashamed of the watery stew or the burned hash or whatever it was he was sore about, feeling pretty abused too and scared because I didn't seem to be making out much better with Al than I had with Aunt Mame and Uncle Frank. "They were crazy about me, Aunt Mame and Uncle Frank were!" I lied. "They begged me to stay on. They never wanted me to marry you at all, and I don't know why I wanted to so much if this is the way you're goin' to treat me!"

Then I burst out crying. The first time that happened, Al came over and put his arms around me and kissed me and tousled my hair with his rough hands that always smelled of oil. I don't know whether I mentioned that Al was good-looking, dark hair and bright-blue eyes and kind of a sweet smile—when he was feeling good.

I kissed him back and whispered, "Don't be mean to me." Then I laughed to show it was a joke. If he'd been older he might have known I really meant it.

I was like a kid who thinks she's found a new trick, a cute way of getting around people. The next few times Al got mad at me I tried crying and it worked fine, but then he got tired of it.

"Aw, quit it! Cut off the water works," he'd growl, frowning at me, his face dark, with anger. "A guy don't want to sit around listenin' to a dame sniffle all the time. Grow up!"

That was a good one. "Grow up," he says to me, and I was all of 15 then.

Timmy was born the next year, a month after my sixteenth birthday. When the doc at the clinic told me he was really on the way, I thought about how I could break it to Al. I guess I'd been seeing too many movies. You know—the ones where they open a big bottle of champagne and everybody drinks toasts to the little stranger. I went and bought a rattle at the dime store and laid it by Al's plate that night. He picked it up as though it was a loaded gun and stared at me.

"What's this?" he asked, dumblike.

"Whaddya think?" I said, smiling. "We're going to have a baby, Al!"

I hadn't expected any champagne, of course, but Al looked as though I'd said a family of boa constrictors were coming to live with us.

"A baby! In this dump!" he yelled. "That's all we need. How the heck can we afford to have a baby? They cost money, and once you start having 'em, they never stop. We'll wind up with a dozen like your Aunt Mame and Uncle Frank!"

I got good and mad then and blew off some steam and it ended with Al going out and staying out all night, for the first time. He'd never been much of a drinker, just a few beers once in a while, but he started in on stronger stuff after Timmy was born. Timmy cried a lot and had trouble with his formula, and his stuff was all over the flat. It sure wasn't any place a man'd want to come home to.

Al began to lose his jobs and drift from one thing to another. He was earning less money and paying more for booze. So pretty soon he was giving me almost nothing. I fought about it for a while, but then I saw it wasn't any use. I went to work, washing dishes, waiting table, short-order cooking—wherever I could get in. I left Timmy at Aunt Mame's house whenever she'd let me, or parked him with a married friend who had so many kids she never even knew when he was around. After he was old enough to go to school it was easier. I could work all day and Timmy made his own lunch and supper and played out on the streets with the other kids.

Then we got into the war and Al came home one night, looking pretty happy and bright-eyed. I could smell the whisky on him, but I didn't think that the reason for all the good cheer. He didn't say a thing, just got all his clothes out of the dresser and began wrapping them up.

"Checking out?" I asked. "Not that I care, but just to keep the record straight."

"You bet I am," he said, giving me a look as though he dared me to stop him. "I've enlisted in the Army. Boy, it'll be swell to get out of this dumpy one-horse burg."

"Yeah, I hear those fox holes are pretty cozy," I said, dryly. "Don't forget about the allotment, will you?"

He made out like he didn't hear me. Timmy came in just as Al was going out with his bundle, and said, "Hey, Pop, where're you going?" But he didn't answer Timmy either. He'd never thought the kid was anything but a nuisance anyway.

I got the allotment for a while but then I got a divorce from Al, because I'd met Clint and hoped he'd marry me. What happened to Al? Where is he now? Search me. People like us don't keep track of each other much.

"*Your mode of living has been disgraceful, drifting from bar to bar, living in transient hotels with a man to whom you are not married, allowing your 14-year-old son to leave school and to lead an unsupervised, irresponsible existence. . . .*" Judges certainly knew how to load it on, I thought as I listened.

It didn't seem to me at the time that I was doing anything wrong. I met up with Clint Arnold right after Al enlisted. I suppose I was lonely after Al left, even though I didn't know it. Al wasn't much of a husband but I was used to having him around.

Clint was a lot older than me, ten or maybe fifteen years. He never told his age. He was funny that way, vain and proud of his looks. He kept thin by working out in a gym and he was always shining clean and well dressed. When he gave me his order at the counter that first time he looked at me nice and friendly—not the way some people acted, as though I was a piece of equipment like the coffee urn, nor was he a wise guy, either.

He ate his hamburger and drank his coffee without saying anything, but I could feel him watching me as I moved around behind the counter. After he left I found a dollar bill tucked under his saucer.

"Like to see a show when you get off tonight?" he asked next time he came in.

Well, why not? I thought. He looked a lot better than most of the lugs who asked me out, even though I didn't know anything about him.

"Sure, what've I got to lose?" I said, but I noticed my hand was shaking when I turned the spigot on the coffee urn. Clint did something to me right from the start. He was kind to me for one thing—never a mean word or a slap out of Clint. His being so much older, too, gave me a kind of looked-after feeling. Heaven knows, I'd never had that before!

Clint said to me one night, "How about laying off this hash-slinging and letting me take care of you, Ivy, honey? We can be together all the time then, and I won't have to hang around, waiting for you to get off work."

He patted my hand and I got all warm and tingly inside. It was swell to feel that somebody cared what happened to me. I thought how nice it was that the juke box was playing something soft and sweet. Sure, Judge, we were in a bar! Where would you think a hash-slinger and a cheap gambler would spend their time anyway? At the Ritz Towers?

I snuggled real close to Clint and sniffed the shaving lotion he always used. His shoulder felt solid and strong next to mine.

"Gee, Clint, that'd be swell," I said gratefully, "but I haven't ever gotten my divorce from Al, you know. He won't care, he'll be glad to get rid of me for good, I guess. I'll get started on it right away, huh?"

CLINT cleared his throat and looked kind of embarrassed. "Well, Ivy, honey, it's like this. I wasn't thinking that you and I'd really get married, though I'd like to. Thing is, I got a wife in Jersey and she keeps pretty close tabs on me. I don't hardly ever see her, but I have to send her money and—well, there it is, honey."

"But, Clint, divorce her!" I said indignantly. "Whatta nerve she's got, hanging onto you. Just tell her you're through."

"Can't be done, Ivy." Clint's voice was still soft, but I could see he meant it and he didn't want to talk about it either. "Rita's my wife and as long as she wants to stay that way, I can't do anything about it."

"You mean she's got something on you," I guessed.

"Put it that way if you want to," Clint said. "Forget her. How about us?"

I said yes. Who wouldn't have? Maybe the life Clint offered me wasn't any bed of roses, but it was a lot better than standing on my feet frying hamburgers all day. *And I thought I loved him.* I got my divorce anyway, hoping maybe Clint'd change his mind about divorcing Rita, but he never did. Clint earned his living in all sorts of shady ways, "fixing" for gamblers, drifting around and picking up information on fighters and race horses, maybe even passing on stolen goods once in a while. I don't know everything he did. Clint was close-mouthed, but somewhere along the line Rita had gotten something on him and he was under her thumb, but good.

We spent a lot of time in bars, like Judge Burton said. They were Clint's clubs, I guess you could say. He carried on his business in them. I tagged along to be with him. Sure we drank. What else can you do in bars? I guess maybe I drank more than I should have, but Clint pulled me up short now and then.

"You'll spoil your good looks, Ivy, honey," he'd say, mildlike but firm. "Drinking is all right for some but not for my pretty girl."

Clint himself never drank too much. Clint never did anything that would be bad for Clint Arnold—looking out for number one all the time, twenty-four hours a day. I found that out later.

I saw Timmy pretty regularly, maybe once or twice a month. He'd been spending most of his time at Aunt Mame's. She was dead now and most of her kids were grown up and gone and Uncle Frank took a fancy to Timmy. That seemed strange. He'd never treated me right, but he was good to Timmy. He was a queer kid, seemed to me, tall as a man, but skinny as a string bean by the time he'd reached 13. I never did feel that I could tell what he was thinking, the way you can with most kids. He never seemed specially glad to see me and never talked much—just answered the questions I asked him and didn't ask me any.

Clint never had seen the kid so he went along with me one day to visit him. Nobody but Uncle Frank was home.

"So you finally came around to see Timmy," Uncle Frank said in a nasty way. "He's over at my cousin Sam's bowling alley. Works there now."

"Works?" Clint asked. "How about school? How old's the kid?"

Uncle Frank looked at Clint as though he'd like to tell him it wasn't any of his business, but he didn't dare.

"Timmy's almost 14," I said quickly. "Come on, we'll go over to the bowling alley and see him."

Timmy was there, setting up pins for some bowlers. He pretended he didn't see us till I called to him. Then he got one of the other boys to take over his alley and walked up to us slowly, not saying anything, his face dead-pan.

"Hello, Timmy," I said, feeling a little funny for the first time about Clint. "This here's Clint Arnold. He's a friend—"

"Sure. I know," Timmy said and he gave Clint a sullen, sidewise look.

"I didn't know you were working here, Timmy," I went on, trying to make conversation. "We stopped over at Uncle Frank's to see you. He said you've quit school."

"Yeah, I wasn't gettin' anywhere," he answered. "I earn good money here, and I don't have to listen to no teacher yapping her head off at me."

"But where do you live, Timmy? Uncle Frank acted as though he hadn't seen you for a long time."

"Right here." Timmy nodded his head at one of the long benches running along the wall. "I got a bedroll. I just bunk there at night."

I noticed how close and smoky the air was. I looked at Timmy and he sure was white and unhealthy looking under those bright lights.

"You don't ever get any fresh air, Timmy," I said. "That ain't good for you—"

CLINT broke in, then. "You oughtn't to quit school before you're sixteen. The law says you can't, anyway—"

Timmy looked down at Clint—he was almost half a head taller—and his blue eyes blazed with sparks.

"Shut up! Don't *you* come around here shooting off your mouth and tellin' me what to do!" Timmy yelled.

"Why, you—" I caught Clint's arm as Timmy turned his back and walked away from us. I called after him but he never turned his head.

Clint was so mad he was fit to be tied. "C'mon, let's get out of here. Can't tell a little wise guy like that nothin'."

So I went with Clint. Timmy didn't seem to want to have anything to do with me.

I didn't see him again until we met at headquarters.

Your son, left to his own devices, came into possession of a deadly weapon and with it wounded a police officer, who narrowly escaped death from his injuries..." Judge Burton was repeating the facts of Timmy's story then.

Clint and I had been eating supper in a grill when the policeman tracked me down. Clint saw him first. His jaw fell open and he looked like he was frozen. I remember he was pouring some ketchup on his steak, and he just kept the bottle upside down until the sauce was all over his plate.

HE BEGAN talking before the officer could open his mouth. "You haven't got a thing on me, Horan. I don't know what you think you're up to, but you're wasting your time—"

"Shut up, Arnold," the guy said, looking at Clint as though he didn't like what he saw. "I'm not after you. It's the girl friend I want."

"*Her?*" Clint said. He looked at me across the table and there was a glint in his eye I didn't remember seeing before—cold and kind of suspicious. It scared me, and because I was scared I stuck my chin up in the air and got hard. Nobody was going to push me around.

"What's the charge, officer?" I asked coolly.

"Contributing to the delinquency of a minor," he said, short and snappy. "Your kid's been playin' around with guns and somebody's got hurt."

"Timmy? Guns?" I gasped. "But what's that got to do with me? I wasn't there. I didn't know—"

The cop looked disgusted. "I'll say you weren't there, but you shoulda been. You shoulda been lookin' after your kid. He's just barely fourteen and the law's got some funny idea that parents are responsible for what their minor kids do. Get it?"

I didn't get it, not then, but I knew there wasn't any use talking any more with him. I put on my coat and picked up my bag.

"Where're you taking me?" I asked.

"To the House of Detention. Your kid's locked up, too, and you'll both stay that way till we see how this shooting comes out."

"Who'd the kid shoot?" Clint asked in a thin kind of voice.

"Oh, nobody much," the other said, sarcastic. "Just the officer on the beat."

Clint let out his breath in a long whoosh. "Why, the fool, the crazy little fool!"

He sat staring in front of him. He almost seemed to have forgotten I was there. I touched his arm.

"Clint," I said, "You can do something for me, can't you? You know people. You got connections. Gee, Clint, I don't want to stay locked up."

"Oh, sure, sure, Ivy honey," he promised. "I'll get busy, see what I can do right away."

When I got to headquarters they took me into a room where Timmy was. There was a police sergeant at a desk and some newspaper reporters. Timmy was sitting in a chair and he kept his eyes on the floor. When they asked him something he answered, but he never looked at me once.

They told me that Timmy and another kid who worked in the bowling alley had gotten hold of two guns, probably picked them up in a pawn shop. The night before, after the alley had closed and they were alone, they'd staged a game of cops-and-robbers. Hiding back of the counters and behind the benches and dodging around the posts, the crazy kids shot it out the

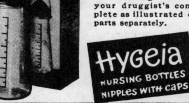

way they thought real cops and bandits did. They might have killed each other! The cop on the beat heard the shooting and came in to see what was going on—just in time to get a bullet from Timmy's gun in his chest.

"But it was an accident, then," I said. "You can't blame Timmy for it. He didn't mean to shoot him."

The sergeant gave me the cold and fishy eye. "Sure, it was an accident. A bullet can kill just as good, whether or not it's meant to. If this officer dies, I suppose telling his wife and kids it was an accident is going to make 'em feel just dandy." He slapped his hand down hard on the desk. "You're his mother, aren't you? Why'd you let him quit school and hang around that bowling alley? It was your business to look after him. We're not blamin' the kid as much as we are you."

I shut up like a clam. It wasn't ever any use jawing with police.

Clint'll get me out, I thought hopefully. *He'll go to bat for me.*

The reporters had been scribbling on their pads all this time, and when I left the room the photographers outside blasted me with their flashlights. They plastered my picture all over the front pages with dramatic headlines.

MOTHER BLAMED FOR ACCUSED BOY'S CRIME! DELINQUENT SON OR DELINQUENT MOTHER?

They really went to town on the story. And if you think that Clint Arnold with his shady dealings and his fear of the law walked into that mess to help me, you're as crazy as I was. After a week I knew what had happened. He'd run out on me in a tough spot—just the way everybody else had, all my life.

So Timmy and I sweated it out in jail while the policeman fought for his life. I never asked to see Timmy. I didn't know what to say to the kid.

Luckily for everybody concerned, the policeman pulled through and was considered out of danger after a month. But Timmy was still guilty of a crime—and so was I.

"I find that you are guilty of contributing to the delinquency of your minor son by neglecting the duties and responsibilities of a parent. I hereby sentence you to serve...." Yes, Judge Burton sent me to prison with those words.

I bet all you women who read them in the papers, sitting in your safe, comfortable homes with your husbands right by you and your kids asleep upstairs, nodded your heads and said, "Serves her right! A woman like that shouldn't be a mother."

Maybe you're right. Maybe, being raised the way I was and going through all the things I did made me so I wasn't fit to be a mother. But whose fault was that? Did I ask to be deserted by my own father and mother and kicked around and never given an even break? Was it my fault that I wasn't ever strong enough to climb out of the gutter where I was born and raised?

Well—no use arguing about that. Everybody felt the same way, Judge Burton, the people in the courtroom, the reporters. Even my lawyer thought I was a Grade-A heel and put up a poor fight for me. So I acted the way an animal does when you've got it in a corner and it doesn't know how to get out—mean and defiant, fighting back even though it knows it's no use.

I looked straight into Judge Burton's face when he sentenced me. I held my chin high and there was a sneer on my lips. He shook his head and sighed as he turned from me to speak to Timmy.

Timmy stood up and though he was so tall, he looked awful thin and young. His face was white as paper and his eyes were big and scared as he looked up at Judge Burton.

Why, he's just a kid, a little kid, I thought, surprised. I'd grown up so fast and so early myself, I guess I'd just figured Timmy would do the same. I began to wish I'd done more for him, tried to get closer to him somehow. When he was really little, there'd never been any time with me working most always, and worrying about Al's drinking and where our next meal was coming from. But I guessed maybe I was just making excuses for myself. I was no good. Everybody thought so.

Timmy was told that he was to go to a training school for boys where he would learn a trade and live until he came of age.

"They can call it whatever they want," I thought bitterly, "but it's still a reform school. Whenever he tries to get a job and

comes to the question on the application blank that asks about being in any institution, he'll stop and wonder if he can get away with a lie."

An attendant took Timmy's arm to lead him from the room. When they reached the door, Timmy looked around at me—it was the first time he'd really looked at me since the mess started, and his eyes were like a little kid's—scared and lonesome, and begging me to help him.

"Wait!" I almost cried out. "Wait! Don't take him away—"

Then I shut my mouth, remembering. There wasn't anything I could do for Timmy now—too late for that.

I started my sentence in the women's prison. Maybe I wasn't a model prisoner, but I didn't make any trouble. I was like an animal who'd been dragged out of the corner and shut up in a cage where I sat glowering and dreaming of freedom. Only it was Timmy I dreamed of. I had nightmares, where the tough kids in the reform school beat him up and he called to me to help him. Like a little kid, he shouted. And I couldn't help him.

The remainder of your sentence is being suspended and you are to be freed on parole. You will be taken to the court chambers of Judge Burton who sentenced you...." It was the warden who said that to me.

I'd hated the warden before, but he looked noble when he said those words

On the way into the city I racked my brains, trying to think what had happened to give me this break. Could it be that Clint had come forward at last to pay the fine that would shorten my sentence? No, I knew better than that. Clint was looking out for number one, the way he always had. He was through the minute the law reached out for me.

The cop outside the door of the judge's chambers opened it for me to go in, but didn't follow. The door closed behind me and I looked around, wondering. There was only one person in the room and it wasn't Judge Burton. It was Timmy.

He walked toward me and he looked different somehow—heavier, for one thing. He'd put on weight in that reform school. He seemed older too, and with something in his face that I didn't remember ever seeing there before—happiness. That was it. Timmy looked happy.

"Mom," he said, and his voice was different, deeper and sounded like he knew just what he wanted to say. "We've got an awful good break coming to us. You're in it with me, if you want to be."

"What do you mean?" I asked, kind of dazed. "What's this all about? How'd you get away from the school?"

Timmy talked fast, running his words together in his hurry to tell me. "It's the superintendent of the school who's done it for us. It isn't like a jail at all, Mom, and the super's a wonderful guy. I told him all about you after I got to know him. I guess I felt pretty bitter toward you. But he kept talking about your background and how you really weren't to blame 'cause you didn't know any better. I didn't think at first, but he spent a lot of time with me, and I finally saw it his way."

"Then you don't blame me, Timmy?" I wanted to hear him say that.

"Naw, not now. Gee, I couldn't see before what a hard time you always had, Mom, what with working and Dad running out on you. But I can now. It wasn't your fault I was such a dope, quitting school and playing around with that gun. I can hardly stand to think of you being in prison, Mom."

"Oh, Timmy," I whispered. The tears in my eyes stung, and I could hardly see him.

"So the super got you paroled," Timmy went on, "and he says you can come and live at the school, too, and learn to do office work. And as soon as he's sure we're ready to go out, he'll let us. We can be together and earn a good living and—oh, gee, Mom, won't it be swell?"

"Swell, Timmy, just swell!" I was crying now, and something inside of me was saying, *Ivy Benson, this is the first time in your life that anyone ever offered you love—love without strings. Grab it. Hold onto it tight. This is the most wonderful thing that'll ever happen to you!*

I held out my arms and Timmy let me hug him. He acted kind of awkward about it, but I think he liked it too.

Things're working out swell for Timmy and me. We'll soon be ready to strike out on our own. Timmy's the best kid in the world. He always was. All he needed was love and an even break. If only I had seen that before. I'll never stop regretting my carelessness and lack of understanding toward Timmy. But I've got the rest of my life to make it up to him.

Do you know what I've found that's made me into the kind of woman I never expected to be? It's something I didn't know existed before. It's something you've all got, you women with your good husbands and your happy homes. And now I've got it too—self-respect. *The End*

hollywood
Undertow

A STORY TO CHILL YOUR SOUL...

BEGIN IT ON THE NEXT PAGE

A COMPLETE BOOK-LENGTH CONFESSION

What had happened to Paula could happen to me! I had to get out of Hollywood...quick!

I'LL start my story on the day when I awoke to the fact that my foolish ambitions and silly pride had brought me not only heartbreak and remorse but now—retribution. The time had come when I had to face Bill and shatter the rapture of our honeymoon by telling him that I was not the sweet, wholesome girl he thought he had married, but one of those parasites that cling to the outer fringes of movieland, leading a precarious existence, lying, scheming, and chiseling in a vain attempt to crash an industry that doesn't want them. Hollywood has a name for my kind—Girl-About-Hollywood. It

When the bright hopes
and promises of a Hollywood career
go glimmering, what
does a beauty contest winner do?
One such girl became known as
the Black Dahlia.
Was that to be Sari's fate?

isn't a pretty label to wear.

And now I had to tell my husband that the bride he adored was Sari Salome!

Bill had brought the paper back to the little bungalow we occupied in the motel at Phoenix before he'd gone to work that morning. So I was alone when I read the screaming headline:

DENTON GETS 99 YEARS

"Oh, no!" I whispered as the paper slid from my nerveless hands.

But the words still blazed before my eyes. I knew that I'd come to the end of my masquerade. I'd have to bring shame and disgrace on my parents, dishonor Bill's name and kill his love forever. I had no other alternative—except to let Carl spend the rest of his life in prison for a crime he'd never committed. Not even I could do that!

I sat there, the paper strewn about at my feet, staring into space. Perspiration bathed my body but it was not the blazing heat of Arizona that caused it. It was the cold, clammy sweat of fear. Presently my whirling mind cleared and focused. *Sari Salome and all she stood for is dead now,* I thought. *Why bring her back to life? Why give up this wonderful happiness? Why bring misery and disgrace on those who love you?*

The voice of temptation hammered away while my mind went back to the time when I was Edna Lawrence, winner of a small-town beauty contest, who had the crazy idea that all she had to do to become a movie star was go to Hollywood where she'd immediately be received with open arms.

Maybe you're one of the girls who have similar crazy ideas about going to Hollywood. If so, I want you to know what happened to me and to another beautiful girl, whose tragedy was so mixed up with my own. Then maybe you'll think twice before you decide to try crashing the movies!

All my life I'd been petted and spoiled by my doting parents. I'd come to Mother and Dad after twenty years of waiting and praying for a child and it was hard for them to refuse me anything. From the moment I could understand words I knew that I was pretty. My parents and relatives, and the neighbors too, kept drumming it into my ears until I began to accept admiration as a matter of course.

I used to sit through every picture that came to my home-town movie theater at least twice, and even as a kid of 14, I envied the glamorous women parading across the screen. I studied their looks, I wore hats and dresses copied from theirs, and tried to do my hair the way they did. And by the time I was 16, I'd begun to ask myself, "What have *they* got that *I* haven't got?"

Dad and Mother had an ice-cream parlor and after school the fountain was always crowded with my friends. They'd argue for hours on the beauty and merits of the stars and often one of them would turn to me and say, "Why don't you go to Hollywood, Edna? You're crazy to stay here with looks like yours!"

Hollywood! The idea became an obsession. *What have they got that I haven't?* That thought was never far from my mind.

Winning the yearly beauty contest sponsored by our local movie house brought things to a climax. I was 18 then. "The most beautiful contestant we have ever had," the Clarion reported.

But the silver loving cup I won didn't satisfy me. My burning ambition to get to the movie capital couldn't be denied any longer and I told Mother and Dad, "I want to go to Hollywood," knowing I was going to have a battle on my hands.

"Your father and I have been expecting [*Please turn page*] this for a long time, Edna," Mother said wearily. "It isn't possible."

"But, Mother! Now that I've won—"

"Sorry, Edna," Dad cut in. "It would break our hearts to have you go so far away from us. Besides, we haven't got the money." His voice held a finality that angered me.

"That's not the real reason you won't let me go!" I cried furiously. "You want to keep me tied to Mother's apron strings till I'm too old to do anything else but jerk sodas in the store! Well, I won't stay in this dead little hole-in-the-wall! I won't! *I won't!*"

I went into one of the tantrums that always made them give in to me when I was a child. But for once, my folks were adamant. No matter how hard I wept and sulked and stormed they wouldn't hear of me leaving them.

The last words I flung at them before I ran out of the house were, "If you think you're going to stop my going into the movies, you're crazy! I'll get to Hollywood if I have to hitchhike there! I'm eighteen and I can do as I like!"

The hands of the little clock on my vanity pointed to 2 a.m. when I placed beside it the long letter I'd written telling my folks not to worry about me. I'd soon be a movie star and then I'd build them a lovely home where they could spend the rest of their lives basking in the California sunshine!

I crept down the stairs, suitcase in hand, passing through the hall like a shadow and had my hand on the front-door knob when out of the darkness came my dad's stern voice, "*Edna!*"

The light switched on and I saw he'd been sitting in a chair by the living-room door. "So you were running away like a thief in the night!" he said sadly.

"What else can you expect!" I cried, defiantly tossing my head. "I'm going to get to Hollywood, one way or another!"

He passed his hand wearily over his forehead, and when I saw how old and tired he looked, I couldn't help feeling ashamed and wanting to put my arms round him.

"I thought you'd do something like this," he said huskily, "that's why I sat watching the stairs." Then he heaved a great sigh of resignation and went on. "It would break our hearts if we knew you were standing on roads waiting for the first stranger to pick you up. So if you're determined—well—I've got a little in the bank and I can raise a loan on the store—"

"Oh, Dad!" I sobbed, and flew into his arms, my heart pounding with a queer mixture of delight and shame. Delight at having got my own way, and shame for the cowardly way I'd made him give in. But I'd make it up to him—when I was rich and famous!

Within a week, I was on my way to Hollywood, with a trunk full of beautiful clothes, $700 in travelers' checks in my bag, and no premonition whatever that my wonderful dream would turn into a ghastly nightmare of misery, degradation and murder.

Six months later I knew what it was the movie stars had that *I* didn't have! I learned the hard way that a girl has to have *talent*, training, intelligence and plenty of spunk to reach even the lowest rung of movie success. Los Angeles is crowded with beautiful girls who have discovered that too late. *And I was caught in the Hollywood undertow.*

During that first six months I didn't even get to see the inside of a studio—not even as an "extra"! I checked into an expensive hotel, registering as Sari Salome, the ultra-phony name I'd chosen to launch me on my career. I immediately had expensive photographs made, then registered at Central Casting. I also fell for some of the phony advertisements of agents who make a living preying on fools like me, paying big fees for nonexistent services and influence.

I'd been in Hollywood two months the first time I met Bill Farwell. Something inside me that wasn't Sari Salome wanted to fall in love with him right away. But I'd just come out of a movie agent's office with my ears ringing from his positive assurance that he was going to make me a great star. For his flattery, I'd cheerfully paid him $50, a registration fee, then gone out into the sunshine of Hill Street treading on air.

My eyes saw nothing but my foolish dreams. That's why I didn't see the grating until it had ripped off the high French heel from one of my shoes. I stood there waving to taxis that refused to stop, and getting angrier by the minute when Bill came out of a doorway near by. He was a tall rugged young man in marine uniform. I was standing on one leg, the heelless shoe in my hand and he took the situation in at a glance.

"Looks like you need a shoe repairer, miss," he said.

"Do tell!" I snapped, mistaking his cheerful grin. I thought he was making fun of my predicament and I froze him like the movie queen I expected someday to be.

"Sorry," he said. "Thought I might help, seeing what a tough time you're having getting a taxi." He walked to an old car standing by the curb, got in, and started the motor. For a minute or two he sat there watching my fruitless efforts to get a taxi, then he got out again and came up to me.

"Look, Cinderella—" he smiled down at me disarmingly—"if you're not too ritzy to ride in my old jalopy, I'll drive you to a shoemaker."

I looked up into his face then, noticing the thick blond hair, the leather-colored skin of his rugged, good-humored face, and the whimsical smile in his gray eyes. The part of me that was still Edna Lawrence went all warm and soft, overwhelming for a moment screen-struck Sari Salome. I smiled back at him. "Well, if it won't take you out of your way," I said.

"Don't worry, kid," he replied. "There's a shoemaker on Figueroa not far from where I live, and I'm going home anyway." I felt his strong hand under my armpit and found myself being almost lifted up while I hopped on one leg to his car.

Kid! Sari Salome, movie queen, thought furiously, *Of all the nerve!*

"Gosh, but you're pretty!" he said candidly when we'd left some of the heavy traffic behind and he could turn to look at me. "It would be my luck to meet you on the last day of my leave." His grin would have melted an iceberg.

"I don't know what I should have done if you hadn't have come along when you did and helped me." I smiled into his nice gray eyes, and felt just like Edna Lawrence—not Sari Salome.

He laughed and I could hear the roll of the sea in his laughter. "I can imagine how you felt. The same thing happened to my sister one time when I was out with her and I had to carry her nearly all the way home."

His deep voice chatted on and it seemed as if my mind was divided into two conflicting parts—one part wanting to listen to him while the other part dwelt on the sweet words of the movie agent I'd just left. "Just put yourself in my hands, girlie, and I'll have the name of Sari Salome in everyone's mouth! What a name! What a personality!"

Presently he pulled up outside a small shoe repair shop and before I realized what he was going to do he had got out, opened the door on my side, and was carrying me across the pavement as if I were a child. For a split second my cheek lay against his and I felt his lips pucker swiftly against my ear. I wanted to turn my mouth round to where his was, I even started to, and then I remembered I was Sari Salome who was going to be a great star and demanded to be put down at once.

He only laughed and carried me into the shop depositing me in one of the while-you-wait booths. "Well, I reckon my good deed for today is done," he said, "so I'll be breezing along." Then he took an old envelope from his tunic and gave it to me. "That's my name and address—" he stopped a second then, went on with sudden little-boy wistfulness— "just in case you'd care to slip a fellow a line. I expect to be out in six months."

"I'll think about it," I said smiling. But there was a promise in my smile.

"You're the sweetest thing I've ever seen in my life," he said softly. "So *very* sweet!" His big hand brushed my cheek for a moment with almost unbelievable gentleness. Then he was gone.

I looked at the envelope. It was addressed to William Farwell, with his number and ship at San Diego. "So very sweet!" I whispered, and let the words drown out for a brief moment the sound of those spoken by the Hollywood agent.

I slipped the envelope into my bag. But I didn't write to him—because there was no room in Sari Salome's life or ambitions for a tall, young Marine. When the time did come, that I'd have given anything to have a real man to tell my troubles to, I couldn't find that envelope. All I could remember was his strong face, the music of his laughter and that his name was William Farwell.

I was down to my last $5, most of my lovely clothes were in the pawn shop, and my room rent at the shabby hotel to which I'd gravitated was due, the morning I first spoke to Paula Casselli. She came into the restaurant where I was having coffee and doughnuts. I'd noticed Paula many times haunting the studios and casting agencies, noticed her more particularly than other girls, because she looked so very much like me. Her hair and eyes were the same color, her nose was small and slightly turned up like mine, and she was my size and build. Her opening remark after sitting down at my table with a glass of milk and a sandwich showed she too was conscious of the resemblance.

"I've been wanting to talk to you for a long time," she exclaimed. "Do you know we're so much alike that somebody mistook me for you the other day?"

"I hope it wasn't the police," I replied jokingly, adding, "I'm Sari Salome."

"Golly!" she murmured. "Where did you think that one up? I'm Paula Casselli." Then she rushed on, "I followed you in here because I've got a proposition to make you. How'd you like to live in a swell furnished apartment up on Sunset Boulevard?"

"*Sunset Boulevard!*" I cried. Apartments anywhere in Los Angeles were as scarce as roses on the desert and getting one on Sunset Boulevard was practically impossible.

"It's true, Sari!" she exclaimed. "A friend of mine who's got a pull with the superintendent of the Ridgeway Arms tells me there's a two-bedroom apartment, elegantly furnished, going to be vacant tomorrow and he can get it for me.

[*Please turn page*]

A recent portrait of
Constance Luft Huhn,
Head of the House of Tangee

WE ARE STILL THE WEAKER SEX

by CONSTANCE LUFT HUHN
Head of the House of Tangee

MANY OF US may be serving shoulder to shoulder with America's fighting men —but we're still the weaker sex . . . It's still up to us to appear as alluring and lovely as possible.

So remember, ask for the aids to beauty made by THE HOUSE OF TANGEE —TANGEE Petal-Finish Face Powder and Rouge and Satin-Finish Lipstick. You'll find you were never lovelier!

Whether you're in or out of uniform, you'll want to be completely appealing and feminine—you'll want delightful satin-smooth lips and all the glamour of a silky, petal-smooth complexion.

THE HOUSE OF TANGEE has created just what you need to keep you as lovely as you should be. For your lips, we have world-famous TANGEE Satin-Finish Lipsticks to give your lips long-lasting satiny smoothness. And with TANGEE Petal-Finish Rouge and the extraordinary new TANGEE Petal-Finish Face Powder, your complexion will take on a silky, radiant petal-smoothness that clings for many *extra hours!*

SAMMY KAYE IS ON THE AIR IN TANGEE SERENADE . . . Listen Every Sunday at 1:30 P. M. (EWT) Coast-to-Coast . . . Blue Network

Satin-Finish Your Lips
Petal-Finish Your Complexion **TANGEE**

It's $200 a month—in advance!"

I smiled ruefully. "That let's me out," I said. "I'm broke!"

"So am I," she sighed. "But it's such a wonderful opportunity. The Ridgeway Arms is full of producers, directors, and all kinds of big shots who can do things for a gal! If we could only dig up that first month's rent, we'd be going places before the next month's was due. I figured I could find a couple of girls who would be willing to put the first month down for my information."

"It sounds super," I said longingly. "There must be some way—"

Then suddenly I thought of Arlene Lamont and Bunny Brabazon, two other movie-struck girls I'd met several times at Central Casting. They shared a room at the Hotel Chatsworth and complained bitterly about how expensive and unsatisfactory living in a hotel was. "But what can we do about it?" Bunny had said once with a shrug of resignation. "There's not even a decent doghouse for rent in this town!"

So now I exclaimed excitedly, "I think I know just the girls for us!"

I hurried Paula over to the Chatsworth, explaining about Bunny and Arlene on the way.

Luck was with us. They were both in and they were just as much interested as I'd thought they'd be.

"It's a deal!" Arlene said after a short conference with Bunny. "It happens our room is up here tomorrow, so we shan't be losing anything." She winked at Paula knowingly and went on, "I think we've all got what it takes to make a go of it."

The next morning we all moved into apartment 221 at the Ridgeway Arms. The $200 took most of Arlene's and Bunny's capital and there wasn't $20 left among the four of us. But that didn't seem to worry the others.

"But how are we going to live?" I asked Paula anxiously.

"You'll find out," she said laughing. "Just wait till you meet Carl Denton and some of the boys. Carl's the guy who got the apartment for me. He's a phony but he's always got plenty of money and, oh, sister! He sure does love to spend it on pretty girls."

Right from the start we four girls knew we were birds of a feather. We all had looks, we'd all come from small towns to Hollywood to crash the movies, and we'd all failed because we had no talent to back up our looks. Our very names, chosen with an eye on movie marquees throughout the country, were as phony as we, a sort of unwritten law sprang up among us which stopped us from ever mentioning our real names or family backgrounds.

I HAD already rented a post office box where my folks could address their letters to Edna Lawrence, explaining to them that the housing situation made it necessary that I move from hotel to hotel as no permanent accommodations were available, so this would be the best arrangement to make sure I'd get their letters. They hadn't liked it, but they hadn't questioned it, as housing conditions were bad even in our small home town so my explanation had sounded plausible enough to them. So now I was all set.

We hadn't been settled in the apartment a half hour before the door bell rang. I opened the door. Leaning against the door post was a man dressed in expensive slacks and a wide-shouldered, wasp-waisted sports coat. His hair was coal black and slicked straight back from his olive complexioned forehead with a dressing that made it shine like polished ebony. His eyes were so dark brown, they looked almost as black as the small trim mustache he affected. He might have modeled himself after any one of a half dozen Latin-type movie heroes.

"So you're in, baby!" he cried delightedly. Before I could answer, he swept me in his arms and was kissing me.

Paula's laughing voice came from somewhere behind me. "Hey, Carl!" she said. "That's my stand-in!"

He released me and stared hard at the two of us. Then he laughed. "Of course I can see the difference now you're together. But you can't blame a guy for making a mistake. Even together you look like sisters."

"Well, don't stand there just staring at us!" Paula said. "Come on in and meet the rest of the gang."

Carl Denton was adept in making himself agreeable. Within a few minutes, he was passing out compliments to all of us and making himself thoroughly at home. Presently he said, "This calls for a housewarming. Stick around, kids, and I'll go out and collect a couple of live wires along with some groceries and stuff."

When he returned he had two other men with him whom he introduced as cameramen. Their arms were loaded down with enough food and liquor for a dozen people, and the familiar way they spoke of big movie stars and directors, mentioning them by their first names as if they were intimates thrilled me. I had at last entered the inner circle of the film world!

The party continued all through the day and well on toward daylight next morning. The men called up their friends and soon the apartment was full of people. Every now and again someone would go out and come back loaded with liquor and delicatessen food.

That party was the beginning of dozens of other parties either at our place or someone else's. But it didn't get me one step nearer my goal. It didn't take me long to find out that the big shots we thought we were mixing with were only washed-up actors, has been-directors and out-of-work cameramen. Most of them were trying too desperately to keep in the game themselves to be able to push a friend along. It was girls like us who actually helped them along—because we were always willing to tag along with them to a party where they had their own particular ax to grind.

These parties were usually given by playboys flashing across Hollywood night life for a short time, throwing their money about under the false impression they were seeing life among the movie folks.

They didn't know that legitimate, hard-working film people despised our kind—just as deep down inside me, I too despised our kind. I guess it was this fundamental feeling that kept Bill's memory enshrined in my heart. He was something fine and decent and honest to think about when I became too disgusted with myself and my crowd. Perhaps if I'd been able to write Bill, and to hear from him in return, I might have found the courage to change my way of life, but when I looked for the envelope he'd given me, it was gone. Once, driven by a need too great to ignore, I did write him, addressing my letter to William Farwell, United States Marines, San Diego. When the letter came back stamped "Address not sufficient," my feeling of loss was almost unbearable.

Our way of life became a constant battle of wits to chisel what we could out of men, without giving anything more than a kiss and a promise in return.

I became, like the others, a Girl-About-Hollywood.

After one of our parties the cupboards and refrigerator were always full of food and liquor. And there was always some man with money we could wangle into a department store on the pretext that we wanted to buy some little thing, then casually lead him to the dress or coat department and go into raptures over a certain garment saying wistfully, "Oh! If only I had the money to buy it!" The gag never failed to work. It was the same way with jewelry, which usually found its way into pawnshops around rent day.

Many, many nights I swore I would quit and get a job next morning. But when late hours make you sleep long past noon, there's not much hope of getting a job then. Once, in a mood of disgust, I did get a job and was supposed to start at 9 a. m. next day. But I didn't wake up till afternoon.

MEN came and went but Carl Denton was always around. Two days after our first meeting, he switched his affections from Paula to me. Not that she cared. Like me, she never really liked him. "There's something sort of sinister about him that gives me the creeps," she said to me. "Heaven knows what kind of racket he gets all his money from. Still, he's always good for a loan when we need it, so you keep him in the family, Sari. But watch your step with him!"

So I played Carl along for the benefit of us all. But you can't play with fire and not get burnt!

I found that out the night Paula and I went to a wild party up on La Brea Avenue. It was a large, noisy affair with more girls than men. When someone wasn't banging away at the piano, the radio or the record-player was going full blast and sometimes all three played at the same time. The din became deafening as the party grew more hilarious and the drinks began to take effect.

The house was on a quiet block and soon complaining neighbors kept the phone ringing constantly. It was about 3 o'clock in the morning when one of the girls answered it and bawled back a lot of insults at the person complaining. The next thing we knew two police vans had arrived and we were all loaded into them.

"Don't tell 'em a thing about yourself," Paula whispered to me. "They'll only get in touch with your folks if you do."

"Okay," I whispered back. I would sooner die than have the folks back home find out how I'd been living.

They let all the others go free on bail, but because Paula and I refused to give any information about ourselves other than the names we were known around Hollywood by, they charged us with vagrancy and disorderly conduct and held us for trial next day. A Hollywood detective, whose job it was to keep tabs on girls like us, gave us bad characters and said we had no visible means of support. And when the magistrate asked where we came from, what we did for a living, and lots of other questions, we just stared at him tight-lipped and refused to answer. So he gave us, and our kind, a tongue-lashing, then sentenced us to fourteen days in jail.

OUR being locked up in the women's prison was the most terrible thing that had ever happened to me. There were women there who had once been young and pretty, women who'd come to Los Angeles with the same burning ambitions that I had. Their stories were written in deep lines on their faces, in the hardness of their eyes, and the coarse language that poured from their thin, tight mouths.

There were other young girls too, as frightened and ashamed as I, and trying to hide their real feelings behind a false front of bravado and defiance.

I'd seen some of these girls before, around Hollywood night spots and bars. There were about a dozen of us, drawn together by the common bond of failure, who made a little circle apart from the downright criminals.

You'd have thought that such an awful experience would have brought me to my senses, wouldn't you? I thought it had and during those ghastly fourteen days I swore over and over that I would cut loose from the life I'd been leading, forget my silly unattainable ambitions, and get a job. I thoroughly intended to do that the morning we were released.

I didn't say anything about it to Paula, as we took the bus to our apartment, because I intended to wait till all the girls were out, then pack my things and quietly disappear. But when we opened the door of the apartment, there was a yell, "Surprise!" and we found the place full of our good-time pals all set for a big welcome-home party. I hadn't the backbone to tell them I was through then walk out on them, and by the time the party was over, hours later, all my good resolutions had been shattered. I was back in the Girl-About-Hollywood groove.

Weeks passed and then the miracle happened. I met Bill again!

Somewhere deep inside me the hope that I'd meet Bill again had never quite died. The thrill of that moment when he'd carried me into the shoe repair shop and his cheek had rested against mine, had planted its seed deep in my heart. Whenever Sari Salome's life became too shabby, Edna Lawrence thought of Bill and felt a breath of sweet, clean air sweep over her.

Now, after that horrible jail experience, my deep need for someone fine and decent and clean in my life was too compelling to ignore. I remembered that Bill had said that he lived on Figueroa near the shoemaker's, and that he'd be out of the Marines in six months. More than six months had already passed and my heart beat painfully the day I took another pair of shoes into the shop as an excuse to see if the man remembered Bill and me. But the shop had changed hands and the new owner didn't know anyone by the name of Farwell who lived near by.

I had already looked in the phone book but there were no Farwells listed, so there was only one other slim chance of my ever meeting Bill. Not far away from the shoemaker's was the Figueroa entrance to beautiful Exposition Park, with its wonderful walks, marvelous museum, and tropical trees. And now, especially on days when my morale was extra low, I'd take a bus and go there, always hoping that a miracle would happen and the million-to-one chance of seeing Bill become a reality.

It was like that the afternoon I was sitting on a bench, deep in my gloomy thoughts. I was hatless and my hair, combed back simply from my forehead, had none of that fresh-from-the-beauty-parlor look it usually had. I was wearing a plain cotton dress and wore no make-up. I heard footsteps coming along the path toward me but I didn't look up, not even when they stopped at the other end of my bench.

Presently I rose to go and glanced idly at the man sitting on the opposite end of the bench. I saw a big fellow in a blue suit, whose face was hidden behind the paper he was reading. Then I saw the thick blond hair I'd seen so many times in my dreams, and my heart skipped a couple of beats. I sank back weakly on the bench.

Bill! My lips formed his name but no sound came from them. I sat there feasting my eyes on him while he went on quietly reading, oblivious of my presence. The big black headlines facing me proclaimed that there had been another sensational development in the Black Dahlia murder case. Presently he lowered his paper to fold it. I turned my head showing only my profile to him. *Will he see me? Will he remember me and speak?* I wondered, restraining myself with difficulty from jumping up and throwing my arms around him.

The rustling of the paper broke off suddenly and the silence told me he was staring at me. My heart came into my throat and stayed there. "For the love of Pete!" I heard him whisper. "If it isn't Cinderella!"

Edna Lawrence looked around at him, her shining eyes matching his delight.

"Remember me?" he asked, his voice eager.

"Hello, Mr. — hello — Bill," I said

HE WAS by my side in an instant, his hands holding mine in a good, firm masculine grip. I wanted to laugh and cry with joy, while I struggled to keep from showing him how pleased I was to see him.

"Bill! You called me Bill!" he exulted. "Cinderella, I've searched Los Angeles for you ever since my discharge. Why didn't you write to me?"

"I lost your address," I answered.

"Well, now that I've found you, I'm never going to lose sight of you again!" His eyes seemed to devour me hungrily as he went on, "You're even more beautiful than my dreams of you!"

Many men had told me that but none with the decency and honesty that shone in Bill's eyes. A red spot crept into my cheeks—the flush of shame and guilt. What wouldn't I have given to be the kind of girl he thought I was!

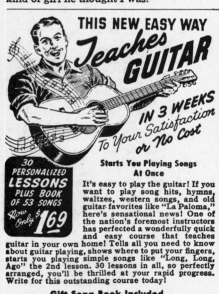

"Why, you're blushing!" he cried, then added, "Maybe now you'll tell me your name!"

I couldn't tell him I was Sari Salome who lived in an expensive apartment, waiting for phone calls from any casual admirer who would take me out and feed me. This man was like the boys I'd known back home—clean and decent, wearing his heart on his sleeve and letting his eyes tell me how much he loved me. I needed that love desperately, had to keep it, no matter how much I lied or what I concealed to do so.

"My name is Edna," I said. "Edna Lawrence!"

"Edna!" He breathed the name reverently. "I knew it would be something sweet and homey like that." He told me many things about himself and I told him that this was my second visit to Los Angeles, the first being the time I broke the heel of my shoe. I told him I was staying with relatives but I didn't give him my address. For the first time since I'd come to Los Angeles, I was able to talk freely to someone about my life and friends back home.

"I SUPPOSE there's a sweetheart there?" he asked wistfully.

"No. Nobody special, just friends."

His hand sought mine again and we drew a little closer. An unaccustomed peace and contentment swept over me just to be near Bill like this. I wished it were night, and there were a moon, and I were in his arms feeling the sweetness of his lips on mine. They would be sweet, I knew, sweet and gentle and loving.

Presently he broke the spell by pointing to the Black Dahlia headline staring at us from the paper he'd dropped. "Isn't that terrible!" he murmured. "Poor kid wanted to be a movie actress and look what she got. Well, maybe her death will do some good by being a warning to other kids. Something ought to be done about all these girls coming here to get in the movies. They find out they're no good at acting and then, instead of going home, they hang around and become cheap!"

Cheap! The word burned itself across my head like a band. That's what I was— *cheap.* But Bill would never know that!

He noted my silence and grinned sheepishly. "Gosh! I'm sorry," he said. "Reckon I was on a soap box. But when a guy puts in a few years fighting all over the world, he gets to thinking about the kind of girl he wants to settle down with when it's all over. And one of those silly, screen-struck beauties just doesn't fit into my scheme of things."

How glad I was then that I had lied to him!

Presently he said, "I've got to go now. I've an appointment to see somebody about a job." He went on to explain that he was a construction engineer but was working temporarily evenings in a filling station until something in his own line turned up. "Things are pretty slow right now," he told me, "with building being held up because of shortages of materials, but I'll find something. And soon—because now it's doubly important that I really get settled!"

His eyes spoke the things he left unsaid.

I walked with him to the entrance and promised to meet him next afternoon. "If I'm not here," he said, "you'll know I've started work." Then a look of alarm crossed his face. "But how am I going to get in touch with you!" he cried. "You say there's no phone at your place!"

"I'll call you tomorrow evening if you're not here in the afternoon," I replied.

"Gosh, but you're wonderful!" he said

writing down both his home phone number—it was a new phone which is why it wasn't listed—and that of the filling station.

As I put the slip of paper away carefully, he added with a grin, "Don't lose it this time!"

But he was there next day, and every day for many weeks to come. And because I lived only for those hours when we met I continued with my old life, for getting a job now would have meant missing those wonderful afternoons when I was Edna Lawrence, whom Bill idolized instead of Sari Salome—Girl-About-Hollywood.

Then one afternoon Bill said, "I won't be seeing you tomorrow. I'm going to San Bernadino to see about a construction job in Arizona. But I'll be back tomorrow night, so how about giving me a ring at home? I told my boss I wouldn't be in tomorrow night."

I promised to call him, little knowing the stage was being set for murder!

It had become a habit for Paula and me to wear each other's clothes because it doubled our wardrobe. That's how she came to be wearing my white evening gown that night.

With Bill away, all we girls were in that afternoon when Carl Denton rang up to ask me if I would go to dinner with him. "I'll pick you up about seven," he said, "then we'll eat and do the rounds till eleven. After that there's a party coming off at Manny Drake's place. So put on your glad rags, baby."

"Okay," I said. Manny Drake gave rather nice parties and sometimes it was possible to meet important people there. The best thing I had was my new white evening gown and I planned to wear it.

I already had it on when Arlene and Bunny went out at 6:30. Paula had gone out about an hour before. It came 6:45, and I was expecting Carl any minute, when Paula rushed in very excited. Her face fell when she saw I had on the white gown.

"GEE, Sari!" she cried, "I dashed home hoping to catch you before you went out. Jack Kramer is going to introduce me to Ray Radford, the director, tonight, and I was hoping you'd let me wear the white dress to meet him in."

"Jack Kramer!" I exclaimed. "Are you still kidding that fellow along?" Kramer was a sullen, bad-tempered man who was very clever at making stage "props" for pictures. But no studio would hire him any more on account of his drinking, and his murderous rage when anyone crossed him on the set.

She laughed at my question. "Why not? I happen to know that Ray Radford is a pal of Jack's, that's why I've given him so much of my time. I knew he'd get me an introduction to Radford someday if I strung him along far enough. Oh, Sari, you've just *got* to let me wear that dress!"

"Nothing doing, Paula," I said. "You know I'm going to a party at Manny Drake's later on, and I want to be looking my best, too!"

"But, Sari," she said tearfully, "I'm only seeing Radford between ten and eleven. You could meet me back here before you went to the party and put it on. Please, Sari darling! Jack says Radford has been looking for a girl my type all over the place."

I wanted to oblige Paula so I said as an idea came to me, "I'll tell you what we'll do. I'll get Carl to take me to The Bucket O Suds and you can meet me there at nine. We can go into the powder room and change clothes. Then you can meet the director, and come back to the apartment about eleven-thirty. We'll change again so I can wear the dress to Manny Drake's party."

"Oh, Sari, you're an angel!" she cried.

We'd no sooner made the arrangement when Carl Denton came in. Down in the lobby of the apartment house I stopped at the desk to ask for mail. The desk clerk chatted with Carl and me for a minute and then we left. That minute's conversation was fatal for Carl.

The Bucket O Suds was one of those dimly lit cocktail bars where you can dine and dance. It was a favorite spot with Carl so I had no trouble getting him to take me there for dinner. We were dancing when I saw Paula coming into the place soon after 9, and I caught her eye over Carl's shoulder and she made straight for the powder room when the dance ended, I followed her in.

There was nobody else in the powder room when Paula slipped into my lovely, filmy white gown and I changed into her black one which had been to too many parties.

"I'll go out the back way," Paula said, "so that Carl won't see me and think I'm you walking out on him."

The phone booth in the corner of the powder room reminded me that this would be a good time to call Bill as I'd promised. "Okay, Paula," I said. "You go on. I'm going to make a phone call."

BILL'S voice was charged with excitement. "I've been sitting by the phone waiting for you to call ever since I got home! Edna darling, *I got the job!*"

"Oh, Bill, I'm so happy!" I cried shakily, knowing it meant the beginning of a new life for me.

"Edna darling, I must see you tonight! I just can't wait till tomorrow to tell you about it. Can you come to the park, dear —now?"

"But, Bill," I stammered. "I—I'm at a party—I can't very well leave—"

"There's a moon," he said softly, "and now that I've got a real job, I want to ask you something, something terribly important—to me!"

Every nerve in me tingled joyously as I answered, "I'm coming, Bill."

There was still no one in the powder room when I stepped out of the phone booth. I went to the door and peeped out.

Carl was sitting with his back toward me talking to another man. I didn't want to explain why I was leaving, so I slipped through the back door into the alley. I rubbed the make-up from my face and eyes, combed my hair out the way Bill liked it, then caught a bus to Exposition Park.

He was sitting on our old bench on Christmas Tree Avenue, I could see his eyes shining in the moonlight as I flew into his outstretched arms. "Oh, Bill! I'm so happy for you!" I cried.

"I start in ten days at seventy a week!" he said, hugging me close. "Oh, my darling, it means much more than just a job! It means that I can ask you the question that's been on my mind ever since I met you here for the first time. You know I love you, Edna. Will you marry me, dear?"

"Yes, darling," I whispered. "Oh, yes, Bill! As soon as you like!" I raised my lips eagerly knowing all the joy that can come to a girl when the man she worships kisses her for the first time. I wound my arms around his neck and let my lips cling to his as if I never wanted to lose the joy of them again. In that moment I swore that from now on I would live up to all the things he thought I was.

The hours flew by and I forgot that Carl Denton was waiting for me at The Bucket O Suds. I forgot everything in the thrill

"I have a war job...and a little mother-in-law trouble"

WHEN JOHN went overseas, I wanted to do *something* to help win the war. So I got an assembly-line job in an aviation plant. Now I realize how important it is for women to work these days.

I COULDN'T be working if John's mother hadn't moved in, to help take care of little Nancy. We all get along pretty well, but I think mother secretly believed I didn't know much about child-raising.

ONE NIGHT when I came home, I found her *spanking* Nancy . . . all because she wouldn't take a laxative! "No wonder!" I exclaimed. "Mother, that's a grownup's laxative and it tastes terrible.

"DOCTORS say it's wrong to *force* bad-tasting medicine on children." I said. "I give Nancy Fletcher's Castoria—it's pleasant-tasting, made *especially* for children. It's gentle and effective, never harsh."

WELL, mother apologized later when she saw Nancy *enjoy* Fletcher's Castoria. "Guess a war job doesn't keep you from being a smart young mother." she smiled. And we've had no trouble since.

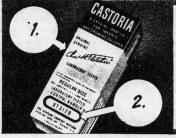

of making plans for a quick wedding so that I could go with him to Arizona.

I couldn't avoid having Bill take me home and I worried terribly as we approached the house. Suppose we met some of my shady crowd! But luck was with me. The lobby was deserted as I kissed Bill good night quickly, murmuring something about being sorry I couldn't ask him up for a nightcap but I couldn't risk waking my relatives. I'd meet him tomorrow afternoon at the usual place.

And as the self-service elevator carried me up to my floor, I was busy making plans. Now that Bill knew I lived at the Ridgeway Arms, I'd have to move at once! The first thing in the morning I'd look for a room some place where I wouldn't be afraid to have Bill come. It wouldn't be easy, either to find a room or to explain satisfactorily to Bill why I'd moved, but I'd manage somehow, because when you want something badly enough, you usually find a way! It would be the last bit of deceit I'd ever have to practice, because in a week I'd be Bill's wife—safe, protected.

As I got out at my floor, I suddenly remembered that I'd told Paula I'd be home at 11:30. It was now well after midnight and the apartment was in darkness as I let myself in. I remember thinking, *Paula must have gone out again,* as I crossed the foyer to switch on the living-room light.

That next moment when the light came on and cold horror poured through me, will never be erased from my mind, no matter how long I live.

Paula was lying on the divan, still dressed in my new evening gown, now torn and crumpled, its snowy whiteness stained with bright red blood. Some fiend had beaten her up so brutally that her face was sickeningly unrecognizable. A heavy bronze book end sticky with blood lay on the floor beside the divan.

HORROR gripped my heart with an icy hand. I knew she was dead. I tried to scream but no sound came from the frozen chords of my throat. How long I stood there paralyzed with dread I shall never know. Then suddenly I found myself shaking from head to foot with long uncontrollable shudders.

"Paula!" I whispered at last. "Oh, poor Paula!"

It was a long time before I managed to tear my eyes away from her and saw the telephone near the bedroom door. Keeping as far away from her as I could, I moved slowly toward it to call the police. As I picked up the receiver my eyes traveled back to her against my will.

Suddenly I thought of the Black Dahlia case, saw the glaring, sensational headlines, the pictures of the girls who had been living with her. *This will be in all the papers, just like that case,* I thought.

Then as I remembered the horrid publicity that had been given the Dahlia's friends I cried out, "Bill" and put the receiver back on the hook. *If the police take me down to headquarters for questioning, my picture will be in all the papers!* I thought frantically. *They'll find out that I'm Edna Lawrence, another screenstruck girl who'd become a Girl-About-Hollywood, and been sent to prison for vagrancy, and Bill will find out the sort of girl I really am and he'll never marry me!*

If I stayed here what had happened to Paula could happen to me! I had to get out of Hollywood—quick!

That last thought drove me into a panic. I couldn't lose Bill, I couldn't! *I'll run away and hide till I can marry Bill and get out of the state to Arizona,* I thought. I raced to the door and then pulled up short. The police would learn about me

soon enough and if I were missing they'd hunt for me until they found me! *They might even think I was the murderer!*

My eyes roved around the room like an animal caught in a trap. Again they came back to Paula, and traveled slowly to her battered unrecognizable face. Then the idea struck me. Somehow I nerved myself to go over and look at her closely. She *was* unrecognizable. *With my clothes on she could easily be taken for me!*

No one knew that I'd changed clothes with her. The other girls had been out when she'd asked me and there'd been nobody in the powder room when we changed. Even Carl didn't know, because I hadn't seen him since that last dance. It was a desperate, irrevocable decision to make, but I had to make it—if I wanted Bill's love, the joy of becoming his wife!

QUICKLY I packed Paula's things in her suitcase. I took her hangbag from the table on which she'd placed it and put mine in its place. Before I did so I took out everything that might enable the police to trace where I came from or who I really was. Then I destroyed all my pictures and left my clothes hanging in the closets. Not a trace of Paula Casselli did I leave in the apartment, and only the things that would identify the murdered girl as Sari Salome. I spotted Arlene's portable typewriter open on the desk. It gave me the best idea of all, and I went over and started typing. But I put on Paula's gloves first. I'd read about finger prints on paper. I wrote:

Dear Bunny and Arlene,
I found poor Sari like this when I came to the room. Have packed up and left town. If you are wise you will do the same and leave someone else to find her. Remember the Dahlia case and the publicity the papers gave to the girls sharing her apartment? It'll be the same this time. Take all photographs and papers with you. Good luck and it was swell knowing you.

Paula Casselli

I rolled the note up high in the roller and left it there. Then I went to the door and peeped out. Not a soul was around on our floor although I could hear a noisy party going on two floors above. I took one last glance at Paula and whispered, "Good-by, Sari Salome!" Then, my eyes blinded with tears, I switched off the lights, closed the door quietly and, carrying Paula's suitcase, I crept down the service stairs and out the basement door which led to the Ridgeway Arms parking lot. I hugged the shadows as I hurried away.

What was I going to do now? Where was I going to hide? Not till I was a long way from the Ridgeway did I start to think that out. I went into an all-night restaurant for some coffee and to think. The clock said 1:30 and I wondered if Bill was awake and thinking of me, or asleep and dreaming of me. It was thinking of Bill that helped me to decide my next move.

I suppose months of practice in telling men phony stories made it easy for me to weave the tale I told Bill that night. I finished my coffee and took a bus to within a few blocks of where he lived. Then I got off and went into a phone booth.

"For the love of Pete!" Bill exclaimed when he heard my voice. "Where are you calling from at this time of night, darling?"

"I'm in a drugstore on the corner of Thirty-fourth and Flower. Oh, Bill! Some-

thing terrible has happened. I've had a quarrel with the folks I'm living with and I've packed up and left. I've got to see you right away, dear!"

"Stay right where you are, sweetheart!" he said crisply. "I'll be over with the car as soon as I can make it."

Ten minutes later he braked to a screeching stop where I was waiting for him on the corner. I was crying then, crying because of the lies I knew I was going to tell him.

I told him that the relatives I was supposed to be staying with had bawled me out for coming home late. I told him that they weren't going to let me see him again until they'd got in touch with my folks and told them I intended to marry him. "They'd have spoiled everything for us," I said tearfully, "so I waited till everyone was asleep, then I packed my things and ran away!"

He was furious. "Let's go right back there and straighten things out!" he demanded. "What's wrong with us being in love and wanting to get married I'd like to know!"

"Oh no, Bill! I don't want to go back there—ever!" I cried in terror. Then I put my arms around his neck and begged, "Oh, darling, if we could only elope and get married at once!"

"Do you really *mean* that, angel!" Bill hugged me tight, his voice full of incredulous joy.

"It would make me the happiest girl in the world," I murmured fervently. "Oh, Bill! I do love you so very much, dear!"

I really meant that. Yet when Bill kissed me almost reverently saying in an awed voice, "What did I ever do to deserve such happiness? I went hot with shame and agony at the trick I was playing on him. "We'll go to my place first," he said, "and I'll pack a few things and get some money. Then we'll drive to Arizona and get married there first thing in the morning. That'll give us a few days for a honeymoon before I start work."

I flung my arms round his neck and cried my happiness on his shoulder. "You'll never regret it, Bill," I sobbed, "never, never, *never!*"

For the next couple of days, I steeled myself not to look at a newspaper, trying desperately to lose myself completely in my ever-growing love for Bill and the beauty of his love for me.

But I couldn't succeed in forgetting Paula, couldn't erase that poor mutilated face from my mind's eye.

Who had killed her? Was it drink-crazed, bad-tempered Jack Kramer? Did she ever meet Ray Radford, the director, that night? Much as I tried not to ask myself these questions, they kept intruding, even in my most sacred moments with Bill.

I HAD to know what had happened, had to know if Paula had been mistaken for me, had to know if anyone had been arrested, had to know whether Bunny and Arlene had managed to get away. And on the second day that I was Bill's wife, I bought a paper and read the news:

COMPANIONS OF MURDERED GIRL STILL MISSING—MAN SEEN WITH SARI ARRESTED AS SUSPECT

A nation-wide search is on for Paula Casselli, Arlene Lamont, and Bunny Brabazon, the three girls known to have shared the apartment where Sari Salome was found brutally murdered three days ago. Police disclose that both the Casselli girl and the victim served prison terms for vagrancy, but no clue as to the murdered Girl-About Hollywood's real identity has turned up. The name, Sari Salome, is obviously the pseudonym of a screen-struck girl. In fact all four girls are listed at various casting agencies where the police were able to obtain pictures of them. But none of the agencies or studios have any record of any of the quartette ever working in pictures. A man known to have been with Sari Salome on the night of her death has been arrested and is being questioned by the police.

There were four photographs of us spread out along the top of the page. I sighed with relief as I studied the one captioned: "Sari Salome, the Murdered Girl!"

"Thank heaven, Bill won't be able to recognize me from that!" I muttered in fervent relief. I'd had the picture taken when I first came to Hollywood nearly two years ago. I remember how I'd paid an extra $10 to have a movie make-up artist do my hair and eyes and lips so that I'd look like a typical screen siren.

I read that last paragraph again and wondered if the man arrested was Carl Denton. "Well, he didn't do it," I said to myself, "so they won't be able to pin it on him." I refused to think of what would happen if they did somehow succeed in pinning it on Carl and I alone knew he was innocent. Bill's cheery whistle as he came through the palm-shaped court of the pretty motel scattered my somber thoughts. I thrust the paper under a cushion as if it were a symbol of my sordid past I was burying.

I WENT to the door and watched Bill striding toward me, his face alive with the sheer joy of living. His sport shirt was open and I could see the satiny bronze of his deep chest.

What a difference there was between my life with him and the scheming, shabby hand-to-mouth existence of Sari Salome!

He came into the tiny living room filling it with his bigness and I threw myself into his arms, kissing him wildly, my heart overflowing with worship and gratitude.

"Whoa, there! Let's do this in style, young lady!" Bill laughed tenderly, pulling me down with him into the one, comfortable armchair. Bill's lips caressed my throat softly, as he murmured, "Edna dear, I'm so happy I can't believe it's real! It isn't every man who's lucky enough to find his dream girl!"

His words were like red hot barbs pricking my guilty conscience. I thought of that hidden newspaper, then forced my thoughts away from it—to Bill.

And in that first honeymoon rapture when each day was twenty-four hours spent together, I was able to stifle the voice of conscience sometimes by drawing strength from his nearness. But when his job started and I had to spend long, lonely hours without him, it was a different story. And one day I came across the newspaper I'd hidden and, in spite of myself, I couldn't help reading it again. Like a cloud of wasps those questions came swarming into my mind again. *Who had killed Paula? Was it Jack Kramer, the man she met that night?*

Then followed the thought that had lain dormant ever since I'd sneaked away from the apartment. *You might be helping a murderer to go free by not telling the police about Paula's last date.*

But I couldn't do that without giving away the fact that it wasn't Sari Salome who had been killed. I couldn't do it with-

Make Evening in Paris a part of you...

YOUR PERFUME is as important to your charm as your perfect make-up, your shining hair, your exquisite clothes. Make Evening in Paris an always-present part of your loveliness. Remember, daytime, evenings and always, Evening in Paris weaves a magic spell . . . and life can be much more exciting when you wear it!

SCENT SECRET: Put a drop of perfume on your palm . . . smooth it over your hairbrush . . . then brush the fragrance through your hair.

GIFT SECRET FOR MEN: The most gracious gift of all is Evening in Paris. She will love it!

Evening in Paris

BOURJOIS

Perfume . . . 75¢ to $12.50
Eau de Cologne 65¢ to $1.50
Bath Powder $1.25

All Prices Plus Tax

147

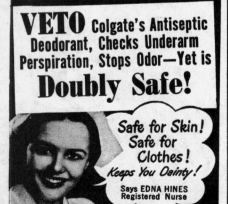
out letting Bill and the rest of the world know that I was Sari Salome! And there were my folks to think of too. They'd been delighted when I wrote them about Bill and me and were planning to try to visit us soon. How could I break their hearts by letting them learn that Sari Salome was their daughter?

I won't do it! I won't do it! I told myself a hundred times a day. *Paula's dead and giving up my happiness, ruining Bill's life and breaking Mom's and Dad's hearts won't bring her back to life!* But no matter how much I told myself those things, a voice inside me insisted even louder, *Your silence is shielding a fiendish killer!*

Then one day while I was out shopping a newsboy thrust a paper at me and I couldn't help but see the front page headline. It shrieked:

CARL DENTON INDICTED FOR SALOME MURDER!

My fingers shook as I gave the boy a nickel for his paper.

It was all there—the damning web of circumstances that fate had woven around Carl. Police investigation of him had disclosed that Carl was a criminal who had already three prison sentences back East. One had been for dope peddling, another for knifing and nearly killing a man in a tavern brawl. But most damning of all was his conviction for brutally assaulting a young girl. The reason he had so much money to throw around was because he was a "caser" for a mob of burglars—a man who went to parties for the sole purpose of sizing up the place for the best way to rob it. He used girls like us to get himself invited and make connections.

When first arrested he'd denied having been out with me that night, and then police had confronted him with the clerk at the Ridgeway Arms who had seen us together and who had described the white evening dress I was wearing. It was that clerk, and others who saw me wearing the dress that night, who identified Paula as Sari Salome. Carl admitted then that I'd been out with him and told how he'd lost track of me at The Bucket O Suds. The medical examiner said that Paula had been killed between 11 and midnight, and when asked where he was during that hour, Carl said he was in a movie. *But he was unable to bring anyone forward to prove he was there!* It was an open-and-shut-case as far as the police was concerned.

LIKE an ostrich hiding its head in the sand, I refused to read a paper after that. But I couldn't hide from the agonizing thoughts that haunted me day and night. The fact that I was enjoying Bill's love by allowing a murderer to go free and an innocent man to suffer for his crime, gave me no peace and robbed me of all happiness.

And then the morning came when Bill went to work and left the paper behind that told me Carl had been found guilty and sentenced to spend the rest of his life in prison.

Sari Salome is dead! The voice of temptation kept saying. *Why bring her back to life and kill your husband's love? All you've got to do is remain silent and you're safe forever!* But I knew I would never again have a happy moment while this awful thing lay like a sword through my heart. No matter what the cost, I had to tell Bill when he came home that night.

I waited till after supper and it was Bill himself who gave me my cue. He picked up the paper he'd bought that morning and reading the headline, said, "Well, I see the man who killed the Salome girl got what was coming to him!"

I took a deep breath and gulped out, "Bill, that man didn't kill Sari Salome!"

He looked up at me and laughed. "We shall now hear from Mrs. Sherlock Holmes," he joshed.

"I—I'm serious, Bill. You see I—I happen to—know!"

The tone of my voice and the misery in my face made him put the paper down and stare at me. "What do you mean, Edna—you *know?*"

"Because I—I'm Sari Salome!" I whispered hoarsely.

HE MADE a funny gesture of closing and opening his big hands, while all the glowing life went out of his face.

"*You!* Sari Salome! I don't believe it!"

I rushed on, "Oh, Bill! I was running away from that murder the night I got you to elope with me. The dead girl was a friend of mine who happened to be wearing my clothes and the police thought she was me!"

"*No! No!*" he kept saying as if constant repetition would make it so. "It's impossible!"

"It's true, Bill," I moaned. "I'd give twenty years of my life to know it wasn't!"

"I've been reading about the case ever since she was killed," he muttered into space. "According to the papers she was everything I despised. And now I find she's *my wife!* The girl I married!"

He slumped down in his chair with a gesture of helpless bewilderment as I went on to tell Bill everything in stumbling pain-wracked words, my heart breaking with the agony of watching Bill's belief that he'd found everything that was fine and good in his wife die before my eyes.

When I had finished he sat there staring at nothing, his face set like a bronze mask, only his eyes dull and alive with pain. I knelt at his feet and laid my cheek against his hand. "Bill," I sobbed. "Don't take it so hard, dear! I'm not worth it!" He flung me away from him in revulsion.

Blindly I got up and went through the motions of putting on my hat. "I—I'm going to tell the police, Bill," I whispered, "and I—I might not see you for a long time." He didn't even look at me as I went on, "Bill, please believe one thing. I love you better than life itself! I shall love you as long as I live!"

"*I never want to see you again!*" he said dully. His head was bowed in his hands as I crept away.

There is no need to go into the sensation I caused when I told that Phoenix police captain I was Sari Salome. He listened grimly to my story, especially to the part when I voiced my suspicion that Kramer was the killer, and his voice was stern when I'd finished. "I suppose you realize your silence has very probably allowed the killer—whether he's Kramer or someone else—to escape. If the Los Angeles Police had known who the girl really was, and who she'd met that night, the case might have been solved by now! Let's hope it's not too late to still apprehend him. I shall have to lock you up till the Los Angeles Police can get here to question you. They'll want to take you back with them." He paused, looked at me hard, then added, "You can fight extradition if you care to, but I wouldn't advise it!"

"I'll do all I can to help," I promised as he reached for the phone.

Detectives arrived from Los Angeles on the next plane and I was flown straight back there. I spent many weeks in prison, held as a material witness pending some break in the case. No mention had been made of the mistaken identity in the papers as the police reasoned that the murderer, thinking the case was over, would come out of hiding.

They were right. Within a few days they picked up Jack Kramer. After two days and nights of continuous questioning, he finally confessed that he'd killed Paula in a fit of rage when she repulsed him. His ruse to get up to our apartment had been simple enough. He and Paula went to the place where they were supposed to meet the director, and after waiting awhile, a phone call (which Kramer had arranged for) came for him. He left Paula to answer it and when he came back he told her the call was from Ray Radford, saying he was tied up for awhile, and he would meet them later at Paula's apartment.

Paula fell for the yarn and when they got up to the Ridgeway, Kramer got fresh, and eventually told her there had never been an appointment with Radford. Paula, angered at being tricked that way, picked up the book end and hit him with it, not hard enough to draw blood, but hard enough to send him into one of his murderous rages. Hardly knowing what he was doing, he twisted the book end out of her hand and started to beat her with it over and over until she was dead. Kramer was sentenced to life imprisonment.

They released Carl Denton from that charge, but brought him to trial again later convicting him of being a member of the gang who had burglarized so many places where he'd been a guest. He got five years.

I thought at first they would prosecute me for my part in the case. But technically I was in the clear legally because I had done nothing more than not come forward to tell what I knew.

But I'm being punished nevertheless—in a way that no man-made law could ever punish me. I'm being punished day and night by my conscience. That torturing inner voice is never still, telling me over and over again that my folly has not only ruined my own life and broken my parents' hearts, but has ruined the life of the man I'll love until the day I die. Not that I ever expect to see Bill again. I don't even know where he is or what he's doing, because when reporters tried to talk to Bill, they found he'd given up his job and disappeared. "The only explanation he gave me," his boss said, "was that he didn't care what happened to him any more. He said he'd never believe in another person or thing again for the rest of his life."

Those are the words that ring in my ears as I go about my humdrum work as a waitress in a town far removed from Hollywood. And those are the words that haunt me in the long, tortured, sleepless nights when my pillow grows sodden with tears of regret—all glamor gone from my life now.

Oh, Bill, Bill! What have I done to you, my darling! I can only pray that someday, somewhere, you'll find a fine, decent girl who'll restore your faith, give you back your zest for life, make you forget that cheap, shoddy Sari Salome ever existed.

It hasn't been easy to tell my story, to reopen bleeding wounds and relive those terrible, tortured months. But if by so doing, I've succeeded in warning away from Hollywood even one other misguided little fool who thinks that a pretty face and shapely figure are a sure passport to movie fame and fortune, then it has been more than worthwhile. *The End*

I Passed as White

I AM Julia Brace, Colored.
I write that now so easily—as though I were saying, "My hair is blond, my eyes gray, and green is my favorite color." I write it proudly, but there was a time when I would have cut off my hand rather than put down in words what I thought of then as my secret shame.

The shame had always been in my heart, and the determination to keep it secret grew as I grew, having its roots in childhood memories that still make me cringe with their sharp, haunting pain.

I was born in the settlement house where my father and mother worked among the New Orleans Colored poor. There was white blood—a great deal of it—in both of my parents. But the light brown tinge in Father's skin showed his heritage from an Indian grandmother. It showed too in his straight black hair and handsome strong-boned face. Mother was partly of Irish extraction. Her parents had met in the West Indies. The dark strain in her blood was evident only in her rich, creamy pallor. I am even fairer than she, with the same dark-lashed Irish eyes and softly curling blond hair.

I couldn't have been 5 when I first began to realize I was different from the other children in the neighborhood. I suffered terribly during my early school days from their spite and resentment. My dark-skinned playmates taunted me with little cruelties—an apple snatched from my hand and thrown rudely away, tweaked curls, slaps and pinches when no one was watching. A new dress or fresh hair bow would be noticed immediately and I'd be punished for daring to wear it with a push that would send me into the filth of the gutter.

My tormentors would chant impishly, "Yaw, yaw, yaw! Yo' dress yo'se'f up fine. Thinks yo'se'f white! Yo's jes a darkie like de bunch a us! Yo' is Colah'd too, Julie Brace. Yo' is jes masqueradin' yo' black soul wid dat yella' hair."

Colored. The word didn't mean just dark skin to me then. It meant hurt, enemies instead of playmates. It meant games in which I wasn't allowed to share, because I was neither white nor black but in the twilight zone between. It meant

This amazing confession of a Colored girl who successfully represented herself as white arrived on the desk of True Confessions' editor without the name or address of the author.

After several months of inquiry the author was located, her story verified. We give it to you as the one story that will live forever in your memory.

At last I was in Chicago. I was born again. No one here knew me. I was Julia Brace, white!

loneliness, unhappiness and puzzled tears which I early learned to shed in secret. I was stubborn and proud and I wouldn't let my tormentors have the satisfaction of seeing me cry.

I've never known a better man than my father, nor a more gentle, understanding woman than my mother. But they were busy, immersed in their work, and they didn't notice how miserable I was. I kept my heartaches to myself, buried deep inside where they slowly festered and poisoned my whole being with feelings of resentment against the world into which I'd been born—neither white nor black.

I LOOKED at the world with the bewildered eyes of a child. To me the other boys and girls were bad. I was glad I wasn't like them. Glad! Glad! Glad! They were mean to me. And because they would have none of me, I wanted none of them. So I played by myself, hunting out nooks and corners where I felt safe from these children who despised me and whom I had grown to fear and hate.

Whenever white people came to the settlement house I would cling to my mother's skirts, my sharp ears tuned to their whispers which weren't meant for me to hear. "That child—would you look at her! You'd never think she was Colored, would you? She could pass as white anywhere." Talk like that—and I heard it repeatedly—gave me hope. I'd run and furtively look in the mirror to prove to myself again and again the truth of their words, and to make sure no sign of my Colored blood had tinged my fair hair and light skin.

By the time I was old enough to think and plan for the future, the knowledge that the choice of race might be mine became a secret, gloating triumph which I hugged to my heart through lonely, brooding hours. Instead of harboring only hate and despair in my young mind, I began to develop a fierce ambition for a new way of life, far away from the place where I'd been born and raised as a Colored girl. I carefully guarded my determination to be white from my parents and from everyone around me. I didn't want anyone to discover and discourage my dreams. Someday I *was* going to e white! I didn't know as a little hild how or when, but someday . . .

There was only a grade school in the Colored section where we lived, but Father had organized night classes at the settlement house for the ambitious young people who wanted to go on through high. He'd found teachers who were willing to give their time and one of these, my biology teacher, was a graduate nurse. She told me what courses I'd need to meet the requirements if I wanted to become one too. I loved her. Her crisp uniform, her capable white hands fascinated me. Mine were just as white, I told myself, and given time they would be as capable as hers. For I was going to be a nurse. I could see myself dressed in white, walking as she did, quiet and self-assured through a white world.

I centered all my dreams around that vision, and after I'd finished my

It's all right to have a train of thoughts, if you have a terminal.

—Bowker

high-school work in the settlement-house classes I made my dreams come true. Mother had decided that I should go north to a school that trained dieticians, as good positions were opening up for Colored girls in that field, she'd heard, and I'd taken science courses that were a prerequisite—the same ones that I'd needed to become a nurse. I couldn't tell Mother I had already decided on my future, because I was going in training as a white girl and of course I'd never, never in the world admit that to my parents!

I'd have to just go off as they planned and then disappear forever from their lives. Oh, it was horribly selfish of me. I can see that now, but it seemed the only way to begin my life over again as I'd vowed I would for so many years—the only way to get rid of and forget the Colored blood I rebelled against.

Father and Mother helped me pack up, not suspecting I had already written to the dietetic school to cancel my registration there. On the train for Chicago, with their traveling checks in my purse to cover my expenses for the year away from home, sorrow swept over me because I'd kissed them good-by for the last time. I was thinking of my own loss, not theirs, and it didn't alter my decision. My love for my parents, deep as it was, wasn't as strong as the hurt I'd suffered because of the blood I'd vowed to disown.

When I stepped off the train I felt a new and wonderful sense of freedom. The city streets looked like boulevards in paradise. It was indeed a Promised Land for me. I stopped and gazed up at the tall buildings and took a long, deep breath that ended in a sigh of relief and joy. At last I was in Chicago. I was born again. No one here knew me as Colored: I was Julia Brace, white!

I went to a first-class hotel. My hand was trembling when I registered at the desk. No questions were asked about my color there, and feeling reassured that I really looked as white as anyone else, I presented my high-school certificate at a large hospital next day and applied for admission as a student nurse. They were badly in need of even inexperienced help and accepted me immediately.

AFTER my first day in training, I wrote Father and Mother what I'd done. My conscience wouldn't let me just disappear as I'd planned. I had to tell them I had arrived safely and why they wouldn't hear from me any more. I told them I loved them with all my heart and always would, but that I would never write or see them again. I said I preferred that they didn't try to get in touch with me in any way. I frankly admitted that I hadn't tried to enter training as Colored, because I was going to be a *white* nurse.

Mailing that letter was like throwing the final clods on an unmarked grave. *There lies Julia Brace, Colored,* I told myself fiercely as I dropped the envelope into the mailbox. *This is Julia Brace, white, and her life is all before her.*

I was starved for happiness, companionship, boy friends, everything I'd never had. I found them all in my new world. The great hospital was heaven to me.

The patients were pathetically grateful for the care they received, and it made me feel that here I was wanted and needed and loved for myself, without the dread barrier of color to interfere. I was proud of being a   [*Please turn page*]

One course they didn't teach her

EVEN though it was Graduation Day Dora felt a little pang of loneliness. What was the diploma compared to those precious sparkling rings that Babs and Beth were wearing? Dora was killing her chances of ever wearing one, too, unless she changed her ways. There was one course* that college didn't teach her.

What do other charms amount to if you have halitosis (bad breath)*? Whether occasional or chronic, it can finish you with a man that quick. Smart girls, popular girls, realize this and are *extra careful* not to offend.

For them it is Listerine Antiseptic night and morning, and especially before any date when they want to be at their best.

Listerine Antiseptic is no momentary makeshift. It instantly freshens and sweetens the breath and helps keep it that way. Not for seconds . . . not for minutes . . . but for hours, usually. Never, never, omit this delightful *extra-careful* precaution against offending.

While some cases of halitosis are of systemic origin, most cases, say some authorities, are due to the bacterial fermentation of tiny food particles clinging to mouth surfaces. Listerine Antiseptic quickly halts such fermentation, then overcomes the odors fermentation causes. LAMBERT PHARMACAL CO., *St. Louis, Mo.*

LISTERINE ANTISEPTIC
the extra-careful precaution
against bad breath

Vacationing? It's mighty comforting to have a good antiseptic handy in case of minor cuts, scratches and abrasions requiring germicidal first-aid.

part of the hospital, willing to take my share of its work as well as its fun—shy at first about its quick acceptance of me and afraid of losing it all, too.

I'd forgotten, in the excitement of getting away from New Orleans, that many of the boys and girls Father had worked with had come north—mostly to Chicago. Now when I remembered that, I became frightened that I might meet one who'd know me. I was haunted by that fear whenever I walked on the streets. I never passed a dark face without cringing for fear I'd be recognized. With my white companions I was at ease. It was only in the race I'd disowned that I felt the great danger of discovery might lie.

Even in the hospital I wasn't really safe, because they employed Negroes in the kitchens, as elevator operators, everywhere, and of course they came as patients in the wards where I worked. I did everything I could to relieve their suffering, yet when their eyes followed me I was in mortal terror lest one would say, "Aren't you the Miss Brace from New Orleans?"

I hadn't changed my name when I came to Chicago, because I wanted my credentials to be authentic when I presented them for admission to the hospital for training. It's a common name anyway, and it wouldn't have helped much to change it unless I'd changed my face too. I just had to take my chances and go on with that fear hanging over me.

But fear, no matter how strong it is, can lose its edge in time. And by the time I had finished two of my three years of training, I'd almost forgotten it in the triumph of my success and continued security.

I've put it over, I told myself. *I've put it over on everyone. I'm white, white, white!* And I felt no guilt then over what I'd done, though I was always sorry I'd had to cause my parents sorrow. I began to understand a little how my disowning them must have made them suffer. But they had become part of the past—an ugly dream that scarcely seemed real to me now.

Dates with the interns, dances, dinners, fun—I had my share. But as soon as a casual flirtation showed signs of becoming something deeper, I was through. That was the bargain I had made with my conscience. *There was to be no marriage for me.*

The nurses called me a heartless flirt. The young interns said I was "loveproof." And I thought I was. I thought the secret I was hiding so well was armor enough against love. I thought so even when I met Dick Rutledge. By then I had nearly ceased to worry about the threat of discovery. Perhaps that's why my defenses were weakened. The days ahead were to prove me terribly wrong!

I was one of the reception committee when our graduating class gave a get-together for a new group of M.D.'s entering the hospital for their two-year internship. I'd heard there was a Colored doctor coming in, not an intern, but a physician from the East who was registering for extra work under one of our staff specialists. He had been invited to the party and there was a lot of speculation as to whether he would show up or not. That evening I was standing a little apart from the others, watching the new faces, curious, and rather dreading his arrival, when I was startled by a touch on my arm.

It was Jim Hawes, a recent "flame" of mine, and he had a new doctor with him —a tall, earnest-looking man in his late twenties, with birth and breeding stamped on his fine, thin face.

Jim was still suffering from my recent "nipping in the bud" strategy, and his "Hi, Julia—a new lamb for the sacrifice, Dick Rutledge from down Georgia way," while it was said with a grin, had a spice of malice behind it. "The guy specializes in hearts," he'd added. "Promised I'd show him a gal who hadn't one." He laughed.

"There she is, Rutledge. Southern, too. New Orleans. Think there's any hope for her?"

I could take my share of kidding but sudden anger flamed in my cheeks then. It wasn't all for Jim. The scrutiny of the stranger's dark eyes that met mine had open amusement behind it. And his "sad case—very sad case, but I might offer a course of treatments that would help if you'd care to try them," made me boil. Oh, where was my professional dignity and self-assurance now? I felt like an embarrassed schoolgirl.

There was only one answer to a challenge like that. Of course I made it.

"Cardiac research is always interesting," I answered, trying to speak lightly, "Suppose we begin by having coffee." Then I led Dick over to a davenport and left him there for a few minutes, coming back well laden with refreshments.

Our friendship got off to a fast and dangerous start. The real reason was deeper than my flush of anger when we met and his teasing. My bitterness always had been for the race I had disowned, never before for the one I had chosen. But standing there looking into the smiling eyes of this man from the Deep South—this man that Julia Brace, Colored, could never have known as an equal—bitterness against both races became mingled and confused inside me. To "put it over" on him as I had "put it over" on these others, to see admiration in *his* eyes, hear it in *his* voice, and turn that admiration into something deeper if I could. . . . Yes, I would do it.

It sounds cold and ruthless and hard. But that's what I was inside. That is the sort of girl I had become then. And Dick made it so easy for me, so pitifully easy. I was pretty and young. To him, my southern birth was a tie between us. My profession was another. We spoke the same soft, drawled words.

WE WERE still on the couch, discussing what Dick laughingly had styled, "The story of my life—The Rutledge Saga —From Wealth to Poverty. From Poverty to Wealth—Still to Come." When the Colored maid came over to collect our empty cups and plates and jarred my arm, I frowned and drew back from her in a movement as uncontrollable as it was involuntary.

I hoped Dick hadn't noticed it, but he

had. He made up for my stiffness by speaking to the girl with extra courtesy, and when she had left he said quietly, "Still clinging to your prejudices, I see. Felt that way myself when I first came North. It's different now. You can see the reason if you'll glance over toward the door. That tall, dark-skinned Negro— that's Doctor Frank Marshall from New York. He rates high—really high. He lectured at one of my classes in college. He wanted some extra work and decided to take it here. So I came along with him for my interning. If he thinks this place is tops, it's tops with me. He is, too. Quiet, reserved. Won't push himself. Had the devil's own time to make him promise to show up tonight.

"Frank! Hey, Frank! Come here—want to see you!"

Frank Marshall!

His friend was Frank Marshall, the Negro doctor the girls told me of. I watched him coming closer. I watched his face grow nearer and clearer, while shock and fear rose in me until I sat there, paralyzed with terror.

Frank Marshall! I would have known his face anywhere even had I forgotten his name. And I hadn't.

I had been a child of 6, perhaps 7, when he had come to Father, a tall, overgrown boy doing a man's work on the waterfront. He was eating his heart out for the schooling he'd never had and dreaming of being a doctor as I was to dream later of being a nurse.

Father had seen the skill in the large, blunt-fingered hands, so gentle and so tender. Somehow, as only Father could, he had raised the money that had sent Frank north to school. Father had heard from him often. He was well established in New York. Dr. Marshall was the last man I'd ever have thought of seeing in Chicago. At last the dreaded danger of discovery was catching up with me! I had been a child. There was a chance he hadn't noticed me—but the name . . . Oh, he was speaking to Dick, and Dick was saying, "Julia Brace, Frank. She's from the city that's going to be proud to claim you one of these days. I'm giving her the chance to boast, 'I knew him when.'"

I don't know what I said. I wanted to hide my face, to run away. All I can remember is sitting there while his eyes searched my face, and I heard him say, "Brace? The name is familiar. I'm sure I've seen you before. New Orleans? I know a man—" He hesitated.

In that instant I saw recognition dawn in his eyes. I stared coldly at him and he didn't go on. I saw him frown and then, with a careless shrug, turn to quick talk of other things. I knew that my secret for the moment was safe, but I couldn't still the hard thumping of my heart against my ribs.

Afterward—I haven't words for that! It was—horrible. Meeting Dr. Marshall day after day as I had to, wondering how long his silence would last, conscious of the contempt I knew he must be feeling for me, knowing that shame and exposure were hanging over my head like an ax— that did things to me. I was a wreck, never knowing what day might be the end.

Each morning I would say, "Today it will happen—today!" And I'd count the hours, each hour I could continue being white.

Little commonplace acts that familiarity had made of small importance to me became big beyond all measuring. To win a smile of approval from a doctor on his rounds, grudged commendation from a stern and watchful head nurse—

the last approval, the last commendation I might ever have from anyone in this white world I'd thought to make my own. I clung to them, treasures that had no price.

And what applied to my work applied to everything else—but most of all to Dick. I had wanted his friendship—even his love, because I wanted an ugly triumph over a white man. I still wanted him to love me, but it wasn't triumph I felt as I watched that love grow in his eyes, it was a cold, bitter joy at knowing that when I was forced from my fool's paradise, I could leave a hurt behind me equal to my own to balance the scales. I wanted to give back pain for pain. But it wasn't until Dick put that growing love into words, that I realized that giving him up was going to be a new hurt, as much mine as his.

Love? What had it ever meant to me? I learned its meaning that night when Dick's arms held me close and his lips found mine, whispering their need and their hunger. And I answered yes.

I suppose my love for Dick had been in my heart all along, growing with his for me. I had been too blinded by despair to know it. The realization surged over me so suddenly, so overpoweringly that I couldn't fight it.

I should have told him the truth, then. I knew it. Perhaps I might have done so if Dick himself hadn't given me the loophole my cowardice needed.

"We'll wait to marry until you graduate, darling," he said. "You'll be on your own then. If you want to stay on at the hospital—swell. We can have a room—a little apartment maybe, and we can go to it during our off-duty hours. With the little I have and what you can make, we'll swing it until I'm practicing. After that—a new line of Rutledges, sweet, strong branches from a worn-out tree."

I didn't want to look beyond the present, nor let him. But even then, I could see his people and mine, back over the generations that had made us—ghostly faces and forms, black and white, but all pointing at me with the same accusing finger.

I had begged to keep our engagement a secret. But Dick was too happy, too proud for that. It spread like wildfire over the hospital. Frank was among the others who congratulated us. His words were quiet, dignified, and to Dick, sincere, but I read mockery and contempt behind them. I thought his silence was only added punishment, that he was just waiting awhile to tell the truth to everyone.

THERE were times when I thought desperately of going to Frank and throwing myself on his pity. Then doubts would creep in, a hope. *I was just a child when he knew me—a child—perhaps he really doesn't recognize me now. Perhaps . . .*

But in spite of what I tried to think, Dick's friendship for Frank meant constant agony to me. I couldn't bear seeing them together unless I was there too so I'd know what was happening. I was braced against it. Where I had avoided Frank before, I cultivated him now. It pleased Dick. He thought I was being broadminded, forgetting my "prejudices" at last. Wherever we happened to be—eating together in the cafeteria, talking during an idle hour in the corridors—his pride in Frank made him draw him out, urge him to talk on his future plans.

That was when I learned about the clinic Frank was expecting to establish in the South, and about the work he was doing even then in the Colored tenement district that surrounded our hospital.

"Got himself an office," Dick chuckled.

VARGA CREATES NEW TYPE OF PIN-UP

Artist Varga, creator of the famous VARGA GIRL, has invented a new type of pin-up picture. It is called the VARGA MOVIE PIN-UP and features the likeness of Hollywood's most beautiful stars. Linda Darnell is the first star honored. Varga's new MOVIE PIN-UP of Linda appears exclusively in September MOTION PICTURE MAGAZINE (now on sale) as a special insert in full color. Get yours today!

LOVELY LINDA DARNELL poses for VARGA . . . Exclusively for MOTION PICTURE MAGAZINE

"Ought to see it, hon. Only thing you can say is that it's on the ground floor and there's standing room on the sidewalk for his patients. It's open every evening, and I'm offering my free hours·as assistant. How 'bout a nurse, Doc? Can't leave Julia out of a setup like this!"

Dick saw the doubt in Frank's face, felt his hesitancy as I did. But the sting behind his answer was all for me. And outwardly there was no sting.

"They are my people," he said softly. "I love them and understand them. If Miss Julia—" and his eyes met mine, holding them in a long, still glance—"feels that she has sympathy and understanding to give I would be grateful to have her whenever her evenings are clear."

I HAD neither. All I had was fear. The sympathy and understanding came later, and not because of me but in spite of me, came with the old and crippled, the sick and ailing who brought not only their bodily miseries to their beloved "Doctor Man" to cure, but their mental miseries as well. The dark-skinned mothers came holding sickly children in their arms, their bodies already large with the soon-to-be-born, they were turned over to me by Frank for the personal advice that the charity clinics were too busy and understaffed to be able to give. And they were so eager for it, and so grateful for the little I could give them.

I think that was what tore me—the way these people stretched out their arms for knowledge and their gratitude when I taught them how to bring healthy babies into the world. Dick could take that in his stride. He was kindly and efficient, full of jokes and always kidding the patients along. But he was more interested in the diseases and Frank's quick and skilled diagnoses, I thought, than in the patients themselves.

He couldn't understand why I took their troubles so hard, why I couldn't leave them behind me when office hours were over, why I worried so over the way Molly Brown's pregnancy was going, or the "crick" in Mrs. Moore's back. And I couldn't have told him, for I hardly knew myself. It was just there—the same sympathy and understanding that was in Frank, and the faint ghostly beginnings of the same deep loyalty to a people who, in spite of everything, still were mine.

I don't know how long I might have fought it down had it not been for Joe, the little black newsboy, and the spot Frank discovered on his lung.

We all knew Joe—everyone in the hospital. He had sold papers on the corner below ever since I'd entered for training, and his mother was one of our cleaning women. But it had taken Frank to find out that there were three children at home younger than he, that he and his mother were their only support, and that Joe had ambitions. "When Ah grows up Ah's go'n to be a doctah!" he'd confided.

I never had seen Frank as upset as he was that night. I'd never heard bitterness in him before. "Doctor!" he said. "Gosh! Unless he gets the care he needs, two years from now he won't be alive.

"You asked me once—" he swung on Dick—"if I ever wanted to be white. I said no. I didn't tell you why. I owe what I am, and what I may be, not to your race but to my own. It was a Negro who took me from ignorance and poverty just as deep as Joe's, and gave me the chance I asked, the chance to be a doctor. His name was Robert Brace. He was neither teacher nor preacher, but had the best qualities of both."

My heart stopped. I looked fearfully at Dick to see if he'd noticed the name. But he gave no indication if he had. Once more I dared to breathe, but I was trembling.

"To be ashamed of my blood," Frank was continuing, "would mean being ashamed of him. I couldn't be. He is the finest and best man I've ever known. What he did for me I wanted to pass along—to Joe if I could—and I meant to, but now . . ."

When Frank left Dick and me that night in front of the nurses' residence I was too sick to wonder if Frank's words had held a warning for me, too sick to care. Shame and guilt, love for my parents, pity for myself, for Joe, for Frank, they were all there in me, crowding at my conscience. But it was Dick who brought my secret out into the open at last.

Dick wanted to talk about ourselves, our love, plans for our coming marriage and for its date, which I had refused so long to set.

I tried to put him off. I said, "I'm tired, Dick, so tired. Let's talk tomorrow." But he wouldn't wait.

"Tomorrow," he cried. "Tomorrow! It's always tomorrow, Julia. I'm sick of it. It's been that way ever since we started helping Frank. If working among those people is going to get you down like this, we're stopping. I'm sorry for them all, sure—Frank included, but after all they're not your people. They're his. I love you and you love me. Let's think of ourselves for a change."

I looked at him standing there beside me, his hands holding mine, his eyes telling me so much more than his lips could possibly say. I never had loved him so much, or wanted him so terribly, as I did when I said, "That's where you are wrong, Dick. They are my people as much as Frank's.

"I am a Negro too, you see. Robert Brace, the wonderful man Frank told you gave him his chance to be a doctor, is my father!"

I told Dick the truth then—all of it. I began at the beginning and went through to the bitter end. I told him about Frank. "He knows I'm Robert Brace's daughter," I said. "I'm sure of it. Perhaps he wouldn't have told. I never meant to, but my shame has been building up inside me for weeks. Sometimes I've felt as though I'd choke if I couldn't tell you—but I couldn't. It took Joe, and the way Frank talked—my father's name and all—to show me that I had to.

"I love you, Dick. I love you so dreadfully, but—it's no use pretending any longer. The blood that's in my father and mother—in Frank—in those poor people we've been working with—it's in me. I couldn't get rid of it and—maybe I don't want to any more. I don't even know that much for sure."

I HADN'T met his eyes while I talked. I hadn't dared. I raised my face then to his, drawn and haggard. I waited for him to speak and when he didn't, I turned toward the steps of the nurses' residence.

That was when he pulled me back and held me with arms so tightly they hurt. The things he said were crazy things. They had no meaning except to tell me that he still loved me and couldn't let me go, that my secret would be safe with Frank, and no one need know—ever.

I remembered afterward that I had heard the wail of the fire sirens and excited shouts coming from the street, but lost in Dick's arms, his kisses, his frantic pleadings, I heard those other sounds only dimly as from another world. We were still standing there in front of the residence when the first ambulance rolled out of the emergency doors and down the drive with Frank sitting beside the driver. The headlights picked us out and he motioned the car to a skidding stop.

"Tenement fire—district where we've been working," he called. "Bad—doctors, nurses needed. Report to Emergency!"

Dick and I were part of the next car out.

And, oh, the sights that met us when we passed the police cordon and swung into our place in the line of waiting ambulances. I had served my time in the emergency receiving room. I had seen my share of death and horror as all nurses must, but never such as this. There are no words to describe the horror of that fire. It's part of Chicago's tragic history.

The world lost a great man that night, and the Colored race a leader whose place can never be filled—Dr. Frank Marshall.

I SAW it happen—all of it. A picture painted against a background of soaring flames and billowing smoke. The dead and dying, the fear crazed, the bereft and the injured. Mothers screaming for missing children, and children sobbing for the parents they would never see again while they huddled, terror stricken at the crash of falling timbers and the shouts of struggling firemen.

We were together, Dick and I, giving first aid to the stretcher cases as they were brought to us, when Frank came hurrying up and told us to prepare for Joe's mother. Their tenement was going with the rest. Joe had brought the children down and he'd gone back after his mother who was too dizzy from the smoke to dare the rickety outside stairway alone. But almost before he had finished speaking, I heard him gasp, and I followed his staring eyes.

The building where Joe lived had been one of the last to catch. But, old and rotten as it was, it burned like tinder and along the rubbish-littered stairway which a few short seconds before had been almost free of fire, the hungry red flames had begun to wind and creep like giant snakes.

Joe and his mother were at the top of the third and last flight, two struggling figures, blackly etched against an eerie crimson glow. Joe, young and thin, fighting his mother's screaming hysteria, dragging her, trying to lift her heavy weight in his spindly arms, while every second of delay was bringing that fiery serpent closer, making his efforts to quiet her harder, and their chances of escape more desperate.

When Frank started up that stairway toward them, Death walked with him, and I knew it.

I went wild then. I screamed and sobbed. These were my people. I had betrayed them. If a life must be sacrificed to save them, it should be mine, not Frank Marshall's.

I would have followed him if Dick's arms hadn't held me back. I was conscious of his quieting, pitying voice in my ears, yet I didn't see him. I saw nothing but those figures on the stairs, Frank struggling up and poor little Joe trying his best to drag his mother down to meet him.

I watched Frank take the mother in his arms while he thrust Joe ahead of him, giving him a push that sent him almost tumbling down the fire-wreathed steps to the safety below. I heard the cheers that met Joe when he reached the ground drown and fade against the groan of horror that swept like a wind over the watching, upturned faces. The stairs had collapsed carrying Frank and his burden with them.

Joe's mother was dead when the rescue squad reached her. Frank died on the way to the hospital. A falling beam had fractured his skull. It was our ambulance that took him, and Dick and I were both beside him. He had been unconscious when we reached him. He was still unconscious when the end came. If he had known my secret he had carried the knowledge with him into death.

It made little difference then. There was no secret between Dick and me, sitting there beside him. I found a certain peace in that, in the fact that I hadn't needed Frank's death to shame me into telling the truth to the man I loved.

I had needed it though, to cleanse my heart of the last trace of my bitterness, and to show me the road my life must follow.

It lay straight and clear before me when we parted, Dick and I, in the light of another day. And there was no place for Dick on that road that stretched ahead of me.

I told him so, my love for him choking my words. I said, "It isn't only ourselves we have to think of, Dick—it is our children. Even if my blood didn't show in them outwardly, it still would be there, and no matter how much you loved them—and me—you'd always be watching for it, and—deep down—fearing it.

"It would ruin your life and mine. It would end in misery and unhappiness for both of us. My love is no excuse for what I've done—I'm not trying to make it one. I'm not even asking your forgiveness. I'm doing the only thing that's left to do, the right and decent thing. I'm going back to my parents and my race.

"I'm Julia Brace, Colored, darling. And for the first time in my life, I'm saying it proudly."

There was nothing Dick could say that he hadn't said, nothing he could do, he hadn't done.

I watched him turn away. I watched him go up the walk, through the hospital doors. Then I went to my room. Less than two hours later my note of resignation was in the mail, and I was on a bus headed home.

That was two years ago. Joe, with what was left of his family, has been with us, with Father and Mother and me, for over a year now. The children are well and happy. Under Mother's watchful care, the spot on Joe's lung has healed and one of these days he may yet be the doctor he yearns to be.

If love and worship for a great man's memory can help, he will be a fine one. Perhaps by that time the clinic Frank had been working for will be a reality, and Joe can take his place in it.

I hope there will be a place in it for me as well. I hope for better things these days than I used to wish for. I hope to be worthy of my father's forgiveness and my mother's gentle understanding, to be able to remember Frank Marshall without the horror of the fire—to pass on to the people for whom he gave his life a little of the love he felt for them.

Shame and guilt are always with me in my thoughts of Dick—and he is never out of my mind—shame and guilt, and lonely, aching pain. The hurt I gave myself will never heal. But Dick deserves to find real happiness—and I hope he can forget me.

I'm sure there is a finer girl waiting for Dick. I am sure of that, sure that the girl who someday will share his work and his life, will be worthy of the love he will give her. *The End*

The 1950's

—— **Truth is Stranger Than Fiction** ——

GLAMOUR-

Why was the piano player looking at me with such scorn as Bob made a pass at me?

THE odd crying sound came again, a sort of muffled whimpering more terrible than tears. My spine crawled with fear, for I'd thought I was alone in the house. Then I realized the sound was coming through the bedroom wall, from my parents' room. Mom crying? She couldn't be!

Hurriedly I slipped the magazine I'd been reading out of sight and rushed into her room. "Mom," I called. "Mom darling. What's the matter?"

She was lying on the bed, her face buried in the pillow. Startled, she sat up and turned her face away. "I thought you were still in the henhouse, Frances. Nothing's the matter, honey. I—I just have a headache."

A headache! I took a good look at her. Oh, no, I groaned inwardly. Not again!

I tried to keep anger and despair out of my voice as I said, "I know what's the matter. You're going to have another baby, aren't you?" The anger was for my father. It was his fault

that we had a new baby almost every year. There were thirteen of us already. My two older brothers had married and moved to farms up the valley, but all the rest I'd helped to raise.

"Don't be cross, Frances child," Mom sighed. "I love babies. And I'm glad, really I am. It's just—I guess I'm just a little tired."

"And why shouldn't you be?" I lashed out, knowing deep down that the despair I felt was more for myself than

CRAZY KID

I wouldn't be trapped in the kind of life Mom had—babies, working on the farm. I was beautiful, talented. And I was going to be somebody!

for Mom. "You work in the barn and henhouse like a hired man. You scrub and cook and wash diapers. And what does Father care? All he thinks about is his prize stock—and having more children. Fourteen! Oh, Mom, it's indecent!"

Mom stood up, and her mouth was grim. "That's enough, Frances. For shame that you should speak so of your father. And what else would a wife be doing if not helping her husband and raising his children? And let me remind you, young lady, that you wouldn't be here to speak so sassy if we'd stopped with two boys. Would you be happier without Alice and George and Esther and—" She named them all.

In my anger I wanted to shout, "Yes!" Then a picture of them all smiling at me flashed into my mind. Could I say, "You should have been born, but you should not"? I did

truly love my brothers and sisters.

Without meaning to I burst into tears, not for Mom but for myself. How could I find words to explain this awful trapped feeling? How could Mom possibly understand what another year of waiting would mean?

I was the oldest girl, nearly seventeen, and Mom would need me. Alice was fifteen and so busy with her junior year in high school that I did most of her work. I didn't mind because I wanted her to have what fun she could.

When a girl comes to the big city, she has to be smart enough to take care of herself. I was dumb enough to think I could— until I found out I was sharing an apartment with a call girl!

It still wasn't the kind of fun we both longed for or that other girls had. None of us was allowed to go to dance or shows. We had no radio, no magazines We didn't own a car. All those things belonged to the devil, Father said.

Oh, I know it sounds incredible. But there are many people in the United States whose religious belief bars all the pleasures that most people take for granted. We lived in Washington, but we had relatives in several states who lived exactly as we did.

When I started to the high school in near-by Elondale, riding the bus that picked up kids along the country roads, a whole new world opened up to me. Thanks to Mom, I was allowed to dress like the other girls and didn't have to wear the long black dress, high shoes, and little white cap our faith required. And I found that my school work required reading newspapers and magazines that would have been banned at home. My father never knew. Even Mom didn't know about the magazines I hid under my mattress. Oh, those wonderful stories of girls just my age who lived in a world of excitement, whose dreams of the right job and the right man always came true!

There was one story I read over and over. It was about a girl with a lovely voice who suffered all kinds of hardships to pay for her singing lessons. Finally, a great producer happened to hear her sing and made her dream come true. The night she became a star, he proposed to her. The picture of his dark head bent over her blonde one in a passionate kiss always set my blood to pounding.

That story became my bible. All that could happen to me, for my dream, too, was singing. If only I could get into the city where someone could hear me, where I could train for the concert stage!

Now, with Mom going to have a baby, the dream shriveled into dust. Not only would she need me, but the money I'd saved from bean and berry picking would be needed, too.

And then I was sobbing out the story of my lost dream on Mom's shoulder, telling her that I'd hoped Father would consent to my living with the Perrys in Seattle. I also told her I planned to get a job in Seattle and use the money I'd saved, almost a hundred dollars, for singing lessons.

The Perrys used to own the farm next to ours, and they were members of our faith.

Mom smoothed my hair and looked deep into my eyes. Hers were so tender, so full of love for me that I was ashamed of my selfishness. "Forget about it, Mom," I said. "I should be sorry for you, not for myself."

"If you're thinking about my tears," she answered, smiling, "it's you who must forget. There are many times in a woman's life when she must go to a secret place and cry alone for a while. You will see when you are a grown woman. But that is not her weakness. It is her strength, for faith returns. For a man, too, comes those times. Then he spades in the garden or pitches the hay."

"Oh, Mom," I said, hugging her, "how can you be so wise, living so far away from life?"

"I'm thinking that wisdom lies closer to us here than in your wonderful city, perhaps. But I will speak to your father. Maybe, after all, you may have your chance. It is seven months before the baby is due. Alice will be out of school in time to help me."

In spite of all reasoning my heart sang with joy. But it was an incredible dream, and I knew it.

That night after Alice was asleep on her side of our bed, I listened to Mom and Father talk together in their room next to ours. I heard Mom say, "For a long time I've been thinking, John. There is no future in the valley for Frances, for any of the girls. In all the valley there is only one boy left to marry."

"And what is the matter with James Turner?" Father's voice was loud and a little angry. Since I was fifteen he'd been planning for me to marry James, who was ten years older than I. Girls in our valley married very young and were usually mothers at my age. But the thought of marrying James, bearing his children, made me physically ill.

Father was saying, "A good farm James has got. And like the old country saying, 'big feet and a big nose are signs of a good husband.'"

"Keep your voice down, John," Mom warned.

After that I could hear nothing but a murmuring that went on and on. Would she win him over? Would I have my golden chance? I got out of bed and stood in front of the little cracked mirror and looked at myself in the moonlight. I knew I was beautiful. I coiled my long red hair up high on my head, and my long white night-gown became a shimmering strapless evening gown like the girl's in the story. Our plain, neat little bedroom became a concert stage, and softly I began to sing a popular song I'd learned in high school. Oh, the dreams I dreamed that night!

The next day I learned that Mom had won out against Father. If the Perrys would let me stay with them I could go to Seattle!

The day the letter came from the Perrys saying they would be very happy to have me and would love me like their own, I skipped about the house, singing at the top of my voice. I hardly noticed how quiet Mom was, or that Father spent all morning swinging a pick in the garden soil.

Alice said, "You look like a fairy princess,

beautiful and shining, waiting for her prince." And that's the way I felt inside. But it was success that the prince held in his hand, not a wedding ring.

Then the day before I was to leave, the mailman stopped at our box. I ran down the lane, then stood staring at the letter he'd handed me. What was Mr. Perry writing for? Just yesterday Mom had received a letter from Mrs. Perry saying they would meet my bus. This one was addressed to Father.

Oh, no, it couldn't be! Yet I knew the letter held the worst possible news. They couldn't take me. Why, oh, why? The agony of waiting for Father to open it was too much. With trembling fingers I tore open the envelope. Mr. Perry had written that he'd just gotten word his mother was very sick in Ohio. He and Mrs. Perry were leaving at once and would probably be there for some time.

So I wasn't going to Seattle, after all. I wasn't going to stand on a big stage, bowing before an audience that shouted, "Bravo!" through a dozen curtain calls. Or was I?

How long I stood there arguing with myself, I don't know. The sound of cow bells coming up the lane finally brought me back to reality. It was milking time. In a few hours, early morning, I could be on a bus for Seattle, fifty-three miles— and a whole world—away.

When I went in the house, I quietly lifted the lid on the wood stove and slipped the letter into the flames. They leaped up, eager to help me deceive the ones who loved me most.

ON the long bus trip to the city the next day, I sat with clenched fists and fast-beating heart. One minute I was filled with a glorious sense of adventure, the next I was appalled at what I'd done. Surely the Lord would punish me for deceiving my parents. Where would I live? How long would my money last? I had just ninety-one dollars. It had seemed like so much when I'd planned to live with the Perrys. Now I knew it was very little.

I thought of Father's last words. They came haltingly, for he didn't talk much to his children, especially the girls. I'd never felt that he loved me. He was always Father to us kids, never Dad or Pop. As we all stood on the highway waiting for the bus, I noticed that his tall frame was a little stooped, his short beard streaked with gray. Startled, I realized that I hadn't really looked at him in a long time.

He said, "We will be praying for you, Frances. You must remember all we have tried to teach you of right and wrong, of faith and humility. You must listen to your head and to your heart not so much."

When I finally arrived in Seattle, I was terribly confused. How different if the Perrys had been there to meet me! But

I'd deliberately set my course, and I was determined not to be afraid. Seattle seemed like the biggest city in the world as I stood on the street with my suitcase, not knowing where to go next.

"Cab, lady?" I looked up, startled. I'd never seen a cab driver or a cab, but I'd read about them. I think I would have gone wherever he told me, I was that dumb. So I'll always be grateful for his advice when I asked him to take me to a cheap room.

He looked me over from head to foot and eyed my imitation leather suitcase. "A girl like you should stay at the Y," he told me. "And you won't need a cab. It's in the next block."

I know now what would have happened to me if I'd asked the wrong man. Other girls, as green as I, have asked the same question. A house of prostitution looks like a cheap hotel from the outside. It's easy for a girl to get taken in. And once she does, she can't get out.

Each day at the Y I'd scan the room-for-rent columns and then go around looking for a job. Everyone wanted girls with experience. But how could I get experience if no one would give me a job? A few employers did suggest that I go to school and learn shorthand and typing, but I didn't have the money for that.

Gone, now, were all thoughts of voice lessons, of excitement and glamour. In my loneliness I felt that I was the only girl in the world hunting for a decent cheap room and enough money to eat on. However, my daily letters home told of my job in a big department store, of my search to find a good voice teacher, bits of news about the Perrys. Lies upon lies—or were they dreams and hopes?

Then two things happened that changed the whole course of my life. I started to night school, and I met Carol. Gorgeous, platinum-haired Carol whom I worshipped at first and then learned to hate.

THERE was an advertisement on the bulletin board at the Y about shorthand and typing classes. For days I looked at it but knew I couldn't afford to go. Then, when my money was almost gone, I decided that it was either sink or swim. Recklessly I enrolled, with a prayer in my heart that somewhere, somehow, I would find the money to live on.

It was Carol who answered that prayer the very first night of school. It was Carol, too, who introduced me to Nick. But that came later, and I want to tell you my story just the way it happened.

Anyway, that night Carol leaned across the aisle and said, "Lend me some paper, kid. I'll pay you back when I get a job."

I handed her a sheet, asking, "Don't you have a job, either?"

"I quit today. Who wants to work in a bakery? You never meet any men. Just women."

She didn't look like the type who belonged in a bakery. I could see her behind footlights, looking a little like the girl I wanted to be. She had thick black eyelashes and a full, pouting mouth. An expensive-looking sweater molded her breasts so closely that I was embarrassed for her and turned my eyes away. The few men in the class, though, stared and stared.

I thought about her job and finally asked her where it was. She gave me the address, saying, "It's just a dinky place, and the pay is peanuts. You're welcome to it, sister."

I could hardly wait for class to be out, and though I didn't expect the bakery to be open, I had to know where it was. When I got to it, the front part of the store was dark, but there was a light in the back, and I could see white-clad figures moving around. I knocked on the door, and someone yelled, "Go away!" But with only eight dollars in my purse I was desperate. Opening the door, I walked in and stood blinking in the bright light.

A DARK little man was kneeding bread at a long table. He called, "Get a load of this, Joe. It's Little Orphan Annie."

"I want a job," I stammered.

The man called Joe came out from behind the big oven. "No job," he said. He paused with a tray of bread in his hands and looked at me. "She's hungry, Bill. Give her some coffee and a doughnut."

The dark man glowered and muttered, "Every piece of trash that blows in off the street—"

Suddenly I was furious. "I'm not trash!" I shouted. "All I want is a job. The job a girl named Carol had. She quit. She told me so."

The dark man sneered, "If you know Carol, you're trash. And she didn't quit. I kicked her out."

"Shut up, Bill," Joe said quietly. He was a big man and younger than the dark one. He poured a cup of coffee from a battered pot and handed me a doughnut. "You a friend of Carol's?" he asked.

I told him how I knew about the job, wondering all the time why they disliked Carol so much. I thought they should have been glad to have anyone so beautiful working in their little bakery.

"You got stung the last time you picked up a tramp," Bill said.

"This girl isn't like Carol, you dope." Then Joe turned to me and told me I could start working the next morning at eight o'clock.

I knew he was giving me the job more to anger the other man than because he wanted me, but I didn't care. That night, with dreams again floating around my head, I wrote to Mom that I had a better job in a bakery. At long last I could tell the truth about something, and you've no idea how it eased my conscience.

"I've licked it," I confided aloud to the mirror as I used to do back home. "At last I'm on the road to success, and nothing can stop me!"

Nothing? If only that mirror could have shown me what would happen in the next few months! I would have run back home that very night.

The work at the bakery wasn't too hard. I cleaned up, kept the cases filled, and waited on customers. If I ever made a mistake, Bill would bawl me out. But Joe was swell. One day I asked him why Bill disliked me so.

"I guess he still thinks you're a friend of Carol's," Joe said.

"But I am," I answered. "I like her a lot. Through her I got this job. And she's so beautiful. I don't see how any one can help loving her."

Joe laughed. "That's what Bill's wife thought. She threatened to divorce him if he didn't fire her. I guess I'm lucky I don't have a wife." Then he added earnestly, "Look, kid, you haven't been around much. Steer clear of dames like Carol. They're poison to little country girls like you."

I didn't tell him that Carol had asked me to share her room and that I'd jumped at the chance. It had happened the night before, at school, and I hadn't been able to believe my ears. Here was Carol, so lovely, so beautifully dressed, wanting me to live with her! Looking down at my cheap clothes, my saddle Oxfords so close to her high-heeled pumps, I asked myself, "Why?" In her place would I be so generous to a dumb little country girl who'd seen only one movie in her life? Then suddenly I realized she probably didn't know how dumb I was. And if I used my head, she need never find out. I could learn from her how to dress and act, how to find the answers for myself.

"I'd love to room with you, Carol," I said. "But we must share the expense half and half."

She threw back her shimmering head and laughed. "We won't worry about that." She linked her arm through mine, and we started out the door. I'd never felt more proud or more humble in my life.

I hadn't realized how lonely I was until I moved in with her. Knowing no one, having no money to spend, I knew little more about Seattle than the day I'd arrived. Just one movie the first week. Oh, what a thrill that had been! I'd wondered why everyone around me looked so bored. Could it be that they'd seen so many that one more didn't matter? I vowed that I'd see a show every day for the rest of my life. But even if I could have afforded it, working all day and going to night school left me no time.

Living with Carol changed all that at first. Almost every night after school we went to a late show. More often than not, one or two of Carol's boy friends went with us. What an exciting life it was, I thought. Though I was often shocked by their swearing and the frank way they all talked, I was learning fast.

The movie was just the beginning of the evening for Carol. But I had to be at work at eight in the morning, so I went back alone to our room to write my letter home and go to bed. How far away home seemed! Sometimes it scared me. And there was always a lot of straightening up to do. I soon learned that my roommate never hung up her clothes and would step over them forever if I didn't hang them up for her.

Usually it was almost daylight before Carol got in. I wondered many times where she'd been, what she'd been doing. But, of course, I didn't ask her. It seemed that the longer I knew her, the less I knew about her. She never told me much except that she was working occasionally as a model. She quit night school shortly after I moved in with her. She said, "I don't know why I ever started those dumb classes. I'm not cut out to earn money the hard way."

Then one Saturday she said, "I bought a new sweater today and some red pumps, so I can't pay the rent. If you'll pay it again, I'll rustle up some folding stuff by next week for sure."

For a moment I was stunned. For three weeks I'd paid the rent. But what could I say? "I guess so," I answered reluctantly. "But this week I thought—"

"I know. You'd take singing lessons." Then angrily she said, "I'm sick of hearing about them. I'm sick of being broke. I'm sick of all this penny-ante stuff. I thought once you and I could team up on a good thing, and we'd both make dough. But after living *(Continued)*

Glamour-Crazy Kid

(Continued)

with you, I've changed my mind. You're not dumb enough, and you're not smart enough."

"If you mean modeling," I retorted, "I'm not interested. I'd rather have steady work. The bakery is okay until I finish school. Just so I can sing."

"Then why don't you sing? Cut out the long-haired stuff you're always warbling and try for a band job." Then with one of her sudden changes of mood she sighed and said, "Forget the harsh words, kid. Jump into this dress of mine, and I'll take you to Nick. If he likes your voice, he'll help you land a job."

And that's how I met Nick. Before that he'd been just a name she mentioned now and then.

Carol took me to a place called the Zero Club. It was very dark and full of smoke and smells and laughter. Half-filled glasses and smoldering cigarettes littered the tables. The dance floor was crowded with couples who swayed with eyes closed, as if they were one body instead of two. It all seemed sinister and threatening, and I knew I didn't belong there. Carol seemed to know everyone.

We sat down at a table, and almost immediately two boys who'd taken us to a movie once left the bar and came over. The one called Pinkie said, in his high-pitched voice, "Well, you finally decided to bring your little virgin to our den of sin. How sweet!"

Carol said angrily, "Shut up, Pinkie! You're drunk!"

The other one—Bob—was even drunker. He put his arm around me and nearly fell into my lap. "Don't let it throw you, sweetheart. You're in good company. Why, through these portals walk some of the best—" he hiccuped—"girls in the business."

I was completely beyond my depth, and I was ashamed, angry, confused. I didn't want to believe the insult in his voice because his words made no sense at all.

Carol said, "Go get us some drinks, Bob. And, Pinkie, tell Nick I want to see him after this number. Fran wants a singing job, and we need his help."

I watched Pinkie push his way unsteadily across the dance floor to the piano just as the music stopped. I saw him gesture at our table, but the piano player only shook his head and didn't look around. Pinkie whispered something in his ear, and this time the piano player turned slowly and stared right at me with a sort of weary scorn. He was young and thin and dark, with a strange hardness about him. Then he turned away, running his right hand over the keys, and shook his head again. I felt as if he'd slapped me. Did he think I couldn't sing? Didn't he like my looks? His eyes had said far more than that. But what? Glancing at Carol, I knew she, too, was hurt and angry. For herself or for me?

"Drink up, kid," she said bitterly, an odd brightness in her eyes. "There always has to be a first drink in everybody's life. A first time for everything." She lifted her glass and drank it all. Then she added, "Nick's the first guy I ever knew I could really go for. And he can't see me for dust."

It was funny, but I suddenly felt very close to her, not worshiping or envious as I usually was, but deeply sorry because she'd been hurt. Who did this Nick think he was? I hated him.

I drank my drink without even tasting the liquor, without realizing that it was the first drink I'd ever had, the first of many more to come.

How quickly we slip from one pattern of life to another. Is it just an inevitable part of growing up? Or do we guide our own destiny, straying from the course we've set because we're weak and lazy?

I wonder about that now. But at the time, in Seattle, it was easy enough to drift into the life at the Zero Club and to think of my life on the farm and everything I'd been taught as something that had happened to me in some hazy past.

The family letters seemed to come from a distant planet, they were so far removed from the world I was living in. The cow, Susie, had had a calf. James Turner was going to marry one of the Peterson girls. I wasn't interested.

My letters to them had got further and further apart, and I'm afraid they didn't tell much of what was actually happening to me. But at least they weren't full of lies any more. I'd explained that the Perrys had been called to Ohio and that I was sharing a room with a nice girl I'd met at night school. I didn't mention that she'd quit. I didn't say that the worship I'd once felt for her was vanishing, like the bleach along the part in her hair, that I was disgusted when she did things like using perfume instead of soap. However, I did tell them that I liked my job at the bakery and that, at long last, I was taking singing lessons on Monday, my day off. Oh, I made it sound as if everything was fine.

I didn't tell them that the first four teachers told me quite frankly after a lesson or two that I would never be a concert singer, for my voice lacked the quality and volume necessary for the stage. And I never mentioned the fifth teacher, who promised me great things, but whose hungry eyes seemed to undress me as he talked.

Oh, I wanted so much to believe him! I thought I'd learned enough about men since coming to the city to keep him at arm's length while I took my lessons. But the second time I went for a lesson he pulled me against him and ran his hands over me.

"Oh, Frances," he whispered, breathing his hot breath down my neck, "do not be so cold. Love me a little. Loving will make you sing like the angels."

"Let go of me," I said quietly. "I came for a lesson, not to be mauled."

But the big professor, although he was old enough to be my father, was filled with a passion beyond all reasoning. His powerful arms held me like a vise while he rained sickening kisses on my neck. He pulled my dress away to bare my shoulder, and the buttons gave way as if they were made of paper. I struggled and fought, trying to hide my growing panic as his hands slipped inside my open dress and his repulsive mouth moved from my lips to my throat. In sheer terror now I tried to reason with him. Slowly but surely he was forcing me toward the divan—we were almost there. I begged and pleaded. But his eyes were glazed with passion, his ears deaf to everything but the desire within him. "Oh, my beautiful one," he crooned, "I will make you so happy."

In desperation I kicked him with all my strength. He let me go, bellowing with rage and pain. "You cat!" he yelled. "You she-dog with the voice of a cow!"

I grabbed my coat and ran, thankful that I had something to wear over my torn dress. Once I was out on the street, the numbness left me. I began to shake as I recalled my terrible words to Mom about Father and about how awful it was for them to have another baby Bu. Mom

and Father were deeply in love. They shared something good and beautiful, and it was only natural for them to want children. I realized that now, for now I knew, too, what plain unadorned sex looked like, and it was so different from what my parents shared. And my father was a good man. He loved his family and he was gentle with his many children in spite of his strictness. Oh, Dad, I thought, I'm sorry I thought anything mean of you. I'm truly sorry. And there on the street in Seattle, with strangers going by, I suddenly knew my father as I'd never known him before. And for the first time I thought of him as "Dad."

When I got home, I took a hot bath, trying to cleanse myself, and my thoughts moved from my mother and father to Nick. What would he say if he knew about the professor? He was so unpredictable, strange. Would he despise me?

For a long time I'd been both fascinated and repelled by Nick Tursone. But I no longer hated him as I had the first time I'd seen him. Sometimes I imagined I was a little in love with him, or with the wild, sad music he played between dance numbers when no one seemed to listen.

I'll never forget the first time we talked. I was sitting alone, waiting for Carol to come back from the telephone and worrying about my shorthand grades. I should be home studying. I shouldn't have taken another drink. But being alone in one drab room seemed so dismal that I couldn't have studied anyway, I told myself. The Zero Club was a familiar place now. Dropping in after class to dance and listen to the music had become a habit. Still I didn't seem to be a part of it. The men I knew were friendly enough, sometimes too friendly, but except for Carol, the girls seemed to shut me out.

Suddenly someone slipped into the chair beside me. In amazement I saw that it was Nick. Without even saying hello, he said, "Never cut your hair. Always wear it long like that."

"I'm surprised you like it," I answered coldly. "I got the impression a long time ago that you disliked everything about me."

His dark face twisted in a weary grin. "I did," he said. "But I've been watching you, and maybe I guessed wrong. Don't you ever get any phone calls?"

What an odd question! "Why should I?" I asked. "I don't know anyone in Seattle."

"Hasn't Carol introduced you?"

"Of course. I've met a lot of people here. But I haven't much time to meet people and go places."

He seemed to think that was funny, and the bitterness left his face. He kept asking questions, and I told him about the bakery and night school and even about my family and meeting Carol. I was beginning to like him.

"Do you really sing?" he asked. "Or was that another of Carol's cheap tricks?"

I bristled. "What was cheap about it? She only wanted to help me. But I can manage nicely alone, thank you. Pretty soon I'll be able to take lessons, and someday you'll know I can sing because you'll be standing up and cheering with the rest of the audience."

He looked into space, his face twisted and bitter again. "And someday," he said softly, "Nick Tursone's records will be in every home, heard on every radio." Then he stood up, glaring at me. "Oh, you fool! You silly little fool! Why don't you go home!"

I was still smarting from his insult as I waited on customers the next day. I

163

didn't know whether I was glad or angry when the bakery shop door opened and I saw him standing there. At first I hardly knew him, for his face was smudged, and he wore grease-stained coveralls with "Bailey's" written across them in red letters.

"Get your coat," he said. "I'll take you to lunch. We've got to talk."

I called to Joe in the back room and threw my coat over my white uniform.

Nick and I drove away in a tow car with "Bailey's" painted on the side. Neither of us spoke. I was waiting for an apology, but it never came. After we sat down for lunch, Nick reached across the table and took my hand. "I meant every word I said last night," he told me earnestly. "Why don't you go home while you still have your dreams? Before you get like me?"

Always before he'd seemed hard and cynical. Now there was a pleading in his voice, as if he were reaching out for understanding and afraid he'd be laughed at.

"What's wrong, Nick?" I whispered. "Doesn't everybody have dreams? Don't you?"

"I did have," he answered, studying his grimy hands. "When I left home, I thought the world was my oyster. All I had to do was work hard and pretty soon everybody would be talking about me. I'd met a sax player who told me there were some good openings in Seattle. So I came up here from my father's truck farm in California, rented a room, and bought a piano. Success was just around the corner."

"And wasn't it?" I asked.

He lit a cigarette and studied the smoke. "My landlady said I made too much noise, and the piano had to go. That was blow number one. And I couldn't find any other place where they'd let me practice. Also, night-club business was bad, and the joints were folding for lack of money. Blow number two."

We ordered hamburgers, and Nick went on with his story. "Music was my whole life. My fingers ached for the touch of the keys. I got a few jobs here and there, but not enough to eat on. Yet I hung on, sending home for money. Pretty soon I owed my father over a thousand dollars. That's a lot of money to him. But I still had my dream. Someday I'd pay it back, with interest. Someday he'd be proud that he'd helped me."

"But you're playing steady now. You've got your own band," I said.

He pushed his uneaten food away. "Yeah," he sneered. "Nick Tursone and His Boys. In lights even. But this is the end of the road. I'm just a fifth-rate hack playing in a dirty dive for peanuts. That's a long way from the dream I had, isn't it?"

His wry grin tore at my heart. "But why do you feel that way, Nick?" I cried. "This is just the beginning, the chance you've been waiting for."

"Oh, sure. Just like it happens in a book. Like you think it will happen to you. Now is the time for the big band leader to go slumming, hear me, and sign me up for top billing. Nuts!"

"What's to stop you?" I demanded.

He pushed up the sleeve of his work shirt. "This," he said, running his finger over a red ridge that crossed his wrist and ended in a bump on the back of his hand. "I was in a cast for three months, and I had to learn to play all over again—if you can call it playing. You see, when I finally got sick of sponging off my old man, I got a job at Bailey's garage. The very next day I got a chance to play steady at the Zero. Not much of a place, I thought, but all right for a springboard. That was two years ago."

"Go on," I prompted.

"Honey, I was walking on air. Just to know that I'd get my hands on a piano every day brought back all my hopes. With both jobs I could pay back the money I'd borrowed and show my folks I wasn't the washout they thought. But you can't work all day and all night, too. And any dumb cluck knows that a piano player shouldn't work in a garage. My hands got so stiff and battered up at work that I'd need a drink or two to loosen the joints. Before long I found out that benzedrine was better than liquor. It made my fingers fly. Then I'd have to take sleeping pills because I was too hopped up to sleep the four hours I had left after the club closed. At the garage I'd take more benzedrine to keep from falling asleep on the job. The stuff makes you feel like you could tackle anything. They say it isn't dope, but it was the way I took it. I began to have accidents. I forgot to finish what I was doing. I didn't realize how pickled my brain was until I did something wrong and a motor fell and crushed my hand. Well, that's all there is to the story, Fran. That's the way dreams end."

I took his twisted hand in mine and held it tightly. Poor Nick. The stirring in my heart was more than pity. "Not all dreams, darling," I told him. "Just because you got a bad break is no reason that I should give up my dream and go home. You haven't gone home in spite of everything."

"I can't," he answered. "After all my loud talk about fame and success, could I go home with my tail between my legs? But you could because you haven't failed yet."

"But you haven't heard me sing," I cried. "How do you know I'll fail?"

He lifted my hand to his lips and kissed my fingers. "Honey, you're a soprano, aren't you? Sopranos just don't fit with a hot band."

"I don't want a band job. I'm going higher than that. And I'm going to have my chance in spite of what you say!"

Suddenly he was angry. "And I suppose you'll find it sitting around the Zero every night, getting stuck a little deeper in the mire?"

I couldn't tell him then that the reason I was there so much was to hear him play. "I've got to get back to work," I said coldly, standing up.

And that's how our strange romance began—one minute feeling so close, the next minute quarreling and as far apart as the poles.

After he heard me sing, he liked my voice, but he still begged me to quit trying for "the top of the heap," as he put it. "You're just like me," he said. "You're good enough for the top, so you'll end up on the bottom, without guts enough to go home."

"I'll make you eat those words, Nick," I said.

I was determined to find a teacher who believed in my voice. I told you what happened there.

Nick and I quarreled once about Carol. He tried to tell me she was no good. I couldn't see anything wrong with modeling, so I refused to listen. Although the glamour had worn off, and there were times when I wondered about her myself, where she went when she was out so late, I'd never seen her do anything really bad, and I wouldn't let him run her down. Besides, since I'd started going with Nick, she had seemed to avoid me. We just went our separate ways.

In spite of our quarreling I was deeply in love with Nick. Sometimes I thought he loved me, too, in a funny sort of way. Oh, he kissed me, and there was a light in his eyes that said more than words, but he acted as if I were too precious and fragile to be held tightly. I wondered how a man as tempestuous as Nick could love so quietly, demanding nothing more than to be with me. It was sad that I longed to have him crush me in his arms, kiss me deeply, when everything about sex had always repelled me.

I thought of that as I lay in the tub after my horrible experience with the music professor. How grateful I felt for Nick's gentleness. And suddenly I knew I wouldn't tell him. Why take the risk when I needed him so? He'd been right all along, and I'd been wrong. My bitter tears stopped, and I jumped out of the tub and hurried into my clothes.

Maybe I couldn't sing. Maybe my dream was lost forever. But in spite of all my disappointments I had more than I was entitled to. I had Nick. Everything would be all right once his arms were around me.

The Zero was almost empty when I got there. Nick came over to me, and when he saw my face, he took me in his arms, just as I'd known he would. "Come in here," he said, pulling me into the checkroom. "Now tell me what happened. Here's a handkerchief."

I told him, leaving out the shameful part, explaining only that I'd been to five teachers and that the last one had convinced me that I couldn't sing.

"I told you the concert stage was aiming too high, Fran," he told me gently. "Is it really so important, darling?"

"You know it is," I cried. "I've nothing to show for all the months I've been here." Nothing but my love for you, my heart whispered, and you haven't said you loved me."

"Would you like to try a number with the band?"

I stared at him. "Do you really mean that? I thought you said I wouldn't be any good with a band."

"It won't hurt to try, honey. Maybe it will ease your heartache. There's hardly anyone here on Monday night, so it won't matter if you go on without a rehearsal." There was a deep tenderness in his eyes. Then he kissed me, long and sweet, and every part of me thrilled with ecstasy. In his arms the horror of the afternoon with the music professor faded away, and I knew, without his telling me, that I mattered more to him than anything else in this world.

"This is the bottom of the heap, sweetheart," he said huskily. "But maybe for you it's a beginning. Right now you're the only one here who's still sweet and clean and good. Stay that way, honey, because I need you so."

We clung together, and I knew he was thinking, just as I was, that out of all our mistakes and failures we'd salvaged one shining thing—our love for each other.

Nick began to play a song I knew, and I gave it all I had for his sake. He didn't want me to sing in this place, but he was giving me my chance. In his eyes had been the message that if I succeeded where he'd failed, he wouldn't stand in my way. Did I want that? If it were possible, would I trade Nick's love for fame?

"Good going," he whispered when I finished. "Try another one."

"It didn't go over, Nick," I said. "Nobody listened."

"They never listen. They don't come here for that. You'll get used to it."

But I didn't. After four nights the little triumph I'd expected was still not there. Standing before the microphone, I began to see the club through Nick's eyes—the cheapness, the tawdriness, easy kisses, roaming hands. Why hadn't I seen it before?

I was trying to find the answers to that question Friday morning as I went about the familiar tasks in the bakery. "Joe," I said, "did you ever want something with all your heart and when you got it, it wasn't what you expected at all?"

"You sound like the kid who finally got his chance to eat his weight in doughnuts. He didn't like what he got, either."

I had never talked to Joe, and certainly not to Bill, about my private life. But Joe had been swell to me. His common sense had saved me lots of times when Bill had made me mad enough to quit. Now I needed impersonal advice, someone to help straighten out my tangled thinking.

I began at the beginning. I told him about the girl in the magazine who'd started my dream, about the new baby who'd threatened it, about the scene I'd raised and how I'd burned the letter, about the music professor and Nick and the club.

When I'd finished, he asked a strange question. "How old are you, Fran?"

"Seventeen."

"You've been here five months, haven't you? So you were sixteen when you came. A child trying to live a fairy tale."

"At home," I told him, "you're a woman at sixteen and usually married."

He went on, "And you've been in Seattle five months. Did you think success would come so quickly? Do you know many singing stars at seventeen?"

"But in five months," I argued, "I should at least have made a start."

"Heaven isn't reached in a single bound, you know." He put his arm around me. "You came too soon with too little. All kids are too impatient, afraid life is going to pass them by. Why don't you go home now? Just chalk it up to experience, pick up your marbles, and leave that dump you're singing in."

"With nothing to show but failure? I've wasted all my money. I've learned a lot of things I'm not so proud of, like smoking and drinking. What do you think my folks would think of that?"

"How did you ever get started going to a place like the Zero Club?" he asked. "Last year it was raided three times by the narcotics squad. They were looking for marijuana. It's the worst dive in town."

I was startled. "Nick says it's bad, but I just thought he was bitter. I didn't know other people thought that. And what's marijuana?"

Joe stared at me. "You mean you really don't know? Didn't you learn anything in school or from your folks? Don't you read the papers?" He looked me straight in the eye. "Are you lying to me?"

I shook my head.

"My Lord!" he said, running his fingers through his hair. "A newborn baby playing with dynamite! So you think you're too worldly wise to go home, eh? Sister, I'll bet you don't know anything!" He turned away in disgust. Then he came back and stood with his hands on his hips, glaring at me. "Since I seem to be the only one around here to teach you the facts of life, I'll ask you some more questions. Do you know what a prostitute is?"

I flushed. "Of course. They had those in the Bible," I retorted. "And I'm not as dumb as you think. You can't live on a farm with animals around or help raise a flock of brothers and sisters without knowing something about sex. But I don't see what all this has to do with the club."

"No? Well, do you know what a call station is? A call girl?"

"No."

"Kid, for five months you've been practically living in a call station. And if I'd known it before, believe me, I'd have had the police send you home. You're under age. Carol's a call girl at the club. There are half a dozen or so regulars, and some of them are dope addicts. They hang

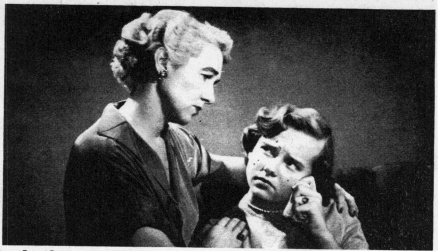

Is there now a
"WONDER DRUG" FOR PIMPLES?

around the club waiting for calls, usually from bellhops. Then they sell their bodies to a guy in a hotel room. High-school girls and even housewives pick up spare cash that way. That's a pretty rotten picture, isn't it? A different kind of sex from what you see on the farm. Now do you feel so darned smart?"

There was nothing I could say. I was terribly shocked; I felt sick. Yet all the things I'd overheard, all the remarks Nick had made, began to fit in. And from the first night I'd gone to the club, hadn't I felt that something was wrong? But how could I have known for sure if someone didn't tell me? Even my folks knew nothing about call stations or marijuana. I was sure of that.

"Are you going back to that dive?" Joe asked.

"No, Joe, of course not," I answered. "I'll tell Nick when he comes to see me to lunch." Oh, Nick, did you think I knew all this, my heart cried.

Joe finally went out for lunch, and I was alone in the shop, waiting for Nick. I was still dazed by what Joe had told me. The bell over the door tinkled, and I looked up, expecting Nick. But it was Bill. Why was he coming in the front way, I wondered. And why was he here at all? He didn't usually come to work till three o'clock. He shut the door and locked it. Then he pulled down the shade with "Closed" painted across it. All this without a word to me.

As he came toward me and I saw his eyes, I started to back away. The man was mad. His face was black with fury, and his eyes were bloodshot and staring. "So you played me for a sucker, eh?" he snarled. "You said to yourself, 'I'll be smarter than Carol. I'll pretend I'm a little country girl working my way through school.'" He kept coming toward me slowly, like a cat stalking a cornered mouse. I backed into the other room. "Every night you'd lie in some man's arms and laugh at me. Maybe many men every night. But never me. Why? Don't you think I can pay for it?"

One hand shot out and grabbed me by the throat. "Stop it, Bill!" I cried. "Stop or I'll scream!"

"With my hand around your pretty throat? Last night I saw you. I heard you sing. You sounded like an angel. You looked like one." Then his voice rose. "But you're black inside. You're rotten, or you wouldn't have been there. Well, I'm not a sucker any more. I'm taking what I want!"

I fought like a wildcat, clawing at the fingers around my throat. But his short, powerful arms pushed me back across the table as he choked me. His mouth, hard on mine, pinned me down. I couldn't cry out or even breathe, and a darkness swirled up and over me.

Then, all of a sudden, there was an odd noise of heavy panting, of grunts and blows landing, and at last a loud clatter. I sat up to see Bill sprawled under a cascade of baking pans, his head against the bottom of the cupboard. Nick stood over him. Blood ran from Nick's nose and covered the front of his coveralls. A cut on his head dripped blood into his eyes.

I covered my face with my hands and started to cry, dry, hard sobs. I couldn't talk. All I wanted was Nick's understanding arms about me. But they didn't come. Instead, through his ragged breathing came a torrent of words that seared my soul. Nasty, ugly words like Bill had used. But Nick was the man I loved!

"If that's what you wanted," he finished, "I'm sorry I butted in. I don't know why I knocked him out. Next time, remember to lock the back door." And then he was gone.

I ran to the door, calling, "Nick! Oh, Nick!" From his seat in the tow car he gave me one long, contemptuous look, as if he wanted to remember, and hate me, for the rest of his life.

I watched the car go out of sight, all my love going with it, while an aching despair filled my heart.

Back in the bakery, I slipped out of my white uniform and into my blue linen dress. I could hear Bill out in the front part of the store, groaning. I didn't even go out to look at him. Mechanically I combed my hair. All I could think of was getting away, not home, just some place where I could hide, where there would be no Carols, no Bills, no Zero Clubs, and no Nick.

When I got home, I found Carol in bed. The blinds were pulled down to shut out the sun. "Gee—" she sat up yawning—"is it time for you to be home? Thought I'd get a little sleep. No sleep for a whole week." Then she saw my face. "Say, what happened to you?"

"Carol," I said, wondering if that cold, hard voice was really coming from me, "how do you really earn your living?"

"Look, baby," she frowned, "I told you I was a model. Let it go at that."

"I want the truth."

She was suddenly very angry. "Okay, you can have it. I go out with men. I get paid for it. Even you ought to be able to take it from there. But it's none of your business." Then she added sarcastically, "My sins don't rub off on your lily-white skin."

"Yes, they do," I told her. "They did today. And you're going to sit right there and listen to me." I told her what had happened, coldly, without emotion. My hate for her only added to the numbness in my heart.

She threw back her head and laughed. "That's rich! That's wonderful! So the great Nick walked out on you!" Then she sprang out of bed, her face contorted with anger. "Listen to me, you mealy-mouthed little fool. For a long time now I've hated you. I wanted Nick, and I couldn't get him. I'm tickled to death you lost him. Don't look to me for sympathy."

"Why did you pretend to be my friend if you hated me?" I asked.

"Because you're a soft touch, and you look so respectable, you stupid nitwit. You make me look respectable, too, and I like living in one place. I admit I had other ideas in the beginning, but I got afraid you'd squeal to the cops. I always said you weren't smart enough to team up with

me. You were just dumb enough to be useful."

She went on jeering at me while I got my suitcase from under the bed and packed it. Her laughter followed me down the stairs and into the street.

At the bus depot I studied the board that listed cities and prices. I had enough money to get to San Francisco. I might as well go there. What did I have to lose?

I gave the ticket agent my money and asked him when the bus left. "Next bus at eleven-forty-five. You just missed the four o'clock."

I had hours to wait. I sat in the station watching the people around me, laughing people who hitched their wagons to stars within their reach. None of them looked as if they were knee-deep in broken dreams. I felt as if mine were piled around me for all the world to see.

The hour hand moved slowly around the clock. It was nine-thirty now. In the Zero Club, just four blocks away, Nick would be running his fingers idly over the piano keys, his damaged left hand stretching painfully for the bass chords. Oh, Nick, my darling, I love you.

Suddenly something gave way inside me. I couldn't leave like this. He had to know the truth—that I was just a dumb girl who had thought she knew all the answers, a dumb girl who'd let herself be caught in this mess because she didn't really know the first thing about life.

But there was no dark, beloved head bent over the keyboard as I entered the club. "Where's Nick?" I asked Pete, who played the drums.

"Not here yet. I thought he was with you."

"No."

"Well, Stan can double for him till he gets here. Your song arrangements are on the piano."

The minutes dragged by. I ordered a drink from habit and looked around the club. It seemed just the same. People I'd never seen before were at most of the tables, and they were still pretty sober. It was early yet. But toward the end of the bar were four of the girls who were regulars, the ones who'd hurt my feelings because they'd seemed unfriendly. And there was Pinkie, laughing in his girlish voice at something Bob had said. Just the same—but, oh, so different. And I'd become a part of this. Why? You must listen to your head and to your heart not so much, came the answer faintly in my father's voice, and I could see his sober,

bearded face in the bottom of my glass.

Stan touched my arm. "It's time for your first number."

"I'm not singing," I told him. "I only want to see Nick for a minute."

"It'll be a long wait, kid. He called from the bus depot and told the boss what he could do with the job. He's gone back home."

Gone! Oh, if only I'd stayed at the depot! Now, all his life, he'd think I was like Carol, after all. He'd never know the truth. I felt the tears dripping in my heart, but my cheeks were dry. At least my heartache didn't show. What had Mom said about every woman needing a secret place to cry in? Well, I was a grown woman now. I knew what she meant.

The farm and all that it stood for came sharply into focus for the first time in months. Tonight my brothers and sisters would be laughing together while they popped corn in the kitchen. No glasses of liquor or trays of smoldering cigarettes would be on the table. Instead I could see a bowl of nuts that I'd helped gather last fall. Oh, how I longed to be there this minute, to cry out my heartbreak on Mom's understanding shoulder.

I got up and walked blindly out of the Zero Club. I walked along the dark street, and now there were tears in my eyes, making a mist before me. A figure was coming toward me, but I didn't pay any attention to it. There was no one I wanted to see, to talk to, any more in Seattle. Nick was gone; there was nothing left. I kept on walking, but the figure suddenly grabbed me, and I heard Nick's dear voice crying, "Fran! Oh, Fran, I thought I'd lost you! I was coming back—I couldn't leave—" Then, right there on the street, Nick was holding me and kissing my eyes, my lips. And I was clinging to him, the tears running down my cheeks.

"Sweetheart," Nick was saying, "after those terrible things I said today, can you forgive me—maybe in a thousand years?"

"Then you don't believe they're true, Nick?" I asked softly.

"Oh, honey, I never did, not really. But I was in a blind rage. Later I went back to the bakery, but you were gone. I didn't need Joe to tell me the score then about you, but he did. I thought I'd lost you forever, Fran, and I couldn't face the thought of going on here without you. But when I got to the bus depot, I realized I couldn't leave without trying to see you once more."

"Oh, Nick, I'm so glad you came back! I was an awful dumb bunny about Carol and the Zero Club," I told him. "But today I realized something, too. Nicky, I don't want fame any more, I don't want to stay here, either, unless I can be with you. Darling, I love you. Please marry me and take me with you wherever you want to go."

And so, two months later, I'm writing this in the little room I shared so long with my sister Alice. Nick is asleep in the white iron bed Alice and I slept in for so many years.

Nick and I were married in Seattle as soon as the law would permit us. Then, after visiting Nick's folks in California, we came here to watch over things while Mom is in the hospital. And Nick is as proud of the new baby as Dad is.

Soon Nick and I will be going back to Seattle and to his job in the garage. But we're not going back to the Zero Club. And we're not making plans ahead; we're not building dream castles in the future. From now on we're going to live our dreams day by day. They'll grow with the years as our love grows. But they'll never be so high that we won't be able to reach out and touch them with our fingertips.

THE END

IN EXCHANGE FOR A BABY

"I should never have let you do it!" Jim moaned. A chill went through me, and I feared for my unborn child. . .

I loved my husband with my whole heart, and it was a bitter blow when he couldn't give me the child I longed for. Yet it wasn't completely hopeless. There was still _one_ chance for motherhood left to me. . .

I THINK the most heartbreaking words in the world are these: "You can never have a baby." They shatter so many hopes and dreams, and they can even weaken a wonderful love with bitterness and misunderstanding. I know, because that's what happened to Jim and me.

Dr. Evert had tried to be kind when he told us the results of all the tests and examinations. He had done his best to find the right words to soften the blow. He said lots of men were sterile. It was just one of those mistakes of nature that nobody could help.

But it all boiled down to the fact that our dearest hopes would never be realized. We'd never have the family we'd talked about and planned for ever since we got married.

Dr. Evert had suggested adoption, but I didn't want anybody else's baby. I wanted to bear a child myself. I had to feel that it was part of me. An adopted baby could never be that.

Jim put his arm around me after we left the doctor's office. "Honey," he whispered, "I wish there was something I could say—something I could do. I feel terrible about this."

I could tell how stricken he was, and I wanted to comfort him. I wanted to tell him that nothing mattered as long as we had each other. But I was so miserable that the words wouldn't come.

All the way home I dreaded walking into our quiet house, because I knew it wouldn't ever echo with the sound of children's voices. The room we had set aside for a nursery would be empty. Our lives would be empty too—and the years ahead lonely and without any real purpose.

Ever since I could remember I'd been crazy about children. I'd always planned to have a big family, because growing up with my four brothers and sisters had been such a wonderful experience for me. Mom and Dad were sensible, down-to-earth parents, and even though there wasn't enough money to go around, we had so many other things to compensate. My folks didn't believe in the modern way of raising children. We got slapped plenty when we needed it and rewarded when we rated it; but we always knew they loved us, and that was the most important part of it all.

I was the youngest in the family and I had just started high school when my two older sisters, Louise and

Beth, got married. My twin brothers had a double wedding a year later. When my nephews and nieces started coming along, I had plenty of baby-sitting to do, but I never minded it. Mom used to say I was wonderful with children. I guess it was because I loved them so much.

When I finished high school, I went to work in the aircraft plant in our town, and that's when I met Jim Hanson. I liked him from the very beginning. Once we began dating, I didn't want to go out with anybody else. Jim loved to come to my house, especially when the whole family was there. He had no folks, no ties of any kind, so when Mom and Dad and the rest sort of adopted him, he thought it was grand. We only knew each other a few months before we got married. We bought a little house near where my folks lived, and at first we were completely happy together.

I was disappointed after a year had passed and I didn't become pregnant, but it didn't really worry me because Jim and I were young—we had plenty of time to start our family. At the end of the third year though, I went to Dr. Evert for a complete examination. He found nothing wrong with me. Finally he suggested that Jim and I both have sterility tests, and Jim was perfectly willing to go along with it. But knowing the truth hit us both very hard. It seemed so wrong, so unfair for other people to have babies—people who didn't even want them—while Jim and I were denied the joy of being parents.

When we got home, Jim took me in his arms. "We'll just have to accept it, honey," he said, raising my face to his. "But I feel like I've let you down, Alice. I feel like I don't measure up as a man or a husband—"

"Oh, no," I whispered. "You mustn't feel that way, Jim. It isn't anything you can help. It isn't your fault."

But that night, when we went to bed and Jim turned to me for reassurance and love, I couldn't respond to him the way I usually did. For the first time since our marriage, there was no answering need in me. It seemed as if knowing that the power of creation was missing had taken away something that was vital and meaningful.

THE FEELING PERSISTED as the days went on. I couldn't seem to overcome it. I grew moody and depressed too. I wanted to be by myself all the time. I stopped going over to Mom's house because I was afraid she would guess that something was wrong, and I couldn't bring myself to tell her about Dr. Evert's report.

I avoided my friends too, particularly the ones with babies. Now that I could never share their interests, I decided it was better to stay away from them. I got so nervous and run down

finally that Jim insisted I see Dr. Evert.

At first I didn't want to go. "What can he do for me?" I asked. "What can anybody do for me?"

"Maybe he can talk a little sense into you, Alice," Jim said. "Maybe he can make you realize what you're doing to our marriage."

He looked so worried and upset that I agreed to go to the doctor's. And when I told Dr. Evert how despondent and blue I'd been ever since I found that we couldn't have a baby, he looked at me for a minute and then he said, "Have you given any more thought to adopting a child?"

I shook my head. "That wouldn't be the answer. I want my own baby."

"Then the only other suggestion I can make is the AID plan," Dr. Evert said. "That's artificial insemination by a donor. In most cases, it works out very well."

"But not in all cases?" I asked, and Dr. Evert said it depended on the reaction of the husband to a great extent. "Some men have a mental block against the whole procedure. Even though the donor remains anonymous, they feel that another man has taken over their husbandly rights. Of course, in many instances, the husband is just as anxious for the plan as the wife. Anyway, we insist on his written consent."

I leaned forward in my chair eagerly. "I'd like to know more about it," I said.

Dr. Evert told me that the donors were carefully selected, that they even were chosen to have many of the physical characteristics of the husband so that the test-tube baby often resembled him. Nobody knew, except the persons involved, that the child's conception was anything but a natural one.

"The idea of the plan is that the wife of a sterile man can bear her own child," Dr. Evert added. "That seems to be very important to most women."

"I know," I said. "Because that's exactly how I feel. Oh, Dr. Evert, I'm so glad you suggested this to me. I don't believe Jim will have any objections once I explain it to him."

"Talk it over with him," Dr. Evert advised. "But don't pressure him into it. That wouldn't be fair to him or the baby."

I could hardly wait for Jim to get home from work that evening. For the first time in weeks there was hope in my heart. Jim just had to agree to let me go ahead with AID. He had to!

The minute he got in the house I told him about Dr. Evert's suggestion, and when I got all through he stared at me in disbelief.

"You aren't serious about this, are you, Alice?" he asked. "You'd actually be willing to have another man's child?"

"Jim, we wouldn't even know who the man is!" I cried. "He wouldn't know who we are either. And nobody else would have any idea that the baby wasn't yours!"

"I'd know it," Jim said. "Every time I looked at the kid I'd know he didn't belong to me. I think Dr. Evert had a nerve to put those ideas in your head. I don't want any part of it. You can tell him I said so."

I was so disappointed I burst into tears. "I thought you knew how much I wanted a baby," I sobbed. "I thought you loved me enough to want me to be happy. If it works for other people, why wouldn't it work for us?"

Jim was silent for a minute, and then he said, "Maybe because I'm a funny kind of guy. But the whole thing sickens me. It's unnatural and wrong. Babies weren't meant to come out of a test tube! They're supposed to be born because two people love each other!"

"But in our case there can't be any babies—no matter how much we love each other," I said.

Jim came over and put his arms around me. "Don't make me feel any worse than I already do," he pleaded.

I was stiff and unyielding in his arms. "If it really mattered to you, you wouldn't be so stubborn," I said. "You'd at least talk it over with Dr. Evert. You—"

Jim let me go. "That wouldn't change my mind," he said. "I'd still feel the same way. I don't want to talk about it any more, Alice. And I wish you'd stop thinking about it."

But I couldn't stop thinking about it. I lay awake for hours that night wondering how I could talk Jim into giving his consent.

DR. EVERT HAD WARNED ME not to pressure Jim into saying Yes, so I didn't bring up the subject for quite a while. But I was terribly depressed. I cried myself to sleep night after night. I knew I was making myself sick over the whole thing, but the more I thought about it, the more important it became to me. I wanted a baby so much it was like a crying need that had to be satisfied. My bitterness toward Jim got worse all the time, because I felt that he didn't even try to understand.

One night my sobbing woke him up and he put the light on. "Alice," he said, "you've got to cut this out! You're making yourself a nervous wreck. I can't stand hearing you cry like that!"

I caught hold of his arm. "Then let me have my baby," I pleaded. "It won't make any difference between us, Jim—except to bring us closer."

Jim sat on the edge of the bed and his shoulders slumped dejectedly as he said, "You're forcing me to agree to something I'll never believe is right, but if it's what you want so badly, Alice, we'll go to Dr. Evert tomorrow and I'll sign that paper. I'll try to go along with it for your sake—"

He turned and took me in his arms. "I love you," he told me. "You'll never know how much I love you. I want to feel close to you again. I want my wife back."

I was clinging to him then, half laughing and half crying. "Oh, darling!" I whispered. "You'll never be sorry, I promise. Oh, Jim, you've made me so happy."

Jim kissed me with passionate hunger, and I gave myself to him completely. I had never loved him more than I did at that moment. We were closer than we had ever been before.

We went to the doctor's the next night and told him what we had decided. There were a few bad moments when he asked Jim if he was sure this was what he wanted to do. I held my breath until Jim said, "That's what we're here for, Dr. Evert."

Then Dr. Evert took a legal-looking document out of his drawer and handed it to Jim to sign. Jim hardly glanced at it before he put his name at the bottom of the page. "There," he said. "That takes care of that."

When we got in the car, Jim sat staring straight ahead for a minute. Then he said, "I don't want to know when it happens. That's up to you and the doctor. Just leave me out of that part of it, Alice."

"All right, Jim," I said, but then I moved closer to him. "Try to feel that you have a share in this, won't you, dear? Try to think that this is *our* baby—not just mine. It will make it so much easier for everybody if you do."

"Sure," Jim said. "I said I'd try, didn't I?"

I didn't tell Jim when the date was made for me to go to Dr. Evert's office. There were three visits in all, and when the procedure was completed, I hardly dared breathe as I waited to see if I was pregnant. When I found I was, my heart nearly burst with joy. Soon afterward, I went to Dr. Evert for an examination and he told me there was no doubt about my pregnancy.

I remember sitting there in his office with my heart so full of thankfulness I couldn't even speak. Dr. Evert said I was in good condition and he was sure I'd have a fine, healthy baby.

I waited until we'd had our supper that night before I told Jim my news. He tried to be enthusiastic about it, but when I suggested we walk over to Mom's and tell my folks that we were going to have a baby, he said, "Won't it wait until tomorrow? You can tell her yourself in the morning."

So I was the one to tell Mom, alone, and it took some of the edge off my happiness. Mom hugged me and said

she was so glad for Jim and me. She insisted that we come to dinner that night and announce it to the rest of the family.

Jim went, but he didn't enjoy himself. It was the first time I'd ever seen him ill at ease and uncomfortable with my folks. He changed the subject whenever the baby was mentioned. But I kept telling myself that it would all be different later on. He would get over his doubts once he held the baby in his arms.

My pregnancy would have been completely normal and easy if Jim had shared it with me. And he tried—I know he tried. Once or twice he went to the doctor's with me, and when I first felt life early one morning and woke him up to tell him about it, he tried to act like it meant something wonderful to him too. But I knew it didn't. I remember how I told him that I wanted him to look forward to being a parent just as much as I did. I said the barriers were all in his mind, but they seemed to grow bigger as I grew bigger with the child.

The day we went to pick out the furniture for the nursery, Jim stood with his hands in his pockets, looking at a small white crib with blue roses all over it.

"We'd better stick to plain white, hadn't we?" I said, smiling. "We don't know if it will be a boy or a girl."

"That isn't the only thing I feel uncertain about," Jim muttered.

I pretended I hadn't heard him, but my heart sank at the expression in his eyes. I knew he was still thinking about the baby's real father, wondering who the man was who had fathered my child.

OUR WHOLE RELATIONSHIP seemed to change as the months went on. Jim had always been loving, but now he didn't want to touch me. Once I asked him, "Don't you love me any more? Is it because of the way I look?"

I remember how he turned away and shook his head. "I guess it's because I had nothing to do with it," he said.

One night I heard him get up and go downstairs, and I followed him. He was slumped in a chair, his head in his hands. I went and put my arms around him. "You'll be worn out in the morning," I told him. "Please come back to bed."

"I can't sleep," he said. "I lie there and toss around, and then I get thinking—"

"About the baby?" I asked him. "Oh, honey, please don't let it bother you like this!"

Jim's face was dark with misery. "I never should have let you do it," he said. "If I feel this way now, it will be worse afterward. I feel as if I'd let you commit adultery—it amounts to the same thing, doesn't it?"

I was close to tears, but I tried to talk reasonably to him. "Jim, this was a completely impersonal thing," I said. "Whoever the donor was doesn't matter—it's the baby who counts! It's the baby you ought to be thinking about and planning for."

Jim shrugged his shoulders hopelessly. "How can I plan for a child that isn't any part of me?" he demanded. "How can you expect me to love him?"

I stood there twisting my hands in despair. "You promised to try," I reminded him.

Jim stood up and started for the stairs. "I guess I didn't know what I was letting myself in for," he told me. "I guess I thought I'd be able to take it. But lately, every time I look at you I think of that other guy. It's a hell of a blow to a man's pride, Alice. But I don't suppose you even know what I'm talking about, do you?"

I knew what he meant, but I couldn't help thinking that he could control his feelings if he really wanted to. Instead, it seemed to me that he was deliberately closing his eyes to all that was precious and wonderful about expecting a baby. . . .

I didn't complain when he started working late at the plant. In a way, I was relieved. I'd go over to Mom's for supper those nights, and when I was with my family I could talk about the baby as much as I wanted to.

I was in my seventh month when I noticed that Jim was working much too hard. He was hardly ever home, and there was an air of tension about him that worried me.

One morning when he was about to leave for his job, I was struck by his pallor and the dark rings under his eyes. I begged him to come home early that night. He shook his head. "I have a job I want to finish," he said.

I followed him to the door. Suddenly I wanted to bridge the gap between us. I wanted to say something that would bring him back to me. I reached up and drew his face down to mine. "I love you," I told him. "I wish you'd believe that, Jim."

He kissed me, but his lips were cold on mine and he didn't take me in his arms like I wanted him to. "But it wasn't enough—just loving me—was it, Alice?" he asked. "You had to have something more. You had to have a baby, even if it couldn't be mine."

He didn't wait for me to answer him. He just went out and closed the door behind him. I remember how I cried after he left me that morning. By then I realized that the baby I was expecting would never bring happiness to our house. Jim's attitude wasn't going to change. It was the first time I admitted that I'd made a terrible mistake.

Jim was late getting home that night, and he worked every night for the rest of the week. I knew he was driving himself, but I couldn't stop him.

And then one day, toward the middle of the afternoon, the doorbell rang. I went to answer it. Ted Murphy, Jim's foreman, stood there, tense and white faced, and the hand he reached out to me was trembling. "I have bad news for you, Mrs. Hanson," he said. "Jim has been in an accident. He fell off one of those big cranes—"

I backed away from him. Lights seemed to be exploding in my brain. There was a sudden terrible weakness in my legs, and pain ripped through my heart as I whispered, "Is he dead?"

Ted came inside and put his arm around me. "You'd better let me call your doctor," he said. But suddenly I was fighting him off, pushing him away from me, knowing all at once what he was trying to tell me, knowing in that second that Jim had been killed. And then I began screaming in horror and realization, and I beat my fists against Ted's chest as he tried to quiet me. Then I couldn't scream or fight any more. I slumped in his arms, and that's all I knew for several hours.

Mom was in the hospital room when I opened my eyes. "Oh, Alice," she cried. "My poor little girl—"

I remembered everything then. Jim was dead. I'd never see him again. I'd never be able to tell him how sorry I was for the misery I'd caused him. He'd never know how much I really loved him. I couldn't prove it to him now—it was too late.

I felt the tears streaming down my cheeks as I lay there. Mom bent over and smoothed my hair. "We nearly lost you too—and the baby," she said. "He's premature, but he's going to be fine. Thank God you have him, darling. He'll be a great comfort to you."

I couldn't answer her. Any words I might have said were swallowed up in a well of pain and heartbreak. Because even then I was thinking: *If it wasn't for the baby, Jim would be alive now. It was because he hated it that he drove himself the way he did. He never had an accident before.* . . .

I turned my face to the wall. Mom couldn't help me. I was beyond her love and sympathy. Guilt and remorse lay so heavy on my soul that the burden was more than I could bear.

After Mom left me, I lay there sobbing hopelessly. It was my fault that Jim was dead, just as much as if I'd pushed him off that crane with my own hands. How could I forgive myself— how could I go on living—how could I even look at the child I had wanted so much? "I've got to stop feeling this way," I told myself over and over. "I mustn't—it's wrong—the baby can't help what happened."

But I was glad that he was in an incubator. At least he wouldn't be brought to me right away. I wouldn't

172

be expected to hold him in my arms. I don't think I could have stood that, because I didn't want him now. I knew he should never have been born. I'd been so selfish, so anxious to satisfy my desire for motherhood, that I hadn't let myself see what I was doing to my husband.

I was too ill to go to Jim's funeral. I begged to be allowed to see him, but Dr. Evert said the ordeal would be too much for me. "He didn't suffer," he told me. "Death was instantaneous."

I didn't find out until later that Jim's neck was broken in the fall. Somehow he had lost his balance and plunged to his death. Jim, who was always so sure footed, so proud of his perfect safety record!

I WAS IN THE HOSPITAL for several weeks. During that time I only saw my baby at a distance. He was a tiny, thin, fragile little boy. He had dark hair and eyes like Jim, and maybe someday he'd even look a little like him. But I stared at him as if he was a complete stranger to me, as if I had never carried him in my body at all. And that's how I felt inside. Because he wasn't a symbol of the love Jim and I had for each other. This baby was something out of a test tube. A medical miracle that had nothing to do with Jim and me.

When I was well enough, Mom took me home with her. The baby had to stay in the incubator until he had reached the proper weight, but I felt no grief at leaving him behind me. I knew Mom wondered about my lack of emotion the day I left the hospital. And I knew she thought it strange that I didn't name the baby after Jim. But I called him Peter. I couldn't add to the injustices I had done my husband by giving his name to a child who had no right to it.

I dreaded bringing Peter home when the time came. And even when I held him in my arms, I felt none of the warm glow a mother should feel when her own baby is close to her I felt only a sadness, because there was no love in my heart for him. I was sorry he was an unwanted child, but I didn't try to change the situation.

Long after I was physically able to take care of Peter, I let Mom take over for me. But sometimes just his presence in the house brought on hysterical crying spells, and I'd go to my room and close the door and refuse to see anybody for days at a time.

At first Mom thought I hadn't got over the shock of Jim's death. She was sure that eventually I'd turn to my baby and let him bring me help and consolation. But when that didn't happen, Mom begged me to tell her what was wrong. Finally, one day, I broke down and sobbed out the whole story.

After I finished, Mom said, her face

white with shock and disbelief, "But you can't blame Peter for any of this! I can understand how unhappy you feel because you did a great wrong to Jim, but don't put the burden on this little baby, Alice!"

"I can't help the way I feel toward him," I said. "It seems to get worse all the time."

Mom shook her head. "I don't understand you," she said. "You always loved children—anybody's children. How can you turn against your own flesh and blood?"

She wanted me to see Dr. Evert. She thought he might be able to help me with my problem. But I didn't want to talk to him. By then, I hated him for ever suggesting the AID plan. It had brought me nothing but grief and misery.

"Maybe if I went away for a while," I suggested to Mom one day. "Maybe if I got a job in New York and got away from the whole thing—maybe later on I'd feel different about it."

Mom looked like she couldn't believe her ears. "You mean—just walk out on your baby?" she demanded. "Alice, you couldn't do a thing like that!"

But once the idea had crept into my mind, the more I felt it was the only answer. Finally I persuaded Mom to keep Peter with her and give me the chance to pull myself together. I knew the rest of the family thought it was terrible of me to leave home like I did. But I felt as if some of the burden was taken from my shoulders the day I got on the train for New York. It was like I was leaving the evidence of my guilt behind me, and now I could forget what I had done and start all over again.

I took a furnished room and got a job as typist in an insurance company. I was very lonely at first, but I forced myself to get used to it. I liked my job, and my nerves quieted down after a while. I sent part of my salary to Mom every week to take care of Peter's needs. But I never said anything about going home to see him. Mom stopped suggesting it after a few months had gone by. I guess she felt that he was better off without a mother who didn't love him.

Two years passed, and then my life took a different, unexpected turn. Vince Gregor came to work for the insurance company. He was in the same department I was, so we were thrown together quite often. I enjoyed working for him from the beginning.

Vince was a warm, friendly man, but I was sure there had been some tragedy in his life. Every so often I'd see an expression of sadness cross his face, or a smile would start and then disappear as if some remembered grief made it impossible for him to be completely happy. I knew what it meant to feel like that. Maybe that's why there was a bond between us even before he asked me to go out with him

for the first time.

I accepted that first invitation of his eagerly. Both of us were lonely, and I felt that we could be good friends. But that night was the beginning of a relationship I never dreamed would be mine again. Because in Vince Gregor I found someone to fill the void that Jim's death had left in my life. Someone who needed love as much as I did.

Of course I didn't realize all that on our first date together. But even then we found we had a lot of things in common. Vince told me he'd lost his wife several years before, and then I understood the reason for his sadness.

"At first I didn't want to go without her," he said. "But I had Penny to think of." He smiled suddenly and drew out a picture and handed it to me. "She's my little girl," he said. "She's almost four now. My sister lives with me and takes care of her."

I looked at the picture, and for some reason it brought tears to my eyes. "She's a pretty little girl," I said. "She looks just like you."

I told Vince that I was a widow, and he asked if I had any children.

I hesitated for a minute, and then I said, "I have a little boy. My mother keeps him with her back home."

"It must be very hard for you not to see him often," Vince said.

I felt a flush come into my cheeks and I avoided his eyes. "It seemed better not to bring him to New York," I said. "This way, I'm sure he's happy and well taken care of."

Then I changed the subject. But Vince brought it up again when he took me home that night. "It seems odd, doesn't it, that both of us were married before—that both of us have children," he said. "It makes it easier for us to understand each other."

I wondered what he'd say if he knew that the similarity of our situation was only on the surface—that there was a world of difference in our lives beyond that. Vince loved his little daughter dearly. You could tell that her happiness was very important to him. On the other hand, I was trying to forget that I had a son. I sent money to buy him toys at Christmas and I paid for his board. But I was glad somebody else was taking care of him, because I didn't want him near me.

I knew I had to keep Vince from knowing all that. He would never be able to understand my attitude. And as we grew to know each other better, I was constantly on guard for fear he'd discover how I really felt about my little boy.

When I met Penny for the first time, she was full of questions about Peter. "Daddy says maybe he'll come to New York sometime and we can play together," she said. Then she added, "Haven't you got a picture of him so I can see what he looks like? Daddy carries mine with him all the time."

I promised I'd bring one along the

next time I saw her. I didn't tell her I didn't even have a picture of Peter.

Vince and I had been going out together for several months when I got a telephone call from Dad telling me to come home at once because Mom was seriously ill. I left New York right away, but I got there too late to see my mother alive. I was deeply shaken when I realized how long I'd been away, how terribly I had neglected her. To make matters worse, I found that my whole family had turned against me because they said I had broken Mom's heart by the way I treated Peter.

Louise was the one to tell me off first. She met me at the station and gave me the news of Mom's death, and when I burst into hysterical crying she said scornfully, "I don't see why you're so upset. You didn't care anything about Mom or you would have come home long ago. You don't care about anybody but yourself, Alice. You don't even care about your own child —you went off and left him for Mom to look after. That was one of the things that made her so sick—she never got over your walking out on him like you did."

"I'm sorry," I whispered. "I couldn't help it. Mom knew why I had to do it—Mom understood."

"Mom knew you went through a terrible time when Jim died," Louise cut in. "But that's over now. And you'd better make up your mind to take care of your child from now on. Mom's gone—and none of the rest of us are going to relieve you of your responsibility. It's time you acted like a real mother."

When I walked into the house, I felt everybody's eyes on me. Peter came running over to me, and he was so much bigger than I'd thought he'd be that I stood there and stared at him in amazement.

"Well, say something to the child, can't you?" Beth snapped at me. "He knows you're his mother. Aren't you even going to kiss him?"

I leaned down and kissed Peter on the cheek. He put his arms around me and looked at me uneasily. "Mommy?" he questioned. "You're Mommy?"

"Yes, I'm Mommy," I said, and then I pushed past everybody and ran up to my room. I knew they all hated me just then, but not as much as I hated myself. Seeing Peter again had brought all the old feeling of guilt back to me. How could I pick him up and hold him close to me? How could I pretend to love him when I could only wish I'd never brought him into the world?

I went through the funeral somehow, but I was in such an emotional upset that I couldn't think straight. I didn't want to take Peter back to New York with me, but I knew nobody in my family would keep him for me. I knew they thought that once Peter was with me for a while, I'd learn to love him. They didn't understand what was behind the way I felt. And I couldn't tell them. I was too ashamed of what I had done.

I tried to convince Louise and Beth that Peter would be better off with one of them. "I have a job," I said. "I can't be there with him all day."

But Beth said other women managed somehow. "You can find somebody to take care of him while you're at work," she said. "At least he'll have his mother part of the time." She softened enough to put her hand on my arm as she whispered, "Oh, Alice, he's such a sweet little boy. Give it a chance, please—he needs his mother. All kids do!"

I turned away from her. "I'll take him," I said. "What else can I do?"

The day Louise packed his things, she cried over him. "You be good to him, Alice!" she said. "God will punish you if you're not."

She made me suddenly angry, because she was acting like I was a monster—like I'd mistreat Peter and be cruel to him. "I'll see that he has what he needs," I told her. "You don't have to worry about him."

Louise stared at me through her tears. "Everything he needs!" she said. "Everything but love. Oh, Alice, I hope you wake up before it's too late!"

I took Peter back to New York with me. He was very quiet on the train. Mostly he sat with his face pressed against the window. But when he fell asleep, he put his head on my lap and I felt a surge of pity toward him. He was only a little boy—not quite three years old. He didn't have anybody who was close to him. He'd never know who his father was, and his mother felt like he didn't belong to her at all.

I took the next few days off from work to look for a foster home for Peter. I finally found a family named Taylor who were willing to take him. They had good references, and there were several other children in the household. I was sure they would be kind to him. When I left him there, I breathed a sigh of relief. But I wished he hadn't cried when I said good-by to him. It was almost as if he knew I didn't want him with me.

On my first day back at the office, Vince asked me to have dinner with him. Almost as soon as we were in the restaurant, he reached across the table and took my hand in his. "I'm so sorry about your mother, Alice," he said.

His sympathy brought tears to my eyes. Then he asked what I was going to do about Peter, and I told him about bringing him to New York and finding a place for him to stay.

"You must have hated to leave him with strangers, no matter how nice they seemed," Vince said. "Poor little fellow. He needs his own home."

He looked at me steadily, and his grip on my hand tightened. "I missed you very much while you were away," he said. "But it gave me time to think about a lot of things. I thought how wonderful it would be if you and I got married and made a real home for both of our kids. They'd have parents who loved them, and you and I would never be lonely again."

He stopped and smiled suddenly at me. "I haven't said the most important thing of all, have I?" he asked. "I haven't told you I love you. I haven't even asked if you love me."

I wanted to tell him I did. I wanted to say it so much that my heart almost burst with it. But I knew I couldn't marry him and let him think that I wanted Peter to share in our happiness. I had to tell him the truth. As ugly and unpleasant as it would sound,

Vince had to know that I didn't want Peter to live with us.

"Vince," I said, "there's something you have to know—" I looked around me, suddenly conscious that we were in a crowded restaurant. I couldn't tell him my story there. "I'm not very hungry," I told him. "Can't we go someplace where we can talk?"

We left the restaurant and got in Vince's car. We drove to a place where we could park. Vince put his arm around me and drew me close to him. "There," he said. "Does that make it easier to tell me what's on your mind?"

I was trying very hard not to cry. I wanted to get it all said as quickly as possible. "You thought it was hard for me to be separated from Peter all this time—you thought I wanted him with me. But I didn't. I've never wanted him—not since the day he was born!"

Vince stared at me. "I don't understand," he said. "You're his mother. How can you say you never wanted him?"

"It was all a terrible mistake," I said. "He wasn't Jim's child. He—"

"You mean—there was somebody else in your life, Alice?" Vince asked in stunned disbelief. "Is that what you're trying to tell me?"

"No," I said. "Jim and I couldn't have children. He was sterile. I talked him into agreeing to artificial insemination. I thought—I was so sure that once the baby was born Jim would accept him and love him. Instead of that—"

The tears came in spite of my efforts at self-control. I was blinded by them as I told Vince the rest of the story. I didn't leave out any of it—how shocked I'd been at Jim's death, how bitter I'd felt toward Peter right from the beginning.

"I never got over it," I said. "I was glad when my mother agreed to take care of him. I didn't want to bring him back to New York with me. My family forced me to. And even if you and I got married, I'd never feel like a real mother to him."

I was trembling like I had a chill, and I couldn't bear to look at Vince. I was afraid of what I'd see in his eyes. But the silence was even more terrifying. I felt it surrounding me, smothering me in its emptiness. I realized that Vince no longer had his arm around me. He had moved over to the other side of the car.

Finally I couldn't stand the stillness any longer and I cried, "Please don't hate me, Vince. Please try to understand! I had to be honest with you. It was the only fair thing to do."

"Understand?" Vince said. "Understand that all this time you've been making a little boy pay for something you did? You and nobody else, Alice! And instead of realizing that you were responsible for his birth, instead of giving him twice as much love and attention because of it, you turned away from him—you left him—you even hated him!"

He reached over suddenly and turned me so I had to look at him. Then he shook his head. "I don't seem to know you at all," he said. "How could you be so cruel and selfish? How could you use a child to get rid of your own guilt? My God, Alice, what sort of a woman are you?"

He let me go and I sat huddled against the seat. I knew Vince didn't want me any more. My heart was breaking as he started the car to take me home.

Before he left me that night, he said, "No matter how much I loved you, there'd still be Penny to think of. How could I trust her to you—when you rejected your own little boy? What kind of mother could you be to my child when you don't want your own child anywhere near you?"

I couldn't answer him. But when I went to my room that night, I cried out in the darkness, asking God why I had to lose everything I wanted just because of one mistake in my life—just because of one wrong I had done!

I was too full of self-pity to take stock of myself right then. It wasn't until several days later that I began to see the light. And even then, it didn't come all at once. It took many nights of sitting in my room alone, searching my heart and soul for hours at a time—thinking back to the beginning of my unhappiness—before I realized that instead of asking forgiveness for the first mistake I'd made, I'd gone on making new ones. I knew it had been wrong to have Peter. I'd gone against God's pattern and insisted on having a baby by a method that was against every natural law of the universe.

But the sins I had committed afterward were even worse. I had deliberately stifled my maternal instincts and refused to give my child the love and tenderness he deserved. I had broken my own mother's heart, shocked my family, and finally I had turned Vince away from me because I had shown him the full extent of my hatefulness.

But the worst harm of all had been done to my little boy. How could I forget my own happy home and childhood, the love and warmth that had surrounded me ever since I could remember? I'd always been so sorry for children who didn't have the things I'd grown up with—but I kept them all from Peter. I wouldn't let myself love him. I just wanted to get rid of him because he made me feel guilty.

It was as if some artist had drawn a life-size picture of me and hung it on the wall for me to look at. And the things I saw sickened me. "I'll make it up to Peter," I whispered over and over. "Just give me a chance, God!"

Friday night when I came from work, I went to the foster home where I'd taken my little boy. I told Mrs. Taylor I wanted him to stay with me for the weekend. He gave me such a sweet smile and tucked his hand in mine so trustingly, you'd think he had been seeing me every day.

I took him to my furnished room, and it was there that I really began to get acquainted with my son. It didn't take very long for that to happen. Because once my heart was open to him, Peter crawled right in and then there wasn't any room for bitterness and guilt and all the other mixed-up emotions I'd been storing up.

After that, I took him home with me every weekend, and just to see him watching for me Friday nights was a wonderful experience. Peter was too little to question the why's and wherefore's of his love for me. He just knew he belonged to me. I was his mother. He wanted me and needed me, and, thank God, he had me at last!

I guess it was knowing that I had changed so completely that made me begin to hope Vince would come back to me. I had been seeing him at work every day, but we had barely spoken to each other since the night he had walked out of my life. But one day I found the courage to walk over to him and say, "I'm taking Peter to the zoo on Sunday. I thought maybe you and Penny would like to come with us."

Vince looked up in surprise and I added, "I've been trying to make up for lost time. I'm so glad I didn't wait until it was too late." Then I said, "Maybe it isn't too late for us, Vince. Maybe we could try again—"

I saw sudden joy leap into his eyes. I saw something else there too—his love for me that hadn't died after all. A love that could be my crowning happiness now that I was ready to make a new start and forget the mistakes of the past.

T HAT WAS A LITTLE over a month ago. Vince and I are getting married in a few days. I know we will have the kind of home that our children will cherish all their lives. I want to be as good a mother as Mom was, and maybe she'll know how sorry I am that I didn't try sooner.

Vince and I are planning to take the children to visit my family when we come back from our honeymoon. I want them all to see how happy Peter is now. I want them to know how much I love him.

I'm never going to tell him the secret of his birth. That's something I will keep locked up in my heart. But I'll never forget that none of us has the right to play God. His will must be done, and we should bear whatever cross He gives us with courage and with faith. *The End*

You can
live down
a bad reputation

A MAD, IMPULSIVE MOMENT—and then, an awful mess! That is Carol's story. Because she was crazy about Don, she said she'd go with him to his family's lake cottage. Don's car broke down, Carol's worried parents went to the police when she didn't return home—and the whole thing came out! Now Don is back at his out-of-town Army base—and Carol is facing a scandal.

Dodie's story is a different one. Bad company was her downfall—a girl friend who didn't care what she did or who knew about it. Dodie was devoted to Francie—until suddenly Dodie realized that the nicer boys had stopped dating her and that the boys who did date her expected her to behave like Francie. "Birds of a feather—" people say about Dodie, and her old friends leave her out of things.

Jean—well, Jean comes from a broken home. Nobody ever cared much about what she did. In a desperate search for love, Jean made the mistake of going too far in the quest for popularity with boys. "Easy," they called her. They're still calling her that, though Jean now wants desperately to be "nice" and have the opportunities that come only to girls with good reputations.

The question that all of these girls ask is this: "How can a girl live down a bad reputation?"

P ERHAPS THE FIRST RULE is the hardest one. Don't apologize or explain or try to "cover up" with little excuses that nobody is going to believe. Words are only words, but actions speak for themselves. Your future actions can come to your defense much better than anything you can say.

Be very careful of your behavior. A girl with a good reputation may take a drink or tell a risqué story in a daring moment without provoking much comment. But a girl whose reputation has been hurt can't afford to do anything that might make people say, "Well, those stories about her must be true! Just look at her!"

Once you've been talked about, it's important not to give people the opportunity to revive the old gossip. In fact, for a while, it's a good idea to model your behavior on your prissy maiden aunt's. Once people have had the chance to see that you've changed—or that you aren't really as wild as gossip said you were, they begin to wonder if the talk couldn't have been exaggerated. And you've reached the first goal in your climb back to people's good opinion.

Avoid the company of people whose reputations aren't good. Barbara is a "good kid," you say, even if she is a little wild, and you enjoy her so much that you'd hate to give her up. Bill has the reputation for drinking and chasing, yes—but he's so much fun, and he'll respect your dating rules, if you insist. It's easy to find excuses for seeing the girls and boys whose reputations are shadowed. But if you're trying to regain your own good reputation, you're defeating your purpose in being seen with friends who have bad ones.

G ET YOURSELF into some worth-while activities. It isn't enough to stop doing what you shouldn't do—you have to replace a bad reputation with a good one, earned by doing what you should do. Try out for a school athletic group—or offer your services to some student project. Try a job as a baby sitter—or join some class in handicraft or swimming. And whatever you do, work at it—your object is to gain the reputation of a girl who can be counted on.

Get right with yourself. You can't expect other people to respect you if you don't respect yourself. And you can't respect yourself if you let your thoughts keep dwelling on mistakes you've made—and reproaching yourself for them.

Many people let their emotions run away with them at some time. Many people make mistakes in judgment. But it isn't what has happened that matters most —it's done with. The important thing is the future—and that can be a happier one, if you work at it. A bad reputation can be forgotten when you've earned a good one to take its place. ■ ■ ■

Like me, Johnny is sick with guilt over that weekend...

IT WAS STILL DARK when I woke up, but the dark was fuzzy, as though morning was about to come. My mouth tasted awful, and my head felt dull and heavy, like it did almost every morning.

Something was wrong. I could feel it, but my head was too muddled to think. I reached for Johnny, and for a minute I felt better, knowing he was there, and then suddenly I jerked my hand away and my breath stuck in my chest. My eyes had got used to the dark, and across the room where our dresser was, there was a window instead!

Where was I? Panic squeezed my stomach as I made out a door where there shouldn't be any door. And then I saw the bed was set wrong. It should be across from the window, not next to it.

My head throbbed worse and my body felt stiff, every muscle, every joint aching. *Remember!* something inside me said. *Remember!* But I couldn't remember anything.

I moved to turn toward Johnny, but all of a sudden I was scared to. What if— The night before was blurred in my mind. I remembered the first part of the evening —and then I calmed down a little and my breath came easier. Of course. Johnny and I were in that cabin up in the woods that we'd been planning to go to. We had got there early the night before with Nora and Frank Carter.

Was it right after supper I'd had the first drink? I couldn't remember. I could hear again the laughing and joking getting louder and louder. One of us had turned the radio up—I couldn't remember which one—and we'd danced. How long had we danced? What had happened afterward? I tried to think, but I could only remember music and a blurry face next to mine. The face of—

I turned my head slowly toward the man beside me, my fists clenched up tight. But it was Johnny, my husband, lying there. Of course it was Johnny! Why had I been so scared to look? Had I thought it would be somebody else lying with me? I shuddered, and my eyes stared into the dawn.

What had happened to Johnny and me? It didn't used to be this way. Up till a year ago, we didn't know anything about party weekends in cabins and drinking and things like that.

I remembered the evening back in Littleton—I guess the evening when it all started. Johnny had looked up from his supper plate and said, "There are jobs up in Haverly. The shoe factory up there's hiring. Jed Miller heard about it down at the station this morning."

I remember how I looked out at the street. Littleton was the only place I'd known in all my sixteen years. I grew up only two streets from where Johnny and I lived.

Johnny and I had been sweethearts for years. Johnny started working at the sawmill when he finished school, and as soon as his first pay check came in, I quit school and we got married. Only a couple of months later, the sawmill closed.

"I hate leaving Littleton," I said.

Johnny's hand closed over mine across the table. "Me, too, honey. But we got to eat, and we can't pay the rent on this house now."

We moved to Haverly soon after. Johnny got hired at the shoe factory for more money than he ever made at the sawmill. We rented a little apartment by the factory so Johnny could walk to work. It was an ugly neighborhood, being by the factory and all, and I didn't go out much except to buy food and the things we needed. Folks in the city didn't want to be friendly like back in Littleton. I mean, you couldn't go in the store and talk for an hour like you did at Clem Green's, where you ran into almost everybody and heard all the new gossip.

We came to the city in September, and in January the factory started laying off. Johnny was laid off first because he was so new there. We were really scared those few weeks. Every day we looked through the papers, hoping there'd be some kind of work open, but it didn't seem anybody was hiring. We'd lie in bed nights holding each other tight, telling each other that the next day's paper would have a job for Johnny.

"I'll take care of you, honey. It'll be okay," Johnny would whisper in my ear, and his breath would feel all warm on my neck.

"I know," I'd answer, and in his arms I'd feel sure things would come out all right. But the next day there wouldn't be any job in the paper.

ABOUT TWO WEEKS after Johnny was laid off, we found an ad for a salesman to sell a baby table from door to

Setup

Frank's eyes seemed to be burning right through me. Suppose I lost the next hand—Could I be a good sport?

for sinning

door. Johnny didn't say anything. He just sat looking at it.

"It kind of scares me," he said finally. "I never did anything like that. I wouldn't want any door slammed in my face."

That would be awful! I knew I'd never dare go selling from door to door.

But Johnny was looking at that ad. "We got to get money soon," he said. "I think I'll just ask about it."

And so the next day he went to see Mr. Atkins. He came home with a smile clear across his face.

"Honey," he said, and he sounded so proud, "I'm going to try it out. Carl—that's Mr. Atkins—is going to go out with me the first couple times so I can see how they do it."

I snuggled up close to him. "I knew they'd hire you," I said. Johnny was so handsome, and his eyes crinkled so cute when he smiled. I knew anybody'd hire my Johnny. He smiled at me, and I felt good right down to my toes. And we stood there in our little apartment, almost no money in our pockets, hugging each other and feeling happy as anything.

Of course, it wasn't just as easy as all that. We had to buy a car, because Johnny had to take a baby table around with him to demonstrate. And Johnny couldn't get a loan because he was only nineteen. But his boss said he'd sign for him, and so we bought a 1950 used car.

Things moved along pretty good after that, and we thought maybe we'd really started living. Johnny liked his job and he sold real well. I knew he would. I knew with Johnny sitting in their living room and smiling and talking about the baby table, people would just like him so much they'd have to buy. And it really seemed like that. Why, that first year Johnny made five thousand dollars. It just didn't seem possible, us having as much money as that.

The next fall, we decided to buy a house. I knew just where I wanted to live. It was a development called Crestmont, and it had the cutest little houses you ever saw. The house we bought was white, and it had two bedrooms and a big window in front. I thought it was the prettiest house on earth. We moved in in November.

That winter I hardly went out at all. Johnny drove me to the stores because they were too far for walking, but outside of that I hardly left the house. Johnny worked all hours and lots of evenings, but we had a TV and I just stayed home looking at the programs.

Johnny wanted me to meet some of the neighbors, but I didn't mind being alone, because alone I wasn't scared I'd do something to make folks laugh at me. I mean, the women on our street all looked so different from me. They wore clothes that looked like the ads in magazines and their hair was fixed fancy and—well, they just looked like they knew what was what. I knew they wouldn't want to be bothered with me. I talked kind of different and I didn't know how to dress like they did.

I did go out one time with Johnny, the night his boss invited us over. That night I just wanted to die, I felt so awful. Johnny made me go, and all the way over I kept saying to myself that maybe it wouldn't be so bad. Maybe if I was quiet they wouldn't notice me much. But as soon as we got in the room, I knew I couldn't feel easy in a place like that. The furniture was pretty, but it looked like maybe you'd better put a paper under you when you sat down so's you didn't mess it up any.

And then, before I'd hardly got used to being there or anything, Carl asked me what I wanted to drink, and I didn't know what to say. Finally I said I guessed I'd like some lemonade. Carl laughed and said, "No, Corrie, I mean what would you like to *drink*? We've got gin and whisky and Coke—"

I felt like I was blushing all over. I knew I had said something wrong. "I'll have Coke then," I told him quickly.

And then Carl's wife cut in and said, "Maybe Corrie doesn't drink, Carl."

Carl raised an eyebrow and looked at me.

"Oh, no," I exclaimed, feeling grateful to her. "No, I don't." And I felt more scared than before. Of course I didn't drink. And I didn't like being in the house of folks who did. And then, just as I was sitting there trying not to look so uncomfortable, I heard Johnny say he'd have a beer.

Both Carl and his wife went out to the kitchen, and I whispered to Johnny, "What did you say about having a beer?" I couldn't think that he meant that. No one drank in Littleton—no decent folk. And Reverend Tucker—oh, you should have heard him go on about drinking. As long as I could remember, I'd listened to his sermons about how only the wicked tasted liquor and about how you went to hell for drinking. And now I'd heard Johnny asking for a beer!

"He's my boss, Corrie," Johnny was whispering back. "It's like it was busi-ness. I mean, what if he fired me because he thought I didn't approve of him? He'd probably think that, if I didn't take a beer."

"I don't care!" I whispered back. "It's wrong to drink, Johnny. You know that."

"Shhh!" Johnny hissed. And then Carl was back with my Coke and his wife brought a dish of potato chips.

I tried to talk that evening, but I couldn't seem to make my mouth open. The Atkinses were very polite, but I felt sinful, sitting in that room, watching Johnny drink that beer and the Atkinses talking about things I didn't know anything about. When they made jokes, I couldn't see what was funny, but I tried to laugh anyway, and you know how awful you feel when you're just *trying* to laugh. Mostly, I just sat back and watched the others. Johnny laughed a lot. He seemed to have a pretty good time, and I felt lonely watching him, he was so different from my Johnny.

When we left, Carl said to Johnny, "Is your wife always so quiet?"

Johnny clapped me on the back and said, "Oh, Corrie's a good wife, but she's kind of shy with people." And that wasn't true. Not back in Littleton. But back home I felt like I fit in. I wasn't scared I'd do something to look silly.

THAT NIGHT, Johnny's arms reached for me. "I'm sorry I upset you, honey," he whispered in the darkness. "But we got it so nice now—all that money I'm making and all. We can't take chances on things. I mean, we got to look like we fit in." Johnny sounded like he felt sort of bad.

"*You* sure acted like you fit in," I whispered back, remembering how he'd been so different from his real self.

"It's the way you have to do," he said. He pulled me close, and for a moment I felt happy and loved, like I always did when he held me tight. But then he kissed me, and his breath was horrible in my face—like the smell in front of the saloon at home on the end of Main Street.

I pushed him away. "You smell of the devil!" I cried out. "Like a saloon!" And I crept over to my side of the bed and lay there, feeling more scared than I'd been in my whole life. What would happen to Johnny? I dreamed all night about hell and all the terrible things Reverend Tucker used to tell about people who sinned.

After that, I didn't want to see anybody. Just Johnny, I was scared that if we got with other people again, Johnny might be the way he was at his boss's, and I loved Johnny the way he was.

But I guess Johnny liked being out with folks, because he started pushing me to meet the couple next door. Of all the people on our street, they were the ones I most didn't want to meet. Just their house scared me, painted all pink instead of white like most of the other houses on our street, and the man and woman who lived there looked as glamorous as movie actors. Oh, no! Of all the people on our street, they were the ones I wanted most to stay away from.

But one afternoon Johnny came home with a paper sack.

"I met Frank Carter, the guy next door, this morning," he said. "I gave him a lift to the bus stop, and he was real friendly. He said we should get together sometime, and that he and his wife had been noticing us. He said he thought you were cute." He looked at me kind of proud, like it was pretty wonderful that the folks in the pink house had noticed us. "I asked him

and his wife over for tonight," he added.

"Oh, no, Johnny!" I cried out.

"Yes, I did," Johnny answered.

"But what if I don't want them?"

"Now, Corrie, if we waited for you to want folks to come, we'd never meet anybody." His face had a pleading look on it. "You'll like the Carters. I know you will."

I guess I hadn't realized how much he'd wanted to make friends. I tried to swallow back the lump in my throat. But it stuck there, so I just nodded and didn't say anything.

Then Johnny started taking the things out of the sack. "I thought I'd get the eats for tonight," he said, not looking at me.

For a minute I felt a little easier. I wouldn't have known what to fix. Back in Littleton I'd have known, but not here.

Johnny was taking bottles out of the sack. "What have you got there, Johnny?" I asked.

"Stuff to drink." His voice was apologetic. "They'll expect a drink, Corrie. That's how folks do here. We got to offer them something—"

But I interrupted before he could finish. "Oh, Johnny!" I cried. "How could you bring that here? Into your own house?" I was crying and stamping my foot. How could he? He knew about liquor! He knew it was a thing of the devil! I could almost smell the evil in our kitchen. I could almost *feel* awful things in the air waiting to happen to us.

"Get it out of here!" I screamed. "Take it out! What would your mother say? What would she say?"

But Johnny just stood there watching me. I couldn't seem to make him understand, so I screamed louder and then I grabbed a bottle. If he wouldn't throw it out, I would!

His hand clamped on my wrist. "Corrie!" he said sharp—so sharp it was like he'd slapped my face. "Now listen to me!" He shoved me onto a chair, his hand so tight on my wrist I thought he'd snap it in two. "Liquor isn't as wicked as all that. Your family was fussy—"

"Fussy!"

"Shut up! I say your family was fussy. Other folks went to church as much as yours [Continued]

I didn't go out on the porch deliberately, but Frank thought I did. He began kissing me

did. They heard the Reverend, too, but they *did* have liquor in the house. Lots of folks did."

I was so shocked I could hardly think. "But—"

"Honey, folks talked good back home, but they did some of the things they were against. And drinking was one of them. Up here it's a thing we got to do if we're going to be like other people. I've been in their houses and I've seen how they do. Folks live fancier than back home. So—we can live like that too."

He turned back to his bottles and the other stuff he'd shopped.

"I bought ginger ale for you," he said.

I couldn't eat supper that night. I was too upset about what Johnny had said. How could people say drinking was a sin and then drink anyway? Even if they kept it secret from everybody, wouldn't God know? Wouldn't they still go to hell?

But after supper I started thinking about the Carters coming, and that just shoved everything else out of my mind. I stood in front of the closet looking at my clothes, but nothing looked good enough. Besides, no matter what I put on, I'd still look like me.

Johnny came in and said I should wear my black skirt and blue sweater. "You wear sweaters good," he said, trying to cheer me up some, but it didn't help. I started dressing and combing my hair, but my stomach ached so I could hardly move. It ached so much I couldn't even think straight. Maybe I was sick.

Johnny's hands pressed on my waist and he pulled me against him. "Scared?"

"I've never been so scared in all my life," I whispered.

"They won't eat you up," he said, but I thought he sounded scared himself. *They won't eat me*, I thought, *but they can laugh at me—they can stick up their noses at me!*

I buried my face in Johnny's chest. "Johnny, I can't! Tell them not to come!"

Johnny cuddled me and said to pull myself together, but I trembled and shivered in his arms like I was freezing.

"A drink of ginger ale would make you feel better," he said suddenly. "You've got to go through with this. We've got to start living like other people." He left me standing there and I heard the icebox open and shut.

"Here," he said, coming back and handing me a glass of ginger ale. "You'll feel better now."

It did feel good on my dry throat, and I drank the glassful in one gulp. I panted a little from drinking so fast.

"Now you just sit down and try and feel easy," Johnny ordered.

I did like he said, and all of a sud-

den I felt warm inside. My muscles eased up so they didn't ache so bad, and my throat didn't feel like it was getting set to scream. I felt almost good.

Johnny came back. "Feel better now?"

I nodded, and even smiled back at him. "That helped a lot," I said.

Then the doorbell rang. Johnny went and let the Carters in, and when we all said "hello," I was surprised I didn't feel scared at all. We talked a little, and then Johnny offered them a drink and he brought me another ginger ale. I drank it fast, hoping it would feel nice like the last one. I remembered Mama used to give me ginger ale when I was sick, and I decided that was why it made me feel so good. Because ginger ale was a sort of medicine.

I felt myself smiling often then, and when Nora and Frank said funny things, I laughed like anything—even when I didn't really know what they meant. Everything was so funny and happy that evening.

By nine o'clock I just knew I'd never had so much fun in my whole life, and when Johnny got up to fill the glasses, I giggled and held mine out and said, "Give me some of the bad stuff." I was feeling so good that I hardly felt wicked at all—more excited than anything, I guess.

Johnny looked a little surprised, but he'd been feeling happy himself, and he laughed and said, "That's the big girl." Then he told Frank and Nora about the scene I'd made that afternoon, and instead of being embarrassed like I would have been any other time, I thought it was the funniest thing I'd ever heard.

When Johnny brought me back a glass with some ice cubes in it and a couple inches of liquor in the bottom, I said, "That's an awful little mite when you're thirsty."

Everybody laughed and laughed. I didn't really know why they'd laughed, but I was proud I'd said something funny. I took a gulp, and I thought my throat would scorch straight through. Tears jumped in my eyes and I coughed and tried to get my breath to scold Johnny for giving me something so awful, and then suddenly my throat was soft and warm and a wonderful limp feeling went right down my arms and legs. I slid down a little on the couch so I was resting on the end of my spine, and I twirled the glass around and giggled. Everyone was watching me, and they laughed then fit to kill. Laughing because I was funny! I was so proud. I was a real success.

I DON'T REMEMBER MUCH that happened after that. Johnny said the Carters left around twelve and that he helped me up to bed, but I couldn't remember it.

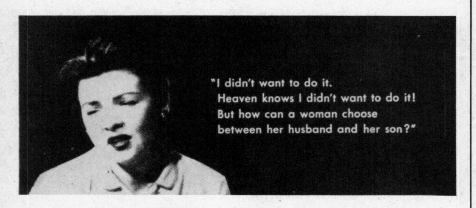

I sure remember the next day, though. My head throbbed, and every time I moved I thought it would bust in pieces. My mouth tasted awful and my stomach felt sick. I dragged around the house, more scared than I'd ever been in my life.

What had happened during those hours I couldn't remember. I remember thinking how good looking Frank was and kind of leaning toward him. Had I—had I flirted with him? I turned cold at that, but then I remembered Johnny saying I hadn't done anything bad. And he'd have been mad as anything if I'd made up to somebody else.

I suddenly sank onto a chair. Made up to somebody else! How had such a thought even come into my mind? I wasn't that kind of girl. I started to cry, and even though it made my head pound so I could hardly stand it, I kept on crying. I never felt so unhappy, and I made up my mind right then that I'd never, never touch a drink again. *Never!*

But I did. The next week the Carters asked us over. You'd think after one evening with them I wouldn't have

been scared any more, but I was. Because it was like somebody else was in my body that last time—the girl who giggled and said funny things and drank whisky. That hadn't been me.

When Johnny got in around seven o'clock from making his deliveries, I told him I was sick, but he knew different.

"I'll fix you a drink and you'll feel better," he said.

"No!" I could never, never do that again. "Just give me some ginger ale." I remembered how good that had made me feel.

Johnny looked at me for a minute. Then he said, "I didn't play fair with you, honey. I put something in that ginger ale you had last week."

I think, underneath, I must have known about that, because I wasn't mad at him for fooling me—only for telling me. Why couldn't he just have gone out and fixed it again? I'd have pretended that I didn't know anything was in it and I wouldn't have felt bad. My stomach was squeezing up till I almost cried out.

"Please, Johnny, don't make me go," I begged.

But Johnny shook his head. "I'm earning good money now. We got a nice house. We're going to have some friends to go with it all."

I fought with myself a little longer. Really fought. I remembered Reverend Tucker's words about drinking and about hell—and what he'd said hell was like. But just before time to go, I said, "Fix me one, Johnny—please." I knew I couldn't go over there without something to help me—not to the Carters' pink house.

Again the drink made me feel good. Not high; not like I was drunk. Just easier and relaxed.

We had a nice evening with Nora and Frank, but I broke my vow over and over again. I had to. And, really, it was so much fun. We laughed and laughed, and everybody got so friendly, and once Frank told Johnny right in front of me that he thought I was cute. I felt so proud, because I knew a man like Frank really knew what was what. Both he and Nora did. You could tell.

And one time in the evening when I was feeling extra good, I leaned over and kissed Johnny—not the way you kiss your husband when folks are around, but a passionate kiss. Everybody thought that was funny too. But when I remembered it the next morning, I felt so cheap. It *was* just Johnny, I kept telling myself. It wasn't wicked to kiss your own husband, was it? But that didn't make me feel any better. I knew it hadn't been right.

From then on, things just moved along, and after a couple months I stopped even promising myself things. I knew if we went out in the evening, I'd drink.

We didn't make friends with any of our other neighbors. I guess we were with Frank and Nora so much we really didn't have time for anybody else.

Johnny met a few of the neighbor men. Once I asked him why the Carters didn't have other friends in the neighborhood when they were so smart and so much fun. Johnny said he didn't know, and then he looked puzzled and said that folks didn't seem to like the Carters—they talked like they thought Frank and Nora were kind of wild.

"Of course, they don't say much of anything," Johnny had added. "It's just a feeling you get. I noticed they act a little different around me now that we're such good friends with the Carters."

"They're jealous," I said, sticking up for our friends. How could people not approve of Nora and Frank? Why, Johnny and I thought everything they did was just right. I'd started buying clothes that looked like Nora's, and I even tried to make our house look as much like theirs as I could.

"Nope, those neighbors must be a bunch of cornballs," I said. I'd got those words from Nora. She and Frank really laughed at stuffy people, and so did Johnny and I.

183

Johnny chuckled. "Honey, you sure have changed."

But I wasn't the only one who had changed. Johnny had changed a lot too. Sometimes I felt lonely for the old Johnny, but mostly I was proud of him. I liked him to act like Frank did. Frank was about the sharpest man I'd ever seen.

THE CARTERS taught us to play cards. One night Nora suggested we play poker.

"Good idea," Johnny said. He was always ready for anything.

I didn't know how to play, but they said they'd write out the hands for me.

Then Frank said, "How about playing strip poker?"

My head was fuzzy from two highballs, but I looked up in surprise.

"Oh, that's lots of fun!" Nora exclaimed, and she clapped her hands together.

"But—" I started to protest, and I felt my face flush. I looked at Johnny, and he looked like he didn't know what to say either.

"Oh, you two funny little babies!" Nora said, giggling. "Not *real* strip poker. Just with rings and watches and shoes and all. And we give everything back afterwards—so you won't lose your watch." She added that last with a big laugh because I was so proud of my new watch.

So we played, and it was loads of fun. I lost both shoes and all my jewelry, and Johnny lost his tie and a shoe. Nora lost the most. She finally slipped off her skirt, and we laughed like anything at her.

Johnny and I drank a lot that night, and the next morning we both got up groggy and sick looking. Neither of us wanted any breakfast, and we sat across from each other drinking coffee. For some crazy reason I felt like crying.

I put down my cup. "Johnny, what do you really think about Nora and Frank?" I was suddenly lonesome for Littleton and the life we were used to and the old Johnny who didn't joke around so much.

"They sure are a lot of fun—and they know the score," he said, staring into his cup. "Don't you think so?" He didn't look up.

"Oh, yes," I said, but I wasn't sure I meant it. For a minute I just felt empty. But it was like that so often in the morning. I drank another cup of coffee.

"I guess I've just got morning-after blues," I said, but the words sounded bad to me. Me—Corrie Howard—having morning-after blues. "Yeah, the Carters sure are fun, aren't they?" I said.

It went on and on like that. Some mornings I'd wake up scared, not remembering much of the night before, feeling that maybe something awful had happened during the time I couldn't remember. Sometimes I was scared to ask Johnny what I'd done, but I knew if it had been bad he'd sure tell me. And the Carters were so much fun.

Then we'd decided to rent a cabin in the woods for a weekend. Just the four of us.

And as I lay there in our room at the cabin that first morning, watching it get lighter at the window and listening to Johnny's heavy breathing, bits of the night before came back to me.

We had got there around nine o'clock, and I remembered we played cards for a while. I remembered, too, the thrill of being alone with Johnny finally in the strange bedroom; but instead of feeling happy at remembering those moments in his arms, I felt scared—like maybe it was bad or something. And the rest of the night was blank. . . .

Then I suddenly remembered standing outside the cabin, feeling the cold air on my bare arms. Why did I think of that? Had I gone out? When? And then the memory started filling itself in. I saw again a shadowy face close to mine, eyes half shut. I felt strong arms around me—and I remembered the face! It was Frank! We had stepped outside because I wanted to look at the Big Dipper, and Frank said he'd show me where it was. Nora was inside showing Johnny how to do the rhumba. We'd stood outside in the dark for a minute, and then we were in each other's arms. He kissed me, and I remembered how I had returned his kiss.

I tried to push the memory back, to put Johnny's face there instead of Frank's, but I couldn't. I had kissed a man who wasn't my husband, and in the cold light of early morning, the thought made me sick inside. We couldn't go on like this, Johnny and me! We had to stop. But even then, guilty as I felt, I knew we couldn't.

I started drinking early that afternoon. I didn't want to be myself and think about the awful things I had done. I laughed hard and talked loud. Anybody looking at me would have thought I was happy as anything, and in a fuzzy way, I thought I was too.

That evening we decided to have a party. We'd brought dress-up clothes along in case we went out dancing, but it seemed like it would be more fun to stay right at the cabin.

I put on my new dress. Nora had helped me pick it out. It was red, with a full skirt and a low neck.

"Boy, you sure have a good figure," she'd said when I put that dress on, and it did make me look good—nothing at all like the Corrie who had lived in Littleton. I felt proud as I saw myself in the mirror, and the men whistled when I walked back out in my dress. I felt a kind of thrill when Frank whistled. I mean, he knew all about women and clothes.

TC MEDICAL REPORT

by Morgan Deming

SMOKING AND COLDS. Will you have fewer colds or get rid of a chronic cough if you give up smoking? This widely held belief was tested by Dr. W. C. Boake of Western Reserve University in a study of respiratory illnesses that occurred over a five-year period among 118 healthy men and women, smokers and nonsmokers. "Nonsmokers had more illnesses, but, on the average, fewer coughs than heavy smokers. Sore throat was significantly less among heavy cigarette smokers than among nonsmokers. Results indicated that there is little, if any, true difference between the incidence of common repiratory infections in smokers than in nonsmokers."

PREGNANCY TEST PILL. A new pregnancy test that uses no animals and is less expensive than common rabbit, frog, and mouse tests has been made available to doctors. The test consists of Pro-Duosterone tablets that contain progesterone, the ovarian hormone that prepares the womb to nurture a fertilized egg, and a small amount of other female hormones. A three-day program of four tablets a day, one at each meal and one at bedtime, answers the "pregnant or not pregnant" question. Nonpregnant women will begin to menstruate two to seven days after taking the last tablet, while pregnant women will have no menstrual activity.

MIXED-SEX HAZARD. The true sex of a newborn child examined at Children's Hospital in Cincinnati could not be determined since its malformed external sex organs combined some aspects of both sexes—a condition known as pseudohermaphroditism. Surgery revealed that internal organs were female and entirely normal. The mother's medical history indicated that her baby's sexual malformation was probably caused by doses of testosterone (male hormone) given during pregnancy for another condition. The Cincinnati doctors suggest that male-hormone treatments of a pregnant woman may cause abnormal development of a female baby. ■ ■ ■

We danced all evening. Nora taught us new steps, and we tried to learn them and laughed when we stumbled. The evening got hazier and hazier. I remember dancing with Frank and thinking how good looking he was. I pulled him closer against me, and he laughed in a funny way and said, "Hey, little girl, don't let Johnny see you dancing like that." But he held me even tighter after that.

Later, we all sat on the sofa. We passed a bottle around, and there was lots of kissing and giggling. My dress slipped off one shoulder, and I laughed and slid the other shoulder strap off too. Somebody kissed my bare back, but I can't remember who. Johnny?

Then all of us started talking at once, and the next thing, everything was quiet. We were alone in the bedroom and I was struggling to slip out of my dress. Then I was lying on the cool sheets, lost in a kiss, in a thrillingly demanding love. . . .

I woke up early the next morning and lay there, my eyes wide open, staring into the early gray of dawn. Something awful was wrong—I knew it. But my head pounded so I couldn't even think. I lay there, trying to remember, and at the same time trying not to remember. Dimly I heard heavy breathing beside me, and for some reason my whole body went rigid.

Remember! I told myself. But my head ached so hard that the pain seemed to be filling my mind so I wouldn't have to remember. I saw myself again in my red dress. I heard our laughter and the music. And then suddenly I went cold all over—ice cold. My breath stopped and then came back in quick gasps—and I knew I *couldn't* turn my head to look at the man beside me. I knew it was Frank Carter!

I GUESS THAT WAS the most awful minute of the most awful day of my life. I crawled out of the bed feeling sick and dirty. I got dressed and sat huddled on the sofa in the living room, watching the dawn turn into a gray, cloudy morning. It was cold in the cabin because the stove had gone out, but I hardly noticed. I was cold straight through anyway. Cold to the middle of my bones—and I knew nothing could make me warm.

I looked up as Johnny came slowly into the living room. I couldn't look straight at him after the first quick glance, and I don't think he looked at me. We just sat there across the room from each other, not saying anything.

When Frank and Nora got up, they acted just like always, just like nothing had happened at all. I couldn't look at either of them, but they didn't notice—or they pretended not to. I helped Nora fix breakfast, all the time feeling like I should go wash—wash over and over again.

I couldn't eat anything. I just stared at my plate and wanted to throw up. After breakfast, I told them I was sick, that I had to go home.

Frank and Nora protested. "You just had a little too much last night. You'll be okay," Nora said.

"Yeah," Frank added. "We're just starting to have some fun." He put his arm around me and pulled me close to him. How could he touch me!

"Take your hands off me!" I screamed suddenly.

"Let her alone!" Johnny snapped at the same time. "I'm sick too. We're going home."

"Well, what's wrong with the babies?" Nora said in a real snippy voice.

But we all packed up and got in the car. No one spoke the whole way home. . . .

How did we manage to live after that terrible weekend? Well, we kept out of Nora and Frank's way, and we sold our house as soon as we could. Neither of us could stand to keep on living in Crestmont, and we didn't want to see the Carters ever again.

It was a long time before Johnny and I felt easy around each other. It wasn't that we blamed each other. How could we, when we'd both done the same awful thing? But we were both so sick inside, we both felt so dirty, like we'd never be able to be around clean people again.

For months we hardly spoke to each other, and at night we'd lie quiet over on our own sides of the bed. Johnny didn't kiss me—he didn't even touch me—and I didn't want him to. I couldn't have stood it.

Through the long, horrible months, I wondered over and over if we would ever feel clean again. If we could ever live a normal life again? But gradually the horror eased. My stomach didn't gnaw constantly and my skin didn't crawl for thinking of what I'd done. There were even times when I could almost forget about it.

It must have been the same with Johnny, because the day finally came when we could talk about it to each other. Not all about it—neither of us has ever mentioned that weekend—but about the drinking and the trying to be different from what we were.

Johnny's still working for Carl; he's still earning good money. But Johnny and I will never be the same as we were. I think we both feel scarred inside. But at least we learned from our awful mistakes. We grew up lots since the time in Crestmont, because we're not ashamed to live simple now and to be ourselves.

The End

We want your story

THE NEWSPAPERS MADE A BIG THING out of it, even though they had it all wrong. They said Harry wanted that tractor so bad he offered to trade his baby son for it—and Warren Johnson took him up on the deal. Well, we did give the Johnsons our baby, and they did give us the tractor, but none of that was Harry's fault.

I'll tell Harry's side of it first, the side the papers wrote about, anyway.

Harry's a dirt farmer. There are rich farms in our state, with beautiful houses and modern equipment. Farms like Warren Johnson's. And then there are run-down places like the one where we lived, where about all we could raise was the rent—if we were that lucky.

"But we could get more out of the land if we could work it right," Harry kept insisting. "I could do as good a job pulling an old hen by the tail and letting her scratch up the ground as I'm doing with that busted plow and Jen and Ned."

Jen was a flea-bitten mule Harry'd bought for twenty dollars because she had a terrible temper, and Ned was a wheezy old horse.

So you can see how Harry needed the tractor. But he never even considered getting it the way they said he did. That part of it just happened, and by then our minds were so fogged up by grief we didn't even know what we were doing. . . .

But I want to go back a long time before that. I'd been better off than Harry in one way, for I'd had folks once. But they were fruit pickers, traveling from state to state with the crops. I hated that life, so when a woman offered me a job doing light housekeeping and baby-sitting for my board and the chance to go to school, I begged my folks to let me do it, even though I was only fourteen.

"I can't hardly let you stay behind, Luly, I'll miss you that bad," Ma said the day they left. "But I know it will be better for you."

Then she kissed me, and Pa kissed me too, but as he drove off he was crying when he said, "We'll be back this way next year, so be looking for us!"

Nothing turned out the way I figured, though. Mrs. Webber, the woman I was staying with, made me work so hard I was ready to drop. Besides, my schooling had been so sketchy the principal said I'd have to report to the classes that taught the things I'd missed. Me, fourteen years old, sitting in the fourth grade with a batch of little kids who snickered every time I opened my mouth! You can bet I stayed out every day I dared—and Mrs. Webber encouraged me.

"It's just foolishness anyway, Luly," she said, "you going to school. You may not know your arithmetic, but you're real good at cleaning and taking care of kids."

After I met Harry, he said she'd talked that way so I'd have more time to work for her. It was the truth, and I guess I knew it. But because I hated going to school with such little kids, I pretended Mrs. Webber was really advising me for my own good.

Anyway, I didn't go to school any more than I could help, and when I was sixteen, I quit altogether. I'd have got another job too, one that paid me a wage, except I was still looking for my folks to come back. But they never did.

"The car wasn't much good," I reasoned. "Maybe it broke down and they couldn't get another, or maybe they got sick and died." It was an awful thing to think about, but I knew it could have happened.

"Two people don't usually die at the same time," Harry pointed out. "Even if one of them died, couldn't the other one write you?"

"Ma and Pa can't write," I had to admit in a shamed voice. "That's why they were so bound I was to get educated. I'd sure hate to tell them I quit school, but they just didn't know how much there was I hadn't learned."

"I wish I'd been there to teach you." Harry had his arm around me then, and I leaned against his shoulder. It sure felt strong and solid. "I'd have helped you, and you'd have caught up in no time. You're smart, Luly, I know that. You just never had a chance."

It was wonderful, hearing him say I was smart. There'd been times I'd had my doubts, even though I

nd DESPERATE

We traded
our baby
for a
tractor

knew I always could understand things if people only took time enough to explain them to me.

"Not smart like you are, though, Harry," I said.

Harry pulled me closer. "Much good it ever did me," he said.

I KNEW HOW it had been with him. He'd been a foundling, living in an orphanage until Mr. Harvey took him out when he was eleven to work on his farm. But Harry had learned all the things I was so hazy about, so he started teaching them to me. And every time I learned my lesson well, I got a kiss.

Mrs. Webber let me see Harry in the kitchen after my work was done at night. In return, I had to get up an hour earlier each morning. But I was glad to do it. Because I was crazy about Harry. I had been since the first time I met him at the church bazaar.

Harry wasn't handsome. He was taller than me, but thin, and his cheekbones were kind of sharp, making him look like he'd been hungry for years—and I guess he had. But his lips were soft and warm and sweet—and sometimes, if I jollied him long enough, I could get him to laugh.

I liked the sound of his laughter, liked being able to make him feel happy, even for a little while.

Harry was five years older than me, twenty-two. He'd gone in the Army when he was eighteen, and he'd saved his money. When he got out, he started working as a farm hand, because farming was the only thing he really cared about. Then he got a chance to rent a run-down hill place, and with the money he had and the money he could borrow from the bank, he could just about swing it.

"It's nothing to offer you, Luly, but years of hard work—and all my love. But I'd like to marry you."

"I'd like to marry you too, Harry," I whispered and went into his arms. "And I'll bet the work won't be any harder than it is right here!"

Harry held me away so he could look into my eyes. "Yes, it will be, Luly," he said. "It'll be harder than anything you've ever done before."

And it was. From three-thirty in the morning till as late as we could see at night, we worked over those hilly,

Harry and I were scared when the district attorney called us into his

worn-out acres. Then we crawled into bed, almost too tired to think, but not too tired for the warming love that was our marriage.

Harry subscribed to a farm magazine, and while he was eating he used to keep it open on the table beside him, running a finger down the page to look at the ads.

"Luly, look!" he'd say, pointing to a tractor. "If we had that and a set of gang plows, think of the furrows we could turn! We'd turn the ground over deep, like we can't do with our old equipment. If we could do that, I bet we'd have as good crops as Warren Johnson raises."

The Johnson farm was the show

place of our county. Everything on it grew fine and high and handsome, and I knew Harry was right when he said our place could produce just about as good crops if we had better equipment.

Most of all, we needed the tractor. We needed it to work our ground, but more than that, it was kind of a spiritual need with Harry. It was just about the finest thing he could think to want, and with it he figured he could get most anything else we'd ever want. He went to the store in town and looked their tractors over, and he talked and talked of owning one.

But Harry couldn't really hope to own a tractor. We never made money enough to pay for one, and the bank

office. We knew it wouldn't do any good to lie. We'd be found out . . .

wouldn't loan him any more, especially after we had to borrow more money to pay for our first baby.

We had Jackie the first year we were married, and I guess I shouldn't have worked so hard in the fields while I was carrying him. But I didn't know any better, and I thought I was getting along all right until I had that sudden, awful cramp in my stomach while I was pitching hay. Harry dropped everything and rushed me to the doctor.

We were married seven months then—and Jackie was a *real* seven-month baby. Anybody looking at him could tell. He was scrawny and puny, poor little thing, and so tiny the doctors

wouldn't let us take him home for several weeks. He had to stay in an incubator until he gained some weight. That's what cost the most, I guess. But it cost for me too, because I had to have transfusions and expensive medicines, and the whole bill was just huge.

BUT JACKIE WAS WORTH IT. He was fragile, but darling—and all ours. He was a part of each of us, brought to life by the love that was the only rich and lovely thing we had.

"My first-born son!" Harry said, running his rough hands gently down Jackie's thin little legs. "Won't be long till I have a helper around the place."

I loved seeing the way his face lit up when he looked at his son. He was that proud.

It was a good life, for all its hard work and not much money. But, like I said to Harry, "You can't have everything. I'll bet Mr. Johnson—with all his fine farm and machinery—would trade anything he's got for a son like ours."

Maybe I shouldn't have said that. Or maybe I'm just being superstitious when I remember those words. I don't know. But Harry agreed with me then.

"The way I heard it," he said, "not having kids is the one big disappointment of the Johnsons' lives."

Cuddling Jackie close against my heart, I said, "If they can't have their own, I wonder why they don't adopt one?"

Harry shrugged. "Folks say they've tried. I don't know—maybe they're too old."

I kissed Jackie, thinking how lucky Harry and I were. I honestly didn't know what I'd do if I didn't have a baby.

Yes, we were blessed, because not long after that we were expecting our second baby. This time, Harry had me see a doctor right away, and he explained what things I should do and what I shouldn't.

And, of course, while I was picking up all that information, I was learning lots of other things about the care of children. It was fascinating and frightening too, because I was finding out there was so much I didn't know. "It's almost the same as it is with farming," I told Harry. "You never learn enough, do you?"

A quick smile flashed across his face, but it sobered off again as he agreed. "You never learn enough—and the more you learn, the more tools you find out you need."

That was awfully true. I'd sterilized Jackie's bottles in a pail, but I knew now that a regular sterilizer would do it better—if we could afford one. When I first brought Jackie home from the hospital, the doctor loaned me a thermometer. Now I realized how important it was to have one handy all the time—and yet we didn't have the price of one.

It was a little thing, I tried to tell myself. A mother's loving intuition and her hand **[Continued]** across a fevered forehead had been good enough for plenty of families. Other things—wholesome food and vitamins—we'd try to manage, but we'd just have to do without the frills.

We made out too, and Richie, our new baby, was round and plump, and whatever we needed and didn't have for him seemed to make no difference.

With the two youngsters to care for, I wasn't much help to Harry. Most of the time he even had to do the hen chores. But Jackie took such an excited interest in the new baby that I was afraid to step outside without taking him with me.

"He wants to share everything he has—toys, food. I even caught him trying to push a piece of toast into the baby's mouth," I said to Harry. "He's too little to understand that the baby

will choke on those things."

"We don't want to scare him away from Richie," Harry said. "It's good to want to share. We just have to watch him till he learns what the baby can have."

I knew Harry was right, and I was proud of my generous little son—and scared to death of his generosity, especially when he found a pencil and put it in Richie's hand.

"Oh, honey, no!" I shrieked in alarm, and I snatched it away before the baby could harm himself with it. Richie had merry, wide eyes, dancing with excited interest in everything around him, and the thought of that pencil being jabbed into one of them sent such a shudder of fear racing through me that I grabbed Jackie and shook him hard.

"Don't give the baby sharp things

like that!" I shouted. "And don't you touch them either. You could get hurt too!"

It was the first time Jackie had seen me angry. Frightened, he turned from me and ran to the bedroom, where he crouched against the wall, sobbing.

I realized at once what I'd done, and I ran after him and caught him up in my arms. I held him close to me, trying to explain that I didn't mean to be so cross, that I loved my big boy.

He put his little arms around my neck, but he couldn't seem to stop the sobs that racked his trembling body. Even after the storm of weeping had passed and I finally had to put him down so I could fix supper for Harry, he lay on the cot in the living room and gasped shudderingly now and then.

By the time Harry came in, I was crying harder than Jackie. "I just don't know what got into me," I told Harry after I'd explained what had happened. "But when I thought of Richie's eyes—"

Harry's face looked more lined than usual, but he took time to pat my shoulder before he picked Jackie up and started to cuddle him. "I guess maybe every mother gets scared out of her wits sometimes," he said. "You know how that old duck of ours quacks and fusses when one of her brood gets through the fence!"

Sniffing back a sob, I smiled. Any time one of our ducklings managed to creep out of the pen, the mother duck always went into a tizzy until we caught her baby and returned it to her. So maybe human mothers weren't the only ones to become frantic now and then.

Safe in his daddy's arms, Jackie's sobs quieted down to occasional shivers, and finally he fell asleep.

"I suppose it was a shock to him," Harry said as he carried him to bed. "But probably he won't even remember it when he wakes up."

I wasn't so sure, but I promised myself I'd be so gentle and loving and tender I'd erase it all from his mind as soon as possible. I tucked him in and pulled the covers close. He stirred and whimpered, and he looked so flushed that I touched his forehead.

"He's awfully hot," I said to Harry. Harry touched him too. "Probably all that crying gave him a temperature," he said. "He'll sleep it off."

BEFORE HARRY WOULD SIT DOWN at the table, he had to make a trip out to the barn. When he didn't come back for a while, I took a quick look at the boys, who were sleeping soundly, and then I ran outside to call Harry before his supper was ruined.

My moment with God

Dear God: As I start down the long road to womanhood, guide my footsteps in the pathway of righteousness and protect me from all evil that awaits along the wayside.

Help me to remember from day to day my mother's teachings about Thee. Let me always be thankful for a wonderful mother who, even when tired and discouraged, always found time and strength to teach me right from wrong.

Help me always to know the good from the bad so that I will not break her heart or make the sweet smile vanish from her face. Help me to be good and kind, to help others in time of need, and to be ever grateful for all Thy blessings. Amen.

B. M., Ohio

I found him standing in the barn, talking to Jen, the mule, who was stretched out on the floor of her stall and tied there with heavy ropes.

"Easy now, Jen," Harry was murmuring. "Easy there, you'll get used to them—"

Jen's eyes rolled as she tossed her head. Then, furiously, she lunged against the ropes.

"Harry—what in the world?" I gasped.

"She broke her leg," Harry said, and pointed to a rough splint he'd made for her from two lengths of boards and strips torn from an old piece of canvas. "She was chasing a calf and stepped in a gopher hole. I got her in here and fixed her up. Now if I can just keep her off the leg until it heals—"

"Oh, Harry," I moaned as I went over and put my arms around him. Most farmers shoot an animal like Jen if it gets a broken leg, but Harry couldn't afford to shoot her. He had to try to patch her up.

"Once I saw a picture of a race horse with a broken leg," Harry said. "They ran straps under his belly and fastened them to a pulley overhead so he could stand up, and it took the weight off his foot—"

Looking upward at the rotting ceiling over the stalls, I said the first thing I thought of. "These beams probably wouldn't hold Jen's weight, even if we had straps and pulleys and things."

"No," Harry agreed. "I guess they wouldn't." Then, taking my arm, he turned toward the house. But he didn't eat much supper—and I didn't either.

"How long do you think it will take her leg to heal?" I asked him.

"Oh—six weeks, maybe," Harry said. "With luck, maybe I can work her some then. But crops won't wait six weeks, not in this weather. If only I had a tractor—"

"Maybe you could mortgage the crop," I suggested. "Being it's sort of urgent."

"It sure is," he agreed, and going to the phone he called the tractor dealer and tried to arrange a purchase. But I guess we'd both known it was only wishful thinking on our parts. You have to have a down payment—some kind of down payment—before you can buy anything big like a tractor. And, of course, we didn't have it.

I couldn't even cry myself to sleep that night. I was too conscious of Harry, lying sleepless and unhappy beside me. He'd tried so hard, against such heavy odds, to make our hilly land into a decent farm, and everything had worked against him. If it wasn't sickness and doctor bills, it was broken-down machinery, and if it wasn't that, it was an old mule with a broken leg. No matter how he tried,

everything went wrong. And from the silent way he was lying there, I knew he was thinking the same thing.

For a long time, I lay quietly beside him, not wanting to disturb him. But then I couldn't stand it any longer, so I slipped out of bed to check on the boys. Richie was sleeping soundly, but Jackie had thrown his covers back. His little body still felt too warm to my touch as I tucked him in again, but I prayed that his unhappiness would be forgotten by morning and that I'd be more controlled the next time something happened.

Then I slipped back to bed, and Harry turned to take me in his arms. "Darling," I murmured, "somehow, we'll manage."

"Sure we will!" he said, drawing me close.

So we still had our love—and we still had our two little sons. . . .

It was barely dawn when Harry's cry awakened me. "Oh, my God!" I heard him shout.

Throwing back the sheet, I got out of bed and ran to where he was standing by Jackie's bed. I looked at Jackie's face—and even before I touched him, I knew. He was so quiet. . . .

In the other little crib, Richie began to stir and chuckle, seeing us up. I remember thinking, with half of my mind: *He needs changing. He needs his bottle.* But with the other half of my attention, I was still staring at Jackie in unbelieving horror. Suddenly I screamed, "He's dead, Harry! He's dead!"

"Yes," Harry whispered. Then, putting his arm around me, he pulled me into the living room and held me close while he called the doctor.

After that, while we waited, somehow we got out in the kitchen—Harry and Richie and I. I tried to warm the baby's bottle, but it slipped out of my hand and broke on the floor—the last bottle we had. I'd meant to buy more, but we just hadn't had the money.

I started to cry suddenly—wild, hysterical tears that wouldn't stop. We didn't have *anything* we needed, not even an extra baby bottle! And now Jackie was dead. I could still feel his little arms clinging tightly around my neck, the way they'd been last night. . . .

The doctor and the coroner arrived finally. They talked to us, and then they said something about an autopsy. After that, they took Jackie away with them.

I couldn't stop crying and screaming when I saw them carrying off my precious baby. I wanted to grab him away from them and hold him close to me. But Harry came over to me and held me back. He put his arm around

me and tried to comfort me, but nothing could ease the awful pain in my heart. Nothing would ever bring my Jackie back to me.

Wearily, brokenly, Harry and I did the things we had to do that morning. Between us, we fed Richie and got him freshened up and comfortable. Then, carrying him, I went along with Harry while he did the chores.

Jen had some of her ropes tangled, but she didn't seem to have hurt her injured leg, so Harry got her straightened out and carried feed and water to her.

With the baby in my arms, I fed the chickens while Harry milked and carried down slops for the pigs. Then we went back to the empty house.

"Why was I so mean to him, Harry?" I asked. "I broke his heart and killed him!"

"Don't, Luly," Harry said. "That couldn't have done it."

"It did," I insisted, and bitter tears spilled out of my eyes again.

After a while, the doctor came back to explain the cause of Jackie's death. "It was virus pneumonia," he said. "It was fast and vicious, and, of course, Jackie was never too strong. Did he seem sick or run any temperature?"

"He was hot," I said, "but I thought it was because he'd been crying so."

"Didn't you take his temperature?" the doctor asked.

"No," I said, and I didn't tell him why I hadn't, that we couldn't afford a thermometer, that we couldn't afford the proper things to take care of our babies any more than we could afford the tools to farm our land properly.

Somehow, we got through the funeral. Even though we didn't know them well, Mr. and Mrs. Johnson sent a spray of roses. Jackie would have loved the flowers. I was thinking how he'd have wanted to touch them too, but I was so choked up I couldn't put it into words. Harry must have been thinking the same thing, though, because after the service, when they gave us a final few minutes alone with the tiny casket, Harry broke off one of the roses and put it in Jackie's hand. . . .

Work on a farm never stops, not even when tragedy strikes, and after we returned from the cemetery that day, we did our chores together, carrying Richie along with us. And the next day, Harry was back in the fields, plowing.

"Ned's too old to pull the plow if I set it as deep as I should," Harry explained. "But, one way or another, I've got to get this work done. Maybe, if we have a good year, it'll come out all right."

I knew enough about farming to

know what he meant. If we had lots of rain, we could still get a fair crop. But if we had a dry year, the crop would be a failure.

And if we had a crop failure, how could we live for another year? How could we give Richie even the few things a baby needs?

The torturing thoughts were on our minds, but we didn't talk about them in the days that followed. We worked hard because we had to and because it kept us from thinking about Jackie. We gave Richie all the love we could, but there wasn't a minute that I didn't worry about how little else we had to give him.

Three months after Jackie died, Harry and I met Warren Johnson and his wife in town. We were on our way to buy groceries.

"Hello, Luly. Hello, Harry," Mrs. Johnson said, walking up to us and peeking inside the blanket I had wrapped around Richie. "Can we see Richie?"

I moved the blanket back, and Richie's face broke out in a smile.

"Oh, you darling!" she said. "You adorable, beautiful darling!"

Behind her, I heard her husband's chuckle of approval. "Handsome boy," he was saying to Harry. "Wonderful kid!"

I thought of it then. *Richie ought to belong to them. They have everything. They could take care of him the way Harry and I never will be able to. They wouldn't let a child of theirs die the way I did. . . .*

Mrs. Johnson held out her arms, sort of clucking in her throat. Richie cooed gleefully. "Oh, Luly," she said, and when she looked at me I could see the longing in her eyes. "May I hold him?"

"Sure," I said, and I handed him over to her. Then I stood there, sort of shivering as I watched the joyous way our baby went to her.

Mr. Johnson held out a finger, and Richie reached out and curled his hand around it.

"Look at that!" Mr. Johnson marveled. "What a grip he's got! Boy, what I'd give for a son like him. Why, I'd trade my new tractor and all my gang plows for that boy!"

It happened so suddenly that I didn't know I'd spoken until I heard my own voice. But, holding tight to Harry's arm, I said it. "We'll take you up on that, Mr. Johnson."

"What did you say?" Mr. Johnson asked.

"If you want, we'll trade our baby, won't we, Harry?" I said.

Harry didn't answer. He just stood there, looking stricken.

Mrs. Johnson was holding Richie tight in her arms, but her eyes were on me, beseeching. "You don't mean that, Luly?" she asked. "Oh, if I could have this baby, I'd be the happiest woman in the world! But of course you don't mean it."

I saw the tears in her eyes, and I said, "I do mean it. I'd like you to have him."

Then I turned to Harry and whispered, "They've got money enough to raise him—and I'm sick with worry over what might happen to him the way we've got to live. Please, Harry—it's his only chance! Let him go."

"Oh, Luly," Harry groaned. I could see I was tearing out his heart because he couldn't deny the truth of what I was saying. His fingers closed around my hand so tight I felt the pain shoot up to my heart. He started to turn back to the car.

"Hey," Warren Johnson called out, and I saw people along the street turn to listen to him. "You really want to trade this baby for our tractor? You'll let us adopt him—let us take him home right now?"

I had a kind of foggy, dizzy feeling inside me then and I couldn't talk any more, but Harry said in a whisper, "Yes, that's what my wife wants." Then we got in our car and started back home, not even stopping for groceries.

On the way home, Harry spoke only once. That was when we were passing the Johnson place. I was looking at the yard and thinking what a wonderful place it would be for our little boy to play. But Harry was looking even further ahead. Out beside the barn, some calves were frisking around in their pen.

"Those are pure-bred calves," Harry said in a strange, tight voice. "Any one of them would sell for enough to send a boy to college for a year."

I broke down then and cried. For the first time, I realized what I had done. I'd never hold my baby again, never hear him call me Mommy. But it was best for Richie. It was for his own good, and that's what I had to think of.

As soon as we got home, Harry went out to start the chores. I peeled some potatoes and put them on to cook, not even looking in the direction of the other room. If I pretended, maybe I could make it seem like the baby—both our babies—were still there, sleeping in their cribs.

It didn't work, of course, but maybe someday I'd get used to the awful, unnatural silence. That's what I told myself as I slipped outside to feed the hens and gather the eggs. Then I went down to the barn to see what was keeping Harry so long.

He was sitting on the straw in Jen's stall, with the mule's head on his lap, and he was stroking her gently.

I caught my breath as I watched him. He looked so beaten, so completely defeated. The sight broke my heart, because it made me realize for the first time what I'd done to him.

I'd been thinking only of Richie and how he'd be better off. And maybe, deep down, I'd wanted to punish myself for Jackie's death. But suddenly I saw that Harry was being punished too. I'd made him feel that he wasn't a good father, that he hadn't been able to provide for his own.

"Oh, Harry, ·what have I done to you?" I cried as I knelt beside him. "I was only thinking of myself—how I'd feel better if Richie had it easier and I wasn't scared all the time I'd do the wrong thing for him. But I should have had more faith in you, Harry. I should have known you'd take care of us, that things would get better—"

"I don't know how things could get better," Harry said. "And don't blame yourself, Luly. I'm not blaming you. I just don't have what it takes."

Sitting together out there on the floor of the stall, we tried to console each other and talk our troubles through. But there wasn't much we could really settle with talk. We loved each other, we'd loved our babies dearly, and maybe someday, if we could ever get a decent crop, we could get out of debt and build our farm up. Then we could have another child. . . .

After a while, we went outside. Somehow, without us hearing anything, the tractor had been delivered.

"I can't look at it," Harry said.

But I didn't feel that way about it. "Mr. Johnson wants you to have it," I said. "Go ahead and use it. It will help us get a new start."

So, the next morning, Harry drove the tractor into the field and started working. That's when the sheriff arrived, with warrants for our arrest. Mr. and Mrs. Johnson had already been arrested, he told us, and Richie had been placed in protective custody.

"Humans can't be sold or traded," he told us. "It's against the law."

"But we didn't—" I gasped. "We didn't mean it that way. They could take care of Richie. We couldn't—"

"And your husband wanted a tractor so bad he had to have it, no matter what it cost."

"No" I cried. "It wasn't that way!"

But the sheriff wouldn't listen to me. He took us both to jail.

Mr. Johnson got a lawyer and we were all free on bail that day. But by then the newspapers had the story, and the way they wrote it up, Harry and I sounded like heartless flesh peddlers.

The district attorney, though, was a wise, kind man who insisted on knowing all about us—how we lived, how we'd lost Jackie, why I felt I'd been responsible for his death, how Harry and I thought we couldn't possibly give Richie all the things he needed—and how the tractor trade came about.

"Mr. Johnson sort of jokingly said how he'd trade his tractor for a baby like Richie," I explained, "and I'd already been thinking that they could give Richie such a good life. I thought I was doing something good for my baby. The tractor wasn't what made Harry and me do it. It was thinking it was right for our baby."

The district attorney then told us we should have asked for help. He said nobody has to go without real necessities like thermometers and medicines and the proper doctor's care—not when there are agencies to turn to and kind people to help you out.

When the Johnsons heard how things had been with Harry and me, they were shocked.

"If you'd just talked to me," Warren Johnson said, "I would have lent you the tractor. You people are neighbors. Neighbors shouldn't be so full of pride they won't ask for help. I thought you just didn't want your baby—"

By then, he and Mrs. Johnson were just sick over what they'd done. But the district attorney understood their side of things too. He knew how even though they'd done a bad thing, taking me up on my offer, their motives had been good.

I'll be grateful till the day I die to that district attorney. He listened to us and he believed us, and he gave us another chance. He even saw that we got Richie back right away, even though he gave the Johnsons and us a stern lecture and ordered us all to report to him once a month for a year.

We've had a lot to report. Harry had lots of help from the neighbors and he had the use of Mr. Johnson's tractor, so he raised a bumper crop. But just as important have been the warm friendships we've made with people we hardly knew before.

There's just one more thing I could wish for, though. I'd like all the people who read that story about us in the papers to understand how it really happened and not to think bad about us any more. Harry and I were desperate and frightened, not heartless. God knew that, I guess, because He gave us this new start.   *The End*

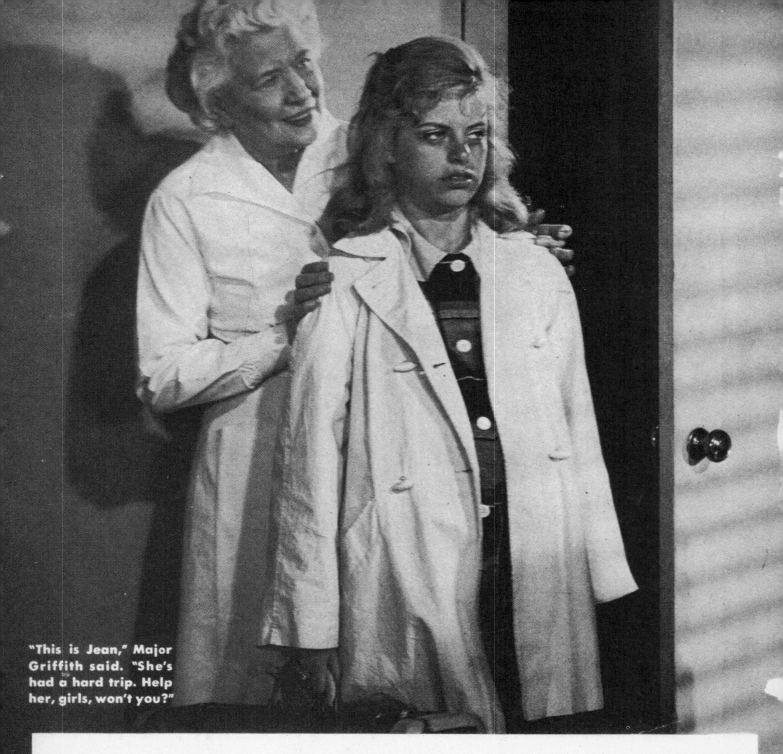

"This is Jean," Major Griffith said. "She's had a hard trip. Help her, girls, won't you?"

As soon as I gave the address, I could tell that the cab driver knew the place I was going to. He glanced at me—at my swollen body that not even my loose coat could hide any more.

"I've driven lots of girls there," he said, as though he was talking to himself.

I met his eyes defiantly in the rear-view mirror. "They didn't get there by themselves," I said coldly.

"No, ma'am," he agreed, and there was pity in his voice. "But that's the way they have to go there. Alone."

I stared out of the window, fighting back the tears. He didn't have to tell me that. Nobody could be more alone than I was. Nineteen, in a strange city, almost broke, and seven and a half months pregnant. Hazel

was the only one who knew where I was going, and she thought the whole thing was a joke. Nobody else knew—or would have cared, anyway. Not my mother or my stepfather. Certainly not the father of my baby.

The cab stopped in front of an old-fashioned brick building with a high board fence around the back. The driver carried my bag up to the porch. I paid him and he drove away.

And there I was, with less than a dollar to my name, standing in front of a Salvation Army home for unwed mothers and not even sure that they would take me in. I knew I should have written first, but I'd let the months drift by till suddenly I was in a panic to get out of town. Hazel, my roommate, had lent me the money for my

Party Girl

—NOW I'M PAYING!

195

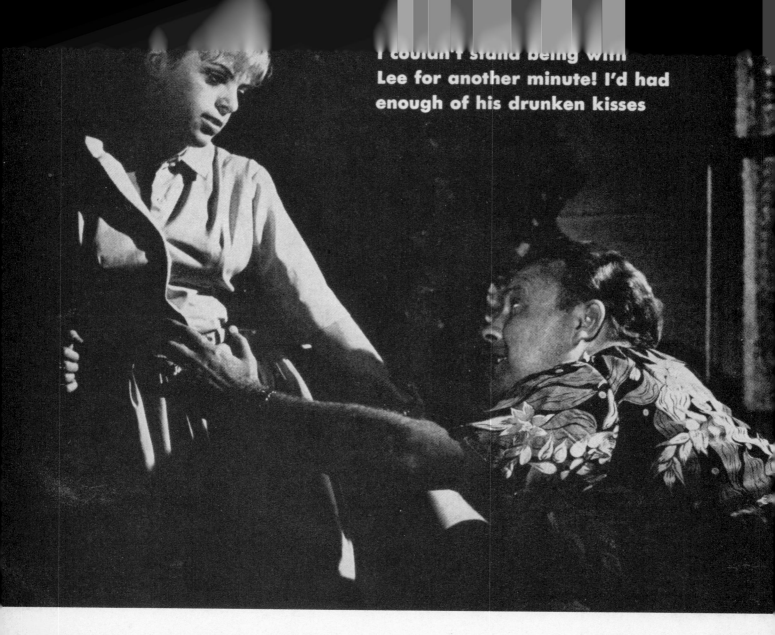

I couldn't stand being with
Lee for another minute! I'd had
enough of his drunken kisses

bus fare, and I'd left without a word to anybody.

I pressed a shaking finger on the doorbell. Then suddenly I panicked. What would I do if they turned me away?

The door opened and a white-haired woman smiled at me. "I—I just came," I blurted out. "I know I was supposed to write first, but I got scared. I'm seven and a half months along—"

"I see you are," she said, and her eyes softened. "Come in, and we'll talk it over. I'm Major Griffith."

I followed her into a small room that was furnished like an office. I sat down across the desk from her and answered her questions—mostly with lies. I didn't dare tell her the truth, because then she might get in touch with my folks. I told her I was an orphan and that I'd been living with my older sis-

ter, Hazel Tey. I laughed at that secretly, imagining my stepfather's face if he could hear me claiming Hazel as a relative.

To the questions about my baby's father—his educational background, his religion, his occupation—I kept mumbling, "I don't know," till I couldn't stand it any longer. Then I confessed that I'd only seen him once.

When I got up enough nerve to look at Major Griffith, I saw that her face hadn't changed. It was still soft and pitying. I clenched my fists. "I don't have any money to pay my way," I said, sure she would put me out. Why should anyone want to help me?

The major's face remained serene. "We have funds to take care of girls without money," she said. "Tomorrow is the doctor's day in the home. He'll give you a checkup and take your

medical history. Now I'll show you to your room."

I followed her down the hall and into a small, neat room with twin beds. There was a girl sitting on one of the beds and another girl standing near her. For a moment, I stared at them. They were both even bigger than I was. Of course I had known that all the other girls in the home would be pregnant too, but still it was a shock meeting the first ones.

Major Griffith introduced us. The girl on the bed was Betty. The other girl, Vicky, was my roommate. Betty left with Major Griffith, and Vicky showed me where to hang my clothes and which drawers in the chest were mine.

I took a shower in the bathroom down the hall and changed into the maternity skirt and smock I had made

signed my seat. Major Griffith gave the blessing, and we sat down to dinner. The food was served in big bowls, and it was wholesome, tasty food. Some of the girls had terrible manners. They put their elbows on the table and talked with their mouths full.

I smothered my feeling of scorn. I didn't have any right to criticize them. We were all guilty of the same sin. The only difference between us was that I'd had a mother who taught me manners. *And not much else, I thought bitterly. She didn't teach me how to live, or I wouldn't be here now.*

I dragged my thoughts away from Mom. It hurt to think of her, to remember how close and loving we'd been in those far-off days when my father was alive.

At eight o'clock, everyone gathered in the recreation room. Major Griffith read a passage from the Bible, and we said the Lord's Prayer. Major Griffith told me then that my work assignment would be in the hospital on the third floor. Every girl in the home had a job, she explained, whether she paid all her way or none of it.

I was glad that I'd be helping to take care of the mothers and the new babies. Once, I'd hoped to be a nurse. I'd even sent for booklets from hospital training schools and figured costs. But all that seemed so long ago.

VICKY AND I TALKED THAT NIGHT, after the lights were out at nine-thirty. "Are you going to keep your baby?" she asked me.

"Oh, no!" I said. Keep Vince's baby? I'd never even thought of doing that. It didn't seem like a real human being to me. I just wanted to bring it into the world, get rid of it, and forget about it.

"I'm not keeping mine, either," Vicky said, her voice sad. "I couldn't do that without my folks finding out, and it would break their hearts. They don't know I'm pregnant. They think I came here to work and to be near Jerry."

She told me about Jerry then. He was a soldier she'd met when he was stationed near her town. "I sure fell for him," she said. "If he had told me to stand on my head in the town square, I would have done it.

"After he was transferred to the Army base here, we wrote. I guess he thought it was safe enough, five hundred miles away. When I wrote that I was pregnant, he didn't answer, so I came here. At the base they told me he was home on a pass, and one of the soldiers gave me his address. When I got to his house, I saw his wife and two kids. Cute little kids—a boy around two and a darling girl around five."

"Did you tell his wife?" I asked.

"Of course not," Vicky said. "It's not her fault. I wouldn't break up anybody's home. It's my tough luck. I guess I asked for it, anyway, going overboard that way."

I didn't volunteer any information about myself, and she didn't ask questions. That's the way it was in the home. If you wanted to talk, okay; but if you kept quiet, nobody pried into your past.

I was awake for a long time after Vicky's even breathing told me she was asleep. People on the outside would classify us as the same kind of girl, but I knew better. Vicky was decent and good, while I—

What kind of a girl am I? I wondered. How could I have messed up my life so completely? I was only nineteen. . . .

I thought of my father, who died when I was ten, and the old grief ached in my throat. I had worshiped him, and I never got over his death. When Mom married Max Howe two years later, I thought the world had come to an end. Oh, I knew Mom had been going out to shows and parties with Max, but I never dreamed she'd marry him.

And then they came home together that day. Mom's cheeks were pink, and she looked like someone had just given her a million dollars. "This is your new father, children," she said. "We've got someone to take care of us now."

*Who needs him? I thought, glaring at Max. He was a big, heavy-set man, with a rough appearance and manner. My father had been slender and handsome, and he had always dressed just so. How could Mom love a man like Max when she'd been married to Daddy? It made me sick to think of it. Maybe Mom had forgotten how sweet and kind Daddy was, but I never would.

My little brother, Bobby, who was only seven, shouted with joy and threw himself on Max. But I squirmed away when he bent to kiss me.

"Jean!"   [*Continued*]

by hand before I left for the city. Then Vicky took me into the recreation room and introduced me to the girls by their first names. Nobody in the home ever used last names. There were about thirty girls, all pregnant, bulging under maternity smocks. It was like seeing myself reflected in a mirror every time I turned around. The girls were all ages: some younger than I, some around my age, many in their twenties, and a few who looked even older. They were playing cards, sewing, reading, talking, watching TV.

I played canasta with one group till a bell rang. Then the room emptied like magic. Vicky laughed at my startled expression. "Chow time, Jean," she said. "Pregnant girls are always hungry. Didn't you know that?"

I followed the group into the dining room across the hall, and I was as-

PARTY GIRL—NOW I'M PAYING!

Mom said, and she looked really hurt.

Max laughed. "Give the girl time. She'll get used to me," he said.

But I never did. I vowed he'd never take my father's place, and I wouldn't call him "Daddy," the way Bobby did. I called him Max, and when he went to court and legally adopted us, I wouldn't accept that, either. Bobby took Max's name, but I didn't. I was still Jean Burl as far as I was concerned, and I told everyone so. I swore to myself that I'd never change, even if Max beat me for it. I guess I hoped he would, so I'd have another reason to hate him. But Max never laid a finger on me. He just talked about my duty to my mother.

How about her duty to me? I'd think. *Why weren't Bobby and I enough for her?* But I didn't talk back. I clammed up because I knew that made Max mad. His heavy face would turn crimson as he tried to hold onto his temper.

Mom talked to me too. Max was a good man, she said. He was a fine husband, and he wanted to be a father to me. Why wouldn't I let him?

"I hate him!" I burst out once. "You ought to be ashamed of yourself for marrying him! If you really loved Daddy, you never would have!"

Mom's eyes filled with tears. "I did love your father, Jean," she said. "I loved him very much. But he's gone now, and the rest of us must go on living without him. I'm only thirty-five, dear, and a woman gets lonesome alone. I loved your father, but I love Max too. Try to understand."

I felt my face twisting into a hateful sneer. "I understand, all right. You just wanted a man."

Mom gasped and slapped me across the face. Then she cried and said she was sorry, but I didn't forgive her. She was siding with Max against me, her own daughter.

When I started dating, Max set the time for me to be in. I'd have stayed out later and defied him, but the way he talked to my dates scared them. They brought me home right on the minute. I boiled with resentment. Max was nothing to me—*nothing*—and he acted as though he was my father.

I decided to quit school when I was sixteen and go to work. Then I could support myself and leave home. I wasn't trained for anything, but that didn't stop me. I told them at school that I wouldn't be back in the fall, and then I told Mom I was quitting. Of course, she told Max, and he blew his stack.

"You're staying in school till you graduate!" he roared. "You're a minor and I'm responsible for you. How do you think you'd support yourself?"

I shrugged. "Oh, I can get a job clerking or waiting tables. Maybe I can be a bar girl at Grady's."

The bar girls at Grady's had a reputation for making money on the side. I knew I wouldn't work there. I just said that to be smart.

Mom went into hysterics, and Max had an awful time calming her down. I should have been ashamed of myself, but I wasn't. Watching Mom crying and Max fussing over her satisfied a dark, ugly bitterness deep inside me. Mom and Max and Bobby—they were a happy family together. They didn't need me or want me, but I sure could make trouble for them!

Afterward, Max talked to me tougher than he ever had before. He threatened me with the State Training School if I didn't behave myself. That scared me, but I still wasn't giving up. It was a contest between Max and me, and I was out to show him he couldn't boss me. The only way to be free of him, I decided, was to get married. Then he couldn't tell me what to do!

I was dating two boys then—Bruce

Hanes and Casey Theron. Bruce was my age and in my class at school. He seemed awfully young to me, because he still thought you should do what your parents and teachers told you. But I liked him, and I always came home from our dates with kind of a good feeling. We didn't do anything exciting, just a movie and a hamburger afterward, and our good-night kiss was a brush of his lips against mine. Still, I went to bed with a happiness inside of me that lasted till the next morning—when I had to look at Max in my father's place at the table.

Casey was different. Like me, he was restless and bucking the world. When he wanted to do something, he did it— no matter what the consequences were. "Everybody has to look out for himself," Casey said.

I thought so too, and that's how I got the idea that Casey and I could do it together. We could get married, and then I'd be free.

I wouldn't have been allowed to date a wild kid like Casey except that his parents were friends of Max's and Mom's. Casey had quit school in his junior year, and he was working for his father. He was a big disappointment to his folks, who kept hoping he'd settle down. Maybe they thought that going with me would help. That was a laugh.

Casey's kisses weren't any brush on the lips. They were real, asking more than I'd ever give him—unless we were married. That idea kept eating at me. It would be easy, I figured. Casey would do anything for a kick.

One night I was feeling especially mean and bitter. It was Bobby's birthday, and Mom had fixed a big dinner for him. I felt like an outsider, watching him blow out the candles on his cake, with Mom and Max beaming.

Casey and I went to a drive-in movie that night. He started petting the minute we were parked, and I let him go farther than he ever had before. "Say, honey, you're okay!" he said in surprise.

I pushed his hands away. "Let's get married, Casey," I said. "I'm sick of going to school. I'm sick of Max. I want to get out."

He jumped at the idea and began planning. There was no waiting period in our state, so we could get married that very night. There was a justice of the peace twenty miles down the road who never asked any questions, Casey said. He turned the car around. "The old man will have to kick in with more money after I've got a wife," he said.

I wasn't listening to him, though. I was thinking about Max. *He'll turn purple when he finds I've got out from under his thumb!* I told myself.

The justice of the peace *didn't* ask

any questions. He got the license clerk out of bed for us. Within ten minutes, we had filled out the papers, the justice of the peace had mumbled a few words over us and collected his money, and there we were—married. I came out of the justice's house feeling confused and sorry already, but Casey didn't give me time to think. He rushed me into the car and over to a motel. He registered, showing the clerk our marriage certificate when he questioned us. Then we got a room.

Casey locked the door the minute we were inside. Then he came up to me, his eyes glittering. He pulled me to him and kissed me roughly. Suddenly I didn't want any part of Casey or marriage either. "Please, Casey," I said, pushing him away, "I'm tired out. Let's just sleep."

"You crazy or something?" he exploded. He grabbed me, and I fought with him. He threw me on the bed, and my head struck the metal post. I was dazed and my stomach was churning, but I still knew what was happening to me—and I hated every minute of it.

I woke up at daybreak. Casey was sprawled on the bed beside me. My head was throbbing, and I wanted to die. Somebody was pounding on the door. Barefooted, in my slip, I stumbled over to it and opened it. Max and Mom stood there, with an officer from the highway patrol. When I hadn't come home, they'd phoned Casey's parents and tracked us down through his car license.

Casey woke up and slunk into the bathroom to dress. I faced Max, bound he'd never know I was sorry.

"We got married last night," I said. "What's everybody so excited about?"

Mom began to cry, and Max put his arm around her. "Don't cry, honey," he said. "We'll have the marriage annulled. They aren't either of them legal age."

That drove me wild, the way they stood there, clinging together, the two of them against me. "You can't have it annulled," I said. "We stayed here together last night. We—"

Max's eyes raked me scornfully, and my voice died in my throat.

"It probably wasn't the first time," he said. "But that doesn't matter. You're under age and I'm your legal father till you're eighteen. You'll have to wait till then to go to hell in your own way."

Casey drove home alone, and I went back with Max and Mom. The annulment was put through, and I had to go back to school that fall. I refused to talk to Mom about it, though she begged me to. We'd grown too far apart. It seemed to me that Max stood between us, barring us from any understanding or love. I saw Casey on the street sometimes, but we both

looked away without speaking. I hated him for what he did to me that night. And I guess he hated me too.

Time crawled by. My school grades weren't good, but what did that matter? Nobody expected anything good of me. Then, in the spring of my senior year, I met Hazel Tey. She worked at a drive-in where lots of the high-school kids went to eat. Hazel was divorced, with a two-year-old boy, but she looked no older than me. Her child was being cared for by her ex-husband's parents, and Hazel was free. She did just what she wanted. I was fascinated by her gay chatter and carefree attitude.

I began dropping into the drive-in after school for a Coke and chat with Hazel every chance I got. She was sympathetic when I told her about Max.

"I know the type," she said. "My father was like that, always throwing his weight around. That's why I married young, but I picked wrong. Kenny can't earn as much as I can, but he expected to tie me down in one room with a kid. Nuts to that, I told him."

Hazel had a three-room apartment that she shared with a roommate when she could find someone she liked. At that time, though, she was living alone. She told me that I could move in with her when I finished school and got a

job. "We'll have a ball," she said. "Lots of dates, lots of laughs, lots of kicks."

"I don't have to wait till then," I said. "I'll be eighteen April fifth. Then Max can't tell me what to do. I can walk right out of the house and he can't stop me."

"But don't you want to wait till you graduate?" Hazel asked. "That's just two months more."

"No," I said. "I don't." I guess I knew that that was the way to hurt Mom and Max the most: to cheat them out of seeing me graduate; to leave home the very minute I could.

Oh, there was a scene, all right! By then, I'd lined up a job as relief waitress at the drive-in, with the promise of a full-time job soon. Then, on my eighteenth birthday, I packed my things and told Mom and Max I was leaving.

Mom cried—as hard as if she really cared. "I baked a birthday cake. Your presents are all wrapped," she sobbed. "Oh, Jean! Don't do this to us! Don't ruin your life!"

"Eat the cake yourselves," I said. "You'll never miss me."

"Oh, yes, we will," Max said. He was keeping pretty calm. "We'll miss your meanness. We'll miss your trying to make your mother miserable, and trying to spoil our home. We'll miss you all right!"

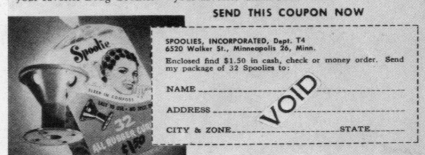

"That goes double," I said, glaring.

"If you walk out of here now, you can't come back," Max warned me.

"Oh, Max! You don't mean that!" Mom cried.

I just shrugged and walked out. Bobby was crying when I kissed him good-by, but I knew he wouldn't cry long. He had Max and Mom. And what did I have? Just myself. *That's all I need,* I thought, feeling brave and strong.

I moved in with Hazel, and I learned to live the way she did. We worked hard on our shift at the drive-in, but it was fun. New people all the time; guys trying to make time with us and leaving big tips. It was exciting, and I lapped it up.

I went out on double dates with Hazel. She knew a lot of men, and they always had a friend who wanted a date. Hazel said double dates were safer, that a guy couldn't pull any really rough stuff then.

We went driving and dancing and drinking. A lot of drinking. I'd had only beer before, and not much of that. But I liked what hard liquor did for me. It made the lights softer and the music sweeter, and the fellow I happened to be with looked a lot better after a few drinks. I didn't really like men. That night in the motel with Casey had done something to me. When a man put his hands on me, I shivered. I had to fight myself to let a man even kiss me.

I began to wake up some mornings with a hang-over. Hazel laughed at me.

"You're turning into a bottle baby, honey," she said.

I'd stare at myself in the mirror, puffy eyed and pasty looking till I got my make-up on. I hated the way I looked, and yet it gave me a kind of twisted satisfaction. I wished that Mom and Max could see me because it was all their fault for not loving me and wanting me—for forcing me out of my own home.

Hazel began dating a fellow named Skip Berton. He was cute and Hazel was crazy about him, but she wouldn't date him alone.

"I'm scared of what might happen," she said. "I want Skip to marry me, and the only way to do that is to keep him dangling."

When she explained it that way, I

Are you adored—or abhorred?

Your disposition makes the difference!

★ ARE YOU FUN to be with? Or are you the kind of person people hurry to get away from? No matter which group you fit into, it's your disposition that puts you there!

A person with a good disposition does not necessarily share all the viewpoints or opinions of those with whom he maintains contact, but he has learned to be "agreeable" with them. A person with a bad disposition has not learned the art of disagreeing "agreeably." Rather, he lets people annoy or frustrate him. He responds to them with angry words or a snobbish action.

What about you? Are you in hot water "dispositionally speaking"?

Such an admission is painful. It indicates you are having considerable difficulty in getting along with your boy friend or husband, your relatives and associates, and that much of the trouble is your own fault.

If you really want to "sweeten" your disposition, you can. You'll have much to gain by the effort, and nothing to lose—except unhappiness.

How do you start? Ask yourself, "Why do I have a bad disposition?"

If it is something that has developed fairly suddenly, you may be ill without realizing it. Some sicknesses creep upon us and play havoc with our disposition. In a case like this, play safe. Consult your physician.

If your bad disposition is of long duration, it may be traced to your growing-up years when you found you could handle your doting parents by sulking or showing anger whenever they failed to give you what you wanted. Such conduct will bring you only unhappiness in an adult world.

Maybe you feel you were the loser in a romance or marriage, or you may be clinging mentally to some other disappointment. Are you going to permit such an experience to sour you for

life? Surely it'd be wiser to accept the experience as one of those things that happened—and then resolutely dismiss it from your thinking. To find any real degree of happiness, you must prove yourself superior to any heartaches that have come your way.

Here are additional "steps" to help you improve your disposition:

1. Place yourself in the other person's shoes. How would you like to be on the receiving, instead of the giving, end of one of your bad temper displays? You wouldn't, would you?

2. Resist the temptation to try to get people to conform to the standards you think they should maintain. Everyone is entitled to his own beliefs.

3. If you can't take criticism gracefully, never criticize anyone.

4. Steer clear of controversial topics in conversation.

5. If you must disagree with a person, do so inoffensively. Don't say, "You're wrong!" Tone it down to "Doesn't it seem to you that this is the way it could be?" You offend people when you are too cocksure of yourself.

6. Learn to appreciate the good qualities about a person while overlooking the flaws.

7. Concede easily in unimportant matters. Sally says the color of Edna's living room is sky blue. You know it is ocean blue. Don't rush to the phone to call Edna so you can prove Sally is wrong. Just forget it. The matter is trivial—compared to your friendship with Sally.

Every honest effort to improve your disposition will pay off. Keep trying, and you'll become one of those agreeable women everyone will enjoy being around. ■ ■ ■

couldn't refuse to go out on double dates with her, though I didn't like the fellows Skip brought for me. Till the night he brought Vince Robbins. Vince was about thirty, and he had a very smooth way about him. He didn't grab me the minute we got in the back seat of Skip's car, and he didn't push drinks at me. He was an easy, relaxed kind of guy, handsome in a dark way, and I found myself letting down the bars.

I stopped counting my drinks and just had fun. I guess I trusted Vince because he was older. He was a terrific dancer, and I floated around the floor in his arms, liking the feel of his cheek against mine. The clouds of cigarette smoke in the cheap little joint seemed like a rosy haze. . . .

I don't remember eating anything, though Hazel said that we had hamburgers and French fries before we headed back to the apartment. In the hall, Skip put up an argument because he wanted to come in. Hazel and I were afraid of the new building manager, who'd been giving us some very suspicious looks. Skip got so loud that the only thing to do was to let him in. I leaned against the wall, laughing. "Crazy Skip! He needs a cold shower," I giggled. "Hazel—"

But Hazel had disappeared, and Skip too. I looked at Vince. He smiled and nodded toward the closed bedroom door.

"Those kids are in love," he said. "Let's give them a break."

In love! What was going on behind that door was a million miles away from love, but I wasn't thinking straight. I wasn't thinking at all. I nodded, and sympathetic tears filled my eyes. I let Vince settle me on the sofa, and I drank what he brought me from the kitchen. He said it would sober me up. It looked like water, and it went down easy. I was so numb from all the drinks I'd had that I didn't even suspect it was straight vodka.

That was lights out for me. Oh, sure, I know when somebody says, "Everything went black," people snicker, but that's the way it was. When I woke up the next day, I knew what had happened, all right. Vince and Skip were gone. I was lying on the sofa, and my clothes were thrown over a chair. Hazel was just crawling out of bed. She had a hang-over, and she was afraid Skip wouldn't marry her. He had what he wanted.

We were working the night shift then, so we had till four in the afternoon to pull ourselves together. I took a long, hot shower, and then turned on the cold water full blast. I put on my make-up with a shaking hand, avoiding my eyes in the mirror. I was beginning to remember Vince's hands on me, his harsh kisses, his voice whis-

pering, begging. . . . It made my flesh crawl, and I hated myself.

When Vince called me at the drive-in two days later, I wouldn't even go to the phone. I hoped I'd never have to see him again. I just wanted to forget how low I'd sunk. But six weeks later, I was frantically trying to reach him to tell him I was pregnant. I finally got hold of him at the plant where he worked.

"Tough luck," he said. "I thought you girls knew how to take care of yourselves."

"What do you mean?" I screamed into the phone. "You've got no right to talk like I'm a—"

"You're no innocent child," he came back at me. "You've been married, and there must have been lots of other men besides me. How do I know this is my kid?"

"It is! It is!" I was crying hysterically. "That's the only time—"

"Try and prove it," he snapped. "I'm a married man. Try and hang anything on me, and I'll have you run out of town!" The receiver banged down.

I told Hazel, and she tried to help. She knew an abortionist, but I didn't have the money to go to him and I was terrified of abortions, anyway. She got some pills from a fellow she knew who worked in a drugstore. They made me

so sick I missed two days' work, but nothing happened.

I was desperate, half crazy with fear. What would happen to me when I was too big to go on working? How would I live? Hazel urged me to ask my folks for help, but I said I'd kill myself first.

I shudder to remember that I actually prayed to God to destroy the life He had created. But my pregnancy continued, and the baby began to move, stretching and kicking. I didn't feel any tenderness for it, only resentment. This tiny, living, growing thing had me fast in its trap. I couldn't get rid of it, and somewhere, somehow, I had to bring it into the world.

My girdle got so tight I could hardly breathe, but I zipped myself into it every morning. I had to go on working. How else could I live? But when I reached six months, I had to quit at the drive-in. I was so thick in the waist and short of breath, I could hardly manage the trays. Besides, the customers were beginning to stare at me.

Hazel said I shouldn't worry, that I could stay at the apartment. She brought me leftover hamburgers, and milk and fruit that wouldn't keep. She was the one who saw the ad: "Any girl in trouble or in need of a friend, write Major Griffith." The address was in a city in a nearby state.

Hazel said "major" meant a major

in the Salvation Army, and that it was probably a home for unwed mothers. She asked around and found out about such homes. They were all over the country, and they'd take care of a girl and let her have her baby there free, if she didn't have any money. Then they'd see that the baby was adopted into a good home.

I knew that it was my only way out, but it took me a while to make up my mind to take it. I'd never been out of my home town, and I was scared. In the year since I'd left home, I hadn't heard from Mom and Max. They'd cut me right out of their lives. I told myself that that was what I wanted, but still I felt terribly alone. Sometimes I longed to get on a bus and rush back to Mom, to throw myself in her arms and beg her to forgive me and help me. The thing that held me back was the memory of Max's face the time he found me in the motel with Casey—the way he told me to go to hell in my own way. I'd done that all right, and I couldn't stand to think of him gloating over me. I wouldn't give him the satisfaction.

Hazel got behind in her rent finally, and I realized I couldn't let her go on supporting me. We both cried when we said good-by. She wasn't a "good" girl, but neither was I, and she'd stood by me in my trouble. . . .

My first morning in the home, I woke up to the ringing of a bell. Breakfast was at seven-thirty. Then we did our work assignments and straightened our rooms. Later, everyone had to exercise for thirty minutes in the fenced back yard. Then we had lunch. The afternoon was open for whatever we wanted to do: sewing, talking, reading, or writing letters. We had prayers every night, and we were allowed to watch TV at certain times.

It sounds dull, but it really wasn't. All of us had the same problem, and that made a close bond between us. We got to know each other fast, meeting in each other's rooms in our free time. The thing every girl talked about most was whether she should keep her baby or give it up.

Lieutenant Hopkins was the case-worker in the home who talked to the girls about it. A few of them had parents who were willing to let them bring their babies home. Some of the older girls planned to go back to their jobs and put their babies in boarding homes so Lieutenant Hopkins helped them plan to do this, to figure if they really could manage it. She worked out budgets, and talked to them about the problems that would come up when the baby was old enough to

realize that he didn't have a father.

The girls who decided to give up their babies for adoption were allowed to stay in the home with them for six weeks if they wanted to. Then the mother signed a temporary release paper and the baby was placed in a boarding home till it was three months old. During that time, she could still change her mind about giving up the baby. If she didn't change her mind, she signed a final release paper and the baby was put up for adoption.

I couldn't understand why any of the girls wanted to keep their babies. Hang onto a baby whose father didn't care anything about it? What kind of a deal was that? Some of the fathers were married, like Vince, and there were others who were too young to get married or who just didn't want to. A few of them were helping with the girls' expenses, but most of them slapped back with the same thing Vince had said to me: "How do I know it's my baby?" After talking to all the girls, I was convinced that there wasn't a decent man in the world.

Lieutenant Hopkins didn't have to talk very long with me. I wanted to give up my baby. When she tried to get me to talk about my own future, I couldn't find much to say. I still pretended that I was an orphan. I said I'd go back to live with my sister and work at the drive-in or somewhere else.

Lieutenant Hopkins was young, and she had a sweet, soft way about her. She looked at me anxiously, as though she really cared what happened to me. "This is a hard experience, Jean," she said, "but you can use it to help, rather than to hurt you. If you can understand *why* this happened to you, then you can build on your mistake. You can grow into a fine person, who can make herself and others happy."

That sounded crazy. *Me* a fine and understanding person? I looked down at my hands, knotted tight together, and the tears ached in my throat. *If only Daddy hadn't died,* I thought. *This wouldn't have happened if I'd had my own father to love me and to take care of me.*

I worked in the hospital with another girl under the two nurses, Lieutenant Burns and Lieutenant Curtis. We gave baths and carried trays to the girls who'd had their babies, cleaned the delivery room, and prepared instruments for the sterilizer. It was hard work, but I was always busy and didn't have too much chance to brood.

About a month after I went to the home, Vicky had her baby, a husky boy. She stayed only two weeks before she signed the papers and left for her home town. The day she left, she stood over the baby's crib a long time, looking down at him. Then she smiled at me, tears sliding down her cheeks.

"No use prolonging the agony," she said. "Oh, Jean!" she sobbed. "He's so sweet, so perfect. Someone will want him very much, won't they? They'll love him and be good to him—"

I comforted her and told her of course her baby would have a good home. I meant it too. Major Griffith and Lieutenant Hopkins had told us many times that adoption agencies had long lists of good people, happily married couples, who couldn't have babies and were eager to take someone else's baby and give it a good home. We knew that the people at the adoption agencies were very careful about where they placed our babies, always thinking of the child's welfare first.

I trusted the Salvation Army people, and I believed what they told me. I knew Vicky did too, so I couldn't understand why she felt so bad about giving up her baby. There wasn't any problem, the way I saw it. Vicky could go back to her home town and her family now. She could get a job and someday marry a good man. All she had to do was forget that she'd had a baby by a man who wasn't worth a second thought. It would all be so easy, I figured. . . .

I WOKE UP ONE MORNING around four, a week later, feeling queer. There wasn't any pain, just a feeling that something was about to happen. I lay quietly, waiting till a sudden keen stab in the pit of my stomach made me sit up straight in bed. *This is it,* I thought, and I wasn't afraid. All I felt was a deep sensation of relief. At last my time had come. In a few hours, my baby would be born. I'd be rid of it, and I could start living again.

I got up quietly, not wanting to wake Corinne, who'd moved into my room after Vicky had left. I put on my robe and slippers and got two clean nightgowns from the drawer. Then I walked up to the third floor. Lieutenant Burns was on duty. "What are you doing up here?" she asked.

"I'm going to have my baby," I said.

"Well, bless your heart," she said, and she put her arms around me as she led me into the labor room.

I didn't have a bad time. It was only an hour or so before I was transferred from the labor room to the delivery room. The doctor was there, and I trusted him and did as he told me to. There was a big clock on the wall in the delivery room. I watched the hands move from five to six to seven to seven-thirty. Then they gave me gas, and I drifted into a hazy sleep. From far off I heard a wail, like the mewing of a kitten, and the doctor's voice, saying, "It's a girl." And then Lieutenant Burns's gasp, "Oh, Doctor, look! God help us!"

When I came to in my hospital bed, it seemed like a dream. I put my hand on my flat stomach and thought how wonderful it was that it was all over. I ate a little breakfast and a good lunch. I waited for Lieutenant Burns to bring in my baby. Not that it really mattered to me, but from working in the hospital I knew it was the customary thing.

The day wore on and nothing was said about my baby. I began to feel nervous.

"Don't I get to see my baby?" I asked Lieutenant Burns, trying to keep my voice from shaking.

She kind of jumped. "Yes, of course, Jean," she said. But she didn't come back.

I was really uneasy then. I knew I'd had a little girl. Had she *died?* Betty, who was in the room with me, was up and walking around, and I asked her to bring my baby from the nursery. The girls weren't supposed to do that, but Betty understood that I was anxious.

She brought in a tiny bundle, wrapped in a pink blanket, and laid it on the bed beside me. I stared down at my baby—my daughter—hardly believing my eyes. I'd gone through all the sickness and heaviness of pregnancy, and yet I'd never quite realized that at the end there would be a real human being. I'd never dreamed that the instant I saw my baby, I would love her with a yearning tenderness and a longing to protect and cherish her. It wasn't like anything I'd ever felt before.

My baby was like a lovely jewel. Starry, dark lashes brushed her creamy skin, and her small head was covered with soft, dark hair. I hardly breathed as I looked at her. A miracle —one of God's beautiful miracles. Why had He sent her to me?

I drew back the blanket and touched her tiny pink hand. Her fingers curled around mine, tugging clear through to my heart.

"Oh, sweet, sweet!" I whispered, and pulled the blanket farther open. I wanted to see every bit of my precious baby. Her little arms waved in the air, freed of the blanket. I looked at

them—and suddenly I felt as though I'd gone mad. My baby's left arm ended at the wrist—*she had only one hand!* I clutched at her little arms, comparing them, babbling, screaming in horror!

Lieutenant Burns came running in. She took my baby away and gave me a sedative before I could ask any questions. But it wasn't any easier when I came to again. My baby was imperfect, and no amount of talking by the doctor or the staff at the home could change that.

"We don't know why these things happen, Jean," the doctor explained. "Sometimes we think we can trace it to a shock to the embryo—an accident, or anesthesia during surgery in the first months of pregnancy. But not always. Don't feel guilty. Don't feel that you're to blame."

Oh, but I was, I was! I remembered the pills that had made me so sick, the other things I had done, the way I had prayed for a miscarriage. I had maimed my own child!

Everyone was kind and tried to help. Lieutenant Hopkins said that when the baby was two or three, she could be fitted with an artificial hand. Growing up with the handicap, she'd learn how to live with it. Her life could be normal and happy.

"And who's going to do all this for her?" I cried in despair. "That good, kind couple who adopt her? You know she's not adoptable. Nobody will want her."

"There are always public funds for children," Lieutenant Hopkins said. "She won't be neglected."

"You mean she'll live in an orphan asylum all her life!" I burst out. "You mean she'll be a ward of the state, and the state will clothe her and feed her and buy her the artificial hand! What kind of a life is that for a child?"

Lieutenant Hopkins tried to comfort me. "Maybe it won't turn out that way, Jean," she said. "She's a beautiful baby and perfectly healthy otherwise. Some people have big hearts. She may find a home."

But I didn't believe that. I knew nobody would want her. She'd grow up in loneliness, feeling rejected, thinking that her own mother had abandoned her because she wasn't perfect. But that wasn't true. I loved her all the more because of it. When she was a week old, I began taking care of her. I bathed her and fed her. Then I'd hold her for a long time, looking down into her lovely little face. When my eyes strayed to the left sleeve that hung limply over her wrist, I'd ache all over with love and compassion.

"My beautiful little girl," I'd whisper to her. "Your mother loves you. Oh, please don't ever doubt that!"

She'd look up at me with her big eyes that were already starting to darken. She seemed to be studying my face, as though she wanted to remember it. "Don't hate me when you grow up," I'd beg through my tears. "Try to understand. Try to forgive."

If only I could keep her! I'd have done anything if I could have had her with me. Lieutenant Hopkins and I talked about that, but it was hopeless. I told her the truth then—that I had quarreled with my mother and stepfather and had no home to go back to. I had no job and no sister to live with. Hazel would take me in if she could, but I couldn't keep a baby in her apartment. Who would take care of her while I worked? How could my pay as a waitress, if I was lucky enough to get a job, cover food and clothing and medical care for a tiny baby? Lieutenant Hopkins said that she couldn't encourage me to try it.

She suggested that I tell Mom and Max, and ask for their help. But I remembered the way I'd walked out on my eighteenth birthday, coldly and heartlessly, and I knew I'd forfeited the right to ask anything of them. Now that I was a mother myself, I realized how much I had hurt Mom. I named the baby Elizabeth after her. She'd never know that somewhere she had a granddaughter with her name, but it gave me a little happiness to do at least that much for her. . . .

A few days later, the newspaper carried a feature story about the State Home for Children. The page was full of pictures of the children—standing in cribs and playpens, sitting in little chairs. All of us girls read the captions and stared at the pictures in silence. This was what every girl who had to give up her baby feared—that he wouldn't find a good home but would be raised in an institution.

The children were looking into the camera with eager, bright-eyed little faces. They all had the same expression of longing in their eyes. They were like a windowful of puppies in a pet shop: each one jumping up, beating at the glass with his little paws—begging you to choose *him.*

After I read that story, I rushed to the nursery and took Elizabeth in my arms. I wanted her to feel loved and secure as long as she could. I knew what her future was going to be. The days, the weeks, the months, and the years would pass, but no one would ever want her. And after a while, the eagerness would leave her face, and the hope in her little heart would die. What kind of a person would she grow up to be? It certainly wouldn't be her fault if she turned out as bad as me or even worse. The guilt was all mine, and I'd have to live with it for the rest of my life.

I left the home after six weeks.

Major Griffith and Lieutenant Hopkins both told me that the longer I stayed, the harder it would be to give up my baby.

"You've been a fine resident, Jean," Major Griffith said. "I'm glad we were able to help you, and you can trust us to do the very best we can for your baby."

I trusted them, but what could they do? Only God could perform a miracle and make my baby whole and perfect. I gave Major Griffith Hazel's address, and she said she'd send the final papers there for me to sign. I said good-by to the girls, and we all cried. We didn't expect to see each other ever again, but we had lived together and shared the experience of motherhood, and we'd never forget each other.

The day I left, I gave Elizabeth her bath and her ten o'clock bottle and tucked her snugly in her crib. She dropped off to sleep, beautiful and sweet as an angel. Before I could force myself out of the nursery, I went back three times to look at her. She slept peacefully, knowing only that she was warm and clean and fed. Later, she would realize how life—and her mother—had cheated her. I tore myself away, blinded by tears. I didn't need any photograph of Elizabeth, her beautiful little face would stay with me till the day I died.

Major Griffith drove me to the bus station. I felt queer, being out in public again, looking like any slim young girl. I boarded the bus and stared out of the window all through the trip, amazed by the green trees and the blooming flowers. The year had turned to summer while I'd been shut up in the home.

I'd been paid a small wage for my work in the hospital, so I had enough for my bus fare, with a few dollars left over. I'd written Hazel that I was coming, and she'd got rid of her roommate so I could move in with her.

Hazel was working as a bar girl at Grady's when I got back. She told me that her reputation had got a little too much for our old boss at the drive-in and he'd fired her. She said she'd spoken to her boss at Grady's about me and that I could have a job there if I wanted it. I didn't see what else I could do. Probably my reputation wasn't much better than Hazel's, and I had to eat.

NOTHING SEEMED TO MATTER to me any more. I worked at Grady's from four in the afternoon till midnight. Then I went straight to the apartment and stayed there. I didn't give the time of day to the guys at Grady's who tried to date me. I'd had enough of men to last me a lifetime.

Hazel kept after me, though. There

wasn't any use moping for a baby I couldn't have, she said. I didn't tell her about Elizabeth's hand. I was afraid she'd be horrified, and I couldn't bear to have anyone feel that way about my precious baby.

Elizabeth was never out of my thoughts for long. I knew she must be in a boarding home, waiting till she was three months old. And where would she go then, my sweet, tiny, helpless Elizabeth? I prayed to God to do what only He could—to find a couple who'd adopt her and love her even though she wasn't perfect. I'd lie awake at night, looking into the darkness, and talking to God. "Don't do it for me, God, but for Elizabeth," I'd whisper. "It doesn't matter what happens to me, but she's Your baby too, isn't she? It's not her fault that her parents are bad and weak."

In the happy days when Daddy was alive, I'd gone to Sunday school. I remembered a Bible text I'd learned, and I'd repeat it, trying to comfort myself with Jesus' words: "Suffer the little children to come unto me, and forbid them not; for of such is the kingdom of God."

When the final relinquishment order came, I put off signing it. I felt that when I wrote my name on the paper, the doors of the State Home for Children would close forever on Elizabeth.

Then came the weekend that changed my life. Hazel begged me to go on a double date with her that Saturday to a cabin at Lake Ossippee. Skip was out of the picture by then, and she was crazy about another fellow, Doug. He'd bring a fellow named Lee for me, and we'd make a weekend of it, she said. I didn't want to go, but I felt that I owed Hazel a lot.

"Okay," I said finally. "But he'd better know what the setup is. I'll drink with him, but I won't party."

Hazel shrugged. "That's up to you, but don't cramp things for Doug and me. We're in love, and we're going to get married. He's already asked me, and—well, you know how it is."

Sure, I knew. I remembered Hazel and Skip behind the closed bedroom door, and Vince and me in the living room, and a sick disgust burned inside me. Love! Girls like Hazel and me didn't know the meaning of the word. I didn't say anything, though. I just packed my overnight bag and followed Hazel out the door. . . .

I soon realized that if I was going to stick out the weekend, I'd have to drink a lot. My date was hard drinking and thought he was a lady killer. I couldn't manage to be civil to him till I'd had a couple of drinks. The boys had rented a furnished cottage. Hazel and I made supper out of cans on the little oil stove, and then we started drinking again.

Along about midnight, we all got the idea it would be funny to take the place apart. We dragged out the stove and the table and chairs and built them up in a pile in the front yard. We roared with laughter, imagining how furious the owner would be.

And all the time, we were drinking. Drink after drink, till the outline of everything swam before my eyes.

Suddenly I realized that Hazel and Doug had disappeared, and Lee was pulling at me, trying to get me down on the porch settee. I don't know what came over me then, but, drunk as I was, I knew I couldn't stand to be with Lee or any other man like him for another minute. He pulled at my dress, and I struck him in the face. When he drew back, I jerked free and ran into the cottage. I stumbled through the darkness and found a door. I slammed it and locked it behind me. Then I sank to the floor.

Dimly I heard Lee raging through the cottage, calling my name, cursing and threatening. He hammered on the door, but I kept quiet and he went away. I guess I passed out then.

When I came to, it was morning, and I found that I'd locked myself in the bathroom. I struggled to my feet and splashed cold water over my face. My stomach was churning, and my knees kept giving way. Finally, though, I felt strong enough to unlock the door and go out into the main room. Hazel and Doug were nowhere in sight, and I supposed they were behind the closed door of the bunk room. Lee was snoring on the couch.

I tiptoed around him and went out on the porch. The sun was coming up, and the dawn air was the freshest, sweetest thing I'd ever smelled. It was clean and pure and good—everything I wasn't. I was still shaky. I wound my arms around the porch pillar and stood that way for a long time, watching the sunrise and suffering the blackest despair a human being can know.

I realized that there wasn't enough liquor in the world to drown the guilt and the remorse that tortured me. In my fear, I had maimed my baby, and in my weakness, I had rejected her. I couldn't face a lifetime with that bur-

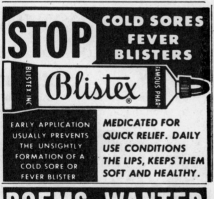

den on my soul. I had to do something to help Elizabeth, or I had to kill myself. There wasn't any other way.

I walked down the dirt road to the highway and hitched a ride with a farmer, going in to market. He was a nice old man, and he didn't ask any questions. He just wanted to know where I was going. And without thinking, I gave him Mom's address. He let me out two blocks away from my home.

My home? I stood on the corner with an empty feeling in my heart. It hadn't really been my home for so many years. What would they say when I told them and asked for their help—Mom, and Max, and Bobby. I wouldn't have done it for myself, but for my baby there wasn't any humiliation that was too much for me to endure.

I opened the door and walked in. They were eating breakfast. When they saw me, their faces went blank for an instant, and then filled with emotion. Mom tipped over her chair and ran to me. She had her arms tight around me, while Bobby tried to hug me and Max stood by uncertainly.

"Oh, Jean, Jean!" Mom sobbed. "You don't know how I've missed you. How I've prayed you'd come home!"

But I did know. I understood, because I was a mother too. I let Mom fix me breakfast before I told them my story—about Vince and the Home and Elizabeth.

I choked up at the last. "She's so sweet and beautiful except for her hand," I pleaded. "It's—it's not fair to her. She'll spend her life in an institution—"

I was crying so hard I couldn't say any more. Mom was staring at me, her face twisted with sorrow and pity. I'll always remember that Max spoke first. His voice was rough, as always, but to me he sounded like an angel speaking.

"She's not going to do that," he said. "She needs her mother and she needs her grandparents, and that's your mother and me. We'll get her and bring her home. She belongs with us."

"Oh, Max!" I cried. "Thank you, thank you!" I put out my hand, and he took it in his. His hand felt like a father's, big and warm and strong. I thought, with shame, that this was the first time I'd ever touched Max's hand —the first time I'd gone to him as a daughter.

"I'm—I'm so sorry for everything," I said, looking from Max to Mom. "I was hateful and mean and wild, but I've changed. If you can forgive me—"

Mom was smiling through her tears. "That's what parents are for, dear," she said. "To understand and to forgive."

They were wonderful, good people and their home was full of love. I'd resented their closeness when I was a bitter, mixed-up young girl, but now I saw how precious it was and what it would mean to my baby. I could bring her into a home where she'd be loved and cherished and made to feel wanted. They'd tried to do that for me too, but I hadn't let them.

The next day Max and Mom and I drove to the Salvation Army home. Major Griffith was happy that I could have my baby with me, and she sent Lieutenant Hopkins to the boarding home to bring Elizabeth back. When Lieutenant Hopkins returned, Mom held out her arms eagerly for the baby.

"Grandma's sweet little girl," she crooned. Elizabeth gurgled and waved her arms. Mom caught the pitiful little left arm and held it against her face.

"She's sure a beauty," Max said.

So we brought my baby home, into a family where everyone loved her and wanted her. Those first weeks, the happy tears were never far away as I watched Mom cuddle Elizabeth and saw Bobby hang adoringly over her crib. The day Max brought home a beautiful baby buggy, I broke down and cried in his arms.

I quit my job at Grady's, and soon after that, Hazel married Doug and moved away. I wished her well, but it was a relief to know that the last link with my former life was broken.

To protect Elizabeth, I took Mom's maiden name as my married name and wore a wedding ring. Of course, there was some gossip, but I faced it down, feeling the loving strength of my family behind me. I was anxious to work for my baby; I wanted to make a good future for us both and to prove to Max and Mom that I was no longer the selfish, headstrong teenager who'd caused them so much unhappiness.

I trained for practical nursing, and that's what I'm doing now. It's hard and exhausting work, and sometimes when I leave the bus to walk the two blocks home, I feel I can hardly make it. Then I think of Elizabeth, who's the happiest and sweetest three-year-old in the world, and my steps quicken. As I turn up the walk, she runs to meet me, her face shining with joy.

I pick her up and hold her soft, trusting body close against me, and suddenly I'm not tired at all. She's my reason for living. She's the second chance that God gave me to grow into a good and unselfish human being. And through loving her, I've learned one of His eternal truths: The happiness that we all long for isn't found in self-seeking indulgence and shallow pleasures. The truly happy people are those who live for others.   *The End*

The 1960's

TRUTH IS STRANGER THAN FICTION

Write US MAIL to be BEAUTIFUL

Dieter in Distress

"I have a terrible problem, and I hope that if you print my letter, my parents will change their minds. I am fifteen years old, and about twenty pounds overweight. I have tried over and over to diet, but I just don't have enough will power. Both my parents and my two brothers are overweight, and they just laugh at my dieting attempts and tell me that I'm meant to be fat, that it runs in the family. I read recently about a summer diet camp for teens nearby that sounds wonderful, but my parents won't let me go because they think it would be a waste of money. My weight problem is ruining my social life, and depresses me so much that my school work suffers."
Miss A.McG., Atlanta, Ga.

Contrary to popular belief, being fat does *not* "run in the family." In almost every case, families are overweight because they overeat. A tiny proportion of overweight people do have glandular disturbances, however, so you should have a complete checkup and talk with your family doctor. If at all financially possible, we think the teen diet camp is a wonderful idea. It brings you into contact with girls who have the same problem, and forces you to follow a low-calorie diet. Some girls have returned from camps such as you mentioned looking so wonderful that they've inspired their parents to diet, too.

If your parents are absolutely opposed to the idea of the camp, have your family doctor prescribe a diet for you. Perhaps if you explained the situation to him, he would be willing to tell your parents that losing weight is essential to your health. If your mother won't cooperate by serving well-balanced, low-calorie meals, learn to pass up the gravy and mashed potatoes, and settle for meat and vegetables. Keep carrot sticks, green pepper, cottage cheese in the refrigerator for munching if you get hungry between meals. If you can lose even five pounds, the difference in your looks will inspire you to keep at it.

Don't Be A Square

"My face is an almost perfect square. Can you give me any make-up tricks on how to make it look more oval?"
Mrs. Y.M., Brooklyn, N.Y.

Try one of the new blushers to slim down your jawline. Apply it under the cheekbone and continue down to the jawbone, blending it carefully so that no definite color lines remain. A muted shade is best. Pale pink looks natural with fair coloring, tawny coral with olive skin.

Try a change in your hair style, too. One that swings or waves toward the cheeks on each side usually is flattering. Avoid straight-across bangs or a "square" silhouette.

Eyes Full

"My eyes are brown, and unfortunately, not what you could call large. I've read a lot about eyeshadow and how to apply it, but when I follow instructions my eyes appear even smaller. Why?"
Miss A.T., Oklahoma City, Okla.

There could be two reasons for your dilemma. First of all, are you using eyeliner in addition to eyeshadow? This is a must! Using a dark brown cake or liquid, always draw fairly wide eyelines as close as possible to the lashes. The effect of an almond-shaped eye can be achieved by extending the line a quarter-inch past the outer corner of the eye with an upward tilt.

Secondly, use brown shadow to elongate your eyes, too. But instead of smoothing the shadow over the eyelid only, sweep the color past the outer curve of the eye and blend it up and out toward the brow. Lightly please! This is not an exercise in stage makeup.

To finish, lightly blend pearly shadow above the lid and under the outer curve of the eyebrow. Apply mascara as usual, and you'll be surprised at how much larger and more luminous your eyes will appear.

Beady-Eyed

"Whenever I wear mascara, my lashes stick together. I've tried several different types and brands, so I must be applying it incorrectly. Can you help me?"
Mrs. N.A., Benton Harbor, Mich.

Mascara usually beads and causes eyelashes to stick together when one thick coat is applied. Instead, apply one thin coat, let dry, and apply another thin coat. When lashes are dry, separate them with a clean dry brush. If you powder lashes before and after each coat, you'll find that they look thicker and much more luxurious.

Smiling Through

"I know it sounds silly but I'm afraid to laugh. My teeth are in fairly good condition; at least that's what my dentist tells me when I go for a checkup. But because I can't brush after every meal, I feel self-conscious about my smile. What can I do?"

Mrs. J.D., Boston, Mass.

Of course, you must brush morning and night to have beautiful teeth. But equally important is maintaining healthy gums. Developed by a dentist, a new product, meant for between meal cleansing of the mouth plus instructions for use, is now available by writing Stim-U-Dents, Inc., Dept. TS; Detroit, Michigan 48238.

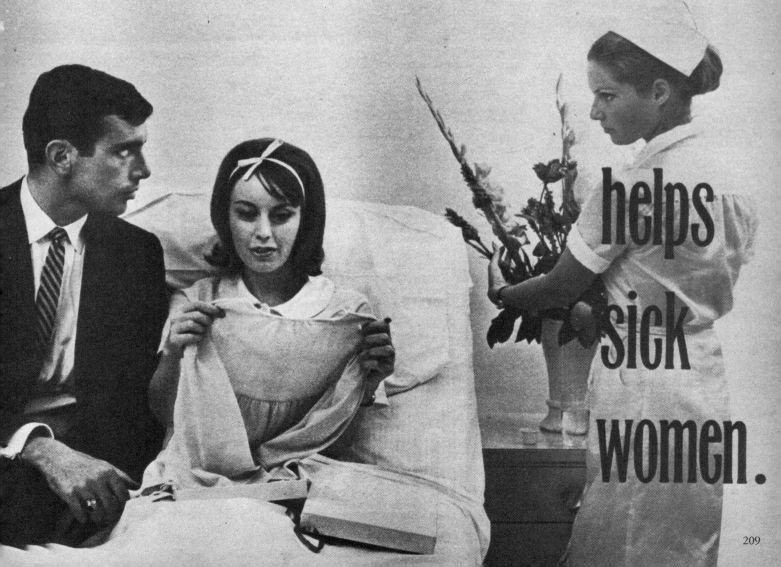

By
day
she

helps
sick
women.

...by night she helps

RESTLESS NURSE

■ It was seven o'clock. The evening visiting hours at the hospital had just begun, and in another thirty minutes I'd be off duty. Suddenly, as I walked down the hall, I heard old Mr. Preston call me. For the past week he'd been asking me to meet him downstairs at eight, so he could drive me home after visiting his wife.

I refused him again tonight. Mr. Preston always stared at me with such an obvious leer that I preferred waiting for the bus in the bitter Chicago wind to riding home with him.

Usually, though, I was very happy to accept a ride. In fact, I often got lifts home from my patients' (Continued on page   )

herself to their men!

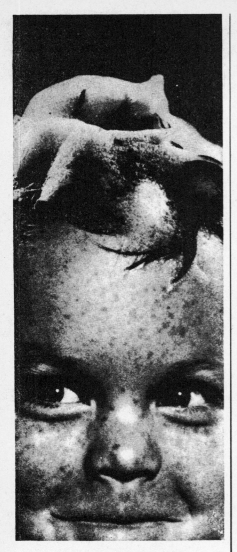

RESTLESS NURSE

husbands. Sometimes we even had cocktails and dinner on the way. But things were aways kept cool and casual, never getting out of hand, because I could spot the troublemakers, like Mr. Preston, ahead of time.

Maybe I accepted more ride offers, more offers for dinner or cocktails, than any of the other nurses assigned to our ward simply because I was the loneliest. Anyway, unless I had to rush home, I enjoyed a nice dinner and some pleasant conversation. Besides, lots of these married men—the husbands of my patients —probably had interesting and attractive friends who weren't married. And I was always hoping that one fine night one of my "dates" would suddenly realize that a friend of his would go for me in a big way. That's what I was really looking for: somebody eligible to fall in love with—somebody who'd love me, too, and want to marry me. So far, my restless search hadn't led to much—but that didn't mean it couldn't happen, did it?

Now, as I hurried down to the nurses' station desk to make sure all my patients had been given their after-dinner medication, I remembered it was freezing outside. But before I had much time to worry about catching my death of cold at the bus stop, I glanced at room ten-fourteen. That was Mrs. Anderson's room. She was a rheumatic heart patient. I always enjoyed chatting with her, and now I suddenly wondered if her husband would be going north—my way. Although I often visited Mrs. Anderson when I had a spare moment, I'd only seen her husband a couple of times. He was a tall, broad-shouldered man with dark hair and warm, intense eyes.

When I entered her room, Ellen Anderson was alone, sitting up in bed, a hairbrush in one hand, a pretty, blue satin ribbon in the other. She looked up at me briefly, then sank back on the pillow, her face pale. A few years older than me, she was in her late twenties— a frail, slender, attractive woman who looked like an angel when she smiled.

"I just can't do it," she said, her lovely eyes misting with tears. "Would you help me, Julie? It ought to be so darned simple—brushing one's hair—"

"Hold still," I told her, feeling a sulden lurch of professional worry because she was so pale. "You'll be getting your strength back before long," I added quietly. "Did you have your shot today?"

As she nodded, I began brushing her soft brown hair.

"I wanted to look especialy pretty tonight. Mike got a promotion at work, and we were going to celebrate." She smiled thinly. "But I'm just—so tired. I'm afraid I really don't feel much like celebrating."

While fixing her hair, I tried to cheer her up. Actually, she was making progress, though her doctor was still a little concerned about her blood count, and she had bad days—like today—when even the effort of brushing her hair seemed to exhaust her.

I told her a few jokes that were going around the ward, and finally she began to perk up a little.

"I guess I've had the blues," she said. "Thanks for helping me, Julie."

"Compliments of the house," I replied

lightly, looking at my watch. "Well, your husband should be here at any moment, and it's time I started scouting around to see if I can get a ride home."

Michael Anderson was just getting off the elevator when I headed for the nurses' lounge, where my locker was. He nodded and smiled, then walked quickly toward his wife's room.

I was wearing my warm winter cape, awhile later, when I passed ten-fourteen on my way to check out. Seeing me, Ellen called my name. She'd put on some lipstick since I'd left her.

"Hey, aren't you the glamour girl!" I said from the doorway, pretending not to notice how tired she looked. "Well— I'm off now. It's getting late."

"Wait," she urged, motioning me inside. "Look, Julie—Mike can run you home. Can't you, darling?"

"I'll be glad to," Michael Anderson said cheerfully. "If you're ready, we can start right now."

I remembered then that this visit was supposed to be a celebration, and he'd just barely gotten here. "Well, thanks," I said uncertainly, "but I still have to sign out and all . . . so why don't you finish your visit, Mr. Anderson? I'll wait downstairs."

"Please—" Ellen said, smiling tiredly at both of us, "please go ahead, you two. I hate to admit this, but I'm awfully depressing company right now. I just want to turn off the light and get some rest."

"I'll try to sneak in early tomorrow to make up for tonight," Michael Anderson said. He kissed his wife's pale cheek, then gently tucked the covers around her.

In the hall, the tall man's face changed. Like many hospital visitors, he'd appeared to be in a good mood at his wife's side. Now he suddenly seemed grim.

"Is Ellen really getting better?" he asked bluntly. "I—I didn't expect to find her like this tonight—as though just talking was an effort."

"I know," I said gently. "But you have to understand that she's going to feel weak and tired a good deal of the time, until we get her straightened out. But all in all, I'd say she's coming along nicely."

He nodded, and I had the impression my words made him feel better.

When we got outside, I shuddered with the cold. We ran to the hospital parking lot, turning our faces away from the rough wind. Once I slipped on some ice and felt Michael's arm go around me. For some reason, I started to laugh at my own clumsiness, and when we finally got to the car, I felt strangely exhilarated.

At first, we talked about the weather, then some more about Michael's wife. He told me how much his two small sons missed their mother even though they'd more or less gotten used to the babysitter who was temporarily taking her place.

Finally, when Michael stopped for a red light near the loop, he turned to me, his intense eyes strangely lonely. "Would you—would you let me buy you dinner, Julie? Frankly I just don't want to go home to an evening of TV. I—I need somebody to talk to. I know I'm being selfish, imposing on you—but—*would* you eat with me?" He smiled wryly. "I guess this is an old story to you—the lonely husband wanting some female companionship. But there are no strings, Julie. And I *do* know a place—Vito's—that has the best darned charcoal-broiled steaks you ever tasted!"

What he didn't know was that I'd already decided to let him buy me dinner if he wanted to. It always secretly amused me when these lonely husbands expected me to be afraid of them. If only

Michael knew how innocent most of my date offers were!

I'm not quite sure when I began to realize *this* date was different, though. I only know that before we'd finished our cocktails, I felt very strongly attracted to Michael.

It was more than his good looks that appealed to me. There was a rugged loneliness about him that touched my heart as it had never been touched before. I knew instinctively the kind of marriage he and Ellen must have, with her never being completely well. When he told me how much he loved the outdoors, and that he planned to take his two little boys on a camping trip that summer—if he could get someone to look after Ellen at home—I thought how sad it was for him that she couldn't go.

Later, when Michael asked me to dance, I began to think how wonderful it must be to have a husband like this, so big and strong and masculine, and yet so infinitely kind and gentle.

When he drove me home, I began to wonder if he was under the same magnetic spell I was. If he was, he certainly didn't show it. He was polite and good-humored as he walked me to my apartment house. He touched my hand briefly, thanked me for a lovely evening, and then he was gone.

I thought about Michael most of the night, promising myself never to accept another ride home from him. By the next morning, he was still on my mind. "Snap out of it, you nut!" I told myself, realizing I was acting like a silly, impressionable schoolgirl. Wouldn't Michael laugh if he knew I'd been so shaken up by our casual dinner date! I simply *had* to stop thinking about him!

Yet, when I saw him step out of the elevator that day, my heart gave a terrific lurch. He was carrying a huge bouquet in one hand and a gift-wrapped package under his arm. For a wild second I wished I could trade places with Ellen Anderson, and that Michael was coming to see me, to bend down and kiss my cheek as I'd seen him kiss hers. True to his word, he'd come early today—a little after five—probably planning to buy something for himself at the snack bar and have supper with her. Though hospital regulations didn't allow visitors at five, all the nurses turned a blind eye.

As I went into Ellen's room a little later, carrying a small medication tray, she was happily untying the gift-wrapped box I'd glimpsed under Michael's arm. The flowers were on the night table. Trying to control my emotions, I put down my tray and arranged the lovely roses in a vase while Ellen took a beautiful blue bed jacket out of the box. Then Michael very tenderly kissed her, and a big lump rose in my throat.

After Ellen took the pill I gave her, she grinned at me. "Your chauffeur came here early tonight, Julie. So you can forget about the bus again."

I forced a bright, impersonal smile. "You're looking very chipper this evening," I told her. "And I'm sure your husband plans to take advantage of it until the very last minute! Right, Mr. Anderson?"

"Oh, but Mike and I still have lots of time together before you get off duty, Julie!" she protested. "I'm sure he'll be glad to drive you. I've just been telling him how wonderful you've been to me. How you always drop by and cheer me

up when I'm feeling sorry for myself. And, Julie—please remind Mike to stop by the gift shop downstairs and buy me some new ribbon for my hair. Look—see how well I managed to fix it myself, today!"

"It looks wonderful," I said, realizing I sounded stilted. I carefully kept my face turned away from her as I adjusted the pillows on her bed. No need to make a scene, I thought. Later I'll tell him I don't want a ride. But I don't have to make an issue of it right now.

Michael was waiting for me near the elevators shortly after seven-thirty, when I'd already checked out.

"I want to ask you a favor," he said, looking down at me with those deep, fascinating eyes.

"I'm sorry, but I can't—"

"I want to buy a nightgown for Ellen. Since you're supposed to remind me to pick up some hair ribbon anyway—I thought you wouldn't mind helping me choose something you think she'll like. It's for her birthday tomorrow, so it has to be very special."

I couldn't refuse him. It seemed so innocent—the two of us going down to the main floor together, looking at the pretty things in the gift shop, and finally choosing a delicate, peach pleated nylon nightie, with some matching ribbon for Ellen's hair. I kept telling myself I'd insist on taking the bus home, once he had his package gift-wrapped, but somehow, when he took my arm and guided me toward the door, the words stuck in my throat. And when we got outside, I let him lead me to the car. He slid in beside me, reaching across me to flick on the heater, and suddenly an electric current seemed to pass between us.

Halfway to my house, Michael said, "I don't have to get home this early. The kids will be asleep by now. I've already eaten—but you haven't. Let me buy you another steak."

Sitting across the candle-lit table from Michael that evening, my conversation sounded forced. He wasn't very relaxed, either, and every now and then, his eyes would meet and hold mine until I had to look away, my breathing shallow and uneven.

We were silent on the ride to my house.

"I—I'd better go on in," I said when we got there. "It's late."

Slowly Michael turned to me. "You might as well know, Julie—I planned this evening," he confessed guiltily. "I told the sitter I'd stay late again." He sighed. "What I'm trying to say is—I wanted to be with you tonight." He moved close to me then and drew me into his arms.

"Julie," he said softly, "you're so warm, so lovely."

His kiss was just as wonderful as I'd known it would be. Wild and deep and full of want. For a little while, I completely forgot everything but the thrill of his closeness, the beating of his heart against mine. I'm in love with this man! I thought wildly. In love, in love, in love. . . .

I slept very little again that night. I tried to tell myself that I had no business getting involved with a patient's husband. Besides, I knew all about the emotional and physical frustrations of a man with a sick wife. Wasn't Michael—like the husbands I usually avoided—just seeking someone to comfort him temporarily, to ease his fears and loneliness only until his wife came home? Wasn't it very unlikely that he had any kind of deep feeling for me? Once and for all, I promised myself I wouldn't see him again. I would even avoid his wife as much as I could

It was the only way to pull myself back to sanity.

I succeeded fairly well for awhile. Then, two weeks after Michael kissed me, I ran into him. I'd just gotten off duty and had decided to have supper in the hospital cafeteria. As soon as I walked into the large room, I saw him sitting at a corner table, drinking coffee.

He stood up the moment he spotted me, and I had no choice but to walk over to him.

"Julie," he said, looking pleased. "I was beginning to think maybe you'd quit your job here. Can I get something for you?"

I nodded wearily. All right, I thought, I tried to avoid him. I really did. And now here he is again! Maybe if I just let this work itself out, I'll realize it's only a silly crush!

He bought us both sandwiches and sat down, putting his hand over mine. "I've nearly been crazy," he said thickly. "Up there in Ellen's room, trying to talk to her, and all the time waiting for you." His fingers tightened on mine. "I've missed you terribly."

Several minutes later, inside his car, I kissed him as naturally as if I had the right to be in love with him.

Beginning the next day, we began to follow a kind of pattern. Michael took a late lunch hour at work, so he could visit Ellen every afternoon. In the evening, he came again and stayed until eight. Usually, by five after eight, he'd be downstairs, where I'd be waiting in his car—he'd given me Ellen's key. Then we'd drive around. Often we went to Lake Michigan and parked and clung together, giving each other wild, sweet, hurting kisses.

During these passionate times with Michael I began to believe what I had not dared believe before—that he truly loved me—that I was more to him than just a woman to be with because he was lonesome for his wife. And I knew, too, that before long we wouldn't be able to stop with those wild kisses in his dark car.

On a Friday, after I'd been seeing Michael for several weeks, I was assigned to take Ellen down to Therapy, where she was to work with her hands and walk around a little. She seemed so much better than last month, so bright and happy and talkative, that an immense feeling of relief went through me. Because, if Ellen was improving, what I was doing with her husband somehow didn't seem so wrong—even though I realized we were about to get more serious than ever.

That night, when Michael joined me in the car, he kissed me and said, "Sorry I was a little late. Ellen wanted to know every last detail about the school play the boys were in." He pressed my hand. "Want to go to Vito's for dinner again tonight, honey?"

"I—I thought," I began slowly, "that it might be nice for us to have dinner at—at my place."

I could feel the shock go through him, then the pleasure. He glanced at me briefly and began to drive.

My overheated apartment was stifling when we walked inside. After I took my cape off, I opened one of the living-room windows. Then I fixed us both some drinks and plopped myself down on the floor. Ever since I was a little girl I'd preferred the floor to the most comfortable chair in the world. With a smile Michael sat down next to me.

"It's cold," I said suddenly, feeling a blast of wind. "I'd better shut that darn window again."

Before I could get up, Michael put his arms around me. I started to say some-thing about dinner then, but the words never left my mouth. For, when he kissed me, I forgot about everything except him.

"Oh, my darling," he said, pulling me even closer. I buried my head against his chest and heard the wild pounding of his heart. "Julie, Julie!" He tilted my face upward, his wonderful liquid eyes burning into my very being. "Let me warm you," he whispered, his hand tracing the outlines of my face. "Let me warm you all over, Julie darling. . . ."

He came to my place every night the next week. Some nights, I'd pull away from him and start crying after we made love. Now that I belonged to Michael completely, I loved him more than ever, but I was frightened too. It was as though we were caught in a tidal wave that could sweep us only to disaster.

"I love you," he told me over and over again. "You've got to believe that, Julie. Sure—I still care about Ellen. I can't help it. Don't ask me how I can love both you and her—just believe I do!"

"But where is it all going to end?" I'd ask bleakly. "This—this is something we never should have let happen."

He'd put his face against my breast and cling to me. And once again we'd both be caught up in the overwhelming surge of our emotions, putting the future out of our minds.

And then, on a rainy, gray Monday, when I least expected it, the blow fell. As soon as I came on duty, I checked the medical board. Ellen Anderson was scheduled to go home that Wednesday!

For a moment I felt the world reel around me. Would this be the end for Michael and me? With his wife at home, how could he possibly continue to see me?

"Good news, isn't it?" one of the other nurses said, grinning at me. "We're all so thrilled for Mrs. Anderson. I brought in her breakfast, and she claims that if it wasn't for all the tender, loving care she got from her nurses, she'd still be lying in bed, half dead! Makes you feel as if you're doing something important, doesn't it?"

"Yes," I said, my throat suddenly dry. I turned away quickly and went into the medicine room, pretending to take the morning drug count.

All morning I waited impatiently for the afternoon to begin, and then, I stayed as close to the elevators as I could. Finally I saw Michael get off. "Mr. Anderson? May I speak to you a moment please?" My voice didn't betray me; it sounded professional and calm. "Wonderful news," I said, feeling the tears form. "Your wife will be going home the day after tomorrow."

A look of anguish came into Michael's eyes for the briefest of seconds. "That's—great," he said quietly. "Thank you for telling me." Then, in almost a whisper, "I can't see you tonight, darling. But tomorrow. . . ."

Behind us, my supervisor stood at the door to the medicine room, watching us.

"Yes . . ." I breathed, then turned and walked down the corridor.

The stores were open late Monday nights, so that evening I went shopping, hoping to find a beautiful, perfect dress to wear for Michael. I wanted everything about tomorrow to be perfect—I wanted it to be a night that would make him remember me and keep wanting and needing me, no matter how seldom he could be with me in the future.

The next day Ellen's buzzer seemed to ring constantly. She kept wanting all the nurses to come in so she could thank us. Each time I saw her, she thanked me for having helped her get well.

Finally I told her I was supposed to assist one of the staff doctors on his ward rounds. Actually I'd lied, but I was in a hurry to finish my regular duties, so I could take my time getting dressed for my date with Michael.

After I changed, I couldn't help admiring the lovely, mint green wool dress I'd finally chosen the evening before. It was just snug enough to make me look seductive, without seeming cheap.

I was heading for the elevators and then the parking lot and Michael's car when Miss Hastings, my supervisor, stopped me.

"I didn't get the medication tray and glass back from ten-fourteen, Julie. Did Mrs. Anderson take her usual pill?"

I felt my face flush in embarrassment. "I—I'm sorry," I stuttered. "I guess I forgot to bring back the empty glass and tray."

Her gray eyebrows went up. "I'm surprised at you, Julie. Please get them before you leave the floor."

I would rather have taken a beating than go down to that room now, but I had no choice.

I could hear Michael talking to Ellen before I tapped at the door. He was saying something about having to leave right away. When he turned his head and saw me, he looked startled for a moment. Then his eyes flicked quicky over me, as if in approval at what they saw.

"I'm sorry," I said. "I forgot to take the tray back, Mrs. Anderson."

"I've never seen you all dressed up," she said, looking from Michael to me, in a way that set me trembling. "I'll bet you have some kind of a special date tonight. You look very pretty."

"Thank you." My heart was beating so hard that I wondered she couldn't hear it. "I—I do have a date—and I don't want to be late so . . . if you'll excuse me, I'll see you tomorrow, for the send-off." And before she could say anything else, I bolted out of the room. Then, as I hurried down the hall, I thought I heard her ask Michael not to leave so soon.

I'd been sitting in his car for more than twenty minutes when I saw him hurrying toward me. He put his arms around me and kissed me as soon as he got inside. "I'm sorry," he said, his breath warm against my cheek. "Ellen gave me kind of a hard time. Maybe—maybe I shouldn't be seeing you tonight—but I had to. It's all we'll have for awhile—I guess you know that." He kissed me again, almost desperately. "Where would you like to go darling?" he whispered then.

There was only one place we both wanted to go—my apartment. We wanted to be as close as possible tonight, to shut out the unhappiness that lay ahead for both of us.

It was a wonderful night. If I had any other thoughts or feelings beyond the fact that I was in love with Michael, I didn't let them come through. When he had to leave, at last, I hung my pretty green dress way back in my closet, tears sliding down my cheeks. I'll never be able to wear this dress again, I thought. I'll never even be able to look at it again. I crawled into bed then, and cried myself to sleep.

When the phone rang, it was still dark. "Hello—" I said foggily.

"Sorry to wake you, Julie," my supervisor's voice said briskly. "Can you come in on extra duty? We're terribly short-handed here—and we've had seven emergency admissions, plus a bad relapse case."

"Be there," I said. Then, for some reason, a finger of fear touched my heart. "Did you say—'relapse?' Everybody

REMEMBERING A SPECIAL FRIEND

As I look back on childhood days,
I find that I recall
A special little friend I had
And liked the best of all.

We played together every day.
We ate together, too.
And shared our toys and picture books
Like best friends always do.

I trusted her with secrets
And poured into her ear
The private thoughts nobody else
Was privileged to hear.

But when I started growing up,
She disappeared one day.
She didn't even say good-bye . . .
Just quietly slipped away.

You see, this special little friend
Who meant so much to me
Was someone I'd created
In a childish fantasy.

And once my need of her was gone,
I guess somehow she knew
The make-believe was over—
So our friendship ended, too.

But I never quite forgot her,
And every now and then
Remembering my childhood
Makes her very real again!

by Alice E. Chase

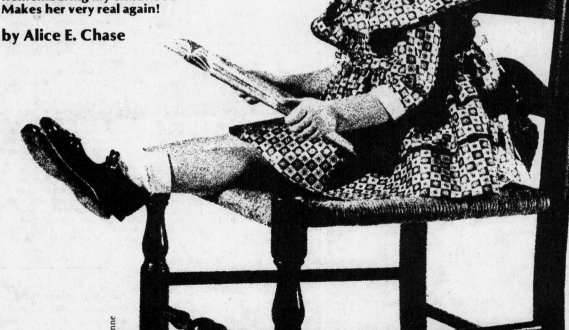

Vivienne

215

seemed to be fine when I went off duty."

"I don't understand it either. Mrs. Anderson's supposed to go home today. Her doctor has been here most of the night—even he doesn't know what caused it. Look—hurry along, will you?"

"Yes," I said faintly, and hung up. For a few seconds I just sat there, holding on to the edge of my bed, trying to keep my teeth from chattering. But all the while I thought, *I know—I know what caused her to have that relapse! She must have found out about Michael and me!*

The ward was a beehive of activity when I got there, and I was put on desk duty, trying to find space in other hospitals for three of the emergency cases we had no room for. Between calls, I watched the door to Ellen's room. I'd heard one of the other nurses say that her husband had finally been reached at his home, and he was with the doctor now.

A shudder went through me. They'd probably been trying to reach him when he was at my place! I tried not to think that Ellen might be dying. All I could do was pray and go about my job.

Around six-thirty, shortly before the day shift began, Ellen's doctor came to the desk, looking at me tiredly.

"Mrs. Anderson . . . how—how is she?" I faltered.

"She won't talk to any of us. Something has upset her—started her heart racing, started up all the old pain again. But I'm dammed if I know what? She seemed fine yesterday." Suddenly his eyes narrowed. "Maybe you could help," he said.

My breath caught in my throat. "I couldn't do anything. If she won't talk to anybody else, I'm sure she won't want to see me."

"But she's always been particularly fond of you. She just might talk to you, give us some clue. It's worth a try, anyway. Will you go in and see her, Julie?"

As a woman—a woman in love with Ellen's husband—I wanted to turn and run the other way. But as a nurse, I knew I had to do as the doctor asked.

Ellen Anderson lay with her face turned toward the wall. When I went to her bedside, she made no sign that she knew I was there. "Mrs. Anderson . . ." I said softly. "It's Julie—I thought maybe there was something I could do for you." Slowly her pale, stricken face turned.

"I'm sorry you're not feeling well, Mrs. Anderson," I continued, struggling to find the right words. "We're all sorry. You were supposed to go home today, you know. And frankly we need all the beds we can get around here—we've got three poor gals bedded down in the hall."

She closed her eyes briefly. When she opened them, they were misted with tears. "I'm sorry for those women who need beds," she said softly. "I—I just wish I could die and then my bed would be—"

"All right," I broke in. "That's enough of that kind of talk!" I touched her cold hand. "What's bothering you, Ellen? Won't you let me help you?"

Her sad, accusing eyes looked into mine. "Help me?" she said. "That's pretty funny, considering how you've been helping yourself to my husband all these weeks! I—I guess I suspected it almost from the first. Yet I couldn't really let myself believe it. Not until last night." Her mouth quivered. "You looked so—beautiful. So strong and beautiful and full of life. And Michael—I saw how his eyes were all but eating you up. He—he didn't keep you waiting long, either, did he? What could I possibly offer to keep him here?"

Guilt washed over me in sickening waves. When I saw the pain and utter despair in Ellen's eyes, I realized how selfish Michael and I had been. We'd thought only of *our* love, *our* feelings, *our* needs. And each time we'd made love, we had chipped away at Ellen's heart and soul, until now she wanted only to die.

I took a deep, determined breath. "Ellen!" I cried. "How could you even think such ridiculous nonsense? Your husband adores you, and you know it! As far as he's concerned, I'm just a nurse he's counting on to take the best possible care of *you!*"

"I don't want any more lies, Julie. After last night, I know exactly where I stand. And now—well—it doesn't matter. I don't care about anything any more."

"But you're absolutely wrong!" I said, and the lie rolled smoothly off my frightened lips. "I'm *nothing* to your husband—and, believe me, he's nothing to me!" When I saw her eyes deepen with what might have been doubt or hope, I hurried on. "Sure, he's been kind enough to drive me home a few times—but only because *you* asked him to! I—I haven't even accepted a ride from him lately. In fact, I'm going with a doctor now. He's working here at the hospital and I—I'm very much in love with him. *He* was my special date last night. I rushed off because he was waiting for me. I—I'm going to be getting a ring before very long." I added this last as a final clincher.

Her eyes widened. "A doctor? You mean you're going to marry a doctor? Oh, Julie, how wonderful! And how awful you must think I am. Oh, my dear, please try to forgive me."

I could see the color returning to her pale face. "There's nothing to forgive," I said, almost faint with relief. "Just get well and—"

At that precise moment, when I was positive I'd patched things up, Michael came into the room and ruined everything. Half-crazed with worry, he brushed past me with hardly a glance. In two giant steps he was at Ellen's side, leaning over her. "I've been glued to the phone, honey, tracking down another heart specialist to come in on consultation—"

Ellen clung to him like a child. "There's no need of that, Mike." She smiled at him. "Oh, darling, I've been such a silly fool! Last night I thought—" And she glanced at me. "I thought you were Julie's date—and that—that you'd been seeing her a lot—that—you and she were lovers! I even convinced myself that maybe you wanted me to die so you could—"

Even from where I stood, I could sense the sudden panic in Michael. He tried to smile at Ellen, but it was more a white-lipped grimace, full of unmistakable guilt. "I've been driving her home," he said, his voice too loud. "You knew that, honey. Simply giving her a lift home. And that's all I did last night."

Ellen stared at him. "You—drove—her—home—last night?"

"That's right. Matter of fact, I didn't even plan it, but when I saw her standing at the bus stop . . ." His voice trailed off as his wife struggled to sit up.

She looked first at Michael, then at me. "But you told me—" she said, pointing an accusing finger at me, "you told me you had a date with a doctor! He was waiting for you—remember? The man you're supposed to be getting married to!" Her face crumpled. "Lies!" she shouted then. "Why don't you both get your blasted, rotten lies straight?"

The next few moments are a kind of blur to me. But I do remember that Ellen kept on shouting and that she tried to get out of bed, using the supernatural strength that desperate people, no matter how ill, sometimes have. Michael tried to restrain her and so did I. When I touched her, though, she flung out her arm to hit me, and the water pitcher went smashing to the floor. Before Michael could stop her, she'd gotten one foot out of bed and cut herself. Luckily, it wasn't a deep cut, but her shouting grew louder and louder.

By the time another nurse and my supervisor, Miss Hastings, got there, Ellen was hysterical, incoherently babbling that I'd stolen her husband, that all she wanted was to die.

I'll always remember the accusing look Miss Hastings gave me as she ordered a restraining jacket for Ellen. I knew what she was thinking. And it was true. I had done an unforgivable thing—and if this woman died, I'd be no better than a murderess!

No one tried to stop me as I left the hospital. And of course I knew I wouldn't even be allowed the dignity of resigning from my job. I'd get only what I deserved —I'd be fired. But what happened to me didn't matter. All I could think about was Ellen. "God, don't let her die," I kept praying over and over. "Punish me any way you see fit, but let her live!"

Michael came to see me the next day, just a few minutes after my supervisor called to tell me I needn't report back for duty any more. He looked haggard and beaten, and he needed a shave badly.

"I—I just came by to tell you Ellen's going to be okay," he said, avoiding my eyes. "And to let you know how sorry I am that you lost your job. It's all my fault—the whole lousy mess is my fault!"

I shook my head. "I'm just as much to blame, Michael. Maybe even more so. You were vulnerable—and I knew it. I knew what was happening between us in time to have stopped it, but I didn't. I just hope you can somehow make Ellen forget, because I know you really love her."

"I'm going to try, Julie," he said huskily. "But I can't help worrying about you. I know you've lost your job. What—what will you do now?"

I shrugged. "I've always wanted to see California. I'm sure I could get into some hospital out there. And right now the smog might agree with me." I smiled at him. "Good-bye, Michael. Thanks for stopping by."

That's the way it ended, with his shaking my hand and walking out of my life.

It's behind me now, all the shame and the misery I suffered and caused Michael to suffer because of my affair with him. It's not going to help to dwell on it, so I'm trying to forget. But the one thing I'll always remember is the bitter lesson I learned at such great cost to a woman who had shown me nothing but kindness. Never again will my restless search for love allow me to so much as *look* at another married man. In fact, I've given up searching, period. Instead, I'm going to simply work—and wait. Maybe, when I've proven myself worthy, a very special guy, who just might be searching for a very special girl to marry, will find *me!*

THE END

"To let friendship die away by negligence and silence, is certainly not wise. It is voluntarily to throw away one of the greatest comforts of this weary pilgrimage."

—JOHNSON

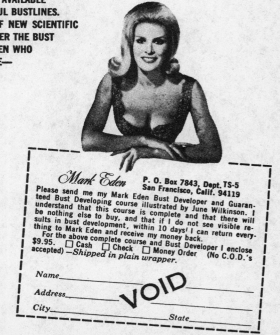

All day I'd been trying to ignore my baby's cries. I had tried to convince myself he was all right, that I needed a coat more than he needed a doctor—

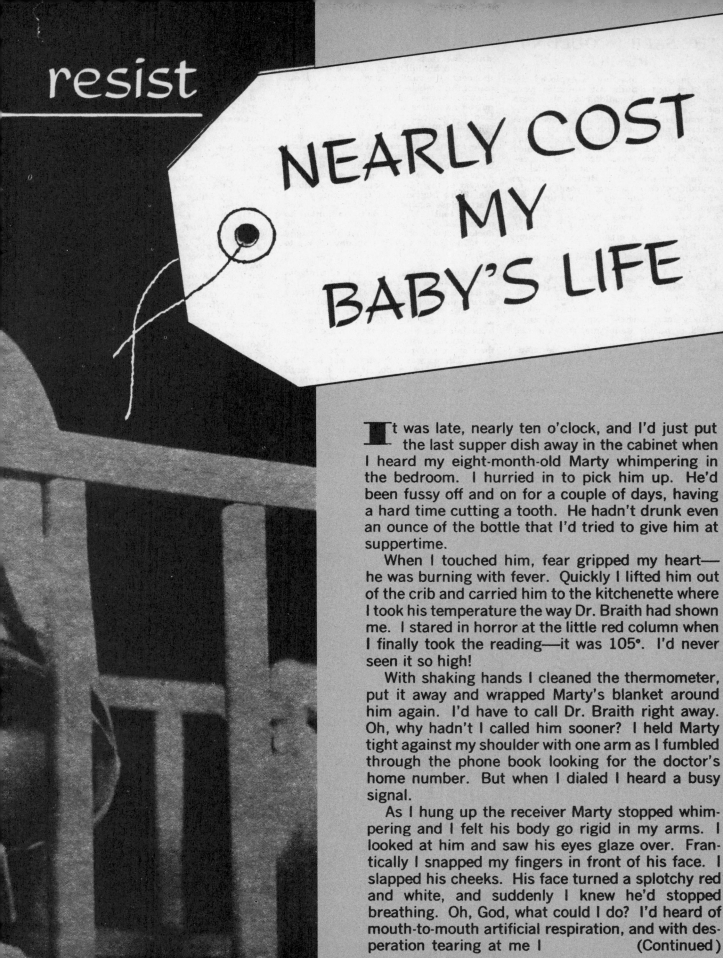

resist

NEARLY COST MY BABY'S LIFE

It was late, nearly ten o'clock, and I'd just put the last supper dish away in the cabinet when I heard my eight-month-old Marty whimpering in the bedroom. I hurried in to pick him up. He'd been fussy off and on for a couple of days, having a hard time cutting a tooth. He hadn't drunk even an ounce of the bottle that I'd tried to give him at suppertime.

When I touched him, fear gripped my heart—he was burning with fever. Quickly I lifted him out of the crib and carried him to the kitchenette where I took his temperature the way Dr. Braith had shown me. I stared in horror at the little red column when I finally took the reading—it was 105°. I'd never seen it so high!

With shaking hands I cleaned the thermometer, put it away and wrapped Marty's blanket around him again. I'd have to call Dr. Braith right away. Oh, why hadn't I called him sooner? I held Marty tight against my shoulder with one arm as I fumbled through the phone book looking for the doctor's home number. But when I dialed I heard a busy signal.

As I hung up the receiver Marty stopped whimpering and I felt his body go rigid in my arms. I looked at him and saw his eyes glaze over. Frantically I snapped my fingers in front of his face. I slapped his cheeks. His face turned a splotchy red and white, and suddenly I knew he'd stopped breathing. Oh, God, what could I do? I'd heard of mouth-to-mouth artificial respiration, and with desperation tearing at me I (Continued)

THE SALE I COULDN'T RESIST

laid him down. My fingers explored the little jaw, the mouth. His muscles were clenched so tight I couldn't get his mouth open.

I snatched him up into my arms again and cried out in anguish when I felt the stiffness of him unyielding against my breast. Oh, God, was he dying? I stumbled back to the telephone, picked up the receiver again and stared at the dial. I couldn't remember Dr. Braith's number; I couldn't even remember George's at the service station. One word leaped up at me from the dial—Operator. I was shaking so it seemed forever before I got my finger in the hole and pulled it around. Two rings, then a crisp voice, "Operator. May I help you?"

"My baby's dying!" I wailed hysterically. "Please help me!"

I heard her voice come sharply back at me. "Give me your name, please."

"Elizabeth Brewster," I gasped.

"Where do you live?" she demanded.

"Sixty-four, Garfield Avenue." My knees started to buckle under me, and I leaned against the wall.

"Mrs. Brewster?" the voice came snapping over the wire. "Mrs. Brewster?"

"Yes?" I whispered.

"I'm sending an ambulance at once. I'll have your doctor meet you at the hospital. Give me his name."

"Dr. Braith," I told her as an overwhelming rush of guilt beat against me. If I'd paid his bill today instead of buying the coat, I wouldn't have worried about calling him when Marty got sick. And I'd known he was sick. I was only trying to put off admitting it, blaming it on a tooth. Had I sacrificed my baby's life for that coat I'd wanted so badly?

The operator's voice cut through the terrible aching remorse that was suffocating me. "Help is coming, Mrs. Brewster." I heard a click, and then the hum of the dead wire. Those next few minutes were the longest of my life. I paced up and down the room, hugging the frighteningly still Marty close against me. Why had I been such a fool? Why hadn't I admitted to myself Marty was sick, and called the doctor? It was that coat, that blue shaggy coat I'd bought with the money meant to pay Dr. Braith's bill.

The whole day had been sort of a nightmare. I'd had to drag myself out of bed to fix George's breakfast. Marty had fussed during the night and I was up and down with him. When George left for his job at Olsen's Service Station, I'd tumbled back into bed to catch forty more winks.

It was late when I woke up, and from then on it was rush, rush the rest of the day. There was laundry, ironing, the breakfast dishes to do. It was the tenth of the month and I had to get downtown and pay the bills, and on top of it all

Marty wanted to be held all the time.

Finally at two-thirty I dropped everything and called Mom on the phone. "Can I leave Marty with you awhile this afternoon?" I asked her. "I've got to go to town, but he's fussy and needs a nap, and I don't want to drag him along."

Usually I took Marty with me, partly because he enjoyed an outing, and partly because George always insisted I pay Mom when I left Marty with her. Mom made her living running a day nursery. "It's only fair," George insisted. "She needs the money as much as we do." That was true enough. Mom had just barely managed all these years since Dad died. The only thing was, I hardly ever had extra money. I was always juggling the budget trying to keep up with the bills.

I took the last bottle out of the refrigerator and tucked it among the diapers in Marty's diaper bag. I'd have to make formula the very minute I got back from town. It was only two blocks from our small apartment to Mom's little house, then eight blocks more to town. George had arranged the bills and the money for me in order; first the water bill, then across the street to the telephone company, then around the corner to the gas company.

I made the rounds and finally stood on the corner of Seward and Park Place. A sign on a building gave the time and temperature—five o'clock; fifteen degrees. I shivered in my thin car coat as I waited for the light to change. I had one more errand to do—go up to Dr. Braith's office in the bank building and pay him the thirty dollars with his bill in my purse.

George had been so excited when he counted out the money that morning. "This does it, Elizabeth," he'd crowed. "After you pay Dr. Braith today, we have only a couple of more car payments and then we'll be square with the world!" Remembering made me shiver again. George thought we would be square with the world. The truth was I still had two payments left on the baby furniture, and I'd only paid five dollars down on the cricket rocker. I'd been juggling the household allowance for months trying to catch up.

The trouble was, George hated to be in debt. He'd wanted us to wait to get married until he finished paying for his car, but we were so breathlessly in love it was easy to talk him out of it. At the time, I was taking the business course at Babylon High, I would graduate in a month, and I convinced him that with me working we could pay the car off in half the time and even put away some. Only of course it didn't work that way. We got married late in May, I immediately got pregnant, and from then on it seemed we never could get caught up with the bills.

When the light turned green I started briskly across the street. Paying Dr. Braith would be sort of an event. Looking back on my year and a half of marriage, I couldn't remember when we didn't owe him. It got so every time I walked in the office I'd get embarrassed wondering what the nurse thought. But with the car payments, the hospital bill, the baby furniture, and the times Marty got sick and had to have penicillin, plus the special formula he needed, well, I was always behind.

Right next to the bank building is Roger's Department Store. As I walked past, a sign in the window caught my eye—Sale! I stopped a moment. Marty's last pair of corduroy crawlers were getting snug. With luck maybe I could pick up a pair on sale. I pushed open the swinging door and felt the welcome warmth. I sort of loved this place—ever since I could remember Mom and I had done our shopping here. We were terribly poor after Dad died and the money Mom made from the day nursery didn't stretch very far. We'd come into Roger's, pick out the things we needed and put them on the extended

"Now pull your top up!"

BOB GUSTAFSON

charge plan. Then we'd save our pennies and faithfully make the payments. I guess we always owed someone; Roger's, the grocery store, or whatever. It was the only way of life I knew. Maybe that was why I couldn't understand why it bothered George so much to be in debt.

There weren't any crawlers left in Marty's size, but as I started for the door another sign in the lady's department caught my eye—Coat Sale! I'd planned to make my thin car coat do for this year —still, it couldn't hurt to just look. But I shouldn't have, because right there, hanging on the front rack, was the loveliest coat I've ever seen, just what I'd wanted all my life.

It was a heavenly blue color, and the fabric was rich and shaggy. It was marked down from fifty dollars, just half price. Blue was the color I loved, it went with my blond hair and matched my eyes. The coat fit like it was made for me and before I really stopped to think, I'd pulled out my billfold and bought it—with twenty-five of Dr. Braith's thirty dollars.

As I counted out the bills my mind was already busy juggling accounts. I could tell George the coat cost a bit less than it did, and I could make a payment on the cricket rocker with the extra five dollars. If I waited a few days before I showed him the coat he wouldn't realize I hadn't paid the doctor and I could tell him I'd paid for it mostly out of my household allowance, and that's what I'd scrounge from to pay the doctor next month. It would all come out the same and I needed the coat so badly.

By the time I stopped at the furniture store and made the payment on the rocker it was nearly five-thirty. I was out of breath from hurrying when I finally got to Mom's house. Marty had just awakened from a nap and was fussing mightily. I'd wanted to show Mom the coat, but there wasn't time. George would be home right after six, and he liked to have supper on the table.

Mom helped me get Marty into his cap and jacket. Her worn hands caressed his forehead. "I think he's running a fever, Elizabeth," she said.

I touched his cheek with the back of my hand. He was warm. "I think it's a tooth cutting that's bothering him," I told Mom. "But I'll check his temperature as soon as I get him home."

"I wish you would," Mom said. "It worries me."

I headed for the door. Mom was such a worry wart! I remembered how she'd worried when I married George. She thought I was too young. I was only seventeen, still a baby, according to Mom. It wasn't that she didn't like George, she did. He was nearly twenty-one and had a steady job. But she was afraid I wouldn't be able to cook, or keep house. Well, I'd showed her. The only times I'd asked for help were times like today.

I heard the six o'clock church chimes when I fumbled the key into the lock and pushed open the downstairs door with my elbow. I dashed up the steps carrying Marty and the big coat box. When I laid him in the play pen he let out a howl. His screams echoed in my ears as I ran back down to get the stroller. As I struggled back up the steps with it I made a resolution—I'd start talking to George about getting a first floor place. I dropped the stroller by the door and leaned over Marty in the play pen. "Hush, Baby, hush," I crooned. "I know that old tooth is bothering you, but Mommy has to fix supper."

Downstairs I heard a car door slam. George was home and I hadn't even started supper. I tucked Marty's cap and jacket under my arm, grabbed the coat box off the daybed, ran for the bedroom and shoved everything under the bed. I was in the kitchen with a sauce pan in my hand by the time George opened the door. He was the sweetest man about almost everything, but he hated to have his meals late. I kissed him hoping he wouldn't notice how breathless I was from hurrying. "It's been one of those days," I told him with the brightest smile I could manage. "Dinner in a minute."

He kissed the tip of my nose. "Well, okay, but hurry. I've got two cars waiting for me to put back together at the station."

I suddenly felt guilty. George was knocking himself out with overtime to get our bills paid and now I'd bought that coat. Even though I needed it and it was such a bargain, I had to stop kidding myself. I knew George would be furious.

The baby was wailing. George picked him up out of the pen, cuddling him in his arms. "I think he's cutting a new tooth," I said as I hurried to open a can of beef stew. I turned the fire on under the sterilizer, lit the oven and popped open a can of biscuits. By the time the table was set and the biscuits were done, the bottles were sterilized and the formula was made. While George ate I'd feed Marty.

When I went to get Marty he was conked out in George's arms, his little face still flushed. Poor baby, he was exhausted from all that crying. But when I touched him his body arched tensely and he started screaming again. I cuddled him against my shoulder. "It's been like this all day," I told George, even though it was stretching the truth a little. "He was so fussy I left him with Mom when I went downtown to pay the bills."

"Did you pay her?" he asked. Oh, why did he have to be so stiff-backed? What did it hurt if I didn't pay Mom every time? Besides, I'd done some shopping for her in exchange.

"Yes," I answered, telling myself it

221

wasn't another fib. I thought of the coat pushed out of sight under the bed, and Dr. Braith's unpaid bill. Oh, why did I do things like that? I felt so bad, tears welled up in my eyes.

George stood there, looking at me and Marty crying and he smiled his wonderful, crooked grin. "You go ahead and take care of Marty, honey," he said softly, "and I'll serve my own supper." I smiled my thanks to him through my tears.

I thought it might soothe Marty if I gave him a quick bath before I gave him his bottle. I slipped off his shirt and diaper, and when I touched his bare skin it startled me to feel how hot and dry it felt. Was Mom right? Was he coming down with something? I'd better call Dr. Braith right away and find out. Yet, I hated the thought of calling the doctor. If he decided he wanted to see Marty, it would be ten dollars for a house call and probably another five dollars for medicine. Added to the thirty I still owed him, well, I couldn't face it.

Anyway, I told myself it was silly to get worried over a little fever. Marty was cutting teeth like mad and I could expect some trouble. I leaned over him and gently pried his mouth open. I ran my finger over his gum, and sure enough, there was the angry red swelling, the point of a tooth my finger touched. Marty let out a yell when I touched it.

George jumped when he heard it. "What on earth, Elizabeth?" he asked.

I felt about a hundred per cent better. "I just touched the sore spot where the tooth is coming through," I told him as I reached for the baby aspirin. I gave Marty the aspirin, then settled down with him in the rocker to give him his bottle. He kept pushing it out of his mouth with his tongue. He was too miserable to eat. I set the bottle on the table and just cuddled him, rocking him to sleep.

When George finished supper he asked, "Want me to take Marty while you eat?"

I shook my head. "I'm not really hungry. I'll get something later." George cleared the table and put the food away. I sat drowzily watching him. How I loved George at that moment. It was so like him to take over at times like this, times when I needed a little extra love, a little extra help. He went into the bedroom. Then, in the stillness I heard a muffled curse.

I sat up with a start, suddenly panic-stricken. What else could make him swear like that except the coat? He came through the door. In one hand he held Marty's jacket, in the other the blue coat. I stared at him. "How did you find that?" I blurted.

"I was making the bed," he said, his voice hard and even. "Where did you get the money to buy it?"

My heart was hammering fiercely. I couldn't tell him the fib I'd planned. He'd know it wasn't true. I told half a fib. "I—I paid Dr. Braith just fifteen dollars," I stammered.

"But, Elizabeth," he went on in that awful voice. "you promised. You promised you wouldn't buy one more thing until we'd paid all the bills."

"I know," I whispered, "but this was a sale. I needed a coat, and this is just what I've always wanted."

"You'll have to take it back."

"I can't," I said miserably. "It was a final sale." I got up from the rocker, put Marty in the pen and went to George. I snuggled my head against his shoulder. "Please, George," I begged, "I did need this coat. It would have been foolish to let it go."

He stood stiff and unyielding. He pulled away from me, then put the coat and jacket on a chair.

He picked up his own jacket, put it on slowly, at the same time looking around the room. "Sometimes," he said, "I think these things you had to have mean more to you than I do." There was the play-pen, the stroller, and in the bedroom the crib and chest. George had wanted to buy them secondhand to save money. But I'd insisted on new things, arguing there'd be more babies to use them.

We'd quarreled over the pretty cricket rocker I'd bought to rock Marty when he had colic, bought when the hospital and doctor bills hadn't been paid. But when you need a rocker to soothe a baby with colic, you need it then. What good would it do later? George just didn't understand. But I couldn't bear seeing him so cold, so angry.

"Please, George," I whispered. "Don't say that. You know I love you more than anything." I tried to put my arms around him again. "Please, I promise—" He pushed me violently away from him, and I stumbled against the daybed and fell to my knees. Tears of shock and pain flooded my eyes.

"You promise?" he cried. "You don't even know what the word means!"

I felt my face crumple up as the weeping started. "Crybaby!" George shouted. "Go on and cry like the baby you are." In the playpen Marty began screaming. George's voice got louder. "Your mother was right when she said you were too young to get married. You're as much a baby as Marty. You've got to have what you want right now. You can't wait for anything."

I put my hands over my ears to shut out the harshness of his voice. I loved him so. What did that have to do with buying a coat? Couldn't he understand? "What a marriage!" he was shouting again. "I've got two babies to take care of. How long do you think I'll be able to stand that? Do you think a man wants a baby-wife?" He jerked the door open. "I'm going to work and earn some more money and pay some more bills. And hear this, Elizabeth, I want out of this rat race!"

He slammed the door and in a moment I heard the roar of his car as he drove off. I wanted to bury my head in my hands and cry forever, but how could I, when Marty was sobbing his heart out? I pushed myself up from the floor and picked up Marty. I cuddled him in my arms and brushed the fair baby hair back from his hot forehead. "Just a little while," I crooned to him, my breath still catching with sobs, "and the tooth will be through and you'll be all better." I sat down to rock him, and the familiar rhythm soothed him into a fretful slumber.

My eyes wandered around the room, noting the disorder. I'd left things half done when I went to town. There were clean clothes on the daybed, folded but not put away. There was a pile of dirty laundry on the floor by the door, ready to go down to the landlady's washer. There was a clutter of little things I hadn't bothered to put away, and the supper dishes waiting in the sink.

At least, there would be plenty to do during the long wait for George to come home—if he came home at all tonight. Once before after a quarrel he'd spent the whole night at the station, trying to sleep in the back of a car. But he'd come home for breakfast, still mad but willing to make up. Maybe, if I put everything in order before he came home, he'd know how sorry I was. And if being out of debt meant so much to him, I'd try again. The thought of losing him made me sick—

But now, it was probably all too late—my baby was dying. Then the wail of an ambulance siren coming down the street sliced through my thoughts, and I cried out with thankfulness. I flung open the door and ran with Marty down into the cold

night to meet it. It was this, Dr. Braith told me later, that probably saved Marty's life. When a baby has a fever convulsion like Marty did, you've got to get the fever down fast. In the few moments it took the ambulance with its flashing red light to turn into our drive, the cold air did its work—cooling Marty's fever, causing the terrible convulsion to ease out of his tiny body.

By the time we got to the hospital the stiffness was gone and Marty was not only breathing, he was crying a little. When Dr. Braith examined him in the emergency room, he beckoned to me after he looked down Marty's throat. "See here, Elizabeth," he told me, "there's the trouble. A cutting tooth couldn't cause so high a fever." Marty's throat was red as fire. Dr. Braith gave him some medicine to bring down his fever and a shot of penicillin.

"You see," the doctor explained, "when the fever goes so high that the body can't handle it, we have a convulsion. Things stop working. You've got to get the fever down fast—with cool water, or cold air."

"Would he have died?" I whispered.

Dr. Braith shrugged. "I don't know, Elizabeth," he said. "He might have. If you had called me when his fever started going up, I would have told you what to do." Hot shame flooded through me and I couldn't answer. "There's no reason why you can't take him on home, now," Dr. Braith went on.

Just then George walked in. I'd called him as soon as we got to the hospital. His face was as white as the sheet on the examining table. I flew into his arms. "It's all right now, George," I told him. "Marty's all right."

When George carried the peacefully sleeping Marty out to the car for the trip home, I hung back to speak to Dr. Braith. "Doctor, I'm so sorry about your bill," I stammered. "I mean, we've let it run so long, and you've been so good about it. I could have paid it today, but—"

He smiled and patted my shoulder. "Don't worry about it one minute," he said. "I know young people with babies can't always pay their bills right on time. It'll wait."

I smiled back at him. Maybe there'd be times again when bills would have to wait, when there wasn't enough money to go around for food or rent or things we absolutely had to have, but I'd never again let a bill wait for a shaggy blue coat. For the first time I began to realize how George felt about the bills. You pay your bills as soon as you could, and you stood straight and square with your world. And you weren't ashamed to call the doctor when you needed him.

On that ride home I did a lot of figuring. There were new bills now—the ambulance, the hospital emergency room, Dr. Braith. We'd have to eat a lot of spaghetti for a while, but we'd make it. Before we went to bed that night I told George the rest of the truth, about the payments left on the furniture, the juggling of household money, and the fibs I'd told. For an awful moment I thought he was going to explode into anger all over again, but instead he gathered me close in his arms. "It's been a long day, honey," he whispered. "Tomorrow will be better."

And it was, it truly was. George knew my promise really meant something this time. And the blue shaggy coat? I wear it still, even if it is getting threadbare. At first I hated it every time I saw it hanging in the closet, remembering how Marty nearly died. But now I look at it with a deep thankfulness in my heart, and wear it like a symbol—a symbol of the day I grew up, the day I learned that sometimes the greatest joy in living is waiting for what you want.

THE END

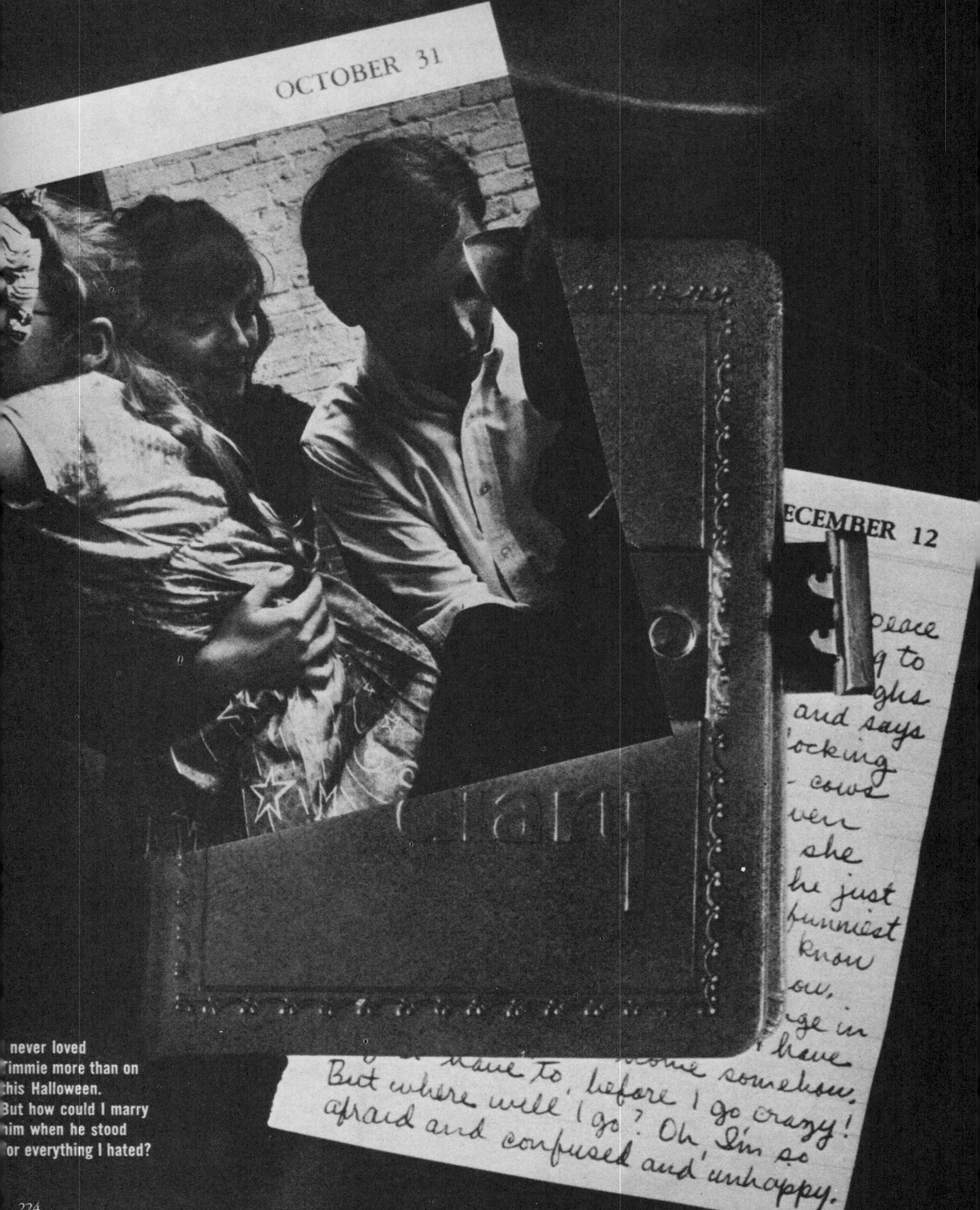

OCTOBER 31

DECEMBER 31

...peace
...g to
...ghs
...and says
...ocking
...cows
...ven
...she
...he just
...funniest
...know
...ou,
...ge in
...have
...me somehow.
...have to, before I go crazy!
But where will I go? Oh, I'm so
afraid and confused and unhappy.

never loved
Timmie more than on
this Halloween.
But how could I marry
him when he stood
for everything I hated?

What kind of a future dare I hope for with

A PAST AT 16!

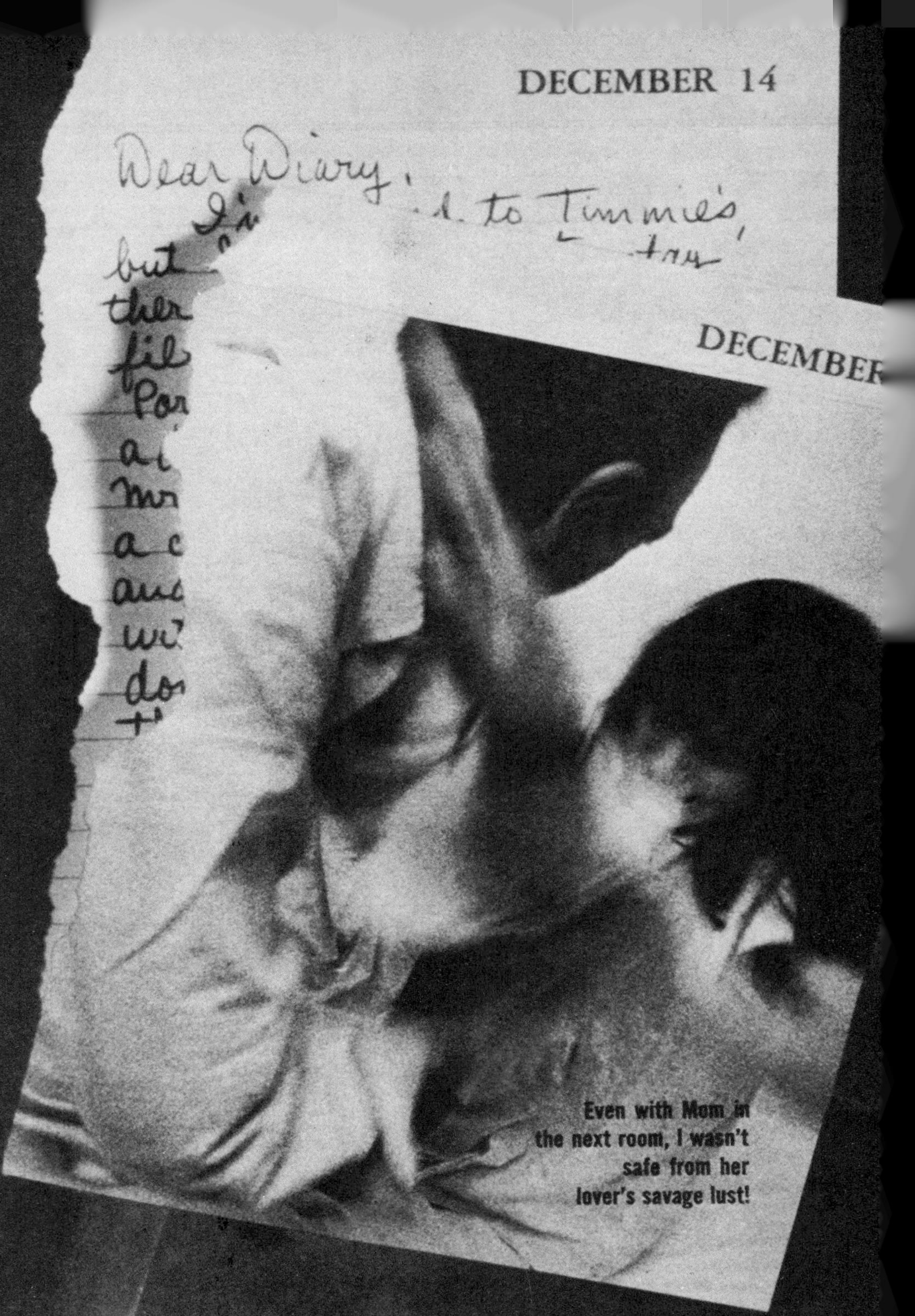
DECEMBER 14
Dear Diary,
DECEMBER

Even with Mom in the next room, I wasn't safe from her lover's savage lust!

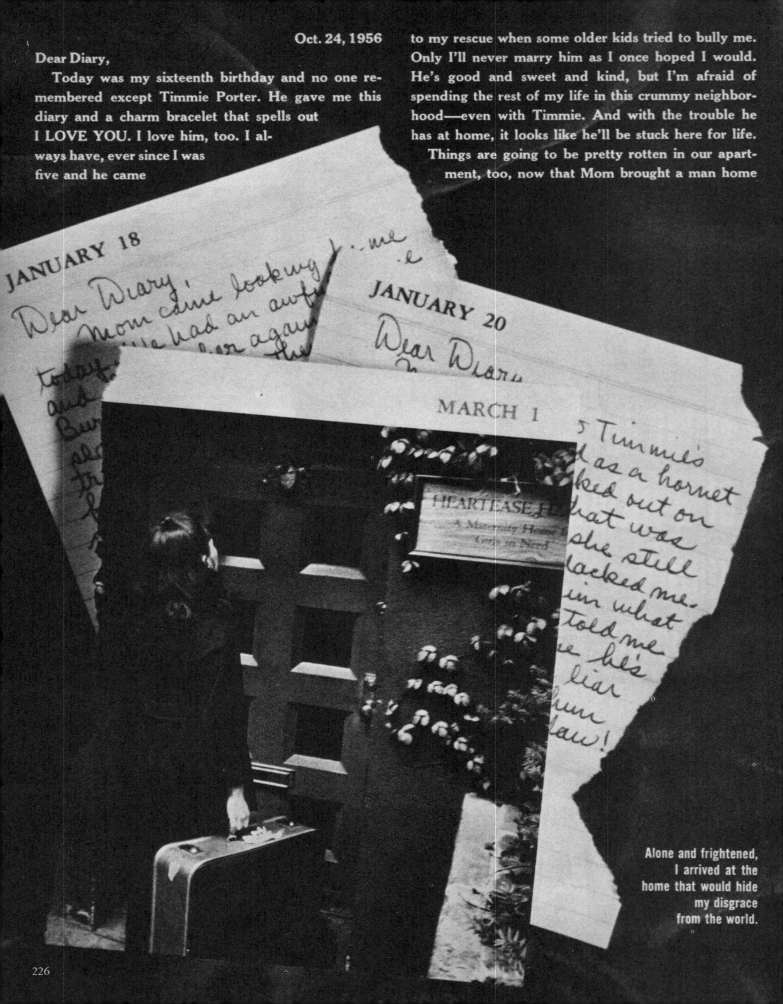

Oct. 24, 1956

Dear Diary,

Today was my sixteenth birthday and no one remembered except Timmie Porter. He gave me this diary and a charm bracelet that spells out I LOVE YOU. I love him, too. I always have, ever since I was five and he came

to my rescue when some older kids tried to bully me. Only I'll never marry him as I once hoped I would. He's good and sweet and kind, but I'm afraid of spending the rest of my life in this crummy neighborhood—even with Timmie. And with the trouble he has at home, it looks like he'll be stuck here for life.

Things are going to be pretty rotten in our apartment, too, now that Mom brought a man home

JANUARY 18

Dear Diary,
Mom came looking f... me
today... had an awf...
and... on again...
Bu...

JANUARY 20

Dear Diary

MARCH 1

5 Timmie's
d as a hornet
ked out on
that was
she still
lacked me.
im what
told me
e he's
liar
him
law!

Alone and frightened,
I arrived at the
home that would hide
my disgrace
from the world.

226

again. His name is Burt, and he's big and mean-looking. Seems like he's here to stay, too, because he brought his clothes with him. Golly, here we go again!

Oct. 25, 1956

Dear Diary,

Timmie and I went for a walk tonight. The stars looked big and beautiful, and Timmie said he'd like to pull them out of the sky and sew them together to make me a gown. Oh, I _do_ love him so much—but I sure wish I didn't. Diary, I haven't told you much about him yet, so here goes. He's the oldest kid in his family —eighteen. There are four other kids, starting with fourteen-year-old Ken and finishing with seven-year-old Marcie.

Last year, after Timmie's father was sent to prison for armed robbery, his mother went all to pieces. But not Timmie! He quit school (even though he was a senior) and went to work to support the family. And, when the welfare people wanted to send his mother to an institution, and put the kids in a foster home, he didn't like it. It would have made everything much easier for him, but he objected. That's the kind of guy he is. He finally made such a ruckus, the newspapers found out and played it up real big. Soon letters came in from all over demanding that the authorities let the family stay together. A doctor and a psychiatrist examined Mrs. Porter and found she was in a prolonged state of shock. The psychiatrist said her chances for recovery would be best at home, in familiar surroundings. So she was allowed to stay home. Now Timmie's carrying an awfully big load on his shoulders, even though the family gets a little money from welfare. He'll be all tied up for a long, long time and he'll never be able to move into the suburbs or anything. But, (Continued on page   )

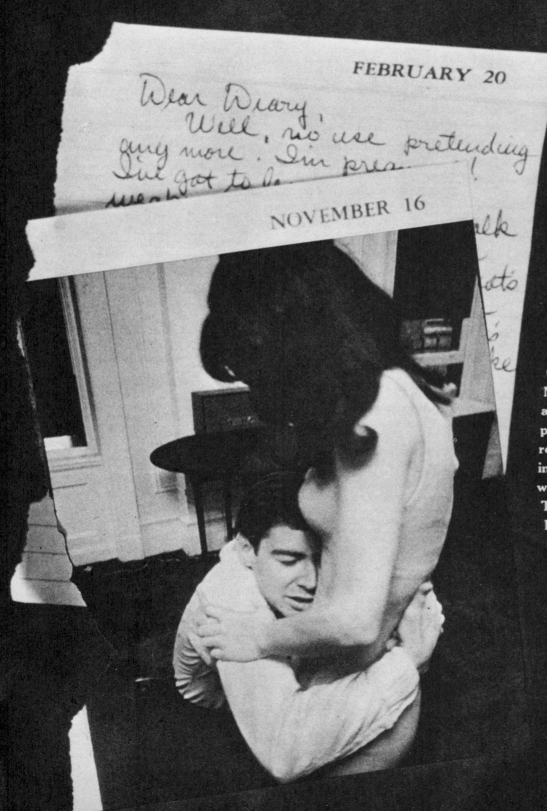

FEBRUARY 20

Dear Diary,
Well, no use pretending any more. I'm pres...
we've got to...

NOVEMBER 16

Marrying Glen was my worst mistake. But how can I desert him when, like a helpless child, he keeps begging me to stay?

227

A PAST AT 16!

oh, how I love him. Still, love him or not, I'll *never* marry him! I've just got to get away from here and I don't care what it costs me.

Oct. 26, 1956

Dear Diary,

Mom finally remembered I had a birthday two days ago. I guess that's because she was sober for a change this afternoon. She asked Burt to buy me a cake, but she only put fourteen candles on it. She must have lost a couple of years somewhere. She gave me a plastic wallet with a five dollar bill in it. I hated it, though, because I know *how* she got the money. I wish she weren't so pretty—maybe then men like Burt wouldn't look at her and she couldn't bring them home to live with us. I wish I knew where Daddy was, too. I sure do miss him. We haven't heard a word from him since he left us four years ago. He might even be dead, for all we know. Poor Daddy. He was an alcoholic and sort of weak, but I loved him.

Oct. 29, 1956

Dear Diary,

This morning I had to fix breakfast because Mom, who drank a lot last night, was sleeping it off. Burt was at the table, in his T-shirt, watching me. Finally he walked up to me and tried to touch me. I stuck him in the hand with a fork. I hate him. I wish he'd die. He's a very nasty man and he scares me. Whenever Mom's away, he says fresh things to me. I don't see how she can stand him.

Halloween, 1956

Dear Diary,

Tonight Timmie and I sat on his front stoop and handed lollipops to "Trick or

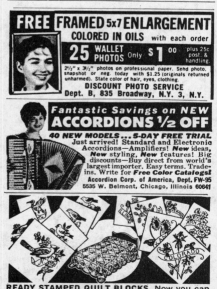
Treaters." It was fun. Timmie and I talked with the kids, and held hands. In a strange sort of way, I felt almost as if I were a part of him. I'd better stop thinking like that!!

Nov. 10, 1956

Dear Diary,

I haven't written for awhile, so I thought I'd catch up today.

Burt is still around and I'm still fighting him off. I'm so afraid of him, I even told Mom about the way he acts. All she did was laugh in my face. She thinks he's only kidding. Hah! Timmie has been giving me a bad time, too—but in a different way. He keeps asking me to promise I'll marry him. A lot of the girls in this neighborhood get married at sixteen, but that's not for me. If Timmie were rich, or at least had a well-paying job, marrying him would be Heaven. He's poor, though. And the girl who gets him will have to stay right here, on Demoin Street—with all the dope peddlers, drug addicts, thugs, and prostitutes. As for me, I'd rather be an old maid than bring an innocent child into a place like this.

Nov. 15, 1956

Dear Diary,

Timmie and I were alone in our apartment tonight. I almost wish he'd made love to me. We were kissing as if we'd never see each other again and crazy things were happening inside me. But he just looked at me, his blue eyes miserable, and said, "No, Annie, it can't be this way for us—I love you too much." When he said that, I almost felt angry with him because I wanted him so badly. Maybe I just don't have enough sex appeal!

Nov. 20, 1956

Dear Diary,

If Burt doesn't leave me alone, I just might kill him someday. While I was doing some ironing this afternoon, he kept looking at me and making nasty remarks. He asked why I wasn't nicer to him. He even had the nerve to say something about "like mother, like daughter!" Finally I got so mad I threw the iron at him—but I missed, darn it!

Nov. 22, 1956

Dear Diary,

Timmie said the only thing he would really be thankful for on Thanksgiving was my agreeing to marry him. Doesn't he know I can't? He's sure not making it very easy for me to stick to my plans to live a better life someday. Maybe I should stop seeing him. Although, if I tried that, I'd probably die from missing him.

Nov. 28, 1956

Dear Diary,

I was never so scared in my life! Burt tried to rape me today! I fought him like crazy, though. Finally I managed to trip him and get away. I was running out of the building when I bumped smack into Timmie. I guess I was pretty hysterical because it took him a long time to calm me down. After I told him all about Burt, he got a funny look in his eyes. That look scared me even more than Burt did. "Okay," Timmie said in a strange voice. "So you won't marry me—and I can't force you—but just you let me know if that creep ever bothers you again. I'll take care of him, all right!" I never saw Timmie so mad before, and I'm worried.

Nov. 29, 1956

Dear Diary,

If I didn't have my heart set on graduating high school, I'd run away from home. Burt pesters me so much I'm afraid I'll panic and marry Timmie. In the meantime, Timmie keeps asking if Burt still bothers me. "No," I always tell him. "Burt leaves me alone now." If I told him the truth, I'm afraid he'd do something terrible to Burt. And if Timmie

ever got into trouble on my account, I'd hate myself for the rest of my life.

Dec. 6, 1956

Dear Diary,

Something so awful happened, I still can't believe it. Burt raped me today! He sneaked into my room, early this morning, while I was sleeping. The moment I woke up, he put his hand over my mouth and grabbed me, saying horrible obscene things. And Mom was asleep in the very next room. Oh, diary, it was just dreadful! After it was over, I became sick.

What on earth can I do now? What if I get pregnant? I can't tell anyone—I don't dare. If I do, Timmie might find out. Then he'd probably kill Burt. Oh, I wish I were dead!

Dec. 12, 1956

Dear Diary,

I'm absolutely *desperate!* Burt won't give me any peace at all now. He keeps trying to get me again. And he laughs when I fight him off, saying things like, "No good locking the barn door after the cow's run off!" Mom doesn't even suspect anything. When she sees Burt "teasing" me, she just laughs as if it were the funniest thing in the world. I don't know what will happen to me now. Timmie has noticed how nervous I've become and he's concerned. I have to get away from home somehow. I just *have* to, before I go crazy! But where will I go? I'm so scared and confused and miserable.

Dec. 13, 1956

Dear Diary,

Timmie offered to let me move in with his family—with no strings attached. Tomorrow I'll look for a part-time job, so I'll be able to help him with the rent and food bills. I asked Mom if I could go, and she said she'd think about it. Then, when she asked me why I wanted to move, I told her what Burt had done to me. But she didn't believe me. She said I was just making it up. "Burt knows what a good set up he has with *me*," she insisted. "He'd only mess himself up by fooling around with a dumb, snot-nosed kid!" Some mother I've got!

Dec. 14, 1956

Dear Diary,

This afternoon I got a part-time job at the local five-and-dime store. Then, tonight, Mom let me move to Timmie's, but I won't be able to stay here long. This place is just filthy! I don't think Mrs. Porter has made a bed, washed a dish, or swept the floor since her husband's trial. There isn't a clean sheet in the house and the place is crawling with roaches. I don't see how Timmie and the kids can stand it.

Mrs. Porter does nothing all day but sit at the kitchen table in her robe and stare into space. She never talks. She isn't even aware half the time that anyone else is in the room. It'll sure be rough going to school, working at the five-and-dime, and trying to keep this place up, too. But I'll just have to do my best, that's all.

Dec. 16, 1956

Dear Diary,

I met Miss Mundy, the social worker, today. She's been making visits to the Porters ever since Timmie quit school. She's awfully nice. You know, diary, she believes that there's nothing wrong going on between me and Timmie. She has more faith in me than Mom. She even said I was a good influence on the children.

Dec. 24, 1956

Dear Diary,

Timmie brought a little Christmas tree home this evening. We popped popcorn and strung it on the tree. We also made some ornaments out of tin foil and cotton. Maybe it isn't much to look at compared to other Christmas trees I've seen —but we're real proud of it. Especially Marcie. I don't think the Porters ever had a Christmas tree before. At least, this seems to be Marcie's first one. She kept clapping her hands and dancing around the tree while the rest of us decorated it.

You know, diary, I've gotten used to living here, except for one thing—staying in the same house with Timmie and not really belonging to him. I've been sharing Marcie's bed since I got here. Every night I think of Timmie in the next room and I can't sleep. I know he isn't sleeping much either. The funny thing is, I *feel* like his wife—cooking for him, doing his laundry, keeping his house, looking after the kids, etc. But I won't make it legal, and he won't have me any other way. We're both too stubborn for our own good, I guess.

Dec. 26, 1956

Dear Diary,

Timmie gave me a bottle of cologne for Christmas. It's called *Toujours Moi*, which means always mine, and it smells simply heavenly. I gave him a tie. I know he couldn't afford the cologne, but I adore him all the more for being so foolishly thoughtful. I wish I had the guts to marry him. I love him so much. But what kind of future could we have? If only he didn't have such a deep sense of responsibility for his family! And yet, if he just forgot about them and went his merry way, I don't suppose I'd love him like I do. How can you ever win?? Timmie'll never be able to leave his family—and I'll never be able to stay here!

Jan. 12, 1957

Dear Diary,

Today was Timmie's birthday, so I baked him a birthday cake. I don't think he's ever had one before. You should have seen him when I brought it to the table. He looked just like a little boy let loose in a toy shop. He was so happy, you'd have thought I'd given him the world on a silver platter. He told me, "Annie, this past month has been the happiest of my life. Everything is so perfect with you here. The house is clean, we all get hot meals, and I don't have to worry about the kids with you around. Marry me, baby, please. I love you and I need you terribly!" But I won't marry him—I can't!!!

Jan. 16, 1957

Dear Diary,

I'm awfully scared. I haven't had a period since I've been here. What if I'm pregnant? Damn that disgusting Burt!

Jan. 18, 1957

Dear Diary,

Mom came looking for me today. We had an awful scene and I told her again what Burt did to me. Then she slapped me and called me a tramp. She also told me to forget I had a mother, because she wasn't going to be *my* mother any more. She acted as if it were my fault that Burt raped me. She seems to think I seduced him. Boy, I sure get all the breaks!

Jan. 20, 1957

Dear Diary,

Mom came over to Timmie's house again, mad as a hornet because Burt walked out on her. She thinks *that* was my fault, too, and she still won't believe Burt attacked me. She said she told him what I'd said. Then she told me that he left because "he's afraid a little liar like you could get him in hot water with the law." How about that?

I didn't tell her I was worried about being pregnant. She'd probably accuse Timmie!

Feb. 20, 1957

Dear Diary,

Well, no use pretending any more. I'm pregnant! I've got to leave before I weaken and let Timmie talk me into getting married for the baby's sake. Because that's just what he'd try to do, even though it's not his child. I sure feel like a traitor about leaving little Marcie. I'm the closest thing to a real mother she's ever had. I have to go, though. I don't know where yet, but I'm leaving—and real soon.

Feb. 24, 1957

Dear Diary,

Bless Miss Mundy! I told her everything today—absolutely everything. And she understands it all, even about the way Mom's just washed her hands of me. At first Miss Mundy wanted to have Burt arrested, but I talked her out of it. I told her I didn't want anyone to know about Burt. That way Timmie couldn't find out about him and harm him. Besides, it would be awfully hard to track Burt down in a big city like Chicago. I also made Miss Mundy promise not to tell Timmie anything about my condition. And, what's more, she'll help me find a home for unwed mothers where I can have my baby. I guess that means I'll have to quit high school, but then, I can't have everything. I hope God gives Miss Mundy His special blessing for all her kindness. I don't know what I'd do without her. For the life of me, I really and truly don't.

March 1, 1957

Dear Diary,

I'm in the home. It's very nice. Miss Mundy arranged everything. I don't know how she did it, but she really came through for me. She's a living doll.

I keep thinking of Timmie all the time. I couldn't bear to tell him good-bye, so I just left him a note that said I was leaving. Naturally, I didn't say why.

Sept. 20, 1957

Dear Diary,

I've been so lonely, frightened, and miserable that I couldn't write a word in here all these months. My baby girl was born yesterday. I don't know how she could be so beautiful with Burt for a father.

I just hate the thought of giving her away. I don't want to. I love her so much—I can't bear it! But for her own good, I'll have to do it. She's so sweet and beautiful that I know the people who'll adopt her will love her. They'll be able to give her a better start in life than I will. That's the only thing that consoles me. Still, I don't know how I'll ever find the strength to sign those papers. Never, ever to see her again—my own baby!!

Sept. 22, 1957

Dear Diary,

Well, its done. I've signed the papers. I gave my beautiful little baby girl away. I named her Eden because holding her in my arms was paradise. I hope whoever takes her will let her keep that name. I haven't been able to cry at all. At least, not on the outside where it shows. And everybody here is worried about me. Because I feel dead, and I guess they can tell. I don't know where I'll go from here, but I don't care much, either. If only Eden had been Timmie's baby! Then I might have married him. I still love him very much and miss him terribly. Funny, but she reminded me of him in a way. She had the same innocent, trusting look in her blue eyes that Timmie has. My poor little baby—I'm going to miss her so much!

Oct. 2, 1957

Dear Diary,

I'm on my own again. I was able to save some money while I worked at the five-and-dime months ago. Timmie wouldn't let me contribute very much to household expenses when I lived with

229

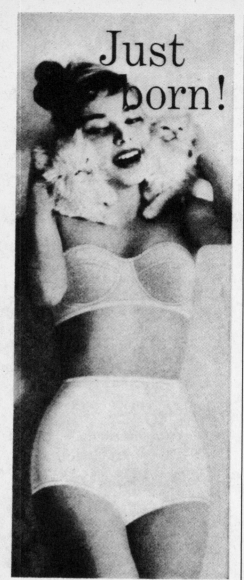

the Porters. But I'll have to find work right away.

You know, diary, I've changed. My looks, I mean. My figure is much better than before, my complexion is much nicer, and my eyes have a sad, dreamy look that's kind of interesting. I've never described myself to you before—I guess now is a good time. I'm five feet three and have black hair, dark brown eyes, and a fair skin. There's a large beauty mark on my left shoulder. Mom told me once that every woman in our family for generations has had the same mark in the same place. Maybe someday I'll see a little girl with a beauty mark on her shoulder and know she's my Eden. But I guess that's just wishful thinking.

Oct. 24, 1957

Dear Diary,

Today is my seventeenth birthday, and I got the best present possible under the circumstances—a job. It's on an assembly line in a metal factory not far from the old neighborhood. I wonder what I'd do if I ever saw Timmie again. It's almost frightening to imagine but it's exciting too. I often wonder what he thinks happened to me. Has he ever tried to find me? Does he think of me as often as I think of him? Or has he found some other girl less greedy than me? Is he married? Funny, but I don't think he is. Somehow I just can't believe he's forgotten all about our love.

Oct. 29, 1957

Dear Diary,

Every time I see a tall, brown-haired man with broad shoulders, my heart skips a beat. Fearing (or hoping) it might be Timmie. I miss him so! But I won't go to him. I mustn't. Life is pretty senseless without him, though.

I have a tiny walk-up apartment all to myself. It isn't much, but it's the nicest place I've ever lived in, and it's out of the slums. I guess I've finally escaped the old life—but, oh, the price I've had to pay! It hardly seems worth it now.

Nov. 4, 1957

Dear Diary,

The superintendent at the factory is very nice to me. His name is Glen Weston and he's real handsome. I guess he's about thirty-five, but he doesn't look it. He's got thick, dark hair and dark eyes, and he's slender and wiry like a Spanish bullfighter.

Nov. 8, 1957

Dear Diary,

Glen has asked me for a date. He's so nice, really, and I'm so lonesome that I said yes. But I was kind of hesitant about it. It just seems funny that a guy with so much to offer has never been married.

Nov. 10, 1957

Dear Diary,

Glen and I went out to dinner. Afterward we went dancing. Glen's a lot of fun. The best thing about him is his sense of humor. It's the first time I've really laughed in a long while.

Nov. 21, 1957

Dear Diary,

Glen and I have been seeing a lot of each other. I've told him all about my past and he was very sympathetic. He said I was the best thing that ever happened to him. I think he meant it, too, because he treats me like a queen. And, though he always kisses me good night after a date, he's never gotten fresh or made a pass at me.

Dec. 22, 1957

Dear Diary,

I ran into Timmie on the street today. My heart almost stopped beating. Oh, Timmie, Timmie, Timmie! I still love him—more than ever. That doesn't matter, though, because his family's still in the same old mess. Yet *he* seemed

changed somehow, more grown up and all. He said he's been working twice as hard since I left. He was glad to see me, too. I could tell from the way he looked at me. I could also tell he'd been hurt by the way I'd suddenly left in March, without any explanation. He said he thought I'd eloped or something. Then he asked if he could see me again and I said yes.

Dec. 25, 1957

Dear Diary,

What a Christmas! Timmie sent me flowers—red roses and white carnations—and a heart-shaped locket. And, best of all, he wrote me the sweetest poem. Glen gave me a beautiful wrist watch that must have cost him a fortune. You see, they know about each other and they're competing for me. Wow, that makes me feel like Cinderella!

Jan. 12, 1958

Dear Diary,

Today was Timmie's twentieth birthday. It's hard to believe he's only twenty. Sometimes he seems more of a man than Glen. He told me the only birthday present he wanted was for me to become his wife. I still can't make myself marry him, though. Especially since I've gotten a glimpse of a better life. I haven't told him anything about the baby—but I want to now. If I were sure Burt was gone I would—but he might still be somewhere in Chicago.

Feb. 4, 1958

Dear Diary,

Glen has asked me to marry him. I told him I wanted to think about it for awhile. He's very good to me and he could give me everything I've always wanted—but I don't know. Because, wonderful as Glen is, he sort of disturbs me—and I don't know why.

Feb. 10, 1958

Dear Diary,

Timmie and I almost lost control of ourselves tonight. I pulled out of his arms, breathless and trembling, just in time. Then I told him I never wanted to see him again because I'd decided to marry Glen. "I guess that's what you've always wanted," he said sadly. "Someone who could give you everything you deserve. I just wish I were in a position to offer you as much."

"Oh, Timmie, so do I!" I cried. And I was in his arms again, sobbing like a baby. He stroked my hair, crooning to me till I'd quieted down. Then I murmured, "Oh, Timmie, you do understand, don't you?"

He said, "Yes, baby, I understand. I wish to blazes I didn't. But I know it wouldn't be fair of me to talk you out of this. You'd never forgive me if I did. I just hope you'll be happy." We were both crying when we said good-bye.

April 27, 1958

Dear Diary,

I quit my job, and Glen and I were married last week. I only hope I can be a good wife to him. I hope, also, that I'll get to love him enough to push Timmie out of my mind. Because I can't forget him. Even when I made my marriage vows, it was Timmie I thought of, not Glen. Our honeymoon was disappointing, too—probably because I couldn't forget Timmie.

May 5, 1958

Dear Diary,

Glen doesn't seem to want me at all. Physically, I mean. He's so wonderful in every other way, I guess I shouldn't complain. All the same, I can't help wondering if there's something wrong with him.

June 12, 1958

Dear Diary,

Maybe there's something wrong with *me* because I want Glen so much. But he just doesn't seem interested in me that way. Sometimes it's just maddening!

July 6, 1958

Dear Diary,

I'm sure there's something wrong with Glen. *I've* been making advances to *him*, and I know he starts to get aroused but then he just kisses my cheek, says "good night, honey" and rolls over. What's wrong????

August 8, 1958

Dear Diary,

Things are no better. I really believe Glen loves me, but not like a husband. I spoke to him about it once and he said maybe he just loves me too much to soil me that way. Now I ask you—does that make sense?

Sept. 15, 1958

Dear Diary,

I might as well give up. Glen wouldn't touch me last night, either. And I tried to look as sexy as I could. I put on my sheer white nightgown, the one I wore on our wedding night. My hair was loose and my skin was glowing from a hot shower. But it had no effect on him at all! How much more can a wife take?

Oct. 2, 1958

Dear Diary,

I'm so miserable! How much longer can I live with Glen? I don't want to be unfaithful to him, but I keep thinking about Timmie—wanting him like mad. Sooner or later, something's just gotta give!! Glen swears he loves me and doesn't want to lose me, but what kind of life is this? And just what does he want me for?

Nov. 10, 1958

Dear Diary,

I know what's wrong with Glen at last. We had a long talk last night and he finally admitted he's impotent. He told me it was the result of some childhood disease. He also said he never should have married me. Only he loved me so much he couldn't help hoping I might be the answer to his problem—helping him lead a normal sex life. But now he knows that no woman can do that for him. I never saw such a miserable look in anyone's eyes as I saw in Glen's when he told me. I want to help him. And I don't know how. I just don't know how. Poor Glen.

Nov. 16, 1958

Dear Diary,

We've decided to get a divorce. It's the only way. I feel mostly pity for Glen now, and he knows it. In fact, the divorce was his idea— And yet tonight, when we talked about it, he begged me on bended knees not to leave him.

Nov. 18, 1958

Dear Diary,

I feel wretched. Glen has committed suicide. He shot himself in the head with his old army gun. He left a note behind. A long, pitiful, heartbreaking note full of love and regret and sorrow. Poor, sweet Glen. May God give him peace at last.

Jan. 1, 1959

Dear Diary,

This is a new year and I pray to God it will mark a new beginning for me. I just can't seem to forget Glen. How he must have suffered to end his life that way! And how I must have added to his suffering! I hope I never, never make anyone unhappy again.

Jan. 9, 1959

Dear Diary,

I've applied for a job in the clerical department of a big construction company. I just can't go back to the factory. Too many people there know about Glen and me. And if there's one thing I can't stand, it's pity.

Jan. 12, 1959

Dear Diary,

Timmie came over today. It's his birth-day. He looked me up "as a birthday present to myself." I still love him, but we acted like strangers with each other. Mostly we talked about his family. His brother Ken is seventeen already and working. Timmie says things are really starting to look better for him now. His father may even be released from prison on parole soon. Gosh, I hope things work out for Timmie. He deserves a break if anyone does.

Jan. 14, 1959

Dear Diary,

I've started working at the construction company. I think I'm going to like my job. So far, everyone's been very nice to me.

Feb. 6, 1959

Dear Diary,

I've met a young accountant at the office. His name is Sid Parnell. Nice guy.

Feb. 20, 1959

Dear Diary,

Sid and I have been seeing quite a lot of each other. I'm awfully fond of him. He's so good. But—he isn't Timmie.

March 20, 1959

Dear Diary,

Sid has told me he loves me. He's really a wonderful guy. Of course, there's Timmie—but I think I've lost Timmie for good now. I really don't deserve him, anyway. All in all, I guess I'm pretty lucky to have found Sid.

April 3, 1959

Dear Diary,

Sid asked me to marry him today. I said yes. He has so much to offer a girl— and he *does* love me, I know that. So why do I keep wishing he were Timmie? I must be crazy!!! I know Sid could make me happy. I have a lot of respect for him and I like him very, very much. I'm sure I could be a good wife to him, too. I just know it! But why, oh why, won't Timmie get out of my mind?

April 8, 1959

Dear Diary,

I talked to Timmie today. I called him. I *had* to. I wanted to tell him about Sid and me. But as soon as I heard his warm deep voice, my heart started pounding and I almost forgot why I'd called. Am I making another mistake in marrying Sid? Could Timmie and I possibly make it after all that's happened????

April 12, 1959

Dear Diary,

I can't stop thinking about Timmie. But I'm *definitely* marrying Sid. It's all settled. We're planning on a June wedding. And that'll be that!

April 14, 1959

Dear Diary,

I saw Timmie on the bus tonight and I still love him. I think he still loves me, too. Oh, for Pete's sake—what happens now????

January 12, 1965

Dear Diary,

Well, I haven't written in you for a long, long time.

Almost six years. I guess it's because I've been so happy. You see, I finally found out what was important and what wasn't—and I acted accordingly. I know I did the right thing, too, because I'm gloriously happy. In a few months my husband and I will be celebrating our sixth wedding anniversary. We have two sons and a two-month-old baby girl (named Eden)—with a beauty mark, yet. We live in a modest little three-bedroom house and somehow we manage. Sure, when emergencies come up, we feel the pinch. But our house is full of love, and nothing can be too bad when you have love. Diary, there's so much to tell, but I've got to run now. It's time I started frosting Timmie's cake. It's his birthday, you know, and he'll be home from work soon.

THE END

Bobby Kennedy started my love affair

He was in our town less than an hour. But that was long enough for my whole life to be changed

□ The coffee shop where I worked as a waitress was to the left of the hotel lobby, separated from it by wide glass doors. As I passed the doors on my way to one of the window tables, I could see a crowd gathering in the lobby.

"Who's expected?" I asked Milly, the cashier, as I walked past her.

"Bobby Kennedy. Didn't you read about it in the paper?"

"Oh, I guess I did," I said.

I went on to my table. The man I was serving asked me for his check as I served the coffee, and I heard him urge his companion to hurry along so they could get out and see Kennedy. The dining room was beginning to empty out fast. There was a kind of contagious excitement going through the place. Everyone wanted to see what was going on. Even Milly kept getting off her high stool to peer into the lobby.

Cora, one of the other waitresses, came up to me and said, "Let's duck out for a few minutes and see Bobby Kennedy. I'll just die if I don't get to see him, he's so close and all!"

I found myself feeling the same way. A celebrity was a rare thing in our town. But then I caught a glimpse of Mrs. Donavan, the hostess, frowning at us. *(Continued)*

What Is a Baby?

What is a baby?
Sweet as a rose,
With petal pink skin
And a wee little nose,
With hair soft as snowflakes
And wondering eyes
That seem to have captured
The blue of the skies.
And fingers as fragile
As butterfly wings—
A baby is all
Of these wonderful things!

What else is a baby?
Symbol of love,
Kissed by the angels

And sent from above.
Made for a mother
To cherish and hold,
A treasure more precious
Than diamonds or gold.
Dear little baby—
Touched by a star,
Life's greatest miracle,
That's what you are!

And what is a mother?
Well, that's hard to say.
She might have been anyone,
Until the day
A baby was laid
In her arms to impart
A gentle new wisdom
Of mind and of heart.
God must have whispered
The secret she knew
That this was His work
She's been chosen to do.

Alice E. Chase

Bobby Kennedy Started My Love Affair

"How can we leave?" I whispered to Cora.

"Who cares about *her!*" Cora whispered back. "I'm going. What can she do if we all go out?"

Nothing, I thought, fingers of excitement chasing through me. I liked my job, but it wasn't the only thing in the world for me. As a matter of fact, nothing was all that important to me anymore. I was in a reckless mood lately, one I recognized and was a little wary of now. Dave hadn't made things easier for me the night before. What had started out as a movie date had wound up in a nasty argument. I knew that I'd have to break up with Dave sooner or later because he was getting too possessive, and I'd built a shell around myself two years before that I wasn't about to crack or let anyone else crack.

I finished my customers just as a roar went up from the crowd outside. I didn't wait to see if Mrs. Donavan was around. Frankly, I didn't care. I dashed out through the lobby and to the street, with half the hotel help with me. I had never seen such a mob before. People were pressing against the hotel windows and filling the street in front of the hotel as sirens sounded close by and a small motorcade came inching its way up the street. I jumped up and down trying to see over people's heads. Cora grabbed my arm.

"Let's get closer," she said, pushing against a wall of people.

I lost her as she squeezed in between two men and got swallowed up in the curb crowd. I decided to keep close to the building wall and maybe get a footing on the narrow ledge of window boxes and get a better view. A man was getting out of the lead car by then, and I began jumping up and down when I realized it was Bobby Kennedy.

He looks just like his pictures. That was my first thought. The next was that his hair wasn't quite as unruly as I'd seen in the newspapers. He was quite a good-looking man, now bending toward the crowd, shaking hands, turning this way and that to shake a hand. Something came over me, a desire to be closer to him since I was already within shouting distance. I edged closer to the wall and toward the door. It would be something to talk about if Bobby Kennedy ever became president and I could say I had shaken his hand! I started to move closer. I even heard his voice. He was saying "thank you—thank you" as he pressed closer to the front door of the hotel.

T HEN SUDDENLY I tripped. It was the wide step leading into the hotel that did it. One moment I was upright and next I was pitching forward and downward. I remember a panicky feeling. If I fell, I'd be trampled to death. I screamed and lashed out to grab at something, and suddenly strong arms grabbed me from behind. I felt myself being pulled back and held fast. In that one moment I clung to the hands going around my waist, thankful that I hadn't fallen into the mob. At the same time Bobby Kennedy passed from view inside the hotel.

I turned to thank the man who'd saved me, but even before I could form the words I was gasping and staring up into Frank Madison's hazel eyes. The shock of seeing him like that left me speechless. I tried to find my voice, but it was stuck somewhere down in my chest. I couldn't say a thing because I was remembering. So was he—I could see it in his eyes as we stood with the crowd pushing and prodding and giving us dirty looks because we weren't giving way.

"You okay?" he said, breaking the silence.

I nodded.

"Better wait," he went on, pressing me back against the wall. "They'll be easing up soon."

I stood next to him with people stepping on my feet, shouting, surging like the tide as police stepped in and began dispersing the crowd.

How long had it been since I'd heard Frank's voice? Two years. And two years can change people, change them from kids to adults.

Frank and I had been seniors in high school. It was spring, and Mom said, "If you want a dress for the senior prom, you'd better think about making one because I haven't time to drive up to Cedar City with you and buy one, and you know you'll find nothing you like in the local stores."

I had started dating Frank the night of the senior play. We'd gone to the drama teacher's house for an after-play party, and Frank had been sitting next to me when a girl named Serena decided we should hold a séance.

"Who will we talk to?" someone shouted.

"My dead aunt," Serena said. "I've communicated with her before."

We thought it was a big joke. We turned down all the lights and someone lit one lone candle. We made a wide circle and giggled and whispered and finally were quiet as Serena became more and more agitated at our refusal to take her seriously. Then someone began to snore and it broke up the circle. Wally Fields had fallen asleep on the couch. It was just the touch we needed to break up the party. Frank took my hand.

"I'll walk you home," he said.

At the door we thanked Mr. and Mrs. Marron for the party and then walked the three short blocks to my house. It was April and just beginning to warm up. I hated the thought of going into the house and so did Frank. We sat on my front-porch steps until Mom came down to see what time it was.

Frank called me the next day for a date. What I liked about him was his energy—he was always on the go. We walked or played tennis or he came over and we scored baskets in the back yard with the basket Dad had nailed on top of the garage door for my young brother. Frank and I were together a lot, and I was in love with him before he ever kissed me. My best friend, Lisa, was green with envy. She had few dates, and unless a girl has a boy interested in her—no matter to what degree—by the time she's in the last half of her senior year, she's dead.

I was afraid of losing Frank. I did anything he asked me to do, was available whenever he wanted me to go somewhere. Sure, I chased him, but it was worth it to have other girls tell me how lucky I was to get Frank.

The senior-prom committee set the date for the prom, but we were short of funds. The bake sales we'd been allowed to hold at school had been fine, but the principal hadn't allowed us to hold as many as we needed to make enough money. We were desperate. That was when Frank came up with the idea of holding a car wash on a Saturday right at the high school.

Frank and I spent hours making up posters and carting them around to stores to be displayed. Then we began to pray it wouldn't rain that day.

Saturday morning I was up at dawn looking at a leaden sky and almost weeping, but by eleven o'clock spring sun had chased the clouds away. We converged on the high school at noon and by late afternoon we had not only made enough money to pay for a good orchestra but we had a few dollars left over.

Jubilant, we decided to celebrate at Coker's, a small place on the edge of town where they catered to the high-school crowd.

I SUPPOSE I was riding that high tide of emotion that comes from doing something constructive and adult. All of us were. When it was time to go home, Frank asked his friend Allan to drive us, but Allan told us to take his car because he wasn't ready to leave.

We went out to the parking lot and got in, and Frank turned to me and grinned. "Hey, we're pretty terrific, aren't we?" he said and pulled me close and kissed me.

I trembled in his arms. We were terrific and adult—and emotional, and when he drove off I was sitting as close to him as I could get.

Frank stopped at Point Park and said, "This is a nice place to kiss a girl," or something like that. I wasn't really listening—I was feeling too keyed up. And when his kisses became much more intense and demanding than usual, I didn't pull away. *I love you,* I cried out deep inside me as his lovemaking swept me on and on—till there was no stopping for either of us.

"Are you mad?" Frank asked me later. "I mean, I didn't plan for that to happen—"

"I'm not mad," I said.

But I *was* afraid, and when I got home I felt ashamed too. I had always wanted to love and be loved, but not like that—not stealing love in a car, having to apologize for it. But it had happened. And a few weeks later I nearly died when I realized how dearly I was going to have to pay for that date at Point Park. I was sure I was pregnant, and one morning in the girls' locker room at school I burst into tears because I was so darned afraid and choking with my dreadful secret. Marcia, a good friend, sat down beside me and asked me what was wrong.

I thought we were alone, so I blurted it out to her. "I think I'm pregnant."

"Oh my gosh," she gasped. "Have you told anyone else?"

CHILDREN'S CORNER

. . . When our daughter Susie's pet canary died, my husband gave our heartbroken little girl a cigar box as a coffin for the bird and assisted in its burial in back of the garden.

After the funeral services, Susie whispered, "Daddy, will my little bird go to heaven?"

"I expect so," her father replied. "Why?"

"I was thinking," Susie murmured, distressed, "how cross St. Peter will be when he opens the box and discovers there are no cigars in it."
—Mrs. Joseph Felice, Pa.

. . . My friend's patience with her mischievous three-year-old son reached the breaking point one after-noon. He had had one spanking already for misbehaving. Now he was racing wildly through the house, yelling at the top of his voice. When he refused to stop, his mother sternly said, "Doug, do you want another spanking?"

"I didn't want the first one," was his quick reply.
—Mrs. Joe E. Taylor, Tex.

. . . A few days after my baby was born, my four-year-old nephew Terry came to visit me and found the baby screaming up a storm. Looking into the crib, Terry asked, "Aunt Chris, was this baby sent from heaven?"

Tenderly I replied, "Yes, he was."

"Well," said Terry frowning in disapproval, "no wonder they didn't want him."
—Mrs. Christine Roberts, N.J.

. . . One day my three-year-old daughter, who loves to play with money, asked me for some pennies. I gave her three and warned her that if she lost them, she'd not get any more.

A short while later she came into the kitchen and asked, "Mommy, do you know where my pennies are?"

"I guess they're lost," I said.

"Oh, no, Mommy," she quickly said. "They're not lost; I just haven't found them yet!"
—Mrs. Karen Miller, Mass.

"No, who would I tell?"

"Is it Frank?"

I nodded numbly.

"Well, listen, we've got to get out of here," she said hurriedly. "Why don't we talk about it later? You should talk to your folks, I guess—" That last part trailed off.

I didn't talk about it anymore to Marcia. I didn't even say anything to Frank when he met me at my locker and asked me if I was going to stick around that afternoon for a committee meeting. I said I couldn't and left school as soon as I could.

The next morning I was hit with it in home room. A senior home room is like a zoo, or at least ours was. Being seniors, we were a little cocky, and our teacher, Miss Lazarid, who was also a music teacher, was always off somewhere getting together a program. We did everything but climb out of the windows. Marcia grabbed me as I came in.

"I thought you didn't tell anyone," she said. "The whole school knows you're pregnant."

I began to shake. "I'm not—I mean, who told them?" I whispered.

"Don't look at me," she said. "I didn't tell, if that's what you think."

"Then who?"

"Why don't you ask Frank?" she said and walked off.

I hadn't told Frank—I'd been too afraid to tell him. I stared around the home room. Kids were lounging around, and some of them looked up at me and I thought their eyes were knowing.

I turned and fled. When I got home, I told Mom I was sick to my stomach and I went to bed. I began to think of running away, killing myself, all sorts of stupid things like that. And then I slept from sheer exhaustion.

When I awoke, it was early afternoon. I really did feel sick by then, and it suddenly dawned on me what the matter was. Cramps! I wasn't pregnant at all! I was practically hysterical with relief at first, but then I realized my reputation was ruined anyway—all because I'd been a silly fool and had talked to Marcia. Obviously I'd been overheard, and the eavesdropper had spread the story all over the school. There was nothing I could do now but face the whole thing down.

I HADN'T counted on Frank's reaction. He came to my house right after school. He looked like thunderclouds coming up over Point Park. Just as soon as he was sure we couldn't be overheard, he lit into me.

"What kind of dumb rumor did you start anyway?" he demanded.

"I didn't," I told him. "It was all a mistake. What I mean is, I was afraid—but it's nothing, it's all right—" I burned with embarrassment.

"Well, you'd better straighten out your loudmouthed friends," he said.

"Is that all you have to say?" I asked him, more hurt then than embarrassed. "Don't you care about me and what that kind of rumor can do to my reputation?"

"Sure I do," he said belligerently, "but you could have talked to me first. I mean, couldn't you have at least waited?"

Waited? His lack of understanding of the panic I'd felt made me turn on him. I hated him at that moment, I blamed him for everything that had happened, and I told him so.

He tried to make peace, to apologize. "Gee, what are you jumping me for?" he kept saying. "I didn't start anything. You were the one who talked."

That was the last time I talked with anyone or trusted another soul. I learned my lesson the bitter, hard way. I went back to school and stared down the gossip. I refused to see or go out with Frank again. He tried to see me and he apologized again for hurting me by what he had said, but it was too late. Something sweet and important had gone out of our relationship, and for the rest of the term we pointedly ignored one another.

It wasn't long before the kids in school forgot the rumor, especially when they realized it was false. But I went to the senior prom with a cousin. I asked him to take me because I didn't want anyone to think I was staying home for any special reason. I saw Frank there, but when he tried to talk to me, I turned away. It wasn't a happy night for me, not the way I had dreamed it would be. On Sunday at graduation I received my diploma and

said good-bye to my high-school life happily and almost with a sense of relief that it was over.

That summer I took a temporary job at the hotel as a waitress, and I liked it. I had never been much for typing and office work. Working at the hotel also gave me more time to myself than a strict nine-to-five kind of job would have. I dated now and then, but I was wary. It was as though I'd built a high fence around my heart and no one was going to break through it.

I heard that Frank had enlisted in the Marines, and once in a while when I read about the Vietnam war I wondered if he was there and fighting. But most of the time I closed him out, too, because it was too painful to remember him.

I became very interested in a children's-theater group in our town and worked with a woman who had had a short career on the stage. Mostly I helped keep the youngsters in line, painted sets, and scouted for likely candidates for our group among the parents in town. Once in a while I wondered about myself. Would I be the kind of girl who would never marry, never know a lasting love? It worried me, and when it did I'd throw myself into a flurry of dates. But it always ended up the same—I couldn't really like a boy for too long.

AND THEN one day I left my job for a few minutes to watch Bobby Kennedy—and Frank Madison came back into my life! I stood next to Frank, and the memory of all that had been between us made us both act wooden and embarrassed.

"You work here?" Frank asked, glancing at my uniform.

I nodded.

"I guess it's okay to go in now," he said.

I looked at him. He looked much older,

much more handsome. I shivered in the spring air, and he said, "You'll catch cold." He took my arm and turned me toward the door.

"Thanks," I said. "I got a little frightened by the crowd for a moment."

Cora came rushing up, yelling, "Did you see him? I was right next to him! He would have shaken hands with me, too, if some woman hadn't pushed ahead of me. Hey, we'd better get back—come on!" She grabbed my arm.

"Can I call you?" Frank asked.

I didn't answer. I ran back to my job, so wrought up it was hard to concentrate. I couldn't write down an order, my hands were shaking so, and my mind was whirling. Would Frank call me—and if he did, what would I do?

I went off work at three-thirty that day. Unaccountably, I raced for home, and then I realized why I had rushed so. I expected Frank to call me. And I wanted to see him. In spite of all that had happened, I wanted to see him. He had started something stirring inside me again, and I was limp. In some indefinable way, I felt I belonged to Frank. Don't ask me to explain that. I had never let another man touch me. Now Frank was back, and it was as though I had been waiting for him.

When he hadn't called by eight o'clock, I figured he had taken my aloofness as a brush-off and wouldn't call. And I certainly couldn't call him. Perhaps it was just as well. We'd been thrown together by sheer chance. Frank was the past, and it was dead. But something inside me was dying all over again too.

I was in my room getting ready for bed when Mom called me to the phone. She didn't say who it was, but I trembled as I went to answer.

It was Frank. "I took a chance on calling you, is it okay?" he asked.

"Yes, it okay," I said.

"This afternoon was hectic, wasn't it?" His voice had deepened or maybe I couldn't remember it. "You all right after that scare?"

"It was nothing," I said. "I guess everyone got a little pushed around in that crowd."

"Sure thing," he said. "Norma, will you let me see you?"

"Do you want to?" I asked childishly while my heart started pumping madly.

"I want to very much," he said.

"I'll be through working at three-thirty tomorrow," I said. "I'll meet you in the taproom at the hotel."

"Thanks, I'll be there," he said and hung up.

I felt like crying and laughing and dancing, and I felt, too, a little like I'd come out of a long dream. I didn't really know how Frank felt about me and I wasn't sure that what I was feeling wasn't a rebound emotion, but I did know that I couldn't wait for the hours to pass before I could see Frank again. I was never so eager to keep a date in my life before.

At work, Cora teased me about keeping some kind of secret and wanted to know why I was so tense. I didn't tell her anything. I had learned not to tell people my innermost secrets and thoughts. But the moment I was able to quit work, I dashed for the ladies' lounge where I changed quickly into a blue spring suit. I looked well and I knew it. Did I also look older and wiser? Had Frank forgotten the scared, belligerent high-school senior I'd been?

Frank was sitting at the bar when I walked in, but he moved quickly to one of the small tables to one side. We sat down and I ordered a soft drink, and he grinned and said I was still a Coke addict, that hadn't changed.

"But a lot else has," he said then, his eyes serious. "I have."

"I know. You've been in Vietnam," I said. "I heard."

"That, too," he said. "A couple of times I wanted to write to you. Would you have answered?"

"I don't know," I said. "Why did you want to write to me?"

"Maybe to apologize again. What a stupid ass I was. No, don't stop me, we've got to let it out, Norma. I mean that whole mess was wrong maybe from the beginning. I more than liked you, but when I heard that rumor, it scared me, and I wanted to bug out. That's about it. I was a coward, and you might as well know—"

"You were young," I said. "I was scared too."

"That's the hell of it. We were both too young to face it, but we should have. You should have talked to me and I should have talked with you—"

"Please, Frank, it's over—let's talk about something else. Are you back for good?"

"Not yet," he said. "I will be in a couple of months."

"And then what?"

"I want to come back home," he said. "I'm homesick. Sound silly to you?"

"No. Even though I haven't ever been homesick, I think I can understand."

"Norma." He took my hand. "What I want is something every guy wants, a place that's home, a girl, a life that's normal. Norma, will you be my girl?"

I wanted to cry. We'd come such a long road alone. I was sure and I wasn't. Frank leaned over and kissed me lightly on the lips. There were few people in the taproom at that hour, and the lights were so dim no one paid any attention to us. Frank's kiss was sweet—it was more than that. It was the start of the love affair that should have been.

"Will it work out?" I asked him. "Can we start new, like nothing ever happened?"

"That's the way it's going to be," he promised me. "You'll see, nice and easy. We've got lots of time now."

Frank took me home a little while later. He came in and talked with Mom, and she made him stay to dinner. For the rest of his leave, three days, we were together constantly. We didn't do much. We drove around and we talked and we shared meals and we kissed. When our kisses got too dangerous, Frank pulled away.

"This time we'll do it right," he told me. "I'll be back soon and we'll make plans."

The day he left, I went down to the station to see him off. I couldn't help but notice the posters tied to the posts outside the station. WELCOME, BOBBY KENNEDY, they read. If Bobby Kennedy hadn't come to our town, I might not have gone out of the hotel that day to see him and might not have run into Frank again. *If.* That's such a little word, but it can change so many lives. I clung to Frank for a long moment and thought that it had probably been the luckiest day of my life.

Frank writes as often as he can and calls me at least twice a week. He's asked me to marry him, but I've told him to wait to talk about it until he comes home. I want everything to be corny and right for us this time, the engagement, the families, the bride and the groom, and all the jitters that go with it. I want everything to be right *forever* for Frank and me.

The End

Photo by Richard Avedon

Miss Sophia Loren

□ Hank smiled at me across the table. "Finish your dessert, honey, while I call The Gay Nineties to see what time the floor show starts."

I nodded, feeling the usual pride when I saw the admiring female glances that followed him to the phone booths in the bar. Big, lean, and good looking, Hank was the kind of man every girl dreams of falling in love with, but he was in love with me. And in three months we'd be married.

Feeling giddy with happiness, I smiled when our waiter appeared with the check.

"Your veal scallopini was to your liking?" he asked in a softly accented voice.

"It was just marvelous," I said. Then, because I thought what fun it would be to surprise Hank by cooking him an exotic meal like that myself some night, I impulsively asked the waiter if he could get me the recipe.

He glanced over his shoulder, then bent to rest his hands on the table. "The chef is very busy right now, but if you would give me your name and address I would be glad to mail it myself—"

At that moment I saw Hank heading back to the table. His steps slowed, and the tight expression I'd come to dread settled around his mouth before he strode over to sit down.

Straightening at once, the waiter said tonelessly, "Will that be all, sir?"

Hank nodded. His eyes were steely as he paid the bill. When the waiter had gone he said, "Shall we leave? Or would you rather wait and make friends with the chef and dishwasher too?"

My fingers tightened around my evening bag. "Oh, Hank, really! I merely asked him for the veal recipe, and he was obliging enough to offer to mail it to me. What's so terrible about that?"

"Oh, Lord!" he groaned. "You didn't give him your name and address, I hope!"

"I didn't get a chance," I snapped. "You came along looking like a thundercloud and scared the poor man away."

"For which you ought to be grateful, you naïve little idiot." He leaned forward, his voice intent. "Believe me, Kathy, if you'd found that character on your doorstep some night, it wouldn't have been *(Continued)*

CARNIVAL RAPE DATE

They say you can smell danger. I didn't. Not even when the nice, sandy-haired fellow kept turning up beside me everywhere I went . . .

239

food he had on his mind, not after the way *you* were smiling and yakking with him."

"And you think that's a crime, don't you?"

"I know it can cause a few. The sordid details are listed in the papers every day. In a city like this, Kathy, if a young, pretty girl cozies up to strange creeps, she's asking for trouble." He caught at my left hand, squeezing it hard to emphasize his words. "Getting too friendly with people you know nothing about just isn't wise."

"Says *who?*" My eyes laughed into his serious blue ones. "Seems to me the wisest maneuver I ever made was brazenly introducing myself to a very handsome stranger at a cocktail party seven months ago. As a matter of fact—" I glanced down at my hand. "—I've got a diamond here to *prove* it."

"Okay." He grinned as he came around to pull out my chair. "You made your point, but that was different and you know it. The point *I'm* trying to make is that not all people are the nice, harmless characters they appear to be. As far as that goes, you shouldn't have let me take you home that night. I'm glad you did, naturally—but for all you knew I could have been the biggest wolf in town."

"Ah, but I could tell you weren't," I said. "And I was right."

I had him there anyway, or so I thought until we went outside and got into the car. Then as we drove along toward the nightclub, he said, "And you could tell about Ilona Cummings, too, I suppose?"

Oh, no, I thought, *not that again!* Hank just wouldn't let me live down that stupid mistake. And more and more I resented his constantly flinging it in my face.

WHAT HAD HAPPENED was that right after Hank and I had started to date, the two girls I'd shared a large apartment with suddenly left me flat—one to elope with her boy friend, the other to take a new job in another city. On a secretary's salary, I couldn't handle the exorbitant rent by myself, so I'd run an ad in the paper for a new roommate. I had lots of responses and interviewed many nice girls, but the one I decided to accept was something else. Tall, stunningly dressed, very sophisticated, Ilona dazzled me with her vivid accounts of glamorous jobs, travels in Europe, and the important part she was sure to get in a new musical comedy.

"That's why I can't pay my half of the rent until next month," she explained when I'd tentatively mentioned it would be nice to have a little something in advance. "Not until I get a check from my agent."

Well, I was sure she'd pay the moment she could. I didn't even think it odd when she moved in with only one suitcase. After all, she'd traveled so much it was only natural she'd put a lot of her stuff in storage. So for two weeks I had an interesting roommate who entertained me with her exciting tales of romance and adventure. While waiting for her "rehearsals" to begin, she even cleaned the apartment while I was working all day. And, finally, she cleaned me out too, taking off with most of my clothes, my jewel box, cash, and even the few bottles of liquor I kept on hand for parties.

"All right," I said to Hank in a small voice when he reminded me of Ilona. "I'll admit I was wrong about her, but that doesn't mean that everyone's crooked."

He lit a cigarette. "You accepted her at face value, that's where you made your mistake, Kathy." He parked the car in the nightclub lot, then turned to face me.

"My concern is only for you, you know. When we're married, I'll be traveling for my firm a lot—we've talked about this before, remember? You'll be alone in a city apartment, and with your overly friendly personality, well—how can I not worry unless you tone it down?"

I made a glum face. "Okay, I won't even laugh if the floor show is funny for fear one of the chorus boys might think I'm flirting. Now, will you please stop lecturing me, Hank? I've just about had it for one evening."

He let out a sigh. "I'm sorry, honey. I don't mean to bawl you out all the time, but you're the girl I love more than anything in the whole world and—"

"And so let's forget the nightclub," I whispered, snuggling closer in his arms. "Let's just sit here and discuss that subject a little further. It's one we couldn't possibly disagree on."

Still, for all the lovely kisses that ended the evening, I was deeply troubled when Hank finally took me home. I lay awake for hours after I was in bed, taking stock of myself and him. It wasn't so much that Hank was actually jealous. He was too reasonable for such childish notions, and he knew how much I loved him. But he was so critical of me—of my basically outgoing personality. And what bothered me was that he seemed to expect me to adjust to *his* personality, rather than to try just a little more to understand mine. Lately, our evenings had ended up more and more often with us arguing, and if that tension crackled like electricity between us now, what would our relationship be when we were married?

Just before I drifted off to sleep, though, I had a hopeful thought. Next weekend, when Hank and I were planning to fly to my home town so he could meet my mother and we could announce our engagement, maybe he'd see how naturally friendly people in a small town always are. I burrowed under the covers, confident that after the long holiday weekend Hank and I would be closer and more in tune than we'd ever been.

Hank, born and raised in a big, bustling city, just couldn't realize what he'd missed not growing up in a sleepy little town like Elmsville. Oh, I might not have had a big, roomy house and some of the advantages other kids had—my dad died shortly after I was born and Mom supported us by cooking in the town's only hotel. But living in that hotel was wonderful. I was thoroughly spoiled by the traveling salesmen and regular boarders, and I had two aunts and three uncles, too, and loads of little cousins to make up for the sadness I felt at having no brothers or sisters.

I was on my own a lot, though. While my mother was working, I'd visit the pool hall across the street from the hotel and chatter with the men there, or I'd go down to the creek by the waterworks to watch the workers eat their lunch. They were always nice to me, and they'd often give me a cookie or an apple from their lunchboxes. Those were the kind of people from *my* town, but there were many people just as nice right here in the city. If Hank just smiled and gave a little once in a while, he'd come to realize that.

THAT FOLLOWING WEEK I felt myself getting more excited by the minute at the prospect of going home. Hank caught that excitement too, but when he kept urging me to let Mom know we were coming, I flatly refused. It was going to be a surprise, and that was final.

"But what if your mother has made plans to go out of town for the weekend or something, honey?" he asked. "You're not being very practical."

I hugged him hard, feeling a real pity for Hank who had no folks and just knew nothing about small towns. "She won't be anywhere I can't find her, darling," I said. "My relations don't take trips to fancy resorts or things like that. Mom and the rest of the family will all be right there, believe me."

"Okay," he said, but he sounded doubtful. "If you're so positive, I'll go ahead and confirm our flight reservations."

"I know my people and I know my town, silly," I insisted. "And everyone will be on hand and nothing will have changed. Now stop worrying!"

Friday finally came, and I left work early to go home and bathe and pack so I'd be ready when Hank called for me. We'd be traveling practically all night, for the trip was a long one and involved changing planes in Chicago. But I felt as Hank did that it would be worth the time and expense. I wasn't getting married at home because we'd decided to have just a simple civil ceremony when Hank got his two-week vacation in November. So this trip back home would make up for not having a big wedding.

I was through packing and ready to slip into my pink linen traveling suit when I heard a knock at my door. Thinking that it was Hank, I hastily pulled on a robe and ran to open the door.

But the young man standing there was a stranger. My hands flew to the front of my robe to wrap it around me more closely. "Oh!" I exclaimed. "I thought you were someone else."

A slow grin tugged at the man's lips. He lounged against the doorjamb, his eyes flicking over me appreciatively. "Whoever he is, he's a lucky guy," he said. His voice was rather thick, and I smelled the raw odor of gin as he spoke. He held up an ice container. "They sent me out for ice, and this was the first place I came to," he explained. "My wife and I are having a little housewarming—just moved in."

I could hear the sounds of music and laughter from one flight up, so I opened the door and grinned back at the man. "Well, welcome to the building," I said as I took his bucket and headed into the kitchen to get the ice.

When I brought his bucket back to him, he'd stepped inside the door and was gazing around with interest. "This is real neighborly of you, baby," he said. "Look, why don't the two of us have a short one together and sort of get acquainted—"

He stepped toward me, stumbling on the throw rug by the door, and instinctively I put out my hands to steady him. At that moment, over his shoulder, I saw a woman coming down the stairs from the upper floor. She paused, her eyes widening, then in two steps she was beside us, jerking the man away from me, her face flushed with anger.

"There's always one man-chaser in every building!" she shrilled. "What do you mean luring my husband in here—"

"Now just a minute!" I began indignantly, but before I could explain what had happened the elevator door opened and Hank got out. He walked quickly toward us just in time to hear the woman rip into me again.

"What's the trouble here, Kathy?" Hank demanded.

I backed inside my apartment, burning with embarrassment, and Hank followed. I closed the door with a loud bang, shutting out the woman and her husband. "It was nothing," I said. "They're new tenants and he asked to borrow some ice. She followed him and got hysterical about it. It's as simple as that."

"As simple as that!" Hank repeated. "You mean you let that drunk in here without even knowing him? No wonder his wife was mad! Don't you have a brain in your head? Won't I ever be able to trust you out of my sight?"

"Trust me?" I cried. "I was only trying to be neighborly, but you and that awful woman act like I'm a tramp! Well, I won't be treated this way, do you hear?"

I burst into tears—I just couldn't help it. That shattered Hank completely, and he put his arms around me and comforted me until, glancing at his watch, he reminded me that we only had a little while to catch our plane. Neither of us spoke all the way to the airport, and I was still smarting from Hank's unfair accusations when we were on the jet and taxiing out to the runway. Then his hand found mine.

"Let's forget what happened and not spoil the trip, honey. Okay?" he said softly.

It was easy to forgive Hank when he was so sweet. But, even so, I fervently hoped the long weekend would show him how, in a town like mine, no one was a stranger, and he'd come to accept my openhearted attitude toward people.

It was early Saturday morning when we finally got home. When we stepped out of the taxi, Mom was on the porch of the little house she shared with Aunt Nada. She had her old green robe on, just as I had pictured her in all my homesick longings, and was peering into the shrubs. "Kitty, kitty," I heard her call softly.

"She always has a cat," I told Hank. "She talks to it, and it understands every word."

Hank stood aside when the taxi had gone, waiting for Mom to discover me. When she did and flew toward me with her arms open, my eyes brimmed with tears. Then I turned to take Hank's hand and draw him close to me.

"Why, he's just as handsome as a movie star, Kathy," Mom exclaimed, "just like you said in your letters—and he's going to be my new son!"

Before Hank could say a word, she hugged him hard and, after a moment, I saw his arms go around her too. *Yes, Hank will learn a lot about people here,* I thought, *and he'll see how right and natural it is to be friendly.*

I couldn't wait to find Aunt Nada and show Hank off to her. "I've promised him your wonderful buttermilk pancakes," I said when the flurry of welcome had died down. "With sausage and some of Mom's strawberry jam."

Mom was already on the phone, and friends and relatives began popping in before we were half through eating. I guess I must have introduced Hank to a dozen or more people, and although he was a little stiff at first, pretty soon he was laughing and talking with them all.

"I'm so proud of you, darling," I whispered when I had a chance. "They all love you!"

His fingers found mine under the table. "Nice people," he said with a smile.

The hours flew past that day and the next. I walked Hank all over town, pointing out the creek where I'd learned to swim and skate, introducing him to everyone along the way, and watching him gradually thaw. And Sunday night at a big dinner party in our honor, everyone took turns telling Hank about some of my childhood escapades, especially the one about the old tramp.

"He came to the back door of the hotel," Mom explained, "and Kathy saw him. But instead of calling to me or one of the waitresses to give him a handout there, she led him right into the dining room where he ordered the biggest steak in the house. Well, I fixed it for him, but Kathy had to pay for it out of her allowance."

Hank laughed with the others when Mom had finished the story, then he whispered to me, "Always asking for it, weren't you?"

His smile softened the words so that I wasn't as annoyed as I might have been, but I was glad when someone changed the subject and began to talk about the summer carnival and livestock show. Because of new industry and more people in the county that year, there were more concessions and rides than ever before. So many, in fact, that the carnival was being held well out of town at the lake.

"You're in for an experience you'll never forget, city boy!" I told Hank when we'd borrowed a car from one of my uncles. "There is nothing in the whole wide world like a country carnival."

And that year, like everyone had said, it was bigger and better than ever. Thousands of multicolored lights were reflected in the calm lake waters, and the music from the merry-go-round blasted out from big loudspeakers. A dance floor had been set up, too, beneath a gaily striped red-and-white canopy, and when I heard the band playing, I pulled Hank along impatiently.

"Let's dance first—or maybe we'd better go on the merry-go-round—oh, I want to do everything at once!"

He chuckled indulgently, his arms slipping around my waist. "Like a kid at Christmas aren't you? Hey—look!" He pointed toward the lake dock, all decorated with crepe-paper streamers. A big sign said: BOAT RIDES TO LOVERS' COVE. "How about it, Kathy?"

I shook my head. "Not yet—that's last on the agenda. Come on, I want to show you off!"

On the dance floor, I waved at other couples I knew, stopping now and then to introduce Hank, show my diamond, and catch up on gossip about old school friends. No other man on the floor looked so distinguished and handsome as Hank. Many admiring glances came our way, and I said to Hank, "We look well together, did you know that?"

His arms tightened. "And when we're married, we'll have beautiful children, all girls who'll look just like their mother!"

We danced awhile, and then we wandered around the carnival grounds some more. I kept glancing around me expectantly as we walked along, looking for familiar faces. Once I would have known at least every other person in the crowd, but aside from the few couples I'd spotted earlier, the faces were new to me, the people were strangers. One man, thin faced with blond hair, caught my glance and held it, and I tentatively smiled, wondering if he was someone I'd known as a kid. But he didn't come over to us, so I figured not.

"What'll it be, honey?" Hank was saying as he led me to the rifle range. "A big doll or the panda?"

"I want the biggest and hardest prize to win!" I said, and heard soft laughter behind me. Turning, I saw the same thin-faced man standing there, his hands in his pockets as he sort of rocked back and forth on the balls of his feet.

"That's five bull's-eyes," he said. "A real tough one with those rusty guns."

"Especially when pulling the trigger is probably a bit rusty too!" I kidded back.

Hank tugged at my arm, and I turned to see his set mouth. "Don't encourage that character!" he muttered.

"Look, Hank, I'm not sure I don't know him." I said in a low, angry voice.

"Forget it," he said. "Come on!"

I could feel myself start to do a slow

burn, but I forgot all about my irritation when Hank began to shoot, so far from the target I giggled my head off before he finally gave up with a rueful shrug. "Okay, Miss Smartie, so that's not one of my talents." He gave me a wolfish look, adding, "But just wait until I get you over to Lovers' Cove!"

We rode the tilt-a-whirl and the Ferris wheel, and Hank seemed to be having a wonderful time.

"It's fun showing you my kind of life," I said when we were on our way to a little beer garden. "After all, you showed me the supper clubs and theaters in the city."

He pulled my arm through his and squeezed my hand, all smiles and good humor.

The beer bar was crowded. Every stool was occupied, and Hank held up two fingers to show the bartender we'd take our drinks over to one of the tables in the pavilion.

"Here, take my stool." It was the same thin-faced man. Up closer he was older than I'd thought, sunburned and craggy like a farmer. I figured he was probably exhibiting sheep or a prize steer from his ranch. I smiled and started to accept the seat he offered when Hank cut in angrily. "No, thanks," he said in a grating voice. "She can stand."

Suddenly I was really furious. "Thank you anyway," I said as warmly as I could under the circumstances. "*I* appreciate the offer."

"I see you didn't get your panda," the man said, ignoring Hank who was glaring daggers. "I was watching your boy friend and he didn't hold the rifle steady. Here, take mine." From the floor he picked up a fat panda with a darling smile on its face.

"Why, I—how nice of you!" I started to take the oversize toy, then hesitated, turning to Hank, mutely begging him to see how innocent the little gesture was, how friendly.

"Go ahead, take it!" the farmer insisted. "And let me buy you both a beer."

Hank's voice was too loud, and very angry. "Look, buddy, why don't you take your bear and get lost? I can buy my girl a beer, a bear, or whatever else she wants!" Several people had turned to stare at us. Hank's hand on my bare arm was rough as he dragged me off.

"I'm sorry," I called back defiantly to the stranger. "I'd like to have had the panda—really."

"Now what kind of a crack was that?" Hank said furiously when we were a distance away. "Can't you see that hick's a wolf, trying to move in on you?"

The word *hick* jabbed at me. So that was what Hank thought of all my friends—after all the hospitality they had shown him. He probably thought *I* was a hick, too.

"Oh, you—you snob!" My voice was shaking with tears. "I was just trying to be courteous." Then I burst out, "Hank, I'll never understand you!"

"And I'll never understand you!" he lashed back at me. "That jerk thought you'd flipped over him, so naturally he's been following us all evening. Come on—let's take the boat ride and get out of here."

"If you don't mind," I snapped, "I'll take the boat ride alone! You've ruined enough of the evening for me with your stupid, jealous suspicions."

He started to protest, and deep down I hoped that he would insist on coming with me. But then he wheeled around to the ticket window, his shoulders rigid. "Help yourself," he said stubbornly, "and while you're alone, try to do a little constructive thinking."

I kept my chin high as I marched an-

Nine special reasons to turn to your CBS Radio Station every weekend

ARTHUR GODFREY

RICHARD C. HOTTELET

ROBERT TROUT

BOB DIXON

HENRY MORGAN

HARRY REASONER

GARRY MOORE

JACK DREES

ALLAN JACKSON

(And stay there.)

What a lineup!
The irresistible, irreverent humor of Godfrey, Moore and Morgan. The experts' view of the news from Trout, Hottelet, Jackson and Reasoner. Jack Drees on Sports—scores, standings and sidelights. Bob Dixon introducing the off-beat, the uncommon in lively Weekend Dimension® features.

What a weekend—every weekend!

Special listening? You bet. And there's more. Your CBS Radio station listed opposite offers all this and the best in local programming, too. Have a wonderful weekend. In fact, make it a long wonderful weekend—like all week long.

The CBS Radio Network

grily along the wooden planks to the end of the pier. Couples crowded there, laughing as they piled into the constantly moving stream of little motorboats going across and coming back. I felt foolish and conspicuous by myself, but I wouldn't go back! I was tired of giving in to Hank, of having him bawl me out all the time. Most of all, I was furious with him for spoiling the night.

WHEN I WAS FINALLY in a boat vacated by a returning couple, my eyes filled with tears as I bobbed across the water. Only a few months until our wedding, and Hank and I were still miles apart as far as understanding each other went. The tears overflowed down my cheeks and I hastily brushed them away, determined not to cry. I was sick of crying and of constantly defending myself when I'd done nothing wrong!

I think I would have turned around and gone right back when I got to the other side, but two couples were waiting for a boat and because they looked at me kind of funny, I got out and gave them mine. Besides, it would do Hank good to cool his heels over there for a while, I thought.

On that side of the lake the carnival grounds had been laid out in tunnels and paths, with little bridges leading into groves of trees. There were benches, fountains, cupid statues—it was a real lovers' paradise. *This was to have been the highlight of our evening!* I thought as I sat down on an empty bench. Lovers everywhere, whispering, laughing, strolling past me, while Hank pouted back there and I sat alone.

Well, I'd tried, but Hank just couldn't accept me as I was. What kind of a marriage could we possibly hope to have when he was so unreasonable? With him for a husband, I probably wouldn't be allowed to have any friends at all. *Oh, Hank, I thought, we have so much going for us, but you're ruining it all.*

"All alone like me?"

The pleasant voice startled me until, as the lone figure came closer along the path, I recognized the thin-faced man. I didn't feel like talking to him, but Hank had treated him so rudely that something compelled me to try to make up for it. So, I smiled, and said, "I'm just waiting for a boat to take me back. It's kind of cute here isn't it, the way they've fixed things up."

He shrugged, shifting the panda bear he still carried to his other arm. "I guess so. I haven't looked around much myself. I came over with another couple, but like your friend back at the bar, they let me know I was in the way."

A girl streaked past us, giggling as a boy chased her. When they were out of sight I could hear her pretended outrage and she screamed, "Now, Roy, stop it! I mean it—" and then silence.

"He caught her, I guess, and shut her up," my friend said in amusement. Another pair strolled along the path, their arms and eyes clinging. "A fellow doesn't have much fun if he hasn't a girl along. But—say, would you like to look around some with me before you go back?"

I felt kind of sorry for him. "Well—just for a few minutes. Then I really have to get back across."

I could hear murmurs from the darkness all around us, so it was all right, I told myself as we strolled along. Besides, this hick, as Hank had called him, was sort of pathetic.

There wasn't much to see, really. It was much prettier back by the water with the lights twinkling on the water and the boats coming and going. My companion was so silent that I finally suggested we return.

"No," he said in a thick voice, and his hand closed around my wrist. "There's more down that path there—more to see."

His fingers were biting into my arm, but when I tried to pull away, they tightened. My heart began to thud as sudden fear gave me the strength to jerk my arm and wrench free.

"I'm going back. I—I don't want to see any more," I said.

The man's lips moved in a smile, but there wasn't any laughter in his eyes. "No, I don't want to see any more either," he said, "but that isn't why we came down here and you know it." His tongue slid along his bottom lip. "Come on—come on, baby, don't give me a hard time."

For a frozen moment I was rooted there, held in a grip of terror. This man wasn't some nice, harmless farmer—this was a nut, a sex fiend! Then he took a step toward me, and the movement jarred me to my senses so that I quickly spun and began to run, a scream starting in my throat. He was right behind me, his feet thudding closer. "Hey, here's your panda—don't you want your panda, baby?" he wheedled.

A girl giggled from somewhere nearby, and I heard a man's deep voice mimic, "Don't you want your panda, baby?"

I swallowed the scream. At least I was safe with couples all around us, and I could see the lake ahead, thank God! I'd hop in a boat and be away in another minute—

Then I felt his hands on me again, and I stumbled. In that second, his arms went around my waist.

"Let me go!" I screamed. "Get away from me!"

He twisted me around, crushing me up against him. "Come on back, baby—back with me—" he said, breathing hard.

I tried to beat my fists against his chest. He caught at my hands, and then pinned my arms to my sides. Two couples hurried past us, glancing back in amusement before they scrambled into a boat. "Let me go—someone help!" I screamed again, writhing helplessly against my attacker. It was like a nightmare! People all around us, people across the lake waiting for boats and watching my frantic struggles—watching and doing nothing!

"Let's go—let's go back there in the dark, baby," the man said in a sickening half whisper. I tried to kick him, but my body was smashed against his, and suddenly he slid an arm down and lifted me up. Holding me, he began to run back along the path, away from the other people and into the thick darkness.

I scratched at his face, screaming and yelling for help. I heard answering screams—muffled screams of flirtation, distant screams of excitement from the carnival rides. No one realized that I was in real danger.

Then I was being tossed down on the ground, and the man was muttering obscenities, ripping my dress off, clawing at me. Nausea clogging my throat, blackness tugging at my consciousness, I sobbed, "No—oh, no!"

AND THEN, silently, miraculously, the man was hurled away from me. I heard Hank's curse as he hit him, and then I screamed as Hank's next blow missed and he went over backward. *"Hank—look out!"* I cried. The rapist had a knife in his hand. He leaped at Hank, making a quick thrust with the knife. I screamed when I heard Hank's grunt of agony. The man moved toward Hank again, the knife gleaming cruelly, then he stopped. Pounding footsteps were coming down the path, and at their sound the man froze, then turned and ran into the thicket.

Sobbing hysterically, I crawled to Hank, whimpering his name. I felt the stickiness of warm blood on my hands as I touched his shoulder. *Oh, God, was he dead?* Then

he moved, just a little, and shook his head as though to clear it. "Hank—oh, Hank!" I cried.

Groaning, he raised himself to a sitting position. "Kathy—are you—all right?" he whispered.

"Yes, yes, darling!" I reassured him.

As I knelt beside him, I noticed all the people gathering around us, staring and murmuring. "Why didn't you do something?" I sobbed. "When I called for help, why didn't somebody *do* something?"

A man, his girl clinging to his arm, gawked at me like I was crazy. "How did we know? We saw you and him together, laughing and all, so when you began yelling, we figured it didn't mean anything. . . ."

"I saw the two of them too," a woman piped up. "If you want my opinion, she was just asking for it!"

I felt other eyes on me and turned to look at Hank. I saw his pained, hopeless expression before he slowly shook his head and looked away from my torn clothes and bruised shoulders. *Asking for it.* That was what Hank had been telling me again and again and again.

The crowd moved away, no longer interested in Hank and me, and I put my face in my hands and sobbed in despair. Hank stirred, his hands touching my shuddering shoulders. Then other hands were helping me up—a policeman. Other officers crashed through the brush with flashlights.

We had to go back to the station with them, and once we were there Hank answered the necessary questions. I couldn't even talk I was so ashamed and upset. When a doctor there had treated us both —thank God, Hank's wound was only superficial—the officers told us we were free to go.

"We'll try to find the guy who tried to attack your girl," they told Hank, "but he's probably out of the state by now. He was some drifter, no doubt. We get lots of 'em during carnival time."

Hank didn't say anything until we were outside in my uncle's car. Then he said, "Honey, I never should have let this happen. It was my fault for letting you go off like that and then waiting around before I went to get you."

"Oh, Hank, and if you hadn't—" I drew in a long shuddering breath, love pouring through me that he could sit there and say that any of it was his fault when it was mine and mine alone. "I walked right into it—again! If you never, never forgave me I wouldn't blame you in the least!"

"I love you, Kathy," he said, "so stop talking like that. Now come on, honey, let's go to your mother's and try to sleep for a little while anyway. We've got a plane to catch out of here tomorrow." He smiled wryly. "Back to the big, wicked city." He slipped his good arm around my shoulders, pulling me close. "But maybe it all happened for the best, honey. Maybe you had to come back home to find out that there are nuts and kooks everywhere."

AND MAYBE I DID. Sometimes, though, even now, I wake up whimpering from the nightmare of that carnival, and Hank's arms pull me close as he soothes away my fears. For a long time after our marriage, I was tense and nervous, even about getting into an elevator in our apartment building when Hank wasn't with me. I suppose it was the normal reaction to such a shocking experience, and gradually I'm beginning to relax again. I'm trying to use common sense and a reasonable amount of caution in my relationships with strangers, as Hank has always done. I know there are sick people in the world as well as good, trustworthy people, and you don't open your heart or your home to just anyone who knows. *The End*

SEX GANG

☐ I pretended not to see the slip of paper Jimmy handed to Scott. Instead, I turned toward the bus window and found myself staring into my own scared blue eyes.

"We have the half," Scott whispered to me, slipping the piece of paper in his pocket. He took my hand and squeezed it. "Okay?"

I let Scott hold me
the way he always did
when we were alone,
and I kissed him. Then
I heard the footsteps

IN THE SCHOOL BUS
We made it our private motel

"Okay." I hoped my voice sounded normal. What Scott and I would be doing during the half at the basketball game was wrong. What was worse, it was dangerous. But I was in it now, and there was no turning back.

I turned to Scott. He was still holding my hand but talking to Beezy, who sat in the seat in front of us in the bus that was taking us to the game between our school, Warren High, and Mount Ida High School.

I loved Scott—even he didn't realize how much I loved him. Once, when we'd been kissing, he'd said, "I wish we were four years older and we were going to graduate from college. I'd have something to ask you then."

I wanted him to ask me to marry him right now! I wanted to be with him always. I'd never loved a boy that much before. But then I'd never been anything to a boy before Scott, either. In tenth grade I'd liked a boy named Travis. He'd walked me home from school and shared Cokes and his lunch with me, and I'd liked it because my girl friends envied me. No more than that. Eleventh grade was a bomb. My parents got after me about my grades, and things in general got a bit rough.

I was glad when my junior year ended. I got a summer job clerking in the dime store. It didn't pay much, but it got me away from home and my mother. I love my mother, of course, but she can be a terrible nag. I don't mean just about schoolwork, either. Sometimes I don't know what it is she expects of me. I feel I'm always letting her down, so I rebel and do some pretty stupid things—like with Scott.

The way it started with us, we started meeting on the bus that summer. Scott had a horrible job at one of the beach clubs—he said they worked him to death. I wasn't exactly ecstatic about my job in the dime store, so we looked for each other and found each other. For me, it was a big break. Scott was a boy any girl would go for, and the fact that I fell into his orbit that summer was pretty unbelievable. A girl has to play her cards right. I didn't chase Scott, but I kept him interested. I let him think I went out with other boys, but when he'd ask if we could take in a movie I'd be available and really happy to be with him.

By the time school started in September, we were going steady. I was the envy of my best girl friend, Cathy. She didn't have a steady, and when you don't have a steady by senior year, forget it— you're going to bomb out. I tried to get Cathy into Scott's crowd, but she didn't make it. After a while we kind of drifted apart. She'd call me at home once in a while, and if I was there we'd talk. But there was a kind of strain in our friendship. I was in with a crowd and she wasn't.

Scott and I dated a lot with Jimmy and Fran, because Jimmy could get his father's car. I don't mean we went out every night—parents aren't that obliging—but on a Friday or Saturday night we'd go to a movie or hang around and we always took in the games together. Leslie and her boy friend, Rad, came with us now and then, too, and the six of us did have some good times.

As I said, that fall we took in all the football games together and some that were away, but in November Jimmy's father wouldn't let him have the car at night so when the first basketball game away came up we all went in the school bus.

THE FIRST TIME, Jimmy was in a bad mood because he couldn't have the car, and he kept making cracks about the bus being too crowded. When we arrived at the school, he just sat there saying maybe he'd skip the game, but Pete, our bus driver, said "Everybody out" and he meant it. Pete went in to see the game, too. He'd gone to our high school, and we kids laughed at his gung-ho attitude about our teams. He claimed the school hadn't had a decent team since his class had graduated.

As we were getting out, Jimmy glanced back at the empty bus and said to Scott, "Seems a shame to leave a nice empty bus and go in there with all that hollering, doesn't it?"

"Come on, what's got into you?" Scott said. "Since when have you been crazy about buses?"

"Since I got an idea." Jimmy laughed and then he pulled Scott aside and whispered to him, and then both of them talked to Rad. I saw Rad's face flush and he kept nodding. That was all until the end of the first quarter—then I noticed Jimmy and Fran didn't come back with us after we went out into the hallway to get a soft drink provided by the host school.

"Where's Jimmy and Fran?" I asked Scott.

"They'll be back," Scott said and squeezed my hand. He kept watching the

clock more than the game, I noticed. At the half intermission, Jimmy and Fran were back, and Leslie and Rad went out. By then I was really intrigued. When Scott urged me away from the game during the last quarter, I went willingly. We headed right for the empty bus parked down at the end of the athletic field, outside the gates.

"Scott, where are we going?" I asked.

He laughed and grabbed my hand, and we ran for the bus like we were going to miss it. The door swung open and we went inside. It was dark and kind of eerie with all those empty seats.

"How's this for privacy?" Scott said and pulled me down in a seat.

"Scott, someone will see us!" I was getting nervous.

"Who's going to be looking in an empty bus?" he asked. "Besides, don't you want to be here with me?"

"You know I do." I turned to him.

"Beats the car I can't get." He kissed me and then he kissed my again. "Once in a while Jimmy gets some good ideas," he said.

"You mean that's where they've been? I mean, here?" I giggled. "What if we're caught?"

"Shut up and let me kiss you!" he growled. "We haven't got all night, just the last quarter."

I shut up and let him kiss me, figuring that was all it was going to be. Just kisses, I mean. But Scott seemed to be getting other ideas. He kept pressing me down on the seat, and his hands trembled as they touched me.

"I'm so crazy about you," he kept saying as he kissed me. "If you're really my girl, prove it."

"Scott, no—I'm scared!" I felt like crying.

"Don't be. No one can see us here," he whispered. "Don't you want to?"

I wanted to do anything that would please Scott, even that. And so it happened. I remember thinking it wasn't the big deal I thought it would be. I didn't feel thrilled or excited. I was just glad when it was over. I felt embarrassed. So did Scott. He kind of muttered that maybe we'd better go back to the gym.

"I'd rather not," I said. "Let's walk around."

We walked, not even holding hands, and I got chilled in my light coat. Thankfully I saw the doors of the school swing open and kids begin to come out. Pretty soon our gang came back to the bus and we boarded with them. We'd lost the game. Pete was mad as a wet hen at the team, and he kept telling us we hadn't rooted enough. I was only half listening. I glanced at Fran—her face was kind of strained, too. But Leslie was blissfully curled up next to Rad, holding his hand. So it wasn't the first time for them, I figured. They had planned for it to happen. I don't know why I felt so isolated somehow.

At home that night I tried to go right to sleep, but a million thoughts kept going through my head. Cathy and I had often discussed girls who went all the way. We'd sworn we wouldn't be like that. Cathy was still a good girl, but I wasn't. I hadn't dared to say no to Scott. I loved him too much to take a chance on losing him.

When he called early the next morning, I felt a rush of relief. Then it was all right. Scott loved me, too.

I had to cling to that belief in the weeks ahead. I tried not to feel different inside, but I did. When Scott and I met in the lunchroom there was a secret bond between us. When we touched hands or kissed, I felt the desire flare up in him. I knew that there'd be another time for us, and I wondered when. It wasn't easy to be alone. Scott didn't have a car. And when

Jimmy had his father's car and a date with Fran, he didn't ask for company.

THE SECOND BASKETBALL GAME away from home came up, and Scott asked me to go. I guess I knew what was going to happen before we started out in the bus. When Jimmy handed the slip of paper to Scott and he whispered to me that we had the half, I felt embarrassment wash over me. It was like—well, it was like making a game of something sacred and beautiful. I wanted to tell Scott as much, but he turned his face to me and smiled so lovingly I didn't have the heart. I held his hand as we went into the school and found a seat on the bleachers.

I didn't really see the game. I was only aware of Jimmy and Fran leaving after the first quarter, and Scott urging me to follow him at the half when kids were milling around outside the gym to get something to eat and drink. Scott took my hand and we ran, as if we were racing against time.

It was warm in the bus. Scott closed the door and turned to me and laughed. "Our private motel!" he said, and I flinched.

"Oh, Scott, let's go back to the game," I said, suddenly hating the bus, with its smell of wet clothes and rotting leather seats.

"Come on, Connie—we can't do that," he said, sitting down and pulling me down beside him. "You want Jimmy to lose confidence in his ideas?"

"I don't care about Jimmy," I said. "I feel creepy here."

"Okay, we'll go back, but let me kiss you first," he said.

We kissed, and his mouth was soft and gentle. We kissed again. I felt myself whirling in space, and I didn't really want to go back. I didn't want to leave the dark bus or Scott. . . .

We didn't hear the bus door open—it was automatic and when the hiss did get through to us it was too late. Suddenly three boys loomed up at us from the dark. Scott pushed himself up from the seat. "Hey, what's going on?" he exclaimed angrily.

"I told you that other couple came here," one boy said and laughed.

"Baby, what a setup," another guy said. "How long has this been going on?"

"Come on, Connie!" Scott took my hand and started to push our way out of the bus, but the three boys were not going to let us off that easy. To them, it was a big joke.

"Hold on, friend," one of them said and grabbed me. "We won't tell on you. We just want to join the fun."

"Get out of our way," Scott said.

"Sure, pass." The boy made a gesture to Scott, but when I started to follow, he put out an arm to stop me. "Not you, doll. We've got plans for you!" he said.

I slapped the boy's hand away and ran for the door. Someone caught me around the waist and pulled me back. I heard Scott say something and then one of the boys began to punch him. They all went at him, and he didn't have a chance. I began to scream and sob and pull at the boys who had Scott down in the narrow aisle of the bus, holding him there. One of the boys turned to me and grabbed me. When I resisted, he tore at my sweater, trying to pull it over my neck.

I scratched and screamed in a wild panic. I wasn't afraid just for myself, but for Scott, too. I didn't know what was happening to him. When the boy tried to push me down on a seat, I hit him. He flinched away from me for a second, and that gave me a chance to dive toward the door and out.

The parking lot looked a mile wide as I ran toward the lighted school. I didn't

A TRIBUTE TO TINY

☐ *Dear Editor: So many times in all the rush of modern living, we forget a very important member of almost every American home—their pet. In our case, it was a dog. Tiny was a small, blond, shaggy dog who made her home with us for five and a half years. I would like very much to share her with your readers. . . .*

I remember that day. I remember it as if it just happened yesterday. My husband came in from work hiding a little round blond piece of fur in his pocket. That is how I was introduced to Tiny—and tiny she was.

For a whole week, we had to keep her with us day and night because she would cry if we left her alone. You might say she was our first baby. We had just been married three and a half months when we got her—and she was the one who stood by me during all those hard adjustments of the first year of marriage.

Everyone loved her. As she grew bigger, she could outrun any dog in the neighborhood. Smart? Oh, she was smart—she seemed to understand everything we said and felt. After our first child was born, she would whine to me if the baby cried, and she'd stand on the edge of the bed on her two hind legs trying to see what was the matter. A year and a half later, our second child was born. Tiny

wouldn't let anyone she didn't know well come near the children. And when my father got so sick and I used to cry because I was so worried, Tiny would stand on her hind legs and put her front paws on my lap and whine and try to comfort me in her small way.

The beginning of this year, she was struck by a passing car and, because of that, her right leg was completely paralyzed. She didn't give up, though. She could still get around the neighborhood.

It's been five and a half years since that day when I first met Tiny. Now I keep going over all the memories she left me. You see, Tiny was run over last week by some careless, selfish driver who did not have the time to spare to wait while a small limping dog crossed the street. So Tiny was left to die in the street. . . .

We have lost a very important member of our family. There is no one to greet us at the gate, and outside our door is still an empty plate from which Tiny will never eat again. There is someone missing in our home. I can feel it when I go to bed at night, and again there's that empty feeling when I get up in the morning.

A part of my life has gone—a part of my heart. I lost my best friend last week. Nothing will ever be the same!

stop to consider what anyone would think. I was too scared for Scott. I ran into the school. Some kids were in the hallway outside the gym, watching the game from the door and keeping an eye on the refreshments, and I rushed up to them.

"Help—please!" I screamed. "They're going to kill Scott! In the bus—"

A boy I didn't know said something to some other kids, and a bunch of them followed me. The game was still going on inside. We raced back toward the school bus. It looked so quiet inside—no one seemed to be there. Where was Scott? My knees nearly gave way as we got near. One of the boys scrambled onto the bus first. I was close behind, and I heard him say, "He's dead!"

I didn't faint. I just gagged and fell back against the driver's seat. I slumped down near the floor. I could see Scott—like a bunch of rags all knotted up in the aisle. There were more voices then, and pretty soon I saw Pete push his way into the bus. He saw me, but he headed for Scott, knelt by him, and then called out to someone to get an ambulance.

"He's dead!" I screamed to Pete. "They killed him!"

By that time the whole basketball game was a shambles. Kids kept pouring out of the school and running toward the bus, and police came roaring up and tried to take charge.

I wouldn't leave the bus. I insisted on staying with Scott. He looked dead to me, but when they tried to move him, I heard him whisper, "I can't breathe. I can't—"

BY THAT TIME an ambulance had arrived and the attendants cleared the bus while they carried Scott out. It was quite a job, too, getting him out of that narrow aisle and onto the stretcher and into the ambulance. The police wouldn't let me go with him. They said they had to question me. Pete, our bus driver, kept close to me, and Jimmy and the rest stood by looking as scared as I felt.

"What in hell were you doing out here?" Pete kept asking me.

I couldn't answer. I couldn't tell him why we'd come out to the bus.

Rad came up to me and whispered, "Listen, no matter what they ask you, play dumb. Say you were taking a walk, you hear?"

He was just a scared coward, and I hated him at that moment. Jimmy, too. They were both scared for their own skins.

"Scott might be dead—don't you care about that?" I sobbed.

"Don't be dumb." Franny pinched my arm. "Get hold of yourself. You'll only get us all in trouble if you talk too much!"

Get them all in trouble! That was all they were worrying about while Scott was on his way to a hospital or a morgue!

The police insisted on taking my name, of course. They told me they wanted me to go with them to the police station to make a statement. They were going to contact my parents to come and get me. They couldn't hold me for anything, but they wanted a description of the boys who had attacked Scott.

I told the police I had never seen the boys before, and that in the dark it had been hard to distinguish features or anything that might help the police identify them.

"Why did they attack your friend?" one of the policemen asked. "Was there any provocation?"

"None," I said.

"Why were you in the bus and not inside watching the game?"

I knew that question would be asked. "We came out for a walk—and the bus was here—and we decided to just sit in it and wait for the others." It was a lame excuse and lamer explanation.

"You mean you got bored with the basketball game?" one of the policemen asked me.

"Not exactly. We just took a walk at the half and were going back in—"

I couldn't tell the truth. I couldn't for my sake and for the sake of the other kids. It was bad enough that Scott might die. What good would it do to get us all in serious trouble? I suppose the other kids went home in the school bus. I went with the policemen to give my statement and wait for Dad to pick me up.

When he came, he looked white and drawn. I began to cry and he tried to comfort me.

"Will you need her for anything else?" he asked the police.

They said no, not at the moment, but they'd be in touch if I were needed to identify suspects.

When Dad and I got outside, I buried my face in his coat and cried some more.

"Dad, can we go see about Scott?" I asked him. "He's in the hospital."

"We'll stop by," he told me.

Scott's parents had been notified and they were already there. Scott's mother looked like she'd been crying, and his father looked haggard. Scott, they told us, had a broken neck. The doctors were working on him at that very moment trying to save his life.

"We don't even know how it happened," his mother said, biting her lip to control her tears. "You went to the game in the school bus—how could three boys attack him on a school bus?"

Stammering, I tried to tell the same story I'd told the police.

"You mean the two of you got into the bus when it was parked out there in the dark—just to be alone?" Scott's mother asked.

"We didn't do anything. We were going right back to the game—"

She looked at me. She knew, and I knew she knew, and I was so ashamed I wanted to die.

"Oh, God!" she said and turned away.

DAD AND I LEFT. I had an idea Scott's mother didn't want me there. Dad didn't say a word on the way home. Mom was waiting for us at the front door. She hadn't wanted to leave my two young brothers alone, but she was beside herself with worry. She put her arms around me and said, "Are you all right?"

I wasn't—I was a child again, coming to Mom with a scratched knee and a broken doll, knowing she would fix both. I cried and cried. Mom let me cry it out. She sent Dad off to bed and then asked me to tell her everything. I did—that is, what there was to tell without revealing the real reason Scott and I had gone out to the school bus. And I just couldn't tell her *that.*

"Pray for Scott," she said to me then. "We'll go and see him early in the morning."

I said good night and went up to my room. I tumbled into bed and slept because I was exhausted.

The next morning Mom and I drove to the hospital. Scott was going to live, but he'd be on his back for at least two months, his neck rigid in a cast, then he'd be wearing a brace for at least a year. He was lucky, the doctor said, that he had lived. I shuddered to think how close to tragedy we'd come, all of us.

I wasn't allowed to see Scott that day.

I called and I sent notes, but I didn't go to the hospital for a week.

The week was a nightmare. Jimmy came to see me the day after the attack. Mom left us alone in the living room. Jimmy was tense and he kept cracking his knuckles.

"What'd you say to them? Anything at all?" he kept asking.

"You know I couldn't tell them," I whispered.

"Well, these guys could be caught, and then it'd be a real mess."

"It wasn't my idea, remember that," I shot back at him. "Don't you care what happened to Scott?"

"Sure I do, but you know what could happen if anyone found out? I mean, we'd all be shot down!"

"I don't care," I said dully.

"You'd better—you're a senior, too," he said. "Listen, is it okay if I tell the others you're going to clam up?"

"I don't know what I'm going to do—can't you see that?" I said to him. "It all depends on whether they find those boys or not! They saw us—they knew what we were doing on that bus!"

"Oh, great!" Jimmy moaned.

Suddenly I couldn't stand being near him another minute. "Go away, Jimmy," I said. "Go away and try to grow up or something!"

"Okay, okay!" he said, flustered. "I don't know what you're taking out after me for. I wasn't the one to get you into this!"

No, he wasn't. Neither could I blame Rad or Leslie. It was my own stupid mistake, my own stupid weakness that made me think it was the only way to hold Scott . . .

I started going to visit Scott twice a week after school. I'd take the bus and get to the next town in time to spend half an hour with him. Our first meeting was the hard one. Scott was lying in bed, his face lean and white against the sheets.

"I'd have come sooner, but I was told it'd be better not to," I said when I walked into his room.

"Don't I look great?" I could tell it hurt him to talk.

"You'll be fine," I said. I wanted to cry. "I'm sorry, Scott!"

"Come close," he whispered.

I bent my head to him.

"You okay?" he asked me then. "Did they—did you get away?"

I nodded. I was afraid if I spoke I'd begin to cry. I hadn't been wrong to love Scott—he was a fine, decent boy. But we'd both been wrong to go along with the others, and the funny, awful result was that we'd been the ones to get hurt, not they.

I STILL VISIT Scott twice a week in the hospital. He'll be home soon, and I'll ask his mother then if I can bring him homework and help as much as I can. I don't imagine we'll ever be the same with each other again. We're just friends now. I want him to get well and go ahead with his life in his own way. But I will feel responsible for him until he's completely well.

The boys who beat him up haven't been caught yet, and I almost hope they never will. But if they are—well, Scott and I have decided we'll just have to be completely honest about what happened that night. Maybe we won't have to involve the others—Jimmy and Fran and Leslie and Rad—but we'll have to blacken our own reputations pretty badly.

As I said, I secretly hope that will never be necessary. But if it is, Scott and I have grown up enough to face up to it.

The End

THE 1970's

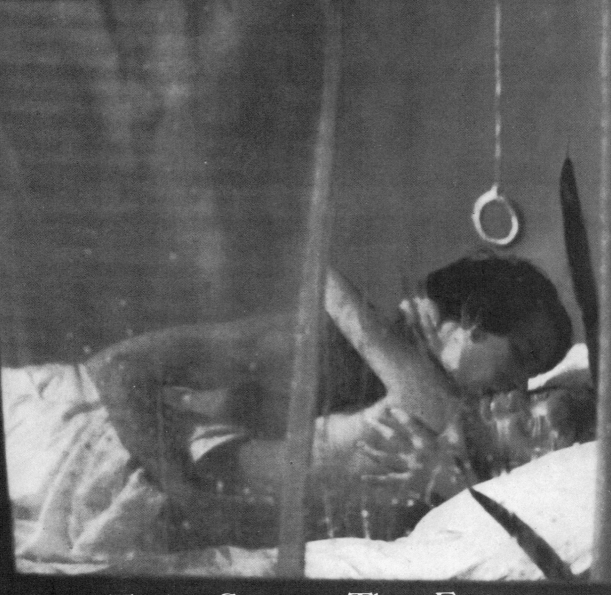

Truth is Stranger Than Fiction

When the phone rang, I thought it would be Julie. She'd promised to call as soon as she was ready. "Hello, sweetheart," I said, picking up the receiver. "All set?" We were going upstate to visit her folks. It would be the first time I'd met them.

"Doug, it's me," a hoarse voice said. It was my father calling from Florida. You could have knocked me over with a feather. I couldn't remember the last time he'd called. Or written a letter. Or showed in any way that he much cared if I lived or died. "What's this you wrote about getting married?" he said. Even though he didn't keep in touch with me, I'd wanted him to know about Julie. "What are you rushing into?" he went on. "You say you know the girl only four months? Listen, Doug, four months is not enough. Don't be an idiot! You hitch up with the wrong woman, and you'll live to regret it, my friend."

Some friend! I thought with a touch of bitterness. All those years after Mom died when I was four, he'd farmed me out to other families, remembering to come see me about once every six weeks.

"Listen, Dad," I said, determined to keep things pleasant, "don't jump to conclusions. I'm not a dumb kid anymore.

And Julie's a wonderful girl. Sweet, sensible, a real old-fashioned girl."

There was a pause. "I didn't know there were any of that kind around anymore," Dad said. "Well, I wish you luck. But if you've really got an old-fashioned girl, you don't need my blessings. You're in luck already."

An old-fashioned girl. I couldn't get the phrase out of my head as I drove over to Julie's about an hour later. It seemed to me I must have been looking for a girl like Julie all my life. After Mom died, I'd never had a real home. It was true I moved back in with Dad after I got into my teens, but we were like strangers. Whole days could pass without him saying two words to me.

I got to be real sullen and nasty during those years. I was unhappy, a real miserable kid. One day I got into someone else's car and drove around for hours till I smashed the car into a light pole. The cops picked me up then. And the next thing I knew I was in the State School for

Delinquent Juveniles, and there I stayed for more than a year.

When I got out at last, I was seventeen, and I entered the Coast Guard. For two years I was stuck on a rock off Greenland monitoring scanning equipment and spending all my time with a bunch of guys and birds. It was hard and lonely, but those two years knocked some sense into me and made me a man.

After I got out, I was lucky enough to get a job with a big business machines company in one of their training programs. But still I was living a kind of crummy life, all alone in a rented room, eating my meals out of cans, and going out with any girl who said yes. And believe me, there were plenty of them. I went a little wild, dating and making love to a different girl almost every week.

Then one morning I woke up and looked around me. My room was a filthy mess. Papers and clothes and empty cans and bottles everywhere. I tried to remember the name of the girl I'd made love to the night before. I couldn't. That's how much she had meant to me.

I closed my eyes and admitted that I hated the way I was living. I was lonely, damn it! I wanted somebody special, somebody of my own.

A month later, I met Julie. I

MY BRIDE IS A MAN!

knew from almost the first moment I saw her, sitting at the reception desk in my dentist's office, that she was *the* girl. It took me another month to get my first date with her. And still another month to get my first kiss! Now it was two months later, we were in love, and we were going to get married.

She was waiting for me in front of her apartment building when I drove up. The first sight of her, small and slender, made my heart beat wildly. I jumped out of the car, and she came flying down the steps to meet me. She was wearing a skirt that showed off her legs to perfection, a white knit top, and a string of coral-colored beads. She loved jewelry and was wearing hoop earrings and rings on both hands.

"Hello, darling." She had a husky voice, and a breathless way of talking. I kissed her. She smelled sweet and fresh, like lemons and soap.

In the car, after the first flurry of talk, Julie got quieter and quieter as we got closer and closer to Evans Mills, her home town. I guess I was more anxious about the upcoming meeting than I realized, and I wasn't saying much, either. I wanted her family to like me. I wanted them to be the family I'd never had. In my mind I was already calling them Mom, Pop, and Sis.

I glanced at Julie as we rolled along the Interstate. She really hadn't wanted to make the trip. "I hate my home town," she'd told me with a burst of bitterness that had taken me by surprise. "I was unhappy growing up there, Doug. I was miserable. You don't know—"

But she'd never given me any details. I couldn't figure it out. One of the things I loved about Julie was that she was always singing or humming under her breath. I couldn't imagine her as an unhappy teenager. "*Now* I'm happy," she'd said to me. "Now I have my own life—and you!"

Well, that had been enough for me. I felt the same way about her. As if my real life had only started when I met her, and everything up till then had been just a kind of crazy dream.

As we drove into Evans Mills, Julie said, "Here it is—home sweet home." She was twisting one of her rings around and around. "Oh, Doug, let's turn around and go back," she said.

I stared at her in dismay. "Honey, are you afraid your family won't like me?" It was the first thing I thought of.

"No, Doug! How could they not like you? It's—it's—" She looked ready to burst into tears. "Oh, never mind—you have to meet my family sometime. Let's get it over with." She took out her compact and comb and freshened her hair and makeup. "Doug," she said in a low voice, "don't expect too much."

I was nervous as hell as I parked the car in her family's driveway and followed her up the stairs to the house. It was a real nice little house with a lot of lawn around it. I couldn't figure how Julie could have been unhappy here!

Her mother appeared, wearing an apron, smiling, and biting her lip. "Julie!" She and Julie kissed, and Julie's mother turned to me, giving me a long look—which was no more than I expected. "So you're Doug." She looked me over, up and down, again. "Well," she said, sort of sighing, "I feel as if I know you already from Julie's letters."

"Hello, Mom," I said. My throat jumped. "Can I call you Mom?" I put my arms around her and kissed her cheek. "I lost my own mother years ago."

"Why, Doug—" Her eyes got moist and she hugged me back. Then suddenly she smiled at Julie and said, "Oh, Julie, Julie! This is a nice man!" She put her arms around us both. It was an emotional moment for all of us.

The tension broke when Julie's younger sister, Liz, came in, holding out her hand to me. "Doug? Welcome. It's great to meet you."

I shook her hand, then kissed her, too. "You're just as beautiful as Julie," I said. "I couldn't resist."

Liz burst out laughing. "A ladies' man! Julie, you've found yourself a real man." Liz made a fist and waved it playfully in my face. "So you think Julie's beautiful? Good thing! 'Cause I think so, too."

I decided I was going to like Liz a lot. I turned around to smile at Julie, but right away I could see she was under a strain, her smile forced. There was something in the air, some kind of tension I couldn't figure out.

Finally, I met Julie's dad, a short stocky guy with a powerful handshake. "Daddy?" Julie said. Her voice sort of quivered. She put out her arms to hug him, but he held her off.

"Hello," he said.

Julie's lips trembled. It was clear as day that Julie was crazy about her father, but he acted like he didn't even like her. Right away I figured that was where the trouble

had been in Julie's life. Her father must have played favorites with the girls. Sure! In the next half hour he ruffled Liz's hair, called her honey, and teased her about a boy who was hanging around her. The difference in the way he acted to Julie was so obvious I felt like a pail of cold water had been dumped on me. The poor kid! No wonder she looked so moody and disappointed. I drew her close and gave her a little squeeze.

"Not here, Doug," she mumbled, pulling free, her face getting red as she glanced at her father.

Believe me, it was a long, long afternoon. Julie's mother was really nice, but I had to control my hostility to her father. When I suggested Julie show me around the neighborhood, her father put the kibosh on it. "I don't want you wandering around," he said—as if there was something about Julie that made him ashamed. I was burning. I was frankly glad when he said something about work he had waiting in the cellar and took off.

Things got more relaxed then, with just Liz and her mother and us. I picked up a photo album and started flipping through it. First thing I saw was a baby picture of "little Julie," lying on her belly, naked as the day she was born. "Look at those eyes!" I said, breaking everyone up. There were all kinds of family snapshots, but I was mainly interested in pictures of Julie, but there weren't that many. A few here and there when she was a little kid, wearing overalls, riding a bike. But none of her as a young girl.

"Oh, we could never get Julie to stand still long enough for a picture," Mom said. She took the album from me. "Anyway, what do you want with pictures, Doug? You have the real thing."

"Do I ever!" I said proudly. I turned to Liz. "Tell me about Julie when she was growing up. She's too reserved to tell me herself. Were all the boys in high school crazy about her?"

Liz was sitting on the couch opposite me. She swung her foot back and forth. "Julie kind of stuck to herself in high school," she said. "Didn't you, Julie?"

"Oh, don't keep talking about me," Julie said, blushing. I'm not that interesting."

"You are to me, honey. I'd like to know every single thing about you. Come on, Liz, you grew up with my girl—tell me something about her."

Liz grinned. "You know what Julie used to do to me?" she said, winking. "Used to beat me up very other day, Doug. How about that?"

"That I don't believe," I said.

"Gave me a black eye once!"

"Not Julie," I said. "You'll never convince me of that, Sis."

"Calling me a liar?" Liz made a mock fist. "Mom! Didn't Julie give me a black eye once?"

"Drop it, Liz," Julie said. Her face was bright red.

"Mom! Wasn't Julie a mean rotten kid when he was living home?" Liz demanded.

"He?" I said. I looked at her, laughing. "Did you hear what you just said, Liz? I'm going to call you dizzy Lizzy if you keep this stuff up."

Liz jumped up. "Did I say that? I didn't say that, did I?" Her eyes filled up. "Julie, I'm sorry!"

WHAT AMERICA'S 200th BIRTHDAY MEANS TO ME

by Cheryl Harris

America's 200th birthday means many things to me, the most important of which is opportunity. Now, when America needs the help of her people the most, this generation has the opportunity to do just that—give real help. We are at a unique time in history. Not since this country was founded has she needed the support of her people more. It is very "in" to criticize her, vilify her, and even try to destroy her. We, you and I, are being challenged as never before to brush aside the apathy that has gripped us for so long.

In this, an election year, we have the ways and means to become involved—from local government to state government to national government. And never before have we, as women, had more influence on which way this country is to go.

What will be our place in history? Are we to be the weak link in the chain of freedom or will we be remembered as the generation that turned this nation back to the Freedom Trail? I say, let us be the generation who gave back the personal freedoms that our forefathers fought and died for so many years ago.

And what will be our reward? The knowledge that we are passing on a better world to our children. We must leave the legacy that we are not the weakest link in the chain of freedom but the strongest.

So in this Bicentennial year, we have another chance, perhaps a last chance, to reaffirm the faith and ideals our forefathers set down on paper two hundred years ago. What better time than on our country's 200th birthday?

We must get involved, meet the challenge, and grasp the opportunity. Challenge! Involvement! Opportunity! Look out, America, we women are ready!

"Hey, hey—easy does it," I said. "No crime committed."

But Liz was getting all upset over a silly slip of the tongue. She was a funny girl! So intense. Suddenly she flung her arms around Julie and hugged her. "You know I love you and want you to be happy," she said.

Later, at dinner, things were quieter. Much quieter! Liz had gone off with her boyfriend, and since Julie's father didn't say a word, and Julie was pretty quiet herself, it was up to Mom and me to carry on a conversation. Mom asked me about my family, what my father did, when my mother died, and stuff like that. Julie was toying with her food, glancing over at her father every other minute. I could tell she was getting more and more upset, and that was upsetting me.

Suddenly her father said, "What's your hurry about getting married?"

"I'm ready to settle down and so is Julie," I said. "I've got a decent job, and we don't see any reason to wait. We're sure about each other." I looked him in the eye. I could be just as stiff as he was.

"There are things about people you can't learn overnight," he said. He looked down at his plate. "You think you know a person, but maybe you don't!"

"Matt," Julie's mother said. "Don't say things you'll regret."

I looked from one to the other. Suddenly the tension was so thick you could have cut it with a knife. "It's okay, Mom," I said. I figured Julie's father was skirting around the baby business. When

(Continued)

we realized we were in love, Julie had told me she couldn't have babies. Sure, I was disappointed, but that didn't change my feelings about her. "Julie and I have talked about everything," I said. "I know all about it."

Well, to look at them, you'd think Julie had told me she was born with a tail like a horse. Her mother's mouth fell open, and her father looked at me as if I were on the FBI's Ten Most Wanted list. "She told you?" he said.

"What's the fuss? So Julie can't have babies. When we're ready for a family, we'll adopt. I'm not that hung up on having my own. As far as I can see," I added pointedly, "being a natural father doesn't necessarily mean a man is going to make a decent job of fathering." I thought of my own father, and the jolt it had given me to realize Julie had been just as shortchanged as me. "I'll tell you one thing," I said. "When we do have kids, I plan to be the kind of father who's not ashamed to show his kids he loves them!"

Julie's father sat back. "Well, maybe people are better off adopting," he said. "At least that way if your children disappoint you, you don't have to blame yourself!" He didn't look at Julie, but who else did he mean? What a bummer! I just couldn't figure this out. How could any man in his right mind be disappointed with a daughter like Julie? No wonder she hadn't wanted to come home!

She was getting more and more depressed. She'd hardly said a word for hours just sat there, kind of sad and drooping. I tell you, it would have given me great satisfaction to punch her father! Sure, it was a primitive feeling, but the way he treated Julie roused a savage anger in me.

Still, he *was* her father and my future father-in-law. I'd be seeing him for the rest of my life. So I controlled myself and made another attempt to smooth things over. "Sir, will you make it to our wedding?" I asked. "We're planning on a month from today."

He got up and walked around. You could see he didn't want to say yes. "It's too soon!"

I glanced at Julie. "We could wait another few weeks if that's more convenient for you. In fact, you set the date," I said. "We'll leave it up to you. Right, honey?"

Well, that did it. I thought I was being tactful, but he blew his cork. "Don't put it on me," he exclaimed. "I'm not marrying you two. As far as I'm concerned, the whole idea is disgusting!" With that, he walked out.

Julie sat there as if she'd been flattened by a bomb. I was seething. That man was a mental case!

"I'll get the dessert," Julie's mother said quickly. "I made your favorite orange cake, Julie."

Julie tried hard to smile, but there were tears in her eyes. As soon as her mother went into the kitchen, she turned to me and said, "Doug, I can't stay here another minute. I want to go home." We'd planned to stay overnight, but I was with her one hundred percent.

"We're leaving," I said, getting up. In order not to put Julie on the spot, I made some excuse to Mom. "It's been wonderful meeting you," I said. That I meant sincerely. "I give you all the credit for Julie. I love her, Mom. I'm going to take care of

her. You don't have to worry about that."

Mom hugged me, searching my face as if she wanted to say something. Then she just sighed, kissed me, and waved us goodbye.

In the car, I pulled Julie close to me. "Your mom's great," I said. "But what's with your father?"

Suddenly, Julie burst into tears. "Oh, Doug, maybe my father's right. You don't know me . . . maybe we should wait . . . it could be a mistake . . . you don't know. . ." She was choking, practically incoherent.

I pulled off the side of the road and took her in my arms. "I know I love you," I said. "And I know that your father must have made your life miserable." I held her tighter. "That's all behind you. I love you, baby. I'm going to take care of you and make you happy." Our lips met.

"Doug, Doug," she whispered.

"Let's get married right away," I said huskily. "What are we waiting for?" I wiped the tears from her face. "I want to spend the rest of my life making you happy."

"Are you sure? Doug, are you really sure?"

The following Sunday we were married in a church chapel. Julie wore a short white dress and carried a bouquet of tiny white orchids. I'd never seen her look so glowing, so beautiful. When I lifted her veil to kiss her, I could barely control the shiver of joy I felt. "Oh, Julie, my love," I whispered for her ears only. "Julie, my bride."

I had invited some of my buddies from work. Julie's boss, Dr. Gregor, and his wife and three daughters came, and Julie's landlady and her husband. We ended up with nearly a dozen people at our wedding supper at a nice restaurant. Julie's face shone with color. "Is that anticipation or wine?" somebody teased. We were so happy. I was only sorry Mom and Liz weren't there to share our joy.

When we finally left, everyone followed us outside to shower us with rice. One of my buddies, probably Marty Shannon, had decorated my car with cotton balls and a "just married" sign. The final touch was the tail of tin cans that set up a clatter when we drove off. Well, just in case somebody missed the point, I proudly honked my horn to let the whole world know I was married, and Julie was mine!

Although we were both taking a few days off from work, we'd decided to honeymoon in Julie's apartment where we were going to live. I couldn't think of anyplace I'd rather start our marriage. Julie had fixed up her apartment into a real home. She'd done things with plants and pots and material that I couldn't have done in a million years. My rooms were just rooms; her rooms were a home, and a home was what I wanted, a home with Julie in it.

It was just dark when we got there. I carried her across the threshold. "I love you, sweet Julie," I whispered. She clung to me for a moment, then she went to change, and I mixed us a couple of drinks. Julie had been very quiet ever since we left our friends. I didn't want her to be nervous or scared. I told myself to go slow. After all, I had the rest of my life to be with Julie.

But when she appeared in a thin, filmy negligee, it was all I could do not to crush her in my arms. "Come here," I said hoarsely. I pulled her down on my lap. I has turned on the stereo to a record Julie loved. She leaned against me. I kissed her lips, then more and more passionately I kissed her cheeks and her eyes and her neck. "I'll be gentle," I whispered, warning myself not to let the excitement that had risen in me dominate me. I wanted everything to be perfect.

"You're so beautiful," I said. I'd waited so long for this moment, this night, the fulfillment that was coming. I loosened the front of her negligee, then pulled it slowly down over her shoulders, baring her small, perfect breasts. As I saw her, naked and pure, as perfect as I'd dreamed she would be, tears came to my eyes. All the other women I'd known were nothing now. I'd never felt this way about any other woman. I wanted to hold her and rock her and kiss her and touch her. I wanted to possess her, yet I felt an overwhelming tenderness. I wanted everything—but, loving her, I was able to rein in my passion.

I caressed her breasts, then kissed them. When I raised my eyes, I saw that Julie was crying. "What is it, darling?" I said, alarmed. "Oh, baby, baby—" I took her in my arms. I could feel her heart pounding. I was sure it was something I'd done. I'd been crude, rough—I'd upset her. "Tell me what it is, darling. Tell me what I've done wrong."

She shook her head. "It's—not -you," she gasped.

"We can wait," I said, smoothing her shoulders. "We don't have to rush anything. We've got the rest of our lives."

"Doug—I'm such a coward—you don't understand." She was choking back tears. "I love you, Doug. I want your love so much. But I'm—so afraid. So afraid!"

I stroked her hair. "There's nothing to worry about. Nothing to be afraid of. I'll take care of you. We've waited till now. We can wait another day—or a week. It doesn't matter."

She was trembling all over. "You don't understand. Oh, God, give me courage," she whispered. She looked tragic and frightened, but when I tried to be reassuring, she drew away from me. "I can't do this to you! I have to tell you!" She buried her face in her hands. "Oh, God, God," she moaned.

"What is it, Julie?" There was a lump in the pit of my stomach, an awful dread. "You can tell me anything. It isn't going to change my feelings about you."

"Doug, I love you. God knows I love you!" Her eyes, huge, wet, stared at me. "Doug, Doug—listen. I—I was born male!"

"What?" I almost smiled. I heard her words, but I didn't understand what she was saying. The words didn't make sense. How could they?

"Listen to me, Doug!" I tried to hold her in my arms again. That sick dread was stirring in me, like a lump of poison. I didn't want to hear her say anything else. She moved away from me. Her face was raw with tears, her makeup smeared. "I was born male," she said again. "Born a boy. Do you understand? I grew up in a boy's body. I had a sex change operation three years ago."

I was sitting right next to her. My hand

254

was raised to touch her, but it froze in midair. Slowly her words penetrated my mind, each one like a bullet. I knew exactly what she'd said, and even what it meant, but at the same time I seemed to understand nothing. My body turned to stone.

"I wouldn't blame you for hating me—" I heard the words from a distance, like background noise. Ice filled my heart. Suddenly I didn't seem to know where I was. I felt disconnected, my mind separate from my body.

"I wanted to tell you before this, Doug," Julie went on, "but I was so afraid of losing you. From the first moment I can remember, I always knew I was a girl, somehow trapped in a boy's body. All my life people have tried to force me to act like a boy, but in my heart and soul I always knew I was a girl. I was miserable growing up. I tried to kill myself. The first time was when I was only fifteen. I was in love with a boy—and he thought I was gay, a homosexual. He hated me. But I never wanted that, Doug! Never! I only wanted to be what I really am—a woman. Doug, are you listening? Why don't you say something? If I hadn't had the sex change operation, I would have killed myself by now. Oh, God!" She began to cry. "Don't you understand? Doug, say something, please!" She raised tear-swollen eyes to my face. Her breasts were still bare, those perfect breasts. But all passion, all desire had left me. I felt cold, numb. I was in a state of shock.

I staggered to my feet. "You tricked me," I said hoarsely. "You lied to me from the beginning." I looked around at the apartment. Now everything in it was abhorrent to me! I'd been taken in, tricked, deceived. I'd married a man. I groaned, a terrible physical sickness rising in me.

"Doug, I love you," she said again. "I'm a woman, and I love you!" She saw me looking at her breasts.

"Yes, look at me!" she cried, and she dropped the negligee to the floor. Now, at this terrible moment, for the first time I saw her body, her seemingly perfect body. But I turned away from her. I couldn't stand the sight of her.

I grabbed my coat and ran out. I heard her calling me, then sobbing. I slammed the door and took the steps two at a time. I thought of getting into the car, but as crazy and shocked as I felt I knew I would kill myself behind the wheel.

I started walking. I didn't know where I was going. I must have walked for hours. Over and over I asked myself the same question. How could the happiest day I'd ever known turn into the most tragic, awful, desolate day of my entire life? Every time I thought of Julie's revelation, I felt sick to my stomach. Now I understood the tension in her family, her father's strange actions, her mother's emotional welcome for me.

"Sham! Fraud! Liar!" I whispered. I didn't know what I was saying. How could this have happened to me? What had I done wrong? All my life I'd wanted somebody close that I could love and share everything with. A woman, a wife, a lover, a friend. My life had been empty till I met Julie. Tears came to my eyes. I couldn't make sense out of anything. I walked to keep from screaming out my

A VALENTINE FROM GRANDMA

I'm thankful for so many things
The Lord has sent my way
That make me glad to be alive
To welcome each new day.

But if I were to make a list
Of blessings big and small,
The fact that I'm your grandma
Would have to top them all!

From the youngest to the oldest,
You've always been to me
As thoughtful, kind, and loving
As any kids could be.

You listen to my stories,
Even those I've told before,
And never make me feel
That I'm a bother or a bore.

The little gifts you give me
All have a special touch.
I like to think they mean
You care about me very much.

I'm flattered when you tell me
I'm looking extra nice,
And doubly complimented
When you ask for my advice.

And yet sometimes we older folks
Forget that kids don't know
Just how we feel about them
Unless we tell them so.

That's why this valentine is sent
In hopes that it will be
The carrier of loving thoughts
To all of you from me!

by Alice E. Chase

pain. My mind, like a skidding wheel, kept throwing up pictures. The first time I saw Julie in the dentist's office, sitting behind the desk, smiling. She'd been wearing a yellow dress. Then I thought of her running down the street to meet me. Fixing me a cup of coffee. Turning in the movies to laugh at something with me.

Suddenly I remembered that long-ago day when I'd been arrested for stealing and wrecking that car. Two policemen had come to the high school for me. It was lunch time, and all the kids were out in front. The police had walked me down the broad front steps of the school, one on either side of me. Not one kid had said a word. Nobody had made a friendly gesture of remark. They had all stared, but that was all. I had felt so incredibly alone. I had felt like nothing. And now I felt like nothing again.

I walked all night. At dawn, I let myself into my old apartment. I still had a month on the lease. Exhausted, I lay down on the couch in my clothes.

When I woke a few hours later, I smelled fresh coffee. For a moment, I thought hazily, with a rush of happiness: *This is the morning after my wedding!* Then I remembered everything. I groaned and slowly got up. The smell of coffee was from another apartment. My head throbbed. My eyes felt like burned-out holes. I washed and shaved, but I didn't know why. Nothing seemed worth doing.

I didn't know what to do with myself, so I went in to work. My buddy, Marty, gave me a funny look when I came in. "How you doing, bridegroom?"

"Doing?" I was so full of bitterness I could barely speak. I walked away from him. What was I going to say? *Marty, old buddy, this is the first day of my honeymoon, but I'm at work because I married a man masquerading as a woman!*

I tried to concentrate on my work, but it was no use. I was making every mistake in the book. I gave it up and left early. I went back to my apartment. That was a mistake. I couldn't eat, couldn't sleep. The phone rang. It was Julie. For a moment her voice made my heart race. Then I grated, "Listen, you forgot to tell me your real name."

"What?" she said, sounding stunned.

"Your real name!" I said harshly.

"Jules," she said, low, after a moment. Then she cried, "No! That's not my real name. Julie is my real—"

I hung up on her. Sickened all over again, I tortured myself with memories of our courtship. I lay down on the bed, I got up, I walked back and forth through the rooms, groaning, pounding my fists against the wall. I began to think that none of this had happened. It was some kind of bad joke, some kind of weird nightmare. How could I have been so wrong? So stupid? I knew the difference between a man and a woman, damn it! And there was nobody as female as Julie. Two days ago I would have been willing to swear to that on a stack of Bibles.

With a kind of crazy hope, I began to think that maybe the trouble was in Julie's head, not her body. I'd seen her completely naked, and what I'd seen was a woman's body. Maybe she had some kind of nutty delusion about being born a boy. A feverish excitement gripped me. It was nearly midnight, but I placed a phone call to her mother.

"Mom, this is Doug," I said when she answered. "I have to ask you something—"

"What's wrong? Is Julie okay?"

"Mom—was Julie born a boy?"

She began to cry. My head slowed down. The pathetic hope I'd been clinging to faded. I had my answer. "Did Julie tell you?" she wept. "Oh, my poor Julie—she's suffered so much—"

A wave of anger swept over me. I'd called her Mom, thought she cared for me the way I cared for her. She'd helped trick me, though. 'You don't care what you do to people, do you?" I said.

"No, Doug, no—it's not that. I thought Julie could have a normal life. She wanted love so much. You don't know how happy she was when she met you! I told her it would never work, but she wanted you so much—"

"Don't you think I'm human, too?" I grated, steeling myself against Mom's tears. "Why didn't you say something? Why didn't you stop it—stop her, or him, or whatever it is!" Yes, I was cruel, but I didn't care anymore. All my hopes and dreams had been smashed, turned into something ugly and sick.

The next days were sheer hell. I lost weight. I had trouble concentrating at work. Julie called me several times, saying, "We've got to talk, Doug," but I was in no state to talk to anyone, and especially her.

Sometimes a few minutes would pass without my thinking of her. Then I'd remember and I'd get this gripping pain like a steel ball ripping apart my insides, and I'd start sweating and shaking. I was a mess.

A week passed. Two weeks. I was living as if there was a brick wall between me and the rest of the world. I went to work every day, but even that part of my life was unreal. After work I was hanging around with Marty, sitting in bars, just to pass the time, to make the empty hours go by somehow.

By then Marty knew that Julie and I had broken up. "Don't ask me anything!" I told him. "Leave me alone!" I sat in those bars for hours, drinking, trying not to think, trying not to feel. Nothing mattered anymore.

One night a girl sat down at my table. Marty was talking to some fellows at the bar. The girl introduced herself. "I'm Sandy," she said. She was cute, dark haired, wearing tight pants, a white sweater. "You look like you lost your best friend," she said. "Unlucky in love?"

"You could say that," I muttered.

She put her hand over mine. "Welcome to the club. I just broke up with my boyfriend. What a rat! He really hurt me."

She sat with me for a couple hours. Why? I don't know. Maybe there's something to the saying that misery loves company. She kept talking about the guy she'd broken up with and urging me to talk, too. "It'll make you feel better," she said. "Get it off your chest." But I didn't want to talk about Julie. It still hurt too much.

We were drinking, Sandy matching me beer for beer, shot for shot. We left the bar together, our arms around each other. At my car, she stopped and said, "Give me a kiss." I leaned against the car, pulling Sandy against me. She kissed me with a

---

A True Story Miracle of Faith

☐ The baby, Faith, is playing happily in the tub as I sit here writing this true story about miracles. My oldest, Donnie, is playing ball down the street with a friend. Matthew and Kevin are out riding their bikes. Patty and Michelle are off somewhere. It's about four in the afternoon, and my husband, Don, has been home for hours with a migraine headache. I'm fine, and in a little while I'll start supper, and then the kids and I will spend a peaceful evening watching TV or reading. If Don wakes up wanting something for his upset stomach, I'll get him some ginger ale.

So what, you say? An ordinary day in an ordinary house with ordinary people. Not so! At least not for me!

Not so long ago this scene was quite different. I couldn't cope with so-called "ordinary" family crises: Children gone in different directions, a sick husband, and meals to prepare sent me into a panic that I had to run from. I would have called all the kids into the house so that I could be sure nothing terrible would happen to them—or I would have gone to bed, hoping to blank the responsibilities out. And in the back of my mind, I would have been planning my "escape."

I would have awakened my husband with the words, "Why do you always get sick when I need you! I swear you do it deliberately just to drive me to the breaking point!" By that time I would have been completely out of control and crying. Of course the kids wouldn't know what was happening and, what was worse, would completely ignore me until I would smash something in my anger or Don would slap me in total frustration and rage.

But thanks to a Power greater than myself, I stumbled into Alcoholics Anonymous. You see, I am a recovering alcoholic. I haven't had a drink in eight years. I know beyond a shadow of a doubt that I am a living miracle! **Mrs. L. M., Ohio**

practiced mechanical passion. "Let's go to my place," she said huskily.

In the car, she lit a cigarette and put it in my mouth. Out of the corner of my eye I saw her pick a bit of tobacco off her tongue. Suddenly I felt cold and sick. What was I doing? What did Sandy mean to me? Why were we together? We'd go to her place and we'd have sex. And then what? Then—nothing. I didn't want her. I didn't want any woman.

I still hadn't started the car. I put my head down on the steering wheel. I felt hopeless, miserable, sick. "I don't feel good," I said. "I better take a rain check."

Sandy shrugged. "Sure, honey. Call me sometime." She slid out of the car and slammed the door.

I drove home. When I walked in, the phone was ringing. It was Julie. "Doug," she said, "I'm coming over. I'm coming over to see you. I can't bear this anymore. I've got to see you!" I thought she was crying. I began to shake. I hung up the phone and wandered around the apartment. I looked in the mirror. I was unshaven, red eyed. I'd been drinking for hours, but I was stone sober.

Twenty minutes later, Julie was at the door. I hadn't seen her since our wedding night. The sight of her hit me like a fist in my heart. She was so beautiful! The old feelings came flooding back, but then I remembered and turned to ice. "What do you want?"

"You're so—so cruel, Doug," she said. Her voice quivered. "Am I so repulsive to you? So ugly?"

Ugly? Even now, she still looked like everything I'd ever wanted in a woman. I couldn't understand it. Maybe there was something rotten in me, too. "For God's sake, why are you torturing us both this way?" I shouted. "What do you want from me?"

"I want you to make love to me," she sobbed. "Oh, Doug, I want that more than anything in the world." She threw her arms around me. Her face was close to mine. "You're still my husband," she choked. Her hair smelled fragrant with that scent of lemons.

"Please," she begged. "Oh, please let me prove to you that I'm a woman, a real woman! Please!" She touched me—she kissed my face frantically—she begged me to make love to her. Tears poured down her face. "I loved you from the first day. I'll never stop loving you. Oh, Doug, love me! Can't you see how I feel about you? Have pity on me!" Her lips trembled. "Just give me this—give me this one night. I swear I'll never bother you again. I'll never ask you for anything else!"

I started shaking. I felt desire flowing through me. It was crazy, but suddenly I was full of an uncontrollable urge to make love to her. My mind was whirling dizzily. I pushed her down on the couch. Wild thoughts were streaking through my head. Now I'd find out the truth! Man or woman, now I'd know! I took her roughly, swiftly. She cried out. It was all over so quickly. I collapsed on her, straining for air.

Her hands stroked my damp back. "I love you, Doug," she said quietly.

And from somewhere deep inside me, deeper than sense, or reason, or mind,

THE MOTHER OF THE BRIDE
by Alice E. Chase

The wedding day is over
And the mother of the bride
Walks slowly to her daughter's room
And quietly steps inside.

The place is full of memories
Of all the years between
That seem to come to life
As if projected on a screen.

The days of babyhood are there—
That first bewitching smile,
The eager outstretched arms
That beg, "Please, hold me
  for a while!"

Memories of the toddler
Who would rather run than walk . . .
Recollections of the joy
When she began to talk!

The early days of school, and then
The teenage years when she
Began to show the kind
Of lovely woman she would be.

Today she took the biggest step
Of any in her life
When marriage changed her status
From daughter into wife.

And though the precious memories
Of all the years between
Will never fade—it's time to put
New pictures on the screen.

And hopefully, with wisdom,
The mother of the bride
Will quickly wipe away her tears
And quietly step aside!

something in me cried out: *And I love you.*

I rolled away from her, my mind reeling. Was it true? Could Julie, who had been born a male, be more to me than any other woman in the world? More than all other women who had always been women? I thought of Sandy, the girl I'd picked up. My body had gone cold and frozen near her. I hadn't wanted her. For three weeks I'd been living in hell, not because Julie was born a boy and told me the truth, but because I had torn myself away from her.

"Thank you," Julie whispered. "Thank you, Doug." Her eyes were full of tears again. She got up and started dressing. "I'll go now, and you can do whatever you think is best about us. I meant what I said. I won't bother you again."

I reached out and took her hand. "Come here," I said. I brought her down next to me and took her face between my hands. "Julie—" I reached into her eyes and saw such sadness there that it wrenched my heart. "Julie, I love you."

"Oh, Doug!" She started laughing and crying.

I saw everything clearly now. I had fallen in love with Julie—not with what

she had been, but what she *was*, the person, the woman she had become. I thought of my own past as a troubled, mixed-up kid, and then as a young man on the make. Would Julie have looked twice at the crazy kid, or that stud with nothing but sex on his mind? The past was behind us both. The future could be whatever we made it.

Julie moved against me, whispering in my ear, whispering her love and happiness. I felt the stirrings of passion returning, and at the same time an overwhelming tenderness flooded me. Maybe it wouldn't be easy being Julie's husband, maybe her past would sometimes torment me, maybe I wouldn't always understand and I'd make her unhappy as well as myself; but looking into her eyes, I knew again that what I wanted was Julie. Nobody but Julie. We'd live together, we'd make our own memories, and hour by hour, day by day, we'd create a new past for the two of us. "I love you," I said again.

"This is the first hour of my real life," she whispered, clinging to me.

"And of mine, too," I echoed. ∎

"You're not the first man I've had, but you're the best"

I believed her. And the next morning the whole town was laughing at me!

■ ■ ■ That particular Friday night started off like any other Friday night. I reported for work at the mall at nine o'clock sharp. My job as night watchman wasn't exactly exciting, but I counted myself lucky to have a job at all. A man with an artificial arm isn't exactly in a position to pick and choose his employment. I knew a lot of Vietnam veterans who couldn't find work at all. The night-watchman job paid okay, and it certainly couldn't be called hard work. In fact, I rather enjoyed it—until that Friday night when all hell broke loose.

From nine until ten, I policed the mall corridor, just keeping an eye on things. There were eighteen stores in the mall. Some of the stores were small, like the jewelry store and the fur shop. Small, but expensive. On my rounds, I hardly glanced at the merchandise in the windows of those two shops. After all, I had no wife or girl to buy jewelry or furs for. Or mother or sisters, for that matter. I did occasionally pause by the sports shop window, though.

When I was a kid, I'd been a hockey nut. I'd dreamed of maybe someday playing professional hockey. Even when I was in Vietnam, I thought about it a lot.

Until the day we were on patrol and I fell against a mine. The dream shattered with my arm, but I still liked to look at the equipment.

That particular Friday, though, I was simply doing my job. I stood at one end of the mall corridor, watching the customers trudging up and down trying to cope with packages and tired kids. Some, worn out by the hassle of shopping, would stop and sink wearily into one of the curved, white benchs placed around the mall corridor.

When the blond girl with the fur hat and the armload of packages walked over and sat down on the bench right where I was standing, I didn't think anything of it. Except to notice quickly that she was very pretty and that her clothes looked expensive. She placed the packages beside her on the bench and then looked up at me.

"Hi," she said casually, smiling. I smiled back, unconsciously pulling my fake left arm closer to my side. "This shopping business is very tiring," she went on.

"That's why these comfortable benches are provided," I answered lightly. "When people get too tired, they stop buying."

She looked at me, her eyes moving slowly up and down my blue uniform. I felt awkward as hell, standing there trying to act nonchalant under the scrutiny of such a good-looking, well-dressed young woman. Before the mine shattered my arm, I'd been okay with the gals. They liked me well enough, and I'd had one very

intense affair with an Army nurse. That hadn't worked out, but I'd looked forward to getting married someday and having kids. Now I shied away from women, period. What woman could love me?

"Are you a cop?" the girl asked suddenly.

I shook my head. "Just the night watchman."

She grinned at me. "You look too young to be a night watchman. I thought night watchmen were only old retired men."

I tried to think of a smart answer, but I couldn't. And I certainly couldn't go into an explanation about my arm. I felt a warm flush creep over my face.

"Why, you're blushing!" the girl exclaimed softly, her eyes still searching my face. "Why?"

I shrugged, hating myself. "Habit," I answered stiffly. "I always blush when I talk to pretty girls."

She laughed. "You're cute, you know that?" she asked teasingly. "Are you married?"

"No. Are you?"

And then she gave a little sigh. "No. I'm afraid not. The right man just hasn't asked me."

"Maybe your qualifications are too tough," I answered, striving to keep my voice light and easy. "What kind of a man are you looking for?"

"Oh, I don't know," she said. "I can't really put it into words. I guess more than anything I'm

waiting for that unmistakable zing that's supposed to zonk you when you've met the right one."

I laughed, feeling almost at ease. The customers paraded by, hurrying now to make last-minute purchases before the mall closed for the night. "Maybe you've seen too many movies," I suggested.

She smiled. "Maybe. What's your excuse?"

I looked back at her. She wasn't smiling now and I had the craziest feeling she was serious, that she really wanted to know about me. I might even have told her then about my arm, but I didn't get a chance. Just then another young woman came rushing up to the bench.

"Oh, there you are!" she said to the blond girl. "I've been looking all over for you." Her voice was very low and husky for a woman, but pleasant.

"Sorry," the blond girl answered. "I was just having a nice chat with the night watchman. What's your name, anyway?" she asked, turning back to me.

"Tod. Tod Wetherby," I answered.

"That's a nice name. I like it. Mine is Greta Lavin, and this is my friend Jill Holson."

Jill glanced at me and then stuck out her hand. I shook it a bit self-consciously.

"Somehow Greta always meets the most attractive men," Jill said, smiling.

I smiled back, blushing again. Jill didn't have Greta's smashing good looks, but she certainly wasn't bad.

Greta glanced at her watch, frowning. "It's almost ten. I suppose we *must* go. The mall will be closing in a few minutes." She picked up her packages and stood up. Her coat opened in front and I caught a glimpse of a well-stacked figure under a white, frilly blouse.

"Good-bye, Tod. It was nice talking to you," she said, smiling warmly into my eyes.

"I hope you come back," I blurted, hardly aware of what I was saying. "I mean—I hope I see you again."

"Who knows?" she said softly. "Maybe you will."

They walked away. I started after them, admiring Greta's legs. And then the stores started closing for the night. I checked the locks after each store closed, making sure everything was secure for the night. I carried several master keys hooked inside my jacket pocket in case I had to enter a particular store in an emergency. In the five months I'd been on the job, there hadn't been an emergency. By a quarter to eleven, the only two people in the place were David, the eighteen-year-old boy who swept and mopped the hall corridor, and myself. At two in the morning, a cleaning crew came in to do windows, clean the rest rooms, and take care of the potted plants. After that, I was alone until six.

David swept up the trash with his big push broom, grumbling as usual.

"As many trash containers as there are around here, you'd think people would use them, wouldn't you?" he complained.

I didn't answer. David asked the same question every night. Besides, just then I heard a banging on one of the big glass outside doors that led into the mall. There were two sets of outside doors, one in the center of the mall and one at the far end of the corridor. The banging was coming from the far end. Curious, I hurried over. Two women were standing at the door, and as I got closer I recognized them both. It was Greta and Jill. I took out my key and opened the door.

"It's our car," Greta blurted out, hugging her coat tightly around her. "It won't start and we can't call a garage because the phone book in the outside booth is gone and there isn't anybody around—"

"Come inside," I said, opening the door wider. They stepped inside and I locked the door behind them. "You can use the phone in the office," I said, looking at Greta.

"Oh, that's very kind of you," Jill answered, rubbing her hands together. "It's so cold out there!"

"What's wrong with the car?" I asked, unable to tear my eyes away from Greta.

"Oh, I don't know," Jill answered again. "We've been fiddling with it for almost an hour. I thought it was just flooded, but that doesn't seem to be the problem. It might just be the cold weather. Do you think someone will come look at it soon?"

"Probably," I answered soothingly. "Come on down to the office and you can call from there."

We started to the office, Greta walking in the center. I glanced at her from time to time. It was nice just walking beside her. David paused in his sweeping and stared as the three of us went into the office. Which rather annoyed me. After all, taking Greta and Jill into the office wasn't any big deal. I'd been called upon before to give stranded customers a hand. The mall was on the outskirts of town, and you couldn't expect people to stand outside and freeze while they waited for a tow truck. Besides, all the stores were individually locked, and there was nothing to steal in the corridors.

We went into the office, and I showed Jill where the phone was and got out the directory. When Jill started making calls, I sat down on the leather-covered divan beside Greta.

"Where are you from, Tod?" she asked.

"Right here," I answered quickly. I could hardly believe that we were actually talking together so soon. I couldn't help feeling happy that they were having car trouble. "This is my home town. How about you?"

"New York City."

"I might have known," I said.

She raised an eyebrow. "Now why do you say that?"

"Just the way you look. I mean, there's lots of pretty girls around here, too, but none of them look the way you do."

"I hope that's a compliment," she said.

"Oh, it is." I assured her. "And if I'm not being impolite, what are you doing here?"

"Visiting Jill. She and her husband have a place just outside Glendover. Do you know where that is?"

I nodded. Glendover was a little town about forty-five miles west.

"Jill's husband was called out of town on business, so Jill and I decided to drive over here for a little shopping."

"Will you be staying long?" I asked hopefully, trying not to stare as Greta crossed her legs.

She shook her head. "I'm afraid not. We wanted to get back to Glendover tonight. I have to leave for New York tomorrow afternoon."

"Oh," I said, trying to swallow my disappointment.

Jill hung up the phone and turned to us, frowning. "That's the second garage I've called that's turned me down," she announced. "I'll have to try another." She went back to the phone book. I turned back to Greta.

"What do you do in New York?" I asked.

"I'm a buyer in a department store," she said. "It's not very interesting work. I rather envy Jill and her country living, although I'm afraid I couldn't put up with her husband long." She paused. "Do you have a cigarette?"

I dug into my jacket pocket for my pack of cigarettes. "They might be a little stale," I apologized, offering her one. "I've been trying to quit," I explained.

She took the cigarette. Her fingers were long and slender, with delicate, pink-tipped nails.

"That's wise of you," she answered. "I've been trying to quit, too, but it's mostly a losing battle."

I lit the cigarette for her, and she leaned back and smiled at me.

Jill hung up the phone again. "Darn," she said, her voice more full of annoyance than ever. "This guy can come, but he said it would be at least a couple of hours."

"But that's awful," Greta exclaimed. "It'll be so late by the time we get back to Glendover. Maybe we should just leave the car and spend the night in a motel."

"We can't do that," Jill snapped. "You know how Frank is about that car. He'd have a fit if I left it in an open parking lot—"

"But it won't start." Greta broke in. "Nobody can steal it."

"Maybe not, but who knows? All I know is that car is Frank's baby. and if anything happens to it I might as well file for divorce."

"You're perfectly welcome to stay here until the garage people come" I put in. "In fact. I'd go out and look at the car myself but I'm not supposed to leave the building."

Jill smiled at me. "That's very sweet of you."

Then I had another idea. "Maybe David could look at the car," I suggested.

There was a little silence.

"Who is David?" Jill asked finally.

"The boy sweeping up in the corridor outside," I explained. "He's young, but he's good with engines. He tinkers with cars all the time—"

"Thanks just the same." Jill broke in quickly. "I don't mean to sound ungrateful, but the car is a custom job and Frank wouldn't like some kid fooling around with it. You do understand?"

I nodded. "Sure. I'm pretty fussy about my car myself. Or rather I used to be . . ." My voice trailed away awkwardly. I glanced briefly at Greta. She was staring at me. I pretended to be looking at Jill. "Well, then, just make yourselves comfortable right here," I went on. "A couple of hours isn't so long. How about a cup of coffee?"

"Wonderful," Jill breathed, smiling again. "Where is it?"

"Right behind you," I said, motioning to the electric pot on the shelf behind the desk. "I put it on just before you came in, so it should be nice and fresh. I'll get the cups."

In the process of gathering cups and saucers and spoons and sugar and the cream substitute, I knew both Greta and Jill must have noticed that my left arm was mostly nonfunctional. When I held the coffee tray in front of Greta, her eyes met mine squarely.

"What happened to your arm?" she asked softly.

"It was blown off by a mine."

Something flickered behind her eyes. 'When did it happen?" she asked, her voice still as soft as a whisper.

"Almost three years ago—in Vietnam."

She nodded and lifted her cup from

A box of memories

My New Year's resolution
Was to go through every trunk,
Each bureau drawer and closet,
And get rid of all the junk
Accumulated through the years
And carefully stored away—
The silly, useless things
That seldom saw the light of day.

I started in by tackling
A box of odds and ends—
Snapshots of my childhood,
Letters from old friends,
Pressed flowers from my first corsage
Complete with rusty pin,
The high-school yearbook with my name
And smiling picture in.

An entry in my diary
That proved beyond a doubt
I'd met the man I really loved
And couldn't live without!
A clipping from the local press
The day that we were wed.
The prayer book that I carried
When my marriage vows were said.

A flaxen curl, a baby tooth,
A favorite bedtime toy
From way back when our grown-up son
Was just a little boy.
Silly, useless things
That seldom saw the light of day,
Yet I couldn't for the life of me
Throw one of them away!

by Alice E. Chase

the tray. Her fingers brushed my right hand, and when I looked into her eyes they were so full and deep I felt I could drown in them.

I served Jill and put the tray back on the desk. Jill sat down on the divan beside Greta. Disappointed, I took the desk chair. After a moment Greta put down her cup and started unbuttoning her coat.

"It's warm in here," she said, smiling at me. "I think I'll get comfortable."

"Me, too," Jill answered. She took off her coat and then looked at me. "Don't you find it warm in here, too?"

I was, in fact, very warm But it wasn't from the temperature of the room. It was because of Greta. She really was getting to me.

"You might as well take your jacket off, too, and get comfortable," she suggested, looking at me. "Or do you have to go back out into the corridor?"

"Oh, not right now," I said casually. "I don't have to be out there every minute. I can relax a bit, too." I slipped my jacket off and hung it on the back of my chair.

Just then there was a knock on the office door. It was David. "I have to go now," he said, his eyes sliding past me over to the divan where Greta and Jill were sitting.

"Okay, I'll let you out," I said quickly. I got the keys from my jacket pocket, walked down the corridor, and opened the door for David.

He didn't go out. He stood there, leering. "Sure you don't want me to stick around?" he asked.

"Now why would I want that?"

"Well, there's two of them. You can't handle two at once, especially with a bum arm—"

He was kidding, but I felt a real surge of anger.

"Get the hell out of here before I break both your arms," I growled.

"Okay, okay. I was just kidding, for Pete's sake," he mumbled.

I locked the door behind him and hurried back to the office. "Sorry," I apologized as I slipped the keys back into my jacket pocket. "Anybody want more coffee?"

Greta nodded and held out her cup and saucer. "Yes, please," she said, smiling. "You make very delicious coffee."

I refilled her cup. A sweet, heady perfume from her hair filled my nostrils.

Jill waved the pot away. "No, thanks, Tod," she said. "I'm not feeling very well. When something like this happens, it makes me very nervous and I get an upset stomach."

"That's because you worry too much about Frank's reactions," Greta put in. "Why don't you go lie down in the ladies' room? There's a couch in there, and it looks quite comfortable. Here—take a couple of aspirin and don't worry about the garage people. I'll come get you when they come."

Jill looked at me. "Would that be all right?" she asked.

"Certainly," I answered quickly, my heart racing at the thought of being alone with Greta.

Jill reached for her coat. "Fine. I think I'll do just that. What did I do

with my purse?"

"It's on the desk," Greta answered.

My chair was by the side of the desk, and I moved it a bit so Jill could pass to get her purse. I really wasn't paying too much attention to her. My eyes were on Greta as she folded her long, slender legs beneath her on the divan. She caught me staring and smiled. I smiled back, feeling warmer than ever.

"See you later, kids," Jill said as she went out the door.

I looked back at Greta. She patted the divan seat beside her.

"You might as well come sit over here," she said. "I'm not sure how much of Jill's nervous upset is real and how much is pretend. I think she's trying to help us get acquainted."

I moved over to the divan. I didn't sit close, but I didn't sit on the far end, either.

"How long have you known Jill?" I asked, making conversation.

"A long time. We used to work together. When I first went to New York, she befriended me and helped me get a job. But now that she's married, she's always trying to get me teamed up with somebody." She paused, her long hair spreading like a fan across the side of her face. "Right now, I think it's you," she added, smiling at me.

"Why should she be impressed with me?" I asked over the sudden tightness in my chest. "I'm a nobody."

Greta's eyes flashed. "Don't say that!" she said fiercely. "Don't ever say that. Everybody is somebody."

I stared at her, startled by the fierce tone of her voice. "I only meant that—well, I'm not sure what I meant," I said lamely.

She looked away, nodding. She sipped her coffee for a moment and then turned back to me. "People make too much of a fuss about money and position," she said softly. "It makes people sort of crazy. Kids start feeling they're not as good as other kids because their parents are poor—that kind of thing. If I had charge of the world, I'd distribute everything equally so everybody would have the same."

"That wouldn't work," I said slowly, thinking about it. "Some people are always stronger and smarter than others. Even if people all had the same to start with, it wouldn't last. The stronger and smarter ones would always wind up with the most."

"Not if there were laws saying they couldn't do that," she broke in firmly.

I looked at her. Was she serious? Her eyes held mine for a moment. Then she smiled and put down the coffee cup.

"Let's talk about you," she said, leaning toward me. She put her left arm along the back of the divan. "You think you're a nobody, but what you are shows all over you. You're sweet and responsible and very, very honest. And kind. That's very important, kindness. Most of the men I've known in my life weren't kind—and they certainly weren't sweet. Or very honest, either, at least with women."

"But I'll bet they had two arms," I blurted out.

Greta's eyes softened. "Oh, Tod, is that so important?" she asked, her eyes

searching my face. "When you have everything else?"

"Yes," I said. "It's important to me and it's important to women."

"Then you've been going around with the wrong kind of women."

"I haven't been going around with any women at all," I answered flatly. "I don't want to ask them, because I can see on their faces what they're thinking. And pity is one thing no man can stomach. Especially from a woman."

Greta's mouth tightened and the softness vanished from her eyes. "That was a very chauvinistic remark, you know," she snapped. "What makes you think women are so different from men? And why shouldn't anyone express pity if that's what she feels? Pity is just sympathy, you know. If I like you and want to be with you and feel what you're feeling, then why should you sneer at that?"

"I wasn't sneering," I began, feeling a bit helpless before her reasoning. "I was just saying I don't want people to feel sorry for me. I don't want anybody's crumbs. I want to be treated the same as any man, especially by women —"

"But that's really not very good, you know," she broke in. "Men and women don't treat each other very well at all. My father used to beat my mother and scream and curse at us kids. But my mother got even. She took lovers—" She paused, biting her lower lip. "I'm sorry," she went on after a moment. "I didn't mean to go into that. But tell me —were your father and mother happy together?"

"Yes," I said, remembering. "Dad depended on Mother for everything and was very gentle with her. When she died I think Dad died, too, although he kept on walking around until I was grown up enough to take care of myself. He died while I was overseas. He loved my mother very much, you see—" My voice trailed away.

There was a little silence, and then Greta touched my arm. "Maybe that explains it," she said, smiling again.

"Explains what?" I asked.

"Why you're so sweet."

"Don't say that." I said thickly, feeling the warm blood flood my face. "You're kidding me."

"Oh, Tod, no," she whispered, looking into my face. "I mean it. I think you're the sweetest guy I've ever met."

And then her softly parted lips were only a few inches from mine, achingly inviting. I would have had to be stone not to kiss her. And stone I wasn't. Her lips opened beneath mine, and—heart racing, head swimming—I drank hungrily. When I raised my head, she clung to me, and then I was kissing her neck until her lips found mine again. I forgot completely about my arm. All I could think of was this fantastic girl, returning my kisses with a passion that was unthinkable, pressing close, so close—

"The light," she gasped softly in my ear. "Turn off the light, Tod."

My brain was aflame with desire, but reason tried to struggle through. "What about Jill?" I whispered back

"And the garage people—"

"They won't be here for hours, and Jill won't come back, I'm sure. Please turn off the light—"

The throbbing desire completely closed down my brain, and I got up and turned off the light and locked the door. In the darkness, I reached for Greta. My heart was pounding with such force my whole body was shaking. She was taking off her clothes, and now there wasn't anything between us. I'd never experienced passion in a woman before. In my experience, women had been mostly passive. Greta was like a fire, a flame, her passion and hunger equaling mine. It was the most exciting thing imaginable. The pleasure we shared was so intense it was almost like pain. Afterward, I lay still, completely exhausted. Greta didn't seem to be in any hurry to get up, either.

"I hope you were taking some kind of precautions," I said finally, remembering.

She laughed softly. "It's okay."

I raised up and looked at her. I couldn't really see her in the darkness. "How often do you do this sort of thing?" I asked.

"Not very often."

"Do you enjoy it?"

"Not usually. I did this, though. Very much. You're the best I ever had."

I laughed. "I think you're kidding me."

"No, I'm not. It was beautiful. Only we'd better get up now. Somebody might come." I got up and slipped on my pants. "Don't turn on the light until I'm dressed," Greta cautioned. I waited a few minutes until she said it was okay to turn on the light. When I looked at her, her cheeks were flushed and her hair was all tumbled. She was completely beautiful.

"Don't look at me," she said, laughing a little. "I'm a mess. I have to go to the ladies' room." She picked up her coat and purse.

I unlocked the door. "Hurry back," I said, smiling at her.

She reached up and kissed me on the lips.

"I meant what I said, Tod," she said softly. "You're the best."

She left before I could answer. While she was gone, I tried to get myself together. It was difficult. I straightened my clothes, but my mind was still shattered. I couldn't believe what had just happened. It was like some kind of crazy, fantastic dream. I plugged in the coffeepot again, drank what was left of the coffee, and then made a new pot. Greta seemed to be taking her time in the ladies' room, but I didn't think much about it. After all, Jill was in there, too, and they were probably talking. About me? Would Jill know what had just happened? Would she say anything?

Don't be a dope! I told myself firmly. *Why should she say anything? She's not Greta's mother. Just act natural when they come back in.*

Only they didn't come back in. When I realized that Greta had been gone almost an hour, I began to get worried. I walked down the corridor to the ladies' room. I knocked on the door, but nobody answered. Feeling vaguely apprehensive, I hurried down the corridor to the other ladies' room. Nobody answered there, either. I shoved the door open and went inside. The place was empty. Feeling a little panicky now, I hurried back to the first ladies' room and went inside. It was empty, too.

I think I knew then, but I didn't want to admit it. And I didn't. Not until I hurried back to the office and checked my jacket pockets. My master keys weren't there. Scalp crawling, I started checking the locks on the individual stores. Two were open, the jewelry store and the fur shop. I had to face it then. Greta, my new love—my exciting, passionate, beautiful love partner—was a common thief. I went back to the office, stared at the phone for a while, and then called the manager of the mall.

He came right out. So did the police. I spent all of the following day at the police station. Greta and Jill were thieves, all right. While Greta had kept me busy, Jill hoisted a dozen of the most expensive furs and fifty thousand dollars' worth of jewelry. I had to tell the police everything, of course, although I didn't go into any details about the lovemaking. The police got the idea, though. And it sounds crazy, but after they were sure I wasn't an accomplice in the deal, they thought my being such a patsy was funny.

The insurance companies didn't think it was funny, though. And of course I was fired. But what the police told me about Greta and Jill made me sicker than anything. While they were thieves, they certainly weren't common. They were wanted in three different states. Neither had served any time, and their operations were always very, very smooth. They made big hauls and then lay low for a long time. They never hit the same vicinity twice. They didn't drink or take dope, and they didn't seem to associate with men other than when they were in the middle of a job. They were, in fact, lesbians.

That last just about blew my mind. I couldn't believe it. If Greta was a lesbian, how could she have been so passionate with me? Was it all an act?

I spent several weeks worrying that one around. But in the end I chose to believe what I wanted to believe. Greta might be a lesbian, but what we experienced together was real. Maybe she would have had sex with any man who happened to be on guard duty that night, but nothing could convince me that the passionate love she gave me was just an act. And believing that, my whole life began to change.

The whole story, of course, was in the papers. Guys I had known all my life kidded me unmercifully, and I had a rough time finding another job. But I did find one. I talked the manager of a used-car lot into giving me a try. I found I was good at selling. Soon I was making more in commissions than I had ever made at other jobs, and I decided to take a bigger step. I decided to go to college. I'd toyed with the idea before, but lacked confidence.

I don't lack confidence anymore. My college work is coming along fine, and I'm still at the car lot part time. The biggest change, though, is in my attitude toward women.

I date when I have time, and when I ask a woman out I'm not crushed or suspicious if she turns me down. My missing arm is no longer the major factor in my life, coloring all my thinking and feeling. I'm partially disabled, yes, but women can accept that or reject it, just as they please. I haven't met the woman I want to marry yet, but I'm sure I will. And I'm equally sure that when I do, she'll be able to love me just as completely as Greta did. Not for just one night, but for forever. ■

66 You'll Love Your New Daddy, Kathy... 99

A family horror story you'll never forget!

My mother was divorced twice. My own father was a boozer, and she put up with a lot before she left him. She didn't have much choice with us three kids to support, so after the divorce she married this guy who had been my own father's friend. He was okay. He liked us kids, and he took us to the shopping centers and bought us stuff and he listened to us when we had something to tell him. But then he started to drift and lose one job after another.

Then my mom got interested in another guy. I came home from school one day, and there was a real fight going on. My little sisters were hiding in their room because of the noise. I guess my stepdad had come home and found Mom with this other guy, and he let loose.

Well, Mom didn't put up with it. Usually she wasn't very strong in her opinions. She always seemed to let the man do her thinking. She was the kind who would go out and work very hard so she wouldn't be on ADC and all that, but she would let a man tell her what to do.

So I just stood there and listened in amazement while she read the riot act to my stepdad and told him where he could head in. The other guy just stood there with a kind of pleasant smile on his face—as though it didn't have anything to do with him. I had never seen him before.

When the fight was all over, my stepdad started packing up his things. By then the other guy had gone, with that nice smile still on his face, a pleasant good-bye to me, and the promise to Mom that he'd be back. While my stepdad packed, he told Mom what a fool she was. He said the other guy was like a rutting goat and she should have more sense than to bring him into a household of little girls.

This really teed off Mom. I never heard her so mad. She was so mad she lost her voice and stumbled over her words. I mean, she was way out. Then she started to cry and ran out of the room.

By the time my stepdad was ready to leave, Mom was in her room with the door closed. He patted me on the cheek and said, "Honey, watch yourself. Poor kids. I'm not much, but I loved all of you."

Later on Mom came out. Me and the kids were having cereal.

"Gee, honey, is that all you could find?" she asked me, but she didn't really care. She went and got herself a cup of coffee, and before she was done with it the kids had gone off to watch television.

"Sit down for a minute, Kathy," Mom said. "What do you think of Hank?"

She looked at me sort of shyly and even a little bit embarrassed. I mean, she was blushing a little.

"Hank?"

"Yeah. You know. He was here a while ago."

"Oh, that guy."

"Yeah. Hank. What do you think of him?"

"I hardly saw him, Mom."

"Yeah. I guess you didn't get much of a look. I hope you like him, though."

She was looking at her hands. She was a waitress and a darn good one, and she had nice hands and she kept them that way. I mean, you'd never know how hard she worked, both at work and home. She liked her hands. She was proud of them.

"Kathy, I think I'm in love for the first time since I was a kid," she told me. "I was in love when I was sixteen, but he didn't love me. So I married your pa—"

I felt awful. Just awful. I didn't really know why. I didn't want to hear about my pa—or about that guy who had been standing there smiling as though that fight didn't have anything to do with him.

But she said, "I'm in love, Kathy, at the old age of thirty."

"You going to marry him?" I asked her, and my heart was squeezed, waiting for her answer.

She gave a funny laugh. "I always marry 'em, Kathy. Your ma is known as a very good woman. I mean that, kid. And I want it to stick. I don't want any talk about the mother of my daughters. But this one I *want* to marry. I mean, I don't really have to. I can support you. I'm not doing all that bad, and in another year or two you can earn your money baby-sitting and help out. We could get by, as far as that goes. No, I want this one just for me—for my own pleasure, Kathy. You'll know what that means someday. Especially if you think back how your ma never had anything."

She sighed. Then she sat back, put her feet up on another chair, and looked at her legs where the robe had fallen away from them. She smiled. "Good legs, too for all the

walking and running I've done carrying heavy trays. Damn good legs. I'm not so bad, Kathy."

I smiled at her, but I couldn't get rid of the worry.

"Well, hon. I said to Hank, 'Hey you got to meet my kids first.' So he came today, and everyone came home a little early. We were just having coffee when your stepdad came in."

Her eye caught mine, and I knew she was lying. She wasn't the type that lied often, and I knew it wasn't comfortable for her. But that made it worse—that she had to lie.

"Well, after all, honey, we *are* going to get married. We'd be married now if it wasn't for Steve. Now that he's gone—Anyway, Hank's going to take us to the amusement park tomorrow. Hank knows how to please a woman. You'll like your new daddy, honey."

He took us to the park the next day, and he was nicer than nice. He took my next youngest sister on the roller coaster. Then he offered to take me, but I wouldn't go. My mom was disappointed, but I wouldn't go. She said, "Just give them all a chance, Hank."

"Sure. They'll all come round," he said.

"You know how to please a woman, Hank."

He smiled at me. "I hope so. I haven't had much experience with them that young."

They both laughed.

Hank lived with us for a while. Mom said it was all right since they were going to be married as soon as they could. Every so often Mom would say, "Kathy, I'm so happy. I hope you are, too."

I said sure, but I wasn't. But then it wasn't too bad, because Hank went to work on the three-to-eleven shift and I didn't see him all that much. And besides he was nice. Maybe, I thought, I was just jealous. I really didn't understand how I felt. But I hated that door closed on them at night. After all, it wasn't his place.

But Mom always said, "Kathy, I'm so happy." She said it about once a week to me. She didn't just say it; it was as though she was asking me something. Asking me to like him, I suppose. My two sisters liked him just fine. His funny smile didn't bother them. They sat on his lap and teased him to find out what he had brought for them, and they all laughed and made too much noise. Mom was pleased.

Sometimes I would feel him looking at me. But when I looked at him, he had that smile on his face—that smile that seemed to say everything was fine and he was above everything.

One Saturday we were out with Mom to buy some clothes, and she took us to Farrell's for ice cream. My sister had on a pretty bracelet. I really liked it. "Oh, Hank gave it to me," she said as she licked the drips on her soda glass. "He'd give you one if you were nice to him."

Mom was looking at me to see what I'd say. I didn't say anything.

"Like him a little more?" she asked me.

"I never said I didn't like him," I answered, so mad inside that I really couldn't enjoy my soda.

I wanted to say I was afraid of him. But I couldn't, because I hadn't any reason in the world to be afraid of him, and Mom was happy. She was so happy that she looked much younger and much softer. She looked like I'd like to look when I was her age.

"Well," I heard her say to Hank one evening after they must have been talking about me, "another month and we'll be married. That may make a difference. After all, sweetheart, she's at a bad age for young girls. You know. Twelve years old."

He laughed. "Late bloomer, eh?"

"Why, no. That's about right."

"Yeah. I suppose so. Thought I noticed her filling out a lot."

Mom laughed, and then they both laughed and their door closed.

I ran to my room, threw myself on my bed, and pulled the pillow over my head. I couldn't believe it! My own mom telling him *that!* I just couldn't believe it. I never cried so hard in my life.

They were married a month later. My mom wore a pink dress with a big pink straw hat with flowers on it. She was very pretty. Each of us girls had a new outfit. There were lots of Mom's friends there, and some of his, I guess. We had all the cake and ice cream we wanted later at the hall they rented. Mom said they weren't going to spare anything to make it a good party.

Once he came over to me to ask me to dance. He was way too tall. I felt foolish and I felt trapped by him. I was always trapped, and yet he didn't do anything or say anything. My little sisters loved him and they wanted to dance with him, but he said no to them. This was our dance, his and mine.

"You don't like me much, Kathy, do you?" he said softly. "I think that is a mistake, and you'll see how nice I can be. Just wait. Give me a chance. Your mom thinks I'm okay, and your sisters, too. But I don't mind a holdout. It's more interesting when you don't give in too easily." He held me a little tighter. "You'll be all right, honey. You're a fine girl."

Then he started to talk about how funny the musicians were, and he made me laugh. That was just as we left the floor, and there was Mom. She looked so pleased. As he danced away with her, I heard her say, "What magic did you use?"

"You should know that," he said.

I turned away with my face blazing.

"Did you like dancing with him, Kathy?" Dely asked. She was eight, and she loved all the fun. She didn't have any sense. She was too young. Anne was only six.

"Let's go have some more ice cream," I said, and that was a great idea. I forgot to think about anything else.

A few months later there was the first problem. Mom had a good job and her boss really appreciated her. She always got good bonuses, and she had the best tables. After all, she had been there longest, and she was the best waitress they had. Her old customers didn't want anyone else.

Her boss decided to go into the nightclub business, and he wanted her to be the hostess. She'd work from four to midnight. And she'd get a good raise. Besides, there'd be no more trays to carry. And no

more guff from the customers. Her boss let her know that he didn't think he'd go ahead with the club unless he could depend on her and the bartender who had been with him for ages. After all, they'd have to run things a lot of the time.

Hank told her he didn't like to be without her so long, but he could get his shift changed. He could work the seven-to-three shift if that would help. Later on, she said to me, "You just don't appreciate what a great guy he is. I mean, he's been doing the night shift for years and he is perfectly happy with it. He doesn't want to change, but he's doing it for me because he wants me to get ahead. I want you to be nice to him, Kathy. There's never been another man like him in my life, and I don't want to lose him."

I wasn't *un-nice* to him. I just tried to stay out of his way. I was polite, and I did the things I always had done, like helping with the ironing and the dishes. I just didn't want anything more to do with him than I had to. I couldn't explain it, but I was afraid of him. I wouldn't have told Mom that for anything. It would have been the worst thing I could do. She might even have hated me. But I was afraid of him, and that's the truth. And I didn't have any reason I could give anyone.

Then Mom started working nights. I hated it. I hated Hank in the house with us.

At the dinner table one night, he was helping the kids with their homework while I did the dishes.

"Got any homework I can help you with, Kathy?" he said.

I shook my head.

He was smiling at me and watching me. Some people thought he was handsome. They said he had such nice gray eyes, and all his features were good, and he had this nice curly hair. My mom loved to put her hands in his hair. When she did that, he would nuzzle her in the breasts and they would both laugh and hug.

I went on doing the dishes. Then I went in to watch television. When he came in with a can of beer, I pretended I was really interested in the TV show. He took a magazine and started reading, but a couple of times I felt him looking at me. Then I got so tired I wanted to go to bed.

"Want the set on?" I asked politely.

"No, thanks. I'll go to bed soon, too."

I was reading when my bedroom door opened a little later. Hank was in the doorway.

"Just checking," he said. "Making sure everything is all right. Everyone comfortable. What are you reading?"

"Something for school," I said, furious that he dared open my door without knocking.

"Oh, what is it? Something I know?" He came over and took the book out of my hand and looked at the title. "Hey, they still reading that? Teachers don't change, eh?"

He pretended to be looking at the book. He turned some pages and laughed a little. Then he read me a little snatch. Then he turned back to where I had been. "Hey, I'm a good reader," he said. "Always was. Some people used to say I should have been a radio announcer. I'll read to you for a while."

He came around the other side of the bed, propped the pillow up, and stretched out next to me. Then he started to read.

He had to put glasses on from his pocket, but he was a good reader. He read about ten pages. Then he closed the book, stood up, kissed me on the forehead, turned off the light, and went to the door.

"Good night," he said, and closed the door.

I hardly slept at all. Every time I started to fall asleep, a sick feeling would come over me. I'd wake up and feel helpless and start to cry.

The next night he did the same thing. And the next. The next night Mom was off, and I was safe. But he didn't stop coming. If I didn't have a book, he'd bring one. If I pretended to be asleep, he'd nudge me gently until I was awake.

"Time for your lesson," he'd say.

It was the same every night. One day Mom said how glad she was I was letting Hank help with my schoolwork. She said he was so smart and I couldn't help but benefit.

Then one night after he was reading for a while, he said, "Turn out the light, Kathy."

I looked at him, scared to death. He smiled that strange smile at me, and he put the book down on the table next to me—which meant he had to lean over me. And he turned off the light. He didn't lie back on his own part of the bed. He lay against me, and he started to kiss my cheeks and to nuzzle my ear and to say things to me.

"Please!" I said. "Please go! Hank, please go."

"You don't really want me to go," he said. "We're good friends now, you and me. We've got to get to know each other. Better than just friends, Kathy."

I wanted to scream, but that would have only scared the little kids. He pulled the blankets down a little way, and he said soft things as he opened my pajama top. Then he began to kiss my breasts. I could hardly breathe because my heart was pounding.

"Poor baby," he murmured, "your heart's going like a little frightened bird. Relax, honey. This is all fun. It's good, and it's good for a girl your age. You need this, honey. Most girls your age get it from nasty boys. Rough kids. Not you, honey. You got me to teach you."

"Oh, Hank, please go."

"No, no. Just relax. You'll get to like it, I guarantee you. Don't be afraid of me. I'm your best friend." He kissed me on the lips, and he kissed my tears away.

"Don't struggle, sweetheart," he said. "You want this to be easy. Now, darling, put your arms around my neck. Go ahead do as I tell you. Stop crying. No need to cry. Put your arms around my neck. Do it. There, that's right. That's how it should be. You see how easy."

He kept fondling me for about a half hour, and then he pulled the blanket over me. "There, that's enough for tonight. You're a good girl," he said.

The next day my mom said to me, "You look awfully pale, Kathy. Taking your vitamins?"

I sighed and I studied her. Could I tell her?

"I work you too hard, Kathy. I don't mean to, but, honey, stick with it for a while. I want to have another baby, and I want to really get ahead before I do. I'll make it worth your while for helping me

GOLDEN WEDDING DAY

The little church was crowded
As the pretty teenaged bride
Stood before the altar
With her bridegroom at her side.

The organist stopped playing
And the service was begun,
The old familiar liturgy
That makes two people one.

They promised to be faithful
In poverty or wealth,
And care for one another
In sickness and in health.

And though they looked like children
Dressed up to play a part,
They made their vows with confidence—
Each word came from the heart.

Still some of those who witnessed
The ceremony said,
"Those kids are much too young
To even think of being wed!"

And lots of others wondered
Once the honeymoon was past
If their love could be depended on
To make the marriage last.

Well, if any of those skeptics
Were in church the other day,
I'm sure their doubts and fears
Were pretty quickly swept away.

For that proud and happy couple
Stood side by side once more
To renew the vows and promises
Made fifty years before.

Their voices rang with confidence.
Each word was loud and clear,
As if they wanted everyone
In all the world to hear.

And though time had lined their faces
And turned their hair to gray,
Their love was still as young and bright
As on their wedding day!

by Alice E. Chase

like you do. I'm so glad you're getting along with Hank. He says it's all roses. Darling, I'm so proud of you."

I left the room and went to my own room and cried and cried. She must have found me asleep when she came in to say good-night, because the next thing I knew my little sister was saying, "Come on, Kathy—make dinner. I'm hungry."

I went out to make dinner, and then he came home. I saw him outlined in the doorway, and I almost got sick. The whole evening passed away in a kind of awful dream, like you knew the earth was going to quake and you didn't know what to do about it.

I went to bed right after my sisters did, and I turned off the light and pretended to be asleep, though I knew it was no good. He came very quietly, and he sat on the bed. I felt his hand on my hair.

"You're not asleep, Kathy." He kissed me. Then he started moving and I opened my eyes to see what he was doing. He was taking off his robe. He had on his shorts and his undershirt. He came around and he climbed into bed with me. He made me put my arms around his neck and he did all the kissing things. Then he started doing something else to me, and he started to kiss me where I couldn't believe. I begged him to stop, but he put his fingers gently on my lips.

"Just relax. You'll see. A few minutes. You'll see."

In a few minutes it was like fire all over, and I was moaning and moaning and saying his name.

Then he came up and lay next to me and took me into his arms. "There. I told you. You see how good it is. Now you can sleep. You'll sleep real good tonight. You're learning fast. You're fine."

The next day I skipped school and I went to where I knew my real father lived. The old lady who rented rooms there told me to go up and see. She didn't know if he was there or not. I went up. His room was almost bare, and it had a funny smell. The only thing I could see personal was a snapshot in an old frame of me and Dely with Mom when we were babies.

I waited all afternoon for him. When he came home, he didn't even see me sitting in the old broken-down armchair that sagged to the floor. He came in holding himself up with the walls and the door, and he swore when he stumbled over his own feet. He went to the toilet and didn't close the door. Then he came out and lurched over to the bed and fell on it. He didn't even take off his shoes.

"Dad," I said, just before he lay down.

He hit himself on the forehead with his fist. "Jeez, I'm havin' the creeps," he mumbled, and he reached for a tattered blanket at the foot of the bed and pulled it over his face.

"Dad," I called. I tried a couple more times and got no answer. Then he began to snore. When I left there, I knew there was nowhere to go but home again.

Mom had left and the rest were waiting for me for dinner. I couldn't meet Hank's eyes. He seemed to understand, and he laughed and talked with the kids and left me alone. He didn't even come in that night, but I couldn't sleep until I heard Mom come home.

The next two nights Mom had off. But after that he came back and he did all that

stuff to me. But this time he told me I had to help him now. He said it would hurt just at first. That night he raped me. He didn't care that I cried my heart out. He held me and said comforting things about how gentle he had been, how it wouldn't hurt after a little while.

At first he came every night. Then he came about three nights a week. He was right. I didn't like him. I hated him, but I got to like what he did. There was no love, just the mechanics. But I did get used to it. I did miss it when he stayed away longer than he regularly did. He told me I would be great with my own man someday because of him. He never was cruel to me or mean. I could never say that.

Now Mom complained that I was too quiet, that I never talked. She complained that she and I had started to be friends, but that now I was different. I *was* different. I went to high school. I was fourteen by then, and I was very pretty. I was more like Mom all the time. Everyone said so. But when boys would like me, I wouldn't do the things with them other girls did—oh, like flirt and say dumb things that are so much fun.

I watched all this stuff, and I wondered about all the girls I knew. Did any of them hide the kind of secret I hid? There was no way I could know. I couldn't trade secrets with them like they all did. When they looked at me to say something, I clammed up. So finally I was sort of alone. I mean, they were afraid I was judging them. That's what one of them told me. She was very frank. She came right out and told me they were afraid of something about me. They didn't like someone who just sat there and looked. She said I should make talk, even small talk. It was funny. So I just kept to myself.

Toward the end of that year, a teacher, Mrs. Carney, the Home Ec teacher, noticed how I was. I really admired her. She had a nice husband and a nice house and two kids—twins. Each kid had a nice room fixed up the way he wanted it. She taught Family Living, so we got to see pictures of all kinds of things concerning her.

But it wasn't that. It was her. I felt she knew what she was doing, and that she was happy. So I began to stay after school to talk to her. She didn't think it was funny or anything. She just treated me friendly like she was to everyone.

I must have stayed talking to her for a month off and on. I got home just in time to make dinner. But that was all right because Mom and Hank thought I was in clubs or something at school. Mrs. Carney never asked personal questions. She just let you be. She was the most comfortable person in the world to be with—and so wise. She was always telling me things the twins were doing to put things over on her and what she did back. I thought they must be the luckiest boys in the world.

I was getting to trust her completely. I knew that one day I would tell her. I didn't know what I would gain from telling her, but I had to tell someone, just one person just once. I needed that. But I didn't say anything. Christmas came and went and it got to be spring, and then one day I heard myself starting to ask her questions and I knew I was going to tell her. I didn't know if she would stop being my friend or what she would do, but I had to tell her.

It didn't come easily. First, I was so awkward she thought I was one of those

kids who do things to themselves and feel guilty about it, but I said no. And then I began to tell her. I told her about my real father and my first stepdad, and then about Mom and how she had married Hank. Then I told her how I had felt about Hank, how something inside me told me it wasn't right with him—and then all the rest.

When she got mad, she got so mad that everyone near her knew it and got out of her way. I only saw that happen once. But it looked as though it had happened again. Her face got flame red and her eyes stared at me. Then she slowly shook her head and looked down. We sat silently for a while.

"I'm sorry," she said then. "This has really upset me. Kathy, you can't talk to your mother?"

"There's no way she would believe it. I know that."

"Well, he must have a 'way with him. We'll have to give him that. I can't do anything at all about this, but I think the principal can. You've put me in a bad spot in a way, because I can't know what I know and not do something about it. Do you want me to do something about it?"

I didn't know.

"We can talk to Mr. Hardin," Mrs. Carney said. "You know whatever he knows stays with him. I can't let you go on like this. We can even get you into a foster home."

"Do you think that could happen?" I asked, really hopeful for the first time that there was an escape for me.

"Can we talk to him?"

"Will you talk to him first?"

"Yes, of course I will."

"I'll see you tomorrow," I said.

All the way home I wondered how it would be without Hank. I mean, I wondered about that more than anything. I wondered if I wanted that now, and I wondered if I got away from it if I would ever want it with anyone again. If I got away from him, would I really be free?

Well, the hope died soon.

It was taken out of my hands. The principal talked to me, and then he consulted the judge he worked with on juvenile cases. The judge told him the court could do nothing unless my mother swore out a complaint. Both the principal and Mrs. Carney begged me to let them talk to her. I think I must have wanted help so much that I agreed to this impossible thing. I was never so scared as the day my mother came in for a conference. She thought it was for something to do with school, but when she saw the principal, Mrs. Carney, and the juvenile officer representing the judge, she knew it was something else.

She sat and listened as the paper was read out to her, for the principal said that would be the best way to let her know what it was all about. I didn't want to watch her face, but I had to. She got paler and paler as she listened, her eyes fixed on the principal's face. When it was over, her eyes came to my face for a long time. She didn't look at me as though she hated me, but as though she didn't know me—like I was someone she was seeing for the first time. Then she sighed.

"I'm sorry," she said. "I didn't know my daughter hated my husband this much. I thought she had gotten to like him."

"After what he's done to her?" Mrs. Carney exclaimed.

"Done to her? Do you believe that? Why, you're as crazy as she is. This girl is crazy. There's no other way to say it. She never liked him, but I thought that was over. He's so good to all of us. I guess if you hate someone, things grow in your head."

"You won't even check this out?" the principal asked.

"Mister, this kid of mine is lying. She's lying as much as though she said that about you. I don't blame her if she can't help herself. But I think one thing is certain. Maybe she should go to a mental hospital—or, if not there, to a foster home. Maybe someone else can help her."

Then she started to cry. "I've worked so hard all my life to make sure my girls had it decent," she said. "I found them a decent father who does all he can for them and who loves them, and now this. You don't know. This good, loving man. To be accused. I've heard that young girls get fancies—" Her look came back to me, her eyes filled with tears. "What happened? Some boy take advantage of you and you're looking for a way out? Is that it?"

I couldn't answer. I just bowed my head, tears coming to me, too. I felt all alone.

"There's nothing we can do unless you bring the complaint," the juvenile authority said.

My mother sat in bitter silence.

"You won't even speak to your husband?" Mrs. Carney asked.

"Lady, I would die before I'd tell him what my own flesh and blood has done to him here. You can believe that. I'll do everything I can to make it up to him. I feel sorry for Kathy. You can put her away if you can. If not, I'll have to take her back, but it'll never be the same again."

"Then may we arrange for a foster home?" the principal asked.

"Yes. I agree to that, though my husband may not. He wouldn't understand. But I'll think of something to make it all right."

Everyone was troubled. I knew that. They had done what they could, what the law would allow. They could see what I had feared was true—that she would never see it, never admit it. But she said she would take me home with her. She had a car now.

On the drive home, she was quiet until we got to a block from our house. Then she stopped the car. ⟶

Coming next month . . .

SOME WOMAN IS MAKING OBSCENE PHONE CALLS TO ME!

"I WON'T LET YOU KEEP A GUN IN THE HOUSE!"

MOVING-DAY ORPHAN

April issue goes on sale March 2. Don't miss it!

QUICK-AND-EASY NEEDLEWORK

799—Instant crochet cape in a design of graduated shells topped by stand-up collar, yoke. Use worsted. Directions, Misses' 8–20 incl. $1.00.

953—Newest look in town—rugged, hooded jacket! Use 2 strands of worsted-size synthetic. Directions for Misses' Sizes 8–18 incl. $1.00.

809—Thrill a child with Spirit of '76 costumes for her 11½–12" girl, boy teen dolls. Easy-to-crochet of bedspread cotton. Directions. $1.00.

529—Give old lamps a new look with decorator-inspired shades. Easy-to-make, low-cost! Step-by-step directions for 10 styles included. $1.00.

7431—Victorian motifs lend a "turn of the century" look to towels, other linens. Transfer of seven 5x6-inch embroidery motifs, color tips. Directions. $1.00.

"I want to talk to you, Kathy," she said. "I'm going to try to forgive you for what you've done. It is the nastiest, most evil thing I ever heard of. We are not going to act funny to each other at home. I want my home to be the happy place it has been for these past three years. So I'm going to pretend everything is okay, and I'm going to talk to you just like I always do. I'm going to try to remember you are just a kid and try to forgive you for what you put me through today. But I'll never forgive you for what you said about Hank. Not in my lifetime. That I cannot do."

I didn't answer. There was nothing for me to say.

"You're hard, Kathy," she said to me. "I sort of saw that a long time ago when Hank was so nice and you always held back. Well, let's get home."

I don't know what she told him about me going to a foster home. I never found out what reason she gave. She didn't say anything at first, because nothing was changed. And then one night at dinner I heard Hank say, "Dely, you like me to read to you?"

"Sure, Hank."

"Well, I will. After you go to bed, I'll read for a little while to you."

I looked at him. He was looking at me. He had the smile on his face. Dely went to see what book she wanted him to read.

"It's going to be lonesome for me here without you," he said, still looking at me. "I thought we got along real good. But Dely's growing up."

I dropped the sugar bowl and the sugar went all over the floor. Hank helped me clean it up.

"Leave Dely alone." I said.

Those cool eyes were appraising me.

"Maybe," he said. "We'll see."

Mrs. Carney gave up on me when I wouldn't go to the foster home. She had found a really good place for me, and when she heard I wasn't going she asked me to see her. Now, I wouldn't tell anyone anything. I had had my hopes up and look what had happened. She demanded to know what the matter was, why I wouldn't go.

"The counselor and I worked for hours to find the right place. What's the matter with you, not wanting to go?"

I simply couldn't tell her. I couldn't even say the horror that waited if I went. And I felt really bad when I saw the look in her face and her helplessness. We were both helpless.

About two years later, two things happened. My mom changed her job to daytime hours. It paid less, but she said she had enough of night work. And a guy I met at a game at school wanted to marry me. He was back from Vietnam and was a nice guy. That's all he wanted was to marry me. I would have walked away from him if my mom was still working nights. But now Hank didn't bother me anymore. Now I wanted to get out of there.

So I went away with Bill and married him. I didn't want any wedding or anything where anyone would look at me.

We get along good, Bill and I. There's something about me that really gets him. It's kind of funny, but I mean everything to him. I never thought I'd marry anyone, if the truth is told. I don't think I can ever really love a man. But Bill doesn't know that. And he's happy, and I'm content. We have a little girl named Sally. I wished it had been a boy, but it wasn't.

One day Mom came over to see Sally. I never asked the family over. Bill didn't understand this, but he accepted it—all part of my mystery, he said. Mystery! He said as long as we got along so well, nothing would interfere with that. I mean, if I didn't want family, then okay.

Well, Mom came over. She seemed to have something on her mind. When Sally was having her nap, I made coffee for us.

"You got a nice neat little place here, honey," Mom said. "I wish you would have finished school, though. Maybe you'll go back one day. Then you'll have something more to fall back on than I had."

I wondered why she was talking like this to me—I mean, sort of woman to woman.

"Kathy," she said, not meeting my eyes, "Kathy, I know. I know how it was."

I just stared at her. "You knew and you didn't—"

"Kathy, I just found out—just before I changed the job to daytime. That's why I did it."

"How did you know?"

"Anne. She said she was sick one night, and when I came home she had thrown up in bed. I asked her why she didn't call Hank. She said Hank was always in your room. She said she didn't think she could bother him. Oh, God, darling! I didn't know what to do. But I couldn't let it go. So one night I came home early and found out it was true."

"Well, what are you going to do, Mother?" I asked.

She toyed with her coffee spoon.

"I did what I am going to do. I changed the job."

"You'll go on with him?"

"I love him."

"I see."

She bent toward me. "You're happy, Kathy, with Bill, aren't you?"

I don't know what made me do it, but I did something nice. I wanted to scream at her and to tell her what a hell she had made of my life, but then I remembered that I did have peace, and I did have a good man.

"I'm happy," I said. "Yeah, Mom. It's okay."

She nodded and gave a great sigh of relief. "I'm so glad, Kathy. I'm so glad. It makes it a little more bearable."

"Yeah."

I was glad I did that, because now I could see all the anguish was on her. It wasn't on me anymore. I was glad I was nice. And for the first time I looked forward to Bill coming home. To Bill. I really wanted him to come home and complete our little circle.

When he came that night, Sally and I were in the window watching for him, and when I saw how pleased he was I knew that sometimes you can patch up awful holes with just simple kindness and forgiveness. I forgave my mom. I'm happier now. ∎

271

The love game I played on my bingo nights out

Nobody told me when I got hooked on the game of bingo that the price of admission might be my marriage. Sure, I felt a twinge or two of guilt each night at seven when I picked up my ink markers and my bingo chips and called out a hurried farewell to my husband. But I told myself that it wasn't my fault.

It was Ken's. Bingo was my substitute for sex and I was entitled.

Thirty-six years old, and lovemaking was over for me. It was Ken's problem, not mine, but it became mine, anyway. There was no organic reason for his impotence at age forty, the doctors said. Not after fifteen years of skyrocketing lovemaking. Not after thorough urological exams and complete physicals. But reason or not, Ken was no longer able to be my lover, and both of us were depressed and miserable.

When Moira, the legal secretary in the firm we both worked for, asked me if I'd like to go to bingo with her, I laughed. "That's for old ladies, Moira. Don't tell me you're looking for a husband there."

"Don't kid yourself, Jen," she said. "There are more eligible men there than at any singles bar. I've met divorced men who are steady bingo freaks. I've sat alongside widowers trying to fill up empty hours and, believe me, it's a whole different world for two and a half hours a night. Besides, there's the thrill of winning cash prizes, and it's a night out, isn't it? Come on, Jen—try it!"

So I went. On my first night, I looked around the hall and saw that Moira was right. This was the place to meet men. All shapes, all sizes, all ages. I found myself smiling at the good-natured bantering between Moira and the fellow who sold specials. There was an easy camaraderie between the neighbors sitting near or around our table, and Moira introduced me.

"This is Jen's first time," she said. "Watch her win—beginner's luck!"

At seven-thirty sharp, the games began. A hush fell over the crowd as each person bent over his boards intent on the winning combination of numbers. As soon as someone called Bingo, the game stopped and the crowd buzzed again. After twelve games, there was a two-minute intermission so players could change their boards, and anticipation ran through the place like an electric charge.

I followed Moira's lead and replaced all my boards. In about fifteen minutes, I realized that all my numbers were covered except one. I started to get nervous and plucked at Moira's sleeve to get her attention.

She glanced up quickly at the board I was pointing to and exclaimed, "Oh, no! Jen! You're waiting! All right!"

I stared hard at the one number left to cover, and I felt excitement shoot through me. A few more numbers were called, and finally one number was mine. I shrieked out, "Bingo!"

The "special" man came over, slid off my red chips on the winning board, and began to call back the numbers for verification. I couldn't believe it. In another few minutes he was back with the $250 jackpot prize I had won. I wanted to tip the man who had brought the money to me, but Moira quickly introduced him to me as Dan and explained that no tips were allowed or accepted. I smiled up at Dan and thanked him for bringing me the money. Again I tried to slip him ten dollars.

"No can do, love," he said, smiling. "How about my taking it out in trade?" It was just the easy banter that the men used on the majority of the women there. It perked up the seventy- and eighty-year-olds, but in my sexless life the invitation threw me a little. I felt myself blush furiously, and Moira and Dan both laughed at me.

The games went on, but I didn't win again.

"What's that bell that's rung every time 066 is called?" I asked at one point.

"Just bingo tradition, Jen," Moira explained. "Any hall you go to, somebody brings along a cow bell just for that one number. At Cranston, when N44 is called, somebody always yells out, 'Quack-Quack.' At Fordham, when G49 is called, the whole crowd repeats it after the caller. Dopey, isn't it? But that's bingo jargon."

Let me tell you about my pet!

MATERNAL INSTINCT

☐ About sixteen years ago, when my children were little, we had a cat named Mittens. She had been missing for about a week when, one day, the clouds of a summer storm began to build up in the sky.

All of a sudden, the children came running to me, yelling that Mittens was trying to get inside with a "big rat" in her mouth. I went to look, and found that it wasn't a rat—it was a baby kitten.

I opened the door, and Mittens came walking in. She put the kitten down, then went to the door and meowed as if she wanted to go back out. I let her out, but instead of going off she kept crying at the door. When I went out, she ran a little bit, stopped, looked back at me, and meowed again as if she wanted me to follow her.

I did follow her, and she led me down a path into some honeysuckle bushes. She then went into a small, cave-like hole. I looked in, and there were four more kittens. I picked them up, put them in my apron, and carried them back to the house.

Meanwhile, the thunder, lightning, and rain had started. As I got back to the house, the sky opened up. Mittens looked up at me and meowed as if to say, "Thank you."

After the storm had ended, the children and I went to see the den where the kittens had been. The storm had washed it completely away! Mittens had had sense enough to know it was dangerous, and I'm sure that's why she meowed for me to follow her. She knew she couldn't have carried all her kittens up to the house and to safety before the storm broke. We were very proud of her for being such a loving mother to her babies.
— **H. R., North Carolina**

BEEP-BEEP

☐ I would like to tell you about the most unusual pet my husband and I ever had. Although we only had our roadrunner for eleven days, "Beep-Beep" will always be remembered in our hearts.

My husband found Beep-Beep in a patch of brambles. When he first spotted the roadrunner, my husband thought the bird was dead because he was being so still. But, on closer inspection, my husband discovered that Beep-Beep was very much alive, unable to move because of a broken left leg.

After bringing the bird home, we called the local humane society, hoping that they could help us. They suggested a local veterinarian. The veterinarian supplied us with splints in order to set the roadrunner's leg, and tranquilizers to keep the bird from being frightened. The veterinarian kindly gave us the supplies free of charge.

After setting the leg, we put Beep-Beep—so named because of his cry—in a padded box in our spare bedroom. This would give him peace, quiet, and darkness.

For ten days, we fed Beep-Beep one tranquilizer in the morning, water from an eyedropper, and raw liver. In the evening we repeated the same procedure.

On the tenth day, we knew that if his leg had not healed we would have to put Beep-Beep to sleep, as roadrunners must catch their prey by chasing it. It was with mixed emotions that we cut away the splints.

His leg had healed! We were so proud and pleased. We kept Beep-Beep an extra day in order to exercise his legs so that his muscles could regain their full strength.

We then took Beep-Beep to a secluded area and set him free. The last time we saw him, Beep-Beep was running into the forest saying, "Beep-beep," and we were standing by the car with tears in our eyes.

— **J. K., Arkansas**

Please tell us about *your* pet! If we publish your story, we will pay you $50. Address manuscripts to: TRUE STORY PET EDITOR, 205 E. 42nd St., New York, N. Y. 10017. No entries can be returned unless accompanied by stamped, self-addressed envelope.

At 10:45 the games ended, and Moira and I gathered our bingo tools together. I turned to put my jacket on and was surprised to see Dan, the special man, at my elbow.

"Going straight home, girls?" he asked.

"What have you got in mind?" Moira flirted.

"Thought I'd take you gals to the diner for a snack."

"You go, Moira," I answered quickly. "I have to get home." I might have imagined the flicker of disappointment on Dan's face, but the gratitude on Moira's was real. I turned and headed for the parking lot.

When I reached home, I was still elated over my big win and fanned out the ten- and twenty-dollar bills to show Ken. He was pleased for me, and when I told him I planned to go again on Saturday night, he said nothing, but I sensed his secret relief. *Sure*, I thought. *Anything to get me out of the house. Then he won't have to feel guilty every time he looks at me.*

That wasn't quite fair, I told myself as I got ready for bed. Ken loved me more than ever, he had said. Particularly now that he could no longer express it. Be patient with him, he had said.

I brushed my hair angrily and stared at myself in the mirror. I took inventory. What would a stranger—Dan, for instance—see when he looked at me? *Not too bad*, I thought as my image stared back at me. Nature had been good to me, but what good did it do me, since the man I loved had already put me on the shelf? How could I not resent Ken for making me so vulnerable to other men? Didn't he know that a woman never strayed when she found satisfaction at home?

The trouble was, I couldn't just start sleeping around. Number one, Ken had been my first and only lover. Number two, I had a strict, moral code that did not permit infidelity.

Well, then, my thoughts churned, *maybe I shouldn't give up on Ken. Maybe I should keep trying to revive his interest.* Okay. Maybe leaving him alone a couple of nights a week would do the trick. If nothing else, it would give him a chance to breathe, to think about me out having fun and maybe miss me enough to make some advances again.

I fell asleep finally to the muted sounds of the television coming from the den. Eventually, after Ken made sure I was asleep, he would feel safe again and come to bed.

Saturday night Moira and I set out again for the bingo hall.

"How was your date with Dan?" I asked. Moira had acted a little cool with me at the office for the past few days.

"Some date!" she snorted. "He spent half our time pumping me about you."

"What did you tell him?" I asked carefully, knowing that Dan was Moira's only real reason for going to bingo.

"Not much," she said, "but I made a point of telling him that you're happily married."

I stared thoughtfully out the car window. Moira was my closest friend, and still I had never confided my personal problem to her. I was too embarrassed to discuss my sex life with her, and too humiliated to discuss Ken's disinterest in me. I didn't want anyone to know that I wasn't woman enough to arouse my husband.

"Penny for your thoughts," Moira broke in.

"You wouldn't get your money's worth," I told her.

Moira jockeyed the car expertly into position in the parking lot. We got out and headed for the entrance. "Jen," Moira said quietly, "hands off Dan, okay? I've got this thing for him. Don't give me any competition."

"Oh, Moira," I said, "what a thing to say! I've got no interest in other men."

"Keep it that way," she said, then walked ahead of me into the card room.

I rounded up my boards blindly, my mind in a dither. *Was it that obvious?* I asked myself. Just because a man had made a remark he'd made to countless other women and I had overreacted— If Moira had been aware of it, surely Dan had picked up the same vibration.

I was embarrassed all over again and tried not to look around for Dan when I took my seat. I couldn't kid myself. I was definitely attracted to him, and that frightened me. But I told myself a mild flirtation might be good medicine for my bruised ego. Moira was a big girl now, attractive and younger than I, and she could handle herself. If Dan were truly interested in her, nothing I could do or say would change his mind. Then I stopped thinking about it and concentrated on my new table mates.

I fell in love with Mama Hess on sight. In her flowered, chintz housedress, with the silver-gray braids piled high on her shapely head, she was beautiful. She was eighty years young, and her eyes twinkled merrily.

Moira introduced us, and I reached out to squeeze Mama's hand as she offered it. I felt as though I had known this woman all my life. She exuded warmth and friendliness.

"So, Jennifer," she said, "you won the big jackpot Wednesday night, yes? Good! I was sitting at the other end of the hall and watched your excitement. Tonight, I sit with you. Maybe your luck will rub off on me, no?" She beamed at me.

"Come on, Jen, pay attention," Moira interrupted. "Here's my boy with the specials."

I turned quickly to find Dan at my side, and I dug into my purse and took out some bills for the special games.

"How many, love?" Dan's eyes raked over me.

"The usual," I said, flustered again by his boldness. "Four for a quarter, right?"

"Sharp-looking outfit you've got on, kid," Dan answered, peeling off the specials. He rushed off again.

When I counted my specials, I realized that Dan had given me four extras, and I called out to him. He looked around at me from halfway down the aisle, winked, and kept right on going. "Moira," I said, "Dan made a mistake and gave me extra specials."

Moira hadn't missed any of it, and she said coldly, "So you made a hit. It sure helps to have friends in high places."

"Oh, Moira, don't be that way!" I said. "Come on, now. Split them with me."

"No way," Moira snapped. "We're here to play bingo, remember? No other games. Got it?"

(Continued)

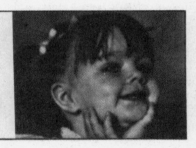

I sure did, and so did Mama Hess. "Give two here, Jennifer," she begged. "I haven't won a game in six months."

The first caller turned up the microphone and made the usual announcements. I gazed around our immediate area, trying to ignore Moira, noticing a familiar face or two, and then my attention riveted on a woman sitting across from us.

She was enormous. In her sixties, I guessed, heavily made up, dyed black hair, her bulk overflowing the chair. The man with her was laughing at something she had just said, and he waved his cigar around as he gestured wildly for Dan and his specials.

"How ya doin', honey?" Dan called out as he neared their table.

"Anybody I can, sugar. You been done yet?" The whole table roared.

"Boy, that Annie is something else!" Moira said. "She makes the bingo circuit with her husband, Al, seven nights a week. Can you believe they've won over $700 this week alone?"

I was impressed. "Legitimately, or on a fix?" I kidded.

"I wonder sometimes," Moira answered. "Some places run crooked games, but I don't think it could happen here."

That night I won the tenth game, which was a double bingo on any one board. My prize was fifty dollars. "Moira," I said, stunned by my win, "I don't believe this. I didn't know it was so easy to win."

"Enjoy it while it lasts," Moira said. "We all have beginner's luck—and then zilch."

I was so exhilarated by my win that I asked Moira if there were any all-night bingo games around anywhere. I hated to quit.

"No, you bingoholic!" Moira said, laughing. "But I'll take you to Cranston tomorrow night if Ken will let you out again."

"He won't mind," I answered. "He's just as happy lying on the couch watching his crime shows."

"Sounds like the honeymoon is over," Moira said.

If you only knew the half of it! I thought

and followed her out the door.

Dan was nowhere to be seen as we threaded our way to the car. I was relieved. I'd practically forgotten about him as my thoughts marched ahead to the game tomorrow night and the Cranston Hall. It was so exciting, such fun, and the money I'd won was just an extra bonus. I loved the heart-pounding moments of waiting for that one winning number to be called, and I was still excited when Moira dropped me off at home.

Ken was elated for me when I told him I'd won again. My excitement had carried over and my mood was still high. "How about celebrating my win," I asked suggestively. "if you know what I mean."

A pained expression spread over Ken's face and he said, "Not tonight, Jen. There's a late movie I want to catch on TV."

I shrugged and headed for our bedroom. After each rejection in the past, I had brooded and resented Ken, but not tonight. I got ready for bed. I tuned Ken out and remembered instead the evening I had just spent. The sights, the sounds of happy people, the smell of hot pizza delivered to the hall during the games, the companionship of people hooked on bingo. I settled comfortably into sleep, and my last thought was of Dan. . . .

When we walked into the card room at Cranston the next night, I was amazed to see many of the same faces from the night before. "Moira," I said, "look. There's Annie and Al. And there's Mama Hess, too."

"Jen, when you get a table, save a seat for me," Mama Hess called. "I want to win tonight." Then she added that she was going to try a new system. She was looking for boards with a different B in every corner and a different O in the other corners. It made sense. Regardless of which of the thirty letter numbers was called, Mama was sure to make it with a chip, and thus gain an advantage, as the corners were crucial.

"Good luck," I told her, and then I went after Moira, who'd gone ahead to find us a table.

I was completely floored when I went in and found Dan sitting beside Moira. "Hello, love," Dan greeted me, "all work and no play makes Dan itchy." Then he pulled out a chair for me.

I sat down weakly, wondering why the small attentions from a complete stranger should heighten my senses so. I was acutely conscious of Dan's presence. His maleness and vitality exuded sex. I was all too aware, too, of his foot nudging mine "accidentally" under the table, and I quickly tucked my feet well under my chair. I tried to avoid his eyes and to concentrate on my boards, but I was really unnerved. I felt like a high-school girl, and Dan knew it.

By the end of the evening we were all in a party mood. Moira, Mama Hess, Dan, and I had each won some money. Mama Hess had won $150, and her rosy face was creased in smiles. Moira had won $75, and she, too, was smiling. Dan and I had won ten dollars on split games, and we were excited, too.

"Come on, women, let's celebrate," Dan said. "I'll take you all out to the diner for coffee and sandwiches."

Mama Hess declined, saying that her husband was picking her up at the en-

trance gate. Since Moira had driven me in her car, I had no choice but to follow her lead and accept Dan's invitation.

When we got to the diner, Dan and Moira slid into the seat across from me in the booth and I sat alone. For an hour or more, as we devoured hamburgers and French fries, Dan entertained us with stories. He told us about his regular job as a used-car salesman and his off-duty hours donating his time at his men's bingo club.

I was fascinated with Dan's stories and didn't realize how late it was getting until Moira pointed to her watch. "Won't Ken be worrying about you, Jen?" she asked.

I gathered my things together and stood up.

When Dan dropped us off at the bingo parking lot to get Moira's car, we thanked him for the entertaining time, and for the treat and drove home.

Moira was unusually quiet and extremely cool, and we spoke hardly at all. The tension between us was thick and I jumped right in. "Moira, I'm sorry I horned in on your date tonight, but I really didn't have any choice, did I?"

"Jen," she said, "I told you before and I'll tell you again. I'm very interested in Dan, and I'm trying to work a few points with him. It didn't help my cause any tonight with you there, hanging on every word he said."

"Oh, Moira, did I do that?" I asked. "I'm really sorry if you're offended. It's just that Dan is so entertaining and I had such a good time. Please, don't be angry with me. Look, Moira, from now on, we'll take my car. That way, if Dan asks you out, I can scoot home and he'll have to drive you back, okay?"

Moira smiled then and reached over to squeeze my hand. "Thanks, Jen, I knew you'd understand."

Ken was furious with me when I walked in the door. "Where have you been?" he demanded. "It's after midnight. Where were you?"

"Playing bingo," I answered coolly, and brushed past him. "Moira's boyfriend treated us to a snack."

Ken spun me around as I walked through the doorway. "Look, Jen," he started, "I know we've got a little problem, but that doesn't mean I want you gallivanting all over the place till all hours of the night."

"Are you telling me that I can't go to bingo anymore?" I bristled. "What's the matter, Ken—don't you trust me? Or are you afraid somebody else might want me?" My tone was taunting.

Ken started to say something, then clamped his mouth shut.

I ignored Ken from then on. The following week I went to bingo four nights in a row, despite the frozen look on Ken's face when I left the house.

I loved the game. I loved the excitement of winning, and I kept right on winning. Sometimes small amounts, sometimes the prize of a single game; but win or lose, I had to be there. There I could forget about Ken and our problem, and there I could use up the energy that drove me.

I knew I was completely hooked on gambling when I found myself annoyed and irritated when I had to give up an occasional night for some affair or other. I accompanied Ken to family weddings and dinner parties as a concession, and our relationship was strained and very polite. I went grudgingly when I had to, but my mind was on bingo. I felt cheated when seven o'clock came and went and I had to be somewhere else. At nine, I'd think: *The jackpot is coming up*—and I'd grow even more resentful of my sterile life.

We were at a dinner party one Saturday night and I glanced at my watch. Ken was furious with me. "Can't you forget about bingo for once?" he demanded. "What the hell is going on with you, Jen? I'm beginning to think it must be something besides bingo—like maybe a secret boyfriend—"

"Are you accusing me of being unfaithful?" I asked. "Is that it?"

"I'm sorry, Jen," Ken apologized, "but it's getting to be too much to take. I don't feel I have a wife anymore—just a roommate. I just pay the bills as far as you're concerned."

His apology didn't impress me in the least, but I didn't want to build our argument into a scene. I moved away from him and started chatting with some friends, but inside I was seething. What right did Ken have to criticize me and accuse me of being unfaithful? That really infuriated me. Here, I'd gone out of my way to avoid the bingo halls where Dan might be, knowing that he spelled trouble to me—but if this was how Ken felt about me, if I was going to have the name, I might as well have the game.

Unwittingly, Moira helped pave the way. In March she decided to take an early vacation and head for California and her folks. If I wanted to encourage her Dan, this was my chance and I took it.

Dan, too, took full advantage of Moira's absence and hovered over me when I went to bingo alone.

"I've missed you, love," he whispered in my ear, his breath warm against my hair. "Wait for me after the game."

"What about Moira?" I whispered back.

"Forget about her," he answered quickly. "She's got wedding bells on the brain, and I'm not ready for that scene."

I went with Dan to the diner that night and stayed for only a half hour. Dan was blunt. "Look, Jen," he said, "we're not kids anymore and I don't want to play games. Want to make it with me?"

I couldn't handle such a direct approach, and I shook my head. "Give me time to think about it, Dan," I answered.

I drove home, my mind whirling. What was I waiting for? Dan's obvious need thrilled me. It had been so long since a man had desired me. But what about Ken?

Resolutely, I pushed all thoughts of Ken out of my mind. He had brought this on himself. He didn't want what I had to give, and Dan was more than eager. I parked the car in front of the house and headed for the back door. Tomorrow I would see Dan again and give him my answer.

The following night I dressed with more care than usual, my nerves taut with anticipation. Luckily, I didn't have Ken to contend with as he had gone out on a business appointment.

When I got to the Bingo hall, Dan was at the entrance greeting some of the patrons. His eyes lit up when he saw me, and the familiar flutter began again in my chest.

"I must live right, Jen," he said approvingly. "You look terrific."

I thanked him for the compliment and whispered that I had something to tell him after the games.

Learn "Secret Male Hypnotism"

And You'll Be Able to <u>Command</u> The Love and Affection of Any Man

By WILLIAM A. LYONS and ALICE GOLDBLATT

NEW YORK - It's been a long time coming, but now, for the very first time ... the principles of "SECRET MALE HYPNOTISM" are being revealed. And now ... you can learn to use these principles to "command" the *love* and *affection* of handsome men.

Never again will you have to lose-out because you might not be the type of girl certain men go for.

Once you learn to apply the principles of "SECRET MALE HYPNOTISM," men will automatically see you as their "dream girl" ... and will be *strongly attracted to you*.

Once you learn to apply these principles, the man of your choice will experience definite feelings of *love* for you. He'll experience a true feeling of *affection* toward you. And ... more than likely ... will be strongly attracted to you *sexually*.

To put it all in a nut-shell: Once you learn to apply the principles of "SECRET MALE HYPNOTISM," you'll have the power to make men do *exactly as you wish*.

To test the power of these principles, we had a friend of ours try them on her boss. The results were unbelievable.

In less than one week, he fell wildly in love with her. She couldn't go anywhere or do anything without him tagging along. And if that's not enough ... he couldn't keep from smothering her with hugs and kisses, regardless of where they were.

That's the strange thing about these principles. They're so powerful that men seem to *lose control* (in an erotic sort of way) when you're near.

In another experiment, we had a more-than-willing young lady try these principles on the gentleman in the apartment above hers (he's a young doctor - and is simply a "living doll").

Here again, the experiment was a huge success.

Not only does she now "command" the love and affection of this hunk ... but (because of "SECRET MALE HYPNOTISM") he actually "worships" her like a queen.

Now you might not have a boss or guy upstairs ... but *we'll bet you a dollar* that you'll have no trouble finding dozens of handsome men to use these principles on. And who knows ... you still may find yourself in the arms of a dreamy young doctor.

"SECRET MALE HYPNOTISM" can be used on any man *without him being aware of it*. When you apply these principles, *you* are the only one who knows about it.

For the above experiments, we purposely used ordinary women. Women just like yourself. They are average-looking girls who make an average week's pay. And ... you could even say that they were a little on the shy side.

That's the interesting thing about "SECRET MALE HYPNOTISM." It makes absolutely no difference what you look like. And you don't need any special talents to make these principles work.

Any woman can learn to use these principles ... *quickly* and *easily*. All you really have to do is "give it a try."

If you do that much ... no more, no less ... there's positively no way you can fail. In fact, we'll guarantee your success.

We guarantee that by the third time you use "SECRET MALE HYPNOTISM," you'll be "commanding" the *love, companionship*, and *affection* of at least one handsome man. If you're not, we'll refund your money at once. All you have to do is return the material.

THE PRINCIPLES OF "SECRET MALE HYPNOTISM" costs only $7.95. And if you ever dreamed about having warm handsome men *touching* you, desiring you, even fighting for you ... send in the coupon now. All you have to lose are some of those dull lonely nights!

NOTE: By using the principles of "SECRET MALE HYPNOTISM," you'll be able to do much more than "command" the love of handsome men.

Unfortunately, we are not permitted to say any more about the subject in this publication. However - we guarantee that you'll be completely delighted when you learn exactly what other exciting pleasures "SECRET MALE HYPNOTISM" can bring you.

by Alice E. Chase

TO A BIG, BEAUTIFUL FAMILY!

In families with a lot of kids
There's very sure to be
Differences in temperaments
And personality.

You'll find a wide variety
In things they choose to do.
There'll be Little League enthusiasts—
Artistic dreamers, too.

There'll be some who like to study
And are never late for school,
While others get in trouble
By defying every rule.

Some will spend their money
Like it's going out of style.
Others with a frugal streak
Will save for things worthwhile.

There'll be kids who'd rather follow,
While others take the lead.
There'll be music freaks and movie fans
And some who even read!

Put them all together
And you have a motley crew.
Sometimes it seems impossible
The bunch belongs to you!

But when the day is over
And they're safely tucked in bed,
And one by one you count them
And pat each sleepy head—

Good or bad or in between,
You know beyond a doubt
There's not a single one of them
That you could do without!

Dan's knowing look and satisfied grin told me he was ready, willing, and able, and my excitement grew.

I spotted Mama Hess at a table and made my way to her. It was only six-thirty—I was an hour early—and Mama had just ordered her supper from the snack bar.

"Come, Jen," she called out to me, "come sit here. I've saved a seat for you. You always bring luck with you. Moira? She's away?"

Before I could answer, Dan was there again. His touch on my shoulder burned through my dress, and I jumped a little when he set down a cup of coffee and a doughnut in front of me. His warm breath against my hair thrilled me as he whispered, "I can't wait, love. Meantime, enjoy."

"Four specials, Dan," I said weakly, and wondered if anyone else had heard what he'd said.

I turned to find Mama Hess's wise blue eyes taking in my obvious discomfort. "Jen," she said, "Dan is a nice man and I never like to poke my nose out—but you're a married woman, no?" She hesitated and then went on. "Here at bingo, no one pries. We play our games and we go home. But most of the people here have something troubling them—something they're trying to escape. Do you have something troubling you, Jen?"

Why is it so much easier telling strangers our most secret thoughts? The warmth and obvious sincerity that was Mama Hess reached out to me and I responded. Before I could bridle my tongue, I found myself pouring out the most intimate details of my marriage, beginning with the strain between Ken and me and ending with the confidence that I was now see-sawing between fidelity and adultery.

Mama Hess listened attentively, nodding her head in understanding. "You've kept all that bottled up inside, eh, Jen?" she said finally. "You felt you were at fault and you were ashamed. Well, you've talked to me, and now you listen to me!" She pulled her chair closer to mine. "I'll tell you a secret, Jen. My Max was like your Ken for twenty years. From age forty to sixty, we had no body touch. My man is eighty-one now, but our love is like when we were first married."

I looked at Mama Hess in amazement. Somehow one never thinks that old people even think about sex, much less indulge in it.

I listened then to Mama Hess explain that most men go through a change of life just like women. At first, she, too, felt that she wasn't woman enough—that Max had someone else on the side. She said she, too, looked for an outlet in those days and found it in knitting.

I laughed out loud when she said, "Oh, Jennifer, when I started to knit, I made blankets that would go from here to Germany. I kept busy, trying to quench the fire inside."

She sipped at her coffee. "Jen, you can do two things. You can play with Dan, but you will hate yourself and lose Ken. Or you can go home to Ken and work to be a good wife."

I started to protest and to defend myself, but Mama shushed me again. "Sure, Jen, you think you've been a good wife, no? You cook, you clean house, you work and bring home money, but that's not enough. That's like a business partner, not a wife. Your man is sick in his soul. Do you show love for his soul—or only his body?"

I felt cheap and small hearing her say those words. It was as though my whole marriage was built on sex only. Maybe if Ken and I had had children, my energies would have been spent more constructively. . . .

I turned my attention back to what Mama Hess was saying.

"Think carefully, Jen. You came here at first to play bingo. Now you think you want to play with Dan. Bingo, you only play for money—with Dan, you gamble marriage. You say you love Ken—how much, Jennifer? Go home. If you really try, you can make him well again."

Mama's words tumbled around in my mind. She was right, of course. I had been more at fault than Ken. He couldn't help what was happening to him, and he felt less than a man. Instead of trying to be patient and building up his self-worth, I had succeeded only in tearing him down. If it had been a physical problem, I would have done everything I could to nurse him back to health. But I hadn't tried to understand this sickness of the soul. I had retaliated by withholding any physical semblance of my love. When was the last time I had shown him any tenderness? When was the last time I had touched him lovingly in any way at all? When had I kissed him last?

Instead of remembering my marriage vows to care for him in sickness and in health, I had cut and run at the first sign of trouble. I had wallowed in discontent and self-pity and had been concerned only with my desires. I saw in myself then what Dan had seen: a discontented, selfish wife ready to betray her husband. No wonder Dan had shied away from marriage all these years. How many other discontented wives had he comforted? How many other women had fallen in the trap I had set for myself?

I made my decision. I slid the chips off my boards, stacked them in a neat pile, and pushed them toward Mama Hess.

She looked at me quizzically. "You're not going to stay for the jackpot, Jen?"

"Mama Hess," I said, "my jackpot is at home."

"Good girl," she said, and patted my hand.

I reached over and kissed her on the cheek. "Thank you, Mama Hess," I whispered.

Dan caught up with me as I started out the gate. "Hey, Jen, what's the story?" he asked. "You cutting out now? I can't leave yet."

I didn't know what Dan's reaction might be as I told him I was going home for good. After all the teasing and half-promises I had given him, any degree of rage wouldn't have surprised me. But I needn't have worried at all.

"Can't win them all, can we, Jen?" Dan said. "Guess I missed by a mile, huh?"

He smiled ruefully and added, "You can't blame a guy for trying, right, love? See you around." He turned and headed for the hallway, pulling out his "specials" pad and already searching the faces of late arrivals as they called out to him.

I got into my car and got ready to go home. Home to Ken, to my marriage, to the only life that really mattered to me. ∎